DANCE OF DESIRE...

Tarifa moved in and out of the shadows around the fountain, her hair a shining black cloud obscuring her face. She wore a thin white petticoat and nothing else. Her throat, her breasts, looked gilded in the moonlight. Her bare feet moved soundlessly over the tiles, her lithe body in sensuous sway to ancient pagan rhythms he had seen once before . . . the night they had stood locked in a deadly embrace trying to kill each other.

He reached for her and kissed her with a savage violence that left them both trembling. She fought against him and yet he did not feel it, did not know the precise moment when she ceased to struggle, her lips trembling under his.

In a surging ecstasy, an engulfing surrender, they clung to each other, transported like ships on a tempest-tossed sea. A sudden primitive fire blazed through Tarifa. Never before had she felt this stark abandonment of her own strength and will. She was enveloped, swept wildly along on a dark tide that had no beginning and no end. On, on, into an eternity of blackness, emptiness, and mad, fierce passion...

TARIFA

Elizabeth Tebbetts Taylor

A DELL BOOK

Published by
Dell Publishing Co., Inc.
1 Dag Hammarskjold Plaza
New York, New York 10017

Dell ® TM 681510, Dell Publishing Co., Inc.

ISBN: 0-440-18546-7

Printed in the United States of America
First printing—September 1978

This book owes a great deal to a great many people—to my father, who initiated my interest in history and letters; to my husband Bob, who during his lifetime spurred me on to complete the book; to Bernard Wirth, who first recognized it as a publishable vehicle and gave me much valuable editorial advice; to the Franciscan padres of the California Missons, who translated old Church records for me; to the living descendants of many of the early California families who generously shared their memories and family histories with me; to the descendants of the early vaqueros, with whom I rode the golden hills and learned a great deal of the art and daring of the real caballero which made California truly the land of the horse that it is to this day; to my sons, Tony, Robby, Ronny, and my daughter Ibby; to my daughters-in-law Lynne and Joan, and my grandchildren Melissa and Anna Marie, and last but by far not least, to my dear Grace Ballew, whose unfailing dedication and two "helping hands," truly made Tarifa *a reality.*

Vaya con Dios,

Elizabeth Tebbetts Taylor
Twentynine Palms, California
September 1978

TARIFA

CHAPTER 1

On the afternoon of the first *corrida* of the Easter season, it seemed to Tarifa that all Seville had crowded into the Calle de las Sierpes on their way to the bullring. And why not? Did not Hobarra fight today? And was he not the greatest torero in all Spain?

Tarifa, too, intended to watch Hobarra when she had collected enough *duros* for a ticket. There was nothing but contempt in her narrowed eyes as she fought to hold her place against the jostling, pressing crowd. *Gorgios!* They reminded her of the bulls she had watched rush blindly into the enclosure of the Plaza de Toros at dawn.

The hot Seville sun blazed down upon her bare head and arms as she danced wildly and with such sultry fire in her long Romany eyes, and such a mad whirling on her small bare feet, such savage abandon, that even the disinterested holiday-makers on their way to the bullring paused in sheer admiration to watch the swiftness of her movements and listen to the rattle of her tambourine. Tarifa knew better than to use it. No true Gypsy made use of a tambourine or castanets to accompany her dancing. Rightfully, these belonged to the awkward-moving dancers in the cafés along the Calle de las Sierpes. But some of them had made fun of Tarifa as she stood on the corner dancing one day, and so she had followed them home and stolen the best of their tambourines while they slept. All the same, her mother Bandonna would have Penti beat her soundly if she knew, for the old Queen of the Gypsies of the Triana was still arrogantly proud of having been the foremost dancer in her *cuadro flamenco* in the Sacro Monte at Granada. Nevertheless, thought Tarifa, the tambourine did help to rivet the wandering eyes of the moving throng upon her.

"Olé!" They shouted. *"Olé, gitanita!"* And occasionally a coin would clatter down between the rapid-moving feet and madly swirling skirts. Tarifa's eyes sparkled brighter then, and her increased tempo showed the *gachos* that she had not missed their gift. But a moment later, as with an arrogant toss of her head and a swift graceful dip, she swept up the coin and dropped it inside her torn blouse, there was no smile of thanks. Her flashing glance seemed to say, I could have taken it from your pocket without your knowing it, rather than have given you a dance in exchange.

She knew all the street urchins' ways to slip into the arena without paying—over the walls, hidden among an unsuspecting family group, by fainting and being carried into the infirmary. But today she meant to buy a seat for the *corrida*. In honor of Hobarra. How her heart raced at the thought of him! For months she had awaited his coming with all the rest of the aficionados of Seville. Now the great hour was at hand. She had memorized the face and name of the famed torero on the colorful posters outside the Plaza and on the walls of the wine shops, and though she could not read the words written in bold type beneath the darkly handsome face, she had lingered until she overheard others reading them aloud to one another, discussing the past victories of the great *espada* in Granada, Cordoba, Madrid. Her heart had gone mad with delight.

For she knew something that these others did not know, with all their ability to read and discuss bulls and the torero's lethal skill. She knew that he was like herself, a *diddikai*, half-Romany, and it seemed to her that this should make them of one mind and one flesh. As a child, growing up in the Sacro Monte in the shadow of the Alhambra, she had suffered the taunts and jeers of the full-blooded Gypsy children who had pelted her with rocks and mud, calling her *diddikai*, half-blood, ash-face, because she was not as dark as they were. And she had screeched back at them, pointing to the Alhambra, that her people were the kings who had built that magnificent palace and ruled all of Spain, while theirs burrowed like rabbits into the mudholes of the Sacro Monte. All her life she had felt that she was alone, until she saw Hobarra's picture on the placards and heard from Penti that he, too, was a *diddikai*. She meant to throw herself at his feet, to offer to serve him for the rest of his life if he would have her. Her passion was the passion of intense pride and loneliness, fueled by a savage determination. He could beat her; he did not even need to care for her, but nothing could stop her from staying by his side.

Already the hour of the *corrida* was approaching and the people were losing interest in the little Gypsy dancer as they crowded toward the Plaza de Toros. Tarifa allowed herself to be moved along by the human sea. As they neared the plaza, the first of the open carriages bearing the brilliantly dressed toreros and their equally colorful *cuadrillas* began to make their appearance. While the crowd pressed in, surrounding them and calling familiarly to their favorites as the *espadas* drove by, Tarifa cleared another small space for herself and began to dance. Much as she wanted to see the toreros approach the bullring, she would not be like these human cattle turning their silly faces all in one direction as if to moo together.

Sulkily, she held her place, once stamping furiously on the toe of an onlooker who had carelessly invaded her little domain. She would make them look at her! There were not enough coins yet inside the flimsy blouse to secure her a seat at the *corrida,* or even standing room. Putting on a savage burst of speed which brought her close to the edge of the tiny circle, she felt herself suddenly taken off-balance and fell heavily against an onlooker.

Strong arms pulled her erect and a laughing voice speaking the purest Castilian, but with a strange foreign inflection, said, "*Hola*, little one, I think the Seville sun has given you sunstroke!"

Tarifa whirled free of the hand grasping her arm, her brows drawing down ferociously over her long eyes, at his laughter, her lips curled from her white teeth like an animal ready to spring. For a moment she stared angrily at the man standing before her and then the scowl faded.

He was young and handsome. Almost as handsome as a

torero, tall and slender, with a grace in his movements to match her own. Light-skinned and sharp-featured in the manner of the true Castilian, he wore his light-colored clothes and wide white Cordobán hat with an aristocratic air, and there were gold rings on his lean fingers, one of them a signet. But Tarifa knew nothing about the garb of a gentleman and cared less. If anything, she thought his dress and that of the plump young man she now perceived to be with him lacking in color. She would have preferred them in the *espada*'s gaudy arena costume.

Momentarily her interest had been taken up in studying the two young caballeros, much as one would study a new breed of horse or cow, and then she saw that they were still laughing at her. The white-hatted caballero had bent gallantly to retrieve one of the coins fallen from her blouse, at the same time making some gay remark to his friend that drew a mocking chuckle from the green-clad fat one.

Tarifa's face whitened with rage, her eyes glittering with anger between her lashes like the eyes of a venomous snake. They could afford to laugh at a *gitana,* these rich *gachos* with gold pieces in their pockets and no doubt a box at the *corrida* from which to watch Hobarra in his triumph. Laugh then, let them laugh! But give them something to remember their laughter by!

"Your money, *gitana mia*—"

The young man was holding out her coin in his fingers with a mock bow. Stepping forward swiftly she raised the heavy tambourine high in the air and brought it smashing down upon the unsuspecting caballero's head, squashing his fine hat over his ears and scattering pieces over his fancy shoe tops.

The young man drew back in amazement, dropping the coin, while his fat friend stepped forward with an oath to grasp the Gypsy. Tarifa snatched up her money and darted into the crowd. For a moment, out of the corner of her eye, she could see the fat one trying to follow her; then he was gone.

She was still panting when she halted at last beside the fountain outside the bull arena. She drank thirstily, cupping her hands to throw water over her head and face and breasts. Then she perched on the edge of the fountain and counted her money. She had made good use of her hasty retreat through the holiday crowd: many a pocket and sash was lighter for her swift flight.

Ai, she thought, I have enough here for the *corrida* and for food afterward. Perhaps that pig of a laughing *gacho* was a good omen. Then hastily she made a strange sign with two of her fingers and touched the amulet Penti had made for her. It hung around her throat on a golden chain that had once belonged to her father—or so Bandonna had told her. Tarifa had no formal religious belief, but believed in the superstitions of her people.

She was a grimy urchin, barely fifteen, but with the ripe figure she had inherited from Bandonna. She lacked the formal Andalusian beauty of soft eyes and voluptuous curves, but there was an arresting grace in her slender symmetry, like that of a wild thing.

Wiping her perspiring brow with the back of a narrow wrist, she began to test the worth of each coin by biting into it with her small, hard, white teeth. A tangle of coarse black hair writhed like twisting snakes over her wide brow, almost covering the oval of her face to a sharply pointed chin. Tarifa was not pretty; her brows grew too thick and straight over her long eyes—Gypsy eyes so dark they were almost black—and her nostrils were too highly notched in the small, high-bridged, faintly curving nose. But the innate grace of her every motion was bewitching, like watching a sultry houri from the court of a caliph.

Tarifa's whole appearance recalled the proud reign of the Moors, as well it might, if what her mother and Penti had told her was true, that her father had been an Arab slaver, descendant of the Moors who had conquered Spain. But one could not always trust Penti, who was a dull fool, and her mother, the Queen of the Triana, was old and ill now, given to passing her time with her cards and her bottle.

She had taught Tarifa, the last of her mixed brood of children, to dance, showing her all of the most difficult and ancient steps of her people. She considered Tarifa alone worthy of it, for from the moment she took her first step she had known that her only interest lay in the dance. Even as a small child she had displayed a certain grace and agility that Bandonna had realized was rare. She had done little else for her daughter; nothing more was expected.

Since childhood Tarifa had danced and begged for her
food and whatever else she required. But even then, in the
poverty of the Sacro Monte, she had done little begging.
There was a hard core of passionate pride in her, unbending and violent, as were all her emotions. Gradually what
she found her dancing could not accomplish she left undone, unless she stole now and then, which was quite within her rights as a Gypsy. It had been necessary to learn
great craft and cunning with that, too, for, fleet as she was,
she had already spent a thief's fortnight in the stinking rat-
infested Seville jail. It had been all but impossble to dance
on the rough straw-littered floor, but dance she had, to the
steady thwack of her tambourine, night and day, until the
distracted jailer threw her out bodily one stormy night,
telling his superiors that she had escaped. Tarifa had kissed
the mud-choked cobblestones and danced around each
puddle, making a bow to them on her way home.

Holding her money clutched tightly in one moist fist,
she got up from the fountain and fought her way through
the crowded lines to the ticket windows only to find that
the *corrida* was sold out. Even standing room was gone.
But the ticket seller said, he would make sure. He left his
wicket and came back a moment later, shaking his head.

"I am sorry, señorita, it is impossible. So many wish to
see Hobarra. If you had come earlier—"

"How could I come earlier, brother of a donkey, when
I was busy earning the money to buy my way inside! I,
too, would see Hobarra! Am I not as good as these *gachis?*"

She waved a small dusky hand with such fluid grace of
wrist and arm that the man was enchanted in spite of himself. She looked a wicked little hellion but there was something arresting about her. And he recognized the fanaticism
of the aficionado in the strangely hard, long Gypsy eyes.

"Señorita! Pass your money to me quickly, then come
inside and run up the stairway to your right." He spoke
without thinking. His superiors would have his hide if they
found out. "At the very back of the shady section there s
a small ledge," he whispered. "I think you will just fit the
spot. But go quickly, little one, and for the love of God let
no one see you! Afterward—" He leered at her meaning-
fully, but she had moved off like a shadow, leaving him
nothing but the odor of warm young unwashed flesh and

the glint of Gypsy eyes in their startling blue-white frames.

No one in the exclusive shaded section of the plaza paid the slightest attention to the ragged nymph climbing on swift silent feet until she found the tiny ledge partially hidden by the soaring wall and scrambled onto it. There was barely room to sit and draw up one's feet, a tight cramping spot, but to Tarifa better than a throne. Was she not actually inside the Plaza de Toros as a paying patron? Would she not watch the toreros come to bow before the boxes below and spread their capes before the whitehatted gentry, while she reigned as a queen from her throne atop the wall? Above all, would she not at long last see the famous Fernando Hobarra himself? There, directly below her, he would make his *brindis* and kill his first bull.

For a fleeting moment she thought of the laughing caballero who had brought her luck despite his rudeness. Then, her eyes sweeping the boxes below with haughty disdain, she felt the breath catch in her throat. Seated in one of the boxes were the two caballeros of the Calle de las Sierpes, the fat one in green, and the handsome young foreigner still wearing his white Cordobán hat with the crumpled crown.

Both were staring straight up at her.

Jorge Narez mopped his plump cheeks with a silk handkerchief. Curse the little imp of Satan. Santiago had just ceased talking about their encounter with the *gitana,* and he had hoped they might watch the *corrida* in peace and now here she was again. He sighed. "The insolent little *gitana,* eh, Santiago? But let her go—time for that later. The entrance is about to begin, we will miss the march."

"Look at her, Jorge. Isn't she like a wild thing? Like a small puma from my own California. We rope them there. Sometimes we tame them as pets if they are young enough."

"And you are fond of wild things," said Jorge wryly. He had been faced with many trying escapades since offering to show this young distant relative from California the sights of Seville. The boy was as unpredictable as a calf and showed as little sense of decorum. The lack of social graces in his colonial relative had been something of a shock to Jorge. California was of course no longer a Span-

ish colonial possession, having espoused the infamous and
traitorous new government of Mexico. But the break was
so recent that Narez and others in Spain still thought of
Mexico and California as possessions of the mother country.

Santiago turned suddenly, a hot glow in his eyes that
was all too familiar to Jorge and made him groan inwardly.

"Why not invite her to sit in the box, Jorge?"

"Are you out of your mind?"

"Why shouldn't we? She will lend a certain verve to the
occasion, which I must admit lacks excitement."

Jorge was momentarily shocked out of his rising anger
by this new affront to his civic and national pride. "The
Plaza de Toros in Seville. Hobarra fighting—and you say it
is lacking in excitement!"

"You do not really call this spectacle wildly exciting,
Jorge? Watching a domestic bull from behind the safety of
these bulwarks?" Santiago tapped the edge of the thick
wall in front of the box disdainfully. "In California we fight
bulls in the open field armed with a knife—or in the plaza
where the crowd takes its chance with the torero."

"That is not the art of bullfighting," said Jorge stiffly.
He was quite sick of listening to this braggart from the
wilderness. Everyone knew that now, under Mexican rule,
California would soon be a useless cow pasture, a waste-
land of crumbling missions and marauding Indians. And
Mexico would soon tire of provisioning and policing a land
that could give her no return in material goods and could
not even feed herself.

"Still," said Santiago seriously, "you must come to San
Diego and see some of my father's Indian vaqueros fight
a bull." The young Californian got to his feet suddenly,
pulling Narez with him. "Come, before she dashes away
again. I swear she moves like smoke! I have never seen
anyone dance as she does. What she could command in a
cantina in California!"

Jorge drew himself up stiffly. "I forbid you to go after
her, Santiago!"

The Californian raised his dark brows. "Is it for you to
forbid, Jorge?"

Narez felt his plump cheeks redden with embarrassment

and shame. "It is true that you and your brother are our guests here, but you go too far, Santiago. And I warn you, Joaquin will not approve of this."

Santiago made a face and laughed. "My older brother is a solemn owl with no sense of humor. Everyone knows that. Coming, Jorge? Or do we stand here until the *corrida* starts?"

Jorge became aware of the snickers and the disapproving eyes watching them from nearby boxes. Furiously he edged around his seat and started up the stairs after Santiago's lithe figure. He could cheerfully have throttled the young man from that despicable wilderness, California.

Santiago moved upward watching Tarifa as she stood poised on the rim of the top step like a small hawk, wary and deadly.

"Do not run," he warned. "If you could fly, you would fly, my little falcon? But you cannot, and I have caught hawks before with my bare hands. I owe you something for that blow you gave me with your tambourine."

Tarifa stood her ground, her high breasts rising and falling, hands bent like talons on her hips. "If you touch me I will tear your eyes out, laughing one!" she spat at him. "I am not afraid of you. You are a pig of a foreigner. I hear it in your speech. I paid good *duros* for my seat, like these others, and I am staying!"

"You see how quick she is, Jorge?" laughed Santiago. "Permit me to introduce myself formally, señorita." His bow, as he swept off his hat, was exquisite, and disclosed glossy black hair, thick and wavy. Tarifa was fond of wavy hair. "I am Santiago Alvarjo, of California. This plump pumpkin is my cousin, Jorge Narez, a native of your own Seville."

"I am not of Seville!" Tarifa snapped, drawing herself up. "I am a *gitana,* born in Granada under the shadow of the Alhambra!"

"Ah. Then we are both more or less foreigners here? Shouldn't that make us friends?"

She disliked being coupled with him in any way, but could think of no apt retort so she continued to frown fiercely down at him.

"I have no wish to harm you." Santiago smiled. "Though you did give me a rousing headache for doing you a favor.

Didn't I do you a good turn when I saved you from a bad fall in the street?"

"And then made fun of me to your friend." Tarifa's eyes flashed with anger and pride. "People do not mock me."

"For that I humbly beg your pardon, señorita, in every language I know." He rattled it off in Latin, French, Italian, while she continued to scowl at him. "I can even do it for you in Indian, of you like." The grunts and squeaks came out like the wail of a pig.

Suddenly she was laughing, a hard, mocking laugh, for there was not much humor in her. But he looked so comical standing there below her, hat in hand like a courtier begging his queen's mercy in that impossible gibbering language. He was indeed an odd one, this caballero from wherever he said he was from, and she still had that odd feeling that he had brought her luck.

"That's better," sighed the young man. "I invite you to share our box for the *corrida,* señorita."

She glanced down at them both suspiciously. "This is more of your mockery." Her breath came hard and fast, staining her cheeks with crimson. "I know your kind. You think because I am of the streets—"

"You are wrong," insisted Santiago. "Tell her, Jorge?"

"Yes," growled the fat man, mopping his brow. "We only wish to do you honor, señorita." He would have liked to have swallowed the words. A filthy Gypsy in his box in full sight of everyone he knew! And the worst of it was, as host, there was nothing he could do but accept it gracefully. The Alvarjos still had powerful connections in Spain, and the Narez branch of the family was deeply in debt to them.

"He does not seem happy," said Tarifa, watching Jorge's puckered brow.

"Pay no attention to him, señorita, he still lives in the days of the Cid. Come, you will see the *corrida* much better from our box, and Hobarra has promised to dedicate his first bull to us. Afterward we will all dine together."

Hobarra!

The bait was too strong to resist. Yet, moving toward him, she paused to ask, "Why do you do this for me?"

"You are a great dancer," said Santiago without hesitation. "The greatest I have ever seen. I must dance with you once at the cantina after the bullfight, just to prove to myself that you are as good as I remember. It is all the payment I ask. Is it a fair bargain?"

"I will come."

In a breath she had passed the two men on the stairs and was running lightly down toward their box, her eyes never bothering to look where she trod.

Santiago stood entranced. "She moves like the wind through the branches of a pepper tree. No one would believe such grace possible outside a wild animal."

"Make no mistake," panted Narez. "She is an animal, and of the most dangerous species."

Santiago laughed and ran down the steps to where an angry attendant stood glaring at the Gypsy, who was attempting to enter the Narez box.

"I cannot permit this—this creature in this section, señor. This box belongs to Señor Narez—"

Jorge came to a puffing, red-faced stop beside the gesticulating trio. Never, never in his life would he be seen in the company of this idiot son of old Don Ygnacio Alvarjo again. No, not if it cost him everything he held dear. This was too much.

"Tell him to let her pass, Jorge."

"People are staring, Santiago, have you no sense of the fitness of things? If she had only slipped in quietly—but now everyone in the place is watching. They stare, I tell you! For the love of heaven, Santiago, tell her to go back. This will be the talk of Seville by nightfall!"

"Bravo! Then Seville will have something interesting to discuss for a change. They only stare at you, my dear Jorge, because you stand here and make such an ass of yourself."

The Californian pushed his way past his infuriated host, dragging the Gypsy behind him, and seated her in the center of the box between himself and Jorge, who stared into the floor of the arena in disapproving silence.

Splendid, thought Santiago, there will be no more argument from Jorge. And he turned himself to the enjoyment of the moment. He found Tarifa surprisingly well-informed on the fine points of bullfighting, as are a great many street gamins concerning a national sport.

Heads together, they watched the black-mantled *alguacils* trot out on their horses to clear the ring, and then return to the main arch from which they would lead the march in front of the *cuadrillas*.

Over the yellowish sand drawn from the banks of the Guadalquiver, the entrance procession began. From the onlookers rose a breathless tension, like a high wind before a storm.

Tarifa leaned so far out over the edge of the box, that Santiago clutched her skirt for fear she would fall. She displayed the delight of a child mingled with a savage joy at the tragedies she was about to witness. Watching her, the Californian felt a sudden apprehension—there was something so fierce about it.

The advancing toreros were indeed magnificent today, each garbed in a different color with richly jeweled arena capes, and each accompanied by his equally gaudy *cuadrilla*, presenting to the onlookers a brilliant mosaic to dazzle the eye.

Hobarra, strutting more regally than the rest, was magnificent in a suit of pale lavender brightly ornamented with gold embroidery and flashing jewels. He bore himself like a king. Indeed, he was king today of all Seville, of all Spain, for he was the idol of the moment in the nation's most dearly loved sport.

Tarifa's heart seemed to stop as he halted before the boxes and after saluting the nobility, turned to make his bow to the Narez group, and spread his cape in front of them in their honor. An extremely slender young man, dark-skinned and wiry, his eyes met Tarifa's in a sudden piercing glance before he turned back to his companions.

"He is the most wonderful man in Spain," Tarifa told Santiago. "He has no equal in the world!"

"I would not say that," answered the Californian. "The world is a very big place, *gitanita*."

Tarifa's thick brows drew together in swift anger. "There are no other toreros like Hobarra!" Her voice was hoarse with passion.

Santiago answered with indolent amusement. "In my country there are Indian peons who could fight these Muiras of yours."

"You lie!" Suddenly, like a whiplash, her hand came up

and caught him squarely in the mouth. It was a hard blow, but he laughed as he caught her hands and kissed them lightly, stilling the sudden fire that had leapt into her eyes.

Patience, he told himself, one tames wild things only with patience.

"I do not lie, little vixen," he told Tarifa under his breath. "Perhaps someday you will come to realize that. And another slap, *carita*, and you shall feel what a man's hand can do. Now watch your Hobarra."

Tarifa turned from him sullenly. He was a strange one, this Californiano. She knew only vaguely where California was, over the water somewhere, in the New World. She had heard sailors talk in the *bodegas* of taking ship for the new lands, but she was not interested. When she had met Hobarra nothing else would ever interest her again. Her eyes sought the slim young figure before her in lavender and gold, and it seemed as if she stood beside him there awaiting the first bull.

Standing in the barrier just below the Narez box, Hobarra was the target for every eye in the arena. Jorge Narez slid deeper into his seat and lowered the brim of his Cordoñan hat. This was disgrace pure and simple. He would never live it down, a filthy gutter Gypsy seated in the place of honor in his box, next to that grinning young hellion.

Santiago was enjoying this moment more than he had enjoyed anything else since coming to Spain six months ago. He had found it a dull, stuffy place for the most part, in spite of the glowing tales of his expatriated parents and the letters of his older brother Joaquin, who had been studying in Madrid for two years. But then Joaquin was more Spanish than the rest of the Alvarjos, more Spanish even than their father, Don Ygnacio himself, who despite his austere Castilian heritage had taken on the easier going ways of the Californianos.

For her part, Tarifa felt more a queen than ever. If only this could last, this moment of ecstasy. If only she might imprison forever this feeling of power and pride, and relive it day by day for the rest of her life. Why, she wondered, did the brilliant, enthralling moments of life pass so swiftly, leaving only the dull, tawdry ones to drag on interminably? She would not let this slip from her. She would make it last.

Tonight, if Santiago had spoken the truth and Hobarra did dine with them, she would dance for the torero. She would dance as she had never danced before, like Ban-donna in her prime, like a cobra turned into a woman, like a houri in Nirvana. Then if he liked her—and he would, he must—she would join his entourage, amusing him on his travels by her dancing. As Hobarra's mistress . . . the vagrant thought sent ice and fire up her spine, for so far she had known no man. A Gypsy guarded her vir-ginity with a fierce passion, bolstered by the unalterable taboos of her people. But for Hobarra . . .

With a sudden clash of trumpet and drum, the first bull was led into the arena, a lean, dark Muira with wicked horns and a powerful neck. It was not Hobarra's bull, for he made no motion, but when a picador and his horse fell heavily under the animal's charge, Hobarra moved into the arena and with his flashing mobility drew the eyes of the crowd away from the frowning, intense matador who finally killed his bull, but with a feeling that it had been Hobarra's victory rather than his own.

The third bull was Hobarra's—big, well-muscled, a magnificent beast. He stood snorting his disdain of the men who dared to oppose him.

The *banderillos* in place, put there expertly by one of Hobarra's *cuadrilla*, the bull pawed the yellow sand, angry at the sudden fire in his neck. The crowd, poised on the edge of their seats, waited breathlessly for the trumpet call that would announce the last act of the drama—the death. It came, shattering the hot air, and with it Hobarra advanced to the royal box, rapier and *muleta* in one hand, *montera* in the other and, standing before the royal family, began his *brindis*. He was dedicating the bull to the Narez box, and, Tarifa realized in sudden elation, to her as a part of that entourage.

Something hot and heady soared up inside her, confus-ing her thoughts and glazing her eyes. This moment would remain supreme in her life forever. The man in the yellow-floored arena putting down his *montera* and turning to face the bull was king of the universe. And she was his queen, poised, waiting, sharing each moment with him. She sat up a trifle straighter and her throat swelled with the words, "*Magnifico*, Hobarra!" and then hotly in Romany, "*Oboro*

duvel atch' paí leste! Me kamāva tut!" The great Lord be on you. I love you! Turning then to Santiago with parted lips: "He is magnificent, I adore him, he is the king!"

"Not quite," said a cold voice behind her. "And it seems a mistake has been made in seating you here, *gitana*."

At first she thought it was Santiago who had spoken, for the voice was like his, held the same foreign burr, but there was an unmistakable ring of authority in it that Santiago's voice lacked. She saw Santiago getting to his feet as he turned to stare stiffly behind him.

"Joaquin," Santiago began haltingly, "you do not understand. There is no harm—she is just a young Gypsy girl, an aficionada—"

"She must leave at once," said the icy voice. "You will escort her to the plaza yourself, Santiago. Immediately."

Turning slowly, Tarifa met the speaker face to face.

She thought, with her swift Gypsy intuition, he has the face of a priest and the eyes of a pirate. He will condemn with one hand, and beckon with the other. I do not like him. I am afraid of him.

"You have heard, Santiago?" The voice, held low, was cutting as a torero's rapier. Santiago flinched and lowered his eyes.

At that moment Tarifa despised him. He was nothing after all, this laughing California caballero. He was afraid of this man, too, and the knowledge erased any gratitude she might have felt toward him. It was hard, with the roar of the watching crowd around her, and Hobarra ready to make his first kill at her back, but her ruthless pride made her rise stiffly.

"I will go, señor. I have already seen Hobarra. The rest of the *corrida* will be nothing."

Joaquin Alvarjo glanced at her oddly, his black eyes inscrutable in his long lean face. He was not handsome in the classical manner of Santiago. Two years older than his brother, Joaquin's features were already too hawklike, his mouth too thin and stern, like the mouth of a judge. Yet one sensed the barely contained emotion in the man, like lava inside a volcano, only held in check by the thin shell of his own willpower. A zealot, scourging himself with his own repressed desires and enjoying it. A dangerous man, the Gypsy knew, because he both feared and pandered to his own emotions. She had not intended to leave the arena but now she moved swiftly away on instinct, to escape from danger.

With head high she stalked by him, shaking off the hand that Santiago attempted to put on her arm, moving so quickly that he had trouble keeping up with her. Where before she had moved like a racing doe, now she bolted like a hare seeking cover. Several times she spat back at him: "Do not follow me! Puppy dog! Hand-licker! Liar!"

At the fountain outside he succeeded in stopping her momentarily, only by pinning her body between the stone-work and his own hard-muscled form.

"Listen to me, you little *gata.*" His eyes were hot on her face, imploring, his hands heavy on her slender waist. She twisted this way and that but found she could not escape, so she prudently gave up the struggle and faced him squarely with blazing eyes and sneering lips.

"You are a liar!" she hissed, watching his face pale at her words. "Your box! You had no right to invite anyone there. You have no rights anywhere. You are a weakling, afraid of your high-and-mighty brother! He is your brother?"

"Yes, my older brother, Joaquin."

Triumphant eyes glared into his. "He at least is a man, while you are still a boy, a puppy dog, to be told what to do, to be ordered outside with the cats and chickens—and *gitanas!*"

"You lie!" shouted Santiago. "I obey only God and my father. If you think Joaquin—"

"Santiago, you will see her from the box," she mimicked. "You little—"

"You promised I would meet Hobarra," she blazed, her small breasts rising and falling under the torn blouse with maddening irregularity.

Santiago clicked his teeth together on a hot retort and said, speaking more quietly, "You shall still meet your Hobarra, and dance for him, little one. This I promise on my honor."

"I do not believe you."

"I swear it by the Queen of Heaven."

Tarifa shook her head and the writhing tendrils of black hair seemed to move with a life of their own, Me-dusa-like, about her wide-browed, oval face.

"I do not hold by the things you swear to. But if you will touch my amulet and swear . . ." She watched him speculatively.

"You little heathen." But his eyes flickered with an amused light as he watched her fish up a little leather sack on a gold chain hung around her delicate neck.

He held it in his hand and asked dubiously, "What is it?"

He knew Padre Cazon would say he sinned in even regarding such a work of the Devil as this must be, yet he found himself genuinely curious.

"Penti, who is a powerful witch, and Bandonna my mother, who is Queen of the Gypsies of the Triana, made it to protect me. It is very powerful," she added darkly.

He laughed, and her eyes blazed at once with suspicion and anger. Santiago knew that she would scratch his eyes out if she could reach him. But this, he had already discovered, was not the way to handle her. And he had made up his mind to tame her as he had tamed the she-bear on his father's Rancho Loma de Oro, by patience and firmness and iron determination.

"What is your name?" he asked soberly and politely.

She hesitated, studying him.

"Tarifa."

"An odd name for a *gitana?*"

"My father named me in honor of the great Tarif who led the first Moorish invasion against Spain. My father was a Moorish slaver." She spoke with haughty pride. "He used to cut women up into little bits, with his knife, when they displeased him. All except my mother. Once she cut him in the throat with her knife."

"Your mother?"

"Bandonna. Queen of the Triana." Tarifa held herself erect, striving to read the expression in his eyes, but they remained only sober and thoughtful.

"You live with your mother and father?"

"My father died when I was a child. He was killed by pirates in the Mediterranean, coming back from Africa."

"But you live in the Triana with your mother?"

He watched her shrug her thin shoulders, and became aware of the layer of dirt and grime on her dusky skin. He moved back a step. She looked and smelled as if she had lain in the gutter most of her brief life.

"I eat when I can, and sleep where I choose. I am free. I am a Gypsy."

"Look," he told her, "I am going to swear on your amulet, Tarifa. I promise that tonight you shall see Hobarra and dance for him, and that you shall be my guest at dinner. Now do you believe me?"

She darted a shrewd glance at him from her odd three-cornered Gypsy eyes, weighing the truth of his words in her own highly suspicious mind. But he continued to speak in such level, convincing tones, utterly devoid of his former levity, that she found herself trusting him. She slipped free of his grasp, moving like a wraith, and he let her go. She stood a little way from him, clasping the grimy amulet in one hand.

"You have sworn on my amulet. If you have not spoken the truth you will die. The amulet is very powerful. I will meet you here tonight. What time must I come?"

He shook his head. "First, you will come with me. We must make you presentable. You would not dance before Hobarra in these rags?"

She drew herself up, fingering the soiled brown stuff of her skirt. "I have no others. He will not notice what I wear when I dance for him!"

"Come," coaxed Santiago, holding out his hand, "let me buy you a dress, a new one, to celebrate our new friendship? You will not still hold it against me because that fat buffoon Jorge laughed at you?" He refrained from mentioning Joaquin, and his smile was very boyish and winning. The one that always moved Tía Isabella from her wrath.

"Perhaps," she said guardedly, "you can buy me a dress." And then in a rush, "A red one, with a yellow shawl with pink flowers—and a new tambourine?" She smiled at him suddenly, a wicked, taunting smile that made his veins swell. "Since mine was broken?"

He took a step toward her blindly, then halted and pulled a leather pouch from his sash instead.

"We will go shopping, señorita. You will see that I am a man of my word." A new idea was taking form in his mind. He would tame this wild little *gitana* to his own satisfaction, and pay Joaquin back in his own coin at the same time. Fate had given him the instrument. Hobarra would be the bait. She would do anything for Hobarra, and Hobarra liked his *vino* following a successful Sunday in the arena. He was also grateful to the Narez and Alvarjo clans to the tune of five thousand *duros* advanced against his latest gambling debts.

"Come, show me where to shop."

She consented to take his arm and was now walking lightly at his side on her small bare feet.

"Señora Gomez!" she exclaimed at once. "She has the finest dresses and shawls and fans in Seville. All the *gachis* of the Calle de las Sierpes go to her for their clothes. Come, I will show you."

"And afterward," said Santiago calmly, "we will go to your mother's so that you can wash and dress properly for the occasion."

Tarifa glanced up, a swift doubt flashing in her long eyes. "I can dress at Señora Gomez's." She was thinking that Penti and Bandonna might try to take the new finery from her. Surely they would steal Santiago's *duros*, but that was no concern of hers, unless it meant that he would then refuse to take her to meet Hobarra.

"No," Santiago was saying, "you must go home and wash first."

"I do not like to wash."

"Do you prefer Hobarra to see an inch of mud under that new dress? I warn you he does not like dirty skins or smelly ones. He told me he bathes himself once a week regularly, and he uses perfume like a court dandy."

Tarifa's eyes widened in disbelief. "*Caramba!* It is a wonder he keeps the strength to kill the bulls!"

Santiago strongly doubted that fat, greasy Señora Gomez, in her grimy basement shop, sharply redolent of garlic, onions, and *manzanilla* of the cheaper variety, was the leading couturier of Seville. More likely she sold stolen property. Nevertheless he stood by, near the door, while Tarifa tried on one gown after another in a fever of excitement.

As far as he could judge, except for the differences in fabric and color, they were all of one pattern: tight-waisted, bouffant-skirted with low, scooped necklines and no sleeves. The accompanying shawls were cheap gaudy affairs, thick with sleazy fringe and bangles. His mother and sisters, he knew, would never have worn such garments.

Tarifa finally selected a cerise silk gown with black-edged ruffles and a thin shawl of red-and-yellow design, heavy with orange fringe. Santiago thought it a hideous combination, but both Tarifa and Señora Gomez, with her pungent garlic-scented breath, proclaimed themselves delighted. Santiago was also cunningly persuaded by the fat Señora to complete the outfit with a pair of high-heeled red-satin slippers, a tortoiseshell comb of great height and clumsy workmanship, and a large beribboned tambourine which seemed to please Tarifa more than all the rest of her newly acquired finery.

She tried once more to dissuade him from going to her mother's home in the Triana, but Santiago remained firm. For all the softness she intuitively sensed in the Californian that set him apart from the true Spaniards she had known, on this one point he was adamant. Her mother, he had decided, was to form an important link in his daring new plan, and since Tarifa half-feared that he would take back his gifts if she refused, she led him reluctantly toward the Triana.

Together they crossed the bridge over the broad Guadalquiver, the ancient Al-Quad-al-Kebyr of the Moors, running between its yellow sandy banks, and past the Torre de Oro, that treasure vault to which the Americas had shipped their fabulous wealth of booty and plunder that had made Spain a power second to none.

Behind them Seville lay displayed like a delicately embroidered tapestry of muted colors, with the imposing mass of the cathedral and its exquisite Giralda dominating the landscape. Here, Santiago knew, were buried Ferdinand and Columbus. Here history had lived, boldly, cruelly, lustily, one segment building itself upon the downfall of the other. But he was not much given to serious scholastic meditation —that was Joaquin's province. For himself he preferred the picturesque if dirty little street Tarifa had led him into, with its crowded row of grimy taverns and shops.

Santiago had never visited the Triana before, but like all hot-blooded youths he knew a good deal of the history of the forbidden Cava, as it was also called. Since the year 1248, when King Ferdinand had captured it along with

Seville from the Moors, it had been linked with the larger city. But no true Trianero admitted that his home was merely a suburb of Seville. It claimed its own place of honor as the first home of song and dance. Even in the days of Ziryab, that peerless minstrel from the court of Harun al Rashiel and Abd-ar-Rahman II, the Triana had been the scene of magic zambras, those fetes of incomparable singing that made Seville the music center of the world in beauty and brilliance of performance. The Gypsies claimed this as their town, and crossing the bridge over the sweep of yellow river which once had carried gold-laden galleons from the New World, one could see every strange and exotic breed of Romany. Peddlers and hawkers of every description, deceptively pitiful old crones offering to tell one's fortune or sell a magic potion, tinkers and acrobats, dancers, singers, and masses of tangled-haired, wheedling children dressed in dirty rags but with eyes as bright and keen as young marmots. A penetrating, musty odor rose from the fetid, enclosed streets, pinching the nostrils with its smell of poverty and squalor. Santiago, used to the wide vistas and balmy clear breezes of his own California, noticed it more acutely than most.

Here, as they wormed their way through the maze of dirty, narrow, rubbish-strewn streets past the closed façades of old houses, there was no echo of soft guitars and voices singing sweetly amid the twitter of caged birds in carefully protected patios, as in the gardens of Seville. Here one heard now and then a true Romany voice, unaccompanied, rugged, fierce, clipping the words and biting at the song, releasing the full tragedy of the particular *Siguiriya* and *Martinete*, as it forced the notes higher and higher, with blatant driving power. And Santiago knew what was meant by the proud metallic harshness of the true Gypsy voice, born to accompany the anvil and hammer and no other instrument. This was indeed *Cante Jondo*—Deep Song—sung by an expert, and something unremembered stood still for a moment in primitive fear and wonder.

"It isn't far," Tarifa told him as they wound up the twisting hilly street. Centuries before, the Moors had built these dwellings in the mysterious style of the East; every front door was alike and unrevealing, empty-eyed façades concealed what lay within. In days past, the rich inner gardens had been works of art and living beauty. Now most were overgrown and neglected by the careless riffraff who had taken refuge in their decaying splendor.

The worm-eaten door where Tarifa paused at last hung crazily by two upper hinges of hammered bronze, which still showed traces of the exquisite pierced work of the Moors. Inside, a tangle of weeds and vines choked the courtyard and fought with each other for a place around the stained pink marble fountain, brown now and empty like the jaws of an old man, its carved lip whiskered with moss and festooned with snails. An ancient, barren rose vine all but obscured the front door.

Tarifa paused nervously on the doorstep, her new finery clasped to her breast. She had refused to let Santiago touch it once it had been paid for. She was taking no chances of having it snatched back from her if this odd young Californian should change his mind once he confronted Bandonna and Penti. And he would be a fool if he stayed once he had met them.

"Bandonna? *Madrita?*"

The reply was dim and laconic. He was to learn that true Romanies usually spoke in a monotone.

"Tarifa? *Avah?*"

"*Sí.* I have brought a *gacho* from Seville—a gentleman."

"Bring him in, little one." There was a sudden spark of life in the voice.

A woman had appeared in the open door, a squat ugly creature of uncertain years with tangled, coarse black hair tied in a green kerchief, and the crafty witch-pointed eyes of the Romany woman that means danger to the uninitiated.

She spoke a stream of biting ominous-sounding words at Tarifa that Santiago did not understand. But Tarifa spat back at her just as vehemently, reaching back and pulling Santiago inside. The Gypsy woman suddenly let out a harsh, derisive laugh like a jangle of taut wires.

"What did she say?" Santiago whispered, as his guide pulled him swiftly from one empty damp room to another. He had forgotten that in Gypsy houses one never enters by a straightforward means, but must ease in and out of passages as though burrowing through a rabbit warren before reaching the habitated apartments.

"She is an old devil, that Penti! She threatened to beat me for not coming home before this. I told her to beat me now, but that I was a powerful witch and she would suffer."

Santiago had a confused impression of gloom, squalor, and stench, and then they came out into a long low apartment that had once held a sunken marble bath, long unused. There were only two pieces of furniture, a small inlaid table and an old carved walnut armchair with a high back.

Both were in use by a gaunt old woman magnificently proud in her straight-backed dignity. Her thick hair, covered by a purple kerchief, seemed more gray than white, as did the thick brows bent like ancient twigs over her long flashing eyes—eyes through which an eagle soul looked out at him. She wore a full black-and-white-striped Gypsy skirt and yellow silk blouse, with a black velvet jacket somewhat the worse for the wine that had recently spilled down the front. Her gnarled fingers and bony wrists twinkled with a clacking array of cheap jewelry, flashing color as she put down the deck of cards she was holding and nodded regally to Santiago.

"*Sarishan, rya.* I welcome you. Be seated, señor. Over there." She waved a hand with something of the arresting grace of Tarifa, and indicated a nearby pile of soiled silken cushions.

Santiago bowed and went to sit down gingerly, his hands on his knees. He was not so certain now that this plan was going to work; this old harridan would see through any subterfuge just like his aunt Isabella. Painful experience had taught him that with such women only one course was possible. Complete honesty—enhanced by his warmest, most boyish smile.

Bandonna held out her arms to Tarifa and he saw the girl fly into them and lie quietly, her head on her mother's breast. Across her daughter's supine body, Bandonna asked, "Who are you, señor? And why do you come into the Triana with my little one? It is not always safe to do so. But rest with ease, señor, you are in the house of Bandonna, Queen of the Triana. No one would dare harm you here."

Before he could reply, Tarifa jumped to her feet. "He promised that I should meet Hobarra tonight. He bought me this dress and shawl, these slippers, and the tambourine." She hid the instrument quickly behind her. "And I sat in his box at the *corrida!*"

Penti, that squat, ugly creature, had come into the room with a bottle and two glasses which she placed before Bandonna. It was plain from her venomous glance that she disapproved of all that was going on, but that like a well-trained if savage watchdog she would hold herself in check until her mistress gave a sign.

"Leave us," said the Queen of the Gypsies to her servant and child. "I will call you later, after the Señor and I have spoken. Go dress yourself, little one, if you plan to go with the Señor."

When Tarifa and Penti had gone Bandonna settled into silence. Santiago could feel her eyes on him as he let his own gaze drift casually about. The floor was made of worn marble slabs, dark with age and filth now, but once milk-white and beautiful. The high, narrow arches that formed the windows still bore the remains of the carved marble fretwork that had guarded them in the days of the caliphs.

"Señor, why have you come here?"

He brought his gaze back to her impassive, wrinkled face. It was impossible to judge her age or her thoughts, yet he felt uncomfortably that she was quite able to decipher his. He decided to be frank.

"I have come to bargain with you for your daughter, señora."

Her reply came at once in the same noncommittal monotone.

"You wish to buy her for your wife, concubine, or slave?"

"No," laughed the young man. "I have come to make you a business proposition. I do not wish to harm her—only to help her. I admit I mean to use her to teach my older brother a badly needed lesson in manners. But in the long run all this will be to Tarifa's advantage."

Suddenly he was blurting out the whole story of Hobarra and Tarifa, and Joaquin's arrogance, telling her, as he might have told Tía Isabella, how he planned to repay his older brother in his own coin.

Without speaking, Bandonna began to lay out the soiled cards on the table before her.

"You must understand—" Santiago began, rising, but she lifted a hand as if to hold back his words.

He sank back on his pile of cushions and watched in fascinated silence as the cards fell one upon the other from her flashing hands, until at last only two remained held down on the table by her thumb. She turned to face him then, her eyes as inscrutable as flecks of obsidian beneath their hooded lids.

"I have no objection to my daughter's leaving my household. She was born a Gypsy—and free. The world is her home, and all that is in it is hers to take if she can. It is the belief of my people. But in Tarifa there runs an older and wilder and darker strain—that of the Moor. It is their belief that to conquer and hold in their own right is their mystic destiny.

"Because you have been honest with me, *rya,* I will tell you this truth. If you take Tarifa from this land to yours, as you plan, it will prove disastrous not only for you but for all you hold dear. It is so written in the cards. You may call it *chovihanipen,* witchcraft, but to my people the cards speak true.

"Tarifa has the witch eye, like a bird's, peaked at the center, the corners turned up like the point of a curving scimitar, the lashes straight and curled only at the ends. She will rule wherever she goes and she will bring dread and unhappiness to many. I have known all this since she was born. I love her in spite of these things. But I warn you, for her sake as much as yours, to go your way and not cross your life with hers. The door is open. You may still go in peace before her spell falls upon you."

Santiago laughed. "I am not superstitious, señora. You have told me the truth of your feelings; I will tell you mine. I have been in Seville as a visitor. I am to accompany my brother home. Joaquin has been at school here these past two years, he feels very superior to us plain, unworldly Californianos. He needs a lesson in humility and I mean to teach him one, with Tarifa's help. When he discovers I have taken a Gypsy all the way to California under his nose without his knowledge, he will have his comeuppance.

"My father, Don Ygnacio, is a great ranchero in California, with a royal grant of over fifty square leagues

near the town of San Diego. I am his second oldest son,
and will in time inherit much land and cattle.

"Joaquin is a serious owl; we have never agreed. I propose to show him that I can make my own decisions, order
my own life, and do Tarifa a good turn at the same time.
What opportunity has she here? This old world is finished
—ours is just beginning. What can I tell you of the beauty
and wealth of my land—a golden, soft land, señora, where
everything grows to twice its normal size! A land of wealth
and plenty, where no one works and all are rich and growing richer. Surely you would have your daughter take up
her life in such a land?"

"She will not go willingly. She is enamored of the torero,
Hobarra."

"But I shall tell her Hobarra will also take ship with us."

"This is true?"

"No. But Hobarra will gladly pretend so—for a price."

"You would trick Tarifa?"

"Only to her own advantage. But I tell you only the
truth, señora. When my brother learns I have smuggled her
on board and brought her to California without his knowledge, when he sees her daily as a symbol of his foolish arrogance and prudery, he will acknowledge his own weaknesses—and that is good. As the Church tells us, I will be
helping him to examine his own conscience and to admit
his sins."

The old Gypsy shrugged. "It is not my business anyway. I grow feeble and she is the last of my brood. She
brings me no money, but I have an affection for her because she is young and dances as I once danced. Only a
rare one dances so! If you have gold, *rya*, and mean her no
harm, then I shall hear you out. What are your plans for
Tarifa in California?"

"I will see that she has a job dancing at the wine shop of
my friend in San Diego. She will be the toast of California;
she will grow rich as a queen."

"And you want only to take her secretly to California to
prove to your brother that you can outwit him? You will
lay no further claim to her?"

Santiago shrugged his elegantly clad shoulders. "Why
should I? I will have shown Joaquin that I, too, am a man
capable of arranging my own affairs."

"And if you should love my daughter?" The obsidian eyes narrowed.

"Then I would love her."

The Gypsy nodded approval. Then the characteristic wheedling tone of the Romany to the *gorgio* came into her voice. "I could not let her go lightly—she is the joy and only prop of my declining years. You see how I live here alone and defenseless? A poor old woman left alone with her tears and her memories, forgotten, unloved. If you take Tarifa, you must agree to take my servant Penti, for I should perish of misgivings for my child's safety otherwise. Penti will send me word of how matters go, and guard my child."

Then suddenly in another tone altogether, she asked, "What is your price?"

Santiago nearly balked at mention of the unsavory Penti, but he had made a bargain with himself. On impulse, he foolishly pulled out his purse. He was aware at once of his mistake. There was a tension in the air. The old woman's eagle eyes glowed in the dusky room like a bird of prey.

"Fifteen *duros*," he said, beginning calmly to count them out in his hand.

A knife whizzed through the air and fastened itself in the wall at his back, a fraction above his right shoulder.

"I could have put that through you, *rya*. I have half a dozen more *navajas* here."

Santiago was shaken but he held himself erect. Not for nothing did the blood of Castile and of the conquistadores flow in his veins.

"Put your purse and jewelry on this table," said Bandonna, and then added unexpectedly, "I will consider your proposal, *rya*. If I agree to send my daughter and servant, how many more *duros* will you guarantee me? I am old and must exist."

So, she meant to help him after all, even if only through greed. His mind sped. "I have a relation, Señor Jorge Narez. His father is a magistrate in Seville. Through him, I will guarantee to send you a monthly sum of ten *duros*."

Bandonna nodded her kerchiefed head. "It is well; I will speak to Penti. But remember if you fail to send the payment, Penti is as expert with a *navaja* as I am, and she will carry out my orders. No come, pour us some wine so that we can seal the bargain in true Romany style."

Santiago rose, moving awkwardly and uncertainly under her beetling gaze. He poured the wine, a smoky amontillado. When he looked up, her eyes were suddenly sad upon him. The unexpected emotion in so harshly dominant a woman momentarily unnerved him.

Bandonna raised her glass with a murmured, *"Sarishan,"* and then lapsed into silence.

The single candle guttered and flickered on the table when the old *faraóna* hunched over her wine.

She said softly a moment later, "You will remember, *rya*, that I warned you not to take her?"

But Santiago had no time to reply and in an instant he had forgotten her words completely. From the shadowed depths at the back of the room, the old servant appeared with Tarifa dancing along behind her.

Even in the dim light Santiago was aware of the change in the girl. She had been bathed and her hair piled high under the tortoiseshell comb. Even the hideous dress and shawl could not hide the strange sinuous beauty of her movements. She walked a bit stiffly in the unaccustomed high heels, but her eyes sparkled in the gloom and a flush of excitement lent dusky color to her thin cheeks.

"How do I look?" She pirouetted wildly about the room.

"As I once looked, little one," murmured Bandonna.

Tarifa stopped in front of Santiago.

"And you, señor, how do you like me now?"

"At least you are cleaner," he replied gruffly, but there was an unaccountable tightness in his chest and heat seemed to rise up out of his throat into his face.

Tarifa frowned at him and whirled off toward the open door, thwacking the tambourine softly to an odd off-beat rhythm of her own.

"You will go with the *rya*," directed her mother, "and dance for the torero. Penti will go with you."

"No! I will not have that filthy lying old *gitana* following me!"

"I have spoken." Bandonna took up her cards and motioned to Penti with a jeweled hand. While her daughter stamped her feet in black rage, the old *faraóna* conversed in a whisper with her servant, the other woman shaking her head and gesticulating wildly, but at last subsiding into a sullen silence.

Santiago rose and went to join Tarifa at one of the windows. A fresh evening breeze came through the open fretwork, a blessing after the stench of the catacomb behind and below them. He attempted to take her arm but she pulled away from him, her flesh sliding away from his eager fingers, and skipped lightly from the room into the dark evil-smelling passageway.

By the Lord, thought Santiago, he would tame her. Tonight!

Stumbling blindly through the gloom of the house after her, he emerged at last into the cool damp air of the patio. He wondered what Joaquin would think of all this—if he would even believe it—and found himself laughing aloud.

"If you laugh at me again," Tarifa said darkly, "I will kill you!"

"But I do not laugh *at* you," said Santiago. "Only at my brother Joaquin, and what he would say to all this. We will show him a thing or two, you and I?"

"I have no interest in your brother. I only go to the dance for Hobarra. As you promised!"

"And you shall, little one, better than you have ever danced before. And Hobarra shall not forget you."

In a moment Penti joined them, toadlike in her black mantilla, carrying a bundle tied up in a dull black shawl. She nodded sullenly toward the gate and they moved forward. As he pulled the broken gate shut, Santiago heard Bandonna's voice from the open window above, followed by her dry humorless laughter. "Remember, *rya,* I have warned you. . . ."

It was not to a public restaurant that Sántiago led his little party, but to an elite, semiprivate café in a little *calle* that formed a cul-de-sac just off the Calle de las Sierpes.

Once, it had been a private residence of imposing proportions, until an enterprising Frenchman, Pierre Santou, had turned its lower apartments and patio into a restaurant for the discerning gourmet, its upper regions into elegant suites for discreet games of chance and other diversions. It was not uncommon for his entire establishment to be taken over—as tonight—for some lavish, private entertainment.

He was pleased that Don Francisco Narez, uncle of Joaquin and Santiago Alvarjo of California, had taken over his establishment to honor his nephews on the eve of their departure from Spain.

Don Francisco sat at the head of the table, with Hobarra as his guest of honor on his right, his eldest nephew Joaquin on his left, and his son, Don Jorge, at the foot of the table. Only the dusky torero did not "belong" in this company gathered under his roof, thought Monsieur Santou, and then his eye, wandering idly down the length of the table, caught another outsider. *Sacre bleu!* How had this creature entered his sacred domain? A girl, dressed in a hideous cheap gown and shawl, sitting on the very edge of her chair beside none other than Don Francisco's younger nephew Santiago!

Santou started to call his maître d' and then, incredible as it seemed, he discovered that young Santiago Alvarjo was discoursing avidly with her, even, it seemed, trying to win her favor. The girl scarcely noticed the young man but sat rudely with her long dark eyes riveted to the mobile face of the famed Hobarra.

Hobarra was too far away from where she sat beside Santiago for Tarifa to hear his words or that of the dignified gray-haired man who was Santiago's uncle and her host. But her eyes could drink in every feature, every movement of the torero. How magnificent he was. How brave! What insipid caricatures of men he made these others seem, as they sat dressed in their somber clothes, laughing politely at his jokes. She laughed also and louder than they did, as a tribute to the torero's wit. She had never been so proud of him. He had replaced his costume of the arena with a bright-green suit, yellow sash, and scarlet cravat. His strong slender hands flashed with jewels. Tarifa worshipped him with a consuming, fiery passion that made her temples throb. It was as if something held her head in a giant pincers. She was hardly aware of Santiago speaking into her ear, but once she turned to hiss at him:

"Why do we sit so far away? Why aren't we closer so that I can hear what he says? Are you still afraid of your brother?"

"We must be cautious," Santiago said uneasily. He had no desire for Joaquin to discover his little plot until it could bear fruit—the bittersweet fruit of revenge. "Wait till the meal ends. I have sent Hobarra a note. He will meet us."

Tarifa watched sullenly, impatient, while the others finished their sumptuous meal. She ate little herself for fear of missing Hobarra's slightest movement or glance. Of the other women present, dressed drably from Tarifa's viewpoint, in plain white or black according to their age, she had only a fleeting impression of soft voices and coy glances around lace or tortoiseshell fans. Such women would not interest the torero, she knew, and she dismissed them from her mind.

After the meal, Santiago led her into the warm flower-scented patio where the women were strolling around the splashing fountain. Most of the men had disappeared up the spiral stairs to the gaming rooms above, among them Don Francisco Narez, his son Jorge, and nephew Joaquin. Hobarra had joined a group of admirers in the patio.

"Wait here," Santiago told her.

In a moment she saw him returning with the torero, their footsteps sharp on the mosaic tile.

Tarifa threw off the shawl, letting it drop to her elbows over her waist. Her palms were wet and her breath caught sharply like a knife thrust in her throat, making her nostrils burn with a sudden dryness. For an instant she stood poised like a wild thing about to bolt, and then, clasping the amulet around her neck, she stood waiting for them.

When they paused before her, she could barely hear Santiago's introduction or Hobarra's polite acknowledgment. She only knew that she trembled violently, could not move or speak. Yet now, within a foot of her, stood the man she would gladly have given her life to please.

Hobarra, still heady with his victory, was in a pliant mood. The rich wines had mellowed his sharp nature, and the rich young caballero at his side had promised to wipe out an old debt and pay him a goodly sum in gold if he would merely consent to play a part with this wild-looking child. Though what young Alvarjo could want with her, Hobarra could not imagine. He preferred his women plump and soft and docile. Still, there was something intriguing in this fiery little *gitana*, and she was as graceful as a swan.

"My good friend tells me you have come to dance for

me," said the great torero, smiling as he held his thin black cigar in one jeweled hand. "You are a *gitana?*"

Tarifa nodded swiftly.

"Do not be afraid of me," he laughed, taking her by the arm. At his touch a shudder ran through her slight frame, and she dropped the tambourine from suddenly lifeless fingers. Instantly the torero bent and retrieved it, bowing low, as he did in the arena when he began his *brindis.* "You dance magnificently, my friend tells me. It is a long time since I have seen a real *gitana faraóna* dance. Once, in Granada, I watched the *Gada.* Do you know it?"

"Yes! Yes, Señor Hobarra."

"Ah, then you must show me. Come, we will find a spot." He glanced around speculatively.

"Upstairs," Santiago said quickly. "I have made arrangements to use Monsieur Santou's private apartment."

He led them into a small room at the top of the stairs, charmingly furnished in the French style, with a bottle of choice wine icing in a silver bucket on the table.

"I knew they did not give you enough of this downstairs," he said, winking slyly at Hobarra. "And with such victories as yours today, there is not enough of it in all Spain in which to toast you properly." The torero, naturally vain, bowed low before his admirers and sat down.

Tarifa wondered that Santiago could make such a bold-faced statement after saying at the arena that Indian peons in his own California could easily outperform Hobarra. He could lie as well as a Gypsy, this strange one. She wondered if Hobarra was taken in.

"We shall enjoy this bottle and many more while the Gypsy dances," said Santiago.

The torero laughed, putting down his cigar. "You are a true gentleman, señor," and lifting his glass, added, *"Saludos."*

A brief knock sounded on the door and Santiago excused himself to usher in a swarthy young man with one gold ring in his ear and a guitar slung over his shoulder.

"Pancho has worked for my uncle," he told them. "He will play for you, Tarifa." Pancho grinned and bowed to each of them in turn, flashing white teeth as he unslung his instrument.

"What will you have first, *miri pen,* my sister?"

"Siguiriya!"

The Gypsy looked surprised that one so young would dare to perform the difficult and ancient Gypsy dance of ritual. The *Siquiriya* had begun as a secret rite evoking pagan gods. It was a haunting and passionate lament of love and death, an outcry against fate, portraying violent grief, hopeless loves, consuming jealousies. Only the most experienced flamenco dancers dared attempt it, for to fail to perform it properly was little less than sacrilege.

While the guitarist hesitated, Tarifa stamped her foot. She had flung the shawl to the floor and removed the high-heeled shoes, and now stood barefooted in the center of the room.

"Siguiriya! Premita Undebe!"

The Gypsy blanched at the powerful and deadly curse. This wild one was indeed a witch. He should have been warned by the bird-peaked eyes, the straight lashes, and hair curling only at the ends.

He struck a chord on his powerful seven-stringed Panormo guitar and the small room vibrated with the sound.

At the first strains of the music a miraculous change seemed to come over Tarifa. Gone was her odd shyness and awkwardness. She closed her eyes, reached up, and pulled the comb from her hair, allowing her long black hair to swirl around her shoulders.

Standing erect and barefooted in the center of the room, arms high above her head, like a young tree beginning to sway gently in a slight breeze she moved gradually into the slow undulations and intricate, suggestive footwork of the ancient dance.

As her fingers wove a spider's web, using the cabalistic signs of ancient enchantment and sorcery, animal symbols of death, the pronged two-headed serpent, the tarantula, and the swift-striking hooded cobra, her body quivered as with the force of evil itself. Her delicate hands, like coppery spiders spinning a web about her entire body, moved ever faster and faster from her knees to her head.

Her black hair fell in a writhing tangle about her face, and she shook her panting sweat-soaked form as if to free it from the evil enchantment of tormented ghosts. Then as the rhythm slowed her hands straightened, fell to her sides for a moment, and opening her long eyes she began to dance jubilantly with a wild fierce joy of living, as if awakening from a deadly trance. Faster and faster, until it seemed the watchers could bear no more movement, no more bending and melting of flesh and bone.

When the last note of the guitar had died away and Tarifa bent low to accept their applause, there was a stinging deadly silence.

The Gypsy Pancho seemed transfixed, his guitar in his hands. Santiago, white-faced, sat on the edge of his chair, his breath coming in short gasps. But Hobarra rose like a walking statue and took two tottering steps toward her. His handsome face was contorted with a mixture of passion and awe and a trace of fear.

Then, stumbling over the unaccustomed tribute, he said hoarsely, "My Queen!"

And Pancho's words rang out, *"Faraóna! Faraóna morena!"* Queen, dark queen!

Hobarra took her shoulders in both hands and kissed her lightly on both cheeks, and he felt her flesh trembling under his fingers. He was only half-gypsy and he thought he had torn himself away from their ways long ago. But the old mystical power of his people began to take hold of him again as he held this child-woman before him.

Santiago had watched the little tableau with mixed feelings, his blood and senses still fired by the intensity and magic—for there was no other word for it—of Tarifa's dancing. He had thought her merely an unusually graceful little girl. But Bandonna had been right; Tarifa was no ordinary dancer. In her the spirit of the dance was a living, breathing thing. A dangerous one, to be reckoned with in its own right, and Santiago sensed with something of a shock that this spirit, whether for good or evil, possessed Tarifa quite as much as anyone who watched her dance. He was a fool to think he could take this creature to California. Mother of Heaven, what had he been thinking of? And yet, the very mystery and danger were a challenge he could not give up.

He knew he would have no trouble with Hobarra playing his part now; he was as plainly bewitched as a man could be. Santiago reached for the bottle and said in a loud tone, to break the spell, "Come, Señor Hobarra, we are here to watch the Gypsy dance! Here is wine and we have the evening before us. Let her dance."

Hobarra, eyes glazed with passion, slowly backed away from Tarifa, who was smiling at him with dazzling desire, and fell into his chair. Santiago put a glass in his hand and nodded to the guitarist.

"Play! We are here to be entertained."

Watching, the men lost track of time, of each other, of everything but the heady beat of the rhythm and the drum-like handclaps of the dancer that have accompanied Gypsy dancing since the Moorish *zambras*—taking the place of the original Moorish drums, driving out the evil spirits. And the swirling, dipping, undulating wraith that was Tarifa herself.

They watched as in a trance the *tango del merengazo*, a mad tango; then the *tango de la flor, tango del candil*— wild, surging dances that eclipsed any others to be found in Spain.

Tarifa let the passion of her dancing run through her like a molten river, yet she herself seemed to be in a dream. Her golden skin paled like a waning moon, as with dilated nostrils and quivering limbs, she writhed like a flaming column blazing itself out by sheer inner force. Yet even in the wild orgy of the *Cante Jondo* her face still held its aloof, haughty, proud expression, like a high priestess performing ancient and sacred rites. As Hobarra said humbly to Santiago later, "You have seen a true *faraóno* of our people— a true Pharaoh's daughter. There is no higher compliment."

When the music ceased and Pancho bent over his guitar in exhaustion, Tarifa stood panting, the thin dress plastered to her high, pointed breasts and slender thighs, her hair dripping with glistening drops, like stars sparkling in a midnight sky.

"You are pleased?" she asked Hobarra. But there was none of the old awkwardness when she addressed him. It was more a taunting reminder that now she, and not he, was to be pleased.

Hobarra drew in his breath sharply and tossed off the rest of his wine. He made a last attempt at preserving his mastery and pride.

"You have not danced the *Gada*. I would like to see the *Gada*."

Tarifa's smile faded, washed away by a fear she had not known she possessed. It was that old devil Penti, who had filled her mind with such superstitious rot. And what had she to fear? She was not a full-blooded Gypsy; she was a *diddikai*. Did not that release her from the curse?

"You have lied to me, little one," laughed Hobarra in some relief, for the whiff of superstition also came back to him this night, as it came sometimes on a bad day just before the *corrida*. One could tempt fate just so far. "You do not know the *Gada*?"

Tarifa drew herself up to her full height and lifted her chin. "I know the *Gada!*"

"But you are afraid—afraid of the old curse? It is well; I asked only to test you. You have pleased me; come and drink some wine. You have earned it."

Tarifa's voice thundered across the room.

"I will dance the *Gada!*'"

Pancho's hand trembled on the guitar and he gaped at her. Like Hobarra, he had thought Tarifa's defiant words a childish empty boast. But if it were true that this little witch knew the *Gada* and would dare to dance it here, then he would have no part in it. He rose, clutching his instrument.

"I must go, señors," he mumbled. "My hand, it is aching from an old injury. I can play no more."

Tarifa whirled to face him.

"You will play, son of a pig! Or I will put the Great Curse on you. Don't you know I am a great *chovihani*, a witch!"

The Gypsy made a cabalistic sign with his fingers and sank back on his chair, his eyes wide with fear. The *Gada*, that forbidden dance known and seen by so few, went back to the earliest history of his people. Further, for all he knew. No matter where a Gypsy wandered or what his tribe, he had been warned of the *Gada's* deadly power.

Originally a sacred dance to the supreme gods of the *gitanos*, *kam*, the sun, and *chone*, the moon, the *Gada* was only recited reverently by the wise men of the tribes, in honor of the mythical marriage of the brother Sun to his Sister, the Moon, on which the Gypsy belief is based. Since the marriage of brother and sister is forbidden in the world's eyes, this belief made the Gypsies outcasts from the beginning of time. Originally descended from the Jats of northwest India, the Gypsies were metalworkers, dealers in horses, farriers, and tinkers of great skill. Since they had no formal religion they were unscrupulous thieves, their women, dealers in fortune-telling and petty magic. Unlike the Hindus, they ate animals that had died naturally, including pork, which made them doubly outcast in the lands of the East. Always they had great skill in music, singing, dancing, and acrobatics, and as they roamed through a hostile world they learned to perfect and turn these attributes to their own advantage.

They observed few rules but certain tabus remained. Death or ostracism from the tribes punished those who broke them.

The *Gada* was one of these tabus. One could dance it in private, in times of great stress as a petition to the gods, or go to a sacred man, and dance it for him while he made petition to the Sun and Moon for the sinner. It was not to be danced in public, and never by an unmarried woman before men.

In the days of the Moors, a bastard form of the *Gada* had found its way into the harems and taverns, thus making it doubly tabu to the Gypsy, who clung to little but the larger beliefs in his Romany life—his gods the Sun and Moon, and his belief in Nature.

At the first strains of the oddly thin Oriental-sounding music with its halting and then quick tempo, Tarifa seemed to change again before their eyes. The other, Moorish side of her nature appeared. As she stood arrogant and solemn-faced with tight-set mouth, she might have been a young calipha. Swaying, shifting from one slender foot to the other, she moved her torso slowly, muscle by muscle rather than limb by limb, as a snake moves.

It was uncanny to watch the smooth expressionless face as calm as an idol's, and yet mirroring an inner force and power that was frightening. The intricate arabesques, casting gigantic shadows across the walls, made Santiago feel suddenly small and helpless as if huge black birds were about to swoop down and devour him. As for Pancho, he played like one mesmerized, in a dream world of his own.

Hobarra sat back grimly in his chair as if braced for the Moment of Truth in the arena. His cigar had gone out between his fingers and there was a fine line of sweat on his upper lip.

None of the men afterward remembered when the music

and movement stopped. When Santiago's numbed senses returned to normal, all of them were staring at Tarifa. She was sitting in a crouching position in her sweat-soaked gown, her eyes flashing up at them and her smile as mocking and wise as that of the Serpent in Paradise.

"Enough!" cried Hobarra. "We've had enough! Come here little one."

Tarifa rose languidly and came to sit at his feet. She allowed him to take her hands, which he put to his lips.

"Never have I seen anyone dance like this," he told her. "Who are you—a sprite from the dark world?"

"I am Tarifa, daughter of Bandonna, Queen of the Triana."

"Ah, I have heard of Bandonna! The great flamenco, best of them all."

"I am as good; she has taught me all she knew," cried Tarifa. "And I am a great witch!"

"Yes," said Hobarra. "Of that I have no doubt." Then, fingering the bag of *duros* in his pocket, he was reminded of his bargain with Santiago. It was a pity to part company with the *gitana* so soon. But he had a feeling she would be a danger to him, and Hobarra did not court unnecessary danger. The bull's horns each Sunday were danger enough.

He said, touching the wet glistening locks on her shoulder, "How would you like to go on a little trip with me, *querida?*"

Tarifa leapt to her feet, her breath making her breasts rise and fall with a rhythm he found enchanting. It was a pity. Perhaps before the evening was over they could be alone in this nicely secluded room. Young Alvarjo would not mind.

"I will go with you," she replied. "Anywhere."

Hobarra exchanged a smile with Santiago.

"You shall not regret it, little one. I leave tonight for Cádiz. From there we will take ship for Mexico, and then to California."

"You go to—California, matador?"

"*Sí.* To see what the New World looks like, to rest myself a little. I sail on the same ship with Señor Alvarjo. Will you come?"

"I have already asked your mother's permission," said Santiago. "She has given her consent, if you will take her woman, Penti, along."

Tarifa started to make a rude reply, then thought better of it. Penti would make a good servant for herself and Hobarra in their travels, and they would not have to pay her anything. Penti would not dare disobey Bandonna.

"I will come, matador."

Afterward, Tarifa recalled her movements only through a haze of joy and confusion. She drank unaccustomed wine from the torero's glass, and later, when Santiago half-carried her downstairs to a waiting coach, she remembered Penti's angry face and Hobarra's smiling one as he pulled her against him on the seat of the coach, which began to jolt over the cobblestones and later to sway from side to side on a rutted roadway. Hobarra addressed her gently, sometimes in Romany, and held his silver brandy flask to her lips.

They saw Santiago again on the quay, where there were many tall masts and a smell of tarred ropes and the sea. Hobarra carried her up a gangplank and laid her gently on a soft bed, while his soft murmur urged her to sleep. She was content. She had never felt as warm and happy and protected in her life. She was with Hobarra; nothing else mattered. He had chosen to make her his own.

CHAPTER 2

It was a typical blue-and-gold spring day in southern California, the day Dona Encarnacion Alvarjo was killed.

She had no premonition of death when she rose at her usual early hour, full of plans on this day of remembered happiness. It was the thirty-first anniversary of her marriage to Don Ygnacio. She had been barely fourteen when she married the young soldier, newly returned from the *frontera del norte* in that vague faraway possession of Spain's, California. In her mind's eye she could still see the soft candlelight in the cathedral in Seville, as she and Ygnacio had stood stiffly before the Bishop, while behind them came the rustle of silk skirts, as her sister-in-law Isabella stooped to straighten the long satin bridal train.

Tonight Encarnacion had planned a surprise dinner for Ygnacio, with all of his old friends present. Invitations had been sent out long ago, carried to pueblo, presidio, and rancho by Santos, the trusted Indian mayordomo of Rancho Loma de Oro with many a strict warning not to let the news reach Don Ygnacio's ears. Of the household only Isabella—Ygnacio's maiden sister who had come from Spain with the bride and groom to make her home with them—and Candelaria, in charge of the household servants, knew of the plans.

Encarnacion felt like a girl again as she dressed in the large square bedroom. It was furnished in heavily carved mahogany that Ygnacio had bought from the Boston brig, *Orion,* the year before at a disgracefully high price in hides and tallow. A gesture of enduring love—but an expensive one. Still, it was delightful to have so many framed mirrors in which to study oneself. And the bed, a vast four-poster affair, was far more comfortable than the first one, made of rough ranch oak laced by rawhide strips, she had shared with her husband.

Their house, too, at first had been a crude one-room adobe built by the Indian peons. The building now served as a kitchen over which Candelaria presided with fat good nature and a high hand. The new fourteen-room adobe had been built when their fifth son, Joaquin, was born twenty-four years ago.

She glanced out the window at the golden land as she did up her still dark, abundant hair under the ornate ivory comb Ygnacio had that morning given her as an anniversary present. He had left at dawn to offer a nuptial Mass for them at Mission San Luis Rey. Now Encarnacion pondered the price she had paid to California for her happiness: their first four sons had died in infancy and lay buried beyond the wall of the family chapel, where Padre Cazon said Mass for them at least once a month.

Joaquin, the first child who had lived beyond a year, and by consequence his mother's favorite, would be coming home from Spain any day now. She could barely wait for his arrival. Encarnacion had thought it foolish to send Santiago, their second oldest child, to return with Joaquin. But Don Ygnacio had wanted at least two of his sons to see Spain. She prayed for their safety daily to St. Christopher, as did Tía Isabella, kneeling at the little shrine in the patio.

Both Encarnacion and Ygnacio came from high-born families. It had been necessary to obtain the King's permission to marry. The Alvarjos were among the very few truly aristocratic families in California. It meant they must live a more restricted life than many of their neighbors. Encarnacion, Tía Isabella, and Ygnacio understood and accepted their position but it had been hard on their children, especially the gay, outgoing Santiago, Encarnacion felt.

She finished her toilet rapidly and turned to kneel for a moment of prayer on the red velvet prie-dieu below the picture of La Macarena. As always, her first prayers were for the safe return of Joaquin and Santiago, and then for the well-being of her family. Encarnacion felt very close to the Holy Mother, for she was essentially and foremost a mother herself. Motherhood had fulfilled and satisfied her greatest needs and desires. She made the sign of the Cross and rose slowly smiling into the face of the painted Madonna. The little candle before the picture sputtered and then went bravely on.

Encarnacion opened the door of her bedroom that led onto the spacious patio. Under the broad red-tiled *galleria* with its long benches and rawhide chairs, fragrant hanging baskets of bright flowers were interspersed with cages of linnets, canaries, and finches, like the bright-plumed birds that had made music in her old home in Seville. She paused to tap gently on Tía Isabella's door.

"Come in." Isabella's voice was low and controlled, always husky in the mornings.

Encarnacion opened the door, smiling. She was a pretty, plump little woman, with a gentleness in her expression that disarmed the most violent opposition before it got fairly started. There had been a time when Isabella Alvarjo had hated her young sister-in-law for coming between her adored brother and herself. But a lifetime under the same roof had changed all that. Now a great bond of affection and sympathy existed between the two women.

"Isabella, dear, do you think Candelaria will remember everything tonight? Nothing must spoil Ygnacio's party. Do you suppose Santos delivered all the messages exactly as I told him to?"

"Of course. Has Santos ever failed you? He worships the ground you stand on. Didn't you save his life when he was a boy and they wanted to shoot him for stealing horses?"

"But that was nothing," protested Encarnacion, coloring prettily. "Nothing whatever. He was a poor misguided neophyte; there were many like him in the early days."

"He has never ceased to be grateful to you. Santos is a good mayordomo, but sometimes I think Ygnacio places too much confidence in him. I do not believe that you can trust Indians to run a rancho the size of Loma de Oro. It is time Ygnacio put Joaquin in charge."

"He will be home soon, God willing," replied Encarnacion. "I pray—I pray—"

Isabella glanced sharply at her sister-in-law. "You do not still have those silly fears?"

"No," lied Encarnacion. "Not anymore. A few days, surely, and he will be back?"

"Of course."

Isabella rose from the stiff high-backed horsehair chair where she had been sitting. She was tall for a Spanish woman, five years older than her brother, as spare and angular as he was, with the proud hawklike profile of the Alvarjos. Her thick hair was beginning to gray and her brows had grown fuller over her heavy-lidded black eyes, giving her an austere look. But the children, especially the gay, irresistible Santiago, had early discovered another side of her, a passionate loyalty to his causes wholly unlike his father's rigid discipline. Tía Isabella was the only member of the household who dared openly defy and criticize Don Ygnacio; she was held in reverence, even awe, by her nephews and nieces.

That did not mean that they found Tía Isabella less strict than their father. Isabella's wrath was more to be feared, for she did not forget an infraction so quickly, and was liable to mete out a longer period of penance. But each child knew that Tía Isabella would stand by him in his hour of need and that the punishment, if harsh, would be deserved.

"Ygnacio rode to the Mission early?" asked Isabella.

"He went to celebrate an anniversary Mass for us, *carita*. He gave me this comb before he left. Is it not beautiful?"

"It is very lovely. I was with him on the *Clara Lou* when he bought it from Capitán Meade."

"You knew it would go with my ivory necklace. It was very kind of you, *querida*."

Isabella turned away, for she loved this little sister-in-law now as she could never have loved a sister of her own. She went to the walnut bureau, opened a drawer, and brought out a wide package wrapped in a white Chinese shawl.

"I bought this at the same time," she said simply. "Open it now."

"But you shouldn't have done this. Everything from Capitán Meade's ship costs a fortune!"

"Open it."

Encarnacion laid the wide package on the high tester bed and unwrapped the exquisite white-lace shawl. Inside a wooden camphor box were layers of fine silk and linen already made into baby clothes, beautifully handworked and embroidered with minute trimmings of fine lace.

"Isabella! How—how beautiful!"

"If it is a girl they will suit her. If a boy, well—we will use them anyway."

Encarnacion came swiftly to kiss her sister-in-law's cheek and there were tears in her large dark eyes. "So thoughtful and lovely of you, my dear Isabella. What would we all do without you?"

Isabella cleared her husky throat and began to smooth the bedcover and replace the infant clothes carefully in the camphor wood box.

"Isabella?"

"Yes?"

"I—I want to ask you something, and you mustn't be angry. Promise?"

"Of course. What is it?"

"If—anything happened to me," Encarnacion spoke in a rush, tumbling over her words, "would you promise to look after Ygnacio and the children as I would look after them? They depend upon you, we all do. Will you promise— now?"

"What nonsense is this?" Isabella began. Then, seeing the strange fey light in her sister-in-law's eyes, she felt a cold fear strike at her own heart. "Of course," she replied stiffly. "And now enough of this, Encarnacion, we have much to do for the fiesta tonight. Have you forgotten?"

Encarnacion, she saw with relief, was herself again. The cloud had passed. "Yes, *querida*, we must hurry. Where are the girls?"

"Dolores and Soledad should be in the chapel."

In the small family chapel built into the east wing of the house that faced the rolling beige and green oak-dotted valley, Soledad was helping her older sister Dolores arrange bouquets of roses and larkspur in silver vases on the small white altar. From the thick-set window, she could see the white pile of Mission San Luis Rey in the far distance, looking to her child's eye like toy buildings spread out a few miles inland from the sea.

Dolores genuflected before the altar and went to light the vigil candles at either end. Though just fourteen, she was tall like her aunt Isabella. And she was that rare type, a true Spanish blonde. Her skin was as fair as a magnolia petal, her hair a light gold, and her eyes under fair brows more gray than blue. Dolores had her mother's devout gentleness with everything around her. She was the peacemaker of the family. When tempers flared as they often did among the stormy Alvarjo men, it was Dolores who patiently tried to turn wrath into tolerance and forgiveness.

Soledad plopped down a vase irreverently and made a scant bow before the altar. She drew the white *rebozo* back on her dark hair. The long braids hanging down her back fell well below the lace.

"It is little enough to do. Why do you always complain? What if you were like Luisa and Margarita Soto; their mother makes them spend one day a week in the kitchen learning to cook."

Soledad made a face. "I would not spend a day in the kitchen with that fat pig Candelaria. Do you hear how she talks to the maids, as if they were her servants and she owned Loma de Oro?"

Dolores laughed and took her sister's arm. They had breakfasted earlier with the other children, but it was the custom for the women of the family to gather in the patio or on the wide *galleria* for a chocolate hour each morning.

Since the weather was fine the two girls rounded the corner of the chapel and entered the patio. It was the favorite spot in the entire hacienda. Enclosed by the house itself, it was open on one end with a vista of the valley and Mount Palomar rising majestically above the serrated foothills.

A horseman, starting at the gate, a full two miles from the ranch yard over gently rolling hills, could trace the eucalyptus-lined avenue to its final destination at the broad steps of the hacienda Loma de Oro itself. A pleasant road brightened in early spring by patches of yellow mustard; and higher on the hills the stabbing white blossoms of the yucca, like ivory candles pointing toward heaven. Live oaks dotted the rounded hills, providing shade for the herds of horses and long-horned Spanish cattle.

Don Ygnacio had laid out the road in 1785 shortly after taking up his grant of fifty square leagues, a royal grant from the King in appreciation of his military service. Don Ygnacio had built patiently and well, as the many substantial houses and outbuildings could testify. With the help of Indian neophytes hired from Mission San Luis Rey, he had erected his spacious home of four-feet-thick adobe bricks with red-tiled roof and enclosed patio, after the fashion of that other home left behind him in his dear Madrid.

Don Ygnacio's house was two-storied, an unusual thing for California houses, and it boasted a tiled courtyard as well as a wide tiled veranda running the full length of the front and supporting a balcony above. In back, away from the house itself, were the outdoor kitchen with its separate covered oven looking like a giant beehive, the huge open barbecue pit where two or three whole steers could be roasted at the same time, the servants' quarters, the sad-

dle room, containing Don Ygnacio's exquisite silver
mounted equipment. The blacksmith's shop, and the leather shop where old Pablo braided his slender rawhide strips
into supple romals, bridles, hackamores, and 100-foot
eighteen-plait *reatas,* including *la reata larga,* that only the
most accomplished vaquero could throw. Beyond were the
vegetable gardens, and the fields of barley for the blooded
Alvarjo horses. Back of these, near the spring that gushed
forth from the rocky ledge of Loma de Oro, that nob of
golden hill from which the ranch took its name, were the
breaking corrals, the bull pen, and the half-mile racetrack,
so popular at fiestas and on Sundays.

Don Ygnacio raised blooded palomino horses. The stud,
golden-coated Khalid, he had brought from Andalusia
himself. Khalid's ancestors were the golden horses of Ter-
razas, sent to Mexico by Queen Isabella. Since coming to
California, the Alvarjo family had collected and bred
horses of that color only for their private use. It was hard
to say which had the more pride in blood or bearing, Don
Ygnacio's sons, or his flashing-eyed palomino horses.
Wherever a golden coat gleamed, a white mane tossed, or
a daring rider swept through the crowd at breakneck speed,
it went without saying that both could only have been bred
on Loma de Oro.

The patio of his hacienda was Don Ygnacio's pride and
joy. The entire floor, save for the flower borders along the
sides; the two splashing fountains, one at each end of the
100-foot quadrangle; and the soil at the base of the huge
feathery pepper tree in the center, was tiled. Not with
crude terra-cotta tiles made by the neophytes that lined the
walks and verandas, but with a delicate Moorish mosaic
imported from Castile. The marble fountains had also
come from Spain. Flowers grew in a riot of color along
the edges of the deep veranda, in jars and pots on the
veranda itself, suspended in pottery bowls on rawhide
thongs from the rafters above. Swallows and doves roosted
beneath the roof tiles, and Doña Encarnacion's little caged
birds sang and twittered from the balcony above. Orange
and lemon trees blossomed in the corners of the patio amid
the flowering shrubs, and an ancient grapevine climbed its
twisting way up the pillars to the balcony and along the
balustrade above like a friendly fragrant serpent.

Dolores and Soledad found their mother and Tía Isabella seated at a table beneath the pepper tree sipping chocolate from tiny Dresden cups, each with a stick of cinnamon floating on top.

Tía Isabella poured chocolate from a matching Dresden pot into two cups and their mother added a sprig of cinnamon from the little dish at her elbow and handed them to her daughters.

"Querida, that white *rebozo* is most becoming. You wear white like an angel, doesn't she, Isabella? We must get you a new white gown and a shawl to match when the next Boston ship comes."

"A satin dress, Mother?" asked Soledad, gulping her chocolate greedily.

"Satin is too old for a child of ten," said Isabella severely.

"Silk, dear. We will get you a white silk one to wear at fiestas," Encarnacion said. "And what would you like, Dolores?"

Dolores lowered her eyes and colored prettily. How long the child's eyelashes were, thought her mother, and how exquisite her profile, like a drawing of the Madonna herself with the same gentle self-effacing manner that the Holy Mother must have had.

"There is nothing," murmured Dolores.

"A new shawl, perhaps?"

"I have plenty of shawls, Madre."

"Well, you shall pick out something. Perhaps even a comb like the lovely one your father just gave me. Soon you will be putting up your hair."

Dolores flushed a deeper pink. Some of the girls of her acquaintance had married already—her own mother had been fourteen when she married—but there was a paralyzing shyness in Dolores, except among her own family, that made her cling fiercely to the protection of childhood.

Tía Isabella, who was aware of this, and who had experienced something like the same emotion herself when she was a girl, said, "It is no longer fashionable for girls to grow up so quickly." She put down her cup and stood, drawing her fine black Canton lace shawl over her high, narrow shoulders. "I am going to speak to Candelaria about the sweet for the fiesta tonight," she said.

"Thank you, *querida*." Encarnacion glanced briefly at her lovely blonde daughter. Someone had already spoken to Don Ygnacio about Dolores—Don Julio Marcos, who had inherited the large and prosperous Rancho Bolsa de los Coyotes in the valley. There was something Encarnacion did not quite like about Don Julio. But, as Isabella had said, girls did not grow up so quickly these days.

CHAPTER 3

Santos Luqueste was disturbed as he kneed his horse into the redwood hitching rack near the kitchen and prepared to dismount. He did not know why he was so uneasy in his mind, as if he had committed a mortal sin and forgotten to confess it to the Padre. But it was there, like a weight on his spirit. He did not like it. His people would call it the Black Feeling. The spreading of the black hawk, Atzut's, wings over the spirit. Santos had not often had this feeling. Only twice in his lifetime. Once, before his mother died, and once when his brother Quito had been killed by a grizzly bear in the mountains beyond San Juan.

He kicked his thick-heeled muleskin *botas* out of the heavy oak stirrups and swung to the ground. The enormous rowels of his spurs, which were seldom detached from his heels, rang and spun on the sun-baked earth as he bent to loosen the saddle. He was always unhappy when forced to tie Marca to the servants' hitching rail outside the kitchen. He never failed to apologize profoundly to the big blond stallion, a Christmas gift from Don Ygnacio two years before, and Santos' most prized possession. The

mayordomo was the only person outside the Alvarjo family who rode upon, much less owned, one of the blooded
golden palominos sired by Khalid. And Marca, so named
for the small white spot on his rump caused by an early injury, was to Santos family friend, companion at work and
play, and the sharer of his innermost secrets.

Santos rubbed the big stallion's muzzle gently with his
rough hand. The first joint of the middle finger was missing, from a careless dally taken on a *reata larga* during his
first days as a neophyte vaquero at Mission San Luis Rey.

Santo was a new type of California vaquero. His father
had been mayordomo in charge of one of the first cattle
herds of Mission San Diego, at the very beginning of the
California Missions. Santos had spent the first part of his
childhood there, living in a brush shelter just outside the
Mission gates with his mother, brothers, and sisters, watching wide-eyed between the spaces of the rough brush and
pole corral, as his father and the other fearless young Indian neophytes were taught by the Padres to ride—hard
and ruthlessly, with complete disregard for danger. But it
was not until his father moved his family to the new Mission San Luis Rey, and Santos' own apprenticeship began,
that he had learned from Father Cazon what it meant to
gentle a fine horse after he had been broken to ride.

Father Cazon, ankle-deep in corral dust, the crow's-feet
showing at the corners of his blue eyes, had shown the
young Santos how to preserve the horse's mouth and teach
him to respond and work without a bit. It was the Padre's
contention that a well-broken hackamore horse could answer to any command as perfectly as a bitted one. Perhaps,
thought Santos, it was Father Cazon's love of all animals
that made him want to spare them the cruelty of the harsh
bit, for the deep-spaded Spanish bits were brutal. Many a
horse bled constantly while his *hidalgo* owner was in the
saddle.

In the Mission corrals young Santos learned his trade,
but with far more skill and understanding than his forebears. Like other Indian children who had grown up on a
pony's back, watching the daily chores performed by the
neophyte vaqueros, Santos himself, had become an accomplished vaquero. These were the men who spent their
lives in the saddle and tended the enormous herds of cattle

spread over hundreds of thousands of acres as easily as if
they had held them in a corral—a long cry from the first
frightened savages who, seeing the mounted conquistadores, had superstitiously worshipped them as some sort
of centaur—half-human, half-beast.

Many of the most intelligent vaqueros were apprenticed
to someone in the nearest presidio. Some became expert
talabarteros (saddlemakers), or skilled farriers and work-
ers in iron. But the cream of the horsemen became mayordomos in charge of the distant ranchos belonging to the
Missions, or as in Santos' case, hired out at their own
request to wealthy landowners who would be responsible
for them.

Santos had first known Don Ygnacio in his boyhood
days when the young Spaniard had served at the San Diego
presidio. He had held the young officer's horse, even in
those days a blooded palomino, and had run small errands
for the aloof yet kindly Spaniard. Never did Don Ygnacio
fail to reward a service or to find time to compliment a
small, ragged Indian boy for a job well done. Santos remembered when Don Ygnacio returned from a long absence with his pretty young bride and haughty young sister, and retired to his land grant beyond the newly founded
San Luis Rey Mission. It was with joy that Santos found
himself ensconced with his family at the new Mission,
where Don Ygnacio was a frequent caller, and from which
he later recruited the Indians to help build the big new
house he would present to his charming wife on their
seventh wedding anniversary.

Santos could still feel the heat of that Sunday in August
when he came out of the church after morning Mass, and
saw Don Ygnacio stepping down from Khalid's glossy
back.

"*Buenos días,* Don Ygnacio." Santos had swept his wide
sombrero and bent his back low in greeting, as the Padres
had taught him. The San Luis Rey Indians were the most
civilized, superior, and well-trained Indians in all the chain
of Missions, the pride and joy of their beloved Father
Peyri.

"*Buenos días,* Santos. I have come to speak with Padre
Peyri about you. Tell me, Santos, would you care to come
and live at Loma de Oro and work for me?"

Santos had felt his heart leap like a bird from a treetop,

the very breath stopping in his lungs for pure pride and joy, yet for the life of him he could not utter a word. He stood a tall, heavily muscled young Indian, his thick black hair tied into a neat queue and gathered up high with ribbons to fit under his wide-brimmed *poblano*. He was thankful that it was the Lord's Day and that he was wearing his best and not his working clothes, for like all Indians he was vain of his appearance. The side seams of his tight, blue, cloth pants buttoned all the way down the leg to his heavy *botas de ala* (winged boots), and the soft buckskin shoe beneath had a neatly turned-up toe that made the jingling spurs more musical when one walked. His red sash, tightly bound below his short jacket, was a new one, a gift on St. Anthony's day, the day of the Mission's founding, from Father Peyri himself. His open-necked white shirt was as spotless as his sister's many washings could make it. Into the scabbard tucked inside his right *bota* was the ever-present long knife, indispensable to the vaquero at work, at table, and to defend himself. Over his left shoulder was folded the muticolored wool serape woven for him on the Mission looms by his mother before she died.

Father Peyri, coming from the private patio behind the sacristy, saved his young neophyte vaquero. "Ah, Don Ygnacio, a pity you did not arrive in time for Mass."

"I shall make a long visit, Padre, and a gift to St. Francis that our coming child may grow to maturity. It is difficult for my wife to believe that one will be spared us after burying our first four sons."

"Faith, my son. One must always have faith in God's divine will and providence. I shall offer up a Benediction and the next morning Mass for your intention."

"*Muchísimas gracias*, Padre."

"Santos, why do you stand there like a statue? Go, *niño*, join the others at the games while Don Ygnacio and I take a cup of wine."

"If you don't mind, Padre," said Don Ygnacio, "it is about Santos that I have come."

Father Peyri's round face lighted up with a smile. "Do you need the loan of my best vaquero, Don Ygnacio?"

"I would like to hire him as mayordomo of Loma de Oro, with your permission, Padre Peyri."

Father Peyri pursed his full lips. "Mayordomo of so

large a rancho is a grave responsibility for a young neo-phyte, Don Ygnacio!"

"I have every confidence in Santos," Alvarjo replied quickly. "I will be responsible for him in every way. Haven't I known him since he was a boy?"

As the priest hesitated, Santos suddenly found his voice and to his consternation, after having been held back so long, the words poured forth like a torrent.

"Padre, if you please, may I speak? It would give me great pleasure to serve Don Ygnacio, if you will give your permission. I have served him before, as a boy in San Diego, when I used to hold his beautiful palomino and run errands at the presidio. I will work long and hard for the Rancho Loma de Oro, and I will ride to Mass every Sunday and say my beads and remember to say all my prayers, morning, noon, and night. And on feast days I will light a candle and go without eating that I may offer it up for all my sins, and for the good of my benefactors."

Santos halted, the breath gone from his lungs, sweat beading his anxious young face.

"Ah," said the Padre lightly. "And Santos has always been considered one of our silent ones. So you wish to serve Don Ygnacio?"

"*Por favor*, Padre."

"You will not forget all that you have learned here at the Mission, my son?"

"No. I will always remember, Padre."

"You understand that the work will be hard, the responsibility great?"

"*Sí*, I understand, Padre."

"Then go, with my blessing. Get your things and say good-bye to your family while Don Ygnacio and I discuss the terms of your hire. And tell the mayordomo I said you might keep your horse and saddle."

Tears sprang to Santos' eyes as he knelt in the dust at the feet of the short gray-robed figure. "Thank you, Padre. Thank you!"

Peyri made the sign of the Cross over him, and a moment later the young Indian fled as much in shame at his sudden tears at leaving the Padre, as at his unaccountable actions before the new master he wished to serve.

But his choice had been well placed. Over the years as

Loma de Oro and the Alvarjo family had prospered and grown, so too had Santos grown in stature and understanding. Though Don Ygnacio took more personal interest in his holdings than most well-born California hacendados, it was really Santos who was responsible for the wide, spreading lands and steadily increasing herds of Loma de Oro. It was also Santos to whom the servants came first with their troubles and problems, and he who presented them to Don Ygnacio for final settlement.

As the Alvarjo children came along (not one of them had died, Dona Encarnacion was fond of pointing out, since Padre Peyri had given them Santos), he taught each of them to ride, pointed out to them the wonders of nature so much a part of his native heritage, and watched over their well-being like a rough but benevolent angel. Their faults he recognized and forgave, their secrets he kept inviolate, their undying confidence and affection were his. In the nearly twenty-five years of his stewardship of Loma de Oro, he had never displeased the Alvarjos by thought, word, or deed.

Santos remembered this as he reached up to scratch the satiny skin under Marca's thick white mane. Never since coming to Loma de Oro had he felt this unshakable gloom, this heaviness of spirit.

"You know I am troubled," he told Marca as the big stallion turned to nibble playfully at his shirt-sleeve. "We have not had days like this, you and I." He sighed and pushed back the sombrero from the black silk kerchief tied over his head and knotted in the back until the braided strap caught against his bronzed throat. He glanced down at his *botas,* which were muddy where he had stopped to examine a drying spring in the hill pasture. Candelaria would scold when he soiled her kitchen floor.

"I have no stomach for food," he told Marca. "Nor for Candelaria. But a man must do what he must do." Of late this had become a catchphrase with him, reflecting a fatalism that until now had been alien to his nature.

He strode around the corner and stepped up onto the long veranda fronting the kitchen, his spurs ringing on the tiles.

Two of the younger, prettier kitchen maids popped their heads out of a nearby window and gave him a giggling greeting, only to disappear like puppets on a string at Candelaria's lusty command.

Santos sat down on a bench near the kitchen door and stretched out his legs. He was tired, and that was something else new to him, never until this year had he known what it was to grow weary in the saddle. True, he was getting old, forty-two his next birthday, and there were many of his friends battered by the elements and crippled by range accidents who could no longer ride and must return to the Indian *rancherías* or the charity of the Missions or pueblos, a sad thing for a man whose life had been spent in the saddle.

Candelaria came outside when she smelled his *cigarrillo*. For many years it had been a little ritual between them. Santos always announced his arrival by clattering his spurs along the veranda tiles, seated himself on the same bench, now grooved and worn satin smooth from the vaquero's leather *armitas*, and lighted his first *cigarrillo* of the day. Then Candelaria would make her studied appearance.

She had been a young kitchen maid when Santos first came to Loma de Oro, a plumply pretty girl brought by the young Alvarjos from Mexico on their bridal trip to California. Under Isabella's tireless tutelage she had become a fine cook and housekeeper, and had taken her place in the hacienda second in command only to Tía Isabella, who took as much of the household cares off her sister-in-law's shoulders as possible. Since Encarnacion was often ill or indisposed or preoccupied with her husband or her children, this meant that Isabella and Candelaria between them ran the Alvarjo household. They made a good team, the quietly efficient Isabella with her sense of duty and decorum, and the voluble, commanding Candelaria.

At thirty-eight Candelaria was, thought Santos, a more handsome woman than when he had first known her. As she came to take her place on the bench beside him, her wide body encased in voluminous skirts of dark calico, a stiffly starched lace-trimmed apron over her ample lap and breasts, he found her air of arrogant confidence more pleasing than youthful charms. Today her dark hair, parted in the center, was drawn up behind a high-backed tortoiseshell comb and she wore large gold hoops in her ears. The earrings glinted in the sun when she held her head sideways.

"Buenos días, mayordomo. You are late. All of the other vaqueros ate an hour ago. You understand that it is impossible to keep food fit to eat when you tarry so. Besides, I have need of the ovens; we celebrate tonight as you know."

"I regret that I am late, señora, but it was necessary for me to see why the spring dries up in the hill pasture so early in the season."

Though Candelaria had been a widow since her first year at Loma de Oro, having married a young Mexican, Don Ygnacio's first mayordomo, who was killed while breaking a wild horse, everyone at Loma de Oro addressed her as señora out of deference to her position.

"If you have taken the time to be late," said Candelaria, "could you not take a moment more to clean the mud from your feet?"

"I will do so before I come in to eat."

"And when may that be?" Candelaria asked in mock anger. She knew perfectly well that Santos would not enter the kitchen until he had finished his *cigarrillo.*

"In a moment, *señora.*"

His brooding glance swept the spacious kitchen courtyard, where servants chattered at their various tasks, and children played.

"What is troubling you, *amigo mío?*"

Santos brought his dark gaze back from the gay, laughing scene in the sunny courtyard to Candelaria's serious brown eyes.

He shrugged his heavily muscled shoulders. "I do not know. A foolishness that has come upon me. Like something weighing me down. I grow old, *amiga.*"

"You are not ill?"

"No. Only in my spirit. Perhaps all I need is to go to confession." His expression changed and he tossed away his *cigarrillo.* "Come. I am hungry."

She rose and preceded him through the doorway but barred his way as he was about to enter. "I thought you were going to clean your *botas,* hombre?"

"Yes, señora, I will only be a moment." When she used that tone there was nothing to do but obey.

Her voice came gaily from the kitchen. "When you are finished, I have some fruit for you to give that beast Marca."

* * *

Don Ygnacio Jesus Maria Alvarjo found that his mind was wandering all during the Mass that he had come this distance, breakfastless, to offer up in thanksgiving. He was profoundly grateful for all the gifts God had bestowed upon him, and all his life he had remained devout, but today, try as he would to concentrate on the ritual of the Mass, on Father Peyri's vestment-clad figure on the altar, on the singing of Father Peyri's superbly trained Indian choir, the finest in all the Missions, he could not seem to keep his thoughts where they belonged. Senseless fears and misgivings besieged him. Worry about his two eldest sons, who were long overdue from Spain. This last child, coming when his wife should be at the end of bearing children. The drought that Santos had shown him was drying up the springs•and water holes earlier than usual this spring. The vague uneasiness that had come over all California since the declaration of Mexico's independence from Spain, and the increasing talk of secularizing the Missions.

Don Ygnacio knew that Father Peyri and Father Cazon would advise him to put all his worries and troubles in the hands of the Lord. But Don Ygnacio was finding faith harder and harder to come by as he grew older. Could it be that he grew too worldly, too far from the simple paths of faith and truth that God had meant him to follow? He wasn't sure.

He left the moment Mass was ended, not even waiting to speak to the Padres or to his young son, Francisco, who was a member of the Mission *escolta* then on duty at the barracks. He mounted El Capitán, and rode out of the Mission yard and into the wide-mouthed valley like one followed by demons.

Work parties of Mission Indians going out to their daily tasks glanced up from the roadside in puzzled astonishment. Don Alvarjo did not often spur a horse so.

Feeling El Capitán's warm sides between his legs, Don Ygnacio knew that the powerful stallion also sensed the odd change in his master, and had no liking for it. He arched his long neck and put back his small, pointed ears flat to his delicate head.

For miles they fled at breakneck speed over the floor of the valley, verdant with spring greenery and fragrant with

a carpeting of wild flowers. It was Ygnacio's favorite time
of year and this his favorite ride, yet hé did not pause to
enjoy it. When at last he pulled El Capitán to a walk he
was surprised to find himself at the entrance to his neighbor Don Zenobio Sanchez's Rancho Santa Teresa.

Conscious of his own hunger and thirst and of the panting stallion beneath him, he turned in at the winding road
that led to the hacienda. Perhaps fate had brought him
here. Often in the past when he was troubled and unable to
unburden himself to the Padres he had found satisfaction
and a sympathetic ear at Don Zenobio's.

Ygnacio walked his horse slowly along the dusty road
that wound picturesquely between giant live-oaks and
crossed a lively stream on a newly built wooden bridge.
At nearly fifty-nine, he was a Spanish grandee of the old
school, his soldierly erect carriage and still-lithe figure clad
in black velvet jacket and trousers decorously embossed
with silver braid, a flat crowned wide-brimmed sombrero,
his thin hawklike features accentuated by long sideburns
and the sharply pointed goatee affected by all Castilian
gentlemen. His hair and beard, though streaked with gray,
were still abundant and the deep-set piercing black eyes
could flash as hotly as ever with their tightly leashed passions. Only pure Castilian blood flowed in his veins and
Don Ygnacio never allowed himself to forget his origin.
He was a man of pride. Pride had allowed him to master
his own emotions and drives, to remain a devoted husband
and father, a loyal soldier and patriot, a kindly, benevolent ruler of his own domain. That he often ruled both
family and friends by a petty despotism, he was completely
unaware.

The Santa Teresa, only half the size of Loma de Oro,
was nestled in an attractive section of the Rey Valley and
spilled over into the rounded foothills and climbed the
tall mountains toward the desert beyond. Don Zenobio, a
bachelor and an old soldier and Indian-fighter who had
come to California with Anza's first expedition, had
chosen to build his small house between two folds of near
foothills.

"Easier to see the Indians when they come to steal my
horses, and pick 'em off the slopes," he had told Ygnacio
gruffly.

The house, a low square adobe neatly whitewashed after the fashion of the houses of the capital at Monterey, where Zenobio had served his last years in the army, was over-shadowed back and front by two huge and venerable oaks. In the early-morning light the little house gleamed against the soft green-and-brown hillsides. No one was stirring. The only live things in sight were the few horses that day or night stood saddled at every ranch door hitch rack: no Californiano would think of walking a step when there was a horse to be had. It was an old joke that a Californian would rather crawl ten yards on hands and knees to reach a horse than walk a yard on his own two feet. Everything possible was accomplished on horseback, and very little that could not be was ever attempted by the *gente de razón.*

As Don Alvarjo rode into the shady ranch yard the three indolent ponies tied to the hitchrack lifted their heads and began to nicker at El Capitán.

The golden stallion gave a short piercing whinny and stood regally, pawing the ground. Don Ygnacio dis-mounted, leaving the horse untied with only the silver-trimmed reins hanging to ground-hitch his well-trained mount.

The hacienda door was suddenly thrust open by a portly grizzle-haired man with a wild, untrimmed moustache and short beard. He was clutching a bottle of *aguardiente* in one hand and a deck of cards in the other.

"*Madre de Dios!* Ygnacio! Come in, come in, *com-padre.* It is long since you honored the Santa Teresa with a visit. What brings you so far from Loma de Oro at this early hour?"

Ygnacio smiled at his friend. Zenobio looked as if he had been up all night, which was in fact the truth. His small, deep-set eyes were red-rimmed, and his leathery, lined face wore a pasty look under its welcoming grin. Zenobio Sanchez was not precisely a gentleman. His family had been farmers and tradespeople on a small scale in Mexico, and he himself had spent his lifetime in the army. He limped badly in one leg, the result of an Indian arrow through the hip received in a skirmish along the Colorado in his youth. But in spite of his lack of birth and polish, Zenobio was a loyal and staunch friend, and his genial nature and shrewd good sense often drew men of higher birth and rank to him, as they had drawn Ygnacio Alvarjo.

Following his friend into the long low *sala* with its narrow, deep-silled windows that made the room seem unduly dark after the brilliant sunlight outside, Ygnacio was surprised to find a stranger seated at the center table. He had counted on speaking to Zenobio alone, unburdening himself of his fears and worries, and receiving Zenobio's reassuring council. Now this would be impossible.

"Amigo mío," rumbled Zenobio's rough voice, "I would like you to meet my young friend, Capitán Bartolomeo Kinkaid, of the Boston ship *Arabella,* which he has obligingly anchored at San Juan to pick up the mission hides and tallow. Capitán, may I present my old and honored *compadre,* Don Ygnacio Alvarjo of Rancho Loma de Oro."

"It is a pleasure to make your acquaintance, sir." Kinkaid came to his feet with outstretched hand. He supposed his Spanish sounded as odd as Zenobio's English. The Captain was still startled to hear his name come out "Bartolomeo Keenkhad" in Zenobio's translation.

Don Ygnacio was doubly displeased. Not only was the man a stranger, but he was an Americano, and Alvarjo distrusted all Americanos. He disliked their push and bustle and the greedy eyes he believed they cast on California. No Americano had ever crossed his threshold nor ever would. But his face was a polite mask as he accepted Kinkaid's hand and made a courtly bow in return.

Captain Kinkaid was young to be the master of a vessel, perhaps no older than his eldest son Joaquin, but there was a strength and purpose in the Americano's sea-tanned face and calm gray eyes that told of a boyhood long forsaken, a quality of confident command that Don Ygnacio found himself reluctantly admiring.

The American, broad-shouldered and well over six feet, towered over the two Californians. Save for his light skin and eyes, Alvarjo thought he had an Indian look. The same beardless face, high cheekbones, black hair and brows, and boldly cut profile. The same lean panther grace about his movements. His wide shoulders and broad chest seemed made for the long, brass-buttoned coat of the sailing master.

It had been a good ten years before, as a lad of sixteen, that Bart Kinkaid had made his first voyage up the California coast as a hand before the mast on one of his Uncle Ephraim's ships, the *Mary Kay*. It had been a voyage to remember, for the captain had gone insane off Cape Frio on the return voyage and cut off the cook's hand with a cleaver, and the mate had been forced to put the captain in chains and bring the ship into Boston Harbor himself.

Kinkaid was no novice to terror and bloodshed and man-killing work. Born and raised in Salem, he had lived there until his father, a mate in the Canton trade, had been lost at sea, and his mother had died in a cholera epidemic. Then he and his younger brother Caleb had gone to live with their only living relative, their mother's bachelor brother Ephraim Endecott, a Boston shipowner.

Endecott was a just but undemonstrative man, and having worked his way up from countinghouse clerk to found the Endecott shipping firm, he expected no less diligence from his nephews. The younger, Caleb, from the first preferred a desk to a deck, and was now the company representative in New York. But Bart Kinkaid had been made for the sea.

In the long hard years of his apprenticeship, there was nothing about the sea and ships that did not entrance him, whether in the doldrums becalmed off Rio or in the teeth of a Cape Horn sou'wester.

"Sit down, sit down, gentlemen," invited Zenobio, carelessly tossing a jacket and sash from a chair for Ygnacio. He added conspiratorily to his newest guest, "The capitán and I have been playing monte all night."

Zenobio poured *aguardiente* into three glasses and handed one to each guest. "A toast, señors, to our glorious golden land—California!"

When they had finished, a little potbellied man wearing the remnants of an ancient sergeant's uniform bustled in carrying a huge tray and proceeded to whisk glasses, bottle, and cards from the table to the accompaniment of disapproving clucks and mutterings.

"Pablo, my guests and I are not finished with the *aguardiente!*" bellowed Zenobio.

The little ex-sergeant, Pablo Rubio, who had served Zenobio Sanchez in the army and out for the past forty years, paid not the slightest attention. With neat precision he spread out his master's breakfast, cooked under his own supervision by Marta, the Indian woman who also did their washing and was the only female Zenobio would allow on the rancho. Frijoles, eggs, beefsteak, and a pot of unsweetened chocolate.

"*Borrico!* Do you not see we have two guests? Bring breakfast for everyone. *Pronto!*" shouted Zenobio.

"*Sí*, capitán."

Pablo left the room briefly and returned with a second tray, but he paid scant attention to serving the guests.

When he had gone, Zenobio asked Ygnacio, "You did not tell me why it is you are out so early, *compadre?*"

"It is the anniversary of my marriage. I went to hear Mass at the Mission to offer it up for our thirty-one years of happiness. Encarnacion, of course, could not go." Ygnacio did not know that Santos had delivered an invitation to the celebration some days past, and not by tone or movement did Zenobio give away the fact.

"Ah, thirty-one years, you say? That is a long time, my friend. How is Dona Encarnacion?"

"As well as her condition permits, I think. She worries that Joaquin and Santiago stay so long in Spain. I was perhaps mistaken in sending Santiago to join his brother for the return voyage. He is still young and irresponsible, but I had hoped the culture of the land of his ancestors might improve him. This new generation has no proper sense of pride and decorum. Perhaps we elders have not been stern enough. My own father used the flat of his sword when I was a boy. I still have the marks to show for it, but I knew what it meant to obey."

In spite of his claims to permissiveness, Don Ygnacio was anything but lax in disciplining his children. Each of them knew only too well what it meant to disobey their father. Just before he had left for Spain, Santiago had felt the lash of his father's long black riding whip rising and falling across his bare shoulders because he had come ten minutes late to Mass. For a week he had taken his meals kneeling on the dining-room floor before a low wooden bench with a crucifix before his eyes, while the rest of the family feasted in rigid silence above him. That his mother,

Tía Isabella, or Candelaria would find some way to smuggle food to him later on, was of little consolation in his agony of pain and mortification. Yet his sons and daughters did not hate Don Ygnacio, for once an offense had been suffered and paid for, it was forgotten completely.

Zenobio, mopping up his plate with a piece of tortilla, said, "Obedience is the first rule of life, and the first broken. Did not Adam and Eve first disobey in the Garden of Eden? And are we not still paying the penalty for that disobedience?"

"But our young today do not seem to remember that," sighed Don Ygnacio. He had swallowed a little chocolate, but his usually robust appetite had deserted him. Perhaps he was ill, for the weight of his uneasiness was still upon him.

Captain Kinkaid had pushed back from the table and was lighting a short-stemmed pipe. He knew that he should be getting back to his ship. Anchoring off San Juan Capistrano was always an uncertain thing, what with the dangerous southeasters that made it necessary to anchor with a slip rope always ready; and the putting off and taking on of cargo from the high hill on which the Mission was situated, lowering the heavy hides from the top of the bluff by ropes, and putting them into the boats to remove them to the dancing ship was a ticklish business and one not welcomed by the sailors.

Besides, he had no right to be at San Juan at all. It was necessary for every vessel intending to trade along the coast to first enter its cargo at the seat of the Mexican government at Monterey before commencing its traffic. And the Mexican revenue laws were very strict, demanding that the whole cargo be landed, examined, and taken on board again. This was not only time-consuming, but costly, and had led to a good deal of open smuggling and double-dealing not only by the vessel owners, but by the Californians themselves. There were a number of ways around the difficult rules and regulations. Ships just in from Boston, as Kinkaid's was, filled with a rich and varied cargo, would anchor off one of the coastal islands, unload part of their trade goods, and make a quick and secret foray into the quieter roadsteads, taking on hides and tallow in exchange for their goods. Then, depositing the hides and tallow at the island hideout, reloading with their own trade articles, they would continue on up the coast to Monterey with only half as much cargo to declare, and reload, before legally continuing their trip from port to port.

Sometimes a sister ship would follow, never declaring herself at all at Monterey, but rendezvousing with the legally declared vessel from time to time and exchanging her load of merchandise for the hides and tallow picked up by the first trader. Thus two shiploads of hides could return to Boston for almost the price of one.

In the beginning, there had been a valid reason for the out-and-out smuggling. As Revolutionary troubles began in Mexico in 1810, income from Spain fell off. The Pious Fund, supposed to support and supply the chain of California Missions, was seized for the benefit of the State treasury, who also soon cut off the revenues of the military of California. The Padres, receiving no further stipends, and unable to collect money for the goods they had furnished the presidios over the years, were thrown upon their own resources. They could exist on their own produce, but that was about all. They desperately needed many items, as did the townspeople, the military, and the rancheros, but with all trading save with the infrequent Spanish ships forbidden, the Missions as well as the people of California found themselves faced with the necessity of smuggling goods to and from whatever foreign ships touched their shores.

This rich plum of commerce was soon seized upon by shrewd Boston shipowners. Whole hides for which they paid a dollar or two in cash or trade could be taken to Boston, made into many pairs of shoes, and returned to California to sell at two dollars a pair. The richer the cargo, the more luxurious the items, the quicker they sold to the comfort-starved people of California. Fine hand-carved mahogany furniture; Chinese fireworks; iron-rimmed cartwheels; boots and shoes; clothing of all kinds; silk shawls, scarves, jewelry, fans, carved combs for the ladies; spirits for the men; teas; coffee; spices; crockery; tinware; cutlery; molasses; silks, satins, and velvets by the bolt; fine linen and china—nothing was too rare or costly to sell at a high price in California. A shipowner could become rich in a season or two of trade, and many of them had.

But Kinkaid, who had come to love California and its

easygoing, warm-hearted, hospitable people, realized that
the real opportunity lay in the land itself. What would it
become if American initiative, organization, and drive
were poured into it? It was an idle speculation, but one
he indulged in more and more with each return visit. He
continued to daydream, dimly aware of the murmuring
Spanish voices of his host and Don Alvarjo, until he suddenly realized that his pipe had gone out. Putting it away,
he glanced at his watch and saw with a start that it was
nearing noon. He got to his feet, making his farewells to
the two Californians in his best Spanish.

"Stay, Capitán," urged Zenobio, "and I will ride to the
ship with you after dinner."

Kinkaid shook his head, smiling. "I have much to do,
Don Zenobio. I must see the good Fathers at Capistrano,
and settle with them, and I must see how the loading goes.
San Juan is a difficult anchorage and there is still danger
of sou'easters. We may have to run for it."

"Then return soon, my friend. My house is always
yours; my door is always open."

"Thank you, Don Zenobio. On my return trip from
Monterey I will stop for your hides."

"*Gracias.* They will be ready after the spring roundup
if all goes well, and the thieving Indians have not stolen
half my herd and left me a penniless vaquero." This was
a hollow threat, since Don Zenobio's cattle numbered in
the thousands. *"Vaya con Dios, amigo!"*

Zenobio and Ygnacio watched Kinkaid mount his horse,
one of the sleepy trio at the hitchrack bearing the San Juan
Capistrano Mission brand on one hip. In spite of his in-
congrous seaman's garb, Don Ygnacio noted that Kinkaid
rode well as he galloped out of the ranch yard waving his
gold-braided cap.

Zenobio put his arm warmly around his friend's shoulders and said in a more serious tone than he was in the
habit of using, "That is a man of stature, *amigo.* He has
done me a service or two while I was starving and in debt
at Monterey, like all the other military in California, and
always he goes out of his way to be of service to the
Padres though he is not a Catholic. I believe he wishes to
settle here someday."

"There are too many of his breed here already," replied

Alvarjo bitterly. "They are all avaricious and greedy. Do
not be misled by his seeming charity, Zenobio."

"I think you are mistaken, *amigo*. You have not lived
as closely among these Boston traders as I have. You have
been isolated in this charming valley of ours. Shrewd traders they may be, that I will grant you, with ways different
from our own, but that they are all men without feeling
or honor I refuse to believe. And there are others who
feel as I do."

"I still say they are not to be trusted," said Ygnacio,
and added loftily, "certainly not to be invited into your
home."

Zenobio threw back his head and laughed. *"Amigo*, I
do not have your high birth and pride to contend with,
por Dios. I would invite a grizzly bear or the Devil himself into my house, if he pleased me! Come, it is time for a
glass of *aguardiente* and a talk about what really brought
you to the Santa Teresa."

Encarnacion paused for a moment on the chapel steps
before leaving the patio, and stood looking down into the
valley.

Like Ygnacio, she loved spring the best, before the valley turned sere and golden brown, as it did soon after the
spring rains. The canyon which led into the valley from
the sea, called Quechinga by the gentiles, in which San Luis
Rey Mission itself was located, had as neighbor to the
south the port of San Diego with its pueblo, mission, and
presidio at a distance of thirteen leagues. To the north lay
Mission San Juan Capistrano, twelve and a half leagues
away. And behind, to the east, lay the frowning jagged
peaks of the Sierra Madre like broken, pointed teeth
gnashing at the soft blue sky.

The countryside between mountain and sea, consisting
of canyons and gently rolling hills, gave the valley a waving undulating look like an ocean bed.

Though the Mission lands adjoined her husband's property on one end, Encarnacion had never been quite sure
where the line of demarcation lay. She only knew that for
farther than her eye could now see everything belonged to
the Alvarjos of Loma de Oro.

Behind and above the hacienda lay the golden nob of

hill for which Ygnacio had named their home. A fully
rounded hillock, visible for miles and at this time of year
a sea of waving gold, covered horse-high with billowing
wild mustard. On top of it, Ygnacio had built a small cabaña with wide veranda, where on clear days there was a
magnificent view of the sea beyond the near foothills. His
Eagle's Nest he called it. Here he spent a part of each
day, reading his favorite books, staring into the distance
across his broad lands. "A man needs a retreat," Encarnacion had told Isabella placidly, "where he can commune
with himself. No one must disturb his privacy when he is
there." And no one but Ygnacio ever went to the top of
Loma de Oro.

Encarnacion took her flowers and walked around the
chapel to the little family burying ground beyond, a pleasant, grassy plot enclosed with a low wall, a fragrant lacy
acacia tree at one end. The four white headstones were
arranged neatly within the shade of the tree, which was
now tufted with plumes of pungent yellow flowers.

Encarnacion knelt down and, taking up the small vases
of water she always left there, began to discard the withered blossoms of yesterday, replacing them with fragrant
fresh ones from her basket.

She was dimly aware of the swift drum of a horse's
hooves on the hard-packed earth of the pasture beyond
the graveyard. Glancing up in idle curiosity she saw a rider
coming at a fast clip, waving his arms and legs. Curiously
she watched him weaving this way and that. Encarnacion
was used to seeing men ride swiftly and in all manner of
careless ways. The vaqueros, even her own sons, could do
anything including standing on their heads while their
horses ran at full gallop. But there was something strange
about this rider. He was still coming fast, far too fast for
safety in that rough hilly pasture, she now realized, and
he seemed to be singing or shouting something. She knew
it was not one of her own family by the color of the horse,
a lean bay that seemed half-crazed in his wild headlong
flight, as did his careless rider.

The pounding of the hooves came louder and louder,
and Encarnacion felt a pang of alarm. No mere vaquero
on Loma de Oro would dare ride into any enclosed portion
of the hacienda itself—that would have been a whipping

offense, and no vaquero would chance being torn to ribbons by Santos' long blacksnake. In the past one or two serious offenders had felt its sting and the loneliness of banishment from the valley. No one would take in a vaquero who had proven himself unworthy to serve on Loma de Oro, for it was known far and wide that Don Ygnacio was a just, if stern, employer.

The hoofbeats were a rising thunder now and Encarnacion could hear the creak of straining saddle leather, the sobbing breath of the laboring horse, while above the din and dust rose the guttural shout and black cursing of what could only be a drunken vaquero.

With a start Encarnacion raised her head again, still kneeling at the graves of her children. Then in one terrorized flash she saw the foam-flecked horse blindly leap the low wall and the madly grinning sweat-streaked face of a half-breed vaquero whom she dimly recognized.

Horse and rider came on like an arrow shot from a diabolically aimed bow. Powerfully, unswervingly, the man's two-inch spurs sunk deep into the maddened, fear-crazed horse's belly.

Straight at her.

She had time to cry out in one piercing, soul-stirring shriek of horror, to see the poor beast try at the last moment to avoid her kneeling body before one flying hoof smashed into the side of her head, another into the softness of her breast.

She fell like a doll, sprawled carelessly among the graves and the scattered flowers.

In the kitchen Santos was just sitting down at the enormous table that ran nearly the length of the forty-foot room, where the Loma de Oro servants usually took their meals in relays. The number of nondependents who enjoyed food and shelter at Loma de Oro was as unpredictable as the weather. Relatives and friends of the servants, travelers, all enjoyed the open hospitality of the rancho. So it was on all the ranchos in this bountiful, hospitable land. Clothing, food and shelter, a fresh horse, a saddle, money—whatever the need, it was as happily and freely given as the host was affluent and able enough to supply. From the highest ranking to the most lowly, no visitor had ever left Loma de Oro without a gift of some kind, one of the prized pure-blooded palominos, a nosegay of flowers, or a stalk of refreshing grapes to speed the traveler on his way. It was said that Don Ygnacio even kept a plate of gold pieces in his guest rooms to save his visitors the embarrassment, should the need arise, of asking for a loan.

Santos had just put a leg over the wooden bench at the head of the table where he and Candelaria always sat, when he heard the scream.

For an instant every cell in his body and brain seemed to stand still. Then he thought, "This is it. This is the horror, the blackness I have been waiting for so long. It has come. It has come."

He pulled back his leg, barely conscious of Candelaria's bleating, *"Madre de Dios!"* and the stricken faces of the frightened young maids, before he plunged out into the yard racing in the direction from which the cry had come.

He ran as he had never run since boyhood, every muscle and sinew of his body taut. He dimly saw others converging on the *galleria*. Servants, Tía Isabella with a face like chalk, Dolores, Soledad, a mute and dreadful question in their eyes.

He was first, tearing into the chapel, seeing nothing, racing out again, and leaping the gate in the low wall leading to the cemetery.

He saw her there, fallen among the gravestones and littered flowers, the ivory comb a few feet away, her dark hair loose on her shoulders. White-faced and still, except for the dreadful red rose blooming on her left temple and spreading across her cheek and her bosom.

He went to her and touched her gently. She was dead. He was certain of that. His numbed brain could accept no other fact for the moment. She had been like a star in his life, brilliant with warmth and kindness, uncorruptible as the Virgin. Now she lay crushed in the graveyard of her innocent children.

Santos' Indian eyes moved swiftly then, noting the hoof marks, the trampled, bloody grass, the chip out of the low cemetery wall beyond. He touched some hair caught on the bark of the acacia tree, noting its color and texture.

The others were upon him in an instant. Isabella, after one horrified look, was trying to send the children back.

Candelaria lumbering behind her, with all the vaqueros and servants who had been within hearing distance, followed dumbfounded in her wake.

There was not an Alvarjo male on the place. Santos straightened his shoulders, knowing he must take charge, bring order out of rising chaos.

But Isabella surprised him. She was not an Alvarjo for nothing. She spoke commandingly to the girls, and instructed Candelaria to take them to their rooms and fetch them their personal maids, then turned to him.

"Dona Encarnacion is not dead?" she whispered softly to mayordomo.

Santos returned her poignant, level look without speaking. He saw her tremble once, violently, before she checked herself with a mighty effort.

Soledad ran forward and flung herself on her knees beside her mother, crying passionately, "She is not dead! She is not dead! *Madrecita—madrecita mía!*"

Then she straightened up with a ghastly expression on her face and fainted.

Tía Isabella spoke sharply to the servants and they lifted the child gently and bore her off to her room, her sister and Candelaria following with tears streaming down their shocked faces. Santos dismissed the others with a few sharp words.

Left alone, Isabella turned to Santos. She had never shared her brother's and sister-in-law's belief that he, an Indian, was fit to act as mayordomo of her brother's vast holdings. But she realized that her only help in this moment of dire catastrophe must come from him.

"Santos, do you know how this—happened?" A strange numbness made her lips feel thick and stiff.

"A horseman, Señorita Isabella. Surely drunk or insane. He came over that wall."

"A Loma de Oro vaquero?" she asked harshly.

"I do not think so. But I will find out. It is important that I go after him now, that he has no chance to get away."

"No," Isabella said firmly. "You must ride at once to the Mission and get Don Ygnacio and Padre Peyri, or Padre Cazon. You must bring Francisco also, and find the boys. Do you understand?"

Santos knew his place. Ordinarily he would not ques-

tion an Alvarjo. But now native instincts, the dark revengeful instincts of the savage, made him adamant.

"I will send my fastest vaquero to the Mission, señorita,
and to fetch the *muchachos*," he said simply. "I must trail
the murderer of my mistress. Don Ygnacio would expect
me to do so."

In spite of her effort to dominate him, Isabella found her
own eyes wavering before him. "Very well. But you must
hurry. And we must carry her inside."

She broke down then and the tears seemed to well from
her very soul. Better I, she thought, far better that I lay
dead there than sweet Encarnacion, with her husband and
family to mourn her, and the child still unborn within her.
Madre de Dios, what have we all done to deserve this?

Santos stooped and gently gathered his mistress' small
form in his arms. Yet in the long walk to her room where
he tenderly placed her on the carved mahogany bed, only
one thought filled his mind.

Revenge. He meant to kill, to commit murder with his
own hands. He was fully aware of the penalty that would
be exacted of an Indian who dared to kill a man of white
blood. In the graveyard he had recognized the hoof marks,
the color of the horse's hair. He knew whom he sought.
Bruno Cacho. A half-Mexican, half-Indian vaquero whom
Don Ygnacio had whipped off the ranch several months
before for attempting to seduce a ten-year-old Indian
girl. Drunk, the half-breed must have come back to seek
revenge from Don Ygnacio. If so, he had also come armed.

Santos knew that once he learned about his wife, Don
Ygnacio would go after the man himself. Not cautious at
the best of times, he was reckless to the point of insanity
when he was really angered. He must not be killed in turn
by this drunken brute of a vaquero, made careless by his
own black rage. Better that Santos himself reach the murderer first, whatever the consequences, than to lose both
master and mistress in the same ill-fated day.

"I will send riders out at once," he told Tía Isabella,
who still stood staring at her sister-in-law's body, her head
bent and a handkerchief pressed against her mouth. She
did not look up, merely nodded, and he left the house of
weeping women and servants.

A dark purposefulness had settled over his spirit as he

rounded the kitchen and took up Marca's reins. As the horse wheeled gracefully and took off at full gallop, his hand sought the coiled blacksnake whip above his *reata larga*, in Santos' hands a weapon more deadly and terrifying than a gun.

He turned the stallion toward the Sierra Madres, back of Loma de Oro. Bruno Cacho, drunk or sober, would have sense enough to make for the mountains where tracking him would be difficult over the stony cactus-strewn ground, and where he could find refuge in a thousand arroyos or canyons. Even so, Santos would find him. He had to.

CHAPTER 4

Zenobio poured more *aguardiente* and said lightly, "Drink, *amigo mío*, and listen to me."

He was glad he had persuaded Ygnacio to take the noon meal with him, for he had noted that he ate none of the breakfast Pablo had served them. "Listen to an old man's advice. I have no wife and family to worry me, it is true, but that does not mean that I do not have other cares and provocations. My creek and springs are also low this spring. If we have another dry season I shall have to destroy half my horses, and if it grows worse, I shall have to slaughter cattle. So it goes! Without the Boston ships we would all starve. What interest does Mexico or the government take in California—except to collect its wealth? You and I, we have both served our country well, both Spain and Mexico, and outside of our ranchos what have

we got to show for it? My pension has not been paid for
the past ten years. They do not pay the soldiers now, yet
they conscript your young sons for military duty. Does not
Francisco serve at the Mission without pay now?"

Don Ygnacio nodded and sipped his *aguardiente*. He
felt better after having discussed his problems with the
crusty old soldier.

"My friend, unless I am gravely mistaken we are in for
a great many more insults. I hear many rumors from
Mexico."

"Rumors?"

"*Sí*. Capitán Ruiz, at San Diego, has heard the same
things. As you know, he and I fought the Indians together
on the Colorado. We will have a new governor any day
now, *amigo*. José Maria Echeandia. Do you know him?"

Don Ygnacio frowned and stroked his dark goatee. "No,
I do not recall his name."

"A lieutenant-colonel of engineers, a desk soldier. You
will forgive my saying it, *amigo,* a well-born popinjay. That
is what they send to rule us. I have not always agreed with
Luis Arguello but at least he is a soldier and a Californian.

"As if this were not bad enough, Echeandia comes not
only as governor they say, but as Commandante General
of the Californias!"

Don Alvarjo was more than disturbed by the news. He
too, had had his differences with the present governor,
Arguello, but that a Mexican of Echeandia's evident rank
and caliber should be sent to rule California was a bitter
blow indeed. Mexico had no interest in California other
than what she could wring out of her by way of revenues
and services. Absorbed in her own political turmoil, she
had scant time or concern for her distant province, and
California was helpless to alleviate matters.

Zenobio chewed savagely on the end of his *cigarrillo*.

"He brings with him Alferez Zamorano, for whom I
have no affection, and there is word he will put Capitán
Portilla in charge of the presidio. Altogether not a nice
picture, *compadre?*"

Ygnacio found that he had almost forgotten his private
worries in his new concern over the coming political upheaval. He was not a man who took much interest in
politics as a rule, considering himself above its petty strife

and backbiting. But ever since the Mexican flag had been raised at Monterey he had felt a sadness that Spain no longer ruled California, that the eagle had replaced the lion. For he still considered himself a loyal Spanish subject, as did the Franciscan Padres, with a few notable exceptions. It pained him to know that Padre Peyri was one of these. Peyri believed Mexican rule would benefit his Indian neophytes in the long run. In his own heart, Alvarjo knew that there would be little benefit for anyone in California from a greedy, conflict-torn Mexico.

"Is there nothing we can do?" he asked sharply. "Could not Arguello call a junta?"

Zenobio looked at him sadly. *"Amigo mío,* you pay no attention to politics, which is a pity, for whether you like them or not they are every man's business. A junta was called, and by majority vote California agreed to do nothing yet, to remain aloof."

"But there must be—"

Alvarjo's words were cut short by the clatter of hooves in the yard and El Capitán's peculiar keening whinny. He was on his feet in an instant, thrusting open the door, as one of his young vaqueros slid from a sweat-drenched horse and stumbled with exhaustion as he swept off his sombrero in a low bow.

"Pedro!"

"Don Ygnacio," the boy panted, "I have been up and down the valley since I left the Mission—seeking you."

"What is the matter, *muchacho?"* A stiffness had gripped Ygnacio's chest like a metal band.

"Patrón," the vaquero sobbed, fear making his eyes roll and sweat glisten on his lean dark face. "There is trouble —bad trouble—at the hacienda. Santos sent me to fetch you, and to send for Don Francisco and Padre Peyri."

Don Ygnacio stepped forward and fear sent the young vaquero to his knees in the dust.

"What is wrong, Pedro? Tell me! *Instantato!"*

"The Dona Encarnacion—" ·

"The child! The child has come? Speak, or I'll whip you on the spot!"

"No, Don Ygnacio. *Muerto.* The Dona is dead. An accident. They have sent me to fetch you at once, Patrón."

Alvarjo stood transfixed, as if he had been turned sud-

denly into stone. A blinding realization had come over him
at the first words his servant spoke, and then a violent re-
jection of all thought and sound made reality mercifully
recede.

Only gradually, from a great distance, was he aware of
the murmur of voices, of hands touching him gently, leading him to a seat on the veranda. They pushed him down
on it. Someone held a glass to his lips and he drank obediently, slowly at first and then avidly of the burning brandy.
His sight seemed to come back from a great distance, too,
as if he had been gazing through the wrong end of a tele-
scope.

"Ygnacio!"

It was Zenobio's voice, rough with sympathy. "I have
sent for the fastest horses. I am going with you."

Alvarjo roused himself. He ached all over, and his
muscles were stiff. He was surprised that his voice sounded
so calm, for his spirit lay curled and dead within him.

"You haven't a horse faster than El Capitán." He got
to his feet and spoke to the frightened vaquero quietly.
"You have told Padre Peyri and Francisco?"

"*Sí*, Don Ygnacio. They are perhaps at Loma de Oro
by now."

Alvarjo nodded. *"Bueno, muchacho.* You will borrow
one of Don Zenobio's fresh horses with his permission, and
follow."

"*Sí*, señor."

"I am coming too," Zenobio said. But Ygnacio seemed
not to hear. He strode to El Capitán, mounted in one swift
motion, and for the first time in his life sank his spurs
without feeling into one of his cherished golden palominos.

An Indian boy clattered up to the veranda a second
later, holding the bridles of two long-legged chestnut stallions, and Zenobio and the vaquero Pedro mounted and
turned their horses in the direction in which Don Ygnacio
had already disappeared.

"Sangre de Dios!" Zenobio muttered violently under his
breath, for the vaquero had told him briefly how Dona
Encarnacion had been killed. He foresaw the danger and
the carnage that would follow.

The riders traveled noisily and carelessly in the manner
of good horsemen, conscious of the superiority of their

mounts and equipment. The horses, all well-groomed palominos, pranced the Spanish walk on the heels of unshod hooves, lifting tender front toes chest-high in the difficult to master and much-admired gait.

Bright sunlight glinted on stamped leather and silver work, on gold bit chains and polished *tapaderos*, on silver- and gold-thread braid and the brilliant silk and lace that adorned their clothes and sombreros. They were young, in the full exuberance and first flush of their manhood, with the exception of eight-year-old Antonio, bringing up the rear.

Handsome youths, black-haired, olive-skinned, and vital, with a show of dashing arrogant pride. They were Paisanos, the first of the true California born.

Life had been kind to them as it had been gracious to their forebears in this hospitable golden land. With no formal schooling to curtail their outdoor activities, no responsibilities to mar their pleasures, no work to be done, the warm wide-breasted inviting land about them became a joyous playground for high-spirited young Paisanos like the sons of Don Ygnacio.

Though he expected something more of his two eldest sons by way of deportment and learning, Don Ygnacio, like the other rich hacendados, was willing for his younger boys to devote their full time to horses, sports, and the charms of fandangos and guitar-playing.

Having spent all morning racing their golden palominos against the fleet Martinez horses and staying to take the noonday meal with their enthusiastic hosts, the Alvarjos were now returning to Loma de Oro, content, well-fed, and gay of spirit. They were returning the richer, for they had won two fine saddle horses. Little Antonio had insisted upon leading them alone. Now he was having difficulty.

Antonio, a startling miniature replica of Don Ygnacio, had his father's same stubborn streak. Sweat stood out on his thin upper lip, and his hand ached where he held the braided hackamore reins of the Martinez horses behind him.

"Let me take them for a while, Tonito," said Luis, wheeling his stallion in beside his little brother's mount. Luis was a slim young man with a lean good-natured face, and a gentle, sympatheic expression in his soft brown eyes.

"No," snapped Antonio. "I'll bring them in myself! I

want to show them to Santos. I helped win them, didn't I?" It was the first time Antonio had been allowed to ride in a real race, and he was supremely proud that his own Concho had easily won the third lap against young José Martinez, who was fourteen. No one was going to deprive him of bringing the proof of his victory to Loma de Oro under his own power.

"Of course you helped win," Luis said patiently. "But we still have a long way to go. Let me take them while you rest your hand, and then I will give them back to you before we get home."

"No!"

"Don't argue with him, Luis," said Nazario in disgust. "He is nothing but a stubborn donkey, everyone knows that! Let his hand drop off."

Antonio scowled in black hatred at Nazario and stuck out his tongue. Nazario, a thin nervous lad of nineteen, ignored him completely and turned to Luis, who was a year older than himself and his usual confidant.

"Antonio!" Nazario muttered. "We should never have let him come. He is too young. Father would not approve if he knew."

"We do not have to tell him," said Luis.

Nazario brushed the suggestion aside with sharp impatience and Luis glanced across at his brother's thin scowling face. He and their sister Soledad resembled each other a great deal. They shared the same restless, whiplash figure, straight hair, and thin-lipped mouth. "You worry as much as Madre or Tía Isabella," said Luis lightly. "Antonio is just a child, and this was his first win. Let him have the joy of bringing them in. If he loses them we will retrieve them."

Privately, Nazario looked with contempt on Luis' calm outlook on life.

"Antonio is a spoiled brat!" he scowled. His stallion shied suddenly at a jackrabbit and danced sideways under him in a move that would have unseated a less sure rider. Nazario cursed and the heavily plaited rawhide quirt at his wrist rose and fell on the startled horse, who began to buck under him, but Nazario sat in his saddle as easily and disdainfully as if he had been in a rocking chair.

The Alvarjo boys were not in the habit of quarreling

among themselves. They were an unusually close-knit family, naturally affectionate and loyal. But since the last fandango at the Martinez rancho, everyone had known that Nazario was hopelessly smitten with Señorita Rufina Corlona, a visitor from Santa Barbara. Unfortunately the señorita had made it quite clear that she returned no such feeling for Nazario Alvarjo. In fact, due to an unfortunate accident on the picnic the day following the fandango, she had slapped Nazario's face before everyone present. Nazario could still feel the sting of her little fingers on his cheek and see the outraged anger in her large brown eyes. It hadn't been his fault that Hidalgo had stumbled and nearly fallen over a boulder half-hidden in the grass, or that he had reached back where Rufina rode sideways behind him and crushed her tightly to him to keep her from falling. Women were completely stupid about such things. For himself, he had had enough of them. He had firmly decided never to marry. As for Rufina Corlona of Santa Barbara—well he had heard that all the Barbarenos girls were impossible, hotheaded, and dictatorial.

Now, glancing ahead, he saw a horseman riding hard and waving his sombrero over his head.

"Who is that?" asked Luis, reining up his big golden-chested Amarillo.

Nazario squinted his eyes against the bright sunlight and pulled down his hat brim. "It looks like old Tomas, no one else rides with such long stirrups."

As one, the boys reined in their horses and stared at each other.

Luis broke the silence first. "Something must be wrong at the rancho," he said, adding quickly, "They would not call Tomas in from the herd to run errands unless it was serious."

"Come on!" shouted Nazario. "Let's go to meet him. *Voy a hacienda!*"

"No me gusta," Luis muttered uneasily, "I do not like it," and gave his horse his head, feeling the stallion stretch powerfully under him as he leaped into full gallop.

Tomas Rivas, a gnarled old Luiseno Indian, one of the first baptized at San Luis Rey Mission by Father Peyri, had seen the palominos coming and wisely pulled his horse into the shade of a small oak tree. He kicked his *botas* out of the heavy wooden stirrups and waited, rubbing his leg where the rheumatism ached. He was too old for open-range work, but his ability with cattle was so rare and indispensable to Loma de Oro, especially at roundup time, that he still acted as chief mayordomo of the cattle herds under Santos.

He watched the youthful anxious faces coming swiftly toward him, and shook his own head sadly. It was a black bitter business—the lovely Dona dead, her household inconsolable, Don Ygnacio not yet returned when he had left hours ago. There had been no sign of the Padres either. Worst of all he knew Santos had gone to hunt the killer with his blacksnake whip in his hand, and murder riding like a brand on his dark face. A day that was to have been a celebration for them all at Loma de Oro would end in horror, despair, and how many more deaths?

Luis on Amarillo reached him a split second before the others, not a hair turned in the stallion's shiny yellow coat despite the long uphill run.

"What is it, Tomas?" he asked, searching the Indian's wrinkled face.

"Don Luis, Santos has sent me to find you. There is a bad trouble. You must come at once."

"What happened?" asked Luis in a harsher tone.

The others, coming up and reining in around the old vaquero's horse, repeated his question.

"What is it? What has happened, Tomas? Tell us!"

"Your *madre,* Dona Encarnacion . . . *muerte* . . . killed. An accident. . . ." He told them the story as far as he knew it. "I—I know nothing more, *muchachos.* You must all come. Quickly!"

Looking at them, Tomas knew that Don Ygnacio would have been proud of his sons at that moment. In spite of the stunning, horrifying news not one, from ashen-faced Luis to little Antonio manfully biting his lips, let out a sound.

Luis and Nazario, the two oldest, seemed to grow in stature before Tomas' eyes. These three had always been the younger ones, the indulged ones, but in a split second boyish irresponsibility and gaiety had dropped from their shoulders like a cloak swiftly tossed aside.

"Now," Luis said quietly, "we ride, *hermanos.*"

Tomas turned his own mount to watch them gallop away. There was admiration in his Indian heart for the animal perfection of both horses and riders. There was no hope he could keep up with the golden ones, but out of duty he put his own tired mount into a lope and followed, wondering what new disaster was awaiting them all at Loma de Oro this fateful and never-to-be-forgotten day.

Padre Antonio Peyri had gone directly from his frugal breakfast after Mass to his small, thick-walled office beyond the Mission *sala,* in order to complete the annual report he was making for the Father Prefecto.

Seated at his rude wooden desk, made for him by one of the neophyte carpenters from slabs of redwood painstakingly hauled, as the beams for all the Mission buildings had been hauled, from the high sierras beyond Pala, the priest found himself wondering why Don Ygnacio had not remained to speak to him after Mass or at least to see his son Francisco.

It was, of course, the poor man's wedding anniversary. Santos himself had delivered Dona Encarnacion's invitation for the celebration. Perhaps Don Ygnacio was emotionally distraught on this day of such warm remembrance?

A smile crossed Father Peyri's round, good-natured face as he picked up his quill and turned to a fresh page in his latest report. In that instant a shadow filled the low deepset doorway leading to the inner court of the Mission.

"Padre?"

"*Sí,* my son, come in, come in."

A ragged, emaciated Indian sidled into the room, holding his torn shirt together with soiled hands.

Father Peyri peered at him more closely, for the interiors of the Mission were always dim due to the thickness of the adobe walls and the narrow deep-set slits that served as windows.

"Who are you?"

"S—Salvador, Padre, *por favor.*"

Peyri's face broke into a welcoming smile. "Of course. Salvador Manti, is it not? You were given permission to visit your people beyond Pala six months ago, and you did not come back. Why, Salvador?"

"I—do not know. Are you going to beat me, Padre?"

"No, Salvador," said Peyri, "but I would like to know why you did not come back when your two weeks' time was over."

"I—wanted to stay with my people. To be free."

"I see. You did not like it here at the Mission?"

"Yes. Are you going to put me in the stocks, Padre?"

"For running away?" asked Peyri. "But you did not run away; you had permission to go; you just failed to return on time."

He was not afraid of Padre Peyri, whom he loved, for the Padres did not themselves punish anyone. The mayordomo meted out punishment when necessary, or the sergeant in charge of *escolta* ordered it, though ostensibly the Padres were in charge of the temporal as well as spiritual well-being of the Indians.

"*Sí*," said the young Indian uncertainly.

"Do you think you did wrong, Salvador?"

"Perhaps. I wanted to be free, with my people."

"But many of your people are here," the priest reminded him gently. "Your brother Nilo. Your cousin Tomas."

"Yes. I wanted to see my grandmother who is a gentile, and very old."

"Of course. That is why we gave you permission to go."

"Will you punish me now, Padre?"

The priest stared at the gaunt, unhappy face, so different from the stalwart youth who had left the Mission six months before so proud of his new clothes and his skill as an ironworker and potter.

"Tell me why you have come back, Salvador, if you do not like it here?"

Salvador's voice broke out like a child's. "I was wrong, Padre! There is no freedom in living in a brush hut and hunting all day for acorns and roots and rabbits to eat. I was hungry and cold. But I was afraid the soldiers would come looking for me and cut off my ears, as I have heard they did to some of the Indians at San Gabriel who ran away, and so I did not return."

"But you are back now, and you wish to stay?"

The Indian fell to his knees, clasping his hands before his face. "*Sí!* Oh yes, Padre! It does not matter if you punish me. I shall understand. I want to work with the bellows again, and the potter's wheel, and join in the games on Sundays and sing again in the choir at church." The man seemed to hesitate and the priest gently prompted him.

"What else is troubling you, Salvador? Tell me."

"Padre, you must help me."

"In what way, my son?"

"My aged grandmother Totilla, she is very sick. Soon she will be gone to the other side. I have talked to her much about the things you and Father Cazon have taught me here at the Mission. I have told her of the holy water and oils and the baptism that alone will allow her to see God and all His angels and His saints, and she begs that she be allowed to see this wonder too. I have promised her that I will bring you to her before it is too late. Will you come with me, Padre? Now?"

Antonio Peyri was, like all of his Order, a zealous seeker after souls for Christ. Not infrequently he had come to cross-purposes with the military and the governor in his refusal to abide by the order never to venture alone, without his missionary guard, the *escolta*, into Indian territory. But the *escolta*, assigned to each Mission to protect the Padres, were also under strict orders never to travel farther than would ensure their return to the Mission by nightfall. Many Indians who lived miles into the wilderness and were willing to accept baptism were either too ill or aged to travel the distance to the Missions themselves. This had become a constant source of friction between the Padres and the sergeant in charge of the Mission *escolta*.

Father Peyri realized that Salvador's people lived too far from the Mission. Sergeant Oliva would not approve the visit. Yet he sorely wanted to save Salvador's aged grandmother for the Honor and Glory of Christ.

"Go to the kitchen," he told Salvador kindly, "and get something to eat, and then ask Padre Cazon if he can spare the time to come here for a moment. Meanwhile I will pray that we may know what to do about your grandmother."

"*Gracias*, Padre! *Gracias*."

"Go, my son, *vaya con Dios*."

More than 2,000 Indians resided at San Luis Rey, and its wealth of lands and livestock, as well as the welfare of its natives, was second to none in the chain of California Missions.

At first Peyri had been alone there, for only two priests

were allowed at a Mission. But since the arrival of Padre Cazon, his load had been lightened immeasurably.

In his late sixties, Antonio Peyri was both a zealot and a highly practical man. In time of drought, he might finger his beads and pray with complete confidence in God's Divine Providence, but at the same time he would continue to dig alongside his neophytes in the marshland in hopes of striking a freshet.

Born and confirmed in Tarragona, Catalonia, he had sailed for New Spain in the spring of 1794, eager for his post in the New World. He had been impatient to leave the college of San Fernando in Mexico for service on the *frontera*, for it was the prayer and hope of all dedicated Franciscans of his day to spend their lives and energies among the natives of upper California. Here a man might start with little else than his two hands to serve God for a decade or perhaps a lifetime, and if he were fortunate and God willed it, might even earn the coveted crown of martyrdom, as not a few Franciscans had already done on the California *frontera del norte*.

Now Peyri prayed that he might have enlightenment as to whether to leave his flock in order to save the one lost sheep. When Padre Cazon came in his mind was already made up.

"You sent for me, Padre Peyri?" Cazon's was a strong voice. There was the unconscious inflection of the aristocrat.

"Ah yes, Padre."

Peyri got to his feet and smiled at his assistant.

Padre Eugenio Cazon was not at all the usual cut of young Franciscan missionary to the New World. His father had been a Castilian nobleman with an enviable military record, and Eugenio had served as a lieutenant in His Majesty's cavalry. As a youth, religion had rested lightly upon his shoulders. He had been a *bon vivant*, a seeker after the lusts and pleasures of the flesh. The army had done nothing to improve his morals or strengthen his faith. He was fond of telling himself that a man was born to a certain place and had little real hope of changing it. If one were born a donkey in life's scheme of things, one remained a donkey. Nothing could change that. If it ever occurred to young Don Eugenio that one might become a good or a bad donkey in the process, the idea did not weigh heavily on his mind.

It was while he lay wounded on the battlefield, left for dead, that a new and powerful thought had come to him. If he had lived, and now was about to die, a good and brave soldier in the service of his King, why had he not seen that to have a good and brave soul in the service of the greatest King of all, was a far more important and difficult thing to attain! Though he had no fear of death, Cazon found himself praying that he might be spared in order to prove that he was as capable of serving a Divine Master as a temporal one.

A Gypsy scavenger searching the battlefield had found the delirious, wounded lieutenant some hours later, and carried him, for no reason that was afterward clear to him, to his rude shelter on the mountainside.

During his long convalescence in the mountain hut Eugenio Cazon thought of many things and came at last face to face with himself. He was not pleased with what he saw. A bold, arrogant young hellion, a trouble-seeker. When he could walk, he gave his ragged benefactor everything he possessed save his sword. Then he borrowed a ragged shirt and pants and made his way painfully to the nearest Franciscan monastery, happier and more sure of himself than he had ever been before in his life.

The Father Prefecto could not quite believe the ragged stranger's desire to become a novice. And he looked with disfavor on the wild, bearded figure and the naked sword Cazon had first laid gently on his desk.

"You have been ill, señor, out of your mind for many weeks. You have been a soldier, a taker of lives, by this very sword? A man does not receive a true calling to the priesthood on the battlefield."

"What better place," cried Cazon, "with death and carnage all around us? Was Christ's own battlefield on Earth unstained by blood? Did He not shed His own blood, before the eyes and hearts of mankind were opened to Him? So it has been with me.

"You claim in your pulpits that we all have a choice of good or evil. So it is with this sword I place before you now. With the blade I have shed blood in the name of my monarch upon Earth. With this hilt"—he held the crossed pieces before the startled eyes of the priest—"I propose to make a cross with which to serve my Master in heaven!"

To say that Eugenio Cazon had turned into a priest of mild and pious mien would have been untrue, but none of his associates questioned the singular ardor of his devotion. A militant priest, driving himself harder than anyone else, he had become a source of wonder and awe to many of his more gentle, devout, and saintly brethren in the Order of St. Francis.

His call to California and the wild untamed frontier was exactly to his liking. Always an outdoorsman, active and exuberant, Padre Cazon had become the inspiration and backbone of the temporal activities of San Luis Rey.

He did not agree with the concept of mortification adopted by many of his brothers. When he practiced penance and self-denial, it was rarely of a physical nature, except to fast or to spend a night kneeling in prayer instead of resting on his rough rawhide pallet in his narrow cell. He was, however, in the habit of creating difficult mental tasks for himself. Concentrating on one particular dogma of Faith for an entire day without letting any other thought distract him, with the penalty for failure a week of alternating nights spent on his knees in prayer. Or he would work an entire day in the fields with his demanding and often unruly neophyte laborers without speaking a word, no matter how great the provocation.

For Padre Peyri, who seemed to exude kindness and patience as a flower distills sweetness, Padre Cazon had an abiding and profound admiration and affection. One could not be long in Peyri's company without absorbing some of his unselfish devotion to his Mission and his Indian flock.

Now the older priest motioned hs assistant to a seat on the wooden bench near the window.

"You have seen Salvador?"

Cazon nodded. "Sergeant Oliva will demand that he be punished."

"I must talk to him and explain the situation," Padre Peyri replied with a worried frown. "He must not be punished as a runaway. He had our permission to go."

Cazon nodded again. He sat tonsured and barefooted in the strip of sunlight from the window, his worn brown robe dusty along the hem from the field where he had been planting corn. The cowl was thrown back carelessly around his thick neck framing his wide strong, bronzed face. The lips were full but controlled at the corners, the brown eyes steady and tranquil.

Here sat no fasted ascetic, no cloistered innocent. Here sat a doer, a worker, a builder of brick, a blacksmith, a farmer, a teacher, a pioneer. A man who, in worshipping God, also administered the simple precepts of his religion to an ignorant and alien people with the same understanding with which he doctored their ills or helped them plant their crops.

That he also was helping to build and civilize a great new land, that he had laid out a highway for others to travel from one end of the country to the other by tramping it tirelessly year after year with bare feet to carry his God and his arts to an adopted brethren without thought of personal reward, that he made it possible for great landowners like Don Alvarjo and his contemporaries— some of whom would soon eye greedily even the sacred pledged Mission lands themselves—to take up rich land grants from the King, and exist on them in a hostile land, this meant nothing to him.

It was enough that he toiled in God's vineyard and that the harvest of souls increased and multiplied.

"I have another problem, Padre." Peyri explained about Salvador's aged grandmother and his decision to go to her.

"Let me go instead," said Padre Cazon quickly. "I can slip away with Salvador and be back in half the time."

"No, my dear brother, I have promised Salvador to go myself."

They were spared further argument by the hasty entrance of a young soldier obviously in a state of high excitement.

"Padre! Padre, *mío!* You must come with me at once! My mother—word has just come that she is dead. Killed —by a drunken vaquero! You must come, Padre Peyri!"

Francisco Alvarjo was a favorite of the Padres, as were all the Alvarjo children, each of whom Peyri had baptized.

"Mother of Heaven! It cannot be true?" The old priest took a step toward the weeping boy.

"They have sent word, Padre; we must go at once."

"To be sure," murmured Peyri, and then remembered his vow to baptize the old Indian woman. He was torn by grief for the bereft husband and children of Dona Encarnacion, for whom he had always entertained the warmest affection, and for the Indian soul awaiting eternal salvation at his hands.

"Go to Loma de Oro," said Padre Cazon into the old priest's ear. "I will take care of Salvador and join you at the Alvarjos as soon as I can. I will leave with Salvador at once."

"But if we are both gone, Sergeant Oliva will ask questions."

"I have told the sergeant that my family has need of you both and he has given his permission for me to escort you, Padre," said Francisco. A small, slight boy, with large melancholy eyes now red-rimmed from crying, he seemed much younger than his eighteen years.

The priests exchanged glances. Padre Cazon said, "I will fetch the holy oils. If you will start, Padre, Salvador and I will catch up with you. While you go on to Loma de Oro, we will go to the mountains to finish our errand. Sergeant Oliva cannot object if we are absent a day or so for the mourning and funeral of Dona Alvarjo?"

"It is well," sighed Peyri, patting young Francisco on the shoulder. "Do not weep, my son, your mother and the little one are already in heaven. Come, while Padre Cazon is getting ready we will light a candle for her in the church and say an Ave Maria and a Pater Noster."

Don Ygnacio had little memory of his ride from Zenobio's house to his own, where a weeping vaquero leaped to grasp the bridle from his nervous hands as Ygnacio threw himself off El Capitán.

His sons and daughters were gathered in the long *sala*, Soledad and Dolores weeping quietly into their handkerchiefs. Only little Antonio cried out at sight of his father and threw himself wildly at his father's knees.

"My mother is dead—dead!" he wailed, and was instantly ashamed of his unmanly outburst.

"Hush, *niño*," comforted Ygnacio. "We must all be brave. She would want you to be brave. Tell me, where is your Tía Isabella? I must speak with her at once, and with Santos."

"She is in Madre's room," came the muffled reply. But the little boy had stopped weeping as he disentangled himself and got slowly to his feet. Dolores came forward to put her arms around him, and Antonio, who as a rule objected to being petted by the womenfolk, drew closer to her.

"Santos?" Don Ygnacio asked his eldest daughter.

"I do not know, Padre. He left some time ago."

Don Ygnacio flung his hat on the nearest table and walked out of the *sala* along the veranda fronting the flowering patio. Grief stabbed at him. Never would Encarnacion walk arm in arm with him here again. He turned abruptly into the large bedroom he had shared with her for half a lifetime.

Isabella knelt on Encarnacion's prie-dieu, her rosary between her fingers, her face so gaunt and tense he hardly recognized it. She rose and came slowly toward him and he took her gently in his arms, muffling her dry sobs against his shoulder. When she had quieted, she led him to the bed where a white lace-trimmed coverlet had been drawn mercifully over the injured remains of his wife.

With a trembling hand he lifted the coverlet, turned it down, and stared. In spite of the frightful head injury, her face was serene, almost beatific, like that of a saint in death.

He fell to his knees and buried his face in the bedclothes, and gave way momentarily to his grief. In his heart rose the age-old bitter question, to which there is no adequate early answer. *Why, oh God! Why?*

After a time he rose to his feet and found that Isabella had again covered the beloved face.

"Tell me," he said simply. And she told him everything there was to tell. All that she knew.

"And Santos said nothing to you before he left?"

She shook her head. "He looked about the graveyard before he carried her in here, and then he left."

"Candelaria?"

"She does not know where he went either."

Don Ygnacio went from the bedroom, across the patio to the kitchen square. He found two vaqueros by the hitchrack, one of them old Tomas.

"Tomas, I want to know where Santos is, and who—did this thing."

Tomas swept off his hat and bowed as far as his crippled knees would permit. "Don Ygnacio, I only know he sent a vaquero to call me from the herd and told me to go in search of the young ones. We passed at a little distance, there to the north, Santos and I. He was carrying his blacksnake whip, and there was the sign of death in his face."

"Do you know who is to blame for the . . . murder of my wife?"

"No, señor, as God is my Protector I know not! But I would gladly kill him if I knew—though the Padres say a man goes to hell who kills in wrath."

"Come with me," Ygnacio said. Turning to the other vaquero, he added, "Saddle two palominos, the fastest in the stables, and bring them here."

"*Sí*, Don Ygnacio!"

Tomas followed as Don Ygnacio walked swiftly down the *galleria,* through the patio, and around the chapel into the graveyard.

Together the old Indian and his master examined the scene of the tragedy. Don Ygnacio's heart contracted at sight of the crushed freshly plucked flowers on his children's graves, on the fallen ivory comb presented to Encarnacion with a kiss only that morning before he left for the Mission. Perhaps if he had not gone— if he had stayed all the day by her side. . . . But such thoughts were worse than useless now. It was over, finished. She was gone and nothing could bring her back. It remained only to find and punish her killer.

"Do you see anything?" Alvarjo's voice was harsh now with anger.

"No, señor. Only the place where the horse came over the wall, and here where he swerved, trying perhaps to avoid the Señora. A horse going at terrific speed. No sane man rides a horse like that!"

"Santos must have seen something. Keep looking."

"*Sí* Patrón."

The old Indian bent, carefully parting the grass, peering at the soil underneath, sniffing like a dog at the print of a hoof in the dust. He brushed the tree bark and limbs gently with his fingers, and turned at last with a gleam of satisfaction in his faded black eyes.

"Don Ygnacio!"

Tomas held out a wrinkled palm. On it were a few brown hairs and some coarse black ones with a curious streak of white across them.

"You know the horse these came from, Tomas?"

"*Sí*. I am sure. Only one bay horse with a white streak down his mane, such as these show, and an injury in the right forehoof, was ever on Loma de Oro."

Don Ygnacio frowned in concentration, but he could recall no such horse. "Tell me!" he ordered impatiently.

"It belonged to the vaquero, Bruno Cacho. It was stolen from the San Diego Mission herds."

Remembrance returned to Ygnacio in a flash, his thin face flushed in anger as he recalled why he had whipped the half-breed, Cacho, off Loma de Oro. He should have killed the man on the spot. But Cacho's father had been a soldier in the first Anza expedition, and had served at San Diego with honor until drink and monte robbed him of his senses and his honor.

Now he told himself with terrible logic that God had meant for this man to die at his hands. He had failed his duty. He should have killed him before. Few would have recognized the aloof, dignified Don Ygnacio Jesus Maria Alvarjo, as he turned his ravaged face and burning eyes upon his aged vaquero.

"*Sangre de Dios!*" muttered Tomas under his breath. Surely this was not his Patrón, the just if demanding Don Ygnacio?

"Come!"

Tomas fled at his master's heels, hobbling wordlessly like a frightened duckling. Ygnacio went into the small room he called his study where he kept some of his precious books and papers, those he had read and reread through the long years of his intellectual isolation on the *frontera*. Here also he kept his weapons and what little ammunition he was able to obtain, for both powder and shot were scarce in California.

From the wall he took down his military saber and buckled it around his slender waist. In a cabinet next to the door he found his rosewood box of dueling pistols, and with a steady hand, proceeded to prime and load both before sticking them in his sash. On a peg under a window

was the coiled blacksnake he used infrequently. Next to
it, the riding crop with which he chastised his sons on the
rare occasions when they aroused his wrath. He eyed both
and finally handed the blacksnake to the amazed Tomas.
Vaqueros did not go armed, save for their own boot knives,
quirts, or *reatas*. It was deemed unsafe to put weapons into
the hands of Indians, even the most trusted neophytes. But
on occasion, Don Ygnacio had chosen to arm one of his
men. Never had he had cause for regret.

"Carry this, Tomas, in case of trouble."

"*Sí*, Don Ygnacio."

Carefully skirting the main part of the house, the two
men made their way back to the kitchen quarter where the
other vaquero waited with El Canario and Calabaza, the
two prime stallions belonging to the absent Santiago and
Joaquin. Don Ygnacio motioned Tomas toward Calabaza,
and swung up on El Canario.

"North?" asked Alvarjo of his servant.

"*Sí*, Patrón. *Norte*."

Zenobio Sanchez was uneasy. He had arrived shortly
after Ygnacio and Tomas had left the hacienda, and now
stood on the veranda wondering what to do. He was unaccustomed to women and children, and though he had
known the Alvarjos all of their lives, he was acutely uncomfortable in their presence with Ygnacio away.

He went dutifully to the bedroom with Tía Isabella to
pay his last respects to the dead, and later he inspected
the graveyard without being able to deduce anymore
about the affair than Tía Isabella had been able to tell him.
He was abashed at her sudden gusts of tears and wished
mightily that he had not come. But it had been his duty as
Don Ygnacio's oldest friend and neighbor. Isabella im-
plored him to find her brother, who seemed to have disappeared, and when Zenobio brought her word that Don
Alvarjo had ridden north with Tomas she dissuaded him
from following.

"I cannot be left alone," she entreated. "Stay at least
until the Padre arrives, Don Zenobio?"

"Of course, señorita. How else can I be of service to
you?"

"If you would take Pedro and see about building a

proper coffin? I do not understand Ygnacio, leaving us alone like this."

As a matter of fact, she understood only too well. Both her brother and Santos had gone out to kill, and because the same Castilian blood burned in her own veins as in Ygnacio's, she could not find it in her heart to condemn their action.

"I will take Pedro and see to everything, Dona Isabella," Zenobio soothed, glad of an excuse to absent himself from her presence even temporarily. When the Padre came he could make his excuses and leave.

Isabella watched Pedro and Zenobio cross the patio to do her bidding. Under ordinary circumstances she abhorred her brother's friendship with this coarse-grained, rough-tongued old soldier, and would have made herself scarce when he appeared at the hacienda. But in her present dilemma Zenobio loomed as her only support.

It was nearly nightfall before Padre Peyri came limping up the road, white-faced and winded, ashamed that the thought of a horse had crossed his mind in his haste to reach the stricken household, as it was a rule of his Order that the Padres use no conveyance in going about their necessary duties. They walked to and from whatever tasks called them.

The Alvarjos, it seemed to the priest's tired and bewildered mind, converged upon him in a body from every window and door. He was surprised and pleased to see Don Zenobio Sanchez present also. Don Zenobio did not often appear at funerals, or at church services either.

Isabella, clutching both his hands, was pouring out the tale of their tragedy.

"We will go to the chapel and pray together," said Peyri, when she had finished. Then gathering the nearest children under his arms: "Has Francisco arrived? I sent him ahead—ah, there you are, my son. Did you tell them we have already lighted candles and offered prayers at the Mission?"

Isabella took Padre Peyri off to her sister-in-law's bedroom. She and Candelaria had already washed and dressed and laid out the body with tapers burning at head and feet. Solemnly the family watched and prayed as the priest anointed the body and said the prayers for the dead. One could never be sure of God's judgment, but this woman, to his personal knowledge, had never sinned deliberately in thought, word, or deed and as surely as one could believe in God's mercy, one could believe that she was now in heaven. So he told the sorrowing family and saw some of the gloom leave their faces.

Supper at the gaily decorated table in the large dining room, which had been laid for a festival meal, was a solemn affair, with the Alvarjos scarcely touching Candelaria's sumptuous repast.

"And all the guests invited for tonight?" asked Padre Peyri. "How did you let them know of the tragedy?"

"I sent many of our vaqueros as soon as I could to tell them all not to come," said Luis quietly.

Studying the young faces around the table Peyri was struck with the sudden look of maturity that had come over each one like a mask. Even little Antonio seemed changed. It saddened him to see them so, and he tried to change the subject in order to lighten their spirits.

"I have word that a Boston brig has put in at San Juan. Yesterday I sent Vicente with a *carreta* of produce to trade for a few items we require. I beg of you all to come to the storehouse at the Mission and pick out a gift when you are able."

As he had hoped, the young faces lighted up in spite of their wretchedness; even Antonio had a faint smile on his lips. It had always been a source of wonder to the Padre that the human mind could concentrate even on despair for only so long, before some other thought came to take its place, even if only momentarily. Such was God's mercy to the troubled spirit.

"What did you send for?" Antonio asked.

"All manner of things," replied Peyri. "Presents with which to reward the neophytes on feast days when they have done their jobs well."

"Is it wise to be always rewarding them, Padre?" asked Tía Isabella disapprovingly. She had always looked upon all Indians, even those who had so long and faithfully served her brother at Loma de Oro, as menials. She understood the Padres' untiring efforts to Christianize and civilize their charges, but was appalled at their attempts to raise them to the white man's stature. Many of the Padres had taught their brighter neophytes to write as well as read. And what need had Indians of books, pray tell?

"Just as one must teach a child to obey by punishing wrongdoing, señorita," said Peyri kindly, "one must also reward willing effort. And the Indians are but children of the wilderness. They come to us to learn of their own accord; we do not go out searching through the brush to find them and drag them to the Mission. But once they have chosen to be baptized, we expect them to live up to their faith. Only kindness can make them willing to do this."

Zenobio, seated between Nazario and Luis, and trying to watch his table manners and not drink too much, was wondering at the difference between Padre Peyri in a social gathering and Peyri in the pulpit. On the few occasions he had heard him preach at San Luis Rey he had come away abashed, for the Padre did not spare the *gente de razón* inside his church. He told them repeatedly and with wicked candor that there was not an Indian present who was not more selflessly devout and sincere in his belief than any white man present, military or civilian. He firmly believed this. It was not hard for a man of God to detect the beginnings of laxness in morals and spirituality among the *gente de razón* of California, or to recognize the growing signs of avarice, greed, and cupidity, which were fast infecting the indolent white population from San Diego to San Francisco. Gone were the old soldiers of Anza's and Galvez's caliber. Lack of discipline, duties, and now funds to support them were fast completing the ruin. The nearness of grog shops and monte games to the soldiers' barracks at the presidios fueled the unruliness of the military, and the priests feared for the young Indian women. This was the real reason for the Padres' nunneries. There, under the supervision of one of the older married women, usually the wife of a trusted mayordomo, Indian girls remained protected until married.

A maid entered the dining room and curtsied in front of Isabella's chair.

"Yes, Rosita?"

The maid bent and whispered in her new mistress' ear.

Isabella waved the maid aside and got to her feet. "Do not get up," she told the others. "The vaquero, Tomas, has returned with word of my brother. I will only be a moment."

But both Zenobio and Padre Peyri rose also.

"You will permit us to come with you, señorita?" asked Peyri.

"No, Padre, stay with the children, I beg of you."

The priest hesitated and then sat down again.

"But I will go with you," said Zenobio, with more command in his voice than he had ever used to a woman of gentle birth. It surprised him as much as it did Isabella, but she said nothing when he held the door open for her and followed her into the *galleria*.

They walked in swift silence to the kitchen square, where lanterns had been lit along the verandas and a small open fire burned near the sleeping quarters.

Candelaria, a candlestick in one hand, beckoned them from the kitchen.

"In here, Dona Isabella!"

The room was warm and fragrant with the aroma of cooking. By the little fireplace where Candelaria was wont to sit and sew of a chilly afternoon Tomas sat cross-legged, his eyes on the small darting flames.

"Tomas!" Candelaria hissed. "The Señorita!"

The vaquero rose awkwardly and bowed. Something in his face held Isabella silent in spite of herself. It was her place to question the man but somehow she could not. She did not really understand these Indians, any of them. If something had happened to her brother, as she feared, then the vaquero would have to tell her of his own accord.

It was Zenobio who broke the silence, speaking a few guttural words to the vaquero. The Indian replied in swift surprise.

"Your brother is safe, señorita," Zenobio turned to tell her and Isabella closed her eyes in thanksgiving.

Zenobio continued continued to question the vaquero, speaking this time in Spanish, but he learned little except that Tomas and Don Ygnacio had found Santos in the mountains and that the other two were returning slowly because one of the horses was lame. They had sent him on ahead to tell the Señorita of their arrival.

"I do not believe he is telling the truth," said Isabella severely. "They all lie if it suits them."

Zenobio fingered his beard and shook his head. Tomas was staring back at them proudly, his chin raised.

"He speaks the truth, señorita."

"Then why doesn't he tell us more? What has happened?"

"We will know in due time. Isn't it enough that Ygnacio is safe and will be home soon?"

Isabella made a sound under her breath and left the room abruptly.

Zenobio turned to face Candelaria, and told her quietly to leave them alone. He dragged up a bench and waved a hand in an inviting motion to Tomas.

The old soldier dug out his *cigarrillos* and offered one to the Indian. "Now, *muchacho, por favor,* I would like you to tell me what really happened in the sierras this afternoon?"

Tomas inhaled the tobacco deeply and coughed on the smoke. He said, "I watched them cut a man to pieces."

CHAPTER 5

Santos hung half out of the saddle as he and Marca left the rim of Loma de Oro and the pastureland began to incline steadily upward toward the sierras. Bruno Cacho, drunk or sober, was no fool. Wherever his tracks had appeared to be carelessly obliterated in an attempt to fool a pursuer, careful examination revealed that he had backtracked painstakingly and taken another direction.

Santos grunted with satisfaction. It was clear that his quarry was heading, by however devious and roundabout a route, for the highest peaks and the long, narrow, needle-like pass that led to the desert beyond the last range. For all his elaborate backtracking, Cacho could not conceal the injury in his horse's right front hoof.

Upward across the flinty sides of the sierras, with here and there a sparse pine or cedar tree and a thickening of underbrush, horse and man moved at a slow but steady pace. They had gone six miles, crisscrossing back and forth as the trail led them, when Marca paused and nickered over his right shoulder. Below them, in the grassy slopes, Santos could see the two palominos coming after him at a furious rate. He recognized Don Ygnacio and Tomas with dismay and a faint resentment. This was to have been his hunt, his kill. Regardless of the consequences. Now he would have to step aside for his master. More men might mean less danger to the hunter, but would also give more warning to the hunted.

Don Ygnacio pulled to a halt a few feet below Santos, and looked at his mayordomo with distinct displeasure. "Why did you not wait for me at the hacienda?"

"I knew that the killer of Dona Encarnacion would get away, unless I followed at once, Patrón."

Though he realized the truth in Santos' words, Alvarjo was in no mood for cool logic. "You should have awaited my orders!"

"I am sorry, Don Ygnacio."

"It is my place to avenge my wife, do you understand?"

"Yes, Don Ygnacio."

"I understand the man is Bruno Cacho?"

Santos exchanged a quick look with Tomas.

"That is my belief, Don Ygnacio."

"He is still ahead of you?"

"*Sí.* As far as I know. I believe he will make for the pass into the desert."

"Let us go on then," Alvarjo said curtly. "I will lead."

He reined El Canario past Marca and began feverishly to hunt for tracks in the bracken and underbrush of the hillside. Soon he was so hopelessly confused by the conflicting trail Cacho had left that he called Santos impatiently to his side and bade him take the lead again. The little party moved to the top of one ridge, down along the sloping sides, and up the next, climbing higher all the time.

"How has he put so much distance between us?" demanded Don Ygnacio, mopping his brown with a silk handkerchief.

"He has been at pains to give himself time, señor," replied Santos. "See how he makes us pause and backtrack before we can go on? He himself makes a false trail in an instant and is on his way. It is only fortunate that his horse's hoof has a mark we cannot mistake. Here, he has gone this way."

In two hours Calabaza and El Canario, unused to the climbing and irritable under the enforced slow gait, were lathered with sweat and nervously fighting their bits.

Presently Santos paused, looked at Don Ygnacio, and pointed below them where a grassy swale filled the gap between two narrow spines of the sierras.

Ygnacio's eye fell instinctively to the small, moving dot against the green. A hard smile played across his face.

"Cacho!"

"*Si.*"

"You will wait here with Tomas." He touched the pistols in his sash but knew it was not pistols that he would use. Emotion mounted in him like a tide. The pent-up rage against the man who had robbed him of his wife. The righteous hatred for the fiend he knew Cacho to be. The destiny that he felt had delivered this man up to him to be killed. Only the shell of Dan Ygnacio sat astride El Canario that afternoon on the hillside, looking down at the man he had come to kill. His mind ran ahead, searching for the best way to take his enemy. Not the swiftest, but the most painful.

"Patrón, if you will permit Tomas and me to ride down from either side, we will bottle him up in the middle, then you can come from the center and take him," said Santos.

"Do as I say! Stay here!"

"*Si.*"

Ygnacio put spurs to El Canario and plunged him recklessly down the mountainside, an avalanche of dirt and rocks cascading behind him. Below, the other rider glanced up briefly in startled surprise and then wheeled, making for the nearest opening at the end of the little swale.

Ygnacio, in a sudden panic that his quarry might yet escape him, plunged his spurs again into El Canario's sides, and the startled horse grunted and stumbled, half unseating his rider. Only a superb horseman could have remained in the saddle and regained his balance on such a powerful, plunging, half-crazed stallion. It was soon apparent that the animal was injured; whether in leg or shoulder, Ygnacio could not tell. He turned and shouted up to Tomas.

"Lleve mi caballo! Pronto!"

As ordered, Tomas tore down the incline on Calabaza. When he reached his master, Don Ygnacio moved swiftly from one saddle to the other without dismounting, and plunged on downhill on his new mount.

Bruno Cacho was not as drunk as he had been some hours before when he had rushed his horse over the grave-yard wall at Loma de Oro, and smashed into the woman kneeling there. He had not been certain who she was, but in his blind hatred for the proud, high-born Don Ygnacio, he would gladly have run down any member of the house-hold.

Cacho's horse, a wiry little mare he had stolen from the Mission *remuda* at San Diego long ago, was not wind-ed, but he knew she would not outrun the powerful golden stallions of Loma de Oro.

Passionately he wished he was astride one of them. Then they would see who was the better rider, he or the high-and-mighty Don Alvarjo! He touched the pistol in his sash, also stolen from the San Diego Mission, where a thoughtless soldier had left it in the barracks with his gear.

As he rode, Cacho weighed the possibility of reaching the pass between the hills before Don Ygnacio overtook him. The golden stallion Alvarjo rode had not yet reached the floor of the grassy swale, and he would come down about midway to where Cacho now rode. Glancing around for the best place to dismount and make his stand, the half-breed made a horrifying discovery. Another rider was plunging down the hillside nearest him, taking savage leaps over the steep, uneven ground. From where Cacho rode, it didn't seem the terrible side bank would give foot-ing to a squirrel, yet the golden horse and rider came on in their wild, mad dash, like a bird swooping into a can-yon.

*   *   *

Before he had fully reached the bottom Santos uncoiled his *reata larga* and swiftly made a loop, passing the bell-shaped end under his thighs, which he pressed close against the saddle to hold it tight.

It took an accomplished *reatero* to turn out a *reata larga* of the sort Santos now held in his hand. Weighted and made of four strands of expertly braided rawhide one hundred feet long, it had a rawhide *honda* at one end through which came the loop, with the bell-shaped terminal at the other. With it, Santos made catches at a distance of sixty or even eighty feet as a matter of course, a staggering distance at which to be able to depend on complete accuracy.

Cacho realized at once what Santos meant to do and reached for his pistol. But there was no time to pause for a good shot. In seconds Santos would be on level ground, and behind him Don Ygnacio was coming along the grassy swale at a ground-eating gallop.

The half-breed began to swerve his horse searching for a crack, a crevice, a boulder where he might dismount and take cover.

There was nothing.

Just the bare little grassy swale before him, and the brush-choked hillsides too steep for his mare. As a last desperate resort, Cacho uncoiled his own fifty-foot *reata* and made a loop. If he could trip the stallion and unseat Santos, he might have a chance.

From his position beside the injured El Canario, halfway up the hillside, Tomas watched the two big blond horses converge on the smaller brown one. Tomas was not sorry to be out of the chase, for he sensed a dispassionate, relentless malevolence in Don Ygnacio and Santos that filled him with an unaccountable and atavistic fear. Were they not riding down a man with the relentless fury of Atzuts, the black hawk of death of his people? A red man and a white one moving in to kill another, whose blood was both red and white?

Below him he saw Santos raise his arm with the long loop of the *reata larga* in his right hand, kneeing Marca forward at a gallop on the flat grassland. At the same instant Cacho threw his own *reata* at Marca's head. The loop fell short, coming only over one ear. A less experienced rope horse might still have been caught by the swiftly and viciously dallied *reata,* but Marca expertly ducked his head to one side and dropped the loop on the ground.

Santos threw his loop with a mighty swing of his arm and a tricky flip of his wrist. Marca set his feet, and the rope settled neatly around the mare's neck with a jar that brought the smaller horse to her knees. Cacho threw himself clear of the saddle and scrambled on all fours into the nearest brush. Santos would have to take time to make a fresh loop and, mounted, he made an excellent target.

Cacho worked the knife from the top of his *bota.* He raised his hand, centering the blade on Santos' breastbone. He smiled through the sweat and grime and hate on his face, for he knew that he couldn't miss from this distance. The muscles of his hand and wrist tightened for the throw. Then a snake struck at him from the bracken, biting into his wrist, making him howl with pain as the knife fell from his nerveless fingers.

He glanced down at the black slithering thing winding itself around his hand and wrist and arm, refusing to let go. He cried out again and tried to shake himself free.

But it was not a snake.

It was made of leather. Black and hard and biting. But not alive.

Fury and fear lit Cacho's eyes as he glanced up into the rock-hard face of Don Alvarjo.

In a flash he pulled the pistol from his sash and fired it point-blank at the mounted man still holding to the whip on the other side of the bush.

Santos shouted and rode in with his own blacksnake smarting down across the half-breed's shoulders.

But fear or anger had made Cacho's aim unsteady. The ball had merely grazed Alvarjo's temple, where a trickle of blood now ran.

Giving his whip a fierce tug, Don Ygnacio brought Cacho crashing to his stomach. Then he turned Calabaza's head and dragged the half-breed roughly from behind the bush into the open. He loosened the whip to free him and watched the man get uncertainly to his feet, massaging his right wrist.

No word was spoken. Only the eyes of the three men communicated their thoughts. Hatred moved and crackled in their glances.

Moving as warily as a wild animal at bay, Cacho backed slowly away from the two horsemen, then turned suddenly and charged up the steepest part of the hillside. Before he had gone ten steps a *reata* settled over his shoulders and plucked him as neatly from the hillside as if he had been a flower. The loop was removed and Cacho immediately dashed up again, only to be once more brought down by Santos' deadly accurate throw. It was useless to try to escape up the mountain, and Cacho knew that he could not outrun two mounted men. But if he could reach his horse —she was standing perfectly still only a stone's throw away. It was plain they meant to kill him slowly, or they would have shot him on the spot. Emboldened by this thought, Cacho stood still and let his lungs fill slowly with fresh air.

Tomas, watching the deadly pageant below, saw Cacho whirl suddenly and leap toward the brown mare. Startled, she took a step backward but the half-breed was in the saddle in one powerful leap, and in the next second was spurring her madly along the flat grassy back of the swale like a hound out of hell.

Don Ygnacio and Santos had been caught off-guard by the swiftness and success of the sudden maneuver. Both came alive at the same instant and sent their horses flying after Cacho's.

Marca was faster than the pasture-fattened Calabaza, and sped by him like a golden arrow, the muscles of his chest rippling powerfully under his satin skin.

The brown mare, infected by her master's terror, fled wildly over the narrow tableland. Neither she nor her rider knew where they were going, only the mindless, urgent need to escape from the crashing, indomitable yellow horses behind them.

Tomas saw Santos' first loop fall short, just grazing the mare's rump. In his anxiety to bring down their prey he had thrown from too great a distance. His second throw fastened on the hind leg of the mare and flopped her down hard on her left side. Cacho threw himself clear and began to run in a blind panic.

The blond horses thundered after the fleeing man. Santos rode several yards past him then turned and flicked out his whip. In a backhanded lash that caught Cacho in the face, he opened a red gap down one cheek.

Cacho put a hand to his face and backed up. From behind him another whip lashed out like an evil tongue, ripping his jacket from collar to sash.

Tomas watched them in fascinated horror as the two horsemen plied their whips, cutting the helpless man between them to ribbons with diabolical method and fiendish skill. Cacho lay on the ground now, a naked bleeding pulp, his cries and moans of anguish reaching even to Tomas on the hillside.

When at last he lay still, Santos dismounted and looked at him, then he fastened Don Ygnacio's *reata* around the man's waist, and his own around his legs. Mounted again, he nodded to Alvarjo and turned in the opposite direction.

Afterward, Tomas only knew that in one moment they had a whole body between them and in the next, each was dragging a piece behind his madly galloping horse.

Don Ygnacio spoke only a few terse words to him when he and Santos finally reached his side. Neither man, he noted, carried his blacksnake whip or his *reata*.

Dismounting and proffering the reins to Tomas, Alvarjo said: "Ride El Calabaza back and tell Dona Isabella I am on my way."

Never in his life had he been so glad to leave a place as he was this horrifying swale high in the sierras. And he knew that nothing, not the threat of death itself nor the Devil's hellfire to come, could make him return.

Padre Cazon trudged at Salvador's side, wearing his wide-brimmed hat and carrying his long wooden staff with the little iron cross on top. Tied to it in a bundle were his prayer book, stole, holy water, oil, and salt, for the administration of baptism.

"How much farther?" he asked Salvador sharply. He did not share Padre Peyri's innocent belief in the goodness and godliness of all the San Luis Rey neophytes. Many a saintly and unsuspecting priest, Cazon knew, had been lured to his death by Indians begging him to come with them into the wilderness to baptize an aged or ailing relative.

Salvador said, "It is not far, Padre. Just a little over that next rise."

They had gone beyond Temecula, where there were several Indian *rancherías* or settlements, and where Mission San Luis Rey maintained one of its largest cattle stations under the care of a mayordomo. Here, the land was wild and remote, broken by numerous small gullies and arroyos, running down from the sierras, that filled with torrential waters during the rainy season.

Cazon glanced casually at Salvador and wondered if he really had a grandmother about whose soul he was anxious.

A small boy appeared suddenly from behind a clump of sumac, naked but for a breechclout, welcomed them shyly in Tamancus. He followed them up over the next hillock and Padre Cazon saw half a dozen crude brush wickiups scattered along a dry gulch.

The Indians who came to meet them were all gentiles. None had the look of ever having been near a Mission, yet they seemed friendly enough and all greeted Salvador as he led the priest to one of the huts.

The interior was hazy with smoke from a small manzanita fire burning in the center. On a pallet of branches and skins lay what seemed to be the skeleton of an old woman. Her hair was as white as powder, her skin like parchment, her fingers bent and twisted like dried twigs left too long in the sun.

Salvador knelt and touched her, speaking softly. To Padre Cazon's amazement he found himself being studied by a pair of curious and lucid black eyes.

He spoke to the old woman in her own tongue. He saw her nod and whisper something to her grandson.

"She is ready to be received into the family of the Great One, so that she may see all His wonders when she dies, Padre."

The priest took off his hat, laid down his staff on the floor, and opened his bundle. He put the stole around his neck and took up his prayer book. Throughout the ritual the old woman watched in rigid and fascinated silence, while her friends and neighbors crowded into the little hut.

"I must baptize her in a saint's name," said Padre Cazon. "We will call her Maria Immaculata in honor of our Blessed Lady."

When he had finished and was retying his bundle, Salvador touched his arm shyly.

"What is it, Salvador?"

"It is a belief among my people that when we accept a favor we must also do one. My grandmother wishes me to thank you for her baptism and she wishes to give you this stone as a powerful protection against snakebite. It is called Xaclul, and as there are many snakes in these parts, it will be of great value to you."

Padre Cazon took what appeared to be a round piece of white chalk into his palm and studied it.

"You must soak it in your mouth if the snake bites you, and then apply the spit to the wound."

Padre Cazon thanked the old woman gravely and put the little stone into his pack to show Padre Peyri as a curiosity. He had long been interested in the natives' medicinal practices and was even compiling a small book on them to send to his brother who was a physician in Madrid.

It was dusk when Salvador followed the priest from his grandmother's hut.

"You wish to return tonight, Padre?"

"I must join Padre Peyri at Rancho Loma de Oro, no matter what the hour. There has been a death in the family."

"I know a shorter way to take you there, Padre."

The priest frowned at him. This was rough country. The coming here had been bad enough. In the dark, would a shortcut not be worse? And though the Indian had told the truth about his grandmother, could he be trusted not to lead the Padre astray on the pretext of losing his bearings in the dark? Somehow Cazon doubted that Salvador was quite the docile, remorseful neophyte that Padre Peyri thought him to be.

"How much time will be saved?" he asked.

Salvador's level stare never wavered. "A good half, Padre. If you are afraid of the dark, I have been that way many times without mishap."

An ex-soldier, Cazon was stung at the challenge to his courage.

"Very well."

The moon rose early and cast a thin white light over the land, making the bushes and trees stand out like thick, sooty silhouettes.

Salvador spoke suddenly in a voice of quiet command, when they had traveled in silence for several miles.

"Padre, be quiet. There is someone coming."

From under a wide, spreading oak two pale horses were emerging, walking slowly, their heads drooping. Padre Cazon could hear the creak of saddle leather and the rattle of bits, chains, and spurs. Then a voice said clearly in an agony of remorse, "You should have let me do it alone, Don Ygnacio. Now we will both go to Hell."

Padre Cazon started upon recognizing Santos' voice. Instantly, he knew what had happened, and he was not surprised. Don Ygnacio, a Castilian gentleman of the old school, could scarcely have been expected to allow his wife's murderer to go unpunished, and it was unthinkable that any but his own hand should have delivered the death blow. Eugenio Cazon understood; he was of the same blood. As a priest he might deplore murder and bloodshed, but he had not quite forgotten the passions of his other life when he himself had killed, often with less provocation than Alvarjo was weighted down with this night.

"Who is there?" called Don Alvarjo sharply, seeing the two shadowy figures on foot.

"Padre Cazon, Don Ygnacio. And the neophyte Salvador. We are on our way to Loma de Oro to join Padre Peyri."

Santos' face under his sombrero wore a haunted look, but Don Ygnacio's was calmly serene, contained, and as remote as a statue's.

"Welcome to my rancho, Padre. I will walk to the hacienda with you, if you will permit your Indian to ride my horse and accompany Santos?"

"With pleasure, Don Ygnacio."

Alvarjo dismounted and handed El Canario's reins to Salvador and the Indian mounted quickly. When the two horses had ambled off into the shadows, Don Ygnacio asked quietly:

"Do you have your stole, Padre? Can you hear my confession? Here? Now?"

"I have my stole," replied Padre Cazon evenly. "I have just come from a baptism. But what is the hurry?"

"I have just killed a man."

"I—see."

Cazon rummaged in his pack for the article he sought, took up his prayer book, and told Don Ygnacio to kneel. The priest blessed him and waited for him to speak.

"I have just killed the man who murdered my wife, Padre. I set out to kill him, and I did so in anger and cold blood."

"Are you sorry, my son?"

"No! He deserved to die!"

"I cannot give you absolution if you feel no remorse for your sin. Only God has the right to give and take a life."

"You were once a soldier, Padre. Did you not take lives —often in anger and cold blood?"

"Yes. But I did it in defense of my king and country. And I have since repented, and asked God's forgiveness, and sworn never to do such a thing again. You also must repent, Ygnacio. Are you not sorry that you have offended God?"

"Yes—I am sorry for that. I regret that I have offended God, but not that a murderer is dead."

"But you repent the anger and wrath that consumed you and made you kill in such a way?"

"Yes, I repent that."

"And you will try never to sin in such a way again?"

"I will try," murmured Ygnacio. All his life he had fought to keep God's commandments, as he had fought to obey his own father and his king. Yet tonight had seen it all swept away in one terrible moment of passionate rebellion. Everything that he had been taught, that he had lived by, had been swept relentlessly away before the tide of his uncontrollable wrath. He knew now the horror of his own weakness and was appalled. His pride was nothing but a sham battlement he'd erected to hide from in his own weakness.

Padre Cazon's voice came as from a distance.

"Then make a good act of contrition and I will give you absolution."

Their voices blended as did their forms in the moonlight with the other shadows about them.

Don Ygnacio was not sure that his confession had been full enough, but at least he had made it, and by great good fortune as quickly as possible. He was also grateful that he had not been forced to make it to Padre Peyri, who was less a man of the world than Padre Cazon.

For his part, after giving the penance, the priest could only pray that Don Ygnacio did truly repent for his sins. And that God would indeed forgive him.

CHAPTER 6

At dawn the ship *Arabella* waited for the fair tide. Day crept in on stealthy fingers carelessly smudging the sky with a lighter gray, like a child's hand rubbing a chalky slate.

Bart Kinkaid, his hands thrust deep into the pockets of his pea coat, stood alone on the quarterdeck anxiously scanning the sky. All night the *Arabella* had lain becalmed off the wooded headland behind which lay the harbor of San Diego. He was hoping for a good breeze which would bring them round the point and through the difficult channel entrance. But this was late July and he would be lucky to whistle up any wind at all.

High hills cut off the harbor to the north and west and lost themselves in the interior. Brown, treeless plains circled the sandy beach where the largest American shipowners each maintained a roughly constructed hide warehouse. The town, hidden behind the first fold of hills, was invisible from the shore. San Diego, for all its difficult entrance, subject to swift currents and a shifting channel, was not a bad harbor. Though only one ship at a time could slip cautiously through its narrow entry, scraping against the rocky sides if the vessel were a large one, once inside they could anchor with ease directly off the hide storage houses.

Since March the *Arabella* had traded up and down the California coast with spectacular success. Now she was ready to deposit her load of green hides at Ephraim Endecott's storage depot for curing, before returning to complete her sojourn in the north. She would stay a year or more on the California coast to collect her allotted 40,000 hides. Now her job was only half done, and her crew was restless and weary from the long hours and hard manual labor.

Made of steel and whalebone himself, with a consuming, tireless, driving energy, Kinkaid demanded a like dedication to seamanship from his men. When he failed to get it, a rare occurrence on the *Arabella,* his discipline was always swift. But his punishments were as rigorously just and fair as they were uncompromising, and for their day were considered mild. He never spread-eagled a man to a grate and left the poor wretch to suffer without food and water for hours on end. He never stood by, coldly counting strokes while a mate cut a man's back to ribbons with the cat-o'-nine-tails. He never left a sailor in port because he was ailing or unable to work. And if he was relentless in demanding the best that body and brain could muster for the service of his ship, his crew could rest content in the knowledge that his demands upon himself were no less severe. The captain was always the earliest to rise and the last to go below. He was never far from the bridge in foul weather, when many a captain holed up in his cabin and let the mate and crew worry the ship through the storm. If he was hard-driving he was also a master to admire. And he gave his men Sundays free, an unusual luxury for sailors on an American merchant ship.

As a consequence, in spite of the grueling life aboard a sailing ship halfway around the world from civilization, in a land where neither law nor redress was to be had, completely at the mercy of the captain, the *Arabella* was known as a happy ship, and sailors seeking a berth in Boston clamored to serve under Captain Kinkaid.

Kinkaid became aware of the man at his shoulder just as a wind began to spring up from the southwest quarter.

"Mr. Banner?"

"Aye, sir."

"It looks like we'll have enough breeze to take her into the harbor. Call all hands to get her under weigh."

"Aye, Captain."

The first mate, Jake Banner, touched his cap and turned to bawl an order in a voice that rang like a rusty anchor chain.

The *Arabella* was fortunate also in her chief mate. A thick-chested, active, ruddy-faced New Bedford man in his early fifties, Jake Banner was said by the crew to have salt water in his veins, crows' nests under his eyes, and a heart covered with barnacles. It was a closely guarded secret aboard the *Arabella*—the truth of which neither the mate nor the crew would have admitted to each other if each had been keelhauled on the spot and flogged—that Banner was also a generous, sympathetic, and protective old hen to his crew, and that in return the men worked with a will and a loyalty for Ol' Jake that was rare indeed.

Banner, for all his solid bulk and craggy, wind-tooled face, was a born worrier. He had sailed on Endecott ships longer than the captain, and in the berth of chief mate to young Kinkaid since the younger man took his first command. He had never ceased to fret properly over the affairs of the Endecott line or the troubles of his young master. His feeling for Bart Kinkaid were those of father, servant, teacher, and protector. Had he been a man of less New England reserve, things might have gone hard for them both.

As it was, Banner never forgot his place, and Kinkaid treated his mate with a firm cordiality that had made of them an able efficient team.

With sailors swarming above and below, Captain Kinkaid stood on the quarterdeck and watched each movement with grave satisfaction. Getting under weigh was a more accurate barometer of the temper of a ship's crew than anything else, and nowhere on the *Arabella* did a man slacken his hold till the chain came only slowly over the windlass, or wield his handspike with a halfhearted rigor.

The men's voices rang out cheerily on the morning air in answer to the mate's lusty, "Heave hearty, lads! Heave ho! Make us a lay and heave ho!" And the anchor came to the cathead with a swiftness and ease that would have amazed many skippers.

The *Arabella*'s sails filled lazily at first and then with vigor, and she soon stood 'round the point, making for the entrance to San Diego Harbor.

The only signs of life in the bay were the men piling hides outside the warehouses, bareheaded in the hot July sun. They could also see the crews on the decks of two other ships that swung at anchor in the current.

Using his glass, Kinkaid recognized one as the small brig, *Camas,* in the Peruvian trade. She had been two years trading on the coast and had a worn, faded look from lack of paint and scraping.

The second ship was a raking long-masted brig, with a sharp lean prow like the jaws of a shark. She gleamed in the sunlight, as bright as new paint and rope and tar could make her. The Stars and Stripes floated briskly from her masthead and gaff end, but Kinkaid could not recall having seen her on the California coast before, or anywhere else for that matter. She was swinging into the wind and he could not make out her name clearly.

He passed the glass to Banner and asked, "Who is she? Do you make her out, Mr. Banner?"

He was surprised at the look of fierce dislike in the mate's faded deep-set blue eyes.

"Aye, I know her, sir."

"Well?"

"She's the *Vulcan,* out of New Bedford, sir."

"I haven't seen her before. Who are the owners?"

"Her master and owner is Captain Titus Judah, sir." He added after a pause, "She used to be the *Melissa* out of New Salem."

"The *Melissa!*"

Suddenly Kinkaid knew a good deal about this handsome ship swaying proudly at her anchor, and he understood the disfavor with which Banner, as an honest seafaring man, now viewed her.

The *Melissa* had been a good and honorable vessel built and launched in New Salem, Connecticut, a score of years before and put into the Canton tea trade. Later she had been sold to a Norfolk owner who sent her round the Horn to Chile and Peru, and afterward used her in the West Indies. There was talk she had foundered and gone down in a hurricane, but later it was said she had only run aground and finally had been salvaged and resold. Kinkaid had heard rumors of her subsequent ill repute. It was reported she had gone to Capetown as a blackbirder, and had been involved in even worse business than slave trading. No respectable seaman would serve aboard her, and at last she had disappeared from sight completely. Now, here she lay at anchor in San Diego Harbor, as smart and trim as a new frigate, with a new name and a new master.

"Captain Judah, you say, Mr. Banner?"

"Yes, sir. Titus Judah. He had her refitted in New Orleans a few years back and renamed her the *Vulcan*."

"You know him?"

"No, sir. But I've heard say he's not an easy man to sail under. He uses Negroes and Kanakas mostly, I hear tell."

Kinkaid nodded and put the *Vulcan* and her master out of his mind for the moment.

"Order the long boat, Mr. Banner; we're going ashore."

"Aye, sir."

Once ashore, Kinkaid stopped first at the company hide house and spoke to Dan Gale, the burly Irishman in charge. From him he borrowed horses for himself and Banner, and rode over the beach toward the little shelf of hills separating the town from the harbor.

He had always thought San Diego the most barren and least attractive of all the anchorages on the California coast. Except for the fine sparkling blue harbor, there seemed little reason for its existence, and yet here Junipero Serra had erected the first of the Missions. The land was not productive; there was little fresh water, and scant food for the stock, yet the Spaniards had built their first presidio three miles from the Mission on a little rise. Below in a square clustered the homes of the *gente de razón* and beyond them, straggling toward the beach, were the rude houses, each with a little garden patch, where the families of the soldiers lived, many of whom had Indian wives.

The houses of San Diego were not as attractive as those of the northern settlements. Their mud-colored bricks remained unplastered or not whitewashed, and many of them had only roofs of tulles instead of red tiles. The Mission and the square presidio were the only impressive buildings, and since the lack of funds from Mexico, the presidio was falling into disrepair.

The captain and mate hitched their horses to the rail outside the smaller of the two stores in the dusty little plaza and went inside.

The shop that Don Pio Pico had opened a few years back had prospered as much from the expansive good nature of its young proprietor as from the quality of the *aguardiente* he sold over the counter.

One of the new order of young Paisanos, the son of Sergeant José Maria Pico, who had come in the second Anza expedition in 1775 and remained to serve honorably in the army of California, he was related to nearly every *gente de razón* family in the territory. Since the death of the old sergeant at San Gabriel some six years back, however, the family had fallen on hard times. Sergeant Pico's landholdings had slipped away from him, and the Picos had been forced to move from San Gabriel to San Diego. It was necessary for all to work to help support the family. While his mother and sisters did needlework, Don Pio Pico opened a small general store.

He was there today, standing in front of the small counter where he dispensed liquor, talking to a tall man in seaman's garb.

"*Buenos días,* Pio," Kinkaid called as he stepped down from the entry onto the hard-packed dirt floor. The damp, musty smell which he had come to associate with adobe buildings assailed his nostrils.

"Capitán Kinkaid!" shouted Pico, and came forward to offer both his hands to the American. "*Hace mucho tiempo que no te veo.*"

"Yes, a long time," agreed Kinkaid with a wide smile that softened the stark planes of his lean face. "Nearly two years. I see you do well, *amigo?*"

"Ah, very well this last year, *amigo.*" The Californian winked slyly. "I travel a good deal now, and always I come home with *mucho dinero* for Madre and my sisters. You did not know I had built them a fine new house last year on Juan Street. A *palacio,* señor! More elaborate than the houses of Bandini, Estudillo, or Arguello. You must dine with us tonight. But come, you must have a drink and meet my new friend."

Following his jaunty host across the room, Kinkaid thought that he looked like an intellectual bear. An uglier man could hardly be imagined. The upper lip of his enormous mouth bent in a U-shape in the center, while the broad, thick underlip hung like a dewlap beneath. The big nose like an oversized plum was made more grotesque by wide deep nostrils. His exceedingly dark Manzatecan complexion gave his face a shadowed look, and made the whites of his eyes, small and set far apart, gleam by comparison.

It was characteristic of him also that though he welcomed Banner cordially and as an old friend, there was a shade less warmth and deference in his greeting to the mate than he had shown toward the captain.

"Come, *amigos!* You are all three Americanos; we must drink a toast to our mutual friendship. Simeon! Open the new barrel of *aguardiente* I just brought from Guadalupe. *Pronto!*"

As they neared the bar, Kinkaid had a chance to observe the third American more closely. Since he wore a captain's cap and sea coat, this could only be the master of the *Vulcan*.

The man stood half-leaning against the little bar. He was tall and well-built, perhaps ten years older than Kinkaid. There was a contained deliberateness in his movements, a quiet watchfulness in his steady light-hazel eyes, and an unmistakable air of confidence. But where Kinkaid's face was open, Judah's was narrow and secretive, his eyes holding a hint of malice and his thin mouth concealing a twist of cruelty beneath the red moustache he affected. His hair, worn long in sideburns beside his small, close-set ears, was of an even deeper auburn, and his brows had an oblique upward slant that gave him a sardonically satanic expression. Kinkaid noted that the large hand resting atop the bar was splay-fingered and covered with freckles like powdered rust.

"Capitán Kinkaid, meet Capitán Judah," said Pico gaily.

Judah took the big hand from the bar to offer it to Bart.

"Titus Judah, of the *Vulcan* out of New Bedford. Glad to meet you, Captain."

"Captain Bart Kinkaid, the *Arabella*, Boston." The red-haired man's grasp had iron in it, and the pressure had been deliberately harsher than necessary for a friendly handshake. Kinkaid held his own hand rock-hard and steady until the other gradually let go.

"A drink, gentlemen! Put the bottle there, Simeon; I

will pour it myself." The Californian reached for a tray of hollowed-out oxhorns.

"Not those!" Judah said quickly.. "Did you think no one had heard of your little trick, Pio?"

Judah reached for a horn and turned it up for their inspection. Wedged neatly inside, a third of the way down, was a wooden plug.

"What poor bastard of a vaquero notices he is getting only a third of a tumbleful for his *dinero,* eh, Pio?"

Pico slapped his thighs in delight at the discovery of his little subterfuge. "You are right, Capitán, I do cheat the customers a trifle, but actually I am doing everyone a service. The vaqueros cannot drink too much, there is less fighting, and the customers are just as well-satisfied."

"And Don Pio grows richer by the hour?" rejoined Judah, not without admiration. In his short time on the California coast he had found the native Californians extravagant, lazy, and profligate. Careless sheep, ready for the shearing. But in Don Pio he recognized, if not a kindred spirit, at least an able adversary.

Judah took four tumblers from the counter and pushed them toward Pico.

Still chuckling, the shop owner filled them to the brim and bowed graciously, offering the first toast.

"To you, gentlemen, and to your long and continued prosperity in the ports of California!"

The Americans downed the fiery *aguardiente* and returned the salutation to their host.

Pico wiped his large nose with a red silk handkerchief. He passed *cigarrillos*, and pressed more drinks upon them and cordially extended his invitation to dinner in his new *casa.*

As he was speaking a young Spaniard entered the shop. He was small and delicately handsome in the manner of the well-born *gente de razón,* dapper in fine brown broadcloth trousers, short jacket, and jade-green sash—the Californians wore no belts—and a wide black sombrero heavily encrusted with gold braid.

"Pio?"

"*Sí*, Macario? Come in, come in!"

The young man seemed to hesitate at sight of the other company, but finally sauntered across the floor to them, a careful smile on his olive-skinned face.

"*Amigo mío,* meet my American friends, Capitán Judah and Capitán Kinkaid, and Mr. Banner, chief mate to Capitán Kinkaid. My friends, may I present to you my old school *compadre,* Don Macario Canejo."

The young man swept off his hat and made them an elaborate bow, while the Americans nodded stiffly.

Macario accepted a glass of *aguardiente* which he sipped with a dainty reserve.

"This is Capitán Judah's first voyage to our shores," continued Pio jovially. "But not his last, eh, Capitán?"

Judah was lighting a *cigarrillo* but he paused to answer, "No, Don Pio. After such a welcome you'll have a hard time keeping me away." He blew smoke through his thin lips and added, "I'll wager you've done well on this coast, Captain Kinkaid. Your ship belongs to the Endecott line, doesn't it?"

"Yes," replied Bart. "Ephraim Endecott is my uncle."

Judah's Mephistophelian brows rose.

"It's fortunate when a relative owns the ships you sail, eh, Captain?"

Kinkaid flushed at the suggestion that he was a skipper by sufferance rather than ability. But he said evenly, "No one is more demanding of his ships or crews than Ephraim Endecott, and that goes for everyone in his employ, from captains on down."

"I know," said Judah. "He is a very successful man."

"The *Vulcan*'s a very sharp-looking vessel," offered Kinkaid. No matter how he might feel about the master, it was not in him to keep from complimenting a fine ship.

"Since I had her reoutfitted in New Orleans a few years back, she's shown her keels to everything we've run up against. My Kanakas and blacks take a bit of driving, but they manage to keep her shipshape."

"What's your cargo, Captain?" asked Banner politely.

Judah's light eyes narrowed a fraction but he smiled when he said, "We've a mixed cargo, Mr. Banner. We're just in from Peru and the Sandwich Islands; devil of a rough voyage it was, too."

While the Americans had been speaking together, Macario Canejo had been excitedly whispering into Pico's ear. A sudden exclamation from Pio caused the Americans to glance up sharply.

"*Nombre de Dios!* You will pardon us, *amigos,* but my

friend here brings me some alarming news. One of my dearest *compadres* has been thrown into the *calabozo* at the presidio. I must go at once and see if I cannot get him released. That a caballero of such esteem should be thrown into jail like a common vaquero is shameful, especially when he has not broken any law! That a son of Don Ygnacio Alvarjo's should recline in prison is unthinkable. You will pardon us, my friends, but the matter is urgent. You will dine with us tonight?"

Judah declined. He was sailing at dawn for San Pedro and Monterey. And Banner, after exchanging a quick glance with Kinkaid, also excused himself: duty aboard the *Arabella* would make his stay impossible. Bart, on the other hand, accepted.

From the moment he had heard the Alvarjo name mentioned he had been intrigued. Recalling the proud, aloof, faintly hostile grandee whom he had met at Zenobio Sanchez's in March, he was curious as to how a son of his could rest in the jail of the San Diego presidio.

Outside, Pico mounted a spirited white stallion, while Macario leaped astride a gleaming, richly comparisoned savino with an odd white eye.

They covered the distance to the presidio on its little hill above the town at a full gallop. To Kinkaid, Californians never seemed to dismount, but to bound from their horses' backs in one fluid movement. And they never seemed quite complete to him unmounted. He got carefully out of his own saddle while the Spaniards stood patiently waiting for him.

Don Pio spoke swiftly with the guard on duty at the gate and they were quickly admitted to the *cuarto* within.

"The sentry says that Commandante Ruiz is not here; he has gone to San Juan," said Pico. "That is a pity, for he is an understanding man. But if you will wait I will speak with the lieutenant in charge."

Pico disappeared in the shadowed arches under the veranda and his companions wandered into the protection of the *galleria* to escape the hot sunlight.

Don Macario Canejo spoke politely of his town, its growth, the Mission visible three miles away, and told how it had been moved from its earliest sight due to a terrible Indian uprising in which Padre Luis Jayme had become the first Franciscan martyr in California.

After a time Bart asked easily, "Do you know which of Don Ygnacio's sons is in trouble?"

Canejo stiffened slightly, but before he could answer, Kinkaid added, "I had the pleasure of breakfasting with Don Ygnacio Alvarjo at Don Zenobio Sanchez's Rancho Santa Teresa this spring."

Don Macario's reserve melted at once and he spoke as if relieved of a physical burden. "It is Don Santiago. It is as if God had laid His hand heavily upon the whole family to crush them. You heard that Dona Encarnacion, Don Ygnacio's wife, was killed by a drunken vaquero last spring? It was in March."

"No, I had not heard," Kinkaid replied. "I am sorry. I only knew that he was upset because his two sons had not yet returned from Spain."

"*Si*. And that was a bad thing, too. They should never have gone. Then perhaps this curse would never have fallen upon them. Even the Padres are afraid to have her at the Mission. They know what she is. A witch! You can see it in her eyes. And the old one is a witch, too. They will put a curse on all of us."

"What are you talking about, señor?"

"That Gypsy infidel Santiago had the bad luck to kidnap from Seville and bring here! You have never seen such a godless creature, señor, eyes that spit fire and fingers like talons ready to tear your heart out. She bewitched poor Santiago, of course, and what Don Ygnacio and the governor will order done about her, I cannot guess." He broke off suddenly at the sound of spurs jingling. "Here is Pio."

Pico swung briskly along the veranda toward them, excitement in his small wide-set eyes and a half smile on his pendulous lips.

"It is all a prank, *amigos,* nothing but a boyish joke. And the joke is on that stiff-necked, pompous Joaquin!" Pico laughed till the tears came to his eyes and he had to use the red silk handkerchief to blow his large nose.

"Come, we will ride to the Mission and I will tell you all about it on the way. It is unbelievable, I promise you! Santiago will never hear the end of it, nor the Alvarjos. But it was all done in jest, and *por Dios,* he brought it off! Can you imagine, kidnapping a *gitana* from the Triana in Seville and hiding her halfway across the ocean from the eyes of his brother, and then planking her out full in his face when nothing could be done about it? Wonderful! Sublime! I could never have done as well myself. Not in a million years!"

He did not add that part of his enjoyment came from the fact that for the first time the proud and powerful Alvarjos were faced with disgrace and ridicule. Though he had never expressed it, Pico harbored a certain resentment and envy toward the few unassailable families of pure Castilian blood who had easily secured immense royal grants for themselves and, whether consciously or unconsciously, looked down their long aristocratic noses at their less wise or less fortunate neighbors.

The Picos traced their lineage from Count Pico, of Italy, whose grandson Pio II had migrated to Spain. His son, in turn, had gone to serve in the army in Mexico, where he had married a Mexican woman.

Since the first expedition to California, only the Padres, the governor, the first commissioned officers, some few sergeants and privates, were of pure Spanish stock. The rest were of varying degrees of mixed blood. Many, like Pio, were born of families whose founders had come to Mexico in the sixteenth century and quite naturally intermarried with the local women. The first California colonists came from good country stock, from Sonora and Sinaloa mainly, and in most cases had some Indian blood.

In Mexico itself such a mixture was something to be proud of; every man was happy to admit his Aztec heritage. But the moment you crossed the California *frontera del norte,* all was changed. Here where Indians were the inferiors universally looked down upon by their conquerors, any admission of Indian blood was obtained only at sword's point. And the highest insult you could offer a member of the *gente de razón* was to hint that he had a dash of Indian blood in his veins. They were all Spanish, pure Spanish, and it was a dueling offense to say otherwise.

It went without saying that the few in California who could still claim pure Castilian blood were hated openly or in secret by the rest of the population. Pico's feeling toward the Alvarjos was not unique—far from it—but it boded ill for the shaky, uncertain government of Upper California. And foreigners were beginning to see the chink

in the armor that could divide and lay waste a rich and
desirable territory, if properly exploited.

As they galloped along the dusty road toward the Mission, Pico had told Kinkaid the whole story of the proud
Alvarjos' disgrace, with relish. The officer in charge at
the presidio had explained to him that Santiago had indeed committed an offense, since it was against the law
to bring an infidel woman into the territory and keep her
there. The governor would undoubtedly have her deported
on the first vessel to leave port.

The Mission lay white in the sunlight, the campanile
ringing out the Angelus. The riders dismounted at the front
gate and tossed their reins to a pair of Indian boys.

The musty Mission smell smote them afresh as they
crossed the arched veranda and entered the *sala*. In the
little dining room beyond, the two Padres rose from their
seats where they had been about to begin their noon meal,
and came forward with a warm welcome.

"Capitán Kinkaid! God is good to have brought you
safely back to our shores again," said Padre Fernando
Martin. "And Don Pio, Don Macario, you are welcome,
my sons." He had grown old and frail in the service of
San Diego Mission, and his toilworn hands gave mute tes-
timony to his unceasing efforts to bring fertility to this
barren land.

Padre Pascual Oliva was a younger, shorter man, with
a soft, shy smile. He said gently, "You are most welcome,
señors. Please come in and dine with us?"

He drew them into the dining room and found them
seats at the table.

Padre Martin poured wine, telling them with modest
pride that it had been made from the Mission's own
grapes, and raised his glass.

"To our young friends and their continued grace in
the sight of God."

There was salad, cold meat, and onions cooked with
Indian peppers and olive oil. There were also frijoles,
guisado, tortillas de maiz, and a large basket of fruit.

"Everything is from the Mission orchards and gardens,"
said Padre Oliva quietly, pointing to the oranges, tanger-
ines, plums, peaches, apricots, and pears.

"We have come to ask you about Santiago Alvarjo, Padre," said Pio when they had finished.

Padre Martin looked stricken and his hand shook on the table.

Padre Oliva said breathlessly, "It is a terrible thing."

"I do not know what came over the boy!" exclaimed Martin. "He has always been a good lad, devout, and obedient to his parents—so Padre Peyri, his confessor, has told me. What Don Alvarjo will do, or the governor, I cannot think. You know all about it, Don Pio?"

"*Sí*, Padre, I have been away a few days, but Macario came to my shop this morning and told me. It is a great pity."

"Is the woman really a witch, Padre Martin?" asked Macario.

"No, my son. She is a Gypsy, she tells me, like her companion. She is no more than a child. But it is true she is a heretic. What Don Santiago can have been thinking of in bringing her all the way from Spain, I do not know."

"She bewitched him," Macario stated flatly.

"We must all pray for enlightenment, my son," said the priest. "And not condemn her without cause."

Pio said, "Padre, I understand you have the two women in the *monjeria* here at the Mission?"

"Alas," said Martin unhappily. "There was nowhere else for them to take refuge. They are not with the neophyte women, however; they are in a small separate apartment we keep for those who are ill."

"Would it be possible for us to see them?" Pio's small eyes gleamed. "I would like to help Santiago if I can, and Capitán Kinkaid's ship will probably be the first leaving California. It might be that between us we can help solve this—disgraceful business?"

The priest hesitated. He was sorely upset by the whole affair. If no ship left soon, he would be forced for charity's sake to harbor the two strange women at the Mission, and their mere presence in the *monjeria* made him acutely uneasy. There was something savage and primitive about them that he had not found even in his contact with wildest gentiles of California.

"Perhaps, if you think you might help, Don Pio," the old priest said, "we might just pay them a brief visit?"

The men rose, Macario with alacrity, and followed Padre Martin's stooped figure out of the dining room, across the sunny square outside where a number of neophytes were sitting or talking in groups during the noon rest hour, and entered a deep alcove leading to a separate wing of the Mission where the nunnery or *monjeria* for unmarried women and girls was located. It was a long, low apartment furnished with rows of wooden bedsteads, and small high windows near the roof. The windows were too small for anyone to climb through, the purpose being to keep recalcitrant girls from leaving, and industrious males from getting in. The heavy wooden door was barred at night and the married woman in charge slept with her bed rolled against it.

They passed through the empty *monjeria*, for the women, by no means prisoners, were only inside at night, and Padre Martin paused before a smaller archway and took a large key from his rope girdle.

From inside the men could hear the dull, steady thwack of a tambourine and the sound of movement on the dirt floor.

Padre Martin turned the key slowly and threw the heavy door back.

There was not a man present who expected to see what he did now, or who was not rooted to the spot, dumb with shock at the sudden spectacle.

A nimble houri danced in the filtered sunlight, the tambourine held high above swirling black hair that twisted in the air like uncoiling snakes. She had her back to them, and it was not until she turned to face them a moment later, that they saw she was naked to the band of her low-hung skirt displaying softly rounded shoulders, small high breasts, and slender supple waist that narrowed to her exposed belly. They saw it all in one flashing glance.

Padre Martin moaned and covered his face with one hand, while with the other he yanked the door shut with such violence that dust and splinters showered down into their startled faces.

The old priest turned the key raspingly in the lock and, white-faced, marched out of the building.

They watched him scurry across the square like a frenzied lizard, and disappear inside the church.

What Bart Kinkaid had seen in that one brief glance of

girating, nubile, coppery flesh and hostile obsidian black eyes had slashed through him like the point of a cutlass, baring his own inner passions in a way he had never suspected possible. He had considered himself, according to his New England upbringing, a carefully contained man, a worldly man, and this Gypsy was little more than a child—a street urchin at that—but he was distinctly aware that somehing in her own hard core of disdain touched a similar natural dominance in his own character with a challenge that left him startled and shaken because it was so unexpected. Then, as he turned to follow the others, aware of the uninterrupted, defiant thwack of the tambourine still coming from behind the thick door, the trace of a smile touched the corners of his mouth. Perhaps Macario Canejo was correct, and she had the inborn power to bewitch all who saw her. He knew one thing: she would linger in his secret thoughts for some time to come, even if their paths never crossed again.

CHAPTER 7

That first night on board ship Tarifa had slept in drugged unawareness of what was going on around her. At dawn, when she wakened, they were already far at sea, and the ship was rolling and tossing like a cork in a fountain.

Tarifa held her belly and felt it rise and fall with an alarming motion, not at all in rhythm with the ship.

"Ohhh!"

The moan came with piteous regularity from the other bunk in a corner of the small, stuffy cabin.

Tarifa got up and reeled across the floor. She bent to peer into Penti's glazed eyes and was startled to find her face a vivid pale green.

"I die," gasped Penti. "I die—on this accursed ship— and they will throw me into the sea."

"Hobarra will not let them," said Tarifa shortly. "You are our servant now."

Penti moaned again and turned to retch on the floor. Tarifa jumped back with the grace of a cat and called her a pig and a dirty old woman in sharp Romany.

Her own stomach was none too easy, but she had the dancer's ability to adapt herself to motion, and she was determined not to make a fool of herself like Penti.

The cabin was tiny, with only one small closed port-hole through which she could detect the heaving sea. There was tremendous noise, too, the creak of timbers and crack and strain of rigging as the ship fought her way sluggishly through the churning waters.

She was not quite certain of how she had got here or why; it all seemed like a pleasantly hazy dream. But she remembered that Hobarra had brought her with him, and nothing else mattered. There was Penti's bundle in one corner, a small trunk, a tiny mirror over an anchored washbasin, the two bunks, and nothing else to be seen ex-cept for the gaudy shawl Santiago had bought her, draped over the end of her own bunk. There was a heavy door set high in the opposite wall of the cabin. By clawing her way from one section of wall to the other, Tarifa reached it and turned the handle.

It was locked.

She was not alarmed. No doubt Hobarra had locked it for safety's sake on his way out. She careened back to the washstand and looked at her face in the mirror. Her hair was disheveled and there was a smudge on her nose and along one cheek. She found some water slopping in a pitcher fitted into a wooden slot, and managed to pour a little into the basin. She washed her face and hands; ran her fingers through her tangled dampened hair; and took a tin cup from a hook, dipped out water from the pitcher, and drank thirstily.

She felt much better when she lay down on her bunk again, and began to toy with the tambourine she discov-

ered against the wall, where someone had propped it for
safekeeping.

She wondered what it was going to be like to belong
to Hobarra, to be his mistress. Perhaps, if he were pleased,
he might even want her for his wife. It made little difference to Tarifa how he took her. Gypsies married by choice
and for only as long as they pleased one another. It was
the only sensible arrangement, she thought. But if Hobarra
had asked it, she would have married him in front of a
priest, and for life. She lost herself in dreams of Hobarra
until she was brought back sharply at the sound of a key
turning in the door.

. The eager smile on her face was for Hobarra, but it
was Santiago Alvarjo who stepped over the high threshold
and closed it quickly behind him.

"Where is he?" she demanded. "Where is Hobarra?
Why does he leave me alone like this for such a long
time?"

Santiago did not answer her question, and he seemed
nervous when he said, "I have a servant coming with some
food for you. What is the matter with Penti?"

"She is seasick. Get someone to clean up that mess on
the floor before Hobarra comes in."

Penti rolled up on one elbow, her pale face giving her
an unearthly, ghostly look. "You will never see your torero again," she chortled. "He left the ship as soon as he
put us aboard—just as he arranged with Señor Alvarjo.
Ask him! I heard them talking. You have been fooled,
Tarifa, fooled!" She fell back, cackling and moaning at
the same time.

Tarifa did not believe a word the lying old crone had
said. It was all pure spite because she had called her vile
names a while back. But she sat up very straight on the
bunk, like a young Egyptian queen and looked at Santiago.

He had never had a face like Joaquin's that could mask
his emotions completely; certainly he could hide nothing
from Tarifa. One look was enough. A moan escaped her
own lips as she realized the incredible, the horrifying truth.
She was not being sped over the seas in the company of her
lover, to a new life of wonder and delight. Instead she
was the prisoner of this lying Santiago, whom she hated

now as she had never hated anyone in her life. Killing would be too good for him; he would have to be tortured, slowly and cruelly, to give her any satisfaction. She wanted to fly across the cabin and tear at his face and eyes with her nails. But the distance was too great, the ship pitching too badly. She would only stumble and fall at his feet and make a fool of herself. And Tarifa made a grim and solemn vow to herself in that moment never to allow herself to be made a fool of twice by Santiago Alvarjo. No! She would find a way to even the score with him.

"You lied to me," she said between her teeth. "You arranged all this to make a fool of me. You tricked me!"

"I had your mother's permission," he said. "Ask Penti. I am to send her money and she agreed for you to come with me. I admit I used Hobarra to get you aboard ship because I knew you would not come otherwise. But I had no intention of making a fool of you, Tarifa. Far from it. I hope to help you. In California you can begin a whole new wonderful life."

"With you!"

He colored. "No. I know you do not want me." He tried patiently then to explain why he had done this thing, tried to make her understand why he had to get the best of his brother Joaquin, to humiliate him just once and bring his arrogant pride tumbling down.

But Tarifa understood only that he had used her, duped her, robbed her of Hobarra, and that from this moment he was her archenemy.

She sailed her tambourine at him, narrowly missing his head, and her eyes blazed with hatred and fury."

"I spit on your California! When I get there I will tell everyone what you are. A liar! A cheat! A stealer of women! I will put a curse on you, and from this instant you will never know a moment's peace!"

Her words were to prove more prophetic than either of them could guess. And Santiago had a moment of stark superstitious fear as her words washed over him, and he met her long, strange, hate-filled eyes. Bandonna herself had warned him that to take Tarifa with him would prove bad luck. In a moment, however, his naturally gay and optimistic nature dispelled the gloom. He smiled at her.

"You will thank me for taking you one day. In California you will live like a queen—*faraóna,* you call it? They will pay in gold to see you dance. You will be rich and famous."

"Get out of here," Tarifa breathed, "and never come back, or I will kill you!"

Santiago stood looking at her uncertainly. He was relieved that she knew, but she clearly needed more time to get used to the idea, or to forgive him, if that was possible.

He opened the door at a faint knock and admitted a cabin boy carrying a tray.

"This is Carlos," he said. "Just knock on the door and call him if you want anything. He will be nearby."

"Premita Undebē!" Tarifa shouted.

The cabin boy, who had picked up a few Gypsy phrases on the wharves, turned pale at the powerful curse.

For Santiago, the voyage was tense and boring. He feared that Joaquin would discover Tarifa before they reached their destination, that the cabin boy or Tarifa herself would give him away, and still he was bored at the endless idle days. He had nothing to fear from the captain or crew, for he had paid generously for their silence before they sailed, the captain accepting the arrangement as just the whim of a rich young caballero. But unlike Joaquin, who spent the days reading in the saloon, the evenings playing piquet with the captain, Santiago craved activity and his young body rebelled at the enforced confinement in bad weather, with only short promenades on the limited deck space to relieve his pent-up energy when it was fair.

In spite of the storms they encountered at first, and again in rounding Cape Horn, they made surprising headway, and they were nearing their first stop at San Blas when Santiago's little house of cards came tumbling down around his ears with such startling suddenness that he was completely taken by surprise.

He had begun taking the two Gypsies up on deck late at night for a brief breath of air while Joaquin was sleeping and most of the crew were below. He should have been forewarned when Tarifa, who had so far maintained a stony silence in his presence, deigned to speak to him one starry night. It was the first time since their walk in the Triana that they had been alone, as Penti, seasick, had remained below.

"Are you warm enough?" he asked.

"I am not cold," she answered quietly.

"Tarifa—I'm sorry about all this, terribly sorry. Can you understand? Will you try?" His eyes pleaded with hers as he turned her with one hand, shyly, to face him.

Her eyes seemed to reflect the sheen of starlight on the black water, like a brilliant film over surging powerful movement beneath.

She walked away from him and leaned against the rail, her hand on one of the ropes. He was about to join her when she bolted with startling swiftness. One moment she was standing before him on the deck, the next he saw her spring to the rail and into the rigging and begin to scramble up the shrouds like a monkey.

"Tarifa!"

She paid no attention to his cry of warning. She went on, up and up, in spite of Santiago's sharp protests from the deck. When she finally reached the yard, she sat down on it, clasped her hands around mast and halyards, shut her eyes, and hung weakly there.

The ship was beginning to pitch and toss more sharply now as the breeze freshened. Unused to such heights, she was growing dizzy. She would have given worlds to be safe on deck again, but was too proud to cry out. Besides, there was solace in the thought that the man below her was suffering for having placed her in this invidious position.

She meant to stay there until everyone on the ship knew of her presence, including Joaquin Alvarjo and the captain. She hoped they would put Santiago in irons.

Below her, Santiago was in a frenzy lest she lose her precarious balance and fall. He knew that his cries must have aroused the ship and that the deck would be alive with people in an instant, yet he couldn't risk waiting for an experienced hand to come. He crawled clumsily into the rigging and began to inch his way upward, keeping his eyes on Tarifa's small swaying figure. If she fell he was responsible for killing her. He had no idea she had become so desperate. He had never been aloft in a ship before, himself, and the swaying motion increased as he climbed. His hands and face were wet with perspiration, yet he kept on, hoping his hold wouldn't slip on the ropes.

Below him he could hear shouts of alarm and the ropes moved as if others were coming after him, but he dared not glance down. One look and he would be frozen with fear, unable to take another step.

On the dizzy height of the main topgallant yard, Tarifa clung desperately to her support. Slowly she became aware of someone coming toward her from below, then a hand touched her shoulder, and a man swung himself toward her across the yard and grasped her by the arm.

"Tarifa! Look at me. No, don't look down! Look at *me*."

"Santiago," said Tarifa weakly. She flung herself into his arms so recklessly that they both nearly fell from the yard.

"Hold on," Santiago said, clutching the girl tightly. He moved down at a snail's pace, a step at a time, praying that help would come from below before his strength gave out.

After an eternity he felt stronger arms relieving him of his burden. Freed, he wobbled and almost fell himself from the shrouds. But someone steadied him and helped him down from the rail onto the deck at last.

The first figure he sought was Tarifa's, where she stood within the shelter of Penti's arms. The old Gypsy was muttering savagely at him under her breath, but it didn't matter. Nothing mattered now that Tarifa was safe.

Joaquin's voice lashed out at him like a blacksnake whip. "Santiago, come with me!"

He turned, saw his brother standing in the light of a ship's lantern near the captain. Joaquin would not upbraid him in public—he was reasonably sure of that, that was not the Alvarjo way. Santiago was quite ready to make an end of it anyhow, now that the whole matter had ended in such a fiasco. He followed Joaquin's rigid back to his brother's cabin and stepped inside. Joaquin closed and locked the door.

There were white ridges of anger around his brother's wire-thin mouth and his narrowed black eyes had the fanatical fury of an Inquisitor. Santiago had no doubt that Joaquin would gladly have watched him drawn and quartered in that instant if it had been possible. In a way, his brother's shock and anger now were the same as he had anticipated experiencing when he displayed Tarifa to him at the end of the voyage. And he found himself enjoying the same satisfaction he had hoped to feel then.

Harsh with suppressed emotion, sharp as a rapier, Joaquin's voice cut at him. "You have disgraced the name of Alvarjo for all time! Do you know that?"

Santiago shrugged, but Joaquin would not let him speak. As he opened his lips his brother cut him off.

"You have lied and cheated! Bribed and dickered with menials! Stolen or kidnapped a filthy Gypsy girl, with the outrageous presumption of taking her to California!"

Santiago's eyes glittered.

"I did it to show you that you are not God Almighty, Joaquin!"

"Now you add blasphemy to your sins!"

"Think a little of your own sins, brother. Arrogance, avarice, and pride. It's time you took a good look at yourself. You're the oldest, so Father has given you the most and the best, but that does not mean that you are to rule the rest of us like a despot, or that your word is law!

"I'm sick and tired of being reminded of your superior wisdom, your education, your authority. If these things are true, prove it, earn them! Then perhaps we can respect you."

"You speak like the foolish, ignorant boy you still are," Joaquin snapped. He reached behind him and picked up a light cane. "In Father's absence I am responsible for your behavior, and it is my duty to punish any—deflection from obedience. Take off your jacket."

Santiago stood still. His eyes were steady and unafraid.

"Take off your jacket!"

"Come and take it off."

With an oath Joaquin leaped at him and lashed out with the cane. It came down hard across Santiago's left shoulder, momentarily paralyzing his arm.

At the same instant Santiago reached up with his right hand and grasped the cane. They wrestled back and forth across the small cabin, crashing into a table, a washstand, the bunk. Joaquin was breathing heavily but Santiago was bright-eyed, eager, and unwinded. This was better than he had expected, hand-to-hand combat with Joaquin. How he ached to plant one blow on that aloof, arrogant face! Oddly, he did not hate Joaquin; he merely wanted to make him aware of his own shortcomings, his own humanity.

"You've spent too much time over your books and the gaming tables, Joaquin." Each was twisting mightily at the

cane with both hands now and Santiago could feel
Joaquin's grip weakening.

"I will punish you as you've never been punished before!" breathed Joaquin.

With a swift surprise lunge, Santiago drove the cane
into Joaquin's chest, knocking the wind out of him. Before he could recover, Santiago tore the cane out of his
brother's loosened grasp and flung it behind them. He
moved in close and lashed out with a hard blow that
landed on the side of Joaquin's jaw. He saw him go down
with a look of ludicrous surprise, sliding along the edge of
the bunk. He got to his hands and knees and waited,
shaking his head from side to side like a bull trying to
free his neck from the *bandarillos*.

Nothing had ever given Santiago so much pleasure, such
pure satisfaction in his life as that one sharp, clean blow.

He had failed to notice that the sea had grown so much
rougher. Everything in the little cabin swayed and bounced
and rolled. It was the large water pitcher, fallen from its
wooden rack where the two men had bumped into it, that
was Santiago's undoing. As he waited for Joaquin to get
up and resume the fight, stepping back to brace himself, his
foot skidded over the pitcher and he fell heavily, crashing
his head against a corner of the washstand. It seemed as if
the ship had cast him adrift in the sea, and he was sinking
slowly but surely into the black watery depths. . . .

Santiago came to on his own bunk. There was a dim
lantern burning above him, and the gray dawn had begun
to make the porthole opaque. His head ached stupendously
and he felt gingerly the back, where someone had tied a
crude bandage over the matted hair and crusted blood.
Sangre de Dios! Could Joaquin have done that?

Then he remembered. Something had been rolling under
his feet. The fall, followed by sudden oblivion.

He got to his feet and walked unsteadily to the door. It
was locked, and he began to shout and pound on it. "Open
this door!"

"I can't, señor," a voice answered from the other side.

"Who is that?"

"Carlos, señor, the cabin boy."

"Why can't you open the cursed door?"

"Because Don Joaquin has ordered it to remain locked

until we reach port. And because he has the key, señor; I am sorry."

"Tell the captain I want to see him!"

"Por favor, señor, he will not come. And he would not help you if he did come. He has taken money from Don Joaquin, and given us instructions to follow his orders."

Santiago swore under his breath. He was worried about Tarifa. If Joaquin should keep him locked up like this till they reached port—

"Carlos!"

"Sí, señor."

"Is—the Señorita all right?"

"Sí, señor. But like you, she and the other one are locked in until we reach port and Don Joaquin keeps the key."

For some reason this information alarmed Santiago more than anything else he had heard.

Never having been close to his older brother, he did not know Joaquin's way with women. But he had seen the unconscious glint of passion in Joaquin's eyes even as he denounced the little Gypsy in the box at the *corrida* in Seville, and he had also sensed her dislike and fear of him.

Joaquin, he told himself, was the oldest son of a distinguished Castilian caballero; he would never so forget his position and honor as to demean himself in the eyes of a woman. But Santiago could not quite convince himself of the truth of this. Certainly Joaquin would be the soul of gentlemanly honor with a lady. But what would he be with a common and defenseless little Gypsy girl?

He tried to tell himself that Tarifa was far from defenseless. Still he had experienced that day the cold self-righteous fury with which his brother could attack. That was the danger in Joaquin. Like Torquemada, Joaquin was capable of any cruelty once he had convinced himself that he was doing it with honorable intent.

"Carlos! Carlos!" He had little hope that the boy was still there, but an answer came quickly from the other side of the door.

"Carlos, tell the Señorita what has happened, that I am also locked in. But tell her that I will try to help her. And ask my brother to come here."

"Sí, señor. *Muy pronto."*

Santiago sat down on the edge of his bunk to wait. But

no one came near him. Not even when he heard footsteps in the companionway and called and beat on the door to draw attention. He cursed Joaquin, and vowed when they reached California he would repay him a hundredfold for every moment of his anguish and embarrassment.

It was night and only the dim light from the swaying lantern showed the outlines of the cabin, when a brief knock came at the door.

"You have my permission to enter," said Santiago with a savage humor.

The door opened and Carlos entered with a tray. Behind him stood Joaquin swaying slightly in the companionway, and smiling his infuriatingly superior thin-lipped smile.

"I have brought you some food, Brother, and Carlos will put up a fresh lantern."

"Let me out of here, Joaquin," Santiago said tightly. "When Father hears of this he will deal with you severely."

"When Father hears my report of your actions he will beat you with his blacksnake, as he did Bruno Cacho."

"You seem to have paid well for the captain's cooperation," said Santiago in a hard tone. "But he is still the master of this vessel and responsible for the lives of his passengers. I paid him for the two women's fares. They are his passengers, not your prisoners. Give him the key to their cabin."

Joaquin continued to smile, a bit foolishly, and Santiago realized with a shock that he had been drinking. Probably all afternoon. He did not often overindulge, but when he did all the pent-up devils within his tortured spirit were let loose.

Santiago rose from his bunk, but before he had taken a step Joaquin reached in, hauled Carlos outside, and slammed the door shut.

"Joaquin! Joaquin, for God's sake give the key to the captain. Now! I'm responsible for those women. Joaquin!"

There was no answer.

Santiago groaned and beat futilely on the heavy door until his fists were numb.

Tarifa sat cross-legged on her bunk, the tambourine in

her lap, and repeated to Penti the information Carlos had just whispered to her through the door.

"Now you have done it, my fine one!" fumed the older woman. "Now you have got the only one who could or would help us locked up himself."

"I am not afraid of Joaquin Alvarjo," said Tarifa flatly.

"Then you are a fool." Penti jerked her bundle of possessions up from the floor and opened it on the bed. "He has the Devil's look, and I have taught you too well for you not to have recognized it, *miri pen.*"

Tarifa looked uncomfortable. She did not like to admit even to herself that Penti was right. Devil take the old witch. Why had Bandonna saddled her with the old fool in the first place?

"It is time that I gave you one of these for your own," said Penti. She drew a small slender *navaja* of Toledo steel from a cloth wrapping and brought it to Tarifa's bunk.

"I do not like knives," said the girl sharply. "I have no need of one."

"Take it. Keep it in your blouse or your sash, or wear it tied to your leg as I wear mine." She lifted her full skirts, revealing the many hanging loops and hooks and pockets by which a Gypsy can secure her stolen loot and then walk away innocently empty-handed. In a garter tied tightly about her ropy thigh she wore a twin to the knife she offered Tarifa.

"I do not want it. Take it away, Penti."

The Gypsy woman shook her head.

"The time will soon come when you will need it, *miri pen.* Keep it safely until the need arises."

Penti returned to her own bed and after a while Tarifa tossed the knife peevishly under her pillow to be rid of the sight of it. She did not need a knife to scratch a man's eyes out, or kick him in the groin, or smash him over the head with her tambourine.

Carlos had brought them supper early and Tarifa had been sleeping lightly for an hour when she was awakened by a sharp Gypsy oath from across the room. Two men stood in the cabin by the open door and Penti had drawn her *navaja* and was crouched between the bunks.

One, Tarifa saw, was the second mate, a beefy, shifty-eyed man who had danced attendance on the rich Alvarjos from the first. The other was Joaquin Alvarjo, smiling his strangely disturbing smile at her. Tarifa scowled back at him.

"What do you want?"

"I am responsible for you now," answered Joaquin, "since my brother is—indisposed. I came to see if you are all right. Was your supper satisfactory?"

"You have locked Santiago up!"

He seemed surprised that she knew.

"He is also under my protection, and he was disobedient. I feel I must explain a few things to you, señorita."

"Santiago has explained."

"Get out—both of you!" cried Penti. "Or I'll use my little friend here."

Joaquin turned to the mate. "Get her out of here. Take her below and leave her there."

The mate drew a pistol from his belt and advanced with it leveled at Penti's breast. The Gypsy rose on her toes, the knife flat in her right hand, but Tarifa cried out.

"No! Put down the *navaja*, Penti. Go with the sailor. I am not afraid."

Penti froze, uncertainty washing over her dark features, but by then the mate had put the gun tight against her body and quickly relieved her of the knife.

Joaquin told the mate, "Send Carlos with glasses and a bottle of amontillado. The Señorita and I will celebrate our new friendship."

The mate nodded, thrusting Penti in front of him, out of the cabin. Joaquin turned the key in the lock and put it in his pocket.

"I am no friend of any Alvarjos!" said Tarifa coldly. "What do you want, señor?"

"To tell you how sorry I am that you have come to this plight through the stupidity of my younger brother. All the Alvarjo men are not so inconsiderate. As soon as we reach port I will see that you and your companion are put aboard the first ship returning to Spain, and,"—he pulled a well-filled purse from his pocket—"that you do not leave empty-handed. Now, can we be friends?"

Tarifa hesitated. She knew it was not safe to antagonize him openly; she was better off to play the game his way as long as she safely could.

Carlos knocked and was admitted with the wine, and

when he had gone Joaquin poured and served it himself.

"To your health and happiness, señorita, and a safe voyage home."

Tarifa eyed him over her glass as she sipped its contents. She did not much like its smoky flavor.

"Tell me about yourself, señorita," said Joaquin. He had seated himself on Penti's bunk facing her and there was a glitter in his eyes and a smell on his breath that told her he had been drinking heavily already. He was not drunk enough to be stupid, but he was drunk enough to be dangerous. If she played for time he might consume enough wine to completely stupefy himself.

"I am a Gypsy, and I dance," she answered simply.

"Ah, I have heard much of the Gypsies who dance in the Triana in Seville. Will you dance once for me, señorita, since we are going to be friends?"

Tarifa put down her glass, reached for her tambourine, and got quickly to her feet. She wore no shoes and she had replaced the gaudy silk dress Santiago had given her with a black-and-green-striped skirt and white low-necked blouse Penti had brought for her in her bundle. A green silk sash was bound tightly around her delicate waist.

At first she moved slowly, cautiously, in a desultory manner, in steps that were not particularly different from those of the other Gypsy dancers Joaquin had watched in Spain. It was true none of them had shown her particular grace of movement or unfailing rhythm, but there was nothing unique in the steps themselves.

He poured more wine and glanced away from her for a minute. When he looked up she had changed completely.

It was as if a different person shared the room with him. She moved like fire along a fuse, every muscle and line of her supple young body quivering with vibrant life. She was electric.

A pulse throbbed in his temple and his hand shook as he watched her. This was something he had never seen, though he had heard of it. A rare one. A true Gypsy *faraóna*, a gifted dancer of the ancient *Cante Jondo*. A sight to make a man's blood run like wine through his veins.

Tarifa had not meant to dance so for him, but she had become bored with herself, and once moving to the rhythm of her tambourine she had forgotten Joaquin entirely in the mysterious self-hypnosis the dance had always exercised over her.

So had she danced, alone, in the jail in Seville. So had she danced in the Plaza de las Sierpas, surrounded by bustling crowds. At such times everything went from her mind but the heady ecstasy of her own movement.

Joaquin, like Hobarra, found himself at first delighted, then entranced, then enslaved by the sultry passion and perfection of her gyrations.

He told himself at first that it was the drink that had befuddled and ensnared his thoughts, not the twisting, turning, fluid female figure before him.

He tore off his jacket and laid it on Penti's bed. He unwound his red sash and let it drop, and when Tarifa bent to the floor, exhausted at last, he went to lift her in his arms and carry her to her bed.

Moments passed before Tarifa came back to herself as from a drugged sleep and, for the first time, became conscious of Joaquin's arms around her. Panic-stricken as she had never been before, realizing the determined purpose in his searing glance, she fought with all her might to free herself from his grasp.

His arms were like iron bands, his fingers like barbs of steel. Her clothing ripped under them and her skin bruised.

She fought like a tigress. Biting, scratching, using her flexible dancer's knees in chest and groin.

He groaned once or twice but he did not slacken his hold. His breath was hot in her face as he forced her to her back and threw her hands up over her head.

He grasped both narrow wrists in one powerful hand, while his other moved downward to the waistband of her skirt, ripping the material away and exposing the frantically undulating coppery flesh underneath. His hand sought the soft inner side of the slender thighs and moved upward.

Blind with fear and hatred, Tarifa felt her hand touch the knife under the pillow. Her fingers closed around it. When he relaxed his grip on her arm she drew it out slowly. His eyes were elsewhere and he did not see. In one swift sure stroke, she brought it up and down like a torero at the moment of truth.

She heard the man on top of her scream with rage and pain as he rolled off of her onto the floor. She took the key from his pocket and like an arrow she flew to the door, unlocked it, and ran blindly down the companionway.

Joaquin lay on his bed of pain and moaned every time the ship's movement caused his body to shift. The mate and Carlos had found him shortly after Tarifa had fled and carried him to his own cabin. The mate had sent at once for the captain, who dressed the wound and, fearing Joaquin might die, released Santiago.

No one yet knew where the Gypsy girl had gone. The captain had ordered the ship searched but they had been unable to find her. They had put the old Gypsy back in her own cabin, thinking it might draw the younger one out of hiding, but so far this ruse had accomplished nothing.

Santiago watched his brother's pale, pain-wracked face with mixed emotions. It was a miracle he had not been killed outright. The little she-devil had sent the knife clean through his shoulder blade. A painful wound but, barring infection, not a fatal one. Joaquin had undoubtedly brought this all on himself. Tarifa must have been terrified indeed to have used a knife. He would have thought the old Gypsy more likely to have wounded his brother, but she had been incarcerated elsewhere, they claimed.

At the same time, Santiago, being naturally fair-minded, had to admit that when all was said and done he was solely responsible for the whole nasty affair. If he had not brought Tarifa in the first place none of this would have happened. It sobered him to think of what his father—not to mention Padre Peyri—would say when he found out. And Joaquin, his mother's favorite, was coming home to her wounded and ill, perhaps dangerously so, due to his own heedlessness.

Joaquin opened his eyes and asked, "Have they found her, Santiago?"

"No. They are still looking."

"Perhaps she jumped overboard."

The thought had not occurred to Santiago, but now that Joaquin presented it, it seemed a very sound one. He recalled the reckless abandon with which Tarifa had leaped into the shrouds and climbed to such dizzy heights on the mast to escape him. To escape what she probably thought was a charge of murder, she might well have jumped overboard.

"If she has," said Joaquin languidly, "it will be good riddance!"

"It is my fault she is here at all," said Santiago. "If she kills herself I am responsible for her death. It's the same as if I had killed her personally. A mortal sin."

"She tried to kill me last night," said Joaquin angrily.

"And you are probably to blame for that. What did you do to her?"

"Nothing," he said sulkily. "We were having a friendly glass of wine. She was dancing for me, when all of a sudden she went into a frenzy. Like a wild animal."

"I do not believe you. She can react like a wild animal, but she does not attack unless she is provoked—or attacked. Did you try to make love to her?"

Joaquin turned away. "What would I want with a gutter Gypsy? You are the Gypsy-lover. You smuggled her on board."

Santiago flushed. "I brought her on this voyage for no such purpose, and you know it. I promised her mother she would have opportunity in the New World, and I mean to keep my promise!"

"Oh, she will have opportunity," retorted Joaquin. "I predict a great success in one of the whorehouses in San Diego."

"Damn you! She is no whore. She will earn money dancing, and they will pay fabulous prices to watch her!"

"You forget," smiled Joaquin, "she will be deported at once. She is a heathen and a pagan. A *gitana*. To stay, she would have to be baptized a Catholic, espouse the faith, be naturalized—and these things she is not qualified to do. What self-respecting priest would baptize such a creature so she might remain and corrupt our young men?"

Santiago wheeled out of the cabin furiously and slammed the door. He could no longer face Joaquin without saying much that he would probably later regret. He had too many offenses to answer for now. Never a deep thinker, he was finding his present problems too complex and disturbing for his simple easygoing nature to analyze. He knew that he must find Tarifa, and reassure her. As for the rest, he would have to handle each problem when the time came.

He went to Penti's cabin and knocked, for the door was

now left unlocked. She opened it a crack and eyed him malevolently.

"I must speak with you, Penti. We must find Tarifa, to protect her from my brother. You must help me, for Tarifa's sake."

She stared at him as if she had not heard, but when he turned in disgust to leave she put a hand on his arm.

"There is a different devil in you than in your brother. I would rather see her in your hands. But I will kill you if you harm her. Come."

He followed her up on deck and back to the crew's quarters in the fo'c'sle. She pointed to some lashed-down sea chests that contained the men's good clothes, put away as soon as the ship left port, not to be taken out until they again reached land. A heavy canvas had been thrown over the pile.

"Tarifa! *Miri pen!*" Penti called softly.

There was a faint rustle under the tarpaulin like mice running, and then Tarifa crawled out on her hands and knees. At the sight of Santiago she started to draw back, but Penti lifted her to her feet, spouting Romany swiftly under her breath.

"You don't need to be afraid, Tarifa," Santiago said. She looked tired and cold and her clothing was torn and dirty. Dust and cobwebs had caught in her hair and her bare feet were filthy. He saw the scratches and bruises on her face and body then, and his anger at Joaquin returned in full force.

"No one is going to bother you again," he told her gently. "Go to your cabin and wash and rest, I will send Carlos with some food and wine. Your door is unlocked. You can go and come as you please. Neither my brother nor I will bother you for the rest of the voyage. I promise. You must trust me."

She stood looking at him for a moment as if weighing his words, then let Penti lead her from the fo'c'sle. But she did not speak. Santiago turned grimly toward Joaquin's cabin. He had indeed used the girl badly and he would pay for it.

But the door was locked.

On a hot July morning they anchored in San Diego bay, and the long uncomfortable voyage came to an end.

Joaquin appeared on deck, his arm in a sling fashioned from a black silk kerchief, his face drawn and pale. Not once did he glance at the two Gypsy women standing by the rail. Santiago followed him but they did not speak.

Tarifa looked curiously at the curving headlands, the sandy beach, with only three or four crudely built wooden houses in sight and she thought it an ugly place. So this was California, Santiago's golden land of promise! It was golden all right; the hills seared brown by the sun seemed made of molten brass from this distance. There was not a tree to cast a shadow over the desolate landscape. A few men in red shirts moved in and out of the wooden buildings on shore, hauling and lifting piles of large flat objects that looked like misshapen logs.

Santiago came over to tell them that they were to go in the longboat with the captain, Joaquin, and himself. His face was stern and he looked worried as he watched Joaquin being helped over the side onto the rope ladder by the mate and another seaman.

"We have many friends here," he said reassuringly. "Everything will be all right once I explain." He was not at all sure of this himself but it pleased him to see that his words had comforted the women.

Tarifa said, "There is no town."

He smiled down at her, "It is straight ahead behind those first hills. No distance at all. We will get horses at the hide houses and ride over."

"The hide houses?"

He pointed. "Those wooden buildings. They belong to the American shipowners who come to trade for our hides and tallow. This is their depot, where they store and cure the hides until they are ready to send them to Boston.

Tarifa had no idea of what he was talking about and was relieved when he led her to the rope ladder and helped her over the side.

The longboat bobbed and dipped in the current and Penti was terrified, but Tarifa enjoyed being sped over the water by the strong-pulling oarsmen.

Joaquin, who sat in front of her, kept his eyes rigidly ahead, and Santiago was silent during their brief journey.

The men at the hide houses seemed like white-faced giants to Tarifa. They were the first Americans she had ever seen and she could not understand a word they said;

even their Spanish was unintelligible to her. But they laughed
a good deal, and the burly sandy-haired man who lifted
her up behind Santiago even winked at her in a bold gay
manner.

All he got for his pains was silence and a dark scowl, but
even this seemed to please him and he laughed uproari-
ously.

Santiago handled his horse with a dash and skill that
drew Tarifa's admiration. He seemed somehow more complete on horseback. The ride was, as he had predicted,
brief.

The sprawling little town of mud-brick houses baked
in the July sun. The square was deserted save for a few
old men leaning in shadowy arched doorways, a scattering of ragged children, and a great many dogs, pigs, and
chickens wandering back and forth across the dusty road.

Joaquin, who led the procession, followed by the captain with Penti behind him, did not stop.

"Where are you going?" called Santiago.

"To the Mission and then the presidio. The Padres can
give the women shelter until we know what is to be done
with them."

Santiago knew that it was the only sensible solution.
There was no inn or hotel in town, and no respectable
woman in San Diego would accept two such guests in
her home, nor could the Alvarjos suggest it even to their
closest friends. Short of staying aboard ship there was nowhere else for them to go. Santiago told himself that they
would be more comfortable and safer at the Mission until
he had spoken to his father. But he was ill at ease as he
watched a reluctant Father Martin lead the women away.

"Why do we go to the presidio?" he asked a moment
later.

"To get some good horses, and see Captain Ruiz. I have
a present for him, remember? The sword from Toledo."

A sentry admitted Joaquin and Santiago to the *cuarto*,
where Joaquin asked after Captain Ruiz and was told he
was not at the presidio. He was just as pleased, for he
had been worried about getting Ruiz to agree to hold
Santiago at the presidio while he himself rode to Loma de
Oro. He had determined that Santiago should not present
his side of the story to their father until his own had been
duly considered.

Joaquin had another piece of luck, two young soldiers—friends of Santiago—who were serving out the term of their conscripted military duty at the San Diego presidio, came from the barracks at that moment and greeted the younger Alvarjo with eager enthusiasm.

Santiago would be kept busy while Joaquin went in search of José Ibana, who must be in charge in Captain Ruiz' absence. He found him enjoying a *cigarrillo* and a glass of wine in his own cubbyhole of an office.

"José?"

"*Sangre de Dios*—Joaquin Alvarjo!"

Tall and thin, with a long chin like a spade, José Ibana leaped up and wrapped his long arms about his friend's shoulders.

"How was Spain, *amigo?* And the little beauties of Seville, eh? Sit down, sit down! We will drink a toast to your safe return."

Joaquin sipped his drink, an excellent Madeira.

"Truly this is wine of the Moor, José," he said, surprised. "Have our California vineyards improved so much since I left?"

Ibana winked slyly. "Of the Moor indeed, full-bodied and unadulterated. Not like Christian wine, baptized with water? As a matter of fact it is from a barrel sent up from San Blas for the comfort of Governor Echeandia, whom I understand is soon to honor us with his presence. He will not miss one small barrel?"

Joaquin related the story of Tarifa to his friend's shocked and sympathetic ears, eliminating only his own treatment of Tarifa, and explaining his injury as the result of a storm at sea.

"It is not possible!" Ibana said. "An Alvarjo do such a mad thing? He must have lost his wits. The governor and Father Prefecto will surely deal with him personally. I should not like to be in his shoes!"

"You can help us," said Joaquin glibly. "Keep him here at the presidio for me until I have explained to my father. He has, after all, brought two foreign infidels into the country, which is against the law."

Ibana nodded but there was uncertainty in his eyes. He did not know how Don Ygnacio would react to such a bold action, and he was quite sure that Capitán Ruiz would never have condoned it.

Joaquin drew some gold pieces from his pocket and laid them on the table. "José, the Alvarjos always pay for a favor—and remember it. The Padres have agreed to hold the women for me; can you not hold Santiago? Believe me, I know what is best for all of them. If I have a chance to talk to Papa first, to explain fully, it may soften the blow and by the time he gets here his anger may have abated. He may not be as hard on Santiago. After all, I am responsible for him still. He has been in my care for these past months. I will have much explaining to do."

Ibana could see the justification in this, and he could certainly use the money Joaquin was offering him. Ibana was a man who never took big risks but was ever ready to take small ones, especially if there was profit in it.

"Very well, Joaquin. I will do it as a personal favor to you. But Santiago will surely raise a row and he has friends here."

"Seize him and lock him up. Keep the key yourself till I return. As for the men—you are in command here?"

"Yes, that is true."

"I will ride to Loma de Oro as quickly as your fastest horse can take me."

"You shall have my own. But for the love of the Holy Mother, return at once, Joaquin? If Capitán Ruiz should return—"

"Don't worry, *amigo,* my father will lose no time in coming here once I have spoken to him."

Santiago and his friends were amazed a few minutes later when two burly armed guards seized him and dragged him off. Ibana watched him locked in and then coolly pocketed the key.

"Let me out! What is the meaning of this, Ibana?" Santiago shouted, enraged.

"I am doing your brother a little favor, Don Santiago," Ibana replied sternly. "You will see that it is best in the long run."

In a frenzy of indignation Santiago watched Ibana march across the sunlit square and disappear inside the barracks.

His friends stood looking at him dumbly, in bewildered astonishment. They would like to have helped him but they did not know what crime he was accused of, and José Ibana was not a man to throw the son of the powerful Don Ygnacio Alvarjo into jail without good reason.

* * *

Mounted on Ibana's swift gray stallion, Joaquin took the road leading northwest up the coast out of San Diego. He skirted False Bay, a shallow arm of the sea three or four miles north of the town, and continued down the road that led among low barren hills.

Joaquin was not a lover of nature like his father and mother, but he noted in passing how dry the land looked and how lean the cattle and horses. After his years in Spain, everything in his native land looked crude and makeshift and much poorer than he had remembered. But now that he held all the cards he was not worried about his interview with his father, and he was as eager as a child to see his mother again, to feel her arms about him and look into her shining, adoring eyes. She was the only thing he had ever loved, and the only reason he had been willing to return to California. She was the reason for his hurry, not Santiago.

The gray stallion sped on through the afternoon's stifling heat and every garment on Joaquin's body seemed to be stuck to him. He had taken his injured arm out of its sling and the wound throbbed and pulsated now.

There was no one in sight on the long front veranda or on the balcony above when he dismounted wearily and tied the drooping stallion to the hitchrack.

He crossed to the open door and bounded into the dim cool *sala,* shouting, "Madre! *Madrecita,* I am home!"

Footsteps came then, running swiftly across the patio tiles and along the inner veranda.

Joaquin hurried to the other door leading to the patio and put out his head expecting to see his mother. Instead he saw his sisters, strangely garbed in black, in this stifling heat. His eyes darted beyond them, looking eagerly for his mother's figure to appear. But only Tía Isabella came out of his mother's room, also in black from head to foot. What was the matter with all the womenfolk? Was this some new fad from Mexico? If so, it was a ghastly one.

Tía Isabella reached him first and enveloped him in her arms with a glad cry.

"Joaquin, *mío!* Your father will be so happy. You must go to him quickly. You and Santiago. He has need of you. Thank God you are home safe! Your father is up on

Loma de Oro, in his little cabaña. He scarcely leaves it these days. You must go up to him at once."

"Where is Mother, Tía Isabella?"

He felt her stiffen in his arms. Her face had an anguished, terrible look, as if it had crumpled from the inside. She backed off from him.

"She is dead. She was killed in March. This house has been nothing but a morgue ever since."

Joaquin stood stock-still as his father had stood at Zenobio's when he first received the news. He heard the words and his mind recorded them in a flash, but his spirit refused to accept them. His mother could not be dead. She was the warmest, gayest, liveliest thing he had ever known. God could never be so cruel as to take her from him when she was still so young, so vital, so necessary to him.

He looked blankly at his aunt, and from her to the sorrowing faces of his sisters, and of Candelaria, who stood by weeping quietly into her handkerchief.

"No!" he shouted. "I do not believe you. She cannot be dead. Not my mother!"

"Joaquin," said Dolores gently, "there was no way for us to let you know. And Father does need you now. Badly. Everything on Loma de Oro has gone from bad to worse. If it weren't for Santos, I don't know what we would do. And even he is changed. Nothing is as it was."

"No!" said Joaquin. He shook his head and said through his teeth violently, "No, no, no!"

A man came through the front doorway, and Joaquin, turning, saw that it was Zenobio Sanchez.

"I'm glad you are home, *muchacho*," said the old man, quietly. "They are in a sorry way here. I do what I can, but it is not enough. Where is Santiago?"

"Yes," said Tía Isabella quickly, anxious to see her favorite nephew. "Where is your brother?"

The mention of Santiago jarred some of the blankness from Joaquin's brain.

"He is in San Diego. I will explain later. Where did you say Father is?"

"In his cabaña," said his aunt.

Don Ygnacio sat idly on the veranda of his hilltop sanctuary and watched the heat haze dance in the valley below.

Since his wife's death he had spent the better part of each day here and often a good part of the night. He remained kind and courteous and considerate of his family, he was solicitous of their welfare, but he no longer took an active part in making the decisions in his household. He left that to Isabella and Candelaria. And Santos, though he often sought advice from his *patrón,* got little of it. For months he had run the great rancho by himself.

He frowned when he heard someone coming up the little path. No one disturbed him here except in an emergency. He was annoyed at the effort he knew it would cost him to face any new crisis.

A man came toward him, young and travel-strained, with a pale ravaged face.

"Papa?"

"*Sí.*" Don Ygnacio squinted into the sunlight. "Who is it?"

"Joaquin."

Joaquin! With an effort Don Ygnacio got to his feet and held out his arms. Tears of weakness were coursing down his cheeks as Joaquin ran into them.

"*Padre mío!*"

"My son, my son! *De donde vines?*"

"From San Diego."

"Santiago?"

"He is still there. I must talk to you, Padre. They have just told me."

"Yes," his father nodded sorrowfully. "The beautiful one. She is gone. She was anxious about you, Joaquin. Each day she asked me when you would return."

The two men supported each other and neither was ashamed of the other's weeping.

A little later Don Ygnacio drew his oldest son to a seat beside him on the veranda, and began in a voice without inflection to tell him the story of Dona Encarnacion's death. At the end of his recital, during which he had spared no detail, even to his confession in the pasture to Father Cazon after he had killed Bruno Cacho, he found that he felt better than he had for months and saw that there was a new color in Joaquin's unusually pale face.

He placed a hand on Joaquin's knee and asked solicitously, "Have you been ill, my son?"

It was Joaquin's turn then to tell his own tale. He

watched with satisfaction the disbelief, anger, and outrage that came and went on his father's face.

At last Don Ygnacio leaped to his feet with something of his old vigor.

"We must go at once. I will deal with Santiago myself, but no son of mine shall spend a night in a presidio jail! You should have known better than to have left him there. I am displeased with you, Joaquin!"

"The officer in charge said that he had committed an offense and was a prisoner. I came to you as quickly as possible. There was nothing else I could do, Padre."

"Come! While I talk to Isabella, go and tell Santos to saddle El Capitán and Calabaza for us, and to come himself and bring El Canario for Santiago."

"Yes, Father."

"Take some food and wine before you leave. It will be a long night."

"*Sí.*"

The party of horsemen galloped away from Loma de Oro just as the sun was beginning to lower in the western sky. On hearing the reason for their journey, Zenobio had insisted on joining them; he also rode one of the Loma de Oro palominos.

They passed the Mission as the sun was going down, and Padre Cazon, recognizing the horses as he came down the church steps, wondered what had disturbed Don Ygnacio from his recent lethargy to ride so swiftly into the sunset.

Santiago paced his cell in the presidio like a jackal awaiting a lion's kill. They could not keep him here for long. They would not dare. Joaquin would have to report to their father at once, and when he did Don Ygnacio would attend to matters for himself.

He was not at all surprised when several hours after nightfall he heard his father's sharp voice outside, followed by swift orders from the sergeant. In a moment he saw lanterns bobbing toward his cell from across the square, and heard running feet.

Keys rattled and scraped against the lock, and then the door swung back and Don Ygnacio stepped into the dank cell.

He looked older, more worn than Santiago remembered

him, but his figure was as erect, his face as proud and
stern as ever. His eyes swept his son with a questioning
look but in the presence of the sergeant and soldiers he
merely said, "It is good to see you, my son, but not in these
surroundings. Come."

The sergeant looked unhappy.

"I do not know what to do, Don Ygnacio. I have been
ordered to keep Don Santiago in the jail."

Don Ygnacio turned on him coldly. "And I tell you to
release him, sergeant. *Muy pronto!*"

"*Sí,* Don Alvarjo. *Sí!*"

The sergeant stepped aside to allow Santiago to follow
his father from the cell. He watched them march across
the square to where Zenobio and Joaquin waited with the
golden horses.

"We will go to the Mission," he heard Don Ygnacio say
when they were all mounted.

At every Mission, rooms were always kept ready to receive travelers, and it was only the obvious importance
of these guests that caused the mayordomo, an elderly
Yuma Indian, to waken the Fathers.

"I desire to speak alone with my son Santiago," Alvarjo
told Padre Martin when they had exchanged greetings.

"Certainly, Don Ygnacio. Take the bedroom on the far
end; you will be undisturbed there. When you have finished, join us in the *sala* for a glass of wine and something
to eat. It will have to be cold, I fear, at this hour."

"*Muchas gracias,* Padre," Don Ygnacio said with grave
politeness.

He led the way into the bedroom, closed the door, and
turned to face his son.

Santiago stood bareheaded, his eyes downcast. Suddenly,
under his father's cold scrutiny, he was ashamed of all the
trouble he had caused.

"I want to hear what excuse you have to offer for your
actions, Santiago."

Don Ygnacio still carried his riding crop and he moved
it through his long fingers slowly as he waited.

Santiago told him the truth, sparing neither himself nor
Joaquin. He had often erred in the past but he had never
lied, and Don Ygnacio wondered at the discrepancies and
omissions in Joaquin's version.

"And you merely offer the excuse of a boyish prank for all this?"

"Yes, my father. I only wanted to teach him a lesson."

"And instead you have brought disgrace and ruin on all of us?"

Santiago said nothing. He was genuinely contrite but to admit it would have been of small comfort to his father in Ygnacio's present grim state of mind.

"I shall whip you," Don Ygnacio said at last, "and when you have repented and confessed, you shall do not only the Padre's penance for your sins, but penance at home as well for a full year. Morning and night you shall kneel in the chapel for three hours, and offer up your prayers for the good of your mother's soul."

Santiago's head jerked up and a questioning horror filled his eyes.

"Yes," said Don Ygnacio dispassionately. "Your mother is dead, her house in mourning, while you disgrace our name from Spain to California. I am grateful that she did not live to know of the dishonor you have brought upon us. I consider that you are also responsible for any sins committed by your brother Joaquin, for you are the cause of putting such temptation in his way. The Devil himself must have inspired you to bring such women here. Take off your jacket and shirt. Kneel down before the crucifix and pray to the Saviour for forgiveness."

Don Ygnacio's crop rose and fell with ceaseless precision as he watched the weals rise and then the blood course down his son's back. Still he did not stop until his arm ached and Santiago, bent double in pain, moaned as he sank to the dirt floor.

Alvarjo turned and left the room, taking his bloody crop with him.

His arms and legs felt like lead as he joined the others in the *sala*. His face was white as paper and his hand shook so badly when he accepted a glass of wine from a startled Padre Oliva that he spilled half of it on the floor.

"I would like," he told Father Martin in a voice as tight as a bowstring, "to speak with the women in the morning."

"Of course, Don Ygnacio. I do hope you can make some arrangement for taking them with you, or placing them elsewhere? I will direct the mayordomo to send them here to you after breakfast. I regret that Father Oliva and I must be off with the neophytes at dawn; we are harvesting the barley." He did not add that he could never face either of the heathen women again, not if his soul's salvation depended on it.

Don Ygnacio slept not at all. Sorely troubled, he paced his room or knelt to pray before the crucifix on the wall. In spite of his severity, his children were very dear to him. And Santiago's gay spirits and warm impulsiveness, so like Encarnacion's, had always pleased Don Ygnacio's own colder, more reserved nature.

Where had he failed in training his son? What had he done to bring about this digrace?

He realized grimly now that Joaquin had not told him all the truth, and he was hotly ashamed that a son of his should have handled a woman—any woman—as Santiago had claimed Joaquin did the young Gypsy girl.

He had no desire to see her at all. But an Alvarjo had never shirked his duty. He must see that she was sent back to Spain. He would give her money and see that she wanted for nothing until she was able to sail, and he would use every influence he had to keep the rest of his family from suffering for the disgrace brought upon them by Santiago and Joaquin.

It was barely dawn when he answered a brief knock at his door and found Joaquin standing on the threshold. He carried a steel-barbed leather scourge with which some of the Franciscans were in the habit of punishing themselves, obviously taken from the wall of the cell in which he had slept. There was an odd light in the young man's eyes.

"Padre."

"Come in, my son. You will waken the others."

Joaquin stood in the center of the room holding the scourge in front of him. He shivered under his short jacket, for he wore no shirt.

"I have lied to you, Padre. Santiago is not all to blame for what happened. I took too much upon myself. I acted like a tyrant, a despot. I refused to understand. I locked Santiago up, and the Gypsy girl. A madness came over me. I drank and I went to her cabin——" He passed a hand over his moist face. "I made her dance for me, and there was something—like a spell, a bewitchment, that came over me. I cannot explain. She was like an evil flame and

I meant to smother her, to quench her. I lifted her to the bed and fell upon her—"

"Stop!" Don Ygnacio's face was dark with blood, his eyes glittering as wildly as his son's. He tore the scourge from Joaquin's nerveless fingers and stripped off his son's jacket with rough urgency.

Then he paused, the whip raised in his hand.

The lean back and shoulders and arms were cut and shredded as if giant claws had ripped and torn them apart in a savage frenzy.

"Madre de Dios!"

Joaquin quivered but stood still.

"You did this?"

"Yes. I shall go on doing this until the Devil in me is gone, Padre."

The whip slid from Alvarjo's fingers and he bent wordlessly to retrieve the jacket and place it gently around his son's shoulders.

"Go to your room and rest," he said in a thick voice. "We will leave soon for the rancho. There has been enough punishment for one night."

Tarifa tensed as she heard the heavy footsteps, the jangle of spurs, and a vivid image of the men who had come to stare at her the day before flashed through her mind, making her shiver.

It had been noon, and stiflingly hot in the small, bare cell when she had begun to dance, slowly, to a somnolent rhythm, feeling the motion relieve the tension she had felt ever since entering this place. She had no trust in churches or priests.

She had just made a full sweeping turn and was standing with her bare back to the door, arms raised high above her head, when she'd heard movement on the threshold and turned to stare at the horrified priest and three open-mouthed men. Two of them were Californians; one, the squat ugly one, must be rich, for he was heavily decked out in gold chains. The third man wore a seaman's uniform and resembled the men at the hide houses.

In the instant that her gaze had locked with his cool gray one, Tarifa knew that the tall stranger's first surprise had turned to amusement.

The door had banged shut on her angry scowl.

He had been laughing at her. Laughing!

She flew across the room shouting curses in Romany and Spanish and beat on the door in her impotent black fury.

Suddenly, without rhyme or reason, the tall cold-eyed stranger had become the embodiment, the symbol, of everything evil she had suffered, everything she detested in this cursed California.

Now, as the door opened, she braced herself for the sight of the tall foreigner, and was surprised to be face-to-face with a Spanish gentleman who might have come from her own Seville.

Oddly, Don Ygnacio's first thought as he entered, followed by the half-breed woman who had charge of the *monjeria,* was not distaste but wonderment at the youth of the sultry little Gypsy.

Why, she was hardly more than a child! He had built up in his mind the voluptuous, deliberately taunting beauty of a practiced demimondaine.

She was nothing like he had expected. She was like a wary young animal flushed from its lair, like a brave but frightened child braced to accept a blow, and determined not to flinch.

To his dismay, he found that he felt sorry for her, and guilty because his sons had been the cause of her fear and discomfort.

"Señorita," he faltered. "I am Don Ygnacio Alvarjo."

Her pointed chin came up and she looked him full in the eyes.

She was not afraid of him! For some inexplicable reason this gave him pleasure.

"I wish to apologize to you and your companion for the unthinking actions of my sons. I want you to understand that you are not a prisoner here; you may go and come as you please, and I will see that you are well provided for. As soon as it can be arranged, I will see that you sail for Spain. More than that, I fear I cannot do. But if you have some other desire I will see that it is granted, if possible."

"This place is a church," Tarifa answered. "I do not like it here. I wish to go somewhere else to await the ship."

Don Ygnacio looked bewildered.

"But there is no place where you would be as safe,

señorita. There is no inn at San Diego. You could not live alone outside of the Mission. We are living on a frontier here."

"I do not wish to stay here, señor."

Don Ygnacio threw a look of bewilderment at Zenobio, who had accompanied him and was now leaning against the wall. The old man straightened and ground out his *cigarrillo* in the dirt floor with his bootheel.

"You could take a small house for them below the town near the beach."

"Leave a child like this alone in the married soldier's quarters? Unthinkable!"

"Then hire a bodyguard. There are many retired soldiers on the beach who would thank God for the job."

Don Ygnacio knew that this was so, yet he hesitated to follow his friend's suggestion. Suppose something happened; wasn't he responsible for the little creature until he got her safely out of California?

He toyed briefly with the idea of taking her to Loma de Oro. But that was impossible. He could not have her under the same roof with Isabella and his children. He could not even chance keeping her in the servant's quarters. Not after he had seen her effect on his two oldest sons. She might look a child and still be a temptation to hot-blooded young men.

Tarifa watched Alvarjo's proud stern face and thought he was the kind of man her father must have been. Aloof, dignified, arrogant, like a fearless eagle. He sat as erect as a king and yet he spoke to her kindly, without condescension. She was not afraid of him as she had been of Joaquin, and he did not nettle and anger her as Santiago did.

"Señorita," he said slowly, "if I could arrange to get you a little house, and a man to safeguard it for you, would you prefer that?"

"I have no need of a man to protect me! Penti and I can look after ourselves, señor."

He shook his head. "No, it would not be safe. You must have a man nearby."

Tarifa shrugged. It mattered little to her whether a man was present or not. She would be free and out of this uncomfortable church, away from its strange-acting, gray-robed priests.

"If you wish it, señor. I will do as you say."

"*Gracias.* Zenobio, do you know of a house we can rent, and a responsible bodyguard for the Señorita—what is your name, my child?"

"Tarifa, señor."

"Ah! You bear the name of the great Tarif of the Moors?"

Tarifa was delighted. "Yes, señor. My father was a Moor."

"Ah, that is most interesting. You must tell me about your father someday."

Tarifa nodded her head briefly but she was pleased. If there were men of such understanding and wisdom as Don Alvarjo here, California could not be such a terrible place after all.

"If you wish to go back to Loma de Oro," said Zenobio to Don Ygnacio, "why don't you let me make arrangements here for the Señorita's comfort?"

Ygnacio's face lighted with relief. He should be getting back to the hacienda, and Zenobio could handle matters here in San Diego better than he could. Were not most of the old ex-soldiers his friends and acquaintances?

He took a heavy pouch from his sash and handed it to Zenobio. "It is a kindness I shall not forget, *amigo.*"

Zenobio laughed as he hefted the pouch. "It would be no trouble to set up fifty such *casitas* with this, *compadre!*"

Ygnacio rose and walked over to where Tarifa and Penti sat on a long bench.

"Señorita, my friend Don Zenobio Sanchez will arrange everything to your liking, and leave you money to provide for your needs. He will see that you have an ex-soldier to watch over your safety while you are here. If you need something else for your comfort, you have only to send word to me at Rancho Loma de Oro."

"*Gracias*, señor."

Up close he noted that her thick black hair curled at the ends, as did her long eyelashes. It was uncanny. Witch eyes, like a bird's, the corners turned up like the point of a curved knife. In ancient mystery lore, he recalled, the enchantress always had a witch-pointed eye like that of this little *gitana.*

Don Ygnacio bowed and left the room with the odd sen-

sation of having been in the presence of a spirit more
inflexible than his own. And yet he had not found it unpleasant. Behind him he heard the old Gypsy mutter,
"*Sar tacho.*"

And Tarifa nodded, smiling to herself at the rare compliment Penti had paid the proud old Castilian: "He's all
right."

Tarifa opened the windows of her tiny bedroom wide to
let in the morning sun and the fresh breeze from the sea.

Everything about her new house pleased her entirely.
She and Penti had been in it a week, and every day for a
week she had fingered and examined and rearranged each
item of her marvelous if temporary possessions.

The house Don Zenobio had finally selected was situated at the top of the little cluster of dwellings that crowded together on a small hill just beyond the town. It belonged to ex-corporal Gaspar Escobar, who had served under Anza and Rivera, and was invalided out of the service
when his horse had fallen with him while he was chasing
runaway neophytes in the sierras. His left leg had been
broken and the bone had never set properly. In spite of
his injury, Corporal Escobar, a powerfully built man in his
late fifties, was inclined to view his position with a wry
good humor. He had known Capitán Zenobio Sanchez for
many years and had once served in his company at Monterey.

"It is not so bad as you might think," he told his old
commander. "I have my house, the sunshine is free—when
it shines—and the monte game always open at Sebastian
Cota's."

A recent widower who had been married to a half-breed
woman, he was not against having women in his house,
and his neighbors would gladly rent him a room next door
while the two Gypsies occupied his abode.

Zenobio explained that word would get around fast
enough and the curious and the troublemakers could be
counted on to flock to the little home of Corporal Escobar.

"Do not fear, Capitán," laughed Escobar. "I will see
that the señoritas are safe. I still have my musket and a
pistol, not to mention my *compadre* here." He patted the
long knife protruding from his boot.

"Bueno. Do not let them go into town alone—or anywhere else for that matter."

"I understand, Capitán." The small, light eyes were curious in the ruddy face. Zenobio had told him only the rudiments of the Gypsies' story but he demanded to know no more. Zenobio was satisfied that Escobar would keep his own counsel.

And despite the interest the San Diegans, in the little house at the top of the hill everything had remained quiet for a week.

Inside the three-room adobe Penti was cooking eggs over a charcoal fire in the crude round fireplace.

Tarifa danced lightly from the bedroom across the *sala* and paused outside the low kitchen door admiring the clusters of dried red peppers and sheaves of corn which hung from the rafters above Penti's head. The late Señora Escobar's cooking utensils hung from the rafters on pegs, or were stacked neatly on the crude chest under the one low-silled window.

"I am starved this morning," Tarifa told Penti. "Why can't you hurry?"

"You are getting too fat as it is," the old Gypsy grumbled. "California agrees with you too well. You grow like a lazy *gata.* Soon you will no longer be able to dance the *Siguiriya."*

Tarifa made a face at her, and to disprove her words whirled into the little *sala* in the ancient dance.

Gaspar Escobar, coming in the *sala* door, was struck speechless at the spectacle. Capitán Sanchez had explained that he was to be guardian over an incomparable *bailaora.* But—

Santa Margarita!—if the soldiers at the presidio or the young bloods of the town should get wind of this, he would have to fight them off with a pikestaff. He must warn her not to dance like this where anyone could see her.

"Señorita Tarifa," he began, "you dance like a living flame and it gives me nothing but pleasure to watch you, but I must beg you not to dance like this where others can see you."

"Por qué?"

"Because it is not safe! Once they see you they will be after you like wolves after a stray lamb. You must listen to me, *niña."*

"I am not afraid." She tossed her head and grinned wickedly back at him. "Besides I have you to protect me, Gaspar."

He groaned. If this kept up his money would be well-earned indeed. He considered sending word to Don Zenobio that he did not want the job regardless of the pay.

Tarifa drew his arm playfully through hers.

"Have you had breakfast?"

"No. And now I have no stomach for it."

"Come and eat and you will feel better. Penti!"

"Patience. I come. Why don't you set the table while you stand about doing nothing but waggle your tongue?"

Tarifa pirouetted daintily to a cabinet against the wall and began to take out plates, cups, and cutlery. The round table in the center of the room bore a blue-checked cloth trimmed with crude lace which Tarifa greatly admired, and a set of glass cruets in a battered pewter stand which she thought magnificent.

Corporal Escobar had a house to be proud of indeed. There were calico curtains at the windows, a bearskin rug on the floor, paper fans and holy pictures and handmade wreaths of hair flowers on the walls. The bedroom had a real bed covered with a bright red-and-green wool serape, and an oaken chest of drawers with a small mirror above. Tarifa never tired of sitting cross-legged on the high bed and looking at herself in the mirror. She regretted it wasn't large enough to reflect her whole figure so that she could watch herself dance. What a delight that would be!

While they sat at the table, breakfasting on eggs, frijoles, and tortillas, the old soldier tried once again to drive home his warning.

"I tell you, señorita, it would be most dangerous for you to let anyone but Penti and myself see you dance until the ship is ready to take you back to Spain. You must promise to do as I say."

Tarifa mopped her plate carefully with a piece of tortilla.

"Señorita, I am here to protect you. You must listen to what I tell you."

"I am listening."

"Then you will promise not to dance except indoors?"

"*Sí.*"

Escobar grunted with relief. He rose and picked up his

hat and limped toward the door. "I have your list, Penti; I will bring your supplies."

"Gracias."

Penti began idly to gather up the dishes and Tarifa disappeared into the bedroom where she slept alone, for Penti made use of a small cot in the *sala*.

Inside the oak chest were the remnants of Señora Escobar's finery which Gaspar had not found it in his heart to dispose of yet. He had given Tarifa permission to wear whatever she wished, and for days the novelty of decking herself out in silk scarves, lace *rebozos,* and brilliant shawls or mantillas over high shell combs or ornately beaded headbands had kept her occupied indoors. Today, however, she felt a surge of restlessness, a need to go off by herself. Gaspar's and Penti's warnings weighed but lightly on her conscience. All her life she had wandered the streets of Seville and the Triana alone and free, and she saw nothing in this bleak open landscape to be wary of.

She took a bright yellow shawl from the chest of drawers and draped it saucily over the shoulders of her short-sleeved white blouse. She put on a shell brooch and a pair of silver hooped earrings belonging to the late Señora Escobar, and climbed out the low bedroom window, confident that Penti could not see her, for the kitchen window faced the other way.

She walked quickly down the hill past the open doors of curious householders. It was a brisk little climb over the hills that stood between the houses and the beach, but once down again she stood with the whole sweep of the blue bay before her.

Boats were going and coming from the lone ship in sight to the hide house nearest her. She would have liked to have walked down there, but, early as it was, the sand was already scorching the soles of her bare feet. She wondered what lay behind the range of mountains there. No doubt that was where Don Alvarjo lived on his rancho with the odd name. She thought idly of Santiago and of the despicable Joaquin, whom she had not killed in spite of her firm intention to do so. But it was mostly Don Ygnacio, with his proud stern courtliness, of whom she thought.

She did not hear the horse walking slowly through the sand until it snorted, and a voice at her back asked politely:

"How do you like California, señorita?"

She whirled and saw him. Anger blossomed in her breast like a bud opening to instant full flower. The tall foreigner still wore his blue seaman's coat and cap, and she detected the same quizzical amused expression in his gray eyes. He sat the bay horse easily, his strong tanned hands folded over the reins and resting on the broad pommel.

She thought of reaching down for a handful of sand to fling in his complacent face, but her Gypsy intuition told her that unlike Santiago Alvarjo when she had smashed the tambourine over his head outside the bullring, this man would not laugh and pass it off. She sensed his authority, his air of easy command, and writhed inwardly knowing that she would be unable to dominate him.

"I am Captain Bart Kinkaid, master of the *Arabella*," he said, pointing to the ship. There was a twinkle in his eye when he added solemnly, "I see you have left the Mission and the care of the good Fathers?"

Tarifa glared up at him, her lower lip outthrust.

"Go away. Leave me alone!"

"I only came to see if I could offer you a ride into town. You'll find it a long hard walk—in bare feet." He glanced down at her toes burrowing in the sand like angry tarantulas. "Tell me, señorita, what really happened after we left the Mission that day? Was Don Alvarjo's son released from the jail?"

Tarifa drew herself up proudly. "Don Ygnacio settled everything. As he will settle you if you keep bothering me! I have only to send word to him. He is a true caballero, a gentleman of honor, as you are not."

Something moved in Kinkaid's gray eyes. He dismounted abruptly and removed his cap, making her a stiff bow.

"You are right, señorita. A sailor's life is a rough one. It is easy to forget your manners. My apologies to you for my past and present lack of them."

His expression was as deadly serious as Don Ygnacio's had been when he spoke to her at the Mission. "If I have offended you in any way, I am truly sorry."

Tarifa knew nothing of Americanos except for what she had witnessed of them at the hide houses on her arrival. It seemed part of their nature to laugh and joke a great deal. Perhaps this man was honestly sorry for having offended her. She still did not like or trust him, but she could understand honesty. It was part of the Romany code to be scrupulously, brutally honest: If you loved, it was with an all-consuming passion. If you hated, you hated to the death. If you swore friendship, it was a sacred trust for a lifetime.

Her long eyes studied the harsh planes of his face. The broad brow, the square uncompromising chin, the flat hard lips, and she knew that this man would live up to his word.

She nodded.

"If you don't care for a ride to town, I will go."

She said lightly, "I will go with you. I have not seen the town."

He was surprised at her tone and change of mind. But he tried his best not to show it as he mounted and then reached down to help her up behind him.

Tarifa sat confidently and deigned to grasp the waist of the man in front of her. It was only the second time she had been on a horse but already she loved the rhythm and movement under her as the animal plodded heavily through the soft sand.

When they reached the hard roadbed Kinkaid turned to ask, "Can you hold on if I let him gallop?"

"Yes."

Then, as the horse surged forward in the first springing movement, she let out a cry and clutched wildly at Kinkaid's coat. He put an arm back of him to steady her but she pushed it away.

"I'll slow down," he told her.

"No! Make him go faster, faster!"

He put his heels into the horse's ribs and they flew up the hill past the scattering of soldier's houses, and came to a sliding stop in the center of the plaza. It was nearly deserted but a few stragglers came to stare at them as Kinkaid dismounted and reached up to help Tarifa alight. She shook her head and slid easily over the horse's rump to the ground. She went around to pat the animal on the nose, and told Kinkaid:

"Someday I will have a horse and ride myself." Then before he could stop her she was gone, rushing up the street. He shrugged and smiled at her retreating figure and flashing legs. She moved with the grace of a fawn he thought. No, that was wrong with the consummate dangerous grace of a stalking leopard. She was the oddest, most arresting child he had ever seen.

Kinkaid visited the homes of the Carillos and Bandinis, sitting long over *cigarrillos* and glasses of wine in their patios, and hearing again the disgraceful story of Santiago Alvarjo's shocking behavior and the dishonor he had brought to his family name. As before, every time he heard the tale repeated by one of the *gente de razón*, Kinkaid detected a note of inner satisfaction that one of the highly born Alvarjos had finally fallen.

Raimundo Carillo told him succinctly, "It will be long before Don Ygnacio thinks of sending another son of his to Spain."

And his brother added conspiratorily, "They say he brought back a *gitana,* full-blooded, a veritable demon from Hell. God grant that she will not put a curse on us all. I would not have my daughters look on her face!"

Dona Maria Carillo was of a more practical nature than her husband or brother-in-law. "They will ship her back to Spain and that will be that. As for looking at her, the poor creature would probably rather be left alone than stared at, and Don Ygnacio knows better than to turn her loose to run all over the town. More wine, Capitán Kinkaid?"

Tarifa, with a little following of curious children who ebbed and flowed behind her like the windblown tail of a kite, was enjoying herself immensely. What odd houses and buildings they had here, so prim and square and all of just one story. Their gardens were sad, dusty affairs, not at all like the luxuriant sweet-smelling, well-watered patios of the elite in Seville.

The shops were small and dingy, and all the goods were piled on the mud floor in a heap or hung from the thick beams in the low ceiling. It would be simple to steal here; one could walk in and carry out half the store before the lazy sleepy-eyed clerks were the wiser. But there was nothing Tarifa wanted at the moment, and she knew that if she was caught it would make more trouble for Don Ygnacio. She did not want that.

The sound of music drew her attention. The blending of a violin, a guitar, and a small harp not played with any particular skill was coming from a building across the plaza.

Tarifa rushed across and glanced inside the open doorway at a long narrow room with windows at either end, all closed despite the heat. A rank smell of spilled wine and *aguardiente* mingled with the musty odor of adobe.

Across one wall two planks had been set up, supported by heavy wine casks on which bottles and glasses of various types and sizes had been stacked. A man in a soiled white apron stood behind the improvised counter, while across the room the three slovenly musicians were still sawing and plucking away industriously at their instruments.

All the rest of the space seemed to be taken up with long benches and tables at which men sat and drank or played cards.

The aproned man came from behind the counter and moved to the door, frowning at Tarifa and the cluster of children who had drifted across the plaza to join her.

"Go away, *muchachos*," he growled, "this is no place for children! Go home and play."

"I want to hear the music," Tarifa said.

"The music is for my customers. Go away."

Tarifa stripped Señora Escobar's silver earrings from her ears. "I will give you these if you will let me come inside and listen."

The man glanced at them held out invitingly in one slender palm but he shook his head. "They are probably your mother's and she would have the soldiers on me if I took them."

"My mother is in Seville. Take them and let me in."

Domingo Chavira rubbed his heavy chin. This was a strange *muchacha*, he had not seen her running with the others before. No doubt she was the child of one of the new soldiers from Sonora. Still she wore an expensive shawl and brooch. It might be that the newly arrived soldier still had some of his travel pay with which to buy *vino* in his cantina. He was tired of carrying the rest of them on credit, and only did so out of expediency, for it did a man no good to get on the wrong side of the law.

"You did not steal the earrings, *muchacha?*"

"No. They are mine. Here, take them and let me in."

"Wait. It is not allowed to let children in the cantina. What would the Padres say if they found out?"

"It is nothing to me; I am not a Catholic. I am a Gypsy."

She forced the earrings into his hand and disappeared into the wine shop while Chavira stood dumbly in the doorway, too startled to stop her. He knew who and what she was now. Gaspar Escobar had been talking about her only that morning, swearing him to secrecy about her presence in the village, explaining the disasters that would follow if she should be seen. And now she was here! In his shop, planning God knew what deviltry in her evil pagan soul. He rushed inside in a panic to throw her out bodily and never let her in again, and found her standing, hand on hip, in front of the three musicians. They continued to play.

"It is very good, this music," she said, as Chavira came to a panting standstill. "But not as good as I have heard in Seville or in the Triana. That is where the music is best of all."

One of the musicians, the guitarist, glanced up at her words and said, "What do you know of the Triana? You are too young, *niña*, to have ever been there."

"I have just come from there."

"Now I know that you are lying."

Domingo Chavira said threateningly, "You will have to get out of here. *Pronto!*"

Tarifa ignored him and waited until the orchestra had finished their piece.

"You must leave, *muchacha*. At once!" Chavira stormed. "If you do not go at once I will call the soldiers—send for the Padres!"

"Can you play an *Alegrias?*" Tarifa asked the guitarist, a middle-aged man with long black sideburns and a black moustache above very white, even teeth.

"What do you know of the *Alegrias*, little one?"

"I can dance it for you. Play it."

"You will not dance a step in here!" Chavira shouted. And in his frenzy to be rid of her he brought disaster upon himself by his thoughtless addition, "Take your cursed earrings and your evil Gypsy ways out of here and never come back!"

There was movement behind him as men rose from benches and tables to come forward.

"Gypsy?"

"She is a real *gitana?*"

"Where did she come from?"

"On the ship from Spain with the Alvarjos."

"Santa Margarita!"

"Is she the one Don Santiago—"

"*Sí!*"

A young soldier who had had a glass too much wine asked with solemn politeness, "Will you honor us by dancing for us, *gitana?*"

"She will not dance here!" Chavira bellowed, but no one paid the slightest attention to him and he went to sit behind the counter with his head in his hands.

The men had formed a circle about Tarifa.

"Is she going to dance?"

"Will you dance for us, señorita?"

Tarifa glanced at the hard dirt floor. "You will have to make room for me. Move some of these benches and those two tables over there."

Eager hands reached out to do her bidding. When the tables and benches had been removed, Tarifa took off her shawl and turned to the guitarist.

"You can play an *Alegrias?* Just the guitar. I want no other music."

"*Sí.* It shall be as you wish, *muchacha.*"

With the first stroke of the guitar, silence fell over the room.

As Tarifa whirled and dipped to the incredible counterpoint of the guitar, the men stood entranced at the wild and varied jubilation of her dance. When she finished in a spirited burst of movement their wild acclaim showered down on her from all sides.

With their shouts of admiration also came coins. Tarifa bent instantly with a grace that delighted her watchers, and began stuffing them inside her blouse with both hands.

Santiago had been right after all. The Californians were willing to pay in gold to see her dance.

A new expression had come over Domingo Chavira's heavy face. If the patrons were willing to pay to watch

the Gypsy dance, why not let her dance for them in his
cantina each night? He could afford to pay her well. It
only remained for him to arrange it with Gaspar Escobar.
Surely he would not turn down an extra *real* a day? And
if he complained that he had been hired to protect the girl
—well, he could take her to and from the cantina himself to ensure her safety.

In the end it was Tarifa herself who made it possible.
Against the cries and warnings of Penti and Escobar she
stood firm in her decision to dance at Domingo Chavira's
cantina, and it was not the gold alone that drew her. She
loved the bravos, the applause, and the genuine admiration that her aficionados showered upon her. And it relieved the terrible boredom of her waiting.

Each night at sundown, Gaspar and Penti accompanied
her to the cantina and sat one on either side of the little
leather-covered chair where she rested between numbers.
She and Penti were growing rich and they had been able
to buy all sorts of fine things at Don Pio Pico's little shop,
dresses and shawls, velvet slippers, fans, and glittering
jewelry. Don Pio had become one of her greatest admirers, and when she moved in a tortuous *Siguiriya,* or
whirled gaily in a *Buleria,* his little eyes would follow
avidly as he called out:

"*Hola!* Little daughter of the sun. Sultana! *Faraóna
gitana!*"

Sometimes he came with his cousins, the Carillos, and
they bought wine for everyone and sent her flowers
filched from their mother's gardens. Señora Pico was
said to be a young stern matron, strict with her sons, yet
she remained completely unaware of Don Pio's escapades.

Don Macario Canejo came also to pay his respects,
and sometimes one or two of the Americanos from the
hide houses. It seemed odd, Tarifa thought, that Capitán
Kinkaid had never once come to watch her dance.

Whether or not they admitted it publicly, all San
Diego was agog at the scandal of Tarifa's presence, and
the shame of Domingo Chavira in turning his wine shop
into a den of iniquity. The *gente de razón* of San Diegan
society were deeply shocked, and had considered writing
to the governor to beg him to put a stop to the degradation of their pueblo. But the wiser ones pointed out that

their ignominious situation would then be known the
length and breadth of California, and San Diego would
become the laughingstock of every rancho and pueblo
from San Francisco to Baja California.

Tarifa, wearing some of her new finery, a white silk
dress with deep scarlet ruffles down the skirt, red velvet
slippers, a high black comb and gaudy bracelets of
Mexican silver, the gifts of a rich ranchero from San
Juan, was ready to start her first dance of the evening
when Don Pio Pico came into the wine shop accompanied
by a tall Americano wearing the blue coat of a sea captain.

Tarifa felt satisfaction. The indomitable cold-eyed
Capitán Kinkaid would at last witness her triumph! He
had thought her nothing but a poor Gypsy to be kept under lock and key at the Mission. It did not bother her in
the least that he had also seen her there half-naked. Like
an animal she had no sense of personal shame. But, childlike, she longed to show off before him, to humble him,
and puncture his infuriating air of superiority.

The two men paused at the counter for drinks and then
walked toward her, carrying their glasses. Don Pio was
dressed in a new suit of dark-blue velvet richly trimmed
like his black sombrero in glittering silver braid, and wearing his usual assortment of large rings and heavy gold
chains.

"What are you dancing for us tonight, *muchacha?*" he
asked.

But she was staring over his head at his companion and
did not reply. It was not Capitán Kinkaid, after all, who
stood beside Pico. This was a stranger. A very odd-look-
ing man indeed. Instinctively, with her Romany knack of
evaluating a person in one swift, penetrating glance, she
knew that he was of the same breed as Bart Kinkaid, and
yet totally unlike him. This man had the same air of confident leadership about him, but there all similarity ended.
The quiet watchfulness in his light-hazel eyes reminded
Tarifa unpleasantly of a cat's.

Beneath his red moustache his mouth was thin and
secretive. Slanting brows and long auburn sideburns made
his eyes appear even more closely set than they were. The
huge splay-fingered hands, the backs peppered with
freckles, looked as if they could crush rock.

"Chiquita," Don Pío was saying, "I have brought you a new aficionado, a slave to your artistry after tonight. May I present Capitán Titus Judah, of the Americano ship *Vulcan*. *Amigo*, I'll bet you twenty *reales* against a glass of *aguardiente* that you have never seen anyone dance like our little Tarifa."

Judah bowed stiffly from the waist. "I have heard little else but your praises, señorita, since I landed today."

Tarifa gave him a brief nod, uncertain what was expected of her.

"What will you dance?" prompted Pico. "A *Soleares*—surely a *Siguiriya* for the capitán?"

"Later," Tarifa answered shortly. "Lieutenant Agraz has asked for the *jota*."

She watched the two men take seats at a nearby table.

As the guitar began the vibrant rhythm, full of gaiety and sweeping impetuous movement, the customers stamped or beat the tabletops with their drinking glasses to keep time to the music.

Pico noted with satisfaction the expression of fixed attention on Titus Judah's face. His light eyes never left Tarifa's whirling, leaping figure, and his glance seemed to center on her tiny undulating waist rather than her vivid face or twinkling red-slippered feet. Now and then he moistened his lips with the tip of his tongue as he watched.

When the dance ended he did not applaud or go forward as Pico and the others did. He sat alone, silently filling and refilling his glass, watching only Tarifa for the rest of the evening whether she sat resting in the leather chair between Escobar and Penti, or moved like a flame across the floor in dance after dance.

Later, when the crowd had thinned, he rose and crossed the room toward where she sat with a cheap red-lace shawl draped carelessly over one bare shoulder. In spite of all the liquor he had drunk, he walked on steady feet and spoke without slurring his words. Only a certain dullness in his eyes betrayed that he was not himself. The members of his crew would have recognized the expression on his face only too readily. It had preceded many a flogging aboard the *Vulcan*.

"Señorita, I would like you to dance with me."

Tarifa glanced up in astonishment.

"I do not dance with anyone, señor. I dance alone."

"Then tonight you will learn to dance with someone, *muchacha.* Me." His smile curved wickedly and brought a frown to Tarifa's dusky face. "I will show you some steps you have never seen before." He held out his hand. "Come. Tell the lads yonder to tip us a waltz."

Tarifa sat very still, her long eyes narrowed slightly. "I have told you, Capitán, I do not dance with others."

She saw a red stain smudge his cheekbones.

"Then it's time you learned different! You work here don't you? It's your job to entertain the customers?"

The few remaining drinkers glanced up in surprise at his tone. Chavira started from behind the counter, though he was not quite sure what he meant to do, and Gaspar Escobar awoke with a start and leaped out of his chair when Penti jabbed him in the ribs with her elbow.

"Here! What's going on?" he demanded belligerently. Judah pushed him roughly back into his chair.

"Sit down, old man, and stay there."

Gaspar, who had left his pistol at home that evening since he had never yet had cause to use it, attempted to draw his knife but Judah tore it out of his grasp. Out of the corner of his eye, the American saw Penti take her own *navaja* from under her skirts and ducked just in time to escape the wicked whistling blade that buried itself in the wall behind him.

The old Gypsy flew at him screeching Romany curses, her fingers bent like talons, but he caught her alongside the head with the back of one powerful hand and she dropped as if she had been poleaxed.

Judah drew a pistol from his waistband and waved it at the stupefied occupants of the cantina.

"You cannot fight in here, señor," Chavira protested from the corner of the bar. "I will call the guard!"

"Call and be damned," Judah grinned. "But not until the señorita and I have had our dance. Tell 'em to play!"

Chavira waved weakly at the orchestra, who began to render a jerky discordant waltz.

Tarifa had run to hold Penti's head in her lap when she had fallen, but now she put the old Gypsy down carefully against her rolled-up shawl and got to her feet.

She walked slowly toward Judah, anger pulsing in every

graceful line of her body. Without speaking, she raised her hands and drew her sharp nails down both the cheeks from eyelids to chin.

He howled in pain and rage as the blood trickled down to his collar.

"You cursed Gypsy cat! You black Satan's whore! I'll fix you—I'll show you something you'll never forget! Scratch, will you? You won't be able to scratch when I get through with you!"

With his free hand he grasped her powerfully and dragged her to him. Her biting, kicking, and scratching had no more effect on him than if she had been a puff of wind blowing against a rock. He yanked her to the far end of the room and backed her against the wall. Putting his other arm across her throat, he forced her chin up and held her pinioned, his body pressed against hers so hard she could scarcely breathe.

"Now you hellcat, I'll show you," he panted. "I'll teach you not to sink your devil's claws into a white man, damn you!"

He bent his head and his mouth found hers and ground against it, bruising her lips against her teeth.

Titus Judah, completely carried away by his passion and fury, was scarcely aware of the first blow that struck his back. But he felt the hand strong as a boathook that fastened on his shoulder and tore him away from Tarifa.

"Swine!" a low voice said. "You damned filthy pawing swine!"

It was Bart Kinkaid who faced Judah, still holding his shoulder, a look of cold contempt on his face.

"I'd like to spread-eagle you myself, by God!"

"See what the little witch did to my face."

"And what did you do to provoke her first?" Kinkaid asked hotly. "What about the old woman lying over there?"

"You're overstepping yourself, Captain," Judah snarled. "This is a private affair between them and me."

"I'm making it my affair."

Judah brought up the gun he still held, but before he could aim it Kinkaid smashed it out of his hand with a brutal chopping motion that made Judah wince with pain.

"You're good in a fight with women, Judah; let's see how you do in one with a man."

Judah's thin face flushed a deep brick red.

"You bastard, Kinkaid, no one talks to me like that!"

Judah tore off his coat and cap and waited impatiently for Kinkaid to remove his. Then the two Americans faced each other on the little square of floor that had been cleared for Tarifa's dancing.

Kinkaid was aware that he had a slight advantage in years and weight, but he was not a boxer. And as they circled each other warily, it was quite apparent to him that Titus Judah was. He would have to stay out of the reach of those long arms and those hamlike hands. All his own fighting had been the rough-and-tumble kind, learned in the fo'c'sle or picked up on the waterfronts as a boy.

Judah could easily outmaneuver him with his clever footwork, or merely wear him out. His own best bet was to wade in, taking whatever punishment came his way, and count on one powerful connecting punch.

Judah, grinning slightly, darted away from Bart's fists like quicksilver and then came back swiftly to land a punishing blow on the side of Kinkaid's neck.

The pain and sudden cutting off of his breath made him fall back momentarily, and to his surprise Judah followed, thinking him worse off than he was. Still slipping backward, Kinkaid blocked a blow to his chest and reached over to smash his right into Judah's face. It glanced off his cheek and landed on his nose. Bart saw blood gushing from his nostrils.

Made incautious by his pain and fury, Judah again rushed in, striking savagely at the other man's chest and stomach.

Pain jarred through Kinkaid clear to his backbone, but he did not go down, and he managed to deliver a fair blow to Judah's right eye that opened up the brow like a split melon.

The two men fought with a silent and brutal intensity that appalled the onlookers, like bull elks tilting back and forth on a mountaintop.

Kinkaid had one advantage that he was unaware of for some time. All the *aguardiente* Judah had drunk was slowing his reflexes. He staggered once and Kinkaid, watching for his chance, rushed in and delivered a tremendous right to his jaw. Judah rocked back on his heels. His eyes glazed but he didn't fall. It was a blow that would have laid an ordinary man out cold.

Judah stepped away, playing for time, sucking air into his lungs like a bellows. He shook his head to clear it, and hooked a jarring left to Kinkaid's chin followed by a powerful right to his chest.

Kinkaid coughed and wiped at the blood on his chin with the back of his sleeve. He would have to end it soon, before Judah recovered his wits and his strength completely. Careless now of consequences, Bart moved in. Absorbing a blow to his midriff and another, heavier blow to his chest that staggered him, he went on, aware only of Titus Judah's cold, hate-filled face before him. He concentrated all his remaining strength on landing one last driving blow to Judah's jaw. His arm rose clean and sure, and his knuckles burst under the explosive force of the contact.

Judah's head snapped back like a broken halyard and his long body went slack. Bart stood over him, his chin on his chest, his mouth open to suck more air into his tortured lungs. He was dimly conscious of the babble of voices rising around him.

He turned at last and spoke authoritatively to Domingo Chavira. "Get some sailors from the *Vulcan* to row Capitán Judah out to his ship. *Pronto!*"

"*Sí! Sí*, Capitán Kinkaid, *muy pronto!* Carlos! Estaven!"

Kinkaid picked up his cap and coat and searched the room for Tarifa, aware of the stiffness settling in his battered body. She stood beside the now-recovered Penti, her long eyes shining with pleasure and excitement.

"You were *magnífico*, Capitán!" she cried, hurling herself into his arms, then stepping back quickly to look at him with bright, flashing eyes. "It is exciting to watch men fight—like the *corrida?*"

He dabbed silently at the blood on his chin. Wicked little heathen. So she loved violence and bloodshed, did she? Well, she might get more of it than she bargained for if she stayed in San Diego much longer. After tonight the town would be up in arms. They would undoubtedly write the governor, and throw her and her Gypsy companion into jail while they waited for his decision. He told her quietly, "You can't stay here, Tarifa."

She tossed her head. "It is late anyway. It is time we returned to Gaspar's beautiful house."

He moved his head wearily. He would be glad to get rid of her. Talking to her was like trying to grasp a smoke ring. But he couldn't leave her to Titus Judah's tender mercies. Once he came to, Judah would be back in search of revenge.

"You and your companion must leave town."

"Leave?" her brows rose. "But where will we go? Don Ygnacio has arranged for us to stay here. I like it here."

"It won't be safe for you to stay now that Capitán Judah knows you are here." He turned to Gaspar Escobar and told him swiftly, "Get three horses, the best you can find, and bring them to your place. We will meet you there."

"But señor—"

"Where are we going?" Tarifa demanded.

"You said you wanted to ride a horse by yourself someday. Well, you're going to get your chance. Now. Come on."

"Where do you go, Capitán?" asked Gaspar. "What am I to tell Don Ygnacio and Capitán Sanchez? I am responsible for the women's safety."

"I will take care of that," Kinkaid replied. "And it's better if you don't know where we are going. If my mate Banner asks for me in the morning, tell him what happened and say I will be back in a day's time."

"Sí, Capitán. I understand." But he did not understand the ways of the tall Americano who fought so viciously with his bare hands. Long after the little party had ridden off he stood scratching his head and wondering if he would have to return all the *dinero* Zenobio Sanchez had given him.

CHAPTER 8

Dolores Alvarjo awoke that morning, for the first time since her mother's death, with a sense of inner joy. The heat of the summer day had not yet risen and her bedroom was fragrant with the aroma of Castilian roses and honeysuckle growing outside the windows. Her room, near the *sala*, commanded a sweeping view of the golden valley and the curving tree-lined avenue leading to the house.

She slipped on a white silk dressing gown, and unbraided her fair hair, brushing it loose on her shoulders, before she knelt briefly to say her morning prayers. As she rose she was surprised to hear horses galloping up to the front door. Only important visitors came to the front entrance of Loma de Oro. Everyone else went around to the kitchen. Who could be coming to the front door in such haste at this early hour?

She went to the deep-silled window that opened onto the wide veranda, and leaned out.

Her startled eyes met head on the cool gray ones of a tall Americano, dressed in the blue coat and cap of a seaman. He had just swung down from his lathered horse.

"*Buenos días*, señorita," he said gravely in good Spanish.

Color swept over her bare neck and throat and up to the roots of her fair hair. She retreated into her room like a rabbit into its hole. What was this bold-eyed Americano doing here? Her father mistrusted them, would never allow one to cross his threshold. Then she recognized Zenobio's gruff voice speaking to a servant. So he was Don Zenobio's friend? That explained a great deal, for everyone knew Capitán Sanchez had strange companions. Dolores dressed quickly in the black garments all the women on Loma de Oro would wear for a full year. Her maid came in to dress her hair in its customary soft loose braids that gave her face a delicate ethereal beauty of which she was quite unaware.

"Do you know who came with Don Zenobio?" she asked when the maid had finished.

"Sí, señorita. An Americano, a Capitán Kinkaid."

"I cannot believe it," murmured Dolores, "an Americano in this house?"

Zenobio was saying, "You must find a way to get them out of the district entirely, Ygnacio. You see what almost happened in San Diego? If it had not been for my *amigo* here, there would have been worse than a scandal to contend with."

Don Ygnacio sat facing his visitors in his study, with the doors and windows tightly shut. He rubbed his temple with one hand where his head had begun to ache, and prayed that he would never have to make another decision concerning anyone else as long as he lived. He was growing too old for this sort of thing. It had not been pleasant to allow the Americano inside his house either, despite his friendship with Zenobio and his service to Tarifa. In his heart he distrusted Kinkaid. Had it not been another Americano sea captain who had caused this whole upheaval? But as Zenobio had pointed out, Kinkaid had acted in the best interests of the Alvarjos as well as the Gypsies. Zenobio looked unhappy and Ygnacio guessed that his friend had not been pleased when the American had come riding up to Rancho Santa Teresa in the dead of night with the two *gitanas* in tow. He was, no doubt, unhappier still to have the Gypsy women quartered in his house.

Kinkaid himself had said nothing, for which Alvarjo gave him credit. He sat quietly in a wide-armed horsehair chair and allowed his eyes to wander over the room's contents. This was clearly Don Ygnacio's sanctum. Kinkaid noted the hunting trophies, the display of guns and whips, the wealth of books and papers filling the ample book-shelves, the heavily carved writing desk.

He admired Alvarjo, recognizing in him not only a gentleman born but also a gentleman of the spirit. He was a fine-looking old boy, too. Handsome, proud, aloof as the Sphinx. It was also plain that in spite of his lavish hospitality and his outward solicitude for Kinkaid's comfort, he disliked his American guest.

Bart wondered if the hauntingly lovely face he had glimpsed at a front window upon his arrival could belong to a daughter of Don Ygnacio's. It hardly seemed possible, she was so fair. She had looked like an angel dressed in white with her pale golden hair loose about her shoulders like paintings he had seen of Cherubim. She must be some visitor to Loma de Oro. But he knew that he would never forget her, with the rosy glow of early morning illuminating the ivory of her breast and throat and outlining the delicate oval of her face.

Don Ygnacio's words roused him from his pleasant reverie.

"Capitán, do you know when the next ship will be sailing from San Diego?"

"The *Arabella* sails in two weeks' time, but we will only be going north to trade along the coast for the next six months. Then we sail for Boston."

Don Ygnacio nodded. "We cannot send them to Boston. We must return the two women directly to Spain. I have given them my word on that. We could perhaps send them to Monterey to await passage on the next Spanish-bound ship?"

"If I may say so, Don Ygnacio," Kinkaid suggested, "Monterey or, for that matter, any other port in California, would be the worst place in the world to send them."

"Why, Capitán?"

"Because Judah is going to be hunting for the girl. His kind dosen't back down easily. He will figure he owes her something, the same as he'll figure he now owes it to me. I can take care of myself, but what about her? Even Gaspar Escobar and her Gypsy companion weren't much good to her."

Zenobio flushed hotly. "The man was a fool! Letting

her go to the cantina to dance in public, what did he expect?"

"He is not entirely to blame I suspect," smiled Kinkaid.
"The Gypsy wench has a will of her own. In all fairness,
she may be a wicked little piece, but I'd hate to see her
fall into Judah's hands.

Don Ygnacio tried to bring his sluggish wits to bear on
the problem. He turned a look of entreaty on Zenobio,
but the old soldier sat with his arms folded and his eyes on
the floor. There was nothing for Alvarjo to do but swallow
his pride and appeal to the tall Americano.

"What, then, do you suggest, Capitán Kinkaid?"

How ready they were all these Californians, thought
Kinkaid, to accept a solution, any solution to their cares as
long as it meant they themselves could cease thinking
about it. It was not a safe policy letting others do your
thinking for you, and Kinkaid felt uneasy for the future
of such men and such a people.

"Well, *amigo?*" Zenobio asked eagerly.

"Set the two women up in a place of their own, as far
from the coast and the pueblos as possible. Between you,
I'm sure you have some safe spot on your lands with a
habitable dwelling, and some servants to spare who can
be trusted? No one else but the three of us, and the servants you send with them, need know of the arrangement.
When the proper ship comes into port, whisk the women
aboard and your problem is solved."

"*Sangre de Cristo!*" Zenobio slapped his thighs. "The
capitán has hit upon the perfect solution, Ygnacio!"

Alvarjo was slower to accept the suggestion.

"I cannot have the Gypsies near my family," he said
slowly, "or where friends or neighbors might discover their
presence. I must also tell the Padres—Padre Cazon at any
rate."

"*Caramba!* Why must you do that?" cried Zenobio.

"Because everything reaches the ears of the Padres sooner or later. It will be better if Padre Cazon knows of it at
once so that he can spare Padre Peyri from finding out
about the matter for as long as possible. Padre Péyri, of
course, would be less likely to approve. Even so, I am not
certain I would be doing the right thing."

Zenobio was disgusted. "If you must go running to the

priests every moment, go ahead. But whether they approve or not, I see little else you can do with them unless you want them to fall into Capitán Judah's hands?"

"Then I will send Santos to ask Padre Cazon to join us at your hacienda, Zenobio."

Sanchez shrugged his heavy shoulders. "If you must. I already have Gypsy females in my house; I might as well add a priest. Santa Margarita, what will it be next?"

While Don Ygnacio excused himself to speak with his mayordomo, Zenobio and Kinkaid strolled onto the veranda facing the fragrant patio. Voices came from the dining room where the family was finishing breakfast.

"A sad household since Dona Encarnacion's untimely death," said Zenobio softly. "And now this."

"Don Ygnacio has his sons at home again at any rate," Kinkaid said.

"Sí. And in what condition? Joaquin keeps to his room, scourging himself like a fanatic, and Santiago has lost his spirit and spends hours on his knees in the chapel, instead of on the back of a horse where a man belongs. It is as if the whole household were cursed since his path crossed that of the Gypsy in Seville."

As his eyes wandered toward the chapel Zenobio had pointed out, Bart saw a slender black-clad figure emerge and walk slowly along the veranda toward them. Her head was bowed as if she were deep in thought or prayer, but he caught the glint of golden hair beneath the black-lace *rebozo* and his heart leaped.

Zenobio peered into the shadows of the veranda as she approached, then called out imperiously, "*Muchacha*. Dolores, come here!"

The girl glanced up, startled, and a prayer book she had been carrying fell to the tiles at her feet. Kinkaid bent to retrieve it for her, and their eyes and hands met briefly as she accepted it from him.

He is tall, she thought, so very tall and fearless-looking. She had never been so close to an Americano before. Her father would never have allowed such a man near her, and yet she felt herself smiling shyly up at him.

Her fragile beauty took Kinkaid's breath away. He stood as awkward and abashed as a schoolboy in front of her.

Zenobio said gruffly, "Dolores, this is my *compadre* and

a friend of your father's, Capitán Bart Kinkaid, from Boston. *Amigo mío,* Don Ygnacio's oldest daughter, Dolores."

Without taking his eyes from her face, Kinkaid bowed stiffly from the waist and hoped that he did not look quite the awkward fool he felt in her presence.

"Welcome to Loma de Oro, Capitán," she said gently, "and to our hacienda. Will you have breakfast—or a cup of chocolate? Or"—she colored prettily, reminding him of his first view of her in the window bathed in the early-morning light—"perhaps a glass of wine?"

"We breakfasted at Santa Teresa, *niña,*" said Zenobio, "but a glass of wine will go well before we ride."

"I will send it to you at once, Don Zenobio," Dolores murmured.

Kinkaid stood watching until she had disappeared through a doorway and he became aware of Zenobio's hand on his shoulder.

"You may well stare, *amigo.* You do not see many like her. A true *rubio.* As fair as a white lily. Probably the most beautiful girl in all the Californias. And Don Ygnacio guards her as the Sultans guarded the favorites in their harems."

Padre Eugenio Cazon was not as surprised or as ill-informed concerning the Gypsies as Don Ygnacio had imagined he would be.

Strangely enough it had been the neophyte Salvador, whose grandmother the priest had gone to baptize on the day Don Ygnacio had made his confession in the pastures of Loma de Oro, who had first brought word to him of Tarifa.

Salvador had gone to Mission San Diego, with the permission of Padre Peyri, to do some ironwork for Padre Martin a few days before the arrival of the ship carrying the Alvarjos and their two strange companions. From the Mission cook, who was related to him by marriage, Salvador learned of the Gypsies' presence at the Mission and of the disgrace of Don Santiago Alvarjo. Padre Martin had requested him, for the sake of sweet charity, not to repeat anything he knew of the affair as he traveled back to San Luis Rey. Salvador had kept his promise. But in confession he had told Padre Cazon what he knew, and asked if he had done right in not relating it to Padre Peyri upon his return to the Mission.

"There is no need to repeat what you know to anyone else, Salvador," counseled Padre Cazon. "It is enough that you have told me. I will do what is necessary."

But Padre Cazon had not expected Don Ygnacio to call upon him for advice so soon. He sat quietly now in Zenobio's *sala* and heard the three men out before he spoke himself.

"You have acted wisely, Capitán Kinkaid. We could take them in at the Mission with the Indian women perhaps, but word of their presence would leak out, and then no doubt there would be more trouble. We have difficulty enough keeping the Indian girls away from our soldiers. The type of soldiers they send us now, unfortunately, are not of the moral caliber they once were."

"Then you approve of Capitán Kinkaid's suggestion, Padre, that I arrange a small *ranchita* on my property?" asked Don Ygnacio.

Padre Cazon glanced out the window toward the blue jaws of the distant sierras. "Do you have a secluded building for them, Don Ygnacio?"

"There is the small cabaña near the corral in the *arroyo seco*, which is only used once a year as a slaughtering-ground, Padre."

"*Bueno.* And you have a servant or two whom you can trust to send there with the Gypsies?"

"*Sí.* An old man and his wife who have been with me many years, distant relations of my housekeeper Candelaria. I will have to tell Santos, so that he may keep the herds and the work parties as far from the *arroyo seco* as possible, and also so that he may act as messenger between the cabaña and Loma de Oro."

"Then everything seems arranged," said the priest, with a warm smile. "Do you wish me to speak with the two Gypsy women before I go?"

"If you would, Padre," Alvarjo said with relief. "Perhaps they will understand the new arrangement better if you tell them."

Tarifa followed Penti into the *sala* when Zenobio sent for them, and was not pleased that they had brought another priest into her affairs. Bandonna had always contended that priests brought bad luck to those of Romany blood.

She listened to the Padre in baffled anger. Now they were to be buried in some hut in the mountains, far from the sea and the pueblo and any life that might be found in this barren, desolate land. And for how long? Might they not leave her there to rot and grow old, forget about her completely, once they had shoved her from their sight?

She was about to refuse to budge a step from the Santa Teresa, when Don Ygnacio said kindly, "We do not wish to make things more difficult for you, señorita, only to ensure your comfort and safety. I have given you my word that you and your companion will be returned to Spain. I assure you that I have never failed to keep my word." He paused, his eyes seeking hers. "I am told you like horses," he added. "Santos, my mayordomo, shall bring you one of my own golden palominos."

Tarifa's long eyes grew less hard. He knew how to tempt her. She had watched the magnificent golden horses that had galloped up to the door earlier in the day, and who now waited, arrogantly pawing at the dust in the front courtyard. To have one of these beautiful spirited creatures, she would gladly have moved into a cave or a hole in the ground, and forced Penti to go with her.

"We will go to the cabaña, señor," she told him simply. "And I will have one of the palominos to ride, no?"

Don Ygnacio smiled at her but shook his head. "No, niña, they are too high-spirited and dangerous for a novice. First you must learn from Santos how to handle them. He will come every day and give you a riding lesson. Then, when you have learned to ride them, you shall come, I promise you, and take your pick of my herd for your very own."

"Gracias, señor!" She would have liked to have thrown herself at his feet and kissed his hands. No one had ever given her such a gift, nor thought of one that would have pleased her restless, rhythm-loving spirit more. He did not mean to tie her down in this miserable land like a bird in a desolate cage, but to set her free to fly over the landscape on four dancing feet instead of two. Truly, there were advantages to be had in this strange California.

* * *

Santos did not know quite what he thought of Tarifa. She was unlike anyone he had ever known before. She was as completely a child of nature, as devoid of modesty as the savage gentiles in the deserts beyond the sierras. She took to the horses with grace and skill, as if she had been born to the saddle, and there was nothing about them, their equipment, or their care that she did not demand to know and quickly master. No one could have asked for a more avid or devoted pupil. And yet the mayordomo feared for her because of her very daring. She lacked any sense of danger. And Santos knew only too well that the powerful palominos were not playthings.

He had begun to teach her on the comparatively gentle mare Estrelita, riding Marca himself. But as soon as Tarifa learned that in California only women or children rode mares and fillies, she would have no more of Estrelita.

In vain did Santos argue that she had not the hand or the seat yet to handle one of the spirited stallions.

"I want you to teach me on a stallion," Tarifa said.

"I cannot be responsible for your death, señorita."

"Then I will go to ask Don Ygnacio myself!"

"No, you cannot do that."

"Will you promise to bring me a stallion then—tomorrow?"

Santos shrugged. If she got killed it would be God's will, and perhaps easier on all of them. There was no need to bother Don Ygnacio.

He selected the quietest stallion in the herd—which was not saying much as each was a prime animal filled with fire and spirit—and the following day he reined up in the ranch yard leading Cobrizo, a bright copper-toned animal. Tarifa was instantly lost in ecstasy over him. She patted and prodded his glistening skin, and picked up one delicate hoof after the other to inspect it.

Santos explained that Don Ygnacio's original stud Khalid had come from Jerez and the Carthusian monastery founded by Obertos de Valeto in 1475 on the banks of the Guadalete, where the knights of Jerez had beaten back the Moors of Ronda and Gibraltar under the command of Zaide.

"How do you know all these things?" Tarifa asked wonderingly.

"Don Ygnacio has been very kind to explain to me all about the horses, for he knows that I love them as he does."

"What else did he tell you about them? I must know these things also."

"When the great Cortes landed in New Spain with five hundred fifty-three men and sixteen horses, it was the horses that made possible the conquering of Mexico. The Indians thought the mounted men gods, since they had never seen men on horseback before, and from the six mares with the Spaniards, the new Americas were stocked. Only the finest horses were shipped to New Spain, and these came from the original stock of the Moors. North African war-horses, Don Ygnacio called them."

"And my father was a Moor," breathed Tarifa.

In the days that followed Tarifa found out many more interesting things concerning Don Ygnacio's prized golden horses. In them, Santos pointed out with pride, could be recognized the same light, wiry, extremely tough conformation; the same wide-spaced eyes, delicate muzzle, and small, pointed ears of the original Arabs.

There was a saying, he told her, that an Arab would rather sell his wife than his horse, and when it was a question of who should find shelter in the tent during a sandstorm, the horse came first and wife and children second. These were horses born and bred to share life with their masters, as much companions as servitors.

The Alvarjo palominos, like their ancestors, were fiery and spirited, but Santos was quick to point out that, unlike the usual fractious thoroughbreds, they were intelligent and dependable. The Arab was slow to mature, but he was seldom vicious.

Don Ygnacio did not, as many claimed, keep a groom for each of his pampered pets. But neither did he allow them to be broken or trained like the ordinary horses on his rancho.

No rough *amansador* mounted his palominos and jerked their noses around with a hackamore and rough mecate reins.

Santos, or an equally skilled and trustworthy horseman, would start to train the colts to a hackamore at their mother's heels. Slowly then, the hackamores gave way to heavier rigs, but a bit was never put into a young horse's mouth until he was a finished hackamore animal, perfectly neck-reined, and able to back fast and straight with his legs well under him, and slide to a clean stop with his hind feet.

When at last the bit was put in his mouth, it was merely hung there for him to play with for several more weeks. Gradually the mecate reins were attached, and for more weeks he was coaxed and encouraged until at last, bitted and perfectly reined, he was graduated, a perfectly trained saddle horse.

The easy, confident stallions, with their soft, unspoiled mouths, responsive to every touch of rein, were a delight to ride and the envy of every caballero who saw them.

Tarifa had been riding Estrelita with a hackamore, as Santos always rode Marca, and she was angered to find a bit in Cobrizo's mouth when Santos brought him to her.

"Why have you bitted him, Santos?"

"Because you could not hold him otherwise. With a bit in his mouth, he will respond as easily as Estrelita with a hackamore."

"You use only a hackamore on Marca."

"Sí. But I have more strength in my arms than you, and Marca is used to me. Cobrizo has never had a woman on his back before. He will be nervous."

The stallion turned his head to nudge her foot in the stirrup with his muzzle, then he put back one ear and stood quietly while Santos arranged the reins at the proper length in Tarifa's hand.

"Remember his tender mouth, señorita. Do not pull back quickly on the reins. We will walk first—to the top of the hill—and tire him out a little."

Tarifa was disappointed. She had counted on starting out at a full gallop, but Penti and the servants were watching and she rode off with her back straight as a ramrod and pride riding in her heart like a banner.

The stallion, his neck curved to an elegant angle and his sweeping white mane cascading down on one side like a dancing waterfall, felt different from Estrelita even when walking. There was a swaying springiness in his longer stride that was exhilarating, and she admired the way he had of snorting disdainfully into the morning air.

Affection had been an emotion lacking in Tarifa. She

had felt no true warmth for Bandonna or Penti, merely a
kinship blended of necessity and a mutual aggression
against the outside world. But now she was discovering to
her surprise that the sight and feel of these wonderful
horses of Don Ygnacio's could bring a warm response in
her heart that it had never known before. She could love
them openly, lavishly, and be loved in return. Short as
their acquaintance had been, Estrelita came at her call to
eat fruit from her hand or nuzzle her cheek, nickering
softly. Even Marca would drop his head on her shoulder
for her to scratch his chin under the hackamore. She had
found a peace and contentment among the palominos that
she had never known before.

"Cobrizo, you call him?" Tarifa asked, patting the arching neck while the stallion put both ears back, alert to this
new strange-sounding voice.

"*Sí*. Copper—that is his color."

"I will keep him for my own."

"That is up to Don Ygnacio, señorita."

"He promised me I could take my pick of the palominos."

"When you can ride like a caballero."

Tarifa gave him a black look from under her sombrero,
and then asked, "Tell me about the others—their names."

"Ah! There is Don Ygnacio's, El Capitán. And each of
the *muchachos* has a stallion."

"And there are others?"

Santos nodded.

Tarifa fell silent until they reached the top of the hill,
where a small stretch of flat tableland was comparatively
free of cactus and underbrush.

"When you start to gallop." Santos warned, "do not
touch his sides. Loosen the reins a little, lean forward like
this, and clamp your knees tight."

Tarifa nodded impatiently, straightened her sombrero,
and jerked the strap tight under her chin. She felt just as
she had the moment before her first solo dance in the plaza
in Granada when she had been six. The palms of her hands
were moist, while a delicious tingling sensation, a mixture
of fear and elation, coursed down her spine.

The sudden explosion of movement was like riding a
cannonball. In the first flash her body was thrown back
violently against the high cantle of the saddle, her hat was

whipped off and only saved from falling by the strap that
jerked chokingly against her throat.

She lost one stirrup, but clung wildly to the reins and
saddle. Hot wind seared her face and blinded her eyes.
Never had she realized that such wild immense power existed. On and on they galloped, until her sides and stomach
and thighs ached from the pounding. Dimly she became
aware of Marca coming up alongside, and of the mayordomo shouting something, but her ears were deafened by
the rush of wind and blood to her head.

A hand reached over and clutched at the reins, then in
a jerking, jarring stop, Tarifa lost her seat and flew over
Cobrizo's head to land with a bone-jolting thud on the
hard-packed ground.

"Little fool! *Idiota!*" Santos' face was black with rage.
"Were you going to let him run clean over the side without stopping?"

He pointed to the rock-filled canyon yawning a few feet
away, where the tableland ended abruptly.

"You could both have gone over. Why didn't you pull
him up gently as I told you to do?"

"I couldn't see, Santos. I couldn't hear. I only know that
it felt like flying—like being queen of the universe!" For
the first time in her life she added the words, "I'm sorry.
Have I hurt him, Santos?"

"No, I don't think so. But you will not do a thing like
that again. In riding, as in life, *muchacha,* it is necessary to
see where you are going. Are you hurt?"

She scrambled to her feet before he could dismount and
help her, and limped over to pat Cobrizo's forehead.

"Only my pride is hurt—but I do not think that I will sit
down to supper tonight."

Santos laughed, oddly relieved that she had not been injured. During their days of riding together he had come to
have a certain respect for her foolhardiness—or courage.
He was not sure which it was. She was like a wild colt that
had never worn a halter. She might turn out good or bad
in the end. She was as unpredictable as the wind.

Tarifa disdained his help and mounted Cobrizo with
more agility than he had thought possible after her fall,
and they rode back to the *ranchita* at an easy and compan-
ionable walk.

Santos asked her, "Shall I tell Don Ygnacio that you

have decided to keep Cobrizo for your own when the time comes for you to prove to him that you are a *caballera suprema?*"

She considered for a moment. "No. You are right, Santos, I am not ready. When I can ride well enough tell Don Ygnacio that I will make my choice. I would like to keep learning on Cobrizo though—if Don Ygnacio will let me?"

This humble acquiescence was something new and Santos eyed her suspiciously. But she seemed sincere enough, if one could trust such a wild godless creature.

"Very well," he agreed. "I will ask Don Ygnacio." But he took Cobrizo back to Loma de Oro with him. Let her practice on Estrelita in his absence. He was determined that she should never ride one of the stallions again unless he was present. It had been a miracle of heaven that he had not ended up responsible for the loss of both horse and rider this day.

On a hot morning in August, Don Ygnacio sent for his mayordomo and asked, "The Señorita Tarifa, how are her riding lessons progressing?"

"She rides like a bird flying, Patrón. Like a burr stuck to the saddle. She is fearless. I have never seen the stallions better handled, though I have not told her this."

Don Ygnacio frowned. He had not been certain he'd been right in allowing her to continue to ride Cobrizo. He would not have thought of letting a woman of his own household mount one of the stallions.

"She has had no accidents—no injuries?"

Santos shrugged. "The first tumbles of a beginner— nothing more. I think she is ready to pick out the horse you promised her for her own. With your permission, Patrón, I will take her to see the herd today?"

"You are sure she is ready so soon, Santos?"

Ygnacio was still amazed that any woman, even a tough half-wild Gypsy girl, could master his beloved stallions. "Wait," he said, "I will go with you."

"You are really going to give her one of the golden ones to take back to Spain with her, Don Ygnacio?"

"I have given her my word, have I not?"

He was not quite sure why he was going with Santos to the cabaña. He told himself it was to make sure she could ride as well as Santos claimed, and was ready for a faster, more demanding mount. But he had to admit also that he was curious for another look at the fascinating catlike grace of the young Gypsy.

Tarifa waited for them sitting astride the hitching rail, her sombrero hanging down her back and her tousled hair glinting like ebony in the sunlight. She was delighted that Don Ygnacio had come also, and hurled herself eagerly upon Cobrizo, throwing her arms about his neck, murmuring to him in Romany.

"What is it you say, señorita?" asked Don Ygnacio, pleased at her show of affection for the stallion but puzzled by her words.

"It is Romany, señor. *Kushto*—love. I have said, 'I love you. My own sweetheart, my darling.' "

Don Ygnacio nodded as he watched her spring gracefully into the saddle. This was a new facet he had not expected to discover in her nature, knowing something of Romany character, this open show of deep affection.

They rode back to Loma de Oro at a gallop, and Don Ygnacio found with satisfaction that Santos had spoken the truth. Tarifa had indeed mastered her seat, and her hands were assured and yet easy on the reins.

She turned in the saddle to admire El Capitán, and asked him many questions about the breeding of the palominos and their training and care.

She seemed to have a quick mind, and a natural inquisitiveness. A very good type of mind indeed, thought Alvarjo, if it were trained. A shame she had been left to grow up in ignorance in the gutter, like an abandoned puppy. He found pity in his heart for her, and was surprised at the depth of his sympathy for the little pagan creature.

He also found it enchanting to watch her ride beside him. On horseback, as in the dance, her body moved with a fluid grace all its own. The dip of her shoulders as she turned in the saddle, the curve of a wrist as she gently neck-reined Cobrizo, were a delight to observe.

In her boy's costume, she might have been little Antonio riding beside him, chattering brightly in the hot sunlight.

The palominos were pastured close to the hacienda, on

the only large enclosed piece of land on Don Ygnacio's rancho. Californians did not fence their property, which was so vast that herds could be easily held by vaqueros at the different locations decreed by their owners.

The sight of so many glistening golden coats filled Tarifa with esctasy, and Don Ygnacio sat his horse smiling indulgently as she darted from one side of the fence to the other demanding that Santos point out the different ones. She seemed familiar with each horse as he spoke its name, and asked, "Which one is Guindilla?"

"That one, señorita, standing alone under the oak tree."

He stood absolutely still with his small pointed ears erect, looking like a golden statue, the most beautiful horse Tarifa had ever imagined.

Though barely two years old, he was big for his age, and his mane and tail already hung long and thick like white floss in the sunlight. Like Cobrizo, he was darker in color than was usual for a palomino, with a distinct reddish tinge to his hide, the reason Don Ygnacio had named him Guindilla, cayenne pepper. The name had proven appropriate. The stallion had a hot, fiery disposition that made him less tractable than his companions, though Don Ygnacio was not particularly concerned. Guindilla's temperament, a defect in a riding horse, mattered little, as he intended to use the stallion primarily for a stud horse. The animal had perfect conformation and he was fond of his color.

Tarifa's eyes never left Guindilla as he lifted his magnificent head and let out a piercing whinny, like a challenge. At the sound she cried out in delight.

"Don Ygnacio?"

"Sí, señorita?"

"That one. I must have him for my own. No other will do."

Alvarjo was startled, "But he is only fit for a stud, señorita. He is not tractable like the others."

"That is why I want him! He has spirit, and he stands so proudly alone—like a Gypsy. We are alike, he and I. We will always understand each other."

Her long Gypsy eyes searched his face. He did not refuse but a look of puzzlement crossed his face. He was thinking that if this horse would make her world less lonely then she must have him, but he wondered also why he had not realized her complete isolation, the isolation of the Gypsy no matter in what land he found himself.

In her anxiety lest he refuse, Tarifa found herself using another word for the first time in her life.

"Please, señor, let me have him? I will love him and care for him as if he were truly made of gold. I will clean him and tend to him myself. I will go hungry, but he never shall. And I will never give him up, not while there is life in my body!"

"Hush, child! Guindilla is yours."

"Gracias! Muchas gracias, señor! May the Great One bless you for all eternity. May——"

"My dear child," Alvarjo broke in uncomfortably, "I have received reward enough in seeing your happiness. Please say no more about it. We must have Pablo make you a fine new saddle and bridle for Guindilla. Perhaps you would like to ride to the hacienda with me now, and tell him what designs you would like carved on it?"

If he had thought to take her mind even temporarily from the stallion he was mistaken.

"May I take Guindilla with me?"

"Santos can bring him to you in the morning. You cannot ride him yet; his training is not completed."

"I will finish it—and Santos can help me," she added quickly for fear of refusal.

"Well——"

"I will do it, señor, with your permission," said Santos. Then he thought, *Sangre,* why am I getting myself into this?

"Very well," said Alvarjo. "Catch him up, Santos, and bring him along."

"Sí."

Tarifa rode contentedly to the hacienda, but with many an adoring backward look at Guindilla walking proudly along behind Marca.

Don Ygnacio dismounted at the kitchen entrance and led Tarifa, who eyed everything with a child's wonderment, to the door of his chief saddlemaker.

Pablo Changarra was as dark and bent and twisted as one of his own strips of dried rawhide. He had come to California as a young soldier in the Portola expedition.

With them had also come the saintly Padre Junipero Serra and his few Franciscan fathers to found the chain of California Missions. Later, when he retired from military duty, Pablo had plied his trade as a saddlemaker, going from rancho to rancho, presidio to pueblo. Loma de Oro had always been his favorite spot, and when Don Ygnacio offered him the position of head *talabartero* on his rancho, Pablo had accepted with alacrity. He had made every saddle on Loma de Oro for the past thirty years.

Changarra's workshop, where he also made fine *reatas* of four, six, and eight plaits of rawhide, and engraved spur-straps, whips, and fancy *botas* for Don Ygnacio and his sons, took up nearly one side of the rear quadrangle directly across from Candelaria's kitchen.

Pablo, a cross-grained old Mazateco, spent his life embroiled in feuds with Candelaria, whom he called behind her back, Señora Entrometido—busybody. Or, if he was unusually angry, Señora Zona—bitch.

Their quarrels usually arose from Pablo's refusal to bathe or to allow Rita, the laundress, to wash his clothes at proper intervals. Then, too, he drank too much *vino* and left his *cigarrillo* butts all over the clean kitchen floor when he took his meals.

It was only the necessity to eat that drove him into the presence of Señora Entrometido at all, Pablo stated darkly to his apprentices. For wasn't it a sin for a man to allow himself to starve, just as much as if he cut his own throat? But it was a crown of thorns to him that he had to take sustenance from such a creature as Señora Zona.

Changarra was rubbing tint into the horn of a new saddle as Don Ygnacio and Tarifa entered.

"Don Ygnacio! You have not come to see me for some weeks. Do you know what the Señora Entrometido across the way has taken it upon herself to do now? She has refused to let me smoke at my meals!"

Don Ygnacio ignored this outburst, as Pablo had known he would do, and went forward to examine the nearly completed saddle.

"Is this the saddle you are making for Don Zenobio?"

"*Sí*, señor."

"It is very nice. He will be pleased."

"*Gracias*, señor."

A young Indian boy was polishing silver conchas in a corner and eyeing the newcomers with open curiosity.

"I have a new job for you, Pablo," said Don Ygnacio. "You will make a saddle and bridle for the Señorita Tarifa here. I have just made her a present of Guindilla."

Pablo's eyes opened wide in surprise under his shaggy brows but he said nothing. Whoever this *muchacha* was, it was clear only the best in his shop would do for her.

Tarifa ran her hand over the smooth leather of the saddle Changarra had been working on, while he and Don Ygnacio felt the texture of various hides and discussed the carving of the saddletree.

A fine saddle was not only a piece of excellent craftsmanship, but beautiful as well. A fiesta saddle, with intricate *talabartería* design in gold and silver threads or colored silks, was a thing of delicate beauty.

The horn, carved entirely of wood, six to eight inches wide and tilted slightly upward to facilitate roping, was often ornamented with silver, as was Ygnacio's. And for Tarifa, Alvarjo had ordered the very finest saddle with a leather *anquera*, a circular piece of leather fastened to the cantle and covering the horse's rump where the rider could carry a fine serape protected from the dust and dirt of the horse's hide.

There were to be *tapaderos* as well, covering the carved wooden stirrups stamped with a design of roses and trimmed with crimson and gold threads.

He had consulted Tarifa and she had told him that roses were her favorite flower, red ones, though she did not add that she hardly knew the names of any other blooms. Unlike the Gypsies of the caravans who knew every flower and leaf from infancy, she had seldom been in the country. Her life had been spent in the caves or squares of Granada, or in the twisting fetid streets of the Triana. Her knowledge was of people, not of flora and fauna.

Though she was pleased with the gift of the saddle and the silver-trimmed bridle Don Ygnacio had ordered, she was in a fever to get back to Guindilla.

She was not pleased that Don Ygnacio ordered Santos to go back with her and lead the colt as far as the *ranchita*, but she thanked Alvarjo prettily and rode off happier than she had ever been in her life.

* * *

Candelaria had seen the visitors to Changarra's shop across the way and went at once to repeat her observations to Tía Isabella.

She found her feeding the birds in their little cages on the balcony above the patio.

"Señorita!" Candelaria panted from the steps.

"What is it, Candelaria?"

"You will not believe it—I did not, though I saw it with my own eyes from the kitchen."

Isabella put down the small basket of seeds she held and frowned at the cook.

"What are you babbling about, Candelaria?"

"Your brother, Don Ygnacio, in that dirty old man's shop. I have told him he can never smoke in my kitchen again. Last week I found a *cigarrillo* in his soup plate."

"What were you saying about Don Ygnacio?"

"He was in Pablo's shop, ordering a fancy saddle for that—creature from Spain," Candelaria whispered the last three words behind her plump palm, and had the satisfaction of seeing Isabella Alvarjo start.

Her voice when she spoke was curt. "You must be mistaken."

"I am not, señorita. You have only to ask that filthy old Pablo the truth of it. I saw her with my own eyes, dressed in a boy's clothes, insolent as you please, looking everything over as if she owned it."

Isabella knew what her brother had told her of Tarifa, but she was not certain that he had told her everything. She knew that the girl was ensconced somewhere on the rancho until a ship could take her back to Spain, but she had not thought that Ygnacio would bring her here to the hacienda or that he would present gifts to her. She understood his sense of shame and responsibility for the girl, and she herself was hurt and baffled that Santiago had brought the creature to California. The Alvarjos would not have done their duty until they returned Tarifa to Spain. But bringing her here! She would have to speak with Ygnacio.

"You may go, Candelaria, and we will hear no more of this matter. Don Ygnacio is master here, and he does as he pleases."

"*Sí*, señorita." Candelaria repeated, surprised and abashed; in the past her morsels of gossip had not been so summarily dismissed.

Isabella climbed thoughtfully down the stairs and saw her brother coming along the veranda carrying his sombrero and riding whip. He smiled at her, something he had not done for a great many weeks, and she waited for him, watching him speculatively.

Voices came from the sala where the girls were sewing with their guest, Rufina Corlona.

"Isabella, come and have a glass of wine in my study."

"Where have you been, Ygnacio?"

"Riding. Come, I will tell you all about it."

He linked his arm through hers and drew her into the study, shutting the door.

Isabella sat down in a straight-backed horsehair chair and said, "Dolores would like to go to Santa Barbara with Rufina Corlona when she returns after Christmas. I have told her it is not suitable with her dear mother dead for so short a time."

Ygnacio poured wine for them both and came to hand his sister her glass. He looked more alert than he had for weeks, more like the old Ygnacio.

"I think perhaps this long mourning and restriction does the children no good. I have spoken of it to Padre Cazon, and he agrees. It is well and proper to show due respect for the dead, but prayers and Masses do more good than wearing black clothes and hiding from the world."

"I am surprised to hear you speak so," Isabella said primly. Things were not going at all as she had hoped. He had changed and it was not to her liking.

"No one could love a wife more than I loved Encarnacion," Alvarjo replied. "But my duty now is to the welfare of my children. She would be the first to say so."

Isabella seized the opportunity.

"Exactly," she said, "and you must continue to think of the children. As soon as you have sent this dreadful Gypsy back to Spain, everything will be as it once was."

"Nothing is ever as it once was, Isabella. Everything moves on—for better or worse."

"Have you found out when a ship will be able to take her away?" asked Isabella desperately.

"No. But the port officials will let me know."

"I pray it will be soon! Dreadful creature—what she has cost this family, Joaquin and Santiago, neither of them the same since that accursed trip to Spain. Encarnacion dead. You a murderer."

"I killed the man who killed her," Alvarjo replied steadily, "and you cannot blame everything on Tarifa— she is a Gypsy, but she is not a sorceress."

"How can you say her name—that pagan name—in this house?"

"You exaggerate, Isabella. She is nothing but a child, a bright but uninhibited child. Would you have been any different if you had been a street Gypsy in Seville?"

Isabella rose. "I cannot discuss her, Ygnacio. And I trust that you will have more consideration than to bring her here again."

She knew instantly that she had gone too far. His eyes widened in surprise and his lips straightened like a rope pulled taut.

"Candelaria has reported to you, I suppose?" he said harshly. "I brought the girl here to give her a saddle. For no other reason. As a charity, because I feel we owe her something. She has nothing. I brought her in through the kitchen square where she could be an offense to no one. I shall bring her again if I choose. This is my house."

Isabella's eyes were bright with anger, but she turned on her heel and left the room without a word. He had never spoken so to her in his life before!

As he poured more wine, Don Ygnacio reflected bitterly that Pablo's definition of Candelaria was not far wrong; she was indeed a busybody and a bitch.

CHAPTER 9

October had brought some relief from the late summer heat and the first rain of the season to the parched sierras and dry San Luis Rey valley. Padre Cazon put down his book and wondered if the rain would cease before it was time to return to the Mission.

He sat in the cabaña across the table from Tarifa who was struggling with a child's intensity to print her name with a scratchy quill pen.

At first he had not approved of the idea when Don Ygnacio had presented it to him.

"I have enough to do teaching the neophytes."

"Yes, Padre, I understand, but surely waste is sin? And she has such a fine quick mind. It will not take her long to learn. If we can return her to Spain able to read and write, and with money in her pocket, surely she can better herself, become somebody? And I will feel I have done all in my power to repay her for Santiago's treatment."

Don Ygnacio had agreed to ask Padre Peyri's permission himself. He told the old priest that he wanted Padre Cazon to tutor the girl at a neighbor's house once a week, and in return he left a large purse of gold for the poor.

So once a week Cazon trudged the distance to the little cabaña to teach his odd pupil, who could not understand why he insisted on walking when she had offered him the use of Estrelita.

From the beginning Padre Cazon knew that Alvarjo had been right. She possessed a quick mind and a retentive memory. Her passion to learn was equaled only by her passion for training and teaching Guindilla. The only trouble was that she was impatient and wanted to do everything at once, yet she wrote and read with the same unique agility that she danced.

"You must master the letters, then you can make words with them."

"But the letters mean nothing by themselves. I want to make words with them, and then I will learn them."

Padre Cazon was putting on his hat to leave when a horseman galloped into the yard.

Santiago Alvarjo, sitting astride El Canario, greeted them by standing up in his stirrups and making a sweeping bow.

"Buenos días, Tarifa. Padre."

"What are you doing here? How did you find this place?" demanded the priest.

"I was riding and I saw Guindilla down here in the corral, so I came to see who was here. I recognized you through the window. Does my father know you are here?"

"Certainly. He arranged the place for the Señorita to wait until her ship arrives. He will be angry when he knows you have been here. You will tell no one else about this, do you hear?"

Santiago raised his eyebrows in surprise.

"May I ask what you are doing here, Padre, since Tarifa is not a Catholic?"

"I have been teaching the Señorita to read and write."

A look of bitterness flashed across Santiago's face.

"My father seems to have gone out of his way to make the Señorita comfortable on our land. I am surprised, after his anger at my bringing her here."

"You did a very wrong thing." Cazon scowled. "Your father, in his charity, is trying to make it right. You will ride along with me to the main road, Santiago, and you will not come back here again."

Tarifa said nothing as she watched them move off, the Padre trudging steadily with his staff, Santiago prancing along on El Canario trying unsuccessfully to hold the stallion to the priest's pace. But she knew she would have no more peace and privacy in which to enjoy Guindilla and her lessons. Santiago, even if he told no one else, would come back himself, and in her nowfound wisdom she knew he was no longer just a laughing boy with a guilty conscience about how he had treated her. He had changed in the months since she had last seen him in San Diego. There was a hardness in his expression and a slyness in his smile that had not been there before.

Luis and Nazario were riding up and down in front of the hacienda, making practice throws with their *reatas* at a tree stump fifty yards away, when Zenobio rode up with Bart Kinkaid. He had arrived at San Juan that morning and ridden over to the Santa Teresa for breakfast, asking his friend to go with him to Loma de Oro. In his pocket was the finest carved ivory fan from Canton in his entire cargo. White was her color, he thought. She was all gold and white, like an easter lily.

Zenobio argued in vain that he was doing the wrong thing, that Don Ygnacio would disapprove of his giving his daughter a gift of such worth, that grand high-born ladies like Dona Dolores did not accept gifts from any male save their own family or intended bridegroom.

Since this was exactly what Bart intended to become, no dire warnings from Zenobio could deter him. He didn't have time for them.

As they hitched their horses Antonio came from the *sala* sucking on a plum, his dark eyes wide. He had never seen an Americano before, let alone a sailor.

When he had greeted the boys and introduced Kinkaid, Zenobio asked, "Where can we find Dolores?"

"She's in the dining room arranging fruit on the sideboard," said Antonio.

"And Tía Isabella?"

"Oh, she drove to the Mission a little while ago to light candles and pray, because she thinks our family is cursed."

"Ho! She does, does she!" Zenobio glanced at the boys, listening quietly but with frank curiosity, and added, "Take Capitán Kinkaid to the dining room, Antonio; he can run my errand while I show you boys a new throw I learned from a *reatero* who came to the house the other day. He was from Sonora. Give me your *reata*, Luis."

As Zenobio had guessed, Antonio deposited Kinkaid in the dining room and rushed back to be in on the roping lesson.

Dolores glanced up with a start as her brother pushed

Kinkaid impatiently into the room and darted out again.

"I did not mean to frighten you, señorita," Kinkaid said when they were alone. He was pleased to see that she no longer wore black, but a sedate gray gown with a pale blue sash and blue silk slippers tied around her slender ankles with ribbons. She put the orange she had been holding into a basket on the sideboard.

"You did not startle me, Capitán Kinkaid. It was Antonio. I fear his manners are not very good since my mother's death. He has grown very spoiled." Then, words that seemed too good to be true: "I'm sorry if you've had your trip for nothing, but my father is away from home, and so is my aunt."

The intensity of his gaze must have warned her for she put a hand to her breast as if to protect herself before he spoke.

"I came to see you, Dolores. May I call you that?"

"I—don't understand, señor?"

He pulled the fan from his pocket and offered it to her with a smile.

"This is for you. The finest carved ivory fan on the coast of California. A friend of mine brought it from Canton himself."

She felt so small, so weak and helpless standing beneath his towering bulk, and yet she was not afraid. He took her breath away, but she sensed that he would die rather than harm her.

"I see. It is a very beautiful fan, Capitán. But I cannot accept it."

"You must! It's for you."

"I understand and I appreciate your kindness, but it would not be proper for me to accept a gift from a strange man. And such a valuable gift."

"But we've met before. I'm not a complete stranger."

She shook her head, smiling up at him. "I would know what I had done something that was not right. Please, try to understand?"

He looked baffled and hurt.

In her natural sympathy and pity for any unhappiness, she said quickly, "I would keep it if I could and treasure it always. It is the most beautiful fan I have ever seen. I could never hope to own one as lovely."

"Then you must take it. Hide it. Put it away. Pretend I

never gave it to you. I'll leave it and you can say you found it?"

She was laughing up at him and he longed to take her in his arms, to hold her close and tell her he loved her, but he knew he could do none of these things. To rush her would be to lose her entirely.

"I cannot take it—"

"Bart," he finished. "Call me Bart."

"Bart?" she said it with a delicious inflection and he knew no one else would ever say it the same way.

"Bartholomew."

"Ah! Bartolomeo, *sí*."

"But you will call me Bart?"

"My aunt and father would not approve—but I shall."

"Will you do one thing more for me, Dolores?"

Her blue-gray eyes widened. "*Sí*. If I can."

"Let me leave the fan at Don Zenobio's for you, and if you ever change your mind he will bring it to you."

"All right, Bart. If it will please you."

They stood looking at each other, neither aware that all embarrassment had ceased to exist between them.

Santiago lay in his bed and felt the fever in his bones. Outside, brilliant moonlight filtered through the wooden grille of his window. His room was the second from the top of the stairs along the *galleria* next to Joaquin's, and he had been wakened by the groans and the sound of the leather flail as his brother scourged himself. Joaquin would go out of his mind soon, and for the same reasons he lay and burned inside.

Tarifa!

No longer did he feel pity and responsibility for her. She lay at the bottom of every horror he had experienced these last tortuous months. Bandonna had spoken the truth when she said bringing the girl would also bring a curse upon him and upon his family.

Tarifa was a witch, she had claimed so herself, and what did you do with witches? You burned them, strangled them, killed them.

He rose from his bed and began to dress himself feverishly. He gathered up his hat, his whip, and his knife from the top of the chest.

Outside the moonlight outlined everything as bright as

day. He stole softly past Joaquin's now-silent room, and down the stairs to the patio. It was safer to go out past the chapel and across the pasture to the palominos' corral.

His soft whistle brought El Canario and he rode him bareback to the outlying shed where the saddles were kept.

Saddled and bridled, he turned the stallion across the hills toward the cabaña.

The little house lay silent in the *arroyo seco* as Santiago approached. It had only two rooms, the larger main one and a small kitchen behind. There was also a shed some yards away where the servants slept.

Penti and Tarifa, he thought, must be asleep in the front room. He had taken off his spurs, and his soft doeskin *botas* made no sound on the veranda. He opened the door a crack and heard nothing but heavy, even breathing with now and then a snore from the old Gypsy, who was lying on a cot directly in front of him. He could not see Tarifa.

He took off his sash and crept forward with it held in one hand, his heavily weighted riding crop held handle-down in the other.

Penti never wakened when he hit her a smashing blow over the back of the head. She only moaned faintly and then lay still. Swiftly, Santiago tied her hands and feet with his sash and stuffed a handkerchief in her open mouth.

He had moved as silently as smoke and yet when he turned Tarifa leaped at him from the shadows like a tigress that can see in the dark.

It was not in her to call for help. She fought him silently, desperately, seeking to stab the knife she held into his breast.

He fought just as silently but with no less determination, and a strength that was slowly overpowering her.

She gasped when he jarred the knife from her hand and flung her roughly on her back across the bed. Moonlight did not penetrate here but he did not need it. He ripped the nightgown from her back and tied her arms behind her with it, tore a strip from a blouse hanging on a nearby chair and gagged her, then threw her back on the bed.

He stood over her and took the knife from his boot. He knew the hate and fury that must be in her curved eyes, though he could not see them. There ought to be a better, a harder way, for her to die.

He watched her strong dancer's legs thrashing on the bed.

There was a better way.

A much better way!

He would finish what Joaquin had tried and failed to do. And he knew, as he stripped off his clothes, that he had had the desire and the intent from the first moment he saw her dancing in the Plaza de las Sierpes in Seville. He pried her thrashing legs apart with his knee and entered her with such force that he felt the membrane tear and break, sending the gush of blood over both their thighs, and still his madness did not leave him until he lay at last exhausted on top of her supine body. He withdrew himself from her and his hand touched his knife, but the desire to kill her had left him and he shoved the knife in his sash. He stood trembling slightly in the silent room, and fear took the place of his passion. He had done better than kill the Gypsy, he had despoiled and conquered her body and spirit. She would not forget this night, if she lived. But he knew his father would hunt him down now, and Santos. From this moment he was an outcast, and he would have to flee just as he stood, depending on the swiftness of his horse.

He turned and left the cabaña, the yard, the *arroyo seco,* as silently as he had come.

Don Ygnacio, awakened by a quick secretive knock on his bedroom door, was amazed to find Santos fully dressed, standing on the veranda with a look of fright in his eyes.

"Santos!"

"I must speak with you, Don Ygnacio—where no one can hear us. Quickly!"

The mayordomo's urgency alarmed Alvarjo. He fell back and the Indian followed him into his room and swiftly shut the door.

"What is the meaning of this, Santos?"

"Today Salvador, the neophyte from the Mission, was here to deliver some spurs to Pablo. He told me that Padre Cazon had seen Don Santiago at the *ranchita* and ordered him away. He had stumbled on the cabaña and recognized Guindilla in the corral."

"You should have come to me at once," Alvarjo said severely. "I will speak to Santiago now."

He reached for a dressing gown.

"He is not here, señor."

"Not here? What do you mean? No son of mine ever left the hacienda at night without my permission."

"He is gone. That is what I came to tell you, señor. I was asleep near the shed when he wakened me saddling El Canario. He had a look on his face—I did not dare to question him. Then he rode off toward the *arroyo seco*. I do not know, but I fear he has gone to the cabaña."

Don Ygnacio stood very still for a moment and then said, "Help me get dressed, Santos. No—go and saddle the horses."

"They are already saddled, señor. Here, let me help you."

The two men rode past the kitchen square at a thundering gallop that roused the servants. Don Alvarjo had no feeling as he rode except a terrible driving need to reach his destination. He had never been impatient of El Capitán's speed before, for he was probably the fastest horse in the territory, yet tonight it seemed to his master that he lagged like a lazy cart horse.

The cabaña still lay silent, bathed in moonlight. Don Ygnacio glanced with sharp suspicion at Santos' face, for El Canario was nowhere to be seen. Only Guindilla in the corral and the mare Estrelita in her further paddock nickered softly.

Upon hearing voices, one of the servants came to the door of the shed, a candle in his hand.

"Who is there? What do you want?"

"Don Ygnacio and Santos," replied the mayordomo curtly. "Has anyone else been here tonight?"

"No, *amigo*, I would have heard them. My wife and I are very light sleepers."

Santos grunted.

"Is something wrong?" called the servant.

"Perhaps, we don't know—bring a light."

The man, José, came a few minutes later carrying a lantern; his fat wife followed with another.

Santos took one of them himself to light Don Ygnacio's way, and thrust back the half-closed door for his master to enter.

One horrified glance showed Alvarjo all he needed to know. He closed his eyes for an instant to shut out the sight while he muttered a prayer, and then opened them resolutely again.

The two women still lay on their beds, but Penti's eyes were open a crack. Don Ygnacio went to stand beside her cot and motioned Santos to untie her and remove the gag.

She moaned and then began to spout Romany invectives.

"Where is Tarifa? What have they done to *miri pen?*" She tried to get up but was forced by her pain to lie down again. She explained to the men that she had not seen who struck her, she had been asleep, and suddenly there was a blinding crash and then she knew no more.

Don Ygnacio went to the other bed and forced himself to look down. She lay crumpled and still, like a broken doll, her black hair tangled over her face and breast in a tumble of bedclothes and a welter of blood. Her hands were still tied behind her back and he bent to release them and to untie the gag that bound her swollen, bruised mouth. There seemed to be no rise or fall of her breast, no color in her pallid face. He took a serape from a peg on the wall and covered her gently. Nothing moved in him; he was like a pool of deep water, so deep that no current could disturb or change him.

Had God abandoned the Alvarjos to the Devil completely? Were they so cursed that nothing could stop them on their road to perdition, nothing keep them from murdering, killing, sinning—again and again and again?

And there was no question about who had done this. He had recognized instantly the red patterned sash that Santiago had worn at dinner that very evening, and that Santos had removed from Penti's arms and legs.

The two servants still stood awestruck in the open doorway.

"Tell Padre Cazon he must come to Loma de Oro at once."

"*Sí*, señor! *Pronto, pronto!*"

He sent the woman for wine and more blankets for Penti; he felt that Tarifa must already be dead. As when Encarnacion had died, one part of him could not wholly accept the fact, though he knew it to be true.

Penti, watching his face, gave a cry of denial and staggered from her cot to Tarifa's bed. She tore aside the serape and gazed in silence at the bent, twisted body, the pale swollen face, and then, with a wail more animal than human, bent and gathered the girl in her arms like a sleeping child.

Don Ygnacio could not understand her Romany mutterings, but her tender crooning tone was unmistakable, the maternal murmurings that speak comfort to the frightened child.

And then as he watched, he saw Tarifa's head move on the old Gypsy's breast, and her purpled lips formed a single word he did not catch.

The old Gypsy looked up at him murderously.

"Your son has done this," she told him shrilly. "Your son!" Her low keening voice rose to a shriek in the classic curse, *"Premita ēndebē,"* followed by the long *oleaje* of curses stringing out like evil beads in a devil's rosary. "May devils keep you and God condemn you!"

Don Ygnacio stood silently absorbing the Gypsy's wrath until the servant returned with wine and blankets. Penti managed to force a few drops of wine between Tarifa's lips then laid her down and wrapped her gently in a warm cocoon of blankets.

Tarifa opened her eyes and glanced once at Don Ygnacio. It stunned him to see that there was no hatred in their depths for him, only a dumb questioning like that of a wild creature that, once befriended, has been hurt and abandoned.

Ygnacio turned abruptly to Santos. "We must get her to Loma de Oro—at once!"

"I will take her, señor," Santos was uneasy about the whole unfair. He could see nothing but disaster ahead for all of them.

"No, I will carry her on El Capitán. Saddle Guindilla for the other woman. *Pronto!*"

"Sí, señor."

"You will not touch her," Penti shrieked. She was hovering over her charge like a crouching lioness. "You will never take her to that place where your accursed sons live!"

With patience and the nearest thing to pleading Don Ygnacio had ever stooped to make use of, he explained that Loma de Oro was the only place where they could be protected, surrounded there by Don Ygnacio and all his vaqueros. He did not mention Santiago.

Tarifa, when he knelt to ask her, nodded her head briefly, and then for no reason he lifted her gently and held her with her head against his shoulder.

She clung to him and her body was suddenly convulsed with sobs, wracking, tearing sobs that shook them both, and he knew a hatred for his son he had never experienced before, a hatred he had never thought to feel again, except for Bruno Cacho's memory.

She was little, so little and fine-boned, and she fitted into his arms like Soledad when she came to cry out her troubles on his shoulder. He had that night lost a son, but perhaps, God willing, he had gained a daughter. Of his household only Joaquin and Isabella would refuse to accept her. But he was still the master at Loma de Oro, and he had determined that never again should this child suffer while he had the power to protect her.

The little cavalcade moved slowly, but his burden was as nothing in Don Ygnacio's arms. She slept fitfully with her head on his shoulder, moaning once or twice when they crossed rough rocky ground.

A faint line of dawn was showing when they halted in the kitchen square, and eager if curious hands came to help them dismount.

There was a private guest room near the chapel, reserved for the Pádres when they came to say Mass once a month for the family. Don Ygnacio ordered her carried there, and a cot set up in the same apartment for Penti.

He sent a scandalized Candelaria to fetch Isabella, before he turned to Santos.

"You will go and find my son, Santos." He gave the mayordomo a purse of coins. "Find him and bring him to me, is that clear, hombre?"

"*Sí*, Don Ygnacio." Their eyes met and held.

Alvarjo hesitated and then took a pistol from his sash and handed it to him. "I want him back. But if you have trouble, use this, and I will be responsible for your actions. *Adiós, muchacho.*"

"*Adiós,* señor. *Hasta luego.*"

* * *

Shortly after dawn Isabella knelt on the cold tiles of the chapel floor and prayed and wrung her hands until the knuckles turned white. She prayed wildly, blindly, not even aware of the words she said, only knowing that this was her last hope of sanity in a world suddenly gone mad.

Ygnacio's cold, terse words, spoken in the dim predawn of her bedroom scarcely an hour before, seemed to have been spoken by a stranger in a hideous nightmare.

He had accused Santiago of a foul and heinous sin. Her own, dear laughing Santiago! It could not be, but if it was, the Gypsy was to blame with her witchcraft and her curses showering upon them all. She had got her just deserts. And because of her, Santiago's father had called him a murderer and a fiend, and had sent Santos out to hunt him down like a dog. As he had hunted Bruno Cacho after the half-breed had killed Encarnacion. With the same look of hatred in his eyes.

She could not believe her ears when Ygnacio told her that he had brought the two Gypsy women here, that they were under the roof of the hacienda at that very moment— and in the room reserved for the Padres!

Infamous blasphemy! But she could say nothing. Ygnacio's frozen, aloof face told her that. To protest would have been worse than useless. He had added pain upon pain, insult upon insult, as if in his own mental agony he could not hurt her enough.

"As head of my household since Encarnacion's death, it is up to you to play hostess to our guests."

"Guests!" The word broke from her lips like shot bursting from a cannon.

"As long as anyone shares my roof and my bread, they are my guests. You will see that they have everything to make them comfortable, and you will see to it personally."

"I will not go near the witch! She has cursed and bewitched you all—Joaquin, Santiago, and now you. I will not go near her!"

Isabella was sitting bolt upright in bed while they talked, her braided hair hanging down her shoulders, her face as austere and haughty as his own, though not as bleak. She had not seen what he had seen. Perhaps he had no right to force her to see it . . . yet, he thought. His instinct had always been to protect his womenfolk.

"Very well," he said with a sigh, "you need not see to

them personally, but send Candelaria with a message. And send a maid to serve them."

Isabella said nothing, but at that moment she disliked her brother actively for the first time in her life. She could feel her respect for him trickling away like sand in an hourglass.

Isabella was roused from her prayers in the chapel by the hurried entrance of Rosita, the little Indian maid she had sent to serve the Gypsy women, as Ygnacio had ordered.

Isabella rose and went to the door where the girl stood nervously crossing herself as she bobbed a curtsy at the altar.

"Mistress."

"What is it, Rosita?"

"If you please, the Gypsy woman, the older one they call Penti, would like to have a pot of charcoal and some food and utensils so that she can prepare their meals in the Padres' room."

"Isn't our hospitality good enough for them?" bridled Isabella.

"The old one says there are medications and concoctions she must cook to make the Señorita Tarifa well again."

"She'll prepare none of her witches' brew in this house! Come!"

Isabella, with the little maid pattering after her, left the chapel and crossed to the room occupied by Penti and Tarifa.

She knocked sharply on the door and instantly found herself face-to-face with a dark, evil-eyed old harridan clutching a sheaf of foul-smelling leaves in her hand.

"What is it you want?"

"I am Dona Isabella Alvarjo, Don Ygnacio's sister. I have run his household for him since his dear wife's death some months ago. The maid tells me you wish to cook in this room?"

"*Sí.*"

"But that is impossible. We have an adequate kitchen in the back of the house. You have only to tell the cook-housekeeper Candelaria what you want and she will get it for you."

Penti eyed her narrowly. "She cannot prepare what I

need. And I cannot prepare them before other eyes. These are secret Gypsy remedies, known and handed down only in the tribe. Bring me a pot of fire of some kind and some utensils. That will do."

"Very well. Rosita, fetch the old charcoal foot-warmer from the storeroom."

During the next few weeks the household settled down into a quiet, if uneasy, routine. Tía Isabella divided her time between the chapel, the kitchen, and her own bedroom, though she ate her meals with the family and sometimes sat briefly with them in the *sala* or patio, sewing or saying her beads. Ygnacio spent less time in his retreat on Loma de Oro, and in Santos' continued absence, was forced to take over the active management of the rancho himself. When he rode out each morning he took all his sons with him, which served the double purpose of keeping them away from the hacienda, and giving them a chance to use up their youthful energies in a useful manner.

He never spoke of Santiago and, when asked, told the family, as Tía Isabella had done, that his son had gone away on business for him and that he had sent Santos along with him.

Only Candelaria was not convinced of the truth of this, for she had seen Don Ygnacio and Santos ride off at breakneck speed in the dead of night and later return with the two women, one of them too ill to walk. She had seen nothing of the two Gypsies after their arrival except for glimpses of the old one walking alone in the pasture beyond the chapel, stooping to dig roots and gather leaves or bark from the oak trees. Candelaria was convinced that she was a witch and that God would strike them all dead if they harbored her under their roof for much longer. The only fortunate thing was that the Gypsies ate all their meals in their room and kept to themselves. Only Rosita came and went from their room freely and, after the first fright of being sent to tend two witches, she seemed to have accepted her routine. She was a stolid Indian girl without too much imagination.

But when Candelaria attempted to question her about her odd new mistresses, Rosita was singularly vague.

"What does the old one cook in there?"

"I don't know, señora. She brews things from leaves and bark. She gives it to the Señorita Tarifa as medicine."

Candelaria could get no satisfaction, even when she repeated her fears to Isabella, for her mistress had a stock answer for everything these days. She sounded like Father Peyri.

"It is God's will, we must abide by His decision. This is my brother's house. He has any guest he chooses."

Padre Cazon had come that day after Ygnacio and Santos had brought Tarifa from the cabaña. He had gone in to see the girl briefly and come out with a face like a stone, and for many hours he had sat and talked to his host in Don Ygnacio's study.

"What will you do to your son if Santos finds him?" asked the priest.

"I do not know. I must find him, that is all. I cannot think what madness brought this on. Santiago was never an evil, sinful boy!"

"Temptation and sin are traps we can all fall into, Ygnacio—even as your own passion led you to murder."

"But I had a reason! What reason had Santiago to harm this child?"

"That, only Santiago can tell us. And repentance and penance are his only salvation. Perhaps you would do well to let him go, to let him face himself for a while?"

"I must find him," replied Alvarjo savagely.

"And what of the girl? Do you plan to keep her here? Dona Isabella seems very upset."

"This is my house, Padre. The Alvarjos owe a debt, now unpayable, to that child. She is only safe here until she can be sent back to Spain."

"And when will that be?"

"How do I know, Padre!"

"She cannot stay cooped up in her room for months."

"No. When she is able, I shall introduce her to the family and she shall live here as one of us."

"Do you think that wise?"

"It is the only solution I can think of. I would like you to continue to give her lessons, Padre."

Cazon nodded. "If you wish it. But I am not sure all this will work out as you think. Your friends and neigh-

bors will get wind of it—and Padre Peyri, I must tell him
something."

"Perhaps it is time you told him all of it," said Alvarjo
slowly. "Secrecy is never a good thing—it has led us to all
this." He waved a hand helplessly. "I shall not keep
Tarifa's presence a secret any longer."

"Then," said Cazon with a note of warning in his voice,
"you must be prepared to face the consequences—whatever they may be."

CHAPTER 10

Tarifa's young body mended surely and swiftly under
Penti's constant ministrations. And her mercurial Gypsy
spirit was not stilled by harsh treatment or fright. The
experience in the cabaña that terror-stricken night she
washed as cleanly from her mind as one would wipe off a
slate. For Santiago himself she felt only abomination and
a vile contempt, but no longer any fear. If he walked
through the door this instant she would not be afraid of
him—or afraid to kill him. Her *navaja* was never far from
her person these days, nor ever would it be again.

Don Ygnacio was the only member of the family who
called on her during those first weeks, but he came regularly once and sometimes twice a day.

They never spoke of Santiago or why she and Penti were
now here instead of at the cabaña. Don Ygnacio brought
her small gifts—some flowers, a book from his study, some
ribbons for her hair, the largest purple grapes from the
vine climbing up the *galleria*—and they sat and talked

companionably, each learning something of value from the other.

Since she had learned to read from Padre Cazon, Tarifa had discovered a whole new world of books, and these she and Don Ygnacio discussed and poured over at great length. None of Ygnacio's womenfolk had ever expressed much interest in his cherished books, none of the boys save Joaquin ever read them, so Tarifa's quick, eager mind delighted and surprised him.

In Don Ygnacio Tarifa had found the first genuinely kind and gentle man she had ever known. Padre Cazon was kind in his way, but he was inclined to be dictatorial and demanding. Don Ygnacio never was, with her.

One day when she was already up and about, exploring the beauties of the elegant room with its carved mahogany furniture and polished Spanish-tiled floor, he came with a servant behind him bearing the new saddle Pablo had just finished making for her.

He set it up on its stand and stood back smiling while she flew to admire it.

"But it is beautiful! The most beeautiful saddle in the world, señor. Guindilla will love it. He is well, Don Ygnacio? It is so long since I have seen him."

Her face, pale and thinner than he liked to see it, looked wistfully back at him surrounded by the curling blue-black hair, like a jet cloud, he thought. She was not softly beautiful as Encarnacion had been and as Dolores was, but Isabella had been right, she was . . . bewitching.

"If you would like to see him," he said, "I will tell them to bring him to the pasture just beyond the wall of the chapel. It will only be a step for you to walk."

"Oh, yes! Tell them to bring him now."

Alvarjo glanced at Penti who crouched over her pot, stirring the contents of a small pan.

"Is she strong enough?" he asked.

The Gypsy gave him a black scowl and a brief nod.

Don Ygnacio stood with Tarifa under the acacia tree near the wall while they brought Guindilla up and held him snorting and pawing for Tarifa to fondle and pet him. She asked the servants to fetch the saddle and try it on him, clapping her hands over his appearance in the regal trappings.

Alvarjo took her back to a seat in the sunny patio and called his children to come out.

Tarifa looked startled but he told her, "You are our guest, señorita; it is time you met my family."

The younger children were frankly curious, but as friendly and courteous as their training had made them. Isabella was as formal and stiff as only a high-born Castilian woman can be but Tarifa seemed not to notice: she was minutely studying the boys and girls grouped around her.

Joaquin came last from his room in the *galleria*. His face turned white and rigid at sight of her. He would have retreated but Don Ygnacio commanded him to remain.

"You have met the Señorita Tarifa, Joaquin," his father said evenly.

Joaquin nodded bleakly, mumbled a proper greeting as he bowed, and added, "I am not feeling well, Padre. Have I your permission to return to my room?"

Don Ygnacio nodded, and turned to listen to the babble of young voices all striving at once to make their strange new guest at home. He smiled indulgently at them as they clustered about Tarifa's chair, and did not even notice when Isabella slipped away toward the *galleria* and ascended to Joaquin's room.

A moment later a servant approached and told them that Santos had just returned and was waiting for him in the study.

With a glance at Tarifa, who was absorbed in listening to Luis play the guitar, keeping time with her fingers on the arm of her chair, he quietly left them—a gay young group near the fountain—and went in to join Santos, with a grim look on his own face.

The mayordomo appeared tired and worn; he had not even paused to change his travel-stained clothes before reporting to his master.

"Well, Santos?"

The Indian handed him back his pistol and untouched purse.

"I did not find him, señor. I hunted everywhere. I asked everyone. It is as if the earth has opened and swallowed him up. From the cabaña he made for high ground on the sierras and I lost his trail. I stopped at every *ranchería* but

no Indian had seen him. It could be that he circled me and
went back toward the Rio Colorado and on to Mexico. Do
you want me to go on looking?"

Don Ygnacio shook his head slowly. Perhaps, as Padre
Cazon had said, it was best for Santiago to be alone with
his thoughts for a time. He could not run away from
them, Don Ygnacio knew, no matter how far he traveled.

Santiago knew if he could reach San Diego by a back
route, disguise himself, and creep into town, there were
those who would help him get to Mexico without betraying
the secret of his whereabouts. Pio Pico or Macario Canejo.
He decided to try it. San Francisco lay too many leagues
to the north for him to travel it on El Canario alone. He
would need fresh mounts, and wherever he left the conspicuous palomino his father would get word of it and put
Santos on his trail. He had no idea what his father could
do to him if he caught him, but he knew that it would not
be a mere whipping this time. If he had killed the Gypsy,
Don Ygnacio was liable to turn him over to the presidio
commandante, or to the governor for punishment. And
though he was a high-born *gente de razón* of the powerful
Alvarjo family, murder was still murder and the new
governor when he arrived might see fit to make an example
of him.

Santiago rounded back over the sierras at nightfall and
left El Canario with an aged Indian he knew who lived
alone with his wife in a distant arroyo beyond the last
ranchería belonging to the San Diego Mission.

He borrowed a worn serape and a horse and rode into
town, leaving the mare at the rack in front of Domingo
Chavira's wine shop where she would be inconspicuous and
crossed the plaza to Pico's less lively shop. He hoped Pio
was not away on one of his frequent trading trips. The
room was dim, with only one candle burning at this early
hour, and seemed deserted.

The clerk nodding over a ledger glanced up idly as he
came in.

"*Sí*, hombre?"

"Where is Don Pico?"

"You have business with Don Pico?"

"Where is he!" Santiago shouted, and instantly regretted

his loud tone, for someone was rummaging in the store-room beyond. He held his breath, ready to run, when the door opened and Pio appeared in his shirt-sleeves and gaudy silk waistcoat.

"Santa Margarita! Santiago!"

"I must see you at once, Pio. Alone."

Santiago's warning look held off Pico's words, and he said cautiously, "You may go, Carlos."

"*Sí,* Don Pio." The clerk closed the ledger and rose to get his sombrero. When he had gone, Pio shut and bolted the front door and turned to Santiago. "What is the trouble, *amigo?* We are alone now."

"I must get to Mexico."

One glance at Santiago's haunted eyes and Pio moved to the counter and poured a large measure of *aguardiente* for his friend. "*Sí, amigo,*" he said. "I will help you get to Mexico."

Santiago's hand trembled as he took the glass. "*Gracias.*"

"Sit down and eat something," Pio said. "There is cheese and biscuits and plenty of *vino.* I will lock the door after me and I will not be long. *Adiós.*"

"*Adiós,*" Santiago repeated, and he went to rummage in the barrels and boxes behind the counter for his supper. His life in exile had begun.

The mesteños roved in great bands of unbranded wild mustangs, and since the recent blighting droughts, the land could not support the quickly increasing herds. Cows were more valuable for their tallow and hides than horses, though many cattle were also destroyed in a severe drought, but it was the surplus of useless horses that were first to be sacrified, in a time when an ordinary horse was worth less than a glass of rum.

Now, with the grass sparse and sere, and water scarce, the time had come to hunt the mesteños, and Tarifa would not be left behind.

"Please let me go," she begged, "and Soledad too. She shall wear a suit like mine."

Don Ygnacio frowned and started to shake his head but the sight of the two eager young faces, happy now in contrast to the sorrow he had seen on both of them so recently, made him change his mind.

"Very well. Hurry, both of you. We are to meet Zenobio and his men in the north pasture."

The Alvarjos left as soon as it was light. The boys and Santos rode ahead with Don Ygnacio. Tarifa and Soledad, like twin slim boys on their dancing palominos, came next, followed by Tomas and twenty Loma de Oro vaqueros.

The October air was crisp and cold, redolent of tarweed and eucalyptus, and the palominos pranced and cavorted like young colts; even sedate El Capitán and the perfectly trained Marca bucked in the delight of an early-morning canter.

"You will have to stop feeding them so much barley," said Don Ygnacio impatiently as he jerked El Capitán out of a crow hop. "This one thinks he is a yearling again."

"And Marca, too, Patrón," said Santos, smiling. "It is the cold after all the summer's heat."

The boys were enjoying the mettlesome behavior of their mounts, and gaily calling back and forth as they rode into the wide saucerlike pasture where the northern edge of Don Ygnacio's property adjoined Zenobio Sanchez's Santa Teresa lands.

Zenobio, his bad leg curled over the wide saddle horn and supported by his horse's neck, was lazily smoking a cigar as they came up. He was surrounded by eight of his vaqueros, mounted and waiting nearby.

He was surprised to see Tarifa and Soledad, but he said nothing at first.

"Where are you going to start?" he asked.

Santos pointed north. "Some of the vaqueros saw a band of mesteños on the other side of the draw. They should be easy to drive down and hold there at the corral till we separate them from the good stock."

Zenobio nodded and gave quick orders to his mayordomo, a round-faced Chumelle Indian named Pino.

"We can go over the top and drive them down to you," said Zenobio. "What are you going to do with the *muchachas?*"

"They will stay here with Antonio, out of harm's way, and watch," said Ygnacio.

"A good many things can happen in a milling band of wild horses, *amigo,*" his friend cautioned. "Better keep them well back."

"They will be all right."

"Where are Joaquin and Santiago?" asked Zenobio before he reined away.

Don Ygnacio put a hand on his friend's knee. "I will ride with you, Zenobio. I have some things for your ears alone."

"Ah. Come then, we ride."

"Where will they drive the wild horses?" asked Tarifa.

"To the far end of the pasture there, where you see the big corral," replied Soledad.

"Then the vaqueros will ride in on their cutting ponies and separate the branded from the unbranded stock," added Antonio importantly. "They will cut out the branded horses and let them out again, and hold only the mesteños who are to be killed inside the corral."

"How will they kill them?" asked Tarifa slowly. Since coming to love Don Ygnacio's palominos she could not bear the thought of any horse being killed. In a way she was sorry she had come on the hunt. The bullfights had never bothered her, even when a picador's horse had fallen or been gored; the more blood there was, the better she had liked it. But since coming to California she had changed in some subtle way. For the first time she had known kindness—mingled with cruelty perhaps—but the first real kindness to come her way, and she found that it outweighed the unhappiness she had experienced. As her mind had filled with learning, so her heart had seemed to fill with a strange new warmth.

"The vaqueros will line up outside the corral gates," Antonio's young voice went on, "armed with lances. As the mesteños run through, one will run after them from each side and bring them down."

Tarifa shuddered, to Antonio's delight, and pressed her hand protectively over Guindilla's shiny neck.

Vaqueros, riding like the wind with careless abandon across the hillsides, were yelling and coming in a huge circle from every direction. Before them thundered a herd of more than one hundred horses, a beautiful sight in the clear October morning with their manes and tails flying and their varicolored hides shining in the sun through the dust cloud created by their flying feet.

"Let's get closer," said Antonio, and his sister called after him, "Not too close, Tonito."

He paid no attention, but rode Concho on at a gallop.

Tarifa pulled abreast of Antonio in a flash.

"This is far enough," she told him, reaching across for Concho's headstall.

Antonio looked at her in surprise. He did not like the news Santos had given him that morning that his father had presented Guindilla and a new saddle to their guest. And no woman had ever laid her hand on his bridle before. His youthful anger was childlike but it was pure and imperious Castilian wrath.

"Let go of my horse!"

"Not until you agree to wait here. Your sister said this is far enough, and your father told you to stay here."

His eyes blazed back at her and his lip curled.

"I don't have to do what you say."

"Right now you do."

"Why?"

"Because you have no other choice."

Soledad rode up and glanced from his rebellious face to Tarifa's determined one.

"We will wait here, Antonio," said Soledad firmly. "If you don't, I will tell father you deliberately disobeyed his orders and mine and were insolent to our guest, and he will whip you and never bring you on a mesteño hunt again."

Antonio gathered up his reins like a young grandee, and retired to sulk several paces away, his eyes turned resolutely toward the corral.

The huge dust cloud was advancing down the draw. Vaqueros rode in and out of it, disappearing, then emerging again, shouting, waving, twirling the ends of their weighted *reatas* to keep the herd in line.

The wild horses converged on the corral and the first few broke loose and evaded the opening, but the vaqueros quickly drove the rest through the gap and then went to gather up the strays.

Through the dust, Tarifa could see Santos and Tomas as they rode into the corral. Marca's golden hide and proud head flashed in and out between the savage fighting mustangs like a bar of gold, as Santos whirled his *reata* again and again, catching a branded colt and hauling it out the closely guarded gate to another herd which was being held at a little distance by a watchful circle of riders. These were the good branded horses that would be kept.

When nothing but the worthless, wild mesteños were left inside the corral, a long double line of vaqueros formed beyond the corral gates, and Santos rode along handing each man a long sharp lance. Since this was not the menial work of the rancho, but considered sport, the Alvarjo boys, Don Ygnacio, and Zenobio had joined the line, each armed with a lance.

At a signal from Santos the gates were flung wide and the wild horses thundered through. Two by two, a man from each side detached himself swiftly from the line of riders and took out after a mustang. Mounted on their fastest horses they chased them down and dropped them neatly with one thrust of their expertly wielded lances.

After the first kill, Tarifa turned Guindilla's head away from the corral. "Why don't they shoot them?" she asked Soledad, who had also turned away, her face pale.

"Powder and shot are too scarce in California," she said sadly, "like everything else that we can't grow or produce ourselves. And there are so many cattle and horses to be destroyed each time there is a drought, so that the best may be saved."

"But there is so much land," said Tarifa. "There should be a way to feed and water all of them."

"You are fond of animals," said Soledad.

"Yes. Although Guindilla is the first one I ever owned." She leaned forward to scratch the top of his head between his ears.

"He is the most beautiful palomino ever bred on Loma de Oro," said Soledad simply.

"And you think your father should not have given him to me?"

Soledad, like Antonio, had learned from Santos of the gift that morning. "I did not say that," she answered. "Father has a right to do as he pleases with his property. I am glad that he has given Guindilla to someone who appreciates him."

Before she could answer, Tarifa heard Antonio's scream of anguish behind her.

"Padre, Padre! He's down between the wild horses—his lance broke off and he's fallen!"

Antonio put spurs to his mount and dashed away, leaving the two startled girls behind him.

"Madre de Dios!" whispered Soledad, her hand at her throat.

Tarifa said nothing but turned Guindilla sharply and lifted him into a ground-covering gallop. She passed Antonio, and came up on the scene of disaster before the men had driven off the remaining mustangs. Don Ygnacio lay face down on the ground, a smear of blood on his cheek.

Zenobio and Luis helped Santos turn him over gently and Tarifa slid off her horse in a flash and joined them.

He cannot be dead, she thought. The only kind friend she had ever had, would probably ever have in this wild *frontera*. He must not be dead!

She bent and touched his forehead softly. It was warm, not cold, and he opened his eyes and smiled up at her before he made a grimace of pain.

"What is it, Padre?" Luis asked anxiously.

"My—leg. It hurts; I can't seem to move it."

Santos ran his fingers lightly over Alvarjo's right leg.

"I feel no broken bones, Patrón," he said.

"Good, good. Then you can help me to my horse."

"But I cannot be sure there is nothing broken, señor. If you will wait we will send for a *carreta*—"

"No. My horse will do. Help me up, Luis."

Tarifa lingered while they helped him around the bloody carcass of a fallen mesteño, with the lance half-broken in his side, to El Capitán and lifted him, groaning and white-faced, to the stallion's back. But when Zenobio and his sons would go with him he refused to allow it.

"Just because an old fool has thrust in his lance too late and broken it off, is no reason why you should not stay and finish the job, *muchachos*. I will ride back with Antonio and the girls."

The way was long and necessarily slow. Tarifa knew that Don Ygnacio was in pain, yet he kept up a gay running fire of conversation that amused them and relieved the fears of his children. But he could not deceive Tarifa. She saw his pallor and the effort with which he held himself erect in the saddle. Her admiration for him rose another notch. He was, as Penti had said, *tacho*—all right.

At the house, Isabella and Candelaria put Don Ygnacio to bed, but could do little for the badly swollen condition of his leg or the pain.

When they knew that the injured man was alone, Tarifa and Penti entered his room. When Ygnacio struggled to rise, Tarifa said, "I have brought my woman, Penti. She will make your leg well in no time."

He protested as the old woman prodded and poked the injury. "A very bad sprain, senor, but this will bring down the swelling."

The next day the old woman came twice to rub in Romany balm, the secret formula of the Rumanian Zingari, of whom Penti's mother had been a tribeswoman.

"What is in it?" asked Don Ygnacio curiously after experiencing the miraculous relief it gave.

"It is a secret, señor, but because of your kindness to Tarifa, I will tell you. It is one ounce of cuttings from the frog of a horse's hoof, one leek, one ounce elder bark, and four ounces of fat from a pig's kidney. You cook it slowly and strain it into a jar."

"It has done wonders for my leg," said Ygnacio. "How can I repay you?"

Penti drew herself up. "A gypsy does not do what I have done for pay, señor."

"I did not mean any offense, Penti," he said hurriedly, "but surely you will accept a gift from—a friend?" He twisted a ruby ring from his finger and handed it to her. "My father gave it to me for luck when I left Spain. Please accept it."

Penti took the jewel as her eyes kindled with excitement. "This is no little gift, sir! May I give you in return the blessing of our people?"

Tarifa entered and glanced sharply at the ring Penti was secreting in her bundle, then addressing Don Ygnacio, said: "Tía Isabella has sent me to tell you that Don Julio Marcos would like to pay his respects."

Ygnacio was not pleased to be visited by a neighbor whom he found bothersome at the best of times, but he refused to use his indisposition as a crutch for escape from his duties as a host.

"Admit him," he told Tarifa.

* * *

Don Julio Marcos left Tía Isabella in the *sala,* after making a great show of gallant courtliness over her hand as he bowed his way out, and followed Soledad's slim, dark-clad figure along the veranda to her father's bedroom.

Julio had hoped for a glimpse of Dolores, whom he thought a ravishing beauty and was determined to marry someday. Now that her mother was dead, his chances might be better, for Dona Encarnacion had never seemed to approve of him. But Dolores was getting to a marriageable age, and Don Ygnacio, for all his wealth and lands, could not be adverse to adding the considerable Marcos holdings to his family's estate.

Don Julio's father Sebastian had been in the army with Ygnacio Alvarjo and had retired to his large rancho near Loma de Oro at about the same time; but, where Ygnacio had married a high-born Castilian bride, Sebastian's wife had come from Mexico with a somewhat dubious past. Julio was their only child, and now lived with his widowed mother at their rancho, Bolsa de los Coyotes. It was a remote place, but large, and it boasted something Loma de Oro could not—an abundance of water and plenty of natural springs. Don Julio was an indifferent ranchero, but his land prospered in spite of him.

He flicked a speck of dust from the gold lace decorating the sleeve of his new snuff-colored jacket, and secretly admired the reflection of his shadow against the sunlit wall of the house.

Don Ygnacio was wearing his dressing gown and sitting propped up in bed, his legs covered with a finely woven serape.

"*Buenos días,* Don Ygnacio. I was grieved to learn of your misfortune. I came as soon as I heard."

"*Buenos días,* Don Julio," Alvarjo replied testily. "It was good of you to come. Please sit down. I do not like to entertain in my bedroom, but will you take a glass of wine, or some *aguardiente?*"

"Thank you, nothing," said Marcos, seating himself in a small brocade armchair that had belonged to Encarnacion.

Don Ygnacio noted that the young man's manner and appearance had undergone no improvement.

It was not that you could put your finger exactly on

what was wrong with Don Sebastian's son. At twenty-nine, he was a tall big-boned man, beginning to grow thick-jowled and heavy-shouldered, something he concealed beneath elaborate clothing and a dandified manner. No hacendado spent more money on his clothes and jewelry than Don Julio, or more time on his toilet or appearance. The scent he used was imported at great cost from France. His leather shoes and gloves from Italy. His hats from Cordobá. He was considered a great dancer, and by the ladies at least, a gallant caballero, but there was some quality lacking in him that jarred Don Ygnacio.

Lack of intelligence? No, the man had a quick, shrewd intelligence. And his father had sent him to school with the Jesuits in Mexico for a year.

Unmanliness? No, Don Ygnacio had watched him fearlessly rush in to put the first rope on a grizzly when they went on a bear hunt.

He gambled and drank too much perhaps, but he was master of his own rancho at twenty-nine, and his mother was indulgent. For that matter, were there not too many other hacendados who found little to occupy their time but riding, women, and liquor? You could not condemn a man with nothing but time on his hands, who had never been trained to the real use of books, or the value of work.

Don Ygnacio was not unaware of why Don Julio had sought him out. He remembered how Julio's eyes had followed Dolores at the Christmas fiesta last year, and how his wife had pointed it out to him with dismay.

"Even if she were of a marriageable age, I could not see her married to a man like Julio Marcos, Ygnacio."

"What is wrong with him?"

"I'm—not sure. Something. Don't you feel it? It's as if he were two different sides of a sphere that don't quite fit together."

Ygnacio had nodded and wondered at his wife's discernment, for Encarnacion seldom spoke of anyone if she could not say something pleasant.

Since then, however, he had avoided asking the Marcoses to Loma de Oro.

He could think of nothing to say to the young man who sat smiling at him, his thin, high-bridged nose and thick black brows giving him the appearance of a hawk. The immense golden topaz he wore on the middle finger of his right hand reflected light from the small fire in the fireplace as he touched his lips with a pale-cream silk kerchief.

"How is your mother?" asked Don Ygnacio abruptly. Anything to end the idiot grin on Julio's wide face.

"She is well, thank you, Don Ygnacio. She is preparing to go to Sonora for a brief visit with a cousin there."

"I did not know your mother was from Sonora?"

"From Mexico City, originally. Her people were very wealthy and prominent."

Don Ygnacio knew quite well that Dona Casimira Marcos had come from Sonora, where she had been born and reared by poor peasant parents, but one did not contradict a guest, or a gentleman's word about his mother.

"I myself was educated in Mexico City," Don Julio went on, convinced that he was impressing his host.

In desperation Ygnacio said, "I believe that I would like a glass of wine; I am feeling faint. In the decanter there on the table, if you will pour for both of us, Julio?"

"With pleasure, Don Ygnacio!" Julio jumped up and busied himself, pouring delicately into two cut-glass goblets and bringing Don Ygnacio's to him with a flourish.

"To your swift recovery, señor," he offered, raising his glass.

Don Ygnacio mumbled and bent his face to his glass. Why didn't the young ass go? Where in heaven's name was Joaquin; he should have been acting as host to a male guest during his father's incapacity. There was no proper sense of duty in young people anymore.

"Don Ygnacio?" Julio had resumed his seat, sitting stiffly forward.

"*Sí?*"

"I have paid my respects to Dona Isabella; I would also like your permission to pay my respects to the other lovely señoritas of the house, Dona Soledad and—Dona Dolores."

That was the cursed part of the young jackanape's fine manners, thought Ygnacio. No gentleman could readily refuse so polite a request.

"Yes, yes," Alvarjo said, waving impatiently. "You will probably find them in the *sala* or dining room or patio. One of the servants will take you to them."

* * *

Julio found no one on the verandas circling the patio, but a cool wind had arisen and no doubt the women were inside. He heard guitar music from the *sala* and hurried toward it only to find Luis playing while Nazario sang in his high clear tenor of the beauties of Alejandra. The sweet mournful melody rose and fell while Julio stood in the doorway unnoticed.

When they saw him the two Alvarjo youths were embarrassed. Don Julio was older than Joaquin, a real hacendado in his own right. They felt shy before him, and neither of them particularly liked him, which made their being left alone to entertain him even worse.

"I have been to see your poor father," said Julio, after they had given him a seat and offered him wine.

"It was kind of you to come, Don Julio," Luis said stiffly, thinking that if Nazario had gone riding with him as he had suggested a moment before, they would not be in this predicament.

"I am going to have a grizzly hunt and a fandango this Sunday," said Julio with a smile for the two boys' sudden interest, "to celebrate my mother's departure for Sonora. Just a few neighbors, the Martinezes, the Cotas, and I hope—the Alvarjos? My mother will be so pleased if Dona Isabella and the señoritas will come to join her early. I realize both your *padre* and Joaquin are unable to come, but surely Don Ygnacio will allow the rest of you to accept?"

"It is very kind of you, Don Julio," said Luis, "but we are not yet out of mourning—and we have a guest."

"A guest? Don Ygnacio did not tell me."

"She has been ill also."

"A pity. But I will send my mother's carriage and they shall come comfortably and in style." Julio was never done bragging about his carriage. It was imported from the United States and one of the few in California.

Nazario, who had heard mention of the Martinez family—and wanted very much to show a certain young señorita from Santa Barbara who was staying at the Martinez rancho what he could do with a grizzly bear at the end of his rope, though he meant never to speak to her again—said, "I will go and ask Padre."

Luis watched his brother hurry out of the room and shook his head. "I do not believe he will let us go. And

Tía Isabella never leaves the house these days; she just sits and prays, like Joaquin."

"Joaquin sits and prays?"

"*Sí*. Sometimes all day."

"*Cristo!* He *must* have the fever."

His words were cut short as Tía Isabella stepped into the room, carrying her sewing box. She seemed surprised to find Julio. But he leaped up to hand her gracefully into her chair, and showed such a charming interest in her handiwork when she unfolded it that she was disarmed. In spite of her tutelage none of her nephews had more exquisite manners than young Don Julio Marcos. She found his thoughtful attentions flattering and pleasant after having been so rudely treated by Ygnacio. She had, of course, no inkling of his interest in Dolores.

When Julio told her of his invitation to Bolsa de los Coyotes—called Bolsa Coyotes by the neighbors—she at first demurred.

"We are still in mourning, Don Julio."

"But this is just a Sunday gathering of a few neighbors, not a grand fiesta, Dona Isabella. My mother has been lonely these last months. She has been nowhere, seen no one. Her rheumatism has afflicted her again; that is why she is going to Sonora for treatment. Your presence will be a great honor and delight to her, and it will do all of the young ones good. Say that you will come? The mourning period is nearly over."

Isabella hesitated. Ygnacio had said he thought long mourning and the wearing of black clothes of little matter. Well, let the neighbors think what they would of the Alvarjos then. They were his children; he was responsible. As he had so rigidly pointed out to her, this was his house; he was master here.

"I will have to discuss it with Don Ygnacio," replied Isabella finally. "It was most kind of you to ask us."

Nazario returned at that moment, a gay smile on his thin dark face. "Padre says we can go! Tía Isabella, Father says we can go to Don Julio's bear hunt and fandango next Sunday."

"Control yourself, Nazario," his aunt said crisply. To Don Julio she said with formal courtesy, "We shall be most happy to accept, Don Julio. You will convey my best wishes to your mother?"

"With the greatest pleasure, dear Dona Isabella. I have a certain rose in my garden—it came from Jerez—perhaps you would like a slip for your patio?"

"Thank you, señor." She put down her workbasket. "Perhaps you would care to see our roses? They are not much now, but my poor sister-in-law cherished them like her children."

Julio had no wish to view roses but he went willingly enough, for he had glimpsed two female forms wrapped in heavy *rebozos* walking in the patio.

"Do you know that Rosita says Candelaria told her Tarifa is a Gypsy and a witch?" said Soledad.

Dolores had been paying only scant attention to her younger sister's idle prattle, her own thoughts occupied by the memory of an ivory fan and a pair of gray eyes as cold and as disturbing as the sea itself. She had never thought to feel this way about a man, wondering where he was, trying to recall his every word and gesture. But her sister's last words startled her out of her pleasant reverie.

"What nonsense are you talking about, Soledad?"

"It's true. She's from Spain, but she's a real Gypsy, and so is that Penti. Why do you think Father has brought them here?"

Dolores, who knew only slightly more of their guest, said firmly, "She is awaiting a ship to take her back to Spain."

"But why did she come here in the first place? I overheard Tía Isabella praying in the chapel for God to take the witch from under our roof."

"You hear too much that is not good for you, Soledad."

Soledad did not reply, for Isabella was coming across the patio followed by Julio Marcos.

Isabella said, "Don Julio was asking for you. He has invited us all to a small celebration next Sunday in honor of his mother's departure for Mexico. Your father has given permission for us to attend."

Both girls expressed their thanks prettily, but it was only Dolores that Don Julio heard or saw.

How she had grown and changed since he had last seen her! How exquisite she was of face and form, looking like a grown woman with her fair hair covered up like that.

How he could dress her and ornament her if she were his!

He bowed low over her slender hand and kept it until she pulled it free with a little tug.

"I am sending my mother's carriage for you," he said. "I hope that you will come early with Tía Isabella to visit my mother?"

Isabella drew him off then to show him the roses, Soledad trailing behind. She admired Don Julio's flamboyant manners and his beautiful clothes.

Dolores took off her *rebozo* and stepped into her father's study. The room smelled musty from having been shut up during her father's illness, but someone had recently opened a window. A shaft of sunlight crossed the room, ending at her feet as she came in, making the rest of the study dim by comparison, and she turned from the doorway almost into the arms of the man standing there.

"Dolores."

She let out a little cry of alarm and then relaxed against the doorjamb, smiling up at him.

"Bart—but I thought you were so many miles away, up north?"

"I seem always to startle you." He laughed, feeling like a boy. "My ship went aground off San Pedro in a sou'-easter, we had a time getting her free, and I had to put back to San Diego for repairs. I'll only be here a short while but I had to see you."

"Does Tía Isabella know you're here?" she asked quickly, fearing her aunt's displeasure.

He shook his head. "Zenobio just brought me. He told me of your father's accident. I am very sorry." Kinkaid did not add that Zenobio had also related the story of Santiago's attack on Tarifa, and of the Gypsy's move to Loma de Oro.

"Are you staying with Don Zenobio?"

"Yes, for a few days. Why?"

Pink stained her cheeks as she said, "Don Julio Marcos is here, from the Rancho Bolsa de los Coyotes, a few leagues away. His mother is leaving for Mexico and he is giving a small celebration in her honor this Sunday. Undoubtedly, Don Zenobio will be going. I thought he might bring you also, as his guest?" She had never been so brazen with a man before, and she could no more have looked into his eyes than have flown to the moon. It was just as well that she did not, for the wild elation was naked in his gaze.

"I'll never speak to him again if he doesn't bring me," he said fervently.

Zenobio sidled in the door and winked at their flushed faces. "The old dragon is about to descend," he said matter-of-factly. "Come, we will pay our respects to Ygnacio first, and that will give Dolores a chance to slip into the *sala* before us, eh, *niña?*"

Dolores laughed. "You are a scheming old fraud, Don Zenobio."

"But you are learning fast, *muchacha?*" He patted her fondly on the head. "Come, *compadre.*"

Don Julio sat on the horsehair sofa between Isabella and Dolores, sipping delicately from a cup of tea, when Don Zenobio and Kinkaid entered from the patio a short while later.

Isabella had not known they were coming this way, having encountered them briefly in the patio with Don Julio, and been told by Zenobio that they had come only to speak with Ygnacio. She disliked seeing the tall Americano in her brother's house looking boldly at his daughters, especially Dolores. But it seemed to do her no good to express her disapproval of things these days.

There was another who did not enjoy the look Kinkaid inadvertently gave Dolores. Don Julio felt his hand tighten on the cup he held. Insolent, greedy Americano to dare look so at a high-born Spanish girl. He would like to have him at a *reata's* end, dallied to the saddle of a fast stallion.

Soledad was explaining to Zenobio about the fandango and bear hunt and Julio, unable to neglect the fine show of manners he was parading before the womenfolk, found himself caught in a trap of his own making.

"You will come also, Don Zenobio?" he asked politely. He did not like the rough old soldier, but politeness demanded he extend the invitation.

"*Gracias,* Don Julio." He added with a twinkle in his eye, "You will of course include my houseguest, Capitán Kinkaid?"

This was a situation Julio had not anticipated but he

replied gracefully, "Any guest of yours is also welcome at Bolsa de los Coyotes, Don Zenobio."

"*Gracias,* señor," said Kinkaid. His quick glance at Dolores was missed by no one in the room.

Sunday was a clear warm day following the first rain of the season, and all the landscape looked freshly scrubbed and polished.

The grooms of Loma de Oro had cleaned and brushed the famous palominos until they shone, and saddled and comparisoned them in their richest fiesta attire.

It was Don Ygnacio who insisted that Tarifa join the party. She declined to use the Marcos carriage and rode her own horse.

Zenobio, dressed in extreme bad taste, Isabella noted, in a heavy leather jacket and gaudy red pantaloons with wide flapping *armitas* of buckskin covering his thighs and legs to his boots, came early accompanied by Captain Kinkaid, to join the riding party. Don Ygnacio, sitting in the sunshine on the front veranda, waved them off, and Penti peered out of a window as Tarifa wheeled by on Guindilla in her blue silver-trimmed riding costume.

Luis and Antonio both carried guitars behind their glittering silver-encrusted saddles, and Nazario was dressed as for a wedding and subject to a good deal of ribbing from his brothers, which he took with ill-concealed displeasure.

"Are you going to catch a grizzly in those clothes, Nazario, or Señorita Rufina Corlona?"

"Like a *novio*—a great lover!" chanted Antonio gleefully, turning to ride Concho backward so that he could watch Nazario's face.

"*Poco duende!*"

Luis laughed and reached for his guitar. He struck up a tune and played, the reins tied over his horn while his horse galloped on.

Kinkaid could not very well ride behind the slower moving carriage but he rode at the back of the group and turned to watch the passengers in the carriage as often as he dared.

He told himself that he was a fool, that Dolores was nothing but a child, too young to be spoken to of love, and yet there was a maturity in her gentle sweet face, a mater-

nal sympathy that made her seem older than she was. If he
could speak to her, ask her to wait and think about him
until he returned again, it would be all he could ask. She
would be older then, know her own mind better, and he
would see that she had the time she needed. Only then
could he speak to Don Ygnacio. He had no desire to rush
her or to antagonize Alvarjo, whom he admired and hoped
to have for a friend as well as father-in-law. Kinkaid had
learned early that the best things come by waiting.

Before noon they were on Bolsa Coyotes land and Kinkaid noted the well-watered pastures and sleek herds of
cattle and horses. At noon when the little party arrived at
the hacienda he saw that it was a large, rambling one-story
structure, built more like a barracks than a house, and set
squarely in the center of a flat treeless plain, the least attractive section of the rancho they had seen.

Wide verandas front and back cast deep shadows over
the doors and windows, giving the house a brooding look,
like a poised tarantula. There was none of the sound of
gaiety or warmth and fragrance about Bolsa Coyotes that
was so much a part of Loma de Oro.

Carretas, carriages, and horses were drawn up at the
front of the hacienda, attended by lazy-looking Indian
boys in ragged shirts and trousers. Apparently Don Julio's
passion for impeccable clothing did not extend to his
menials.

Don Julio appeared instantly upon their arrival, as if he
had been peering out the window watching for them. Quick
as he was, however, Kinkaid was before him, his hand
holding Dolores' as he helped her down from the carriage.
Julio, as host, was left to hand down Dona Isabella and
Soledad, which he did with a great flourish and many
flowery compliments.

His mother waited in the shadows by the open front
door, a squat heavy-shouldered figure in a black gown and
shawl. She had beady black eyes and a thin high-bridged
nose like her son's in a wide dark face.

She greeted her guests warmly and ushered them all
into the large patio. It was wide and tiled, but the flowers
had a dried withered look, despite all the water that
abounded on Bolsa Coyotes, and the paper lanterns and
streamers that had been strung up in honor of the celebra-

tion had a worn tattered appearance, as if they had not been used in many years.

The women were assigned rooms and maids to help them freshen up or change clothing if they so desired, while the men returned to the *sala* for a smoke and a glass of wine before luncheon.

Tarifa, more sensitive to her surroundings than Soledad with whom she shared a small unheated bedroom and a drab thin-faced Indian girl as maid, said, "If Don Julio is as rich as he seems, why does he live in such a poorly furnished house?" She looked with distaste at the crude oak bedstead, washstand, chest, and two rawhide-bottomed chairs which were all that the room contained save a cracked mirror in a tin frame and a crude but highly colored holy picture with a dusty pink paper ruffle around it.

"He does not spend much time here," answered Soledad, helping the maid to fasten her full white-cotton petticoat. "He is usually at Monterey or Santa Barbara or visiting someone at the pueblos. He has many friends."

"I see," said Tarifa. But she did not. If a man had all this land and stock and yet it meant nothing to him, there must be a reason. She could not understand why a man should prefer the crude gaiety she had witnessed at Domingo Chavira's in San Diego to the comfort and luxury of his own rancho.

Luncheon, served to the twenty-odd people who had gathered for the occasion on a very long table in the dim cavernous dining room, was a heavy indifferently cooked meal of frijoles, fried beefsteak, cooked tomatoes and onions, baked corn cakes, salad, wine, and fresh fruit.

When the meal was finished the older women and many of the younger ones retired to their bedrooms to rest for the evening fandango, while the men prepared their gear and horses for the bear hunt.

Tarifa stood on the veranda watching the men mount, piqued that she had not been invited to go along.

"But women never go on bear hunts," Soledad told her, aghast at the thought of such a thing. "It is far too dangerous. Even the men have to be experts." She pointed out that the younger children and boys knew better than to ask permission to go.

"Then let's go for a ride," Tarifa said. "They can't say no to that."

"We're supposed to rest for the dance tonight."

"Rest? To dance? I could ride all day and still dance all night."

Soledad held back. Tía Isabella was in charge of her here. Her father might give in to her himself, but he would be quick to punish any breach of her aunt's authority while Soledad was in her care.

"I can't. Padre would be furious. He made a concession in letting us come, and I wouldn't upset him while he is ill."

"Then I'll go alone."

"No. Don't go, Tarifa. You don't know what a grizzly bear is like. I've seen them tear a horse to pieces."

A half hour after the hunting party had left, Soledad watched Tarifa ride off jauntily on Guindilla, taking the same direction. She thought wistfully that she would have given anything to be that unafraid, that sure of herself in anything she wished to do.

Tarifa found the land green and inviting away from the arid little plain where the house stood. It was not hard to follow the men's tracks as they circled upward toward the foothills. This was a far more rugged and remote area than Loma de Oro lands. She saw hawks and then a few buzzards against the pale blue sky, and high on top of the sierras were thick fringes of pines and cedars and a still taller, bigger tree—California redwoods, the famous Palos Colorados which the Padres had early discovered and requisitioned for the beams in their thick-walled Missions.

Tarifa came upon the hunters after topping a little rise, but stayed carefully out of their sight by taking to slightly lower ground. Most of them kept their eyes upward, scanning the rocky hilltops, and she noted that each man carried a *reata* looped and ready in his hand. There was no conversation.

A dangerous, life-or-death game was about to begin, as men armed with only their tough rawhide *reatas* and their horses' skill faced the fiercest of all North American wild animals, whose terrible taloned paws could disembowel a horse with one mighty swipe.

Tarifa sensed the uneasiness in Guindilla and took a firmer grip on the reins. She saw the bear before the hunters did, behind a rock some forty yards away. She could

see the long grizzly hair, dark along the spine and fading
to a yellowish tinge along his mighty shoulders. He looked
to weigh well over fourteen hundred pounds.

At the same instant Guindilla and the bear got each other's scent. Like a rolling boulder the grizzly charged down
the slope, huge claws distended toward the frightened
horse. Guindilla had never hunted but he recognized the
terrifying bear scent. He plunged wildly, took the bit in
his teeth, and dashed down the rough broken sidehill in
blind panic.

Tarifa hung on, aware only faintly of the cries and
shouts behind her, and of the bear plunging down the hill
after poor, fear-crazed Guindilla. She tried to speak to the
stallion, to turn him from his crazed dash, but it would
have been as easy to control a hurricane with her bare
hands. Everything that Santos had taught her she brought
into play in order to stay in the saddle.

At the first charge of the bear and Guindilla's keening
scream of fear, the hunters had put spurs to their own
mounts, excited now as they too caught the bear scent, and
plunged after him. The severest test of a cutting horse was
to be able to send him charging full tilt into the chase
after a grizzly bear. Yet every horse in the line whirled
and skidded down the hill obediently.

Don Julio led the chase on a deep-chested sorrel with
leather *armas* protecting his legs, but it was Nazario who
made the first lucky throw and caught the bear around one
hind leg with his *reata larga*. He took up the dallies furiously as the grizzly rose to charge him, and Hidalgo backed
swiftly and expertly over the rough ground, his flanks and
sides heaving with sweat.

Zenobio's rope swished out and caught the bear's right-
front paw, and Don Julio's snapped down on the other,
while all three horses backed feverishly to keep the ropes
taut and stretch the bear on the ground. Ropes came like
circling snakes now, over the bear's head, on each of his
legs, till he lay panting and infuriated, stretched helplessly
before them. The huge teeth bared viciously and saliva
foamed from his immense powerful jaws.

Kinkaid, knowing that he was no use as a *reatero*, had
sent his horse down the hill after Guindilla. He saw the
stallion run down the length of the hillside into a bush-

and rock-strewn stream bed and gallop madly on till he finally came out in a grassy meadow. Miraculously, he was still on four legs, but gasping and swaying.

Kinkaid came up just as Tarifa threw herself off the horse and went to press the stallion's muzzle to her shoulder.

"Tarifa! Are you all right? What in God's name are you doing here? Didn't they tell you to stay at the hacienda?"

She looked up at him, a strange fear and awe in her eyes, yet he felt that it was not of the bear that she was afraid.

"I didn't know that it would do this to him," she said in a choked voice. "I might have killed him! Do you think I have hurt him badly?"

Bart got down and examined the cracked, split hooves caused by the horse's run over the stony creek bed.

"I don't know. These cracks may heal up all right, but I wouldn't ride him now. Get up behind me and we'll lead him."

On the hillside behind them the men had begun the slow task of taking the captive grizzly back to the ranch. Some of the ropes were eased up enough to allow him to stand and move a restricted distance, so that the animal could lumber back to the ranch under his own power, since to haul him forcibly would have been to choke or dismember him. This was not without danger or excitement, for a hold might be loosened too much or lost, then another quickly and expertly thrown rope would have to replace it. Too much slack and the bear would make a violent charge at the nearest horse, until pulled harshly back into line.

The younger riders on the swiftest horses rode as near El Oso as they dared, and offered themselves as tempting bait to lure him on. Many a daring caballero had been mauled or killed in such a maneuver, when his horse stumbled or the bear charged beyond the distance the rider had calculated as safe.

The men worked in relays, relieving each other and the horses, but it was dark when they finally dragged their prize to the rancho where he was housed in the stout cage Don Julio kept for bears. The animal would be watered and fed to await the bull-and-bear fight Don Julio had planned for his guests' amusement the next day.

Tarifa and Kinkaid, leading the limping Guindilla, had come in just before the hunters. Tarifa had insisted on showing the stallion's cracked hooves to Don Julio's head groom, who told her that they might be fixed if she could find an old cavalry farrier who knew his business. For himself, Don Julio never asked him to doctor a horse; he had so many—why bother to save one particular one? And Tarifa's opinion of Julio Marcos fell even lower.

Soledad was not in the little bedroom, but there were candles burning and Tarifa's borrowed gown had been laid out with her other things on the bed. The little maid helped her wash, and brush and put up her hair under the high tortoiseshell comb borrowed from Dolores.

The gown pleased Tarifa, though it was not as vivid as she would have liked, a warm raspberry satin, short-sleeved and low-necked, with rows and rows of a darker rose ruffling covering the full skirt. The wide sash was pale pink velvet, and she wore the small gold cross Don Ygnacio had given her when she was ill on a black velvet band around her slim dark throat. But inside her bodice she still had the amulet Penti had given her, and she still carried the *navaja* in a garter high on her thigh.

When she passed along the veranda to the patio she could hear the men in the dining room drinking and congratulating themselves on the fine bear they had captured. No one but Kinkaid had asked her why she had followed them, which was just as well for her. Don Ygnacio, if he heard, would not be pleased.

The patio was abustle with voices and music, servants going and coming among the long tables laden with food and drink, set under the lighted swinging lanterns. A trio of harp, guitar, and violin played from a little alcove built into one wall of the patio, and the younger people were grouped about them listening or singing and clapping their hands in time to the music. The older women were seated in a little circle gossiping over their cups of chocolate until the men joined them for supper.

Tarifa felt no kinship for either group. She wandered off by herself, circling the tables and inspecting the food. There were roasts of beef, lamb, and venison, rice and tortillas, cooked vegetables and salads, sweet cakes and wine. Since each guest was to help himself, plates and cutlery had been stacked at one end, and little tables and groups of chairs had been set out in the large patio.

The men had begun to trickle out of the dining room looking for their dinner partners, and it amused Tarifa to watch both Don Julio and Kinkaid converge on Dolores, where she stood near Soledad among the young people by the orchestra. Kinkaid reached her slightly before the Californian, but even if he had not, courtesy would have demanded that Julio step aside in honor of his guest.

Julio fought hard not to show his anger and chagrin. He managed a stiff bow for Kinkaid and a smile for Dolores, and gallantly offered his arm to Soledad.

Pretty young girls and gay young men quickly paired off —Nazario with the prettiest, Tarifa noted, a saucy little brunette with magnificent dark brown eyes in a small oval face. The corners of her mouth, when she was not smiling, curved slightly downward, giving her a proud haughty expression. She seemed to be coyly flirting with a red-faced Nazario behind her black-lace fan.

Don Zenobio limped along on his game leg beside Tía Isabella, still dressed in his outlandish hunting costume, and Luis came shyly to offer his arm to Tarifa. She smiled briefly up at him.

Of the Alvarjo boys, Tarifa liked Luis the best. He had some of the same sympathetic manner and kindness his father had shown her.

"May I take you to supper, señorita?"

"*Gracias*, Luis."

They followed the long line, serving themselves at the big tables, and found a corner near the orchestra where they were alone.

"You shouldn't have followed us into the bear country," Luis said seriously.

"I was just riding."

"But you should have stayed here. That bear could have killed you."

"He would have killed Guindilla." She told him of the animal's cracked hooves.

"I'll have a look in the morning," he told her. "But old Pablo and Santos at the rancho are as good veterinarians as you can find in the district. I'm sure they will be able to do something."

Comforted, Tarifa fell to studying her supper companions with the frank curiosity of a child.

"Who is that girl with Nazario?"

"Dona Rufina Corlona, a cousin of Señora Martinez, from Santa Barbara. She is nothing but a tease and a flirt, but Nazario fancies himself in love with her. They are both too young to marry, of course. Padre would never permit it. And her family would object."

"Why?" asked Tarifa naïvely. "Aren't the Alvarjos the finest family in all California?"

Luis colored. "We hope we are worthy of being considered among the best," he said modestly.

Tarifa frowned at him. "I have heard in San Diego that there is no family in California higher born than the Alvarjos. If you are the best why do you not say so?"

Luis, beside himself with embarrassment, said quickly, "That would not be proper—to declare yourself better than others. It just isn't done."

"Then you are fools," Tarifa snapped. "I know that I am better than Gypsies like Penti, or even my mother Bandonna. I have the blood of the conquering Moors of Spain in me, and they have not. All my life I have known that I was better than they were, and I have told them so. Why are you so afraid? If I were an Alvarjo living in California, I would bow down to no man. I would make them bow down to me! They would know when an Alvarjo spoke or rode by, and they would not forget it!"

"Tarifa," he pleaded, mopping his face, "they can all hear you!"

"Let them. I do not care a fig for any of them. They are not like you and your father."

"*Por favor,* Tarifa! You are a guest here. You will disgrace us all. Tía Isabella is looking at you."

Tarifa stared across the patio where Zenobio and Isabella sat by Señora Marcos with Don Julio and Soledad, and returned the old woman's stony look with a baleful one of her own.

"*Chovihani!*"

"What?"

"Witch," Tarifa spat. "She is an old witch, like Penti. But they cannot harm me; I am a greater witch than either of them. My amulet is more powerful."

She fished deep in her bodice while Luis flushed scarlet,

and brought up the grimy amulet on its chain to waggle before his startled eyes.

"This my amulet; it will always keep me from harm and allow me to overcome all my enemies. Do you want to touch it?"

"No," Luis flattened himself back into his chair. He would have liked to make the sign of the Cross to protect himself, but hesitated to draw more attention to their corner.

The music saved him, for the players struck up a lively *jota,* and Tarifa's attention was instantly riveted to the dancers.

Because this was considered a small private country celebration, only the Alvarjos and Don Julio were dressed in high style. The older women wore dark clothes with black or dark blue mantillas or *rebozos,* the younger ones flowered muslin skirts tied with gaily colored sashes, white muslin blouses with embroidery on the short sleeves, and velvet shoes to match their sashes. The young girls' glossy black hair hung in long plaits down their backs. The men wore silk or velvet suits, the short jackets trimmed with gilt braid. And with the exception of Don Zenobio, Don Juan Martinez, and a few old men, handsomely embroidered dancing shoes.

Though she had seen *jotas* and *contradanzas* before, Tarifa found the dancers clumsy and dull.

The *jota* as executed in the old kingdom of Aragon was meant to express the energy of a strong people, the couples vying with each other in quick leaps and spins, feet beating together in the air, knees hitting the ground, in a vibrant rhythm of gaiety and sweeping movements to the loud clatter of castanets. There was only one pair of castanets present, held by an old woman watching from the sidelines, who clacked them now and then in a desultory fashion.

The girls stood like wooden posts, eyes downcast, their arms at their sides. There was as little excitement in their limbs or expression on their faces as if they had been carved images.

Around their almost motionless figures, the men moved with more agility and virtuosity, their slender horsemen's figures showing to advantage.

Tarifa was surprised to see that Don Julio danced well,

with an elegant vigor in his leaps and unusual skill in his footwork, but she had no way of knowing that he did little else than dance, drink, gamble, and wench.

Luis sat as still and as far back in the shadows as he could, hoping Tarifa would not suggest they join the dancers, for by this time he knew how reckless and unpredictable she could be. He had no wish to call further attention to his father's strange houseguest.

When the *contradanzas* and *jotas* and *Salmantinas* were over, the orchestra struck up a new rhythm that Tarifa had never heard before. The floor cleared and there was a murmur among the older women behind their raised fans. A slow, gliding rhythm that fascinated Tarifa seemed to fill the patio. Only a few couples stepped onto the floor, among them Delores in her simple white gown with a strand of Loreto pearls around her throat, her light golden hair shining in the lantern light. Tarifa saw her put her left hand on Captain Kinkaid's right arm, and her other hand in his, while he held her only a few paces in front of him. Tarifa had never seen a man and woman dance together like this before. She was overcome with astonishment.

"What are they doing?" she demanded of Luis.

"Waltzing. It's a new dance called the waltz. The Americanos do it a great deal, but the Padres do not approve of it. In fact, Padre Martin in San Diego claims it is a scandalous and lewd dance, and should not be allowed in California."

"I like it," said Tarifa, watching the few gracefully moving figures on the floor. "I shall have to learn it."

"I don't know how to dance it myself," said Luis quickly. If only there were some excuse he could use to get away from the girl!

When the waltz was over the couples were cheered and applauded, and the orchestra paused to drink glasses of wine and enjoy a *cigarrillo*.

To Luis' unspeakable relief, Tarifa rose without a word of excuse to him and hurried inside the house. She had seen Dolores and Captain Kinkaid go in a moment before, and she meant to ask Kinkaid to teach her the waltz at once.

She paused in the deserted *sala,* peeped into the equally empty dining room and began a systematic search through the rest of the house. It was a musty, rambling place, filled, it seemed, with endless little bedrooms. Since none of the doors in the adobe were locked, she threw open one after the other, and discovered that some of them, quite to her own amazement, were occupied by couples locked in each other's embrace who glanced up at her scarlet with embarrassment.

The sight affected Tarifa no more than if she had found two dogs mating in the street. This was no novelty to a Gypsy child who could wander upon any stage of courtship or passion in the caves of Granada.

But of Capitan Kinkaid and Don Alvarjo's eldest daughter, there was no sign.

Tarifa was not the only one who had missed them. Tía Isabella had excused herself from Señora Marcos, for whom she had no great liking anyway, as soon as she was aware of Dolores' absence after the waltz. Now she came down the veranda from the *sala* seeking her niece. She had the discretion to knock on the doors before calling Dolores' name, but she came away as disappointed as Tarifa had been. The Gypsy was seated on a bench outside her own bedroom door when Isabella came up to her.

Each one cordially despised the other, but for the fiesta they had declared a mutual if uneasy truce.

"Have you seen my niece Dona Dolores?" Isabella asked. formally. She held her long hands in front of her with her black fan folded and pressed tightly against her skirt.

"No," said Tarifa. "I saw her dancing in the patio with Capitán Kinkaid. that is all."

"*Gracias muchísimas,* señorita." Isabella inclined her head proudly and went on to her own room, shutting the door firmly behind her.

I would not tell her even if I knew they lay together, thought Tarifa darkly. But she was piqued because she could not find Kinkaid and get him to show her the waltz.

The music had started again, and her feet moved restlessly on the veranda tiles.

Tarifa and Tía Isabella had missed the one place in the house where it was possible to secrete oneself and not be discovered.

Long ago when he built the house, Don Sebastian, who had been a devout Catholic at least in form, if not in practice, had ordered a private prayer booth built beyond his study like the one his father had used in Aragon. It was not a family chapel, for only two or three people could enter it at one time. A cubicle like a long closet, with a prayer bench and a shelf for an altar containing a wooden statue of Saint Sebastian, the old Don's patron saint, it had been built for him to retire into to pray and meditate, to say his penance after making confession in the family chapel at the other end of the building. Or, as the case might be, to get away from his shrewish wife.

Sebastian had added a stout bolt on the inside to ensure the privacy of his meditations, but there were some who claimed he had never meditated there long or without a female companion not of Señora Marcos' proportions, and usually in her absence.

Since his death many years before no one had used the place. Don Julio shunned it because of the lurid tales his mother had told him during his childhood, outlining the sacrilegious use to which the room had been put. Señora Marcos had never gone near the cubicle before or since her husband's death, and had forbidden any servant to open the small door half-hidden by a large cabinet.

Kinkaid had discovered it quite by accident, when wandering about the room alone after Tarifa and he had returned from the hunt. While Tarifa dressed he had gone into the study to admire the hunting trophies—heads of elk, deer, bear, mountain lion, bobcat, and coyote which lined the walls. He opened what he thought was a closet door and discovered the little prayer room, noting the lock on the inside. Certainly he had had no ulterior motive. But with Yankee astuteness he made use of what came to hand. All he wanted was a private word with Dolores. Up to the moment of his discovery, that had seemed an impossibility.

After the waltz he asked her politely if she would go into Don Julio's study with him for a moment. He had something he wanted her to see. She had come with him like an angel, serene and unsuspecting. When he showed her the old prayer closet she had been more curious than fearful and had stepped inside of her own volition.

Kinkaid followed and carefully bolted the door behind him as he stood with his back to the lock.

Dolores, holding her skirts out of the thick dust, stepped to the altar to examine the statue in front of which Kinkaid had left a lighted candle taken from Don Julio's writing table in the study.

"It's a statue of San Sebastian, Bart. It must have belonged to Don Julio's father. Look how old and cracked it is. Don Sebastian must have brought it from Spain. I never knew he had such a room at Bolsa Coyotes. How did you ever discover it?"

"Quite by accident. We don't have such things in the United States. I was interested and I thought you would be."

She turned to face him. "Oh, but I am! I must tell Padre Cazon; he is so taken with the old history of California." This amused Bart, for the entire historical period did not cover more than fifty-six years. No matter what she said, it amused and delighted him.

He said, "Dolores, I want to talk to you."

She could not miss the change in his tone and she instantly lowered her eyes, the lashes making delicate shadows on her cheeks. And the candlelight, Bart thought, brought out delicious hollows in her throat.

"I'm going to be sailing back to Boston before long," he said. "It will be two years before I can hope to return. Even longer if we should be held up rounding Cape Horn."

"We—we will all be sorry to see you go, Capitán."

"Call me Bart. Look at me, Dolores."

She glanced up like an obedient child but he could see that her chin trembled. He hadn't meant to touch her, but he hadn't intended to frighten her either. He moved forward and grasped her gently by the shoulders. She felt as soft and as fragile as a butterfly under his hands, and he was the one who felt himself shaking now.

"Dolores, don't be frightened of me, for God's sake! I'm trying to tell you I love you. I have since the first moment I saw you in that window at Loma de Oro, with your hair around your face like a golden cloud, wearing that white thing. You looked like an angel from heaven.

"I'm a plain man," he floundered. "I haven't the pretty speeches or fancy manners of your caballeros here in California. But my feeling for you runs as deep as the sea. If you could be happy with me some day as my wife, it would be the greatest gift heaven could bestow upon me.

"I know you have to think about all this," he went on quickly. "I want you to have the time to do that; that's why I'm speaking now before I really should. You're young, too young for marriage. But in two years you'll have grown and if you'll promise to wait and think about us during that time that's all I can ask. More than I have a right to ask actually, but I must. Will you do it, Dolores?"

She hadn't taken her eyes from his face as he spoke, and every change of mood or pace in his words had been mirrored in their blue-gray depths, like deep waters with a current rippling over them.

"*Querido,*" she murmured, "you must not suffer so over me."

He drew her to him, held her against him, his chin on her fair head, while his heart hammered like the hull of the *Arabella* in the teeth of a nor'easter.

"Will you wait, and think about me while I'm gone?" he asked after awhile.

"Yes, Bart, if you want me to."

"Do you—care for me at all?"

"I have never been in love, but I think I am now."

He lifted her chin with one finger and gazed deeply into her eyes.

"I want you to be sure," he told her. "And will you be at the end of two years?"

"It's a very long time," she said wistfully.

"Not when you're sailing toward snug harbor," he said jovially.

He told her then of his plans to settle one day in California and ranch, himself. Then he asked:

"Do you think your father will be against our marriage?"

"He hasn't met many Americanos, and for that reason perhaps he doesn't trust them. But I will pray that he changes his mind before you return."

Kinkaid nodded. It was enough that she had promised to wait, that he held her now in his arms. Alone, and apart from the others.

They both started violently when a knock sounded outside the door, and the handle began to turn against Kinkaid's back.

Don Julio was also looking for Dolores and Kinkaid. Occupied with his other guests, he had not seen them slip

away from the dance floor but he knew they had been dancing together and he was sure they were somewhere inside
the house at this moment.

His search was an unrewarding as Tarifa's and Isabella's
had been. Where could the fool Americano have taken
her? And why had the girl not had sense enough to stay
safely in the patio as any decent señorita should and not
allowed her name to be linked with those other *amantes*
who were careless of their reputations. He was not aware
of it, but half of Dolores' appeal for him lay in her spotless
inviolability, and the difficulty of obtaining a high-born
Alvarjo for a wife. He did not propose to have her subject
to word or conjecture until she was his, and then no one
would dare speak against the Señora Dolores Marcos—or
the high-born Marcos heirs she would bear him.

Like Tarifa, Julio had gone first to the *sala,* dining room,
and on to the bedrooms, but on his return he remembered
that he had not searched the study.

Here he came upon a most interesting little tableau, and
his face flushed with anger at the scene when he realized
its significance.

Dona Isabella stood frozen-faced on one side of the
room with Dolores beside her, while across from them, in
front of the half-open door that led to the prayer room,
Tarifa and Kinkaid stood arm in arm calmly facing them.

"What were you doing in that room?" Julio shouted
hoarsely. "No one is ever allowed in there. It is sacred to
my father's memory!"

"I'm sorry, Don Julio," Kinkaid said with a smile. "I
discovered it quite by accident and asked the Señorita if
she would care to see it. I had no idea it was a secret place."

"Sacred, not secret," glowered Marcos. Then turning
his head suspiciously toward Dolores he asked, "Where
were you, Dona Dolores? I have been looking for you for
some time—to come and dance."

"I'm sorry, Don Julio. I felt a bit faint after my last
dance and went for a small walk to get away from the
crowd."

"That is right, Don Julio," said Tía Isabella, covering
quickly for her niece. "I met her here just as she arrived,
and we found—these two coming out of that room. You
should have taken a shawl with you, Dolores; it has grown

cold. Come, we will join the others in the patio before it is time for bed."

She was pleased that Don Julio followed them out of the room. She wasn't blind; she knew only that she had entered the study and found Dolores alone there by the door as if she had just entered. A moment later the small door by the cabinet had opened and Tarifa and Kinkaid had come brazenly out. The Gypsy witch, after any man she could get! She had no conscience and undoubtedly no soul to worry her. But Isabella had also seen the look Kinkaid had given Dolores in the *sala* at Loma de Oro the day before, and again today on the dance floor. She knew which way the wind blew, and Dolores was an impressionable girl. Far better she go to Julio Marcos, with all his family skeletons and shortcomings, than to that bold Americano with his brazen ways. Don Julio was at least a Californian and a wealthy ranchero. Dolores could make something of Don Julio and Bolsa de los Coyotes if she half-tried. She would have to feel Ygnacio out, for it was certain the girl was like her mother Encarnacion, too kind and sympathetic for her own good or safety.

When they had gone Tarifa looked up at Kinkaid. "It was lucky I was the one who heard your voices first and told you they were coming."

"I shall be eternally grateful, Tarifa," laughed Kinkaid.

When he had opened the door at her knock, Dolores cowering behind him, and heard her voice say matter-of-factly, "The old witch and Don Julio are coming this way. You had better let the Señorita wait over by the door as if she just came in and take me in there with you," he could have kissed her with relief and delight. What a cool, clever, little vixen she was.

"Quick, my darling," he had told Dolores, "wait over by the door. Pretend you just arrived, and act surprised when we come out."

"Bart—"

"Go! Quickly, *angelita*."

He drew Tarifa inside and shut the door, both of them smothering laughter. Tarifa's long Gypsy eyes danced with a wicked delight. She's having the time of her life, he thought, and wondered about himself, for he was enjoying it as much as she was.

When they heard Isabella's voice questioning Dolores,

Kinkaid swung open the door and stepped out arm in arm
with Tarifa, looking as surprised and embarrassed as he
could manage. In an instant Julio stood in the doorway
and began storming at them.

"What can I do to make it up to you?" Kinkaid asked
Tarifa.

"Teach me the waltz. Now."

He laughed and she found that she did not mind. This
was the warm inclusive laughter of friendship.

"Of course, you shall learn the waltz this very moment!"
He took her by the hand and led her out to the patio.

The musicians were just finishing a *Salmantina.*

Kinkaid drew coins from his pocket and bent his head
to speak to the leader. When the soft gliding music of the
waltz began he took Tarifa's rigid body in his arms and
showed her how to place her hands. After mastering the
first few steps she seemed to change under his grasp, like
a snake uncoiling, or lava coming slowly to molten life in
the heat of the volcano. She moved with him but he was
conscious that she danced at her bidding. She seemed to
surround him like a flame, and when he caught her flashing impassioned gaze he was astonished at the turbulent
electrifying emotions she stirred in his own breast.

She was a witch, all right. He wanted to free himself of
her but you might as well have asked a flame to cease burning as to ask Tarifa to stop dancing.

He saw with confusion that they were the only couple
now on the floor, the others having all drawn aside to watch
them. Tarifa was as unaware of the onlookers as if they
had been wooden statues, but Kinkaid felt like a fly in a
bottle. The sweat ran down his face, wilting his collar, and
he found himself wishing fervently that he had never seen
Tarifa in his life and that he would never see her again.

When the dance came to an end at last, Tarifa accepted
the adulation like a young unsmiling princess, but Kinkaid fled to the veranda to smoke a cigarette.

He had seen Dolores and Tía Isabella retire earlier from
the patio, and he doubted that he would get another
chance to speak with the girl now before he left. He and
Zenobio were not staying the night like the others, but
were returning to the Santa Teresa. From there Kinkaid
would return to his ship in the morning. Zenobio had
offered to sell him a piece of his land, and now that he

had spoken with Dolores, he meant to take the old soldier up on it. He would never take Dolores far from her home, for he sensed her dependence on it, even if she did not. She was like a delicate mountain trillium that would grow sturdily in its own clime, but perish quickly if transplanted. He recalled the scandal surrounding another sea captain, a friend of Ephraim's, who had brought home a Chinese bride and installed her in a palatial home in New Bedford. He would subject Dolores to no such criticism and narrow-minded bigotry.

A couple came toward him from the direction of the cage where the bear was being kept, and he recognized the voices of Nazario and the very pretty little Rufina Corlona, whose father was an official at Santa Barbara.

"He is a very nice bear, Nazario, and I am very proud that you put the first rope on him," she said coyly.

"You have not heard a word I've been saying, Rufina."

"Oh, but I have, Nazario. I can't possibly marry you; my father has arranged for me to marry Lieutenant Gonzalez of the Santa Barbara Presidio."

"But you can't love that fat ugly old man? I shall kill myself if you don't marry me!"

"How?"

"What do you mean?"

"How will you kill yourself?"

"Rufina, you're a perfect little beast. I don't see how anyone could ever like you."

"But you said you loved me."

"That's different. I do, the Saints help me." He reached out and pulled her roughly to him and kissed her on the mouth.

"Nazario!"

"Are you going to marry me?"

"You're only a boy."

"What do you want—a man twice your age, like Don Julio?"

"He is very rich, but no I would not like to marry Don Julio. There is something about him I don't like. Look, Nazario, you may come to Santa Barbara and speak to my father. But if he says no, and he will, you must not be disappointed."

Nazario held her and kissed her again, and this time she did not protest. A moment later they were gone;

they had not even seen Kinkaid standing quietly in the shadows. Their conversation had sounded silly to him, and yet he knew his own to Dolores, a few moments before, would have sounded no less puerile to anyone who overheard it. He wondered uncomfortably just how much Tarifa had heard before she knocked on the door of the prayer room.

CHAPTER 11

In January, following the New Year, the rainy season began in earnest. Streams and creeks were flooded to overflowing: the entire landscape was a sea of red adobe mud, making the houses smell like the earth they were made from.

Yet, in the beating rain, Don Ygnacio rode the long miles to the Mission to make his confession, and to discuss his problem with the Padres.

He found Padre Peyri in his little office.

"Padre Cazon is supervising the weaving," he told Ygnacio when he had given him a glass of wine. He lifted a letter from his desk and added. "I have here an invitation, if one may call it that, to go and meet the new governor in San Diego, along with the heads of the other Missions and the Father Prefecto. I do not like to say it, *amigo*, but things look bad for us."

"How do you mean, Padre?" Alvarjo stretched out his legs and sipped his wine with delicate enjoyment. It was good amontillado.

"As you know, these past few years all the Missions

have been heavily burdened. It is enough for us to feed and clothe all our neophytes without having to support every presidio and barracks in California. Yet this morning Governor Echeandia sent Lieutenant Ibarra with soldiers from San Diego to take all the grain their mules could carry. They pay us in worthless scrip that tthe Padres cannot collect from the treasury even in Mexico. And the governor talks again of secularizing the Mission! What will the soldiers do then, pray tell?"

Don Ygnacio shook his head. Like all the older hacendados he knew the real worth of the Missions on this frontier. It was the perservering hard-working men of God who had civilized and built California and who now held it together. Take away the skeleton and the flesh would fall as if dropped from a scaffold. Yet there had always been those who eyed the Mission lands and prosperity with greed and envy, never realizing that it was hard work and toil that had built them up in the first place, and that kept them in operation. Work that the envious ones had no intention of copying.

"But you did not come to discuss Mission affairs on such a miserable day," Padre Peyri was saying. "What can I do for you?"

For the first time in his life Ygnacio Alvarjo found himself at a loss for words. He needed advice, but he was afraid to ask for it—or rather, he was not prepared to accept it if it was not to his liking. Peyri was a man of tolerance and understanding, and yet he felt the Padre would neither like nor approve of his next statement. Because he was flustered and annoyed with himself, he spoke bluntly.

"I am going to marry again, Padre."

Peyri opened his eyes in surprise and then smiled.

"That is good news, my friend. Your children need a mother, especially the girls and little Antonio. Do I know the lady?"

"No, Padre."

"Ah, then tell me about her."

"Her name is Tarifa, and she has been my houseguest for the past few months."

Peyri's round face flushed. "Not—the Gypsy girl Padre Cazon has been tutoring?"

"The same."

"But—you cannot be serious, Don Ygnacio? She is not even a Christian, let alone a Catholic? She is to be deported. It would not be allowed, even if you had the governor's permission for her to remain. You must not even consider such a thing!"

"I have considered it very carefully, Padre," Alvarjo replied. "My mind is made up, and she has consented to become my wife."

"But your children—Dona Isabella—how will they feel? Have you thought of them?"

"Most of them like her already," he murmured, though he was not certain that was true.

"But to make her their mother—to put her in Dona Encarnacion's place!"

Ygnacio colored. "No one will ever take Encarnacion's place, Padre. Tarifa will have her own place. I came to ask you to instruct her and to baptize her a Catholic, as the law demands, so that we may be married in the spring. She has agreed to that. And I will get the governor's permission for the ceremony."

"I cannot let you do this thing, Ygnacio. It would be madness! Padre Cazon says she is as young as one of your own daughters."

The color deepened in Alvarjo's lean face, but he said evenly, "She is mature in her own way. She has not led a sheltered life like my daughters, but I shall make it up to her. She shall never want for anything again."

"Your charity should take some other form than marriage," Peyri said. What madness had come over Alvarjo anyway? Surely he could see the impossibility of such a marriage?

Ygnacio got to his feet abruptly.

"It's not charity, I tell you! I love her. I want her for my wife. I don't care what the whole of California thinks or says about it. I am going to marry Tarifa."

"There can be no harm in baptizing her a Catholic, if she desires it," Peyri said, choosing his words cautiously. "You say you do not plan to marry till the spring? That will give you both time to think this over more carefully."

"If you think I will change my mind you are mistaken."

"I believe that you should tell your family of your plan

as soon as possible," said the priest. "It may not work out as you intend."

A hard look crossed Alvarjo's coin-thin face.

"This is not a matter for my children or my sister to decide," he said. "I will bring Tarifa to you for instructions once a week."

The Padre nodded. "As you wish, Ygnacio." But he was thinking that a priest giving ecclesiastical instruction could also give advice on temporal matters. Obviously the Gypsy saw Don Ygnacio as a rich plum waiting to be plucked; she could have no other valid reason for agreeing to marry him. Padre Peyri was determined to protect his friend in spite of himself.

Tarifa had spent the cold December morning riding with Don Ygnacio on the day he asked her to marry him. At breakfast, which she now shared with the family, she had expressed concern for Guindilla and Ygnacio had offered to take her out to the marsh beyond the separating corrals where the stallion was now pastured. When she had returned with Guindilla from Bolsa Coyotes, Pablo had agreed with Santos that the sand cracks could be cured, but only by desperate measures. The two men had cut deeply enough into each hoof just below the hairline till they bled, and turned the horse loose on wet marshland. It would take time, Santos told Tarifa, but Guindilla would eventually shed his present hooves and grow a new set.

Ygnacio had show her the horse and they were on their way back when he asked if she had ever seen his small cabaña atop Loma de Oro.

"I have seen it," she told him, "but only from a distance."

"If you would like to see it now, there is a back way we can ride up there."

"But Soledad tells me you allow no one to visit you there."

"You are no longer just a visitor on my rancho, Tarifa. You are like one of us."

She glanced at him curiously. He was smiling at her and she found herself smiling back because his words had pleased her. Each day that she spent at Loma de Oro, she dreaded the thought that she must leave it someday soon.

There was not an inch of the rancho that she did not know intimately, having ridden over all of it at one time or another with the boys, Santos, or Don Ygnacio. She rode Cobrizo again now that Guindilla was growing his new hooves, and next to her own pet she loved him the best of the other palominos. She had never ceased to look upon Don Ygnacio as her good friend, her benefactor.

"I would like to see the cabaña," she told him.

A small steep hill path crisscrossed the back of Loma de Oro, now faintly green in the winter sun, and emerged by a hitching rack and water trough behind the little house.

Don Ygnacio led her inside and showed her his treasures with the abrupt pleasure of a small boy.

It was just one room, twelve by twenty-five feet, with thickset windows on either side of the door overlooking the veranda and spreading valley below, and another window in one sidewall looking out toward the mountains. Furnished sparsely with a writing desk, armchair, rawhide-strung cot, and some shelves for books, plus a prayer bench and a small painting of the Macarena, it might have been a monk's cell.

Ygnacio put her in the armchair and brought out his books and writings, his poetry which he read with a touching shyness, and his treasured copy of the Moor Al-Tabari's book, *Akhbār al-Rusul w-al-Muluk*, which he told her meant *Annals of the Apostles and Kings*, in Arabic.

Tarifa was enchanted with the book that had been written so long ago by one of her father's people. She bombarded Alvarjo with questions about Moorish history.

He explained that the Arabs had brought their famous thoroughbred horses, *Kuhaylāna*, chiefly from Najd, into Spain in the eighth century. They had written superb medical books and developed surgery, begun a postal system with relay horses, built a paper factory in Spain in 1150. And the first guitar, *Quitār*, had come from them.

"Tell me how to say some of their words," Tarifa begged.

"I am not a linguist, my dear, merely a very superficial student. But I can tell you a beautiful feminine name, Qatr-al-Nada—Dewdrop. I think it would have fitted you."

"Qatr-al-Nada, that is very nice."

"And the Palace of Khumārawayh had a golden hall,

with gardens in the shape of Arabic words, and there was a pool of quicksilver on which were moored inflated leather cushions held by silk cords and tied to marble pillars, where the caliph could rock himself gently to cure his insomnia."

Tarifa laughed and ran her fingers over the strange words in the book she held as if she could absorb them by touch.

"At one time the Islamic Empire stretched from China to Gaul," he said.

"Then why did they lose it all?"

"Because the northern Arabs and southern Arabs could not agree. When the great dynasties fell, many petty kingdoms arose, and so they were conquered one by one, divided and split by their own interior separation."

"If I ruled a kingdom," said Tarifa hotly, "they would never be able to divide and conquer it. I would hold it together by main force if necessary, even if everyone hated me for it!"

Ygnacio was watching the way her eyes slanted under the straight lashes, their deep pigmentation flashing like polished ebony as the sunlight struck them. She was so alive, so charged with passion that he could not be near her without feeling the vibrant force of her personality.

He did not know now exactly when his feeling for her had changed from a protective fatherly one, to his present love that bordered on adoration, and his driving need to make her his. He had no idea how she felt for him, or that she would accept his proposal. He only knew that he must make it.

She had gotten up to look at a painting of the Madonna and he followed her.

"Do you kneel and pray to all the statues and pictures you have, Don Ygnacio?"

"Not to them, my dear. They are not gods, only pieces of wood and canvas, but by looking at them when we pray we are reminded of the person we are praying to; as you would be reminded by looking at the picture of a friend, and they help to rivet our attention—to keep it from wandering."

He indicated the painting. "La Macarena is the patroness of Andalusia. Surely you have seen her statue pass in the

Easter procession in her green cloak embroidered in gold, soaring above the flowers and candles? And smelled the scent of orange blossoms as she passed?"

Tarifa frowned.

"I have seen the processions, but I never knew one statue from another."

"You know, for a foreigner to remain in California, it is necessary for him first to be baptized a Catholic, and then to be naturalized. Would you be willing to do that to stay here?"

She turned to face him, fear and hope mingling in her look.

"Stay—in California?"

He reached for her hands and held them tightly.

"Not just in California, Tarifa. Here, at Loma de Oro." He went on swiftly then because once stopped he knew he would never have the courage to say the words again. "I want you to stay here always, my dear. I want you to share everything that I possess. I would put the world at your feet if I could. I have grown to love you, Tarifa, and though I haven't the right, I can no longer think of you as a daughter as I did at first, but only as my wife. I want you to marry me, if you can consider such a thing. I am old, so much too old for you, but I shall make it up to you somehow."

She stood for a moment, her eyes regarding him as if she had not understood a word he said. Then with a little cry that was more like a moan of relief, she threw heraself into his arms.

"*Querida, querida,* have I upset you? Have I shocked you, made you unhappy?" he asked in bewilderment.

She raised her face from his breast and her eyes were shining with happiness.

"You could never make me unhappy, *kushto;* you have always brought everything wonderful into my life. If I have to be baptized a hundred times and naturalized over and over every year, I will do it to marry you. If it will make you happy."

He bent to kiss her and they were both startled at the passion of the embrace.

"*Querida!* You shall rule as a queen of your own little empire, my *angelita.* Queen of Loma de Oro." Alvarjo felt the life surging through his limbs as it hadn't done since he was a boy.

"And—the others?" asked Tarifa finally, when they sat hand in hand on the veranda looking down at the long valley below.

"I will make all the arrangements before we tell them," said Alvarjo. "I must speak to Padre Peyri about your instructions and baptism first; then I must get permission for the wedding from the governor. When would you like to be married, *querida?*"

"In the spring," Tarifa said promptly. "When the hills are green again and all Loma de Oro is golden with the wild mustard. I want a big wedding, so fine and big they will talk about it forever!"

He smiled. What a child she was in some ways, yet so old and wise in others. But it was well to wait till spring.

The rainy season would be over, and Tarifa would be a Catholic then. He knew that there would be recriminations, undoubtedly a terrible scene with Isabella and Joaquin when he told them, and he wanted to save Tarifa from facing any of it. He still could not believe that she had agreed to marry him, even if she only did so out of gratitude. It was enough. He felt humble in his good fortune.

"You must have a jewel for your engagement gift," he told her gaily, and took a small box from the writing desk where he had left it the day before, hoping for just such an answer to his proposal, but never dreaming it would be granted to him.

"What is it, Don Ygnacio?"

"Ygnacio," he corrected gently.

He opened the little box and brought out a large square-cut emerald surrounded by small pearls.

"Oh! Oh, how beautiful."

He fitted it to her finger. It was a bit too large.

"It belonged to my grandmother," he said. "She was also a woman of strong character; she ran the castle and protected it against the Moors, while her husband was away at the wars. She would have liked for you to have it, my dear."

"It is beautiful—so beautiful, Ygnacio." She raised her hand to the light to see it sparkle. "It is like a green lake shining in the sunlight. I shall wear it forever!"

He kissed her hands and held them to his burning cheek. It was madness, as Isabella would soon tell him cuttingly, a man of his age with these pounding schoolboy emotions. But he was powerless to stop them.

"Soon," he told her, "we must go to San Diego to one of the trade ships, and buy your trousseau. You shall have six complete outfits of everything. No self-respecting bridegroom could provide less, and you shall have the most beautiful wedding gown in all California."

She clasped him around the neck. *"Me Kamāva tut.* In Romany that means, I love you, Ygnacio. This morning I found a red ribbon on the veranda when I went to breakfast; do you know what that means?"

"No, *querida mía."*

"It means you will find your true love. You see, your gods are not as powerful as Gypsy magic?"

He smiled indulgently.

"We will take the best of both to ensure our happiness," he told her. "You must teach me your Romany."

"And then we can talk and no one but Penti will know what we say! And you must have a nickname; all Gypsy men of stature have nicknames."

"What shall mine be, my little love?"

"El Águila—the Eagle. Because you are strong and brave and you keep a nest high up here like an eagle's nest on a crag."

He kissed her cheeks and her brow, and vowed that never would he bring anything but happiness to this wild, enchanting creature, who had come to fill his heart and his mind so completely.

It was late at night. Ygnacio sat alone in his study mulling over his great new happiness, when Joaquin knocked at the door and came in.

Ygnacio had seen little of his oldest son since Tarifa had come to stay at the hacienda. He was startled now when he saw the pale emaciated face and feverish eyes. He got up to pour him a glass of wine.

"Joaquin, you should have told me if you were ill."

"It is nothing, Father." He passed a thin hand over his face. It is an inner fever that will not leave me, perhaps forever. There is one thing to be done. I must leave here—as Santiago has done."

"No! I forbid it."

"I cannot stay in the same house with that—Gypsy. You cannot ask me to."

Don Ygnacio said nothing but went on studying his son's ravaged face. Had he made a terrible mistake? In befriending Tarifa, in trying to do his duty, undo the wrongs his sons had done her, had he failed his own flesh and blood? Made a mockery of Encarnacion's memory?

He said, "If you feel guilt for how you treated her, that is all over. Paid for. You have no reason to leave your home. You are my eldest, Joaquin; I need you here with me. There is your family and Loma de Oro to think of. Have you no sense of family duty? You know that when I die, you will be the head of the house."

Joaquin put down his wineglass with trembling fingers. "This house is not the same since my mother died. None of us are the same. I think Tía Isabella is right. The Gypsy has cursed us; we will all come to a bad end unless we get away from her!"

Alvarjo got to his feet angrily. "Nonsense! You talk superstitious nonsense! Are you afraid of a woman just because she is different from you?"

Joaquin shook his head and said wearily, "I only know that I must get away from her—or perish. Let me go, Father, I beg of you!"

Ygnacio sat down and buried his face in his hands. After a time he asked quietly, "Where do you want to go, *hijo?*"

"To the College of San Fernando in Mexico. I want to become a Franciscan."

"A priest?"

"*Sí*, Padre."

Ygnacio was unhappy. The son he had raised to be his right hand, to protect the family after he was gone, was deserting him.

"How do you know you have a real vocation for the religious life, my son. Isn't it that you just want a place to hide, to escape life's problems?"

"If my vocation is not real, they will find it out in time, and so will I."

"And if you find it is not, will you return then?"

"No," said Joaquin. "I can't promise that. I don't think I shall ever return. Perhaps I will try to find Santiago, and we will go on together, for I don't think he will return either."

Ygnacio bowed his head. He was thankful Encarnacion had not lived to see her favorite son forsake his family, to see another son disappear like a criminal with a price on his head.

"When do you want to leave?" he asked after a time.

"As soon as I can. If there is no ship going south, I will ride overland."

Ygnacio rose and went to a chest, unlocked it, and took out a chamois sack of coins. He gave them to his son along with a painted miniature of Encarnacion.

"Take Calabaza with you."

"*Gracias*, Padre. But I would rather leave him here. I will take another of the palominos."

Ygnacio thought grimly that with each son he lost he was also losing one of his prized palominos. Santiago had taken El Canario. He wondered what Joaquin's answer would be if he offered to send Tarifa away, and asked him to stay? But he could not ask it, for he knew even in this awful moment of losing his son that he would prefer to lose him rather than Tarifa.

Joaquin knelt for his blessing, and then rose while Ygnacio embraced him with tears in his eyes.

"You will write to me, my son?"

"Yes, Father."

There was a more settled look on Joaquin's face than when he had entered the room.

"If there is something that I can do for you, Padre, or for the others, you have only to send me word."

Ygnacio nodded wordlessly through his tears. What would Joaquin say if he knew the Gypsy would soon be mistress of Loma de Oro, and his stepmother as well?

It was with something like relief, mingled with his sadness, that Ygnacio watched his oldest son go. Now, he thought, there was only Isabella to oppose his marriage to Tarifa.

Joaquin had been gone for a month and Tarifa had begun her instructions at the Mission, riding to and fro with Don Ygnacio once a week, when he proposed one day that they ride to San Diego and select her trousseau.

Tarifa was delighted and insisted that Penti, Soledad, and Dolores go as well. The family still knew nothing of the marriage, but Don Ygnacio knew that he could buy all the women new clothing without exciting any comment. He also took Santos to look after the palominos while they were in town, and to arrange for a *carreta* to bring back their purchases.

It was a clear but windy morning when they left, Don Ygnacio muffled in his black velvet collared cape, the others wearing thick cloaks or serapes.

The horses danced along the muddy road, for it had rained the night before, and Santos predicted another rain before nightfall.

"Then we shall stay at the Mission," said Ygnacio.

"No!" said Tarifa with a quick glance at his face. "Not that place—I could not go there again."

"Very well, we will find another place to stay if the occasion arises. I have many friends there."

They had reached the camino and turned south when they heard a call behind them and saw a horseman on a fast-moving bay coming after them.

"Who is that, Santos?"

"I cannot be sure, Patrón, but it looks like Don Zenobio."

"Zenobio? What is he doing here?"

Sanchez slid to a stop in the muddy roadway, his cheeks above his beard red from the wind. He was muffled to the neck over his leather hunting jacket in a coarse vividly colored Indian serape.

"*Saludos, amigos!*"

"What are you doing on the road to San Diego?" asked Alvarjo, none too pleased to have him along on this particular journey.

"I might ask you the same thing." Zenobio winked slyly.

"I am going to the trade ships to buy the women some clothing," said Ygnacio stiffly.

"And I am going for an evening of monte and *aguardiente* at Domingo Chavira's. I can tell you what ships are in also. Juan Martinez was by my place. Yesterday he put Rufina Corlona on the *Galindo* for Santa Barbara."

"The *Galindo?*"

"From San Blas, and without much in the way of cargo,

so they say. A few things for the governor's comfort, a little holy oil for the Padres, and nothing as usual for the soldiers. There is going to be a mutiny one of these days, mark my words. And there is no liking for the Mazatlan cavalry Echeandia brought with him either."

Alvarjo was vexed. If there were no decent ships in the harbor they were making the trip for nothing.

"But you may be able to get something," said his friend with a glance at Dolores' face. "The *Arabella* is loading the last of her hides. She sails at dawn, I believe, for Boston, but Kinkaid may have something left to trade."

Ygnacio brightened, failing to catch the look of joy that crossed Dolores' face like a beam of light and was gone in an instant.

"Capitán Kinkaid will no doubt have something," he told Tarifa. "And you can order anything you like; he will bring it direct from Boston."

"You are very generous, Padre," said Soledad. She had not known him to be quite so open-handed before with his daughters' whims, but she had noted that when Tarifa was around he was inclined to be more lenient. She wondered about her father's interest in the Gypsy girl. She still liked Tarifa but she was not sure she wholly trusted her.

Zenobio chatted gaily all the way to the pueblo, keeping the girls laughing at his wry humor as the little party passed Gaspar Escobar's small house—which Tarifa saw now was nothing but a poor shabby hovel in comparison to Loma de Oro—and rode through the sifting sand to the beach.

"You will stay here with the horses," Alvarjo instructed his mayordomo.

"*Sí*, Patrón."

Again the Americanos came out to laugh and wave, but Tarifa did not mind them this time. Zenobio wished them well and turned his horse back to town.

"Come to the cantina later," he told Ygnacio, but the other shook his head.

"We will go back to the rancho if it is not too late."

Jake Banner came out of the company warehouse when he heard them asking about the *Arabella*, and in his halting Spanish offered to see them safely rowed to the ship himself. The captain, he explained, was on board, as they were sailing at dawn.

While the sailors pulled briskly at the oars, Banner studied the passengers carefully. He knew all about the Alvarjos and the Gypsy. But he was most interested in the blonde girl. A beauty all right. A real beauty. Sweet-faced and trim, like a spanking new brig. He could not blame Kinkaid for wanting her or for hating to leave her, but by the austere look of the old grandee she would not be an easy flower to pluck. It was plain the old gent didn't care for Americans. His eyes were set rigidly ahead and he had not spoken two words since they entered the boat, though Banner had tried politely to make conversation in his limited Spanish. Kinkaid could talk it almost like a native, but Banner found the words as slippery as eels in his mouth and used them only when necessary and then with extreme caution. Once in Monterey he had made what he thought was a perfectly polite inquiry and had his face soundly slapped as he stood in the plaza.

On board ship, Banner led the Alvarjo party to the trade room and introduced them to the supercargo's clerk, a slender, blond young man named Adkins, who spoke excellent Spanish.

There were still some of the more luxurious and expensive trade goods left, for Ephraim Endecott did not believe, as many of the other shipowners did, in dumping all of his goods in port at a loss before the ship sailed in order to load the space with more hides. He had found it better business to hold what did not sell, and carry it as far as Rio on the return voyage, where it often sold at double its value.

The girls went about examining everything with the abandon and shrill delight of children turned loose in a candy store.

Adkins showed them the choicest laces, satins, high-heeled slippers, spangled shawls, velvet cloaks, necklaces, earrings, fans, and several tortoiseshell combs valued at $600 each.

Banner excused himself from Don Ygnacio, and told him that he would fetch the capitan. He ducked up the steep brass-studded steps of the companionway and went to knock at Kinkaid's cabin door.

"Come in."

As his mate entered with a faint smile on his wind-tanned face, Bart glanced up from the logbook in which he was making an entry.

"Sorry to bother you, sir, but there are some customers aboard in the trade room."

"Well? Let Adkins see to their wants."

"I thought, sir, you'd like to greet these customers yourself," said Banner. "There's three young ladies, sir, and an elderly gentleman. One of the young ladies is blonde as an angel, and I heard them call her Dolores."

Light from the open porthole glanced across Kinkaid's high cheekbones and Indian-sharp profile as he raised his head abruptly.

"Dolores Alvarjo? You're sure?"

"Yes, sir. The same. Shopping for clothes and materials and gewgaws, they be."

"Thank you, Mr. Banner, I'll come at once."

"Aye, sir."

Kinkaid straightened his collar and reached for his cap.

Coming into the trade room a moment later he was aware of only one thing, a fair golden head bent above a case of jewelry. She seemed to sense his presence even as he came to a halt, and turned to look at him. For one precious moment they gazed deeply into each other's eyes, and then Dolores dropped her lashes and Kinkaid forced himself to welcome Don Ygnacio and the others aboard.

He invited Alvarjo to his cabin for a drink while the women shopped. Don Alvarjo accepted with cool civility.

"This is a brandy my Uncle Ephraim imported from Lisbon five years ago," Kinkaid told his guest, pouring from a decanter on his own sideboard. "To your very good health, sir."

Alvarjo replied in kind and complimented the liquor.

"I hope that you will accept a cask as a gift from my uncle when you leave, sir?"

"You are most kind, Capitán Kinkaid."

Bart studied the old grandee and found a subtle change in him. He seemed more alert, more impatient, and at the same time tense about something. Perhaps he was worried about leaving his women alone and unchaperoned in the trade room except for old Penti. She was probably helping herself to half the goods in the place, thought Kinkaid with wry amusement. He wished he dared to speak to Alvarjo about his feelings for Dolores, but he had made a pact with himself to say nothing until his return to California.

It was Soledad who finally came with Banner to get her father, asking him to come and check their purchases.

Tarifa had a large carved camphorwood chest before her and was busily engaged, with the help of Adkins and Penti, in folding up silks and satins, velvets and ribbons, and stowing them hastily in the chest. Kinkaid noted the emerald on her left hand and wondered where she had gotten it.

"I must have all of these," she told Alvarjo with an assurance that surprised Bart. Had she so bamboozled the old boy that she had him entirely under her thumb?

While Alvarjo went forward to examine Tarifa's numerous purchases, discarding some in favor of less gaudy but more expensive items, Kinkaid strolled over to where Dolores stood alone glancing out of a porthole toward the open sea.

"Someday," he told her softly, "you will sail out there on the *Arabella* with me, my darling."

She glanced at his face as if she would burn every line of it into her memory.

"I will be waiting," she whispered quickly. "Will it be long?"

"As fast as sails can take me, beloved."

Her eyes clung to his a moment longer and she murmured, *"Vaya con Dios,* Bart," and moved away from him toward the others. Kinkaid noticed that Alvarjo had been watching them, a puzzled expression on his face.

Alvarjo went with him to his cabin to arrange payment for the goods, and Kinkaid offered him the usual credit terms. As he was leaving port and could take no more hides or tallow, he suggested they be stored in the company warehouse after Don Ygnacio held his spring roundup. The next Endecott ship in port would pick them up on her return voyage.

"I prefer to pay for the goods in cash," said Don Alvarjo.

"But it is not necessary, señor." Kinkaid knew how scarce gold or silver was in California. Almost all business was conducted on a barter and trade basis, the hacendados preferring to hoard their money for emergencies.

"It is my wish nevertheless, Capitán."

Kinkaid shrugged his wide shoulders. "Whatever suits you, Don Ygnacio. I will see that the goods are rowed ashore at once."

"*Gracias.* I would also like to order a few things from Boston to be delivered on your next voyage."

"Certainly." It was not Kinkaid's place to take such an order himself—it was the duty of the supercargo or his clerk Adkins—but he obediently took pen and paper from his desk and waited for Don Alvarjo to continue.

"I want a diamond necklace and earrings, the finest you can obtain in the United States, and a full-length mirror in a carved rosewood stand, some gilt French brocade chairs for a lady's boudoir, and an emerald brooch surrounded by pearls."

Kinkaid remembered again the emerald on Tarifa's finger and wondered what the extravagant order Don Ygnacio had just given him meant. He remembered also his own helpless moment of passion when he danced with Tarifa at Don Julio's, and he felt a new uneasiness, not only for Alvarjo but for Dolores and the others as well.

He saw them into the longboat and managed to press Dolores' hand as he helped her over the side, his eyes caressing her face, his fingers aching from the too-brief touch of her flesh. How was he going to hold himself like this for another two years, keep his hope alive on just the memory of her exquisitely gentle face and their few moments alone?

Banner, standing to one side, saw Kinkaid's profile tighten as the boat moved shoreward, and knew that there would be a driving skipper on the quarterdeck this trip. A man was no stronger than the emotions that ruled him, and for the first time Bart Kinkaid was in the throes of the most powerful of them all.

Rain was threatening when they joined Santos on the beach and mounted their horses.

"Stay and see to the loading of the *carretas,*" Alvarjo told the Indian. "We will try and go on since the Señoritas do not wish to spend the night."

Santos nodded and wondered at his master's taut, worried expression. Something was bothering Don Ygnacio, like a mortal sin unconfessed.

In spite of the black skies and cold wind that had arisen, the rain did not start until after they had left Mission San Luis Rey. Then a deluge seemed to come from the skies, soaking horses and riders and reducing their pace to a crawl. They all looked as if they had been bathed in mud when they finally halted at the door of the hacienda.

It was late when Ygnacio called Nazario and Luis to his study to have an unaccustomed glass of wine with him.

"Since your brothers are gone," he told them gravely, "you are my two oldest, and you shall have to try and take the places of Joaquin and Santiago."

The boys eyed each other and nodded uneasily.

"I do not like the way the Americanos are coming more and more into the territory," he told them. "The day may come when they will be a great danger to California. Then you will have to be prepared to defend what is yours. I doubt if the government in Mexico will be able to help you even if they desired. You know the condition of the soldiers and the presidios. And now Padre Peyri tells me there is talk again of secularizing the Missions."

"*Si*, Padre, we understand," said Nazario, feeling his new responsibility like a heavy cloak on his shoulders.

"What would you have us do, Father?" asked Luis solemnly.

"Take over the running of the rancho. Go out every day with Santos and learn what has to be done. You see what has happened to Bolsa Coyotes because Don Julio has left it entirely in the hands of indifferent overseers? The time may come when the land is all you have left to fight with or for, my sons. Guard it well, for the sake of the family."

"Of course, Padre. But these are very gloomy words. Why must we worry when we have Santos?"

"Even Santos will not be here forever," Alvarjo snapped. "You must forget your days of play and buckle down to the responsibility of being men. You are young, but I would like to see you married with families of your own that would help to settle you down."

Embarrassed, the boys looked away. Ygnacio found himself impatient with their callow immaturity. It had been a grave mistake to concentrate on the training of only two of

his sons to manage the family affairs after he was gone.
Nothing was the same, he thought bitterly. Fathers could
not count upon their sons as they had when he was a boy.

"We will do our best, Father," Nazario said earnestly,
wiping his lean face.

Nazario was sincere and kind, a good boy, thought
Ygnacio, but he would be no match for hardheaded traders
like Capitán Kinkaid or others of his ilk. Alvarjo studied
Luis' solemn face over his wineglass and found it stronger,
more purposeful than his brother's. Perhaps Luis was the
one to take Joaquin's place? He would have to watch and
see.

When they left him he sat close to the brazier for
warmth and again thought of the way Capitán Kinkaid had
spoken to Dolores alone. Perhaps, being a foreigner, he did
not know that such things were not done. But the times
were so uncertain and seemed to move with such swiftness
that he could not afford to take chances.

For the first time in months he went in search of Isabella.
He found her sitting up in her room, her missal on her lap.

"Isabella?"

"Yes, Ygnacio?"

"I must speak with you for a moment."

"Sit down," she invited, moving over on the horsehair-
covered love seat. She closed the book and clasped her
long hands on top of it.

Ygnacio was angry at himself for feeling guilty in her
presence, as well as defiant. She had always been a good,
even a doting sister to him, but that, too, had changed.

"You had a pleasant trip?" she asked politely.

"Yes. Except for the rain on our return. We boarded
Capitán Kinkaid's ship. I was not pleased at Capitán Kinkaid's actions toward Dolores. Do you know of anything
between them? I know it is unthinkable—Dolores is a
dutiful daughter—but I do not trust these Americanos.
Kinkaid has done us a favor or two, and I know he went
with you to Bolsa Coyotes for Don Julio's fandango, but
was there anything else?"

Isabella took her hands from the book and smoothed the
silk skirt of her black gown.

"She waltzed with him once, I remember. I told her
afterward it was not quite proper, and then she went for a
short walk—she says alone."

"You did not believe her?"

"Not at first." She explained about searching for her niece and finding Tarifa and Kinkaid coming out of the prayer room in the study of Don Julio's hacienda.

Ygnacio's face grew black with rage but she did not know that it was at the thought of Tarifa alone with Kinkaid, and not his daughter.

Isabella, thinking that this was an advantageous moment, said, "Don Julio gives every indication of being in love with Dolores. She could do worse than be mistress of Bolsa de los Coyotes."

"What is that you say?"

"Don Julio, I believe, would like to marry Dolores. She is young, but perhaps it would be better if she were married. I have noticed that she is highly suggestible and impressionable. Marriage would be a steadying influence."

"No," said Ygnacio impatiently. "Neither her mother nor I ever approved of Don Julio."

"Then some other proper young Californian," suggested his sister, puzzled. "Perhaps I could take her with Soledad on a visit to Santa Barbara or Monterey this spring? I have long thought it would be a good idea. We could visit with the Corlonas. You knew of course that Nazario had been making calf eyes at Rufina Corlona all summer?"

"Nazario?" No, he had not known.

"The Corlonas are a very good family." Isabella went on, "It would not hurt to feel them out while I am there?"

But Ygnacio was not listening. He got to his feet and paced back and forth in front of the high canopied bed.

"What is the matter, Ygnacio? I know you have something else to tell me. I have always tried to stand by you, but of late I confess I do not understand you. You bring a common Gypsy, a heathen, into your household and do nothing when it drives away two of your sons. You subject your family to the evil influence of this creature and her—servant. You demean yourself by making an equal of her, lavishing rich presents upon her as if she were your own flesh and blood. And you will do nothing to end this impossible state of affairs. How long must we go on like this, Ygnacio?"

He had stood perfectly still listening to her words, his face pale and his eyes burning like coals of fire.

"I have done nothing? That is right." He spoke softly.

"But I am about to bring it all to an end, once and for all, Isabella."

"What do you mean?" She was suddenly afraid. Horribly afraid. He was not himself, had never been since Encarnacion died. A demon had taken possession of him. First that terrible withdrawal, and now this driving passion to destroy them all, even himself. She clutched the missal in her lap.

"I am going to marry Tarifa."

A sharp cry escaped her slightly parted lips. Of all the things he might have said this was the last she could have imagined.

"You cannot—you *cannot* mean this, Ygnacio!"

She got to her feet and stood clutching the back of the sofa, swaying slightly on her feet.

"Marry! You must be mad! We must call in Padre Peyri and Padre Cazon—at once."

"They already know. Padre Peyri is instructing her for baptism himself. I have only to get the governor's consent, and we will be married in the spring."

Isabella sank onto the sofa and began to weep bitterly, covering her face with her hands. "You are not my brother," she sobbed. "You are nothing like the brother I knew—and loved. This creature has bewitched you, is leading you straight to Hell, and you do not even realize it. Oh, Ygnacio, Ygnacio, come to your senses and put away this terrible demon from the underworld before it is too late!"

Ygnacio stood as stolid and implacable as Loma de Oro itself looming in the dark behind the hacienda.

"I love her, and I am going to make her my wife." His voice was thick and unrecognizable.

After a time Isabella dried her eyes and stood up, her face as cold and contained as hewn granite.

"Very well, Ygnacio. Then there is no place for me anymore in this house. I would not have stayed in the first place when she came, but for the children's sake. I cannot stay any longer."

"But they need you, Isabella. This is your home for as long as you live." His eyes opened wide in disbelief. He had never thought she would abandon him.

She shook her head.

"Do you think I could see *her* walking in Encarnacion's place, using *her* things, ordering *her* children about?"

"You exaggerate, Isabella."

"Do I? Wait and see what kind of wife and stepmother your greedy, cold-hearted little Gypsy makes! I can no longer stay in the same house with her—or you. A man of your blood and background—a man old enough to be her father—it is worse than disgusting!"

"Isabella, you go too far!" He gritted his teeth but he could not stare down her blazing, contemptuous eyes. They were too alike for either of them to back down, but he found that he could not endure her presence a moment longer.

"Run!" she hissed after him as he turned to go. "Run and hide from your own conscience if you can, Ygnacio! But you cannot, and that infamous harlot will chase you into your grave!"

He banged the heavy door shut on the last of her maledictions. They rang like death knells in his ears.

CHAPTER 12

It had been a wet, cold winter, but spring, when it came, was the most beautiful California had known since the drought of 1820.

In the softly rolling, nearly treeless hills and meadows of the San Luis Rey Valley, water splashed once again in the creeks and streams, and filled the long, dry, small lake beds. Limitless, the plain spread like a varicolored carpet to the snow-topped sierras beyond, a paradise of color and fragrance.

Amid the chameleon velvety chaparral blossomed blue and white lupin, golden poppies, and waving horse-high wild mustard.

Everything had prospered in the wealth of rain that had blessed the parched land all winter. Grass and water would not be scarce this season, and the planted fields of the Mission promised a yield beyond the wildest dreams of the Padres.

Before Easter Padre Peyri had baptized Tarifa into the Catholic faith, and the sergeant in charge of the *escolta* and the wife of one of the soldiers at the Mission had stood up as her godfather and godmother. Ygnacio had gone alone to San Diego that same month and gotten permission from Governor Echeandia to marry, and found the new governor as little to his liking as Zenobio had claimed he would be.

The morning after his quarrel with her, Tía Isabella had called for the carriage, taken only her own belongings and her elderly plump maid, and, after a tearful farewell, left for Santa Barbara, where she had many friends.

Ygnacio tried once more to dissuade her but she ignored his words as if he had not spoken them. After she left he called the children into the *sala* and explained why their aunt had gone.

At first there was a shocked silence, and then Dolores came forward and kissed his cheek, for now she also knew and understood love and passion.

"If it is what you want, Padre, and it will make you happy, we are all very pleased for you. And I know Tía Isabella will return when she has thought it over."

"Thank you, my dear," he murmured, accepting the good wishes of his other children as they crowded around him with tears in his eyes.

The days had flown for them all since then in anticipation of the wedding in the spring. Candelaria, who, unlike Isabella, could not leave in high dudgeon, was forced to accept the unhappy prospect of serving her new mistress and was busy from morning till night helping the girls and the maids sew all the new clothes necessary for the nuptials.

Don Ygnacio cautiously issued invitations to his close friends and neighbors, and was surprised and gratified to find that they accepted the news with a minimum of shock or criticism. But these were people who had known him all his life, simple rancheros for the most part, placid country people. He did not know how the marriage would be received by the more sophisticated *gente de razón* of Monterey, Santa Barbara, or San Francisco. He had not even invited the first families of San Diego to his wedding, but Tarifa would never know that. A large, flamboyant wedding she should have, well attended by the richest gentry in the neighborhood, but Ygnacio had taken care to invite no one who could snub or hurt his young bride.

Tarifa herself was a constant delight to him; he worshipped her with a fire and intensity he would have thought impossible at his age. And only from one unexpected quarter did he get a reprimand now that Isabella had gone.

Ygnacio had been sitting alone in the patio taking in the sun, Tarifa and the children having gone to visit the Martinez rancho, when Zenobio Sanchez came through the door from the *sala*.

Ygnacio had not seen him since Isabella had left, for Zenobio had gone to Baja California with a small herd of mares he wished to sell to the Missions there. Now he stood, hands on his hips, blinking into the sunlight, and Ygnacio saw that he had been drinking.

"Come here, Zenobio! Welcome back."

Zenobio spat on the ground and limped across the patio toward him.

"I have come to ask you a question, Ygnacio, because I believe someone has been telling me lies about you."

"What do you mean?"

Zenobio's little eyes were wary in his bearded face.

"They have told me that you plan to marry again."

"That is correct."

"And that the bride is to be the Gypsy girl you kept at the cabaña?"

Ygnacio colored angrily.

"And that because of it, you have driven off Joaquin and Dona Isabella," said Zenobio carefully.

"That is not true!"

"What is the truth then? That is what I have come to find out."

"Joaquin does not even know of my plans—he left at

his own request to join the Franciscans at the College of San Fernando. Isabella also left of her own accord. I pleaded with her to stay, but she refused."

"And why in God's name shouldn't she!" thundered Zenobio, pacing back and forth in front of the fountain, his long shanked spurs rattling on the fine imported tiles.

"I thought you would understand," Ygnacio said reproachfully. "You are my friend."

"*Sangre de Dios!* It is because I am your friend that I have to speak to you like this! I am not like the others who tell me about you, congratulatory to your face and snickering behind your back. Are you blind, Ygnacio? Don't you see what you are doing?"

Ygnacio stood with his hands clenched at his sides, staring into the belligerent face of the old soldier. Why had he never seen how narrow-minded and ill-bred the man was? Why had he taken him as a confidant, honored his advice? The man was nothing but presumptuous mestizo.

"Is that all you have to say?" he asked coldly.

"*Caramba!* Have you no sense at all? I know Tarifa as well as you do—better perhaps, for she's closer to my kind than yours."

"She loves me."

"She loves herself! And all she can beg, borrow, or steal for herself! She has ruined two of your sons, driven off Isabella, and now she is going to ruin you and the others!"

Ygnacio had taken a step forward, too angry to speak, meaning to throttle the red-eyed accusing face before him, when a quiet voice said:

"Do you think I would desecrate everything that my people believe in, Don Zenobio?"

Zenobio looked at Tarifa standing in the doorway, at first in surprise, then in black fury.

"To Gypsies, Nature is God," she said. "The Sun and the Moon, and the Earth. None of this"—she waved a hand toward the hills behind them—"is ever going to suffer because of me. And Gypsies do not throw love away either, Don Zenobio. I shall not destroy Ygnacio's."

She came to slip her slender brown arm through Ygnacio's and stood with her chin raised, gazing levelly at Zenobio.

The old soldier turned on his heel and limped rapidly

toward the *sala* where Soledad and Dolores stood listening in awed silence.

"I'm sorry for you, *muchachas*," he told them passionately. "If you need me you have only to come to the Santa Teresa. But do not call me to help those two!"

With an oath he stumbled past the two girls, and a moment later they heard his horse gallop out of the yard at a furious pace.

On her wedding day, Tarifa stood at the window of the Padre's room which she would occupy for the last time that morning, and drew the flower-scented May air deeply into her lungs. She felt as gay and free as a bird in flight.

The emerald flashed on her finger and behind her Penti was already assembling the wedding gown on the bed, murmuring over the texture and beauty of the material.

"Bandonna would never believe in your good fortune," said the old Gypsy. "Such a gown is fit for a princess."

"Ygnacio says I am going to rule as Queen of Loma de Oro; why should I not have a princess' dress?"

"Aye. You'll rule, all right," said Penti darkly. "But not quite as you think."

"What do you mean?" Tarifa scowled at her and turned from the window.

"Last night I studied the cards. It is bad, your taking a new god and discarding the old ones of your people. You no longer wear your amulet."

"Padre Peyri says it is powerless—a superstition. I wear this instead." She held out the gold cross around her neck.

"And it is doubly bad for you," said Penti, "to wear that."

"I do not understand you; you talk in riddles," snapped Tarifa, brushing her long hair vigorously. "I do not forget all that I have learned in the past; why should it harm me? If I have studied and allowed the Padres to mumble over me and pour water on me, and give me another name along with my own, Tarifa Ana, what does it matter? I did it only to please Ygnacio, and so that we could stay in California. I care nothing for their teachings or their statues and pictures, but it does no harm to pretend if it pleases my husband."

Penti said stolidly, "You are half Gypsy and half Moor.

Our people do not believe in the Christian cross, and the
Moors believe in the crescent of Islam. You will be doubly
cursed."

"You are an old witch and a devil!" Tarifa shouted.
"Enough of your evil curses. You will not upset me on my
wedding day, or I will flog you." She moved for the braided
riding crop that Pablo had made her.

Penti cackled with mirth. "The truth hurts, *miri pen?*"

Ignoring her, Tarifa ripped off her nightdress and turned
slowly in front of the mirror admiring her nakedness, the
clean line of her high-pointed breasts, the flat oval of her
stomach, her slender dancer's hips and legs.

Penti helped her into her underthings and the voluminous silken petticoats that Candelaria had made for her,
scented with bags of sachet sewn into the hem.

"If you were a virgin and the *piaora* had made sure you
were intact," Penti went on glibly, "tonight she would
sing the *arbola*." Her old voice rose in the ancient lewd
song, "Rise most honored patron; let the feast begin, the
bride has yielded up her maidenhead."

"*Premita Undebē!* Shut your ugly old mouth that is as
full of lies as a fig is full of seeds!"

Dolores knocked on the door and came in followed by
Soledad, to help Tarifa complete her toilet. Dolores carried the box of pink Loreto pearls that were Don Ygnacio's
wedding gift to his bride.

Tarifa, with her Gypsy love of color, had not chosen to
be married in white. Her gown of fine imported satin was
of pale green, like the fresh grass that now covered the
hills of Loma de Oro. Over the full-skirted gown embroidered with roses made from white and pink bugle beads,
she wore a rose-colored jacket trimmed with white glass
beads and silver lace. Her pink satin shoes had silver
buckles, and her black hair was done up behind a high
silver comb with a white lace mantilla drawn over it.

The wedding guests had arrived the day before in order
to accompany the bridal party to the Mission where they
were to be married, and when Tarifa stepped onto the
front veranda, they were all mounted and ready.

The Martinez family, the Cotas, Don Julio Marcos, Don
Ygnacio and his four sons, for Francisco had gotten permission to come home for the wedding.

Don Ygnacio was not wearing his accustomed black, but was decked out gaily in yellow satin knee breeches and jacket trimmed with gold Mexican pesetas, a lavender satin waistcoat embroidered with white roses, buckskin boots tied at the knee with gold and silver ribbon, and one of the hats of yellow vicuña wool heavily covered with gold lace under the brim and around the crown.

Eyes bright with appreciation of his betrothed's beauty, he helped her into the richly carved fiesta saddle on Caminante; Nazario, resplendent in purple satin, put her pink satin slipper in a loop of silver braid.

The Loma de Oro palominos had never looked so splendid nor been more richly comparisoned. Silk and satin ribbons floated from their headstalls and they pranced the Spanish walk like proud, strutting monarchs, each conscious of his own supreme dignity.

Inside the church the perfectly proportioned dome over the chancel and the beautiful groined arches on either side over the altar had a translucent quality in the early-morning sunshine. Light and dark blues, reds and blacks used by the Indians to frescoe the four broad pilasters on each side of the church, gave the only color save for the altar itself and the carved richly painted statues in their niches.

Padre Cazon acted as Peyri's assistant at the Mass. It was he who would bind the white silken scarf around Tarifa and Don Ygnacio's shoulders, signifying that they were bound henceforth temporally as well as spiritually.

Behind them the congregation knelt on the tiled floor, the women on shawls or small rugs they had brought.

Don Ygnacio's hand trembled as he put the thick gold band on Tarifa's finger, and she smiled at him with quick assurance.

When the long ceremony was over, Ygnacio took his bride before him on El Capitán and the whole party rode back to Loma de Oro for a week's celebration.

A huge tent had been raised over the patio, and Don Ygnacio had spared no effort or expense.

Indian musicians from San Luis Rey Mission played continuously from their seats on the *galleria* above the patio, relieved now and then by amateur guitarists who sang love songs or played spirited *jotas*.

In the long afternoon and evening following her wed-

ding, Tarifa danced with every man at the celebration, and
no one had a better time. With Ygnacio she danced the
last dance of the evening, the *canastita de flores*, in which
the dancers circled singing and on the last word each man
rushed forward to embrace his beloved.

She fell into his arms breathlessly, her hair brushing his
cheek, and he lifted her in his arms and carried her into
the large square bedroom he had shared with Encarnacion.

In the week that followed, Ygnacio entertained his guests
with a bear-and-bull fight, horse races, and games of riding
skill. Whenever Californians gathered in leisure there was
sure to be horseplay and hilarity. Their games, played on
horseback, were hard, rough, and dangerous.

On the flat ground in front of the hacienda, Don Ygnacio
would drop a coin and offer a purse to the man could scoop
it up on the first pass. Since the rider must hang from a
galloping horse practically by his toes to do it and since a
good deal of drinking had been indulged in on the night
before, there were some highly edifying results.

Money changed hands rapidly in the next few days, as
everything from roping tricks, to jumping hurdles with a
coin pressed to the saddle between both knees, were heavily
covered with bets.

On the last day of the wedding celebration, Carlos Cota
demanded a *capoteando* to round things out nicely.

"Have you got a bull, Ygnacio, that is *muy vicioso?*"

Alvarjo had Santos bring the black bull to the north
pasture. After breakfast the women rode out on horseback
or in the *carretas* to the large holding corral where the
mesteños had been slaughtered, and formed a bright-hued
circle as they stood outside to watch.

The bull was large and well-muscled with a spread of
widely spaced, wicked horns. Santos and three vaqueros
drove him into the corral and turned him loose. With a
whoop of delight, the men on their fastest cutting ponies
entered the corral swinging their serapes or short capes to
attract the bull's attention.

Ygnacio rode close and brushed his *capa* across the
bull's eyes. El Capitán dashed to one side to avoid the
bull's rush, and the excitement was on. The women called
encouragement and clapped loudly when a rider made a

particularly miraculous escape from the bull's horns. Twice, a horse fell to his knees to avoid the bull's head, and then quickly recovered himself and spun his rider around out of harm's way.

But the wildest part was yet to come. When the bull and riders were both tiring, Don Ygnacio ordered him turned loose, and the animal was driven through the gate at full speed. Outside the enclosure riders pounded after him in a wild melee, vying with each other to be the first to tail him.

Nazario and Luis outdistanced the others and fled over the prairie like twin arrows shot from the same bow.

Watching from Cobrizo's back, Tarifa saw Luis begin to gain a slight lead. Frenzied and reckless they jolted each other. Nazario, on Lagarto, tried to cross in front of his brother and collided savagely with the other horse, grasping for the reins. Lagarto stumbled and fell with a thud that could be heard where the watchers stood, just as Luis grasped the bull's tail and neatly flipped the running bull onto his back.

There was a roar of approval from the men. Lagarto had limped away from the spot, but Nazario did not rise. He still lay where he had fallen.

Luis threw himself off his horse even as the others started toward him and lifted his brother's head. He was white-faced and there was blood on his lips.

"Nazario! Nazario!" He was still calling when Tarifa and Ygnacio reached him. He looked up at them dumbly. Ygnacio quickly felt his son's face, neck, and limbs. One of the legs was turned unnaturally.

"He has a broken leg," he told Tarifa.

She touched Nazario's face, conscious of the silent group at her back. She was mistress of Loma de Oro now. The neighbors would expect a speedy and correct decision.

"We must make a litter, Ygnacio, and carry him back to the hacienda to Penti, at once."

He nodded, noting that Nazario had opened his eyes and was biting his white lips to keep from crying out in pain.

Tarifa bent and looked in his face.

"It won't take long to get you home, Nazario, and then Penti and I will ease your pain."

He said nothing, afraid to relax his vigilance, but his dark eyes mirrored his gratitude.

Tarifa ordered Nazario moved to the Padre's room, where it would be easier to care for him, and when they had given the boy *aguardiente* mixed with laudanum, she helped Penti and Santos set his leg. It was broken just below the knee, a bad place but a clean break, and Penti splinted and dressed it expertly.

"I have not set a human leg before," she told Santos, "but I have set horses' legs in the caravan, a much more tricky business."

In June, Don Ygnacio held his spring roundup. He was usually joined by Zenobio Sanchez on one side and José Martinez on the other, but he had not spoken to Zenobio or seen him since their argument in the patio at Loma de Oro. And so only the Martinez's Rancho Tocayo vanqueros joined those of Loma de Oro for the seasonal rodeo.

A California ranchero could no longer hold a roundup at his own whim and pleasure. The entire affair was bound by the government in protocol. It galled men of Ygnacio Alvarjo's proud temperament, but he was subject to the jurisdiction of the *ayuntamiento*, the municipal government, who had designated that no one might mark or brand or kill stock except on days named by them, and never without permission of the *juez de campo*, field judge, who had first to notify the mayor of the nearest pueblo. Penalties for disobeying the law were stringent and costly. Twenty *reales* for the first offense.

The *juez de campo* who had been assigned to watch over the roundup of Loma de Oro and Rancho Tocayo stock, Fernando Huerta, was a Mexican of enormous girth and great pomposity who had come from the pueblo of Los Angeles.

Huerta was a man who displayed himself with vast importance. He had never been the guest of so high-born a grandee as Don Ygnacio. He approved of everything about Loma de Oro, from its spreading lands and herds to the luxiurious appointments of the house and the charm and beauty of Don Ygnacio's young wife and daughters. Secretly, he determined to make the rodeo last as long as possible.

Dressing to go out to the pastures with Santos and Huerta, Ygnacio told his wife peevishly, "That ass of a

Huerta is going to be nothing but a hindrance. I'll wager he knows nothing about cattle; certainly he knows little enough about a horse. He sits like a sack of meal and saws on the animal's mouth like one of those ship-bred Americanos."

Tarifa came to put her arms about his neck and he held her to him, feeling his own heart pound against her breast, smelling the heavy scent that she had taken to wearing lately that mingled with the warm fragrance of her thick black hair.

"Soledad and I will ride out to the pasture later," she told him. "Ignore Huerta. He is a fool but you cannot hold the roundup without him. It is Nazario I worry about; he chafes because he cannot get about. I have been trying to interest him in books, to teach him to read, to amuse himself a little."

"That is good of you, *querida*. Have I told you how proud I am of the way you have taken charge of the household? Isabella could not do better."

An angry shadow passed over Tarifa's face as she stepped away from him.

"My dearest, you must not misunderstand. I mean that you do better—much better."

"You all miss Isabella."

"No! No, I assure you we do not, *querida*." He reached for her hands and held them tightly. "Isabella, heaven forgive her, is a harsh and unforgiving woman. We are all better off without her."

"The children miss her," said Tarifa. "They do not say so in front of me, but I overhear them talking. They cannot treat me as a mother; they will not come to me with their problems."

"You must give them time," he chided. "You are so young yourself; they cannot realize you are the mistress of this household now."

"Candelaria hates me," said Tarifa darkly.

"She was trained by Isabella, who gave her too many liberties. She is an old and faithful servant. But if you like, I will dismiss her."

"No, let her stay. I do not mind particularly if someone hates me, if it is an honest and open hatred like Candelaria's or Isabella's."

"But this is your house, my dear; I want you to be happy in it."

She smiled at him and disengaged a hand to reach up and pat his cheek.

"I am happy, Ygnacio. How could I be otherwise on this magnificent rancho with you? Do not worry about me—or the others. Go with Señor Huerta and start your roundup."

He kissed her and left the room a moment later with a light step and a smile on his thin aquiline face.

By midmorning Santos, with a hundred vaqueros from Loma de Oro plus fifty from the Martinez rancho, had gathered the great herds on the rodeo grounds, a flattish prairie, part on Loma de Oro, part on Rancho Tocayo land.

Here the parting commenced, separating the cows and calves of one brand from those of the other, to be held in separate herds by a loose circle of watchful vaqueros. Now and then a wild cow or balky calf would escape from the milling herd and make a dash for freedom, only to have a *reata larga* settle over his unwary neck or hind leg and be dragged back to the circle.

When all the stock were separated into two cut herds, the *juez de campo* rode out in deliberate majesty to inspect the cattle.

In his hand Fernando Huerta carried a book with the branding irons registered with the mayor, for Rancho Loma de Oro and Rancho Tocayo. Each ranchero was required to have two, *el fierro para herar los ganados* with which to brand his stock, and *el fierro para ventear*, with which to strike out his brand in case of sale. If the *juez de campo* found these properly used on the cattle held, and approved in the registry he held, plus the correct ear markings which most rancheros used, and which must also be entered in the registry, he would issue the order for the branding and marking to begin.

Instantly *reatas* flashed through the air and began dragging calves, struggling and brawling out of the milling herd, to where the branding fires had been built. Santos and Tomas between them, with a vaquero to tend the fire, branded and cut the calves' ears with the Alvarjo brand and left ear notch, with an ease and dispatch that was astonishing.

In the other herd, the Martinez vaqueros were doing the same to the Rancho Tocayo cattle.

As the freshly branded stock were freed and chased back onto Loma de Oro property, Huerta smoothed his thick black moustache and told Alvarjo, "This is an amazing thing, Don Ygnacio. Never have I seen vaqueros work with such precision and speed, and yet you round up only once a year." He looked suspiciously at his host and saw Alvarjo's face grow rock hard.

"Of course I only round up once a year. I do not disobey the law, Señor Huerta."

"Certainly not, Don Ygnacio! I did not mean—it is only the amazing speed of your men that I comment on."

"My men are well trained. I am also fortunate in having a very able mayordomo."

"To be sure. He is from Mission San Luis Rey, they tell me."

"Yes. But he has been in my employ for many years."

Huerta studied Santos' sweat-streaked back and quick hands. "Is he not still under jurisdiction of the Padres?"

"In a sense. But they gave him permission to work for me, and neither of us has ever regretted it."

Don Ygnacio went forward with his sons to tell Santos which of the cattle he would slaughter that year for their hides and tallow, and which he had selected to be made into *tasajo* or jerky, for sale to some of the merchant ships or traders coming into port. Since there was no other means of preserving the meat, this was the only alternative. He selected several steers to be butchered on the spot and carried to the house for the feast and barbecue that always followed the spring rodeo.

"You should have a very good yield, Don Ygnacio," said Huerta enviously, as they galloped home in the setting sun.

"It is fair enough," Ygnacio answered. He was anxious to get rid of the *juez de campo*. The barbecue and celebration tonight should end their enforced association and Huerta would be on his way. But for tonight Huerta would remain his guest.

"I have been thinking," Huerta said later that evening as he lowered his bulk into the most comfortable chair in the *sala*, "that I would ask the governor for a grant and start ranching myself. There is a little piece of land between San Gabriel and Los Angeles that is not filed on."

"I thought that was all Mission land?" Don Ygnacio said quickly.

Huerta's fat face reddened. "According to the Padres, all the land is Mission land, and is being held by them for the Indians, except for the land the pueblos are built on and that which you rich hacendados hold royal grants own! What of the rest of us *gente de razón,* do we get nothing?"

"The Padres do not claim all the land," said Ygnacio evenly. "Only the territory that was first designated as Mission land, that they and their neophytes have stocked and improved and planted. With all the land in California, why is it that every would-be ranchero can only consider the Mission lands suitable for him to settle on?"

"That is not true, Don Ygnacio. But you must admit the Padres selected all the best of the land and water first?"

"Do you think Loma de Oro was a rich and prosperous rancho when I came here to settle?" Alvarjo asked. "It was a raw land, water was scarce as it is all over the south-land, but this was my grant and I built it up. Without the Padres to show me how to deepen my few springs and irrigate properly, it would have been a futile undertaking, and without the help of their Mission-trained neophytes, physically impossible.

"You have a like opportunity. But you cannot start by claiming Mission land, and failing to treat the Indians you borrow from the Missions well or to pay your mayordomo a fair wage."

"But the Indians work for their keep—just as at the Mission," said Huerta. "You cannot mean that you pay them?"

"Some of them. My mayordomo, Santos, and Candelaria, my housekeeper, though she is not Indian, nor is Pablo my saddlemaker. I also pay a stipend to Tomas, my chief herder, and to my *amansador.*"

"But we are not all as wealthy or fortunate as you," Huerta said, smoothing his moustache.

"There are other ways of paying for services, Señor Huerta."

"*Cómo?*"

"A cow or a horse which your servant may trade. Food-stuffs, *aguardiente,* wine, which he may sell. Whatever you have in your storehouse that he may barter for money or other goods in the pueblos."

Huerta smiled thinly. He knew of other benevolent rancheros, but none who were such idealistic fools as this proud, arrogant Alvarjo, claiming to pay them in money, no less! Huerta wondered how much wealth was buried on Loma de Oro. Perhaps right here in the house, in one of those heavy locked chests over there?

Alvarjo did not miss the greedy look on his guest's fat face. What was California coming to, he wondered, that a gross, selfish individual like this should hold a post of importance and honor in a pueblo?

A servant came to announce dinner and Huerta bestirred himself to escort the charming red-silk-gowned Dona Tarifa to the table, while Don Ygnacio followed with Dolores and Soledad.

Nazario, with the help of a crutch made for him by Pablo, had managed to hobble to the table. He could no longer endure his imprisonment in the bedroom, and he hoped to hear of the day's activities at the rodeo. He listened in morose silence, however, as Luis related the day's adventures.

"You will be riding soon," he told his sad-faced brother. "It's not so bad as all that."

But Tarifa noted that Nazario made no reply.

In early July the Alvarjos received an invitation on thick official stationery to attend the governor's ball to be held in his newly completed mansion in San Diego.

Tarifa and the girls, as well as the young men, were entranced at the prospect of so much pomp and elegance. Once only the capital at Monterey could have boasted such festivities; now that the new governor had declared his intention of making San Diego his capital such regal celebrations might be expected as a matter of course. But Don Ygnacio hesitated to accept because of Tarifa.

As his wife, she had been accepted easily enough by his local friends and neighbors, with the exception of Don Zenobio. But what sort of reception would she find among the better families of San Diego? Particularly the matrons who had already snubbed her as an outcast for her public dancing in Domingo Chavira's cantina? Many of the women had been friends of Encarnacion and were undoubtedly shocked at his marriage.

He tried to explain all this gently to Tarifa in the privacy of their bedroom, but all he succeeded in doing was to make the governor's ball appear doubly attractive, a personal challenge as well as a brilliant social affair.

"I am not afraid of the old hags," she laughed, dancing like a nymph before him in her thin nightdress and bare brown feet. "I shall have the most beautiful gown, the most wonderful jewels there, and I shall dance as they have never seen anyone before, Ygnacio!"

"It will be a very prim, formal affair," he warned her. "You are now Dona Alvarjo; you will have to behave with the dignity and decorum expected of you."

She laughed.

"I think it is time someone stirred them up; San Diego is a dull place. I don't see how the governor can stand it. What is he like?"

Ygnacio frowned. He had only met Encheandia briefly when he had secured his permission to marry Tarifa. The man had seemed well-bred and jovial enough, but there was something about him that made Alvarjo wary. Perhaps it was because Encheandia had seemed to be trying too hard to please.

"We are going to the ball, Ygnacio?"

"If it is what you want, *querida*," he replied uncomfortably.

"Yes! And I will start Candelaria and the maids sewing at once. No one at the ball shall be finer than the Alvarjos!"

"Your Excellency, may I present Dona Tarifa Alvarjo of Rancho Loma de Oro."

Tarifa curtsied deeply as Dolores and Ygnacio had instructed her to do, and looked up into the face of José Maria Echeandia, first Mexican Governor, *jefe político*, and Commandante General of the Californias.

A tall slender man in his forties, with a white face, very black hair, and scanty beard, he made a low bow as he kissed her hand and murmured, *"La casa es suya,* Señora."

She noted, as he spoke with Ygnacio, that he affected the Castilian pronunciation.

He had a pleasant if apathetic manner, but seemed petulant with his underlings.

Beside him, presenting the guests as they arrived, stood his secretary, Agustin Zamorano. Both men, Tarifa knew, had been officers at the Mexican College of Engineers. Zamorano, however, seemed a man of energy as well as diplomacy.

"You must grant me a dance later in the evening, Señora," said Echeandia.

"With pleasure, your Excellency."

Ygnacio led his wife from the reception line near the door, to the large *sala* beyond, which had been converted into a ballroom. The governor had built himself a pleasant and roomy house and furnished it with imports from Mexico and United States. A ten-piece orchestra played on a raised dais at one end of the long room which let out on one side to the tent-covered patio, where couples also danced on the tiled floor, and where long tables covered with fine white linen cloths and glittering silver were laden with the best food and drink the province afforded.

Everyone who was anyone had traveled for miles to take part in the celebration. But it was quite obvious many were present without benefit of an invitation. For one thing, Tarifa noted, there were quite a few Americans. Those who were not in seaman's garb wore the colorful costumes of the country, but looked odd with their light skins, hair, and eyes.

Don Ygnacio glanced at the older women in their dark gowns and black or white mantillas, who sat in chairs against the walls. He knew that they were whispering about him behind their tightly held fans, and his skin crawled at the prospect of facing them in this crowded room with Tarifa on his arm. But to delay would only make matters worse, and Alvarjo had never been one to shirk a duty just because it was unpleasant.

"Are you ready to meet them?" he asked his wife, indicating the women across the room.

Her long eyes gazed up at him, a wicked light dancing in their black depths. "Are they ready to meet me?"

Ygnacio wanted to warn her once more to be cautious but somehow he could not bring himself to do it. He was very proud of her as she stood beside him. She looked every inch a lady in her new full-skirted red satin ball gown embroidered with black thread, a fine black lace mantilla thrown over her bronze shoulders, and her hair done up under a high black comb with one red rose tucked in front of it. She wore a necklace and earrings of jet, and her flashing square-cut emerald winked like green fire next to her wedding band. She had been right. No one had a finer gown than she did, and no one looked more regal or attracted more attention than the Alvarjos of Loma de Oro. Ygnacio squared his shoulders under his black velvet jacket. What did he care about their reception from a lot of old crones?

With Tarifa's hand on his arm, he led her across the floor to where the older women sat.

"Buenos noches, señoras. *Hace mucho tiempo que no te veo."*

Five pairs of eyes greeted him coldly and completely ignored Tarifa. Dona Paula Lugo fanned herself furiously as she replied with curt politeness, "Good evening, Don Ygnacio. We were so desolated to hear of dear Encarnacion's sudden death so short a time ago."

Ygnacio's cheeks reddened but he replied evenly, "It was a sad and unfortunate thing for all of us. May I present my new wife, Dona Tarifa. My dear, Dona Paula Lufo. Dona Maria Estaquia Pico, Señora Estudillo, Señora Carillo, and Señora Canejo."

Tarifa flashed them an engaging smile and curtsied politely, receiving only disapproving stares and barely inclined heads in return.

"You must show me your garden sometime, Señora Pico," Tarifa said sweetly. "Your son, Pio, used to bring me such lovely bouquets each night when he came to watch me dance at Domingo Chavira's wine shop."

Señora Pico had turned a dull brick red and her small eyes, so like her son's, glittered dangerously.

"My son does not frequent such places, señora. You must have him confused with some other gentleman."

"Ladies do not dance in cantinas in San Diego, señora," said Señora Canejo bitingly. Her thin wrinkled face had the look of a judicial adder.

"No?" said Tarifa. "But I have noticed that the sons of all the better families spend most of their time and money there—at least here in San Diego? I believ it is your son Macario who was there every night I danced? He was also at the Mission with Pio in the *monjeria* where I was held by the Padres, the day I had taken off most of my clothes because it was so hot. It was unfortunate that Padre Martin brought the young men in unexpectedly."

There was a gasp of horror from the women. They rose as one person and stood glaring at Ygnacio and his bride.

"This is infamous!" cried Señora Canejo.

"You dare to bring this—this person here into the decent society of San Diego, Don Ygnacio?" rasped another angry matron.

"She has done nothing but tell the truth, señora," replied Alvarjo stiffly.

"She has told lies about our sons—nothing but lies!"

"Ask them," Tarifa answered with a wicked grin.

Her harsh Gypsy laughter followed them as they stalked from the room, pausing in their retreat to speak behind their fans to other women as they passed.

"That was not very wise of you, my dear," said Ygnacio ruefully. "They will cause you nothing but trouble."

Tarifa shrugged. "Would it have helped if I had bowed down to them and made a rug of myself for them to wipe their feet on? They would not have liked me in any case; at least now they will not bother to cross swords with me so soon again. Let us go and dance and enjoy ourselves, Ygnacio?"

"You are right," he said with a laugh. It did not matter if they said Alvarjo's wife was not a lady; he was in love with her and he was proud of her. There was nothing they could do to humble a spirit like Tarifa's.

The music, the fine foods, the color and richness of the beautiful gowns and jewels delighted Tarifa. If the women were scant in their civilities, the men were certainly not. Her magnificent dancing, the whispered stories about her, had whetted their masculine appetites, made her a much sought-after partner.

Juan Bandini, the best dancer in the room, claimed her for a waltz, and together they moved with such intricacy and grace that gradually every other couple withdrew. Bandini, a small, slender gazelle of a man, came only slightly above Tarifa's head. His small feet in thin moroccan slippers moved as precisely as Tarifa's own, and she sensed his inner passion and abandon in the dance that she herself possessed.

They danced for half an hour and when they finished the delighted governor led the wild applause and came to claim her for the next waltz.

Echeandia danced well, but not with the same fire and spirit as Juan Bandini.

"Your husband is a most fortunate gentleman," he said, "to have such a dancer in the family. He tells me you came recently from Spain?"

"Yes, your Excellency."

"There are many beautiful things in Spain, but Mexico City is also beautiful. Have you ever been there?"

"No, your Excellency."

"I have some lovely paintings of it. You must come and see them sometime soon—with your husband."

"Thank you, your Excellency."

Echeandia would not allow them to depart that night but put them up in his spacious house. Though they did not see him at breakfast when they rose early to return to Loma de Oro, he had left a message for Don Ygnacio, asking him to call again with his charming wife.

"You have made a conquest of the governor at least, my dear," laughed Ygnacio. "Perhaps you will have no need of the good opinion of the ladies?"

"The governor will be more useful to me," said Tarifa with a calculation of which her husband did not quite approve.

"I have been thinking," she said slowly, "how nice it would be to travel north and visit all the other ports and pueblos."

Ygnacio shook his head.

"You would not find things the same in the north. Society is much more rigid there, *querida*. Be content with your conquest here."

"You think they would not permit me in their homes? Because of the wagging tongues of these old women in San Diego?"

"I am afraid so, my dear. Those women are related to almost every other family of class in California. That is why I warned you they could make trouble for you. And have you forgotten, Isabella herself is in Santa Barbara?"

"She will not allow her own nieces and nephews to be snubbed."

"But she will welcome it for you and for me," he sighed.

Tarifa hummed a little tune to herself, thinking of something the governor's secretary had said the night before when he danced with her: "We will be going north shortly; the governor is going to visit the northern pueblos—Santa Barbara, Monterey, perhaps even San José and San Francisco."

"Ygnacio," said Tarifa, "promise me that we will accept the governor's invitation to call again soon? He said that he had some paintings of Mexico to show me."

"Paintings?" said Ygnacio in surprise. "I didn't know you cared much for paintings."

"I would like to see these."

"Very well, my dear."

Don Julio rode all the way to Loma de Oro with them, though none of the Alvarjos was pleased at his presence. At the house, Don Ygnacio was forced to ask him inside for refreshment and, when he showed no disposition to leave in spite of the hour, he found it necessary to invite him to luncheon.

The young man attached himself to Dolores like a burr and paid her elaborate court which brought a blush of shame to her cheeks. She felt an actual physical nausea when he was near or when his hand accidentally brushed hers.

Tarifa recognized her antipathy for Marcos but did nothing to draw him away from her. Let her learn to handle her own men, she thought. It was time she stopped being a child.

"My mother has returned," Julio told Dolores as they walked in the patio. She had found that walking was far safer than sitting beside him and feeling his hands and legs press against hers. It alarmed her that there was no one else in the patio at the moment, but all the doors were open and her call would bring everyone running. Tía Isabella would never have allowed her to remain alone with a man like this, but her father never seemed to notice all the niceties, and Tarifa forgot, or chose to ignore them.

"Mother has asked to see you again," Julio went on. "She is lonely and ill, poor woman, and she so enjoyed your last visit, and that of your aunt. Did you know I saw her while I was in Santa Barbara recently?"

Dolores raised her eyes. "How is she, Don Julio?"

"Well but sad, I think, to be separated from her loved ones."

"It was her choice to leave us."

"Being a high-born lady, she could do little else."

Dolores flushed and Julio felt the blood race through his own veins. *Dios*, how beautiful she was!

"If you see my aunt again," Dolores said, "please tell her we are all well and send our love?"

"Of course, señorita. But tell me, will you come to see my mother soon?"

"If my stepmother agrees to come also," replied Dolores. She had no desire ever to visit his home again, though it was there Kinkaid had told her he loved her.

They were nearing the chapel and on impulse Julio said, "Would you go into the chapel with me and offer up an ave for my poor mother's health?"

It was said with such simplicity, compared to Julio's usual mode of speech, that she believed he was sincere. He seemed a devoted and dutiful son no matter what else he might be.

"Of course, Don Julio."

He took her arm to help her up the steps, and waited while she drew the white mantilla over her fair head.

Inside the chapel was cool and quiet, only the redly winking vigil lights on the altar gave a semblance of life to the thick-walled tomblike structure.

Julio crossed himself and knelt next to Dolores. He never knew afterward whether he started to pray or not; he only knew that a sudden madness seemed to overtake him at the knowledge of their privacy and of her nearness.

He put his arms about her as they knelt and turned her to him while his hoarse voice rattled out passionate words that made her face turn deadly pale.

"I love you, Dolores! I know I have no right to say it now, until I have spoken with your father, but I had to tell you! I have loved you for a long time. *Madre de Dios,* how I love you! I must have you; I must make you my wife. You shall have everything, everything you desire. Everyone in California shall look up to the wife of Don Julio Marcos."

Dolores, frightened half out of her wits, struggled with him in silence before the altar. But she might as well have struggled with a giant or a madman; his strength overcame hers like the relentless coils of a boa constrictor.

They stared into each other's eyes, his flaming with passion, hers glazed with fear, and his lips closed over hers in a fiery, devouring kiss.

Dolores never knew clearly what happened after that loathsome, disgusting kiss. One moment she was in his smothering embrace, the next she had been ruthlessly torn from his arms, and she could scarcely recognize her father's voice as he shouted hoarsely:

"Get out of my house! Never show your face here again or I will kill you! If you were not my guest at this moment, I would whip you off the rancho and drag you all the way to Bolsa Coyotes with my *reata*. Get out!"

Julio crouched, looking dumbly up at the old grandee with the chalk-white face, quivering with rage like an ancient eagle. But Julio was not a fool; he knew danger when he saw it, and he read the hatred and contempt in the other's eyes that told him all too plainly he was fortunate to leave the premises with his life.

He scuttled across the floor and out the door like a crab. He passed other members of the surprised family without bothering to make his farewells on his headlong flight to his horse.

CHAPTER 13

Governor Encheandia was not popular with Californians. And, in bypassing Monterey in favor of San Diego, he had added further fuel to the feud that had always existed between Monterey, San José, and San Francisco in the north; and Santa Barbara, Los Angeles, and San Diego in the south.

Indian attacks persisted in spite of the efforts of the Mazatlan cavalry he had brought with him, and the governor found the Missions hostile, despite the fact that in April the Padres had met with him and signed pledges of allegiance to Mexico.

The military found life not better but worse under Echeandia, who replaced the beloved Captain Ruiz, Commandante of San Diego presidio, with Captain José Estudillo.

In July Echeandia had issued an edict for the Missions to release all Indians qualified to become Mexican citizens in the San Diego and Santa Barbara area. He was completely baffled that only a few chose to leave the Missions despite their newly won freedom, and that all his edict accomplished was to make the natives who did leave restless and disorderly.

No money or supplies came from Mexico, and the plight of the people grew worse as Echeandia closed all ports to foreign trade, with the exceptions of Monterey and Loreto.

Smuggling became a necessity even among the best and most loyal citizens. And the governor's dislike for Californians increased as much as their displeasure with him.

Echeandia was peevishly signing the reports his secretary put before him one broiling August afternoon, when a servant announced Señora Alvarjo.

He was childishly pleased to escape the monotony of his work, and requested with enthusiasm that the Señora be shown in at once.

She was a delight to behold in her thin muslin gown of pale mauve, with a cream-colored mantilla over her ebony hair and high white comb. She wore long jade earrings and a jade necklace, and she seemed to breathe life into the exhausted governor as she stood in the doorway.

"My dear señora, I am delighted to see you!" He rushed to take her hand and lift it to his lips; she was as electric as lightning to the touch, and as graceful as a beautiful leopard as she took the seat he provided. "Where is Don Ygnacio? He is with you?"

"No, my husband was unable to come; he had business to attend to at the rancho," she said demurely.

"Ah, that is too bad." If his words were false, his tone was properly sympathetic.

After that, neither of them bothered to pretend that they regretted it, and Tarifa did not need to add what he already suspected, that she had come away quite without Don Ygnacio's knowledge.

Echeandia dismissed his secretary, and, when Zamorano had gone, led her to view a series of large oil paintings in thick gilt frames on the walls.

Tarifa pretended interest in views of gloomy cathedrals, flamboyant parks, sparkling lakes, and ancient Aztec ruins.

"People in California have so little culture," he complained. "Nothing that cannot be done on horseback amuses them. I am glad to see that you appreciate art, señora. Come, I would like to show you something else."

He led her to his desk and sifted through a pile of papers until he found what he wanted.

"Sit down here at my desk," he pulled out the carved rosewood chair for her, then placed a crude sketch before her.

"What is it, your Excellency?"

"It is my own design for a new state seal of the Californias!"

Tarifa recognized the figure of an Indian wearing a plume and carrying a bow and quiver, in the act of crossing a stream.

"You see," he explained eagerly, "I have suggested to Mexico that we change the name of the state to Montezuma instead of California. And here you see the proper symbol, the Indian crossing the strait, to remind the people that the first man to enter California came to find the Strait of Anian!"

"It is very well executed, your Excellency." She had no idea what he was talking about and very little conception of what a strait was. "And what does Mexico say of your clever suggestions?"

Echeandia's face reddened under his pale skin. "They refuse to accept them, but only because they are men of little perception or interest in what is not right under their noses."

"It is a very good idea nonetheless," comforted Tarifa, and seizing her opportunity asked, "When do you plan to pay a visit to the north, Governor? I had heard that you were going?"

He sighed. "There is nothing but trouble there. I have never seen such a place. Monterey is jealous because I have chosen to make my capital here in San Diego due to my delicate health, and they spread untrue stories about me from one end of the land to the other."

"Then your visit to the north should serve to end such rumors, your Excellency?" Tarifa said. "I have never been north, either; I would love to see Santa Barbara, Monterey, and San Francisco."

Echeandia brightened at her long glance of speculation. "Why should you not see them now also, Dona Tarifa? If you and your husband would care to join my entourage going north, it would make the trip much more enjoyable for me. Do you think Don Ygnacio would agree?"

Tarifa smiled up at him seductively and sweat broke out on his temple. He wiped it daintily with a white silk kerchief. What a little vixen she was, but how enchanting, despite the local rumors of her lurid past. It would be exciting to have her along, and how he would enjoy forcing her upon the best families of the north, with their stiff-necked pride and their open dislike for him.

"I will ask my husband," said Tarifa, getting up from her chair. "Perhaps it can be arranged. You have been most kind, your Excellency."

Again he raised her hand to his lips and this time they exchanged a frank glance of mutual respect.

"I shall send a note to Don Ygnacio as soon as I know the date of my departure, señora."

Don Ygnacio felt uneasy as he dressed for dinner in the home of his old friend Diego Novato, in Santa Barbara, where the governor and his party were quartered. Against his better judgment, Ygnacio had allowed his wife to persuade him to come on this journey to the north. They had left by ship from San Diego a few days before and only arrived in Santa Barbara that afternoon.

Ygnacio put on his black velvet jacket with the silver lace on sleeves and lapels, and glanced at Tarifa in her white satin gown, beginning to put up her hair. She wore pearls at ears, throat, and wrists, and a high mother-of-pearl comb lay on the dresser before her. She had never looked lovelier, more hotly vivacious, and his heart contracted at the reception he knew she would get this evening from the *haut monde* of sedate, prim Santa Barbara.

"You are not ready yet, *querida*," he told her, "I think I will smoke a *cigarrillo* in the patio."

"Yes, go ahead, *kushto*. I will be out when I am dressed."

To Ygnacio the Novato patio, deserted for the moment, was a haven of quiet peace before the storm. A fountain splashed languidly in the center and a riot of fragrant flowers bloomed along the edges. He sank down on a bench and allowed the silence to envelope him. He had found out from Novato that Isabella was staying with the Corlona family and that they had all refused his invitation to attend the banquet Novato had felt obliged to give for the governor.

The Novatos were an old and honored family in the southland, and Diego's family tree was as aristocratic as Ygnacio Alvarjo's. Ygnacio knew the rumors concerning Tarifa must have preceded them weeks before and yet Diego had given no inkling of it as he greeted his guests warmly with old-world courtesy. A majestic figure, tall

and erect even in his seventies, with a full beard and
snowy white hair, he lived alone in his spacious hacienda
near the beautiful Mission Santa Barbara now that he
was a widower and his numerous children were married
and scattered all over California.

While Ygnacio was sitting there his host came into the
patio from another wing of the big, square one-story adobe.

Like Ygnacio, he wore discreet black velvet with a
white sash and held a brown *cigarrillo* between his fingers.
They had been friends for many years and had served together once at San Diego.

Novato sat down beside his friend and shook his white
head.

"This will be a night to remember in the *casa,* Novato,
amigo mío."

"You think no one will come?"

Novato raised his thick brows.

"No, they will come, all right, all but the most stiff-
necked ones will not dare to openly defy the governor.
That is the beauty of it. Everyone who comes will have
to issue the governor and his party an invitation to their
homes in return. And your little wife was clever enough
to think of that? She will see the gossips hoist by their
own petard? She is a clever one, Ygnacio."

Ygnacio looked startled. It had not occurred to him
that Tarifa had had any other motive than to bask in the
governor's reflected glory and to enjoy the sights. That the
whole thing might have been a deliberate plot seemed
absurd, and yet as he considered Novato's words, he realized it was true. He felt doubly embarrassed in front of
his smiling friend and host.

"You have married a clever woman, Ygnacio," said
Novato, with a smile. "She will not bend to the will of
California society; she will bend California to hers."

"But she's little more than a child," said Ygnacio. "They
have said cruel things about her and she wants to strike
back. Once she has had her revenge, she will forget all
about it. She will be off on another tangent."

"Ygnacio," his friend said kindly, "I am older than
you, and I am not smitten by her, although I admit her
charms are powerful, so perhaps I can judge her more
dispassionately? You have not married just a beautiful

woman, you have married a houri. She will lead you a merry dance, but it will not be dull. And you do not have to be afraid for her—be afraid for those who cross her."

Don Diego Novato's prediction had been correct. Only a few of those who had received invitations to the banquet in the governor's honor failed to appear, or on leaving failed to extend an invitation to the governor and his party to visit their homes.

Often the invitation was given with chilly reserve and these both the governor and Tarifa, like twin conspirators, made a mental note of.

For Tarifa the long banquet was a dull, stodgy affair, followed by an equally dull recital by a stringed quartet who played classical music in the square thick-walled *sala*. There was no dancing, and few young people made their appearance. Everyone left as swiftly and discreetly as it was polite to do.

Don Diego chuckled over a final glass of brandy in his study with Ygnacio, after the others had retired.

"You see, *amigo,* it went as I said it would? And your little wife was completely bored but triumphant. They cannot dare snub her to her face now when she pays those return calls with the governor, as she fully intends to."

"I shall not permit it!" said Ygnacio hotly. "She shall not make a spectacle of herself, nor add to the embarrassment of anyone in Santa Barbara."

"Oh, you must not stop her, Ygnacio. I have a feeling it will be good for some of them. Charity is an odd and rare thing, *amigo.* So few of us show any real charity in our lives. It is the most difficult of all virtues to practice, because true charity means giving away a piece of ourselves, which is contrary to nature. And how often we pass by the chance to make use of it?

"It was not necessary for those women in San Diego to behave as they did. A little understanding, a little charity for a poor ignorant little waif brought to our shores, and none of this need have happened."

"You are right, Diego. Tarifa was uneducated when she came, but since then she has learned a great deal. Padre Cazon himself taught her to read and write. She has used my library, and both my daughters and I have instructed her in proper deportment."

Diego put a hand on his friend's shoulder.

"Ygnacio, suppose she has been clever as street urchins often are, and absorbed a veneer of knowledge and culture? A leopard does not change its spots just because it appears docile when caged. I tell you this, whatever is her destiny you will be powerless to alter it, even if she loves you. And perhaps that is just as well? She is strong, Ygnacio, and California is in need of strength and purpose in her people. I see bad times ahead for us all. And Mexico has proven she will be no help. Regard Echeandia, such a popinjay sent to rule us!"

"You sound like Zenobio Sanchez," Alvarjo said irritably. Were all his old friends losing their reason in their dotage? He was as impatient with Novato as he had been angered at Zenobio's gloomy predictions.

"Don Zenobio is a man of perception," Novato said.

"He is a presumptuous old fool! He thinks our only hope lies in more trade with the Americanos."

"That is also my outlook, Ygnacio."

Alvarjo stared at him in astonishment.

"You would allow more and more of them into our country to settle and marry our women? Eventually they would take over the entire territory."

"We have had no such experience with them here in in Santa Barbara. They have traded fairly with us, and those who have been naturalized and married have remained loyal citizens. And good Catholics, I might add."

"They are pushing and greedy. You make a mistake to trust them too far, Diego," Ygnacio said sharply.

Novato sighed and put down his glass.

"It grows late, Ygnacio, and we are two old and weary men. Let us argue this another time, *amigo?*"

Ygnacio found his wife still awake, seated before the dressing-table mirror wearing a thin white dressing gown. He closed the door quickly and went to stand behind her, putting his hands on her shoulders. With her cloud of curling jet-black hair loose around her small pointed face, she looked more like the child he had first seen at Mission San Diego.

"My dear, I would like you to tell me something, very truthfully."

Her long Gypsy eyes regarded him levelly in the mirror.

"What is it, Ygnacio?"

"Why did you insist on coming on this trip?"

Her eyes widened in surprise.

"To see the rest of the country, of course."

"But you and I could have journeyed here by ourselves. Why did you insist on coming in the governor's party? Was it because you knew society would not be able to refuse you if you came under the governor's protection?"

"And if I did, what harm is there in that?"

"It was not an honorable thing to do," he said gently. "You are an Alvarjo now. You must learn to protect your good name. I do not wish you to visit these people if it is against their wills."

"It is to protect our good name that I came here!" she said passionately. "Would you rather I took their insults and slunk off in a corner, never able again to raise my head? I am going with the governor to visit them, and they are going to receive me politely whether they like it or not!"

"Tarifa, Tarifa, my little love, I do not like to see you like this." He pressed her head back against him. "I can only tell you when you are wrong, but if you refuse to listen—"

She moved free of him and got out of the chair, coming to put her arms around him.

"*Kushto,* I cannot hurt you whatever happens. But tell me, if I go alone without the governor, would it be wrong?"

He was surprised and again fearful for her. "But they will snub you, my dearest."

"Would it be wrong for me to go?"

"No—but you cannot think of it."

"I am not afraid of them. I want them to know that, Ygnacio. It is important that they know it—for all our sakes."

Alvarjo knew raw courage when he saw it. He drew her closer to him and buried his face in her fragrant hair. He was constantly amazed at how much wiser and braver she was in some things than he was. She was right. Santa Barbara society might hate her effrontery—for that is what they would call it—but they would be unable to help admiring her courage in coming alone and unprotected by the

governor, to beard them in their own dens. If she was
animallike and savage in many of her approaches to life,
was she not also as straightforward and basic in her drives
as Nature itself?

That night as they lay in bed, Ygnacio loved her as passionately as if it had been their wedding night, or his first
wedding night with Encarnacion so many years ago.

The next afternoon while the governor attended a horse
race and a bearbaiting on the edge of town, Tarifa ordered
the Novato carriage for herself and her two stepdaughters.
She dressed in her most sedate dark gown with no jewelry,
and put a black *rebozo* over her head and shoulders. Both
of the girls wore white and looked as fresh and demure as
young nuns.

The carriage stopped first at the oak-shaded adobe of the
Alvisos. An Indian servant girl showed them into a small
anteroom with nothing in it but a long sofa, a table, and
a stand containing potted flowers and vines. She disappeared down the short, thick-walled entry that led toward
the patio.

Tarifa and the girls sat stiffly on the sofa and the female
voices from the nearby patio came embarrassingly clear to
them all.

"They are here, Rosita? You have shown them in?"

"*Sí*, señora." Spoken with a quaver.

An older feminine voice asked, "How was the poor girl
to know, Carlotta?"

"But, Madre, here in our own house? You say the governor is not with her?"

"No, señora. Only the two young señoritas."

"Ah. I am sorry for the two girls, Madre, but I cannot
receive them—or her. The woman's vast nerve in coming
here!"

The older voice said, "Did you not invite her?"

"No! Naturally José and I asked the governor to call
at his convenience during his stay. The members of his
party were included in a general way. But we only did
what was proper—what everyone else did. Now for her to
come here alone, brazenly like this?"

The older voice chuckled. "She has nerve and courage,
niña, like we used to have in my youth. There is no real
daring among you young people anymore. I am curious to

see her. I never saw a Gypsy before. Is she anything like an Indian, Carlotta?"

"Madre! I cannot invite such a creature publicly into my home."

"You have already, my dear daughter. Last night at the governor's ball. And now she is here. What would be more disgraceful, to permit her to stay a few quiet minutes in our patio, or to have her thrown publicly into the streets from the Casa Alviso for all Santa Barbara to see?"

"Madre!"

"You cannot have it both ways, Carlotta. If you receive her she will shortly go her way satisfied."

"But the scandal—I could never live it down that I had received her, and that the others had not!"

"How do you know they will not? You are undoubtedly the first she has called upon, at this early hour. It is in your hands to set the precedent. The others will follow suit. Do we want another public tongue-lashing like they claim she gave poor Señora Pico and Señora Canejo in San Diego? Those women should never have given her an excuse to quarrel openly with them. Let the governor see that we know better how to smooth over such trying matters."

Dolores touched her stepmother's hand timidly. "Do let us leave before they come? This is dreadful!"

Tarifa sat without moving a muscle, only her eyes seemed to smolder like hot coals. She looked as poised and deadly as a cobra.

"We will wait," she said flatly.

The servant returned and asked them to follow her to the patio.

Soledad and Dolores rose more slowly at Tarifa's commanding nod, but Tarifa marched smartly down the entry and into the warm fragrant patio, head up like a stalking lioness.

The two women seated in chairs on the veranda overlooking the patio looked much alike, one a younger edition of the other. Tarifa remembered Dona Carlotta, the wife of José Alviso, from the reception. A short plump woman with strong features and white teeth, her deep black hair drawn low to cover her ears, and the narrow black silk headband with a jeweled star in front, affected by most well-bred Barbareno women.

The older woman was heavier, with gray hair, but her

deep brown eyes had the same contained intelligence and confidence as her daughter's. Both wore dark muslim gowns and fine white-lace shawls.

"*Buenos días,* Señora Alvarjo," Carlotta Alviso said politely. "Welcome to my home. May I present my mother, Señora Galvez? The Señora Alvarjo, and her stepdaughters, Señoritas Dolores and Soledad, *madrecita.*"

The old woman acknowledged the introductions with a regal nod and waited, gazing curiously at Tarifa as she sat relaxed but erect on a straight wooden chair.

"Are you enjoying your trip north?" Señora Galvez asked abruptly, while her daughter poured chocolate from a silver pot and handed cups and small cakes around.

"Yes, señora," replied Tarifa. "I am learning a great deal."

"Ah. One never travels without learning something, Señora Alvarjo. When I was a bride my husband and I traveled across the Colorado River to come to California. I have always regretted that my children never had such an experience. One learns self-reliance, adaptability. I think the young ones today are too protected. Don't you agree, Señora Alvarjo?"

"Mother," Carlotta flushed. "I am sure Señora Alvarjo and the Señoritas are too young to have an opinion on such matters." She was furious that these people were in her house, angry at her mother for having talked her into receiving them, and only anxious that they leave at the first possible moment.

But Tarifa had no intention of cutting her visit short or of avoiding any of the old woman's deliberate thrusts. She disarmed them with truth. "Dona Carlotta is quite right. I am no judge of such things. I went into the streets of Seville as a Gypsy child, and I knew no protection of any sort until I married Don Ygnacio."

Carlotta Alviso's face flamed. Then, incredibly, she heard her mother ask with frank curiosity, "And how do you find your life now, señora? Is it to your liking?"

"Señora Galvez, would you ask a kicked cur if he approved a master who had picked him up and treated him with gentle care and loving kindness?"

The proud old woman stared back at the unflinching young one, and she found neither condescension nor insolence in the long Gypsy eyes. Merely a natural dignity without pretense. She said quietly and with sincerity, "Don Ygnacio Alvarjo has always been noted for his courtesy and his honor. I am glad to see that you appreciate him."

Carlotta was scandalized at the turn the conversation had taken. Her mother must be bereft of her senses, but she herself tried valiantly to speak in a normal manner with the two Alvarjo daughters while her mother questioned Tarifa more closely about the life of a Gypsy, as if she were genuinely interested in the wicked little harlot. For the girl could be nothing else, even if Alvarjo had married her.

When Tarifa rose at last to leave, old Señora Galvez insisted on walking to the door with her and stood where every passerby could see her speaking to Tarifa.

"When you are in Santa Barbara again, my child," she said, "come and see me?"

"With pleasure, señora. And if you journey south you must be our guest at Loma de Oro?"

"Very prettily said." Señora Galvez laughed, while her daughter stood helplessly by congealed with ill-concealed horror.

"You learn quickly, child," said Señora Galvez patting Tarifa's hand. "Continue to do so. You remind me of one of the old conquistadores my father used to tell about. His men hated him thoroughly, but he drove them to victory in spite of themselves."

In the carriage Dolores said, "I never would have believed it. Old Señora Galvez liked you, Tarifa, and she is a dragon in Santa Barbara society!"

Tarifa's smile was thin but satisfied. "As I told your father, it is not important to me whether they like me or not—most of them, like Dona Carlotta, never will, but I am determined that the Alvarjos shall be received everywhere, in spite of me."

"You are brave, Tarifa," said Soledad with a grin. "I would never have dared face them as you did."

"What is bravery, Soledad? Everyone has their own kind of courage. Even a mouse will fight when he is cornered."

"But you are never afraid of anything," marveled Soledad. "I wish I could be like you."

Tarifa said nothing, but she remembered her fear of

Joaquin on board ship, and her later wild terror in the
cabaña the night Santiago had nearly killed her. Fear was
like a live thing. Having known it once you never quite
forgot it. And you recognized its face forever afterward
in no matter what guise it accosted you.

From the moment their ship rounded Point Pinos and
entered the wide entrance of the beautiful bay at Monterey,
Tarifa was enchanted with the place. She was struck with
the well-wooded headlands, the succession of green-clad
gently rolling foothills and valleys stretching parklike to
the water's edge, free of underbrush and dotted with oak
trees. The ship came to anchor between two large brigs,
one bearing the Union Jack, the other the American flag
anchored only two cable lengths from shore.

The town lay directly in front of them, the red-tiled
roofs of the numerous buildings contrasting prettily with
the white plastered walls and green lawns upon which each
one was set.

The most conspicuous building, a spacious square one
near the landing, Ygnacio told her, was the Custom House.

From the presidio, the Mexican flag floated in the clear
morning air and across the water they could hear the
drums and trumpets of the soldiers coming to order in
the square to receive the governor. Beyond the presidio,
a short distance from the barracks, nestled the Mission San
Carlos, founded on the Carmel by Padre Junipero Serra,
where he now lay buried.

"We must go and say a prayer there," Ygnacio told his
wife and daughters.

The officers and officials who came aboard to welcome
Echeandia were more sedately and better dressed in their
dark blue or black broadcloth cloaks with black velvet
collars and their dark sombreros than the *gente de razón*
of the south. They were also chilly in their reception of
the new governor, who had chosen to ignore the time-
honored capital of California in favor of that mud-heap,
San Diego.

Nevertheless certain formalities had to be observed, cannons boomed from the presidio and the townspeople
flocked to the beach to watch the soldiers line up to present arms to the governor.

Tarifa and the girls were delighted with the dragoons' short round jackets of blue cloth with the scarlet cuffs and collars, blue velvet breeches open at the knee to show the white stockings, wide red sash, and embroidered deerskin leggings. The officers looked resplendent at this distance with their gold lace-trimmed jackets and wide gold epaulets. It was not until the little party came closer that the shabby patches and darns on their uniforms were woefully apparent.

But in spite of the general poverty, Monterey, Tarifa knew, was the center of California culture. She had discussed it thoroughly with the governor.

Monterey, alone of the pueblos, maintained a rigid caste system. Here were both the Customs House and the Treasury, and here ships of all nations were received and made their declaration of cargo. Monterey set the styles and surpassed all the other ports and pueblos in public functions. Monterey supported a school for the "better classes," and tolerated the rowdy element of the waterfront with its cockfights, gambling, wine shops, and public fandangos.

Gentlewomen were seldom seen on the streets except on the way to Mass, and here they went attended by servants carrying their embroidered kneeling mats, and wearing the plainest of dark clothes wrapped in their unrevealing black *rebozos* like women in purdah.

After their official welcome, the governor's party was taken to quarters in the presidio while Echeandia himself, with his secretary, was quartered in what Monterey felt should have been the gubernatorial residence nearby.

Don Ygnacio, however, received an invitation from his friend Pedro Lopez, a ranchero who preferred to leave the running of his rancho to his mayordomo, like Don Julio Marcos, and live in town.

"*Amigo,* I have a large house and staff. You must bring your family and come and stay with me," he said cordially. A small, fat man with round brown eyes and bushy sideburns that gave him the look of an inquisitive gopher, he added with a sly wink, "My wife and children reside at the rancho; it makes a nice arrangement when I have business in the pueblo."

"And that is nearly all year?" asked Ygnacio.

Lopez chuckled. "Why not? The rancho is a very dull

place except for rodeos and bear hunts. It is for raising children and cattle, eh? But you do not agree with me; you have always preferred the pastoral life. No matter, perhaps we are both right—or wrong. Who can say? Come and stay with me. I can make you more comfortable than this drafty presidio that is going to fall down about their ears if they don't get some funds from Mexico. Did the new governor bring anything with him besides his dandified self?"

When Alvarjo told him that Echeandia had helped the San Diego presidio as little as he was about to help this one, Lopez threw up his hands.

"It is as I thought. If the new Financial Agent, Herrera, brought anything with him to enrich the treasury with, he is sitting on it like a hen on an infertile egg. And there is as much chance of its doing us any good."

Pedro Lopez lived near the center of town in a comfortable square, one-story house, tastefully furnished with imported furniture, but bearing the marks of his pseudo-bachelorhood. He assigned the Alvarjos pleasant rooms off the patio court and sent servants to help them unpack.

After a well-cooked dinner of fresh salmon, wild ducks, rice and tomatoes, and a rich dessert of honey cake, Lopez proudly showed the women the new pianoforte in the *sala*, just purchased from one of the brigs in the harbor at a tremendous cost in hides and tallow.

"I will have it carried to the rancho," he said, "and my daughters shall learn to play. You should have one, too, Ygnacio. There is another aboard the trader."

"Yes!" cried Tarifa, looking at her husband. "We must have one, Ygnacio?"

"It is a great deal to pay for an instrument, my dear."

"I know, but how many other families in California can boast of such a thing in their parlor?"

Dolores and Soledad added their plea to Tarifa's, and Ygnacio bowed his head in agreement simply to halt the entreaties.

He was greatly troubled at his friend's attitude which seemed to him unwise and dangerous in the extreme.

"Pedro," he said when the women had left them, "it is easy to say rule ourselves, but how? The north and south even now bicker over which shall contain the official capital. Would you see civil strife split them completely? And how are we to protect ourselves from the watchful greedy foreigners who ply our coastlines or come overland from the Colorado? Half the guns in your own presidio are spiked as they are in San Diego. The soldiers have no clothes, food, or pay, let alone powder and shot. We have no ships to protect our shoreline. What then do we do— rope the invaders with our *reata largas* and drag them behind our *caballos?*"

Lopez looked sullen and unconvinced. "There are those who would help us," he said. "The northern provinces of Mexico have offered us an alliance."

"And how much can they help? They are as impoverished as we are."

A servant appeared on the veranda, and Lopez called, "What is it, Gervasio?"

"An Americano, Patrón. The capitán."

"*Bueno.* Show him out here."

"*Sí,* Patrón."

"Another American sea capitán?" growled Alvarjo. "I have no liking for them."

"This is the one from whom I purchased my pianoforte, *amigo.* He is a friend of Señor Ortegas."

Alvarjo said nothing, for the Ortegas were known to engage in smuggling from their isolated rancho, El Refugio, conveniently situated on the coastline south of Monterey.

Captain Judah's tall figure seemed to overshadow the two Californians as he strode into the patio. His shrewd eyes took in the aristocratic bearing and expensive if decorous clothes of Alvarjo. Here was a much richer pigeon to pluck than the fat, toadlike Lopez.

"I am happy to make your acquaintance, Señor Alvarjo," Judah said when Lopez had introduced them.

"*Buenos días,* Capitán."

"Don Ygnacio and his family came north from San Diego with Governor Echeandia's party," said Lopez.

"I am a great admirer of San Diego," said Judah, accepting wine from the tray Gervasio had brought out to them. "It was my first port of call on the California coast. At the time I did not know it was necessary to report first at Monterey. And now that the governor has closed all ports but Monterey to foreign trade, it is devilishly hard for us."

"Don Ygnacio's wife and daughters are much taken with my pianoforte, Capitán," Lopez said. "They would like to purchase one like it though they will have a weary time getting it to San Diego by *carreta* or muleback."

Judah said quickly, "I carried two pianofortes from Norfolk. You must allow me to make a present of the remaining one to you, Senor Alvarjo."

Ygnacio was startled and annoyed. These infernal Yankees thought they could buy or bribe their way anywhere.

"I could not accept such an expensive gift, Capitán," he said coldly. "If my wife decides to have one she will purchase it in the usual way, and at the price Don Pedro paid—unless the remaining one is more expensive?"

Judah was angry without exactly knowing why. He would like to have flogged the insolent old devil with a cat-o'-nine-tails, but his own smile was as firm and cordial as if he had received a compliment instead of a slap across the face.

"The price will be the same, Don Ygnacio. And I will be glad to show you and your lady over my ship. I carry a good mixed cargo, as I'm sure Señor Lopez can tell you?"

"The best of its kind I have seen, Ygnacio. Guillermo Hartnell himself has brought in nothing finer."

Alvarjo had no desire for his wife and daughters to meet this man, and he was greatly relieved when Lopez excused himself to accompany Judah to the pueblo on a business matter.

It saddened Ygnacio to discover one of his friends had been won over by the breezy open-handed Americanos and refused to recognize the danger of the situation.

The following afternoon, while Don Ygnacio and Dolores visited the Mission, Tarifa went with Soledad and Pedro Lopez aboard the American ship *Vulcan* in the harbor, and though Tarifa saw the name on her prow under a gilt figurehead of a pouting woman it meant nothing to her. The long-faced mate received them on board and took them to the storeroom where the supercargo showed them the delightful wares in the drawers, shelves, and glassed-in showcases.

"But we have come to see the pianoforte," said Tarifa, "like the one Señor Lopez bought from you."

"Certainly, señora, this way." The supercargo whisked a canvas cover off a square object in a corner and the women exclaimed at its gleaming mahogany beauty and black and white ivory keys. It was identical to Senor Lopez's save for two gilt candle brackets fastened on either side of the music rack.

"How much is it?" Tarifa asked, although she already knew and Ygnacio had told her to think it over carefully before she made the purchase. It was a great deal of money.

"A thousand hides, señora."

Soledad gasped. Even her mother had never spent so much on a single item.

"It is a very high price." Tarifa frowned, running a finger over the gleaming wood.

"You are correct, Señora Alvarjo," said a voice behind her.

Tarifa turned in her correct dark clothes and mantilla, and came face-to-face with Titus Judah.

He was as startled as she was. Here was the little Gypsy from the San Diego cantina washed and curried like a prize horse, and married to the sedate old grandee he had crossed swords with at Pedro Lopez's.

"Capitán Judah!"

"The same—señora." His bow was derisive but correct. "It would seem that your fortunes have improved? My congratulations."

Tarifa eyed him levelly. His red brows slanting over his cat's eyes made her think of a watchful cougar she had once seen crouching on a tree branch in the *arroyo seco*.

"Would you care to come to my cabin to discuss terms, señora? I understand you want the pianoforte?"

He thinks I'm afraid, Tarifa reasoned; it is better to have this out once and for all. A challenge could only be met with a challenge; to retreat always invited disaster.

"Yes, Capitán. I shall be most happy to discuss terms with you."

"This way, señora." Judah turned to the supercargo. "Show the Señorita and Señor Lopez the shawls we brought from Manila, Morse."

"Aye, Captain."

Judah's cabin was larger and more luxuriously appointed than Kinkaid's. A young Negro boy was polishing the copper and brass lamps as they entered.

"Get out, Noah," Judah ordered, and the boy scampered away like a frightened puppy.

Judah gave Tarifa a chair and poured wine from a silver cruet on the carved mahogany sideboard.

"Tell me, how did it happen?"

"What?"

"Your fortunate—alliance. Or is it really marriage?"

Tarifa glared at him. "We were married at Mission San Luis Rey by Padre Peyri."

Judah's brows rose and he lifted his glass.

"Then I do most heartily congratulate you, Tarifa."

"My name is Señora Alvarjo."

"Of course. And you want my pianoforte?"

"Yes. But the price is high."

"The merchandise is rare, señora. A good many in California would gladly pay the price if they knew about it."

"But," said Tarifa shortly, "you cannot show your wares anywhere but here—or in Loreto."

"Legally. But there are ways of getting around such stupid and uncomfortable laws."

"You take a great risk, Capitán. Did you know the governor has ordered the ship and cargo of a certain capitán who landed goods at Refugio held in San Diego?"

Judah looked thoughtful. She had come with the governor's party, she undoubtedly knew the truth of what she said, and under no circumstances could he afford to have his ship or cargo seized.

"Señora, I offered to give your husband the pianoforte, but he refused unless it was paid for in the full amount of Señor Lopez's purchase."

"That is right."

"But what you pay can remain a secret between the two of us?" He flashed her a knowing smile. "You and I are both people who know what we want, and what we are willing to pay for it."

"What are you trying to say, Capitán Judah?"

"There are some things more important to me than mere profit, señora."

"You want something other than the thousand hides?"

"Goodwill, señora. Something more precious than money. Something you cannot buy even from these hard-pressed, stiff-necked hacendados. California is not through trading, she has just begun. When this ridiculous embargo is lifted trade will flourish. But only the men who have trade agreements, like Hartnell, Begg & Company, or the Endecotts, will really grow rich."

"So it is profit you want, after all?"

"In the long run—not now. I want a trade agreement with enough Missions and rancheros to ensure my future. In the meantime, it will take time to build up the fleet of ships I need."

"And you want me to help you for a pianoforte? I have not forgotten San Diego, Capitán. If it had not been for Capitán Kinkaid—"

He flushed. "I apologize to you for my actions that night. I had been drinking. You maddened me with your damnable dancing. Be fair. I cannot be the first it has driven out of his head. Is it not a compliment in a way?"

Tarifa smiled languorously, enjoying his discomfort, his pleading.

"Why should I help you?"

He came to stand beside her chair, but she knew she was safe. He had something more powerful on his mind now than her body.

"Because you are as ambitious as I am. And California cannot exist forever on only her hides and tallow."

Tarifa's eyes widened. "Why not? I see no sign of the trade falling off. In fact it increases each year."

"Perhaps, but a bad drought plays havoc with it, and if, as they speak of doing, they secularize the Missions, the Indians will leave and the stock will die off for want of care. I give them at most five years after the fall of the Missions."

"That will not happen!" said Tarifa angrily. "The Missions will not fall, no matter what Mexico orders."

He sighed. "I have just come from Loreto. The California Missions have served their purpose as far as Mexico is concerned. The Pious Fund that is supposed to support them is too big to be administered honestly by a government in need of money. Even Spain filched from it to finance her wars with Portugal and England, and now that Mexico has the chance she is following suit. Already they have sold whole estates, pocketing the price, and farmed out other valuable holdings for the benefit of the state treasury."

"So that is why the Padres here can collect nothing, even on their presidio drafts? Padre Cazon mentioned it."

"They will never collect the money for goods given the presidios. That is another reason why secularization is inevitable. The amount owed the Missions now is so high it could never be repaid."

Tarifa was suddenly concerned, not for the Missions, but for Loma de Oro. "But secularization will not affect the ranchos," she said.

Judah finished his wine and put the glass on a silver tray on his desk.

"The Missions are the backbone of California economy, señora. When they fall they will sooner or later take everything else with them. Secularization will free most of the Indian peons, will it not? And if the Indians can leave the jurisdiction of the Missions, what is to stop them from leaving their employers as well? Who will work your great ranchos for you then? Cheap, plentiful labor has made you prosperous here just as it has the plantation owners in the southern United States. There a man buys his slaves and owns them, but are not your Indians indentured slaves?"

Tarifa frowned. She knew little about slavery except that her father was said to have been a handler of slaves, and therefore she could see nothing wrong in it.

"But our vaqueros and servants will not leave Loma de Oro," she said quickly. "They are devoted to Don Ygnacio and the rancho."

"Have you any idea what the notion of freedom can do to a slave? It drives them berserk, wipes every other thought from their minds. I have seen slaves revolt, and wallow in their newly won if temporary freedom for months on end while the land writhed in utter chaos. When they are captured again, or come to their senses, it is usually too late to recover from the destruction they have wrought."

"It will not happen here!"

"Those are the last words of a great many ex-patriots."

"I don't understand you," she said impatiently. "You talk in riddles. It's time I left."

"Wait! I'm trying to tell you that no matter what happens you can save your rancho if you want to."

She sat back in her chair and waited, watching his face narrowly. If he was tricking her he would find he had picked the wrong person. But if there was truth in what he said she would listen, for next to Ygnacio, Loma de Oro was the only thing that mattered to her. Like her love for Guindilla when Ygnacio had given him to her, at first her affection and pride had been in ownership alone, but had grown and taken roots as deep as her soul.

"Tell me what you mean," she said.

He dropped into a chair across from her and spoke earnestly. She had respect for the clever way his mind worked if she had none for him as a man.

"When secularization comes you will need two things. Men to work your stock and a steady market for your wares. I can guarantee you both."

"How?"

"Sign a contract giving me exclusive trade rights with your rancho, delivery to be made at San Diego. Get me contracts with as many ranchos in your area as you can, and I will agree to keep you supplied with labor."

"With these black boys and brown-skinned ones you have on board? What would they know about working cattle?"

Judah shook his head. "I can bring you help from Mexico, experienced riders. I have connections with those who wish to settle in California—secretly, let us say."

"Convicts," Tarifa said with scorn. "I have heard of the plan to foist ex-criminals on California to make it a clearing ground for undesirables."

"Undesirables?" Judah smiled thinly. "They will come whether you use them or not. But I can guarantee you a labor supply that may make the difference between success and failure."

Tarifa stood up but her face was thoughtful. "I will think over what you have said, Capitán. Don Ygnacio will have to decide; he controls Loma de Oro."

"But you can put in a word for me with your neighbors?"

"Perhaps. I will see. I can do nothing about it at the moment."

"May I call upon you the next time I am in San Diego?"

"You may send a message."

"Very well." He stood also, towering over her, the sunlight glinting on his red hair. "I will send the pianoforte to you within the month."

"It has not been paid for yet. I will arrange with the supercargo."

"I make all such arrangements here, señora." His eyes held hers, unwinking as a cat's.

"A thousand hides you said?"

"One dance."

"What?"

"Worth a thousand hides, if you are not afraid to do it."

"You want me to dance for you—here?"

"Not here, at the governor's ball tonight. The dance you did at the cantina that night. I would like to see all their smug faces when you have finished. If you are not afraid?"

They gazed at each other for a moment and suddenly both of them smiled, a wicked conspiratorial smile.

"Be at the ball, Capitán Judah," Tarifa said, and released her hand before he could raise it to his lips.

Ygnacio was unable to attend the governor's ball. Something he had eaten at luncheon at the Mission had disagreed with him and he lay on his bed at Pedro Lopez's in acute discomfort. Tarifa wracked her brain to think of what herbs Penti would have used for such an affliction, but could remember nothing. In the end she accepted Lopez's remedy, a mug of hot brandy with peppermint and clove.

Ygnacio dutifully drank the concoction his wife brought him but was too ill to take anything else. He insisted over her protests that she attend the ball for both of them, escorted by Pedro Lopez.

When both Soledad and Dolores insisted that she go and agreed to stay with their father, Tarifa dressed herself for the ball.

As she came in to kiss him good-night, Ygnacio thought that he had never seen her so dazzlingly vivacious, so like a haughty young Egyptian queen. He had never seen this gown before, and it seemed a bit brilliant even for so young a matron, but it became her well and set off her wild dusky beauty and passionate clear-cut Romany face, reflecting color in her high cheekbones and curved lips. The gown, of cerise silk, glittered with embroidery and a myriad of brilliants. She wore a necklace of gold links and large gold hoops in her ears, and many thin gold bracelets upon each arm. She wore no comb in her hair but had left it to fall loosely to her shoulders about her face. It gave her a younger, a more seductive look, that her husband was not sure he approved of, but when she kissed him sweetly and assured him that she would much rather stay with him he told her firmly, "No, my dearest, you must go to represent the family. Soledad and Dolores will be with me."

The largest room in the presidio had been cleared and decorated for the ball with crimson, green, and yellow streamers. When Tarifa arrived on Don Pedro's arm, the dancing had already begun and the room presented a kaleidoscope of brilliant color as everyone of quality in Monterey, elegantly dressed, moved and whirled in rhythm to the band.

Tarifa and Don Pedro paid their respects to the governor and she explained Ygnacio's absence, noting the flicker of excitement in Echeandia's eyes as he looked at her opulent low-cut gown. Later when he claimed her for a waltz he said, "We must dance again, after I have done my duty by all the other ladies present. Will you have a little midnight supper with me, at the governor's house across the square?"

"It would not be proper, your Excellency. My husband is not here. And I must leave early."

Echeandia frowned. "He could not object to your having supper with me. If you like I will ask that fat fool Lopez also."

Tarifa glanced up at him. "If you still want me to, after the ball is over, your Excellency, Señor Lopez and I will be glad to accept."

Echeandia beamed at his easy victory. His hand was moist through the fabric of her dress as he released her from the dance.

On Pedro Lopez's arm, Tarifa met the leading citizens of Monterey and found them more sophisticated and more remote than those of San Diego or Santa Barbara, like emotionless wax figures. But slowly she began to put names to the faces present. Old Don Dolores Pico, grantee of the Balsa de San Cayetano rancho, who told her he was an uncle of Pio Pico's and an old friend of her husband. He said nothing of her quarrel with his sister-in-law at San Diego, but gallantly danced with her and released her with a courtly old-fashioned bow.

The names, though Tarifa did not know it, were the oldest and best in California—Aceves, Castro, Soberanes, Montano, Padillo, Torres, Estrada. Padre Narcisco Duran with his pious, firm-jawed face was present in his gray robe, and several Americanos. One, tall with a dignified bearing, was introduced to her as Don Guillermo Hartnell, who represented the leading trading company on the coast. He spoke Spanish fluently and dressed and acted so like the Californians it was difficult to distinguish him from them, although Lopez told Tarifa that Hartnell was an Englishman who had arrived from South America five or six years before. Two other foreigners Tarifa found intriguing because she had never met their kind before were a burly thick-necked Scotsman, Dr. Jock Muir, and Karl Krantz, a small German who had recently arrived, and told her in broken Spanish while they danced that he had jumped ship from a whaler when she put in to San Francisco for supplies and was held for having disobeyed the law.

"And I'm going to settle here," he told her eagerly. "I'm a Catholic already, so all I need is to be naturalized, ask for a grant of land, and settle down to ranching with some charming señorita, if she'll have me. A mill is what I'd like on my land, a nice gristmill like my father had in the old country."

When the dance ended, Tarifa found herself standing by one of the long refreshment tables.

"Let me get you a drink, señora?"

Tarifa turned and found Captain Judah at her elbow, one red brow raised quizzically over his yellowish eyes.

She smiled up at him, "Thank you, Capitán."

He brought her a glass of punch and led her to a chair slightly apart from the others.

"Are you enjoying this brilliant if dull affair, señora?"

She nodded.

"Don Ygnacio is not here?"

She explained about his indisposition.

"That makes it more convenient for you? To earn the pianoforte, I mean."

Tarifa glanced about the room, decorous and orderly in spite of the gay music and milling throng.

"They call this dancing," she said scornfully. "You should see the *cuadrillas* in the Sacro Monte at Granada!"

"When will you do your performance?" he asked softly.

Her bosom rose and fell rapidly and she waved a hand at the band playing a lively but uninspired *jota*.

"I cannot dance to that. Get me a tambourine or some castanets."

He rose, heading toward the orchestra, and Tarifa went in search of the governor. It gave her a wicked exultation to make him a part of her wanton act.

Echeandia was talking politics with a group of men, a look of polite boredom on his face, when Tarifa caught his attention.

"Thank heaven you have saved me from those bombastic old bores."

"Your Excellency, I would like permission to do a special dance of my people for you. Have you ever seen a true Romany dance?"

His thin face brightened. "No, but I should be much honored to do so."

"If they will clear the floor then and you will announce me?"

He studied her for a moment, a faint suspicion in his eyes, but she smiled back at him so frankly and with such warmth that he dismissed the uneasiness from his mind. What could be wrong in letting her dance a Gypsy dance? These people had all watched the savage gentiles of their frontier dance, hadn't they?

"What shall I ask the orchestra to play, señora?" he asked.

"Nothing. They do not know my music. I will use none. I have sent a friend to borrow a tambourine or some castanets for me."

She watched the governor march toward the bandstand and bend to speak to the leader. A roll of drums and Echeandia's petulant well-bred voice brought instant silence followed by a longer, more startled pause before there was a patter of restrained applause.

Echeandia nodded to Tarifa and she selected a tambourine from the three Judah had just brought to her. She had untied her satin slippers and stood barefooted, her body swaying slightly to the light rhythm of the tambourine.

She began in the ancient Zorongo style, and then as her flexible body became a symbol of the tree of Paradise, her arms moving like the branches writhing in a fiery wind from below, she tossed the tambourine from her and her coppery weaving hands became the two-headed serpent of the Evil Temptor. Then the fingers began to weave a cabalistic enchantment of their own against the writhing evil hands, symbols of enchantment and death to the evildoer. The spider, the tarantula, the cobra—the Evil Ones succumbed to their deadly poison, and trembled in agony as they died, and the tree of Life, freed of its enchantment, shook itself from its trance and moved in jubilant exultation.

She was panting when she finished and stood for a moment with her arms at her sides, her eyes still closed, her hair a wild tangle about her shoulders.

The silence in the room seemed like a spell that could not be broken. She opened her eyes and found the guests staring at her as if mesmerized. Then, as she jerked back her head, the tumult broke as the Latin blood in the room responded with a tremendous roar.

The young men leaped on the chairs and applauded wildly and raced forward to form a circle around her. But the women, she noted, began to file slowly out of the room.

Echeandia stood with clenched hands near the door, not knowing whether to applaud or escape. He had not expected this spectacle. He was convinced that the undulating dance had been both lascivious and indecent, but the other men had applauded, perhaps in spite of themselves. He was incensed that she had subjected him to this humiliating uncertainty. It undermined his dignity; she should have realized that. Truly she was a little savage and he should never have brought her in his entourage. Perhaps that is why they applauded, they were afraid of offending him? He decided on the spot to be publicly displeased with her.

He turned to Señora Aceaves and said angrily, "I had no knowledge that you and the other ladies present would be subjected to such an outrage, señora. I most humbly beg your pardon. I shall see that amends are made."

Señora Aceaves nodded gravely but she did not speak. Would the old idiot explain what he had said to the others? A fine way for his most important social function of the trip to end!

Tarifa, still surrounded by Judah and her new admirers, had seen Echeandia's action and smiled to herself. It was rewarding to watch him sweat and bow and scrape to the statue-faced women. Don Diego Novato was right; he was nothing but a popinjay, bobbing and darting like a puppet on a string. She turned to Judah and asked, "Will you tell Don Pedro I am ready to go, Capitán Judah?"

"Let me see you home, señora?"

"No. I came with Don Pedro, I must return with him."

Judah said speculatively, "You have won your bet, señora. I promise delivery in a month—and you will consider my other offer?"

"I will consider it, Cápitan."

Lopez came to get her with a very red face, and eyes darting like mice to escape the amused catlike glances of the crowd. He would never live this down. Never! And his wife would hear of it and order him to close up the house in Monterey and move permanently to the rancho. Curse the wanton woman with her uncouth Gypsy ways. He hadn't believed the tales about her but now he knew only too well they were all true. Ygnacio must have gone out of his mind, temporarily at least, to marry such a creature of the Devil.

As they turned to leave, Tarifa paused and, picking out the most aristocratic-looking and elderly man present, said in her hoarse Gypsy voice, "Would you do me a favor, señor, and tell the governor for me that I will be unable to keep the appointment I made earlier to have a midnight supper with him in his house across the square? Please explain that my husband is ill, and that I will have to keep our appointment another time?"

"Of course, señora," the old man said stiffly.

Tarifa was roaring with laughter inside as she walked demurely from the presidio at Pedro Lopez's cringing side.

Neither Tarifa nor Lopez said anything to Don Ygnacio about the final moments of the ball. But the following day as Alvarjo was walking with his host in the patio after having made a swift recovery from his malady of the day before, a group of the town's *gente de razón* called to see him.

Lopez, shaking with acute misery, led his callers to the *sala* and shut all the doors and windows. In simple and restrained language, the elders of Monterey requested in the name of their affronted womenfolk, that Don Ygnacio take his wife out of their pueblo at his earliest convenience.

White to the lips, Ygnacio marched out of the *sala* and went directly to his bedroom where he found Tarifa glancing at a collection of shawls and fans Soledad had bought aboard the *Vulcan*.

Tarifa looked at her husband's face and told Soledad to leave them.

When they were alone he said, "What have you done to deliberately disgrace my name in this pueblo?"

She stood calmly in front of him.

"I danced a dance of my people, with the governor's permission."

"You disgraced him as well. He had no conception of what you meant to do."

Her eyes flickered with contempt. "I told him the truth, that I would dance as my people do. If he does not know what a Romany dance is, with all his superior knowledge, and now feels disgraced, that is not my fault."

Ygnacio's voice rose and fell like a whip. "You knew what it was, and what these people would think of such a thing! You had no right to do it, and to choose a time when I was not even present!"

"Then they cannot blame you," she said calmly, "and I have saved you further embarrassment."

"Don't you understand yet what you have done? Oh, I was a fool to ever bring you on this trip "

Her pride stung, Tarifa said, "You did not think that in Santa Barbara."

He threw out his hands in despair. "What madness

came over you to act in such a way here in Monterey, Tarifa?"

She drew herself up and he was surprised at the flash of anger in her eyes, the first she had shown him.

"I am your wife, Ygnacio, and I love you," she said, "but I am also a Gypsy and I was born to be free. My freedom is something you cannot hope to take from me. I may willingly become a slave to you, but you cannot shackle me into bondage. You cannot tell me when to dance or not to dance. The dance is life to me. It is the breath in my lungs and the blood of my heart. When you understand this you will understand me as well as a *gorgio* can understand a *gitana*.

"What I give you I give you freely because of my deep feeling for you, but you cannot buy it, frighten it, or shame it out of me."

Alvarjo stood very still, his eyes on her flushed animated face and he realized the truth of her words. Was it not the very thing he had learned to adore in her, the wild, untamable courage that could stand up under any onslaught, superb and unafraid?

He came forward and with a groan swept her into his arms. What did it matter what Monterey or the whole of California thought or said of him? Hadn't he used those very words to Padre Peyri when the priest had tried to dissuade him from marrying Tarifa? He would take her home to Loma de Oro and live for her and with her for as many years as were left to him. They needed no one else.

"*Kushto,*" Tarifa murmured presently, "you are no longer angry?"

"No. It does not matter. But we must return to Loma de Oro."

"Yes," she said, "I would like that. And Capitán Judah has agreed to send the pianoforte in a month's time."

Ygnacio said nothing. If she wanted it and it was coming, that was enough. He had made up his mind never to quarrel with her again. His hands tightened on her arms and drew her close to him. His lips were as firm and eager as a young man's.

CHAPTER 14

They had been back at Loma de Oro several months after
their long overland journey on horseback from Monterey
—for there had been no other ship but the governor's
going south and this Ygnacio had refused to take—when
Tarifa awoke feeling ill.

Ygnacio touched her hot head and went in search of
Penti.

"I will take care of her, *rya*," said the old woman, shoo-
ing him out of the bedroom. "She will be all right."

"How are you sick?" Penti asked as she examined her
patient.

"I am hot all over and I have a bad feeling in my
stomach. Mix me something quickly."

"In good time," mumbled Penti. "You eat like a pig
lately; maybe that is what is the matter."

"I eat less than you do, *chovihani!*"

Penti poked about in her bundle of medicines and
made up an evil-smelling brew which seemed to help, for
Tarifa was able to rise later in the day and walk in the
patio and even eat a light dinner with the family.

But the next morning she was pale and listless and
Penti was again called in.

Tarifa was irritable at her strange indisposition for she
had never been ill, except for the time Ygnacio brought
her here from the cabaña.

"What is the matter with me, you old witch?" she demanded.

Penti cackled with laughter.

"You are pregnant, *miri pen.*"

Tarifa went very pale and her black eyes grew wicked with hate.

"You lie! You thieving, abominable, cursed old devil-witch, you lie!"

Penti sat gleefully rocking herself back and forth in her chair beside the bed.

"Did you think you were different from the rest of womankind, *miri pen?* You are pregnant. You are going to have a child."

Tarifa, breathing very hard, felt her heart flutter in her breast and suddenly she leaped from the bed and dashed to the basin on the washstand.

Behind her Penti continued to laugh harshly as she gathered up her bundle of herbs.

Ygnacio was both humble and elated to learn that he was to be a father again at his time of life. Slowly his joy took hold of Tarifa and she felt a strange new emotion growing in her. This thing that had happened was most wonderful in a way. A part of her would go on living, no doubt after she was gone, and perhaps in a different land, but it would go on like the ecstasy of the Romany dance, on and on, passed down from generation to generation.

And her child would be a true Alvarjo, with the blood of aristocrats and grandees in his veins as well as that of the proud, free Romany. What a man he would be! For she had made up her mind she would bear only a son, and she would teach him all that she knew and he would be wiser and more beautiful than all the Alvarjos. Then let the Californians try and laugh at the son of Dona Tarifa of Loma de Oro!

And Loma de Oro assumed new proportions in her freshly maternal eye. This would be his domain, his realm. He would rule it like a king. It would be the finest, richest rancho in both the Californias. She found pleasure in endless discussions with Ygnacio about how they would improve the rancho and what part was to be her son's exclusively.

As they sat in the little cabaña atop Loma de Oro in

the wintery sunlight Ygnacio told her, "I have always hoped that the rancho would remain intact after my death. That way everyone is ensured of ample water and pasturage. Naturally, Joaquin, as my oldest son, should have had control of it and watched over the welfare of his brothers and sisters and their families, whom I hope will settle on different parts of the land—but all will share in the work and income."

Tarifa nodded, "But with Joaquin and Santiago gone, who will handle the rancho?"

Ygnacio took her hand in his. "All my children shall share equally, our little one with the others. But the hacienda I leave exclusively to you, *querida,* for as long as you live and you can pass it on to your child for himself —or herself."

Tarifa was not satisfied even though she knew it irked Ygnacio to discuss business matters with a woman. He had the old-world idea that women should be protected from all such mundane affairs.

"Padre Cazon has told me that such things must be written down in a will and signed before witnesses and a lawyer?"

Ygnacio smiled indulgently at her preoccupation with the matter. "And who is to dispute the way I leave my holdings, *querida?"*

Tarifa frowned. "I am not sure, but you yourself have said that things are changing here. May the time not come when such a written document will be useful, Ygnacio?"

"My dear, leave such things to me. I do not know of a person in California who has a properly written and attested will."

"Then let us be the first? It can do no harm to call upon the mayor and have it properly drawn up and signed? I would feel easier in my mind, for our child, and it would safeguard the others."

He patted her hand and lifted her fingers to his lips. She was so young and vibrantly lovely and she was giving him a child. She should be humored.

"Very well, *querida.* We will go to the mayor in Los Angeles and do as you wish. It can do no harm."

A week later Don Ygnacio and his wife set out for Los Angeles. The alcalde, Juan Rivera, was flustered at their request. It took a good deal of digging into his dusty, seldom-used law books, before he found the proper way to draw up and execute a will. He also discovered that it was usual for the remaining parent to be named executor of the estate, until his death, when the property reverted to the children.

Don Ygnacio hesitated to make such an addition to his will, for he still felt strongly that the oldest male of the family should administer the estate, but because Tarifa wanted it and told him that she would always look after the others he named her administrator of his entire estate, to be held in trust during her lifetime for all the children. He also added purely as a personal thought, and not as a condition of his will, that he hoped the children would not see fit to divide the rancho, but that such a decision should be theirs alone. He signed the document in his flowing hand, and the mayor gave him one copy and sealed the other and placed it in the chest with his official documents.

In April, all the Alvarjos, with the exception of Tarifa, due to her condition, and Don Ygnacio, who remained with her, left for Santa Barbara, where Nazario's marriage to Rufina Corlona was to take place.

The hacienda seemed quiet and lonely with all the children gone and after luncheon while Tarifa napped, Don Ygnacio ordered El Capitán saddled and went for a long gallop over the hills of his rancho. He had come down into the *arroyo seco* when he saw two horsemen cantering toward him.

In spite of the clear April day there was a brisk wind blowing and Ygnacio could see the bright-colored serape of one of the horsemen flowing behind him. The other wore something dark but they were still too far away to distinguish faces.

El Capitán pawed the hard ground impatiently. He had not been ridden lately and was eager to be off. Ygnacio held him with a steady but light rein. There was no reason why he should stay here waiting for the two men. They were on his property, and if they wanted to see him they could come to the hacienda. He half-turned the stallion ready to gallop off, when he heard his name borne on the breeze.

"Ygnacio! Wait!"

Zenobio! Ygnacio's face hardened. He had sworn never to speak to the old fool again. But habit dies hard, and whoever was on his land was his geust.

He sat his horse like a graven centaur, noting with distaste that the other man was Bart Kinkaid.

"We must speak with you, Ygnacio," called Zenobio as they galloped up. He looked older and more ragged than ever, his toe sticking through one of his deer-hide *botas*.

"What can I do for you, señors?" Ygnacio asked formally.

"Capitán Kinkaid has brought word from Mexico. They have ordered immediate secularization of the Missions!"

Ygnacio glanced at Kinkaid's boldly chiseled face and saw him nod.

"I am sorry to hear such news," Alvarjo said quietly. "But there is nothing we can do to prevent it."

Zenobio spoke with impatience. "We must try to do something! Get the governor to call a junta. California cannot just sit by. What's the matter with you, Ygnacio, don't you realize what is about to happen? Everything we have, everything we've worked for, will fall in chaos about our ears!"

Ygnacio did not relish discussing California affairs in front of Kinkaid. There was a watching, waiting look about the Americano that he mistrusted.

"We cannot go against the government, Zenobio. But I do not agree that secularization will be accomplished at once, or that it will affect our holdings."

Zenobio flung up his hands in despair and Don Ygnacio said coldly to Kinkaid, "I thought you had returned to Boston, Capitán?"

"We had a bad blow rounding Cape Horn, señor, and while the ship put in to Rio for extensive repairs I got passage on a brig headed this way. I would like very much to speak to you in private about a certain matter."

Alvarjo was surprised, but he said, "Of course, Capitán. If you would care to return with me to the hacienda?"

"Thank you, señor."

Alvarjo wheeled El Capitán and looked uncertainly at Zenobio. There was a wistful look in his old friend's eyes, like a dog that has been warned off but still wants to come to you.

"Come and have a glass of brandy with us, Zenobio," he offered stiffly.

"With pleasure, Ygnacio! We are two old fools, you and I, to let anything come between us. I have explained to Capitán Kinkaid our little disagreement."

Alvarjo did not reply as they started off. He was not happy that Zenobio took the Americano so much into his confidence. But Zenobio was elated to be going back to Loma de Oro. He had missed his friend and the Alvarjo family.

When Kinkaid had ridden up to his house that morning he had been unable to believe his eyes. "But what are you doing here, *amigo?* I thought you were halfway to Boston?"

Kinkaid had explained about the ship, but Zenobio had a feeling he would have returned anyway. Kinkaid's next words proved him right.

As he paced back and forth in the *sala* on his long legs the younger man told him, "I was a fool to have thought I could leave her, Zenobio. I prattled on to her about waiting and now I am the one who cannot wait. I want to marry her now, young as she is. I want to take her back to Boston with me, as my wife. I have a feeling that if I leave her now I will never see her again."

"The foolish superstitions of a lover," laughed Zenobio. "But what of Don Ygnacio?"

"You must take me to him and add your plea to mine. You will help me, Zenobio?"

The old man explained his quarrel with Ygnacio, and Ygnacio's marriage to Tarifa.

Kinkaid was startled at the odd alliance, but it pleased him, for as he told Zenobio, now that Alvarjo was himself a new bridegroom, he might look more kindly upon the other's request.

Sanchez shook his head. "I don't know, *amigo.* Don Julio Marcos asked for Dolores' hand and was booted off the place."

Kinkaid's face darkened. The thought of that oaf near Dolores made him writhe inside. It was imperative now that he get her away from here. He said flatly, "I've got to ask him. Will you come with me? Now?"

Zenobio shrugged his shoulders and put down his wineglass. "If you want me I will come, but I am not sure of my reception. How do I know what that Gypsy has turned him into by now? Come, we will get the horses and on the way I will say a prayer for you to Saint Jude, the patron saint of impossibilities."

The hacienda was quiet as they dismounted and tethered their horses at the front door.

Ygnacio led them to the dining room and poured brandy for them at the sideboard, the same sideboard, Kinkaid recalled nostalgically, where he had first been alone with Dolores. The thought filled him with an intense longing to see her.

When they had finished drinking, Don Ygnacio led Kinkaid to his study, leaving Zenobio to sun himself in the patio.

It was good, Don Ygnacio thought, to hear his old friend's voice again in his patio. He was surprised to realize how much he had missed him.

In the study he offered his guest a seat and sat down across from him in the large horsehair chair Isabella had always favored. He was aware now that he missed her, too. Could it be that he was in his dotage? Or was it that so many of his family had changed and slipped away from him lately? Since his accident Nazario failed to show the same interest in the rancho and horses that he had before. He even seemed afraid of his mount these days, and for a Paisano Californiano to fear his horse was worse than sacrilege.

"What do you wish to discuss with me, Capitán?" he asked finally when Kinkaid seemed at a loss for words.

Bart looked at the proud old man and wondered how best to approach his subject. In the end he chose blunt truth. Alvarjo was himself a straightforward, truthful man, he would expect nothing less in a prospective son-in-law.

"I don't know how these things are done properly in your land, señor," he began, "and I do not wish to seem presumptuous, but I must talk to you about your daughter Dolores."

Alvarjo was too surprised to speak for a moment. Of all the subjects Kinkaid might have chosen to discuss with him, this was the last he'd expected.

"My daughter?"

"Yes. We are in love, and she has done me the honor to promise to become my wife."

Alvarjo felt the blood drain from his face.

"You do not even know my daughter, señor."

"I know her enough to love her above all other women. I have spoken with her alone only a few times, but in that time we came to an understanding. At Don Julio Marcos' fandango I asked her to marry me and she accepted. I told her that we would wait the two years until my return from Boston, that she was to think about it, and then I would speak to you. But I found that I could not wait. If my ship had not been wrecked off the Horn, I swear I would have turned her 'round and sailed back to California."

"It is impossible," said Don Ygnacio, realizing bitterly that still another child had hidden part of her life from him. "Dolores is young, still a child," he said sharply.

"I realize that, sir, but if you will send for her now and ask her she will tell you of our deep love for each other. I can make her happy, protect her, love her for a lifetime. Will you just ask her?"

Alvarjo got to his feet.

"I cannot ask her."

"What do you mean, señor?"

"She is not here. And I do not intend to tell you where she is. You are not of our blood or our faith, Capitán Kinkaid. Even if she were not too young, when Dolores marries she will wed a Catholic and a Californian. I wish to discuss the matter no further. You will not see my daughter again."

Kinkaid flushed and stood up.

"That is something I cannot promise you, Señor Alvarjo. I have tried to act honorably, but I intend to marry Dolores. And I will."

They stared at each other.

"You spoke of faith," Kinkaid said at last. "I will become anything Dolores would have me become. As for blood, there is nothing in mine to be ashamed of. It would seem, however, that you do not practice what you preach. Your new wife is not of your blood, is she?"

Instantly Alvarjo picked up the heavy crop lying within reach on top of a chest and smashed a heavy blow across Kinkaid's face, laying the cheek open below the left eye.

Bart took a handkerchief from his pocket and dabbed at the blood, feeling furious and ridiculous at the same time. He hadn't meant to say that but the old boy had acted so high and mighty he had wanted to take his pride down a peg. Now he had isolated himself from him completely. Before he could speak a voice from the door said:

"This is a pretty picture, Ygnacio."

Both men turned to face Tarifa. Kinkaid was surprised and faintly shocked to find her with child.

"A guest, Ygnacio, and you treat him like this?"

"You do not understand, my dear," Alvarjo said, throwing down the crop. "This man offered me an insult. He is no guest from this moment on. He is never to set foot on Loma de Oro again. You will oblige me, señor, by leaving at once."

Kinkaid bowed briefly to Tarifa. "What I said to your husband, señora, was not intended as an insult, merely an illustration. I have asked for Dolores' hand in marriage, and Señor Alvarjo has refused on the grounds of my faith and nationality. I merely pointed out that he himself had married a person not of his own faith or blood. Am I not correct?"

"You will address no more remarks to my wife," Alvarjo said, his voice threatening.

"You are correct, Capitán Kinkaid," said Tarifa. "But if my husband is opposed to the match, then the matter is settled, and you would do us both a favor by leaving."

Kinkaid felt the anger rise up in him again. She was learning to act as coldly dictatorial as Alvarjo, but she owed him a favor for coming to her defense in San Diego.

"I am leaving," he said evenly, "but I have a right to ask one favor of you. Where is Dolores now?"

She glanced from him to her husband.

"You do not wish him to know, Ygnacio?"

"No."

"Then, Capitán, I cannot tell you."

Kinkaid picked up his cap, turned abruptly, and left the room without a word.

All the way back to Zenobio's anger beat in him like a tom-tom. He cursed the Alvarjo pride, the stiff-necked old despot who controlled them, and the sloe eyed Gypsy who had dismissed him in so smug and high-handed a manner.

Kinkaid had not known that he could hate a woman with such intensity.

After the first brief explanation Zenobio had not asked any questions. But when his guest began to down *aguardiente* until a dangerous glitter lit his gray eyes, he said mildly, "It is not just the words of Ygnacio and Tarifa that bothers you, *amigo*. What is the matter?"

"She is gone—Dolores. And they won't tell me where. How am I to find her, Zenobio?"

The old man smiled through his grizzled beard.

"You should have asked me."

Kinkaid took hold of his shoulder and swung him around.

"You mean you know? Where is she, tell me for the love of God!"

"I went out to talk to Pablo, the saddlemaker, and he told me she's in Santa Barbara, at her brother Nazario's wedding to Rufina Corlona."

Kinkaid thought bitterly that Don Ygnacio would approve the marriage of his young son, but not his daughter. He took his cap from the table.

"Where are you going?"

"To Santa Barbara, of course. Lend me your fastest horse and tell me the quickest way to get there?"

"Patience, *amigo mío*. How do you know she is still there? She may have left."

"I'll find her, and I'm going to take her with me."

"Wait. Think a bit before you go off like a mesteño with a burr in his tail. You might take her, marry her someplace else, but what then?"

"I will make her happy," Kinkaid said harshly.

"Will you? This is her home, the place she loves best; she will never be able to return to it once she leaves it with you. Her marriage will be considered illegal unless you are a Catholic first and can show that you were married properly by a priest in a church. And the Alvarjos are a close-knit family; she will miss her brothers and sisters, if not her father."

Zenobio grabbed his arm.

"Let me tell you of a similar case I once knew of. A sea capitán married one of the Chicos against her family's wishes, and took her with him to Boston. She could not stand the climate, the loneliness. In two years he brought her back here, a pitiful little creature all skin and bones, and she died within a few months of consumption."

Kinkaid's mouth was tight. "That will not happen to Dolores!"

"Perhaps not. I can see nothing will stop you, so I will not waste my breath. I do not think it is a bad thing, if she loves you. But I will ask you this as a favor to an old friend?"

"Yes?"

"Let her make the decision, whether to go or stay?"

"Of course," Kinkaid said. There could be no question of that. He was confident of her answer. All he had to do was find her.

"I will go with you," said Zenobio. "I know the short-cuts, and where we can get fresh horses."

The Corlona house lay behind the Mission toward the mountains, with the front veranda facing the roadway. The wedding and five-day fiesta had come and gone, and Nazario, with his young bride before him, had already started back for Loma de Oro. The others had lingered at their new relatives' insistence, and the visit had been brightened for them by a warm reunion with Tía Isabella, who was a houseguest of the Corlonas.

She asked avidly for information about all the children and neighbors, even the servants, but of Ygnacio and his new bride she inquired nothing. If one of her nieces or nephews inadvertently mentioned them, she found some excuse to leave their presence.

Dolores had just experienced this vexing reaction on her aunt's part as they sat on the veranda sewing.

Isabella had been asking about the palominos, and Dolores said, "They are getting fat. Neither Padre nor Tarifa ride like they used to since she is to have a child."

Isabella's face grew bone-white, then mottled with fury as she rose. But her voice was emotionless as she said, "I've forgotten my pink thread. I believe I'll just sew in my room for a little while."

Dolores continued to sit on the deep cool veranda and her eyes wandered idly toward the roadway. Two horsemen were coming at a furious pace, clouds of dust kicking up behind them. The sunlight glinted on the clothes of one of them and as they drew closer she saw the brass buttons and blue coat. Her heart lurched and she rose, staring like someone in a trance.

It couldn't be Bart.

But it was!

He leaped from his horse, his face and clothes powdered with dust, his teeth a white slash between his wind-burned cheeks as he saw her.

"Dolores!"

"Bart, Bart!"

She flew across the veranda and felt herself swept up in his arms, arms that felt as strong as the branches of an oak tree. He kissed her not once but many times there in the open, and she felt no shame, only a great tingling joy.

She hardly saw Zenobio, even when he patted her head in passing as he went on to the house.

Bart led her away from the veranda to a small path that led into the woods, and though she knew it was wrong for her to go alone with him she could not have turned back.

They found a shaded spot under a giant live-oak and he spread his coat for her to sit on and sat beside her with her hands in his.

She listened with concern to his recital of his shipwreck, his return, his talk with her father. With the tip of one finger she gently touched the red scab under his eye.

"Padre has a very bad temper when he is really angry. But he shouldn't have struck you."

Kinkaid had not spared himself or Alvarjo in the telling. He had lain the whole truth before Dolores and now he was shocked to see her eyes fill with tears.

"I cannot go away with you like this, Bart."

"But why not? You love me, don't you? That is all that matters."

She shook her head and the dark leaves above made patterns of light and shadow on her fair hair.

"I love you, but I cannot run away. I was not brought up to disobey my parents, Bart. I could not be happy that way. I love my padre, too. You do not know him as I do, his kindness, his patience, and affection."

"But he is unreasonable! He can't keep you penned up like one of his prize palominos forever!"

"He doesn't intend to, Bart. He thinks I am young and

he is right. You asked me yourself to wait. I know he will change his mind about you if we wait."

Kinkaid groaned and drew her to him.

"I can't wait. I'm afraid to wait. There's something—I can't explain. But I can't leave you here."

She smiled up at him. "What is there to be afraid of, Bart? I will not change my mind. I will wait for you, no matter how long it takes. Can't you wait a little for me?"

He looked into her face for a long moment as if memorizing every feature.

"If you ask it of me I can do anything," he told her, "but don't ask me to do this."

"I must, Bart. I will go home with the others and speak to Padre myself, then I will write to you—at Zenobio's?"

"If you go back he will not let me see you and he will not let you communicate with me. He has said so."

"My padre is not an ogre, Bart. He will not keep me a prisoner against my will, no matter what he has said."

"You will not consider going away with me now? There is a British ship sailing tonight that can put us ashore at Rio. We can be married on board by the captain, and later by a priest in Rio. Then we can take the *Arabella* back to Boston."

"No," her voice was sad. "I cannot go like that without speaking to my padre."

"And if he refuses when you speak to him, will you come with me then?"

She shook her head, and at the flash of pain in his eyes, kissed him quickly.

"Be patient with me, my darling; if we wait a little I know everything will be all right."

He plucked angrily at the grass. He could not move her, no matter what he said, and the fear rose in him anew at the thought of leaving her.

"Bart, you are not angry with me?"

He turned and took her shoulders in his hands.

"No. I could never be angry with you, my dearest. If this is the only way that will make you happy, if you think you can talk your father around in the two years I'll be gone, then it will have to be. I—promised someone to abide by your decision. Is this it?"

She took his face between her hands and smiled at him.

"It will be the best way in the long run. You will see."

He sighed. "I hope so. But I tell you one thing: when I come back I am done with waiting. I am going to marry you then, with or without consent, come hell or high water."

She laughed and her cheeks were vivid with color.

That night Dolores, accompanied by a frightened maid, went down to the beach to see Bart off.

They clung to each other, and Kinkaid's eyes devoured her face as a starving man consumes his food.

"I will wait," she said, "and pray that you return safely."

"Take care of yourself," he said tersely, unable to trust himself to say more. Again a fear of losing her haunted him and when the boatswain called to him from the longboat he put her from him almost roughly.

"*Adiós, querido,*" she whispered. "*Vaya con Dios!*"

All the way to the ship he kept his eyes on the shoreline. For as long as he could still see her small white-clad figure she did not move.

On a hot morning in June, Tarifa awoke in an agony of pain and Ygnacio went in his dressing gown to fetch Penti and Candelaria.

Penti put a glass to Tarifa's lips when the pain abated, and when Candelaria and Ygnacio wanted to know what it was she replied, "*Sangría.* Wine and fruit juice."

Next she anointed Tarifa's body with butter and explained that it was an old remedy in childbirth to ease the stretching of the skin.

Ygnacio wanted to stay but Penti finally drove both Candelaria and Alvarjo from the room.

Tarifa panted and clenched her teeth, for she knew Gypsies did not cry out in torture, and she would not give Penti the satisfaction of hearing even the smallest moan from her lips.

The old woman seated herself cross-legged on the floor and began to clap her hands and sing the birth song, ending with a loud *Ay* as she finished each stanza. Tarifa repeated it from the bed and slowly the rhythm began to take hold of her and as her body labored in time to the music, her pains miraculously lessened until they all but disappeared. Through the hot morning and into the afternoon the women chanted, Tarifa only weakly now with a beading of perspiration on her lip and brow, but though her body was wracked with movement she felt little actual pain.

At three o'clock she seemed to drift off to sleep and when she opened her eyes Penti was peering into her face and holding another glass of *sangría* to her lips. Tarifa rose on her elbow to drink and was astonished to find a tiny brown face beside her pillow.

She looked up quickly at Penti and found her laughing.

"It is all over. You have your babe. Is he not handsome?"

"A boy?" Tarifa bent and examined his wrinkled face and touched his thick black hair. He was indeed beautiful, and seeing him she felt a great wave of elation, a smothering adoration.

"Call Ygnacio. Quickly!"

"Very well, *miri pen*."

Ygnacio bent over the bed to kiss his wife and son and to take the child's tiny hand in his.

"Is he not beautiful, Ygnacio?"

"He is magnificent, and so are you, *querida*. What shall we name him?"

"He must have a Romany name as well as a Spanish one."

"If you like."

"Piramus," she said, "no—Lasho."

"What is that, *querida?*"

"Luis, you call it. We shall call him Lasho, and he shall be named Ygnacio for you, too, *kushto*."

Later in the day when the other members of the family, including the house servants, Candelaria, old Pablo, and Santos, came timidly in to inspect the newest Alvarjo, it was young Rufina who lingered longest and showed the most interest in the baby, for she and Nazario were to have a child in the next winter.

Tarifa recovered from the birth with the speed of a healthy young animal, and she greatly admired her regained lithe figure with a few interesting curves here and there that she had not had before.

Don Ygnacio assigned a young Indian boy, Poco, to be his new son's body servant, but Tarifa insisted that the baby, whom everyone called Lasho, be given into Penti's care entirely. Ygnacio did not object, for he had faith in the old Gypsy's abilities as a nurse.

When the child was a few days old Alvarjo said that they

must take him to the Mission to be baptized, and he sent Santos and his sons with invitations to all their friends and neighbors to attend the ceremony and the fiesta to follow.

To the Californians, birth was always considered a great joy, and the choosing of the *padrinos,* or godparents, a great honor in itself, was done quickly. After consulting with Tarifa, Ygnacio asked his old friend Zenobio to stand as godfather to his new son, and Dona Carlotta Galindo, a very pious woman, as godmother.

Candelaria and the maids had made exquisite christening robes of the finest embroidered and lace-trimmed linen and silk, and Zenobio had given a large white-satin gold-tasseled pillow on which the infant was to be carried.

The procession, complete with musicians playing gay tunes, left the hacienda early on a pearl-pink June morning, with the heavy scent of wild mustard and lupin and poppies in the air, and wended its way slowly toward the Mission.

Padre Peyri officiated at the baptism, christening the child Ygnacio Jesus Maria Lasho, as the parents had requested.

Lasho wiggled in his long white robes, but Tarifa was immensely proud that, Gypsylike, he did not cry out when the salt was put on his tongue and the cold water poured on his tiny black head.

After the ceremony the entire party gathered outside the church where the Mission neophytes rang bells and serenaded them with music and song, and the members of the *escolta* fired their muskets while the proud new stepbrother Francisco Alvarjo set off rockets and fireworks especially ordered for the occasion.

Don Ygnacio gave gold pieces to each of the Padres, and reminded them that they would be expected at the fiesta.

The christening party returned home at a full gallop, and Tarifa pointed out to Ygnacio proudly that Lasho never cried once.

At the hacienda, Candelaria had outdone herself in providing a feast fit for kings. There was the special *panecito* bread used for christenings, *chorizos,* cold chicken and beef, rice and green peppers, *salsas* of every variety, stuffed eggs, frijoles with pimento, salads, smoked fish, sliced watermelon, and baskets containing oranges, peaches, plums, and pomegranates.

After the feast each guest came up to a table beside

Tarifa's chair in the patio where she held Lasho on her lap, and presented him with a gift, until the table was piled high and Candelaria brought another smaller one.

Zenobio, beside the christening pillow, gave his godson a fine saddle blanket woven by the Yuma Indians, a pair of silver spurs, and a tiny pair of kidskin *botas* delicately embroidered with cow heads.

The fiesta and ball that followed were the gayest the people of the valley had seen in a long time.

Rufina, despite her condition, danced every dance, proud of her new matronly appearance with her dark hair piled high under an ivory comb.

They were at the height of their merriment when Salvador arrived from the Mission with a message for the two Padres. When they returned from the front veranda where they had spoken to the neophyte, both priests looked grave. Don Ygnacio went to them at once, concern on his own face.

"What is the matter, Padre Peyri?"

"A word with you in your study, Ygnacio."

"Of course."

The old priest faced his friend with dignity and a faint bewilderment.

"It has come, *amigo.*"

Ygnacio said simply, "Secularization?"

"*Sí*. As you know, I alone among the Padres hailed Mexican independence with joy, as a step forward for our poor Indians. I thought Mexico, being closer physically and by blood ties with the Californianos, would help us better care for our poor charges." He laughed wryly. "Even I began signing my communications with '*Dios y Libertad.*' I gave readily whatever was asked by the new government. Yet I had to beg Governor Echeandia for permission to sell fifteen hundred hides I had already contracted to sell from our rancho, Las Flores. I was only successful because, having served over my required ten years on the *frontera,* I had requested a passport from the governor to leave."

"You would not leave us, Padre?"

The old priest bowed his head. "I can see the day coming when I shall be of little use to anyone here. Our hands are tied, *amigo*. The beauty and wealth that we have built up with God's help and our hands will be desecrated in the name of freeing the Indians. And what will happen to my poor children? The few who have chosen to leave under Echeandia's earlier decree have come to beg to be taken back, or they lie starving and diseased in the pueblos. What do these children of the wilderness know of ruling themselves? They need another decade at least of learning to work and take their place in the world before we can leave them."

"Can you not appeal somewhere, Padre?"

"Where, my son? To Spain, who has no more jurisdiction over us? To Mexico, who has no interest other than the last spoilage she can wring from us? To the governor, who is as avid as the young Paisanos to confiscate our lands and herds for his own gains?"

"But the people will not let you go."

"The people, my son, do not have either voice or strength to help now. You must hold on to your own lands, my son. You have a royal grant in writing. Keep it safely. They cannot take that from you, or fail to honor it. Yet I fear for you—all of you."

"I will protect what is mine," Ygnacio said grimly.

"There is another thing you should know, Don Ygnacio. Only a rumor—but I fear there may be truth in it."

"What is that, Padre?"

"They say Mexico has issued a decree expelling all men of Spanish birth under sixty years of age, and disqualifying others from holding office. It is said that Don José de la Guerra y Noriega has already been suspended from his military duties in Santa Barbara. They will suspend or sweep away all men of reason, I fear."

Ygnacio was jolted. José de la Guerra, like himself, was a Spanish-born aristocrat, only one of far more worth to California than he had ever been. Guerra had remained in the army, risen from lieutenant to commandante of the Santa Barbara presidio, and was a man not only of intelligence but of high moral integrity as well.

"This is infamous!" Alvarjo cried.

The priest nodded in sympathy. "It will not affect your sons as they are California-born, but you yourself will be asked to sign a new pledge of allegiance to Mexico and declare your lands."

"I will do no such thing! I served my king honorably

and well. I hold a royal grant, and I have reared my children here," he thundered. But Ygnacio had realized at last that the fears expressed by Zenobio Sanchez, Diego Novato, and even Pedro Lopez were no longer surmise, but stark reality.

CHAPTER 15

Upon receiving his orders to leave Mission San Luis Rey and California, Padre Peyri showed the letter of his formal dismissal to Padre Cazon and the Zacatecan Father, Antonio Anzar, who had come from Mexico as assistant a few months earlier. It was decided that he should remain in charge of the Mission, leaving Padre Cazon free to travel to Pala and the outlying *rancherías* as the need arose.

"Before I leave, though," Peyri told them sadly, "I must give one last fiesta for my children and my friends. And not a word of my leaving must leak out."

The whole Mission was astir early in the morning of the unexpected fiesta. And as Peyri stood in the front courtyard with the neophytes bustling about him, he knew a quiet satisfaction in spite of his heavy heart. Because he had come here, they were better off than they had been, better clothed, housed, and fed, with a skill that could command a wage, and with a spiritual belief to sustain and uplift them.

He glanced up at the gleaming white Mission with its vast five-hundred-foot quadrangle, its thirty-two square pillars supporting the rounded arches of its façade, giving it a noble, graceful appearance. From the open *sala* door he could see the large inner patio, tiled and level, around which more pillars and arches supported the cloister which gave access to all the apartments.

How well he knew the richly ornamented interior, the newly gilded pulpit, the earthenware pipe with faucet that he had himself installed to bring water to the sacristy.

And the rooms fronting the courtyard where the unmarried boys lived apart from the others. The storerooms for tools, for looms, the infirmary with its special inside corridor where the sick could enter the church without stepping from cover.

He glanced at the two small buildings beyond the Mission with their flat roofs, designed by himself to accommodate the Mission mayordomos and the sergeant and eleven soldiers of the *escolta.*

Beyond was the wide stairway that led to the orchard with the two tiled ponds in which the Indians bathed each Saturday and washed their clothes. Part of the waste water ran off in an elaborate circuit of conduits to irrigate the orchard and gardens beyond. He thought of the grapes, the color of Porto purgato, the finest vines in California that he himself had planted.

Two hundred yards to the north he could see the scattered, conical straw-thatched huts of the *ranchería,* where two thousand neophytes made their homes, and he said a prayer that all of this should not be swept away by man's insatiable greed.

He turned and went into the church to vest himself for the last High Mass he would ever say in the church he had built with his own hands.

The Indian choir sang the responses more beautifully than he had ever heard them, and there were tears in his eyes when Salvador and Father Anzar helped him off with his vestments in the sacristy.

After Mass and a gay breakfast, the vaqueros brought a large bull into the quadrangle and began to show their skill at escaping from its wicked horns on their fastest horses.

The young girls, who were afraid of the *corrida,* crowded upon the veranda where the Padres sat, their black hair cut to shoulder-length, all dressed in white blouses and bright red serge skirts, and giggled and laughed at the antics of the men and the bull.

When the Indian vaqueros had thoroughly tired the bull they let him go from the enclosure and followed, whooping and hollering until one of them caught up with the animal and, catching his tail, flipped him over on the ground like a tortilla in a pan.

The girls clapped and hooted from the veranda as the bull rolled in the dust, got up shaking his head, and loped off toward the pasture.

In the evening the soldiers fired volleys from their muskets and kindled a huge bonfire in the square to light the feast. Ten bullocks had been roasted by the women in the deep pits in back of the Mission, and now the long tables were laden with food and drink and the Indian orchestra began to play its merriest tunes.

Tarifa, with Don Ygnacio and the Alvarjo children, had come with the other *gente de razón* this evening. They clustered around Padre Peyri and Padre Cazon, each of them wondering why Peyri had held this fiesta. It was no saint's day, no feast of the church, and nothing was being dedicated, but they did not ask the reason. Only Tarifa, with her quick Gypsy intuition, a sense inborn in the Romany like a second sight, knew that something was vitally wrong.

After the meal, while the Indians played the rollicking Quattro Canti or Four Corners, riding from four different directions, armed with long willow switches with which they dealt each other unmerciful blows until the willows were worn to stubs, Tarifa sought out Francisco.

He sat near Luis watching the games, and now and then his eyes wandered to Lisita, one of the prettier young Indian girls with a red ribbon in her hair.

"Francisco, I want to talk to you," Tarifa said.

He rose at once, and followed her to a bench on the long veranda beyond the spot where the games were taking place.

He glanced up, his thin face questioning. He was always friendly to his young stepmother, but he was naturally reserved and shy.

Tarifa faced him and said, "I want to know what is wrong."

"Wrong?"

"Here, at the Mission."

"But nothing is wrong, Dona Tarifa." None of the children called her mother, indeed most of the boys were older than she was, and she had refused to allow the formal señora.

"This fiesta—why does Padre Peyri give it?"

"I don't know—he likes to."

"Have none of the soldiers noticed anything wrong?"

"No. It has been very quiet all week. Only one man visited us."

"Who was it?"

"A messenger—from San José."

"San José?"

"It is routine. The missionaries write back and forth all the time." Francisco was impatient. He wanted to get back to the games, and to watch a graceful Indian girl named Lisita.

"Is the man still here—the messenger?"

"Yes. Over there. The neophyte with the green and black serape."

Tarifa glanced toward the fire where a group of Indian boys sat cross-legged and saw a young native with a green band around his flowing black hair.

"Tell him I would like to speak to him."

Francisco did not care what she wanted of the Indian; he was only too glad to be released. He felt uncomfortable with Tarifa, as if her long Gypsy eyes could look into his most secret thoughts.

The Indian came with a free, dignified walk. He was perhaps eighteen or twenty, hawk-featured with intelligent eyes.

"Señora?" He bowed low as Padre Duran had taught him. He was not used to speaking to white women.

"What is your name?"

"Tomas, señora."

"You brought a message to Padre Peyri from San José. I want to know who sent it."

"Why, the Father Prefecto, señora, Padre Duran."

"Do you often bring messages from him here?"

"When they are sent by Padre Duran. I have ridden very fast to bring this one."

"Why?"

"Because, señora, of its great importance. Padre Duran

said that I must get here very fast so that Padre Peyri may
leave in time to catch the ship. That is all I know, señora."

She let him go and went back to the fire. The others
were watching the Indians throw four-foot sticks through
a ring, two at a time; if both went through together the
man won the pile of ornaments that had been piled in a
glittering mass on the ground.

When the games ended the Indians each passed before
the Padres and received a small gift; one was kindly commended for a task well done, another gently scolded, another paternally admonished for forgetting to wash her
clothes. But each went away contented with a smile, and
the small present clutched in his hands like a child.

Lisita boldly asked Peyri why the married women were
allowed to dance and the girls were not.

The priest listened gravely to her arguments and appeared to weigh them carefully, then he said, "We must
all wait for the good things of life, Lisita, and be worthy
of them before they come to us. When you have cooked
as many meals and washed as many clothes as Juana
there, then it shall be time for you to dance too."

He turned away with a serious expression but Tarifa
noted that he smiled into his cowl.

A moment later the Indians filed obediently off to bed,
the girls shepherded to the *monjeria* by an elderly married
woman, the unmarried boys to their apartment by an older
mayordomo.

Peyri turned to his friends and thanked them warmly
and lingeringly for having come. The Alvarjos, at Tarifa's
request, lingered till last.

"What is it, my dear?" asked Ygnacio.

"Padre Peyri is leaving."

"What!" Ygnacio had not believed that the Padre would
find the heart to leave the Mission when the time came.

"I spoke with the messenger who came from Padre
Duran," Tarifa said. "I thought you would like to know—
to say good-bye. He is your friend. Go and speak with
him alone. I will keep the others here. There may be some
reason they should not know."

Ygnacio went over to Peyri and a few moments later
they entered the Mission *sala* and closed the door.

"I'm getting cold," complained Soledad, "and so is
Rufina. I wish Padre would hurry."

"Be still," said Tarifa. "When it is time we will go."

Ygnacio was gone a long while and when he rejoined them, Tarifa saw that he had been profoundly shocked by what he had heard. Not until they were in the privacy of their bedroom did he tell her what Duran's letter had said and why Peyri felt he must go.

"He leaves tonight; there is little time since the letter traveled six hundred miles to get here. He is afraid the Indians would refuse to let him go, might follow him, so he will sneak away. But nothing will be the same at the Mission again. It is a bad time, Tarifa, a very bad time."

"We will be all right, *kushto*. We will look after Lasho and the others. No one can touch Loma de Oro. No one ever shall as long as I live."

He kissed her gently and knelt to say his prayers. It always bothered him that she had never taken the form of her religion as deeply as she should, refusing to kneel morning or night with him, sometimes making excuses to escape from attending Mass as if it bored her. But he had no idea of the extent of her indifference to the faith he had brought her into. He knew her good qualities—surely God knew them better than he did—and if after her different way of life she was finding it difficult to conform at once to all the demands of Catholicism, then he knew he must be patient with her.

Padre Peyri did not get away completely in stealth after all. Salvador, sleeping on the veranda in a remote corner which he had preferred lately, was awakened before dawn by whispering voices. Instantly alert, he heard the swift heartfelt farewells exchanged by the Padres.

He could not believe his eyes or his ears when Padre Peyri mounted a horse and galloped off toward the Camino de Rial and the seacoast.

He waited till all was quiet again and then slipped away to the *ranchería*. He woke the men he wanted softly, so as to disturb no one else and together they slipped away to the pasture, each carrying a hackamore, and caught their horses. They rode bareback, walking without sound well past the Mission, and then at a signal from Salvador put the ponies into a full gallop.

When the mists of early morning began to clear over

the bay they rode onto the beach at San Diego. A ship with an American flag was just getting under weigh.

With a great cry Salvador spurred his horse into the surf and the others followed him, three hundred voices rolled across the water like the heartrending cries of lost children.

"Padre! Padre Peyri!"

"Why do you leave us, Padre?"

"Come back, *por favor*, come back!"

A gray-robed figure appeared on the afterdeck, hands raised as he gave them his final blessing. His voice came clearly.

"I leave because I must, my children. God be with you always. Remember His teachings. Go back to the Mission, *niños;* go back quickly!"

But the sound of his voice only made their wails rise louder, more pitifully. Many flung themselves into the sea when their horses could swim no further and tried to reach the ship. The two men drowned, their brown hands reaching till the last toward the vessel where the priest stood, arms out-stretched, head sunk on his chest, blinded by his tears.

Salvador swam forward strongly until his hand touched wood, a rope, and they lowered a rope ladder rather than see him drown too.

When he stood on the deck, his breath locked in his lungs, Peyri embraced him, then told him passionately, "You must go back, Salvador. The others will need you because you are strong. Do not desert your people as I am forced to do. Go back, my dear son!"

Salvador drew himself up, looking into the priest's wet, anguished face, and something moved in his black eyes like a flame behind a shutter.

There on the deck he tore off his shirt and pants, all that he wore, and with his hand broke the chain round his neck that bore the holy medal Peyri had given him at his baptism. He fell on one knee and kissed the Padre's hand, then with a powerful running motion leaped over the railing and threw himself into the sea.

They watched his black head bobbing in the distance as he swam with the current toward shore. When he reached it he never looked back. In a flash he mounted the nearest pony and turned its head due east toward the mountains.

Echeandia had declared that all persons of Spanish birth must come to declare their property and to take the oath of allegiance to Mexico. And he noted with anger that Don Ygnacio Alvarjo was not among those who presented themselves. He would like to have confiscated the Alvarjo lands then and there, but he was afraid of the numerous loyal vaqueros of Loma de Oro who would rise to defend him at their master's bidding. Still he continued to harass and embarrass Alvarjo by sending written orders for him to appear at once on pain of immediate exile.

It was unfortunate that the most recent of these high-handed orders fell into Tarifa's hands instead of Don Ygnacio's, for Alvarjo had not seen fit to inform his wife of them.

Tarifa read the stamped red-sealed order in the patio. She had just come out dressed for a ride on Guindilla. The stallion was now fully recovered, having grown a new set of hooves as Pablo and Santos had said he would. As she read, fury flashed through her like a flame, a consuming white-hot flame.

She stalked to the bedroom Penti shared with Lasho and said, "I am riding to San Diego. If Don Ygnacio asks where I am when he returns from the Martinez rancho, tell him you don't know—I am just riding. You understand?"

"Yes, *miri pen*."

Penti looked at Tarifa's face and saw that she had the black look—the Devil rode in her Gypsy eyes—that meant danger for whoever crossed her path this day.

Tarifa did not spare Guindilla as they flashed down the camino, and clattered across the town square toward the house Echeandia still used as governor.

A startled servant had little chance to admit, much less announce her after stammering that the governor was in his office.

Tarifa thrust back the door and stood on the threshold, staring with blazing eyes at Echeandia. He had been seated in a satin-backed chair by the window, reading a gold-tooled copy of Gonzales del Castillo's playlet, *El Soldado Fanfarrón*.

At sight of her he got slowly to his feet.

"What do you want here?" he asked haughtily.

She closed the door with a vicious stab of her spurred bootheel. She wore a man's black velvet trousers and jacket and had a black silk handkerhcief tied over the forehead and the top of her loose black hair.

She tore the order he had sent Ygnacio from her red sash and threw it on the floor. She spat upon it and said with a curling lip, "You dared send this to my husband, you scum of Mexico's army!"

He paled at the fury in her face but replied testily, "It is the law! He has ignored my previous orders, but as governor I intend to enforce this one. Get out of here, *gitana,* before I call the guards."

He backed away from her toward the wall and the bell-pull hanging there and was astounded in the next instant to feel his arm jerked powerfully backward and pinioned there. He glanced up and found a long wicked knife imbedded in the fabric of his coat-sleeve just below the shoulder, pinning it tightly to the wall.

His gasp was more fright than indignation, but he mustered the courage to cry, "Get out of here! You are mad. Guard!"

Another *navaja* whistled through the air and caught his coat by the other shoulder, cutting slightly into the flesh.

He howled with pain as she strode toward him and struck his cheek a glancing blow that blurred his sight.

"One more sound," Tarifa hissed, her blazing eyes an inch from his own, "and I will let you have a *navaja* through the heart. I may cut off your ears, like the soldiers do the runaway Indians."

"You have gone crazy," he whispered. He could feel the blood trickling slowly down his shoulder but he did not raise his voice. He knew she was quite capable of killing him. And he had given permission to Alvarjo for this creature of Hades to remain in California! "What do you want?" he whimpered. "Why are you here?"

"Because I hate everything about you! Your tyranny, your canting little ways, your idiotic pomposity—your ugly pictures on the walls!"

She whirled and drawing a third knife from her boot, began to slash savagely at the nearest canvas.

"My beautiful paintings!" he gasped. "Don't!"

She paid no attention to him and it seemed to his bewildered senses that the canvases fell and disintegrated as snows after a rain.

"There!" she panted, her eyes like a tigress's. "That is what I think of your Mexico and your culture!"

He could only sag helplessly like a pinioned bird.

"You will go to that desk and you will write an official letter stating that my husband is a loyal California subject, and that as such and on your personal honor, you assume full legal responsibility for his failing to sign the oath of allegiance, and that you have personally and officially in your position as governor of California excused him now and forever from further declaring his property or holdings."

"I cannot do that! The Supreme Government would not honor such a document in the first place, and I—"

"You will do as I say! You are the Supreme Government here until they send a new governor, and if you try for a reprisal against my husband or tell anyone how you came to sign such a document, I will find you wherever you hide and slice off your ears as neatly as Candelaria carves a roast."

He did not doubt her. He only knew that if this was the price of her leaving he must do it at once.

"Let me loose! I'll do it. But let me loose!"

She came to jerk the knives away and grinned when he moaned with pain as he moved his shoulder.

"You will pay for this," he said between his teeth. "You will not make a fool of Echeandia for long! And Alvarjo shall suffer too."

"I do not need to make a fool of you, your Excellency, you do that very well yourself everytime you open your mouth. Write!"

He glanced uncertainly at the knives in her hands and scuttled across the room to his desk. She stood behind his shoulder while he drove his quill furiously across the page, sealed it with the official seal, and added his flourishing signature. She took it from him.

"Thank you, your Excellency. I don't believe you will make trouble over this while you are in California. My maid Penti, who is also a *gitana,* is very adept at making poisons. A drop or two in the food or wine that comes from the Missions would do, and they would never be able to trace it. But perhaps this"—she tapped the paper she held— "is a more powerful persuader? Your only hope of remaining until your replacement arrives is to appease the southern hacendados. They would not look kindly upon an official document signed by the acting governor that gives precedence and full protection to a single ranchero, while the others are being forced to comply with your edicts."

Echeandia stared at her. He felt giddy with hatred. The blood seemed to boil to the top of his head and simmer there, burning out every other thought. And because he was barred from spewing his hatred at her by his naked fear of her, he felt nauseated, as if his stomach would pour its entire contents on the rug in a moment. He prayed to Saint Joseph that she would leave. He prayed to Saint Joseph that he would not vomit. He prayed to Saint Joseph that he would not have a heart attack. He prayed. . . .

When he glanced up a moment or an hour later, she was gone. He fell on his knees and began to retch.

In the verge of civil war, with both the north and south vying for the capital, California waited expectantly for its new governor.

Ygnacio Alvarjo was at the Santa Teresa when José Martinez rode in on his return from Monterey. He was gleeful as he greeted his friends.

"The new governor has arrived, *amigos!* I have seen him in Monterey, and all is not lost, he seems like a man of sense and honor."

Zenobio and Ygnacio plied him with questions over their wineglasses.

"What is he like, José?"

"A soldier. There is some Indian blood, I think. He is swarthy, thickset, a little under medium height. The teeth are large, the lips full. Dark hair. A short beard. They say he likes to gamble and keeps a mistress though he has a family in Mexico. But he shows good sense, and the soldiers like him. I believe he will be popular."

"A soldier, you say?" said Zenobio. "What is his name?"

"General José Figueroa."

"Ha! I know him well. I knew him in Sinaloa. You are right; he is a sensible and hard-working man."

"Do you know," mused Martinez, "he brought along a small printing press and type, the first in California? Yes, he is a man of vision and progress."

"Whom has he brought with him?" asked Alvarjo.

"Let me see if I remember all of them," said Martinez. "His brother Francisco."

"I know him, too!" chortled Zenobio, slapping his thigh.

"Ten Zacatecan priests, no doubt to take over the Missions. Capitán Nicolas Gutierrez. Two lieutenants—I forget their names—a surgeon, Manuel Alva, and thirty soldiers. I do not like the look of them; they are mostly cholos and ex-convicts, and I can tell you Monterey is up in arms at being made into a repository for criminals, pardoned or not. California is not what it was, *compadres*."

The men drank in silence, each busy with his own thoughts, and then Martinez said morosely, "There is one bit of bad luck."

Ygnacio leaned forward. "What is that, José?"

"Echeandia will get off scot-free. He is an old friend and political ally of Figueroa's. And Zamorano has talked himself into remaining as Figueroa's secretary. But under the official orders brought by Governor Figueroa, I hear Echeandia is required to report in person to the Supreme Government in Mexico. I hope it is the last we will see of him!"

"Amen!" echoed Zenobio. "Look how he has turned the heads of all the young men who should know better."

Rufina, who was terrified of Penti who often went up and down the verandas muttering to herself in Romany and poking about in the filthy bundle of herbs she always carried tied to her sash, would not allow her in the room when she awoke from a late nap with her first labor pains. The child was not due for another month, and neither Tarifa nor Don Ygnacio was at home, having gone to the Cotas for the funeral of an aged great-grandmother of Señora Cota's. Over a hundred, some claimed she was.

Nazario, who had heard her call, rushed from the *sala* where he had been playing cards with his brothers, and found her with her young face convulsed with pain and terror.

"Nazario!"

"What is it, chiquita?"

"The baby—get someone. Quickly!"

"Penti—"

"No!" It was a scream of dread. "Not—that horrid old witch! Get Candelaria, and one of the maids, Rita." Her own maid was ill with influenza in the servants' quarters. It had been a dry winter but there had been months of freezing weather, and on this day in late January a fierce wind curled round the hacienda like a crushing hand, tearing at the shuttered windows and doors and slashing the trees and vines of the patio with taloned fingers.

Nazario nodded mutely, bracing himself against the wind as he went out onto the veranda, and found himself held and buffeted and played with like an infant.

He was to be a father, he thought dully, and the idea was too enormous to leave him any emotion on the subject.

He wheeled into the warm kitchen and had to take a deep breath before he could tell Candelaria and the maids, in a tongue stumbling over itself like stones in a rushing creek-bed, what his errand was.

"Santa Maria!" cried one of the younger girls.

"*Silencio*, Catalina! Watch the dinner. See that the frijoles do not burn."

"*Sí*, señora."

Nazario and Candelaria fought their way back to Rufina's bedroom and found her doubled up with cramps, tears of fright streaming down her cheeks.

Nazario attempted to comfort her, but Candelaria ordered him from the room.

"Go fetch that Penti, if you want to be useful, *niño*." Candelaria resumed her old nursery-days authority in a crisis.

"But she will not have her!"

"She may be glad of her," muttered Candelaria, pushing him out. "But I will do the best I can. Find Rita and send her here."

"*Sí*."

Nazario sent Rita from the dining room, where she was laying the table, and tried to say a prayer for his wife in the freezing chapel, but he could not recall the words of a single prayer and went on simply making the sign of the Cross until his teeth chattered and he left to rejoin his sisters and brothers.

Every time Rufina's screams were borne along the veranda to the *sala* on the wind, Soledad moaned and covered her ears with her hands.

"Why doesn't she stop? Why doesn't she stop!" she cried, looking from one tortured face to the other. "Why don't they do something for her? I think she's dying."

"Hush!" said Dolores sharply, her own fear plain in her tone. "I think it would be better if we all knelt and prayed for her and the baby. Come."

She knelt down by her chair and took her rosary from her sash, looking like a young madonna herself in her long fair braids and simple blue gown.

The others knelt and followed her through the Glorias, the Pater Nosters, the Aves, through the Mysteries to the final amen, trying not to hear the now weaker, less frequent cries from Rufina's bedroom.

Later when he could no longer bear it, and while the others pretended to eat, Nazario went to rap on the bedroom door and was told curtly by Candelaria that there was nothing he could do. Her ample bosom barred his sight of the bed and its moaning occupant, and he found himself wishing that his father and Tarifa were there. Tarifa did not let things happen, Tarifa knew what to do. Why wasn't she here?

It was after midnight and all but Nazario, who sprawled asleep in the *sala,* had long been in bed when Candelaria herself burst into the room shared by Penti and Lasho.

"What is it?" the Gypsy asked, instantly awake and fully clothed as she lay on her cot.

"Penti! You must come—Rufina. I have tried. She would not let me call you, but now you must come!"

"I knew you would come for me sooner or later," the *gitana* said with grim satisfaction. "The young lady is too fine for me, eh? And yet now she would call me?"

"She has not called you. I have. Nazario and I wanted you when it first began, but she went into hysterics. She is a foolish child, but now she can no longer ask for you or not."

"A coma?"

"I fear so. Come. Quickly!"

Penti rose, peered at the rosy sleeping Lasho, and scooped up her bundle of medications in one swift movement.

Rufina lay half on her side, eyes closed and her skin a queer purple color.

Penti let out an ejaculation and buried her hand in her bundle. She brought out a strange-looking hooked instrument made of bone.

"You are not going to use that?" cried Candelaria, and beside her Rita grew pale.

"Go, both of you! Bring me some hot water, all you have, and more towels. Are you never going to move?"

The two women shrank from her threatening advance and she pushed them before her out of the bedroom and slammed the door.

Candelaria opened the door and put down the steaming buckets she carried. She glanced fearfully at the bed and saw Rufina lying on her back, her braids flat on her chest, her color returned to normal. Penti was bent over the bed poking in her bundle; a strange, eerie mew came from its depth.

"About time!" she muttered. "Where have you been? Bring the linen here and the hot water."

"Rufina, Dona Rufina?" gasped Candelaria.

"She is asleep. I gave her a draught of cowslip. She has lost some blood but she will be all right. It is this one I am worried about; it is premature and awfully small."

Candelaria gaped at her. She had forgotten all about the baby. Slowly she and Rita stole forward and Penti opened the rags of her bundle.

An infinitesimal black head and monkey face, the size and color of a pomegranate, stared back at them while scrawny doll's arms and legs moved feebly.

"Go to my room quickly," she ordered Rita, "and bring me the foot-warmer I use to cook my herbs on." She turned to Candelaria when they were alone and said, "Tear up some linen in small pieces and chew on them to make them moist and warm."

By the time Rita came back with the brazier and had heaped it full of coals from the fireplace according to Penti's directions, enough linen had been moistened to wrap the baby like a tiny mummy. Next Penti took long lengths of linen and fashioned a hammock that could be raised or lowered to just the right distance from the coals to keep the infant warm.

When morning broke and Nazario stumbled into the room rubbing his eyes and heard the tale from Candelaria's lips, he could not believe his ears. He did not say a word when she finished but walked slowly across the room to where Penti stood tending the baby over the fire like a roast on a spit, and without glancing at the child bent and gently kissed her cheek.

Penti turned away, but there was a faint smile on her usually taciturn old face.

Rufina still slept, and so while Penti parted the linen folds for him, Nazario glanced at his child and asked, "What is it?"

Candelaria was nonplussed to find that she could not answer him, for she did not know!

"A girl, señor," Penti cackled. "Small, like her mother, but all there."

"Will she—live? She's so little!"

"I will take care of her, señor, if the Señora permits."

"Yes, of course she will. We cannot thank you enough, Penti."

Later when he told Rufina what Penti had done he was glad to hear her say, "You must beg her pardon for me, Nazario. I was afraid of her looks. But looks don't really mean anything, do they?"

"No, *querida*. And the child, what do you want to do about her?"

"Penti shall nurse her with Lasho."

He smiled. "And her name, when Padre Cazon baptizes her?"

"I think," said Rufina shyly, "that one of her names should be Gypsy, like Lasho's."

"Penti?" asked Nazario, kissing her hand.

She nodded.

"And her Christian name?"

"Encarnacion, I think, for your mother."

"Padre will like that—and his new grandaughter."

Under Figueroa, a certain peace and order returned to California. And the Californians, ever anxious to find the easiest and least demanding way out of a situation, agreed for the most part that General Figueroa was indeed a sensible and popular man.

All ports were now officially open to trade, and this, with the recall to Mexico of Echeandia, lessened the tension. The year had been a very dry one, but all of the ranchos and Missions had hides and tallow to trade, and there were more ships than ever on the coast. A good many more Americanos had come to settle permanently in California, and the Paisanos, though resenting them in many cases, grew to know and like those who intermarried with them and became a part of California.

For the most part, sailors, trappers, and traders, the *ojos azules,* or blue eyes, became popular with the women of the ports and pueblos.

The Americans were coming to California as well as the Russians at Fort Ross, the Germans and English, the Scots and Irish. Though it was a small unobtrusive trickle hardly noticed by the general public, men like Don Ygnacio Alvarjo, Don Diego Novato, and José Martinez were alarmed. The unstable state of the Missions, the presidios and the government made them fearful for the future of California.

Don Ygnacio heard from Joaquin, now a Franciscan priest serving in New Mexico. Matters were no better there. The Supreme Government seemed incapable of taking care of her outlying territories.

As he felt the net of isolation closing around him, Alvarjo concentrated more and more on Loma de Oro itself, and on preparing his sons to defend it if necessary. At times he was highly vexed with what seemed to him their indifference to the rancho. He never thought to blame himself for indulgently allowing them to grow up uneducated, untrained, and without any sense of responsibility. The worst of it was that when he severely tongue-lashed them or even on occasion whipped them to bring them to their senses, they seemed to drift further away from him, like quicksilver.

Nazario was bound up in his new wife and child, though when he rode with his father and Santos he showed some sense in the running of a rancho. His father took a faint hope in this glimmering promise.

Soledad had grown into a coy and bold little flirt, pat-

terning herself after the now again beautiful and brazen
Rufina. Ygnacio was not overly fond of his daughter-in-
law, but he was unfailingly polite to her, and a doting
grandfather to little Encarnacion, who had amazed them
all by growing into a fat chubby baby with a trace of her
mother's petulant arrogance.

The spring was dry and bitterly cold with few wild
flowers to brighten the drab landscape. To lift their spirits,
Señora Martinez decided to give a fandango at Rancho
Tocayo and invited all the countryside.

Ygnacio was recovering from a head cold, but when
Rufina and Soledad pleaded to be allowed to go to the
dance in the carriage, he agreed to drive them. Tarifa and
Dolores were absent on a visit to Los Angeles, and the
boys, with the exception of Nazario and Antonio who
were out helping Santos, were also away from home.

The drive across the barren hills was cold and windy.
Bundled in his heavy black velvet-trimmed cape, Ygnacio
felt the cold to the marrow of his bones, and his gloved
hands were stiff on the reins.

But the two girls were in high spirits, laughing and whispering all the way.

Ygnacio had told them that they could not stay the
night but would have to return at an early hour, and he
insisted on leaving the team in front of the house hitched
and ready. He took a glass of *aguardiente* with Don José
and watched the dancers in the big *sala,* then excused
himself to wait in the carriage for his daughter and
daughter-in-law.

Wrapped in his cape and a lap robe he lay down on
the seat and fell asleep. A hand shaking his shoulder
woke him and he realized it was very late.

Rufina peered at him anxiously.

"We didn't know you were out here all this time, Padre.
Are you all right?"

"Of course. We must go home. Get in."

He started to rise and a pain knifed through his lungs.

"What is it, Padre?" cried Soledad.

"My—chest. It is hard to breathe. Get me a glass of
aguardiente, Rufina, and ask José if he will drive us
home."

They brought Ygnacio into his bedroom, his face as white as paper, the breath sobbing in his lungs.

Penti and Candelaria made him as comfortable as they could. When his breathing was a little easier he insisted that Santos go to Los Angeles to get Tarifa, and sent Nazario to get Padre Cazon at the Mission.

In spite of Penti's remedies, Ygnacio grew steadily worse and when Padre Cazon and his wife arrived, he hardly knew them.

Tarifa knelt by his bed and held his hand while Padre Cazon administered Extreme Unction and gave him the last rites. She could not believe that he had grown so ill so quickly. When she had left him a few days before he had only been suffering from a simple head cold. This was all the fault of those idiotic girls for insisting on going to the dance in the carriage, and she felt a bitter hatred growing in her heart for them both.

In his moments of lucidity, Don Ygnacio talked to her about the rancho and the family.

"You must look after everything yourself, *querida*. There will be no one else. It will all fall on your shoulders. Keep the rancho intact; do not let them divide it or take it from you. Keep the family together whatever happens. Do not let them scatter. Keep them safe. Protect them. You are so strong and wise, *querida mía*. Promise me?"

She nodded her head, but even now there were no tears in her eyes, they were all inside, in her heart. Stripped of his strength and his arrogance, Ygnacio looked what he was, a tired old man.

"*Querida*—"

It was the last word he spoke. Padre Cazon said the prayers for the dead and the family rose from their places about the room and filed out, the girls weeping softly, the boys with a bereft, stricken look.

Tarifa stayed beside Ygnacio a moment longer, mentally renewing her promise to him, then got to her feet, straightened her shoulders, and walked out of the room.

She glanced about the patio and raised her eyes to Loma de Oro and the little house on the hill that Ygnacio had so loved. This was all Lasho's now. She was determined to protect it for him.

Don Ygnacio was buried from his own chapel by Padre

Cazon, and laid beside Encarnacion and his first children.

In leaving, the priest told Tarifa that things were not good at the Mission. Capitán Portillo had been sent to San Luis Rey as commissioner, to emancipate the neophytes under the secularization law. The Padres had little or nothing to say anymore about temporal matters, and the chaos and disorder was heartrending.

"The Indians do not want to work for the soldiers, who give them little or nothing of the fruits of their labors, and take all the rest to the presidio or to sell. And when they refuse to work they are whipped or put into the stocks. The young girls have been released from the *monjeria* and the unmarried soldiers make free with them. Poor Padre Oliva, who came from San Diego to take charge, is melancholy and half-crazed at the evils he faces daily."

"I am sorry for your troubles, Padre. You were Ygnacio's good friend, as you are mine. If I can do anything to help you or the Mission, you have only to ask," Tarifa said.

He smiled at her.

"You are kind, señora. I would ask for my passport and leave if it were not for the poor Indians, but they need us now more than ever. I am only thankful Padre Peyri did not remain to watch the disintegration of his work."

A week after Don Ygnacio's death, Tarifa gathered the family in the *sala* and read them the copy of his will.

"You may as well understand me," said Tarifa. "All of you. I promised your father to keep Loma de Oro intact and to see to your welfare. The rancho will not be broken up. You will all stay here and each of you will do as I say, or you will forfeit any right to your eventual share of Loma de Oro."

There was a smile on Luis' face, Tarifa saw out of the corner of her eye.

"No matter what happens to the rest of California," she went on, "Loma de Oro is not going to suffer. Not if it takes all the energy and every drop of blood in this family. You are through with being petted, pampered, useless creatures. The male servants will go into the fields. The fe-

male servants, with the exception of those needed to run
the house, will work outside also. And each of you will be
responsible for a certain job.

"Luis, you will plant and supervise the crops. We will
plant extra barley and wheat this year."

"What do I know about crops?" Luis asked morosely.

"You will go to the Mission and learn from Padre
Cazon."

He said nothing.

"Nazario, you will be responsible for the herds and will
work with Santos. If I catch you sneaking off to San
Diego again during working hours, I will whip you myself.
That goes for any of you who disobey me. This is your
rancho and I intend to see that you keep it."

"You mean you intend to have us work our fingers to
the bone to build it up so that you and Lasho can keep
it!" cried Nazario with sudden insight.

Tarifa reached over and cracked him across the face
with the back of her hand, her eyes blazing.

"Loma de Oro shall be dealt with as your father wished,
and so shall you."

She turned to Rufina and said, "You and Dolores will
act as housekeepers. You will direct Candelaria and the
house servants, see to the spinning and weaving, the soap-
making, and the sewing."

Antonio raised his eyes and asked, "What do I do?"

"You will go to the Mission every day and study with
Padre Cazon. Between times you will look after the palominos."

In one thing Don Ygnacio had failed his family. Except
for the fair amount of gold and silver coins he always
kept in the chest in his study, Tarifa could find no other
money of any kind. When she asked Santos about it he
said that Alvarjo, like the other hacendados who had no
banks available, kept the bulk of his fortune buried on
the land in a secret place, known only to the father and
the oldest son.

Santos did not know where it was buried, but he did
remember that Don Ygnacio claimed to have reburied his
money after Joaquin and Santiago left; therefore, there
would be no use writing to Joaquin to ask him. Luis also
claimed to have no knowledge of the whereabouts of the
money.

Tarifa told the family that night at dinner that there could be no money spent on anything, that they would have to trade for whatever they needed, and that she would purchase no more luxury items.

"I suppose," pouted Rufina, "I have to write to my father whenever I want a new comb or a fan?"

"You'll do no such thing," Tarifa warned. "You are now an Alvarjo, and you will live as one. When the hides and tallow are sold, I will take part payment in trade goods, the rest in silver and gold. But we will purchase only items of necessity."

"Why should we trust you with our money?" asked Luis.

"Because I am now the head of this house," said Tarifa bluntly, "and because you have no choice."

Santos asked Tarifa to ride out to the pasture with him a few days later and showed her two of the springs that had already run dry.

"It is bad, señora. We will have to kill double the amount of cattle and all the mesteños we can find."

Tarifa looked at the rock-hard adobe soil with its sparse covering of brown grass. Given even a little water it could blossom into verdant life. Where could she get water to save the stock?

"Are all the other ranchos as badly off?" she asked the mayordomo.

"All except Bolsa Coyotes. There is enough water there, no matter how dry the year."

"I will go and speak to Don Julio. Perhaps we can arrange to put some of our stock on his rancho temporarily."

She rode Guindilla to the Marcos rancho that afternoon and found Don Julio and his mother playing cards in the patio.

Don Julio listened to her proposition without comment, but with a good deal of inner jubilation. It was nice to know that the proud Alvarjos were not faring so well. That they needed something from him. They also had something he wanted, and now that Don Ygnacio was dead and Tarifa was the head of the family, perhaps he could make a deal with her. When he spoke it was in his most cordial tone.

"I have not been faring so well either, señora. Times are difficult. Since this accursed emancipation proclamation of Figueroa's, a good many of our Indians have left the rancho, even though I offered to pay them to stay. I understand few have left your rancho? Perhaps some of your vaqueros could look after our cattle also, when they come to tend yours?"

"Of course, Don Julio." This was better than Tarifa had expected. She had thought that he would demand payment in gold. She would have been willing to pay it.

"If you care to ride out with me to look over the pastures, you can select your own site for your herd, señora."

As they rode over the lush, green, well-watered pastures of Bolsa Coyotes, Tarifa was consumed with envy. If she could add this to Loma de Oro, it would make it the most wonderful rancho in California.

As if he had read her thoughts, Julio said lightly, "A pity our two ranchos cannot be combined?"

She glanced at him and found him studying her speculatively.

"You know it would please me if they were," he said. "You would have no more worries about water, and I would not suffer for want of vaqueros," he added lightly.

"I don't understand your proposition, Don Julio."

"It's quite simple. I am in love with Dolores. I always have been. She does not feel the same way toward me, I imagine, but I think she would learn to love me in time. I want her for my wife. If you could speak to her about the matter—after all, you are now the head of the house."

"I see," said Tarifa. "Bolsa Coyotes, for Dolores?"

"You put it very baldly, señora, but that is substantially correct. Do you find it distasteful that I go to such lengths to get the woman I love?"

"No. But if Dolores will not marry you?"

His full face hardened. "Then there will be no water and grass available to Loma de Oro."

Tarifa nodded. "I will think about the matter, Don Julio, and let you know."

"*Gracias,* señora."

A great hope rose in his heart as he watched Tarifa gallop away on the powerful golden Guindilla. He would like one of those horses, too. And he had a feeling that he would have it soon—and his bride.

* * *

It was a beautiful morning, warm and as clear as crystal, showing each dimple and fissure of the distant purple-shadowed mountains. Dolores sat alone in the *sala* making out a weekly menu for Candelaria. Of them all she was the only one who had not complained at the new regime Tarifa had forced upon them. She was actually enjoying the responsibility of her new chore, and she felt a new respect for all that Tía Isabella had done with so little apparent effort when she ran the Alvarjo household. Rufina was less than useless, but whenever Tarifa was around she made a great show of being busy. Now, pregnant again, much to her sorrow and Nazario's delight—for he wanted a son—she could use the excuse of her indisposition to keep her from her work. It seemed to her the only bright spot of her pregnancy. Nazario had his father's hot blood and Rufina was not pleased at the prospect of having as many children as Encarnacion had borne. She was determined not to end up a fat misshapen old matron, with no knowledge of anything but husband and children. After this child she meant to speak to Nazario.

Tarifa came in as Dolores finished her list.

"If you are not too busy I would like to talk to you, Dolores."

"Of course, Tarifa."

"Will you come into the study?"

Dolores, puzzled, followed her stepmother's erect figure into the study that she now used as an office.

"Sit down, Dolores." Tarifa told her quickly of the plight of the rancho and of Don Julio's proposal. She was amazed at the look of revulsion that came over Dolores' face as she finished.

"But I couldn't marry him! Never, never, never! I can't bear the sight of him. Padre would not have wanted me to marry him."

"You would prefer to marry Capitán Kinkaid?"

"Why not? I love him. When he returns we are going to be married. I promised to wait for him, and I am going to."

"Your padre said nothing to me of such a marriage, and I know that he would not have allowed it."

"I don't have to obey you!"

"I think you do, now that I stand in your father's place."

"I'll go to Tía Isabella!"

"That will not be necessary, Dolores."

The voice came from the door. They had not heard it open, and both were startled at the grim-faced figure in the doorway.

"Tía Isabella!" Dolores flew to her and buried her head on her breast.

Tarifa stood straight and still and her eyes stared into those of the old Spanish woman's without flinching.

"I have come back to my brother's house to look after his children," said Isabella calmly. "I would have come to the funeral if I had been informed of his death. As it is, I've just received word of it from Zenobio Sanchez."

"I thought you would not be interested in our affairs at Loma de Oro," Tarifa said shortly.

"My brother told me when I left that this house was open to me for as long as I lived. Now that he is gone I cannot leave his children here unprotected."

"Unprotected! From me?"

"If you like to put it that way. Rufina tells me that you make her work even though she is with child. Soledad tells me you teach her reading and writing instead of the gentle arts of a lady, and says that the boys are captives, not allowed off the rancho without your permission. And now what are you trying to do to Dolores?"

Tarifa flushed but held her tongue.

"She's trying to make me marry Don Julio Marcos!"

Isabella said nothing.

"Dolores would prefer to throw herself away on a foreigner," said Tarifa, "Capitán Kinkaid, even though her padre had forbidden him the house."

"He came to the Corlonas to see you behind my back," said Isabella to her niece. She had no liking for Kinkaid.

"I love him, Tía Isabella."

"What do you know of love; you are like a child. Your padre would not have approved of Capitán Kinkaid."

"He did not," said Tarifa. "Kinkaid came here asking for Dolores, and Ygnacio struck him in the face with his riding crop and ordered him off the rancho."

"And you still want to marry this man?" Isabella said with wonder.

"*Sí.*"

"You will do no such thing. You are an Alvarjo. I'll not see you throw yourself away on a foreigner. You will marry a good upstanding Californian."

"No, no!"

"We will speak of this later. Come to my room, child, and help me unpack."

Tarifa said nothing as they went out. Things were going to be different now that Isabella Alvarjo had returned.

Dolores was no more receptive to her aunt's pleas than she had been to Tarifa's.

"I cannot marry him, Tía Isabella."

"You are being selfish and obstinate, Dolores. I do not like Tarifa, as you know, and I do not approve of most of the things she does, but in this one instance I think she is right. It is time you married, and Don Julio is an honorable and gentlemanly Californian. You could do a great deal worse. Do you realize the position the rancho and all your family are in? Without hides or money, how are we to live?"

Dolores hung her head. She knew how bad things were; she had gone riding and seen the carcasses and bones whitening the plains. She, too, loved the rancho.

"Will you see the place where your parents lie buried go to strangers because of your own stubbornness?"

"No, no!" Dolores buried her face in her hands. "If it is the only way to save Loma de Oro, I will marry him." And she prayed in her own heart, God give me the strength to keep my word.

Dolores' wedding day was hot and sultry with dark scudding clouds and a threat of rain. Before the wedding party reached the Mission, the first large drops fell and a clap of thunder rolled down the valley with startling loudness.

Padre Cazon said the nuptial Mass, but declared that he could not come back with them for the festivities as he dared not leave poor Padre Oliva, who was in ill health.

Because the family was still in mourning for Don Ygnacio, only a few close friends had been invited for luncheon and dinner, with dancing to follow.

Dolores, solemn-faced but ethereally beautiful in white satin, her golden hair piled up under her mother's ivory comb, danced the first dance with her husband.

Julio could not believe she was really his at last. He held her tightly as if she might escape from him, and he was in a fever to leave Loma de Oro and take her home to bed at Bolsa Coyotes.

Sooner even than it was polite to do so, he made their farewells to the family and took Dolores up before him on his richly caparisoned horse. His hand around her waist was moist and heavy.

Thunder rolled across the valley as they rode, but no rain fell. Dolores felt dead inside as if she were going to her own funeral. And the hacienda, when they reached it, had no lights on and looked like a crouching thing under the lowering sky.

Julio lifted her off, whistled to an Indian sleeping on the veranda to take his horse, and led her inside.

"*Caramba!* Why didn't they leave a light?" he grumbled. "Nothing is ever right when mother is away. I am sorry she was in Mexico and missed the wedding, but she will be back soon and she will be so pleased to have you here, *querida.*"

He lit a candle and led her to the largest of the bedrooms which he had ordered prepared for them. The fools had actually done what he had asked them for once. The mahogany bed with the high carved head and footboard was polished, with a new lace-trimmed spread and fresh linen. There were flowers about the room, soap and water on the stand, and embroidered linen towels.

Dolores' things had been brought over that morning and a maid had neatly laid out her nightclothes, as well as Don Julio's.

He took her in his arms, felt her tremble, and kissed her with passion as he had wanted to do the day Don Ygnacio drove him out of the chapel at Loma de Oro. And Dolores held herself very still, accepting his embrace, closing her mind to the repugnance, the hatefulness of it.

"*Querida,* I am going to make you happy," he mumbled.

"Yes, Julio."

"I am going to get us some wine."

"Please, none for me."

"But this is our wedding night."

"Have some yourself if you want to, Julio, and send me a maid to help me with my clothes?"

"Very well." He kissed her again, lingeringly, and went out. A moment later a young Indian girl, who introduced herself shyly as Mariana, came in and helped Dolores into her nightgown and robe.

I am going to die, Dolores thought, I am never going to live through this night. She shivered and the maid asked if she was cold and went to close the window before she left.

Dolores braided her hair and got into the high bed. It was not as soft as her own and there was an odd smell about the sheets, as if they had been stored for a long time in an old chest.

Julio was some little time in joining her, and when he did it was apparent that he was slightly tipsy. Dolores' blood congealed with fear. She felt as if she were slowly suffocating.

He talked to her intimately and jokingly as he got undressed and crawled in beside her.

Dolores could never remember her wedding night except as a blur of horror and degradation. She knew that she would never feel clean again, and she prayed that she would die.

She did not die, however. She found herself the mistress of Bolsa Coyotes and again faced the problems of running a large household. Don Julio kept the place constantly full of guests, and Dolores found that the atmosphere of the house was entirely different from Loma de Oro. There was something strange, an undercurrent here, that she could not fathom. The servants for the most part had a sly, sulky way about them.

There was one room where Dolores never went. The study. She could not face the prayer closet there, where Bart Kinkaid had held her in his arms and told her he loved her. She had no right to think of him, she was another man's wife now, but she still remembered his steady voice and strong arms. Why was life so cruel? Why hadn't she run away with him when he asked her to in Santa Barbara?

Julio also liked to travel, and he took her with him to

Santa Barbara, Monterey, and San Francisco, where he
showered her with costly gifts and took delight in showing
her off to his friends. He knew that she did not love him,
but he was irked that she showed no feeling for him
whatsoever. As time wore on, her continued indifference
grew to infuriate him, and he took to goading her and trying to humiliate her into a response of some kind, even
anger. But she remained aloof and serene, merely bowing
her head helplessly under his tirades.

He began to drink too much and to leave her on the
rancho alone for weeks at a time, only coming home to
sleep with her at night and then be off again.

In her loneliness and misery, Dolores was glad when
her mother-in-law returned, though she was a watchful,
taciturn old woman without much to say. She was glad
that her son had succeeded in getting the high-born wife
he wanted, though he seemed not to find much happiness
with her, and she herself felt little affection for the girl.

When Dolores told Julio that she was pregnant, he
laughed with glee.

"At least I'm going to get something out of you, and
it had better be a boy. I don't want any girls cluttering
up the place. I'm tired of being the only male in the house."

Dolores suffered through the first weeks of her pregnancy, too ill to eat and too nerve-wracked to sleep, and
then she asked Julio if she could send for one of her
sisters.

"No! I'll not have them peeping and prying into my
home life. You have mother and the maids. This is your
home now, and you'll live in it."

"Please, Julio. Just till after the baby is born?"

"No. We won't discuss the matter again."

Dolores tried to bribe one of the servants to take a message to Loma de Oro, but they had been ordered by Don
Julio not to do her bidding, and were afraid to disobey
him.

"He whips us, and does other terrible things," said Mariana breathlessly. "I would help you, señora, but I am
afraid."

As the birth of his child drew near, Julio never left
the house. He drank day and night and watched his wife
like a hawk, with moody, speculative eyes.

Late one night she went into the dining room for a little brandy because she felt chilled, and through the open door of the study she saw Julio and one of the maids embracing.

The sight so sickened her that she felt she was going to faint, but she managed to turn silently and make her way back to the bedroom.

Early the next morning her pains began and she cried out for Mariana. The girl, white-faced and shaken, fetched Señora Marcos and Don Julio. Julio stared at his wife, puffy-faced and red-eyed, but he did not go near her.

"Julio—send for Tarifa or Penti for the love of God!" she begged through her pain.

"No. We will take care of you here." His deliberate voice gave terse orders to the maid. "You are not to call anyone from Loma de Oro for my wife."

As the morning wore away, Dolores' mind cleared now and then from the blur and frenzy of her pain, and she called again for Tarifa and Penti.

Julio, standing in the doorway with a glass in his hand, did not reply. She was taking a devilishly long time with his son, curse her. He wondered now why he had gone to all the trouble to marry her.

When he left the room, Mariana held her mistresses' hand and wept. A fat married woman from the servant's quarters was acting as midwife in a disinterested, unskilled manner. And when the child was born at last, she found herself unable to halt the bleeding.

"You can't let her die!" cried Mariana. "There is a woman at Loma de Oro, she says, who knows of such things. I am going to get her."

"You will be whipped, or hung up by your thumbs," said the midwife without interest.

"It doesn't matter." Mariana climbed out of the window as the other woman placed a blonde, delicate-looking baby next to Dolores.

A little girl as pale as her mother.

Tarifa was in her office when the terrified little maid from Bolsa Coyotes was shown in by Soledad.

She listened to the girl's tale in silence and when she had finished, sent for Penti and Santos.

When Santos entered Tarifa was writing furiously on a piece of paper. Finishing, she folded it and tucked it into her sash. "Get the boys and the vaqueros," she told him. She explained what they were to do and Santos nodded, his eyes flat and hard.

To Penti, who had also come in, Tarifa said, "Bring your medicines, *pronto*. You will ride ahead with me."

Tarifa did not spare Guindilla on the way, and she arrived ahead of Penti, who was riding Cobrizo.

Julio, with his face like a thundercloud, barred Tarifa's entrance.

"I want to see Dolores."

"She is ill."

"I know. I have brought my maid to treat her."

"What lies has that slinking little slut Mariana told you?"

Tarifa held onto her temper with an effort. Dolores was the first problem to be dealt with. Her anger for Julio could wait.

"God help you, Julio, if half of what she has told me is true."

He backed away from the fierceness in her face.

Tarifa marched into the house, opening doors until she found Dolores' room.

"Tarifa!" It was little more than a glad sigh.

"I am here, Dolores, and I have brought Penti. Everything will be all right now." She took Dolores' hand in hers and studied the pale, too-thin face anxiously. She cursed Julio anew at the sight of the wistful weariness in the lovely face.

Dolores shook her head. Already she seemed miles away.

"It is—too late. I know. Tarifa?"

"Yes?"

"The baby. A girl. I want you to take her back to Loma de Oro. Promise—you will not let Julio—have her?"

"I promise."

Dolores smiled faintly and closed her eyes.

Penti came in and busied herself with the patient. But a moment later she shook her head in silence.

"What is it?" asked Tarifa in Romany.

"It is too late. There is nothing I can do."

"There must be something!"

"No. Nothing. And she is so young."

They waited beside her helplessly, one on each side of the bed, and Tarifa felt the hatred and anger for the man in the *sala* rising in her like a tide. The beast who had caused this, who had killed his wife not in one way, but in every inhuman way possible.

Dolores opened her eyes once more briefly, and gazed at her sleeping daughter. As Tarifa knelt to hold her hand she smiled, and the hand Tarifa held grew slack.

"She is gone," Penti said, without inflection.

Tarifa rose. The need for revenge was bone-deep in her and as insatiable as a live thing, a monster clawing to get out.

She left the room, passed Julio, and went out to take her blacksnake whip from Guindilla's saddle. The Loma de Oro men and vaqueros mounted on their horses, grim-faced and silent as icons, ringed the hacienda.

"You will stay here," she told Santos evenly. "No one is to leave the hacienda or enter it."

They nodded and watched her go back into the house. Santos saw the whip and thought of the hours he had spent teaching her to use it. She was as deadly accurate with it as Ygnacio had been. He did not let himself wonder what she was going to do with it.

"Your wife is dead," Tarifa told Julio in an expressionless voice. "You killed her."

"If she is dead it has nothing to do with me," he blustered.

"It has everything to do with you! You said you loved her. You lied. You loved only what she was, and when you found you could not reach it, force it to succumb to you, you killed her. You kept her a prisoner here. You subjected her to every humiliation and torture that you could think of. You left her to the mercies of an ignorant Indian midwife."

"You believe the word of a lying little Indian whore?" he asked insolently.

"I believe truth when I hear it and see it! She begged you to send for me and you would not. I am going to show you what it is like to beg without hope of getting mercy."

She took a folded paper from her sash.

"You will sign this before I leave."

He was startled out of his nonchalance.

"What is it? I will sign nothing!"

"It is a deed for Bolsa Coyotes, naming your daughter Dolores as beneficiary and myself as her legal guardian until she is of age."

A look of contempt swept over Julio's face. "Do you think I am mad? Do you imagine you can enter my house like this and dictate to me?"

"If you will bother to look outside, Julio, you will see my men surrounding the hacienda. They are armed and they have orders to let no one inside or outside. You are my prisoner."

"Do you think such a paper signed under duress would be considered legal?" he asked mockingly.

"This one will. You will leave California as soon as it is signed. And you will not return."

He laughed and turned to pour himself a drink. The bottle went crashing from his hand and his face grew livid at sight of the whip curling about his fist like an oily snake. He disengaged it and threw it from him furiously.

"You've gone too far, Tarifa! Get out of my house, you Gypsy whore!"

The whip cracked like thunder, ripping the sleeve from his right arm, cracked again in a twinkling and opened the skin from shoulder to forearm. Julio roared with pain and lunged at her.

She moved away from him as nimbly as a fawn through bracken, and the whip—there was no stopping the whip. It rose and fell, flicking him on the raw skin, tearing a piece from his ear, slashing at his face and neck and even when he clutched it with his two hands, it seemed to writhe and twist with a life of its own and slip through his clawing fingers like an eel.

Tarifa tripped as she neared the door to the patio and, seeing his chance, Julio jerked the whip toward him and threw her flat on her face.

In an instant he was on top of her, his hands seeking her throat. They rolled over and over into the patio and Tarifa fought him like a cat, slackening her muscles till she seemed to melt and twist out of his grasp like butter.

"I'll kill you!" he panted. "I'll kill you, you devil's spawn of hell!"

Tarifa bit and clawed then raised her strong legs and sank her spurs into his thighs. He screamed with pain and rolled away from her. As swift as light she was on her feet and running. Inside the *sala* where he lumbered after her, his legs dripping crimson like a maddened bull, she had just time to snatch up the whip before he reached her.

She struck him across the temple with the butt and he staggered back into the patio, Tarifa following. She had never known such strength, such exultation. Nothing could stop her, not death itself. She was like a wall of fire, a raging tornado, the avenger incarnate.

He raised his hands to protect his face and clawed desperately at the stinging lash as it still tormented him, biting, piercing, gnawing at his body till he seemed swimming in a nightmare of exquisite suffering.

He was conscious that he ran about the patio like a frenzied animal, seeking escape. But when he tried to run down the veranda or enter a door the whip drove him back, biting and slashing him like the fangs of a maddened dog.

He stumbled and fell on his knees and covered his head with his arms, the breath sobbing in his lungs, and he heard Tarifa's voice as from a great distance, cold as an executioner's ax.

"Will you sign the deed?"

"God damn you, no!" he sobbed. "I will never sign it! Never!"

"Oh yes, you will."

He raised his head in defiance and the whip sprang at his face like a striking cobra. It seemed to Julio as if a hot hook had suddenly been sunk into his eye socket. He felt an immense mountainous pain that dragged him to his feet, and something warm and soft rolled down his cheek and fell to the ground.

He slapped a hand to his eye to stem the gush of blood. *"Sangre de Dios!* You've torn out my eye!" he screamed. He could not believe it. The pain and horror swept over him, leaving him weak and nauseated.

"Now you know how she felt," said Tarifa harshly. "Are you ready to sign the rancho over to your daughter and leave California?"

"Damn you, damn you to hell, you fiend!" he sobbed

shaking from head to foot. "I will kill you for this! Someday I will kill you!" He was shaking so violently his tongue seemed to rattle against his teeth like a stick against fence slats.

"Are you ready to sign? You have one other eye, Julio."

"Help!" he shouted suddenly in a dreadful voice. "Help me, someone! Vaqueros—servants, where are you? Don't you hear your master calling, damn you! Damn you—"

"They are not going to help you, Julio," she said dispassionately. "We will stay in the patio, you and I, undisturbed until the matter is settled. If you prefer to go to Mexico, or wherever you are going, completely blind—"

"No! For God's sake, no! Have pity on me, Tarifa. Leave, take the child, use my rancho but go and let me stay here?" He was sobbing openly now.

"You are never going to set foot on this rancho again," she said. "It belongs to your daughter now. If you ever attempt to come back, I will kill you, Julio."

She raised the whip.

"No! Wait—I will sign. I will go away." He began to cry like a child in misery and despair as she led him to a table and helped him into a chair. She spread out the paper and held his hand around the quill.

"Write, Julio."

He managed to sign his name in a shaky scrawl, his blood spattering the page.

"Penti will fix your eye," said Tarifa, "before you leave, and Santos will take you and your mother to San Diego. I understand there is a whaler headed for Loreto. You will sail on it. And you will not come back."

He hardly heard her as he crouched, holding his head in his hands. Pain convulsed him, throbbing through his wracked body with an agonizing rhythm of its own.

"Don't try to return, Julio."

And Julio knew briefly something worse than his pain and humiliation, the cold paralyzing fear of a woman. Something he would never have thought possible and it shook him to the core. He hated her far more for this than for what she had done to him physically. This would stay with him, haunt him, etched sharply into his brain for as long as he lived.

* * *

They brought Dolores and her child home to Loma de Oro, and laid the mother beside her parents in the chapel graveyard. It seemed to the family that there had been nothing but deaths and burials since their mother had been killed, and in a way none of them were the same since her death. The fun and laughter had gone out of Loma de Oro, and the gentle easy way of life was a dimly remembered thing of the past. Nothing was the same.

CHAPTER 16

In the early-morning light they left the rancho, the un-greased cartwheels of the heavily laden *carretas* screeching behind them like banished ghosts, and Tomas in charge of the teamsters.

Tarifa wore the costume she was seldom out of these days: black velvet trousers and jacket, red sash, her flat-crowned black sombrero jerked tightly under her jaw by the braided black-and-silver strap. Her spurs were seldom off her feet these days. She had almost forgotten that she was a woman.

Since Dolores' death, and the sailing of Julio and Señora Marcos, she had put Nazario and Rufina in charge of Bolsa Coyotes. Rufina's increasing instability had not escaped Tarifa's notice, and though she did not know its exact cause, she hoped that being alone under their own roof might ease the problem. The Alvarjos had been talked about enough; Tarifa was determined for her son's sake that no further scandal touch Loma de Oro.

There were many new houses in San Diego and too

many more Americanos and idle, drifting Indians to suit Tarifa.

"Which is the ship?" she asked Santos, who had arranged for a Boston brig to take their hides and tallow.

Two brigs, both flying the American flag, swung at anchor in the bay, one with her crew still running about the deck and swarming through the rigging, so that it was apparent that she had just arrived.

"The one to the left," Santos said. "The *Marblehead*. The other one wasn't here yesterday."

He stopped one of the men working on the shore and pointed to the new vessel.

"What ship is that?"

"The *Lorelei*, señor. Just in a few mintues ago, from Boston, with a fine store of goods, I hear."

Santos nodded. A long boat was just putting out from the newly arrived brig, two men in blue uniforms and brass buttons in the stern. One of them leaned forward in an odd precarious position and seemed to be speaking sharply to the crew, who rowed with powerful sure strokes that carried the boat through the water like a chip on the tide.

Tarifa stood idly on the beach watching the approaching boat while she waited for Santos to make arrangements for them to board the *Marblehead*. Neither ship was known to her, but there were so many new ships on the coast since the trading ban had been lifted that she was familiar with few of them.

Santos beckoned to her and she turned away as the boat crunched on the sand behind her. She was walking along the beach when she felt a hand close around her arm, halting her in her tracks. She felt herself swung around, gently but firmly.

"I thought it was you—Señora Alvarjo," said Bart Kinkaid. His lean Indian-face was darker than she remembered it, his teeth flashing white in the sunlight. A glint of tightly held excitement shone in his gray eyes.

She stood stockstill in the first shock of seeing him. When she spoke, her words were annoyed rather than angry.

"You have been gone a long time, Capitán Kinkaid."

"Too long, señora. But not of my own choosing, I can

assure you," he said. "Is there some place where I can speak to you alone? It is important."

She raised her brows. She wanted to be rid of him. But sooner or later he would find out about Dolores. Then he would come seeking her. It would be better to have the unpleasant interview over now.

"I have horses," she said. "We can ride to Gaspar Escobar's house. He won't mind. But I can only give you a moment. I have to complete the deal for my hides and tallow aboard the *Marblehead*."

He nodded, grateful that she did not cut him off coldly as Don Ygnacio had once ordered her to do. It never occurred to him to wonder why she, instead of her husband, was completing the transaction, going alone aboard an American ship.

Tarifa spoke briefly to Santos when they approached the *carretas* that he had already set about unloading, and then offered Marca to Kinkaid.

He had never ridden one of the palominos before and he knew the moment he hit the saddle, as he knew a superb ship the minute he stepped on her deck, that this was perfection.

The graceful arching neck and deep chest, the springing, powerful muscles that seemed to move him forward as the sea moves a ship, inexorably, effortlessly, spoke of a crowning completeness of breeding.

Neither spoke as they galloped over the sand to Escobar's little house below the town. Tarifa, frowning, was wondering how to put herself in the best light when she told her story, even as she asked Gasper for the use of his *sala*. And Kinkaid, his jaw hard, was contemplating how to win Tarifa to his side. For he was determined not to quarrel again with Don Ygnacio if he could avoid it.

For the little over three years of his absence, he had been alternately like a man gone mad, and a condemned prisoner coldly helpless in his bonds and resigned to his fate.

In the little *sala* she had once thought so grand, Tarifa removed her hat, as Kinkaid did, and turned to face him. He had changed. The lines of his face were sharper, his level gray eyes, so cold and steady, were more commanding even with the odd feverish light that now shone in their depths. He is through asking us for what he wants, she thought; now he will demand it. She felt a tremor of fear at what his reaction would be to Dolores' death as she waited for him to speak first.

"For old times' sake," he asked smiling, "may I call you Tarifa? It will be easier."

She nodded.

"I have come back for Dolores," he said. "You know I love her, and that she has promised to be my wife? I am sorry if it is necessary to offend your husband again, but this time I will not leave without her. I had hoped you might help us by speaking to Don Ygnacio?" He saw that her face did not change. You could never tell what Tarifa was thinking; she was a maddening creature. But he saw her take a deep breath, as if she were bracing herself.

"I cannot speak to Ygnacio for you, Capitán Kinkaid."

"Cannot?" His dark brows rose. What game was she trying to play with him now?

"He is dead," she said flatly.

"I am sorry to hear that. I admired him very much."

"Then you should respect his wishes, as I do."

"His wishes?"

"You know he forbade you to marry Dolores. It was his wish that she marry a Californian, one of her own people."

"I'm afraid I can't respect that wish any longer. In any case he is dead. The knowledge cannot hurt him."

Tarifa's eyes pierced him. "You have no choice. Dolores married a Californian, as her father wished. She died in childbirth a year later."

He rose and stood staring at her coppery face and long black slanting eyes while words spilled contemptuously from him.

"I don't believe you. You would lie, cheat, anything to gain your own ends or to please Alvarjo!"

He took a step toward her, his fists clenched. "Where is she?"

Tarifa stood up also, her chin lifted. "At Loma de Oro—"

"That's better!" He would shake the truth out of her if he had to.

"—in her grave, beside her mother and father."

His slap cracked across her lips like a cannon shot, and

he saw the blood as her mouth began to swell. She clawed at him cursing in Romany, but he grasped both her wrists and held her writhing and twisting.

"Tell me the truth, damn you!"

"I told you! She's dead, dead, dead! You'll never see her again. And I'm glad. Glad, do you hear!"

A part of him still refused to believe her, but another part, the deep inner core of him that had lived with a similar fear aboard the *Arabella*, felt a cold and suffocating dread that she spoke the truth. But she couldn't be telling the truth. She couldn't! The truth wasn't in the lying little bitch. He was back and Dolores was waiting for him, as she had promised to wait, no matter what her father said or did. She was his, no one else's.

He threw Tarifa from him and she landed on her hands and knees, her hair falling in a tangle around her face and shoulders, a diabolical knife-sharp hatred in her black eyes.

"You are too late, Capitán Kinkaid," she hissed. "She married another man, and now she is dead. If you don't believe me, ride to Loma de Oro and look at her grave. Ask Padre Cazon, who buried her. Ask the neighbors, the family, who attended her funeral!"

He staggered back a step as if she had struck him, then, without a word, turned from the room and threw himself on Marca, wheeling him north up the coast.

Behind him Tarifa's coarse Gypsy laughter rang out metalically, as merciless and inescapable as a death knell.

Tía Isabella stood on the front veranda shading her eyes against the sun. She knew the rider was one of the family, for the horse was a palomino, but no Alvarjo sat so rigidly in the saddle or whipped his mount as ruthlessly as this one did.

It was with an unpleasant shock that she recognized Kinkaid. She turned and called sharply for Luis, who was in the *sala*.

"It is Capitán Kinkaid," she said quickly. "Your father forbade him in this house, and he is riding Santos' horse."

Luis came to stand beside her as Kinkaid threw himself from the exhausted Marca and came at them.

"Where is she?" he demanded feverishly. "Where is Dolores?"

The Alvarjos exchanged a startled, stricken glance.

"Take me to her," Kinkaid cried, moving toward the door.

Luis stood in front of him, barring the way, trying to speak.

"Get out of my way."

"Wait, señor. You don't understand. Stay here——"

His words were cut short by the staggering blow that smashed into his jaw. Luis slid foolishly to the floor and Kinkaid leaped over him.

"Wait!" Isabella commanded. But he was gone. She knelt and called to the servants as she tried to help Luis rise. The Americano was indeed a madman; they were all in danger. She would send for the vagueros.

Kinkaid rushed headlong through the patio, past the chapel, and entered the little graveyard. He searched the headstones wildly, his sight too blurred to read the inscriptions. Augustin, Carlos, Ramon, Encarnacion, Ygnacio, Dolores . . . *Dolores Maria Alvarjo Marcos.*

He stood foolishly, reading it again and again, still not crediting his senses, still believing it some monstrous joke of Tarifa's, until a dry sob rose from the pit of his stomach and shook him. He covered his face. He fell on his knees, bending double with pain as realization flooded him with the bitterness of utter and complete defeat. Too late. Too late. . . . The words etched themselves in his brain in lightning-clear letters.

He would have liked to dig up the hard dirt with his bare hands and smother himself in it beside her. If he'd had a weapon, he would have used it. But there was nothing, nothing but the consuming pain that wracked his body and mind and soul, like a raging brush-fire.

He lost track of time, feeling seemed to recede from him, and a great numbness took the place of everything else. Nothing moved in him.

When he felt the firm hand on his shoulder, he would have ignored it, but it reached under his arm and pulled insistently.

He looked up into Padre Cazon's concerned, sympathetic face, and became dimly aware of the others. Isabella, the Alvarjo sons and daughters, even Tarifa—though how she had gotten here in so short a time he couldn't imagine. And then he saw with a start that the sunlight had faded to a mauve dusk.

"Come, my son," Padre Cazon said. "You have had a bad shock. If you will ride back to the Mission with me, I will try to explain."

Kinkaid got slowly to his feet. He felt drained of everything, as weak and purposeless as a new colt, but he allowed Cazon to lead him gently from the graveyard past the family with their lowered, wondering eyes, past Tarifa, who had no expression whatever save a faint smile of contempt on her swollen lips.

Padre Cazon's cell suffered from damp and a sad unmistakable neglect. The Padres had been given no choice of quarters by the new administrator, who had assigned them the least desirable rooms and the smallest amount of food and fuel possible, in the hope that they would leave. But the Padres had stayed, accepting the hardship and contempt heaped upon them, in order to protect as best they could what remained of the neophytes' spiritual and temporal welfare.

Cazon produced a basket Isabella had given him as he left and set food and wine on the rough table before his dull-eyed guest.

"Eat, my son. You will feel better."

"I can't." The words, the first Bart had dared allow to escape his lips, came hollowly, as from a deep dungeon.

Cazon poured wine and held the cup to Kinkaid's lips until he swallowed. He encouraged him with small words until it was empty. He watched critically as color tinged the American's lips and cheeks and he buried his head on his arms with a groan at the return of feeling.

Padre Cazon prayed silently until Kinkaid raised his haggard face sometime later and said dully, "Tell me, Padre."

The priest told the truth as he knew it. Dolores' decision after her father's death to marry the Californian. The plight of Loma de Oro, following Ygnacio's death, and the reasonableness of joining Rancho Bolsa Coyotes to Loma de Oro in view of the present difficulties. He did not mention the tales he had heard of Tarifa's whipping Don Julio and forcing him to leave California. He was not sure these tales were true, so horrifying were they, and so strangely pleased were the Bolsa Coyote vagueros to tell them. No, he would not repeat such tales. He told Kinkaid only that

Marcos had decided to leave California after Dolores' untimely death, and that Don Julio had left his rancho to his infant daughter Dolores, with Tarifa as administrator.

To Kinkaid's dulled senses, only the fact of Dolores' marriage and death made any impression. What did he care, now that she was gone, what happened to the rancho, the child, the Marcoses?

This terrible void in him was like a canyon into which he was slipping slowly but surely. To save himself he clutched at the wine but it was like pouring water into a sand hole for all the effect it had on him.

After a time he said, "Don Zenobio told me you were once a soldier, Padre. Did you ever feel despair, so deep and black like the sea, that you'd gladly put a bullet through your head to make sure you'd drown in it for good? It's not the void I mind. It's the coming out of it. I can't live without her. What am I to do?"

The priest stood up and folded his work-calloused hands inside his full gray sleeves. The room was cold in spite of the small fire he had managed to kindle in the tiny grate.

Every man knows despair at one time or another, Capitán Kinkaid, for different reasons and to a different degree. I knew despair when I found myself wounded and left to die by my comrades. I realized I was going to die without having done anything useful with my life, without ever having really lived. Mere existence, even if it seems sufficient and pleasurable, is not living. Living is going out of yourself, going forth to meet a personal challenge, doing, giving, building something within yourself. Everything you experience is a part of life, and can be borne, if you are truly intent on building."

"You mean I should put on a monk's robes and offer myself for the good of a bunch of ungrateful heathens, like you," Bart said sardonically.

"I don't mean any such thing!" The priest's anger surprised him.

"I mean each man has his own way to go, his own job to do, his sacrifice to make, if you like. Mine was to come here and work among the natives. Not everyone can do the same—or should. You asked me about despair, and I'm telling you everyone experiences it sometime. Our Blessed Lord knew it at Gethsemane," he said quietly. "You can accept it as He did, or you can spend your life battling against it, or you can escape it physically and mentally if you are a coward."

Kinkaid said nothing. He did not want to think with his numbed, tortured brain; he wanted to wallow in his own misery, to drown in it and not think at all. But this driving outspoken priest was forcing him to think in spite of himself.

"I fancied myself a strong man, too," Cazon continued, his sandaled feet slapping the dirt floor of the cell, his beads clacking at his side as he marched back and forth. "In a way it is worse for the strong when they fall. They have had no experience of depending on others, of asking for or accepting help. You came back here determined to marry Dolores, and now that you cannot you are engulfed by your own pains and inadequacies. You can deal with physical reality. Why are you afraid of spiritual reality?"

"Afraid?"

"Yes. A man is not one thing, but three. Body, mind, and spirit. We tend, all of us, to divide ourselves ruthlessly into two beings: the body and mind that experience all temporal matters, and the soul that hovers in the background, timidly absorbing whatever bits of belief or spirituality we deem worthy to throw it.

"I tell you it is all wrong. You cannot divide them. The body and mind and soul together make up a human being. We are not a spirit walking around in a body—we are a body and spirit, welded together into one, until death. What your body does, your soul suffers for and vice versa, as in my own case. You are a man of perception, Capitán, a man of strength. The loss of your beloved must not rob you of all sane judgment. Dolores herself would not have expected that of you."

Kinkaid gave a hard laugh. "Don't give me that, Padre, drawing upon the thoughts and wishes of the dead. I'm not a churchman. I'm not sure I believe in a soul."

"You loved Dolores?"

"Yes—I loved her."

"And to marry her you would have become a Catholic? For I know she would not have married you any other way."

"Yes. I would have done that—but only to please her."

"Then you believed in her?"

"I believed in her because I loved her. She was my life."

"So is God," said the priest softly.

CHAPTER 17

With the sudden death of Governor Figueroa in September José Castro took temporary charge of the government. But there was little satisfaction in the hearts of Californians. North and south continued to mistrust each other with a growing intensity.

The Indians who had left the Missions and the ranchos found their emanicipation and much prated equality nothing more than a farce. Those who actually got land and a few cattle were soon stripped of them by the shrewder merchants or rancheros, and found themselves reduced to sweeping the streets of the pueblos or performing other menial tasks. Now, for the slightest infraction, they were put into the stocks or bound naked over a cannon and given a hundred lashes. In the past, even for the most flagrant crimes, the Padres had never meted out more than twenty-five lashes to a neophyte offender. Gone was liberty, and what little dignity they had left.

The temporal management of sixteen of the Missions had been taken away from the Padres, and put into the hands of administrating mayordomos, who in turn replaced the first *comisionados*. At San Luis Rey, Portillo had been replaced by Pio Pico.

The drought that the land still suffered from made a large-scale slaying of cattle a necessity. It also made it possible for the wily administrators to stock their own private holdings with the "slaughtered" Mission cattle.

A terrible pestilence and fever followed the massive killing of surplus stock, nearly depopulating the valleys of the Sacramento and San Joaquin. Constant and frightening depredations from the renegade neophytes who had allied themselves to wild gentile bands and unscrupulous white traders kept the country in constant turmoil. Herds depleted by the drought and scattered from the lack of vaqueros to care for them made the receipts of the Custom House far from sufficient to meet the military and civil requirements. Hard times dogged the footsteps of every Californian, no matter how vast his holdings, and in spite of the brisk trade of foreign ships buying hides and tallow.

In the noon heat of the kitchen, Candelaria was ladling out steaming *puchero,* a stew of meat and vegetables which Tarifa had designated as adequate to feed both the servants and the members of the household. Candelaria found herself recalling unhappily the fine meals she had once prepared for the hacienda when Don Ygnacio had been alive.

Unlike most of the ranchos, Loma de Oro had lost few of its vaqueros in the new wave of emancipation. But of late there were increased grumblings about the food and the long hours of work demanded of them to meet the needs of both Loma de Oro and Bolsa Coyotes.

Santos alone remained aloof and uncomplaining. He, too, had a nostalgic longing for the old days. But he knew there could be worse things for a man to bear than hard times.

That morning, high above the *arroyo seco,* he had come suddenly upon Salvador, thin as a lizard and naked save for his breechcloth. Salvador, he knew, had never gone back to the Mission after Padre Peyri left. He was a renegade now with a price on his head for the cattle and horses he had stolen, the haciendas he had looted and burned, and even, it was said, for the soldiers he had killed.

Santos had offered him tobacco and watched sadly as he leaped to take it. "They will give your people food at Loma de Oro, if you will come for it," he said.

The Indian raised his head quickly. "We want no more charity from white men!"

"You did not always feel that way."

"I have my eyes open now. You see what has happened to our people—to the Missions? Padre Peyri left us," he said in a harsh voice. "He did not care. Soon they will all have gone and left our people to be slaves to their new masters."

Santos eased his leg over the horn and stroked Marca's neck. "I am not a slave, nor are those who have stayed to work the ranchos. If we are patient things will be better."

"When? When we are all dead like worn-out oxen! You cannot trust the whites, not even the Padres. They will all deceive you!"

"The Padres have not deserted you, Salvador; you have deserted them. They stay, and lead a dog's life to try and protect our people. They have every right to go. Everything has been taken from them. They stay because they would not leave our people in misery."

"Padre Peyri left!" The old wound, the old scar.

"*Sí*. Because his chief ordered him to go."

Salvador considered this, but the pain, the humiliation of their parting was still too fresh in his memory. He straightened up, his bow in his lean hands.

"My people have only one hope, to get rid of the whites and go back to their own ways."

Santos shook his head wearily. "You will kill and be killed, and still it will not change matters."

"You have lived among the whites too long, working for a woman!" said Salvador contemptuously.

Santos straightened his sombrero and eased his feet back into the stirrups. "Like Padre Cazon and the others who remain, I am doing the thing I was set to do. I will not run away from it. I have not lost my faith, Salvador, like you. And I would tell you one more thing. Don't bring your gentiles or your renegade whites against Loma de Oro. I would cut you in two with my *reata* without a thought."

He turned his back deliberately on the angry face of the naked Indian and held Marca to a steady walk until he was out of range of Salvador's arrows.

When he left the Mission at dawn, Kinkaid had gone directly to the Santa Teresa. He was only vaguely aware of the desolation the drought had wrought on the once prosperous rancho. He found Zenobio a ragged red-eyed old man, but got the warm welcome he sought and the solace he needed.

Zenobio filled him with *aguardiente* and listened sympathetically to his ravings, and when he was finished sat with him in a soul-healing silence worth far more than mere words of comfort.

"*Amigo,* I will tell you," the old soldier said finally. "Ygnacio was a fool, a stiff-necked old fool. I always speak ill of the dead if I think they deserve it. Why not? Is a man any less to blame for his mistakes because he is dead? Ygnacio was a fool to marry that Gypsy wench, though I must give the devil her due and say she has run the rancho well since he died. And he was a fool not to let you marry Dolores. It gave Tarifa the advantage she needed. And Isabella, returning when she did, no doubt helped her too."

"I don't understand, Zenobio." Bart's senses were blessedly dulled by the *aguardiente* and he realized that the old man was thick-tongued, too, and probably rambling.

"Tarifa's cattle were dying for lack of water," Zenobio explained. "The only water available was on Bolsa Coyotes, so she tried to make arrangements with Don Julio. She had some gold—not much, because Ygnacio died without telling any of them where he buried his hoard. But Julio didn't want gold. He wanted only one thing. Dolores."

A great throbbing had set up in Bart's temples as he listened. But Zenobio's voice ground on and on, relentless.

"Dolores did not want to marry him. I am sure of that. But she allowed herself to be persuaded. Tarifa wanted to save the rancho. Dona Isabella was determined that no Alvarjo was going to dilute her Castilian blood by marrying an Americano.

"So they were married, and Julio found that marrying a woman like Dolores can be worse than Hell, if she has no more feeling for you than a fly on the wall." The old man paused to splash more *aguardiente* into the glasses. "I have no concern for Julio. He got what was coming to him, if the tales I have heard are true."

"What tales?" The question struck in Kinkaid's brain like a barb.

Zenobio was startled at the sound of another voice in the room. Lately, he often ranted on to himself when he was alone and in his cups. A powerful hand reached out to clutch his shirtfront and dragged him erect in his chair.

"What tales, damn it? Tell me! What tales?"

Zenobio gaped at him but went on. "Tales of the servants. Lies, most likely, about how he kept her a prisoner there, had other Indian women, wouldn't let her send for her family when she was having the child. . . ."

A black cloud swam before Kinkaid's eyes, and his hands tightened on Zenobio's shirt, ripping the fabric.

"Tarifa! It was Tarifa's fault she died. She killed her, sending her there. I knew, I felt something when she told me. God in heaven, why didn't I kill her then and there!"

"No." Zenobio could not quite recall what he had said but he was aware that it had been a mistake. "Dolores died in childbirth. There was nothing anyone could do."

"Nothing! She was left in that house to be murdered!"

He got up and Zenobio cringed at the look on his Indian-dark face. So might God have looked in the Garden of Eden, he thought in bewildered awe. Condemning, pitiless, inexorable.

Kinkaid went to the wall where Zenobio kept his weapons. He selected a pistol, looked to see if it was primed and loaded, and stuck it in the waistband of his trousers.

Zenobio tottered to his feet. What was the matter with his wits? Why in the name of Christ had he drunk so much that his cursed tongue had run away with his thoughts?

"Wait!" he cried as Kinkaid wheeled toward the door. "You don't understand—wait. *Amigo!*"

But even before he stumbled through the door he heard the clatter of hooves and saw the dust cloud settling in the courtyard like the stirred ashes of the dead. He sank down on his knees in the open doorway. Tears coursed down his weathered bearded cheeks.

"I am old," he said hopelessly, "old and drunk and useless. I don't even kill with my hands anymore, openly, like a soldier should—I kill with my foolish, babbling tongue. *Madre de Dios,* what have I done?"

Tarifa had spent the long hot morning, from sunup till well past the lunch hour, in the saddle riding over the farthest pastures of Loma de Oro with Tomas. Everywhere, she saw the white picked bones or swelling carcasses of dead cattle, cattle with their swollen tongues protruding and their eyes staring sightlessly at the white-hot sun.

She knew many of the Indians were down with the fever that plagued the whole of California, and that Penti was trying valiantly to keep it from spreading on Loma de Oro.

When she turned back alone from her tour of inspection, leaving Tomas to bring in a group of calves they had gathered up, she felt as lifeless as the lion-colored grass. In all the desolate landscape, burned to a dull bronze under the hot blue sky, only an occasional giant oak seemed alive.

Even with the water from Bolsa Coyotes, she could not hope to save all of the rancho. And if the cattle continued to die, what would become of the family and Loma de Oro? Weariness ate into her bones, and each step Guindilla took pounded through her burning skull.

She glanced at the sky and wondered if there was any use in praying for rain—supposing that she believed in prayer? Ygnacio had believed in it, and so did his children and Tía Isabella. But when each of them was really in need what good had it done them? Isabella had not been able to keep her from marrying Ygnacio, and surely she had prayed for that? Ygnacio had not been able to keep Joaquin from leaving, though he must have prayed for his son to stay? And Dolores, for all her prayers, had died.

Tarifa had never prayed except to please the Padres or Don Ygnacio, or during the Mass when it was expected of her. She did not have to pray to her gods; she sensed them all around her in Nature, not confined in a small space on top of an altar surrounded by statues and incense.

I've never asked anything of that God, she thought, perhaps I should? And she told Him as boldly as a child, "I need rain. Make it rain."

She rode on with her head bent and a superior smile on her face. Guindilla moved with more spirit as they neared the hacienda and Tarifa was wondering if she should ride to Bolsa Coyotes that afternoon to see Nazario, when she felt the first drops. As big and glistening as giant tears. She watched them on the back of her hand, on the saddle horn, gliding down Guindilla's dusty neck.

She raised her face to heaven and all the avid superstition of her Gypsy nature rose to torment her. She had prayed, or rather she had simply asked, and this had come about. Could it be that they were right, the Padres and the Alvarjos, and she was wrong? But the idea was still too new, too unproven in her own mind for her to accept it wholly.

At the hacienda she leaped from Guindilla, telling an Indian boy to take him and rub him down well, and strode into the house with her head up and shoulders straight.

Isabella stood in the patio doorway, a white-faced Soledad beside her, wringing her hands.

"What is it?" she asked impatiently, instantly alerted by their silence. Always there was something wrong with these foolish women. "Why don't you speak? What is the matter?"

"The children," said the old woman miserably, "Lasho and Dolores, they have the fever."

A white-hot flame knifed through Tarifa as she swept them aside and raced down the veranda to the nursery.

Penti was bent over Lasho's cot spooning liquid into his small mouth, while little Dolores cried with a pitiful monotony in her crib.

Tarifa knelt and raised her son's head so the liquid would go down more easily. His little body was scorching hot, his dark cheeks reddened.

"When did this happen?" she asked harshly.

"He was restless this morning, and so was Dolores," said Penti, "but I did not think it serious. I was busy with the others on the rancho—"

"You brought this to my son from the others you attended, you evil old woman!"

"No," cried Penti aghast, "no, I did not, *miri pen*. Each time I washed before I returned here. The pestilence and fever are in the wind; there is no escaping it. If it would rain—"

"It is raining." Tarifa scowled at her. "Now you had better save my son."

Penti bent over the boy and Tarifa went to quiet the other baby. After a time when the children slept, she crossed the patio through the rain and entered the chapel.

It was the first time she had ever come here of her own volition. She gazed at the altar with its winking candles, then knelt and blessed herself as Padre Peyri had taught her. Outside, the rain pattered more heavily on the tile roof, and a fresh breeze came through the thickset windows and stirred the edge of the white altar cloth, making the candle flames flicker like small hungry tongues.

Tarifa spoke directly to the altar. She said slowly and stiffly, "I asked for rain and You sent it. Now I ask that my son be made well." She thought for a moment and added, "And the other child. I will believe in You, and I will make Lasho believe, if You do this."

She got up slowly a moment later and went back to her son's room. He lay with his eyes closed, his chest barely moved. Penti was putting wet cloths on his head and torso. There was a worried look on her face which she tried to hide as Tarifa came in. The maid Rita held little Dolores on her shoulder and was humming gently to quiet her cries.

"How is he?" Tarifa put her fingers to Lasho's hot forehead.

"Do not worry, I have tended fevers before," Penti said with a gruff assurance she was far from feeling.

All afternoon Tarifa knelt by her son's side, holding one of his small, hot, dry hands. Surely the God who had made it rain so quickly when she asked could make Lasho well? She had only to trust and have faith, that was what Padre Peyri had always said. She waited, watching Lasho's face and labored breathing, while Penti tried one after another of her Romany medications.

The rest of the family wandered in now and then to glance silently at the children, and left again without saying a word. Tarifa noted that Isabella and Soledad held rosaries in their hands, and she wondered if their prayers would be answered even if her own were not. For the first time she was aware of a faint kinship with them.

At dusk, she went onto the veranda for a breath of air and sank down on a bench near the bedroom door. It had stopped raining but there were still dark clouds in the sky. She was not going to lose Loma de Oro after all. If the rain continued even for a few days, it would work wonders on the parched grass and dried-up springs. But it would all seem as nothing if Lasho was not there to enjoy what she was building for him.

A hand touched her shoulder, and Tarifa rose in one catlike movement and stood facing Penti.

Penti's face was gray under its coppery wrinkles.

Tarifa's eyes widened with fear and she thrust the old Gypsy aside, nearly throwing her to the ground, and raced into the bedroom.

She stared down at Lasho in horror and disbelief. His small face was as pale and gray as Penti's, his eyes closed. His chest did not move.

With a terrible cry she snatched him from the bed, parted his lips, and began to breathe in and out in a hopeless effort to put life back into him.

She held him fiercely to her breast and would not believe the terror in her heart that was curling it to a cold black cinder, ready to blow away at a touch for all eternity.

She kissed his face, his hands, his feet, and in the wild violence of her pain and incredulity blamed everyone her thoughts touched upon. Penti had allowed this to happen, in spite of all her sacred brews!

The servants, with their lax, unclean ways, had allowed themselves to get the fever in the first place, and so endangered Lasho!

Isabella had failed to supervise the household properly; perhaps an unclean serving maid had been allowed to come near Lasho? Or had Candelaria allowed one of them to handle his food?

Because of the Alvarjos, and all in this accursed household, he was dead. She had been away attending to their business instead of here, watching after her child. Then in a blinding flash she knew who was really to blame.

Their God!

The One they prayed to so blindly and so fruitlessly. Because of the Alvarjos and the Padres, she had believed her prayer for rain had been answered, and so she had put her son's life into His hands, instead of into the hands of her own gods. And her gods, the powerful ones, Gandharbavivaha and Vasantasena, had been angered and taken Lasho.

Fear lashed through her misery like a quivering viper, but her desolation was too great to give it room to grow.

She ran to her room, the child in her arms, and snatched up the old amulet Penti and Bandonna had made for her and hung it around Lasho's neck. When she glanced up a moment later and saw Penti and the family gathered around her in saddened silence, the women quietly weeping, she stared wildly at them.

"Get out! Get out all of you. You have killed my son. Get out and leave us alone!"

Penti made a tentative motion toward her, but Tarifa's torrent of Romany invective made her draw back.

When they had left, Tarifa laid the child gently on her bed, undressed, and put on the striped Gypsy skirt, and the thin white blouse she had worn in Seville, loosening her hair about her face. From a chest she snatched up her tambourine and the gaudy shawl Santiago had bought her so long ago. She wrapped Lasho in the shawl and went on bare feet across the wet patio, past the clustered, gaping family in the *sala*. She started up the hill toward Loma de Oro with the rain beating in her face. As she climbed, her bare feet slipped in the oozing adobe mud.

In the cabaña she lighted a candle and laid Lasho carefully on the floor, his face turned up to her. She knelt over him, her tears and her hair brushing his face. She writhed and moaned until there were no tears left in her. She rose then, and stood over him, her fists clenched at her sides.

She took up the tambourine, struck it a sharp blow, and rattled it above the infant's head. Then slowly, as if in a trance, she began to move. Like a cobra rising from its basket at the first notes of its trainer's reed horn, lazily coming to life coil by coil, she began to dance.

As her people used rhythmic incantations to cure the sick and to ease childbirth, so did they relieve their grief with the rhythm of the dance. Older than she could imagine were the movements Tarifa felt herself using, going back to the classic Moslem *nuba*, further still, to Egypt itself, and then changing as she threw away the tambourine and clapped her hands, and the sound became the thunder, releasing the demons.

Improvising, a high priestess at her devotions, springing, writhing. nostrils pale, her whole body trembling in the mad orgy of her arabesques, old as the ancient cabalistic signs that ruled her people, she lost track of time and place. She felt herself in a dream world beyond human existence.

Now and then she swooped low and murmured hot passionate words to Lasho, touching his closed eyelids with her moistened fingertips.

She sang in her coarse unmusical Gypsy voice as she danced the *Chirindin* that followed the Gypsy wake, and tears sparkled on her lashes, but she dashed them away impatiently and went into the mad prohibited *Manguindoy* with its lascivious undulation, and erotic shifting movement of the belly and hips.

She was mad, drunk with the pulsating movement of her body, with the rush of blood from head to toes, when she fell down beside Lasho's body and buried her face in the shawl. From its folds a moment later came the high, keening, primitive wail of bereft motherhood.

In the hacienda, after Tarifa had walked by them barefoot, with her dead child clasped to her breast and a terrible vacant expression on her set face, Dona Isabella crossed herself and murmured, *"Madre de Dios!* She has lost her mind."

Grouped about her, the others could only stare in disbelief. Tarifa did not lose her head. Tarifa had barely wept when their father was buried, certainly not when Dolores had died. She was always aloof, completely untouched by the emotions that afflicted ordinary humans. She was the strength, the bulwark of Loma de Oro, although they had failed to recognize it until now. They might hate and despise her, wish her out of their lives, but each of them knew with a hideous clarity as they watched her leave the house that they had come to depend upon her entirely.

"You must go after her," Tía Isabella told Luis.

"No. Let her alone with her dead." It was Penti who spoke from the doorway. "My people know how to handle their own grief."

"Then go to her yourself," begged Soledad. "You will know what to do. We can't leave her alone on a night like this."

Penti shook her head. "I am no good to her now." She turned back toward the patio, her head bent.

"We must know where she went," said Luis. "I will follow at a distance. We must send to the Mission for Padre Cazon."

"Yes," Tía Isabella said, "that will be best. And for Nazario and Rufina."

The young man hurried out of the room, but though Luis took Amarillo and rode about the rancho, he could not find Tarifa. It never occurred to him to glance up toward his father's cabaña on Loma de Oro, so he rode on.

Long after the others had gone to do her bidding, Dona Isabella sat alone in the *sala* saying her rosary. She became aware of the sharp wail coming from Loma de Oro, and rose on trembling legs to hurry into the patio. She saw the glimmer of light in the cabaña above.

Ygnacio's old sanctuary. So that was where she had gone. Why had none of them thought of it? She considered going to Tarifa, but remembered Penti's words. Perhaps she was better off alone. She was such a queer creature. Isabella could grieve for the loss of the child who had after all been an Alvarjo, but she could feel only dislike for the Gypsy herself. She could never forgive her for marrying Ygnacio, for taking over Loma de Oro by getting her foolish husband to sign such a will, or for the harsh way she had treated Ygnacio's children. But though Isabella was as haughty and coldly unforgiving as Ygnacio had been, she had a good deal of her brother's sense of fairness and duty as well.

She knew that Tarifa had not spared herself since her husband's death. She had tried to keep the family together, protected Loma de Oro, and, acting as head of the family, had avenged Dolores' death and the insult of her treatment at Julio's hands as well as Ygnacio himself might have done. Further, she had provided for the future of Dolores' child. No one could say that she was not an efficient and fearless ruler of her little domain.

Reluctantly Isabella had come to recognize some of the weakness of her brother's children. While she did not agree with Tarifa's methods, she had to admit that they produced results. Secretly, she had come to welcome Tarifa's tyranny.

A shiver went down her spine as the sounds ceased in

the little house atop Loma de Oro. What would happen to them all, she thought in sudden panic, if Tarifa left them—if she had indeed lost her reason? She moved forward again to go up to the stricken Gypsy, but she could not bring herself to climb to the cabaña she had never been allowed to enter. She wept as she lifted the rosary to her lips and began another decade.

Kinkaid left his horse in the shadows a few yards below the house. Someone had passed him riding very fast toward the hacienda a short while before but had not stopped or spoken in the darkness.

He moved forward quietly. On the way to Loma de Oro, only his burning need, like a brand in his brain, and the comforting bulge of the pistol in his belt had been realities to him.

High above the hacienda, a faint light flickered. He paused to watch it but it did not interest him. And then he heard the cry. High and clear, like an anguished animal in mortal pain. There were cougars in these hills; perhaps that was what he had heard. Then another sound captured his attention: spurred feet on the veranda in front of the hacienda.

Two male voices were borne clearly to him on the fresh breeze where he stood in the shadows cast by a large live-oak. He recognized one of them as Santos', low and guarded, but with a hint of urgency in it.

"Dona Tarifa is up on Loma de Oro, in your father's cabaña, señor. But I advise you not to go there."

"Why not?" It was Luis' voice.

"She is like a tigress tonight, Don Luis. I looked in the window and was afraid of her myself."

The two men moved off, their voices and the clank of their spurs growing fainter as they rounded the house.

So she was up on Loma de Oro alone. He couldn't have asked for more. He kept Dolores' face before him like a beacon as he made the steep climb. Around him, the night pulsed and lived, crickets chirping in the freshened grass, a tree frog croaking flatly, in the distance a coyote barking as it hunted rabbits in the foothills. He heard none of it as he moved forward in silence.

The flickering light was dim inside the cabin when he

stepped onto the veranda and crept cautiously to the open door.

He saw her lying coiled, on the floor, her bare arm clutching something bright. Candlelight glinted on her white teeth bared between her lips. Her fiercely blazing black eyes stared up at him and there was something feral about her, like an animal crouched and waiting.

Deliberately he took the pistol from his belt and saw her stiffen, start to rise, and then fall back into her former position.

"I know now why Dolores married Marcos," he said in a tight hard voice. "I know that you drove her to it. You are responsible for her death. You destroyed the only thing I cared about. I'm going to kill you." His voice rose in spite of himself. He felt sweat break out on his face, neck, the small of his back.

Still she lay there, her strange fiery black eyes with their scimitar lids staring up at him unwinkingly.

He swore as he stepped into the room and leveled the pistol at her head.

"Don't you have anything to say?" he shouted.

"Why don't you shoot?" she asked calmly. "You *gorgios* always talk too much. A *gitano* would not waste words. He would have come through the door, thrown his *navaja*, and it would all be over by now." Mockery dripped through her voice like acid. "If I were on the other side of that gun, I would have shot you seconds ago. You are a fool, Capitán Kinkaid."

He crossed the room with an oath she did not understand and dragged her to her feet. She did not resist him, standing erect and still; only her eyes battled his in the gloom.

There was death and madness in both their glances as he threw aside the gun and closed his hands around her slim throat. Still she did not fight him, her arms and hands lay slack at her sides, making him wonder dimly about it when she began to sink under his grasp.

She had welcomed his coming. She had wanted to die and be where Lasho was. But when his hands found her windpipe and she felt the relentless mastery of his action, something in her snapped. The older more powerful instinct of survival took hold of her. Her own indomitable pride and hatred for the man who held her throat between his hands gave her a strength she would not have thought possible a moment before.

She still carried the *navaja* Penti had given her in a garter high up on her thigh. Her sight swimming, she bent her knees, groping wildly for the knife under her full skirt. He was lifting her by her tortured throat, when her hand found and drew the knife and she stabbed straight upward between their twisting bodies. She heard the sharp, surprised intake of his breath with a deep exultation.

Kinkaid's hands moved to her shoulders and dropped away, as he stepped back, staring down incredulously at the knife hilt protruding from his side. He tore it out and let it fall with a clatter to the tile floor. He sank to his knees supporting himself with one arm, conscious of a dull pain and the hot blood rushing down his side like a tide.

When he glanced up there was a thin smile of triumph on her lips. He could see the livid bruises on her throat and she seemed to sway, fighting for breath. But her voice, no more than a faint, rasping croak, was full of cold malice.

"You had a chance to kill me. I gave it to you. But you were foolish enough not to take it." She stared at his white face, bending her head, and asked fiercely, "Why didn't you take it? Why didn't you shoot me?"

He shook his head and eased himself to the floor. His hand touched something soft and yielding. He glanced at it in dull bewilderment, straightening up in spite of his pain and the sudden weakness that had come over him. The face of a child wrapped in a gaudy shawl stared back at him.

A dead child.

He stared up at her in horrified disbelief.

"My son, Lasho," she whispered. "He died this evening. I came here to be alone with him. That's why I hoped you would kill me. There is nothing left. . . ." She bent to take up the child and carried him to the cot nearby.

Kinkaid dragged himself to his feet, using a chair back to brace himself, and stared wildly at her.

"Oh, my God!" he groaned. "Oh—my—God!"

She saw him bend uncertainly and fumble for the fallen

pistol. He fought his way across the space to her and dropped the gun in her lap by Lasho's head and stood swaying above her.

His face looked bloodless. His eyes were haunted in their red-rimmed sockets. The dark stubble on his unshaven cheeks, the lines of pain and suffering etched deeply in his face gave him the haggard condemned look of an abandoned soul.

"Use it," he told her grimly. "Use it now—or I will!"

Her fingers closed silently around the gun butt. Her hand was steady as she raised it.

CHAPTER 18

Padre Cazon was the first off his horse, his gray robe tucked up under his girdle showing the muscular calves of his bare legs.

It seemed ever afterward that the stark tableau that greeted him that night would never fade from his memory.

The guttering candle, the shadows dancing on the walls like malignant wraiths, and the three motionless human forms: Tarifa, seated on the cot with her eyes closed and her head fallen back against the wall holding the dead child in her lap. Kinkaid, lying on his back at her feet his chest covered with blood, and a pistol next to his slack hand.

Cazon went first to Tarifa and reached to take the child from her lap.

"No! Don't touch him!"

It was not her voice, this strange rasping whisper, but he saw that her eyes were open and sane.

"Thank God," he said. "You are not hurt, *niña?* They heard a pistol. They thought—"

"It was him," she said, glancing with disinterest at Kinkaid's motionless figure. "He came to kill me."

"And you shot him?"

She shook her head wearily, remembering Bart's eyes, his harsh demand that she shoot him. She had wanted to do it—until she saw Lasho's lifeless face in her lap and knew that she could not kill even in self-defense over the body of her dead child. She remembered Kinkaid bending forward to pull the trigger himself. She had struck him over the temple with the gun and heard the bullet whiz by them both.

She had watched him lying at her feet with his eyes closed, his dark hair fallen over his forehead, the wet redness of his shirt visible under his unbuttoned coat. She had lain back then, too weary and spent to do anything but clutch Lasho's body weakly to keep it from slipping from her lap.

Luis put the lantern on the table and he and Santos knelt in silence beside Kinkaid. The Indian felt inside the Americano's shirt for his heartbeat.

"Well?" Luis demanded.

"I don't know, Patrón."

"Let me see." But Luis was no more certain than Santos whether Kinkaid lived or not, when he relinquished his place to Padre Cazon.

The priest opened the shirt with careful hands and inspected the knife wound high in his side. It still bled. Knife wounds, he knew, were tricky. Once inside the body, a knife could do any of a dozen different things and there was no way to be sure what it had done. He felt Kinkaid's chest and wrist, and laid his ear above the heart. He held his palm to his nostrils and lips.

He could hear nothing. Feel nothing. But there had been the trickle of blood still coming from the wound. With a sigh he reached for his missal and stole, and was astounded to hear a voice laughing at him in cold derision.

"Are you going to kneel and pray over him with your mumbo jumbo while he dies, or are you going to try and save his life?"

Shaken more than he had ever been in his life, Cazon

glanced up and saw the old Gypsy Penti leaning in the open doorway with a bundle of black rags in her arms.

"Even I can see from here that he is not yet dead," she grinned wickedly, "though he may soon be."

"Then for the love of God come and help him!" Cazon cried, rising. "Do you want this to end in murder?"

Penti frowned and spoke sharply to Tarifa in Romany, receiving a laconic, disinterested reply.

"She does not care whether he lives or dies," said Penti. "But she has no objection to my trying my art upon the *gorgio*."

While the others were busying themselves with the injured man, Tarifa allowed Santos to carry the child for her and help her back to the hacienda. The Indian's face was stiff as a piece of dried rawhide with sorrow and pity he could not express to her.

Because Penti insisted Kinkaid could not be moved, Padre Cazon and Luis lifted him to the cot where Tarifa had been sitting and followed the Gypsy's terse instructions, then watched in fascinated silence while the old woman washed and probed the wound, grunting at her labors, and bound it tightly with a sticky dressing compounded, so she told the priest, of turpentine and Romany balm. She also forced between the wounded man's lips, a spoonful at a time, a wineglass full of boiled cola vera mixed with *aguardiente*.

When she had finished Cazon could detect a faint pulse in Kinkaid's wrist and see the shallow rise and fall of his chest. "I must congratulate you," he said.

Penti rubbed her palms on the sides of her soiled skirt. "Do not congratulate me too soon, Padre, and tempt the gods. He has not been saved yet. This is a bad wound; only once in the Sacro Monte did I see a worse one. A quarter of an inch to the left and he would be dead and in need of your prayers."

Cazon glanced at Kinkaid's pale rigid face. "You will take care of him?"

"I do not know yet all that went on here," Penti frowned. "If Tarifa wishes I will do what I can for him." She stared at the wounded man with a sly smile. "He is big and strong, like a lover I once had. They called him El Monongo, which means The Cat, in Romanes. But I greatly fear the spirit has already left this one."

The priest looked at her inquiringly.

"The fire," she said impatiently. "The life passion. He is ready to die, and so he will make no fight to live. If his will is strong enough he will succeed. Such a feat is easier for primitive people than for civilized ones. I have seen the old ones in the caravan decide the day and hour and place of their deaths, and so it was."

"Yes," Cazon agreed uncomfortably, for it seemed wrong to him for a mortal to take his death into his own hands. "I have seen it among the Indians—the gentiles at least, here in California. But I do not believe in such things."

"Then you are a fool. It is not the spirit that is the most powerful thing in man, it is the mind. The human mind, once made up can stand against anything—even God, if it chooses."

Cazon was shocked but he said quietly, feeling a strange sense of unreality in his conversation with the old Gypsy, "The mind is a thinking, logical organ. But it cannot drive itself beyond its natural powers. Only the indomitable spiritual will, God-given, can give to a mortal more than human ability. I have seen men, mortally wounded on the battlefield, who still fought on though they should have fallen in their tracks instantly, held up only by their God-given willpower. The mind itself cannot do this."

"What does it matter, Padre? We talk at cross-purposes." Penti bent to feel her patient's cheek. "You and I can both do our best for him and still he may die—if he has the wish strongly enough. And it is written in his face: this man has a will of iron."

"Pray God there has been enough dying in this house for one year," murmured the priest, taking up his rosary. He knelt beside the cot and lifted the little metal cross to his lips.

Jake Banner walked the deck of the *Lorelei* with his hands behind his back and a worried expression on his craggy face. The captain had been gone for two nights now, and had sent no word to the ship to explain his delay.

Banner could not investigate matters for himself, for in the captain's absence he was in charge of the vessel. But the feeling that something was terribly wrong would not leave him. Like all sailors, Banner was deeply superstitious in his own heart, though he scoffed at such nonsense among the crew. He was as jumpy as a ship's cat on a galley stove.

The *Lorelei* had done a brisk business ever since her arrival, and even at this early hour the storeroom was filled with buyers and lookers, and the longboat was kept busy plying from ship to shore with customers and goods.

By afternoon, when trade had slackened off and he had ordered the storeroom closed for the day, Banner could stand the delay no longer and ordered the boat to row him ashore.

A stiff breeze made dancing whitecaps on the water, an aftermath of the heavy rain the night before.

Banner walked over to the Endecott hide house to ask if anyone had seen Captain Kinkaid. He found Davis of the *Marblehead*, a small blunt-nosed man with a short spade beard, talking to the hide house superintendent.

"Lost your captain, have ye?" grinned Davis.

"Well, sir, he's been ashore two days and nights without sending me word," replied Banner, and then added defensively. "Not that there's anything wrong, I'm sure."

"Of course not, Mr. Banner." Davis took a short-stemmed pipe out of his mouth and knocked the dead ashes into the palm of his hand. "When I was Bart Kinkaid's age, I used to be gone ten days when we first touched port—no questions asked or answered. Go back to your ship, man, and stop acting like a broody mother hen."

Banner, growing red-faced, was about to do just that when he heard someone call his name. He went to the door and found Zenobio Sanchez sitting on his sweating horse, an odd expression on his face. Banner knew Sanchez only slightly from his previous visits aboard the *Arabella*, but he knew he was a friend of Bart's.

"Señor Banner, will you come with me?"

All Banner's fears rose up in him like flags shooting to a masthead. "Has something happened to Captain Kinkaid?"

"*Sí.* And it is all my fault. I am a babbling foolish *viejo*, without enough wits to come in out of the rain. But there is no time, *amigo*, come. I will explain it all to you on the way." Zenobio indicated a second horse which he led behind his own. "Come. Quickly!"

"Captain Kinkaid," Banner asked as he climbed awkwardly into the saddle and gathered up the reins, "is he hurt?"

"*Sí.* He lies at Loma de Oro. I will take you to him."

"How—"

"The Gypsy knifed him when he went there to kill her with my pistol. *Sangre de Dios,* if he dies I am responsible, do you not see? It was my foolish words that sent him there."

"My God," cried Banner. "Hurry! Can't we hurry?" He drummed the horse's sides with his heels, then clutched wildly at the horn as the animal broke into a spine-jarring gallop.

Pablo made the small coffin for Lasho out of redwood, and Candelaria lined it at Tarifa's request with red satin. She would not allow the child to be buried in the conventional white with a wreath of white flowers on his head as was the Californian custom. Instead she and Penti wound him from head to foot in blue ribbons after the Romany fashion. At the last moment she took her amulet from his neck and put it around her own. Dry-eyed, she watched Penti paint the child's cheeks and lips red to give him the appearance of life.

But when the family friends and neighbors arrived with their children dressed in the funeral white, carrying garlands of flowers to walk behind Lasho's coffin and sing hymns of joy, she drove them away angrily.

In the hope of comforting her, Señora Martinez tried to explain that only joy should reign at the funeral of such a small child, who because of his very youth and innocence had gone straight to heaven. Baptism had removed all taint of sin.

Tarifa stood in front of her, her eyes like burning coals and in her still husky voice said, "You lie. I have taken away his baptism, with this." She touched the amulet around her bruised throat. "He is with my gods now."

Señora Martinez gasped and crossed herself hastily. A moment later after a brief conversation with her husband and Tía Isabella, the Martinez family left, accompanied

by the other disapproving neighbors, with accusing backward glances and shaking heads over the fate of the poor
niño.

Though Padre Cazon had not left, having spent the
night with Kinkaid and Penti in the cabaña, Tarifa would
not permit him to bury Lasho with a Mass or say the
prayers for the dead over him. Santos carried the coffin
to the graveyard and buried it near Ygnacio's grave, where
Tarifa had instructed him to prepare a place. The Alvarjos stood silently beside Tarifa until the grave was filled
in with the still moist earth and the small headstone was
in place.

They watched Tarifa standing straight and dry-eyed,
her amulet in her hand, while her lips moved in a strange
incantation they could not understand. When the brief
burial was over she returned to her room and did not
come out again.

Later, when Padre Cazon tapped on her door, he found
her standing by the window that looked out over the valley.

"I have said a prayer for the little one in the chapel,"
he told her gently.

"He has no need of your prayers."

"No. He has no need of them. He is in Heaven; that is
why we can be glad for him in our unhappiness. He has
won Eternal Paradise with very little effort. But my prayers
may help you?"

She turned toward him, her face twisted with angry
passion. "What sort of religion is it that likes to see children die so that they can be in heaven!"

"We do not like to see them die, Tarifa. But if they do,
we can console ourselves that it has not been in vain."

"Your God is a cruel God. I do not believe in Him!"

Cazon bowed his head. What could he say to her; how
could he make her understand? What words were simple
or eloquent enough?

"There is another, a better life for us than the one we
live here on earth," he said slowly. "But it must be earned.
By suffering, by sacrifice, by having faith in something
greater than we are."

"I don't believe in any other life. I want none. When
I am dead I don't care what happens to me. You are
wasting your time, Padre."

He sighed and sat down on the edge of a chair. "What will you do now?"

Her head came up. "I will stay. Because this land was Lasho's. It would have been his one day, his alone as I had planned it. He would have been the greatest hacendado in all California. Now I shall make Loma de Oro a monument to his name. I will buy the others out when I am able. What do they care about the rancho?"

"More than you are aware of, I fear," the priest answered.

"They will sell out to me, I tell you!" He watched the clenched hands at her sides, the straight line of her lips. "No one else can share Lasho's property. Loma de Oro belongs to him and to his memory."

"And what of the Alvarjos? Did you not promise Don Ygnacio to be responsible for their future welfare?"

"Haven't I looked after them?" she said impatiently. "After I have bought them out they can do as they please. They are not children. What do I care what they do?"

"I was hoping that because of Ygnacio and Lasho you felt some responsibility for them as individuals. They are not trained to look after themselves, I fear, especially in these hard times."

"I have done my best for them," Tarifa snapped. "That should satisfy you. Am I to be saddled with them for the rest of my life when they despise the ground I stand upon?" She was suddenly very tired. Tired of the Alvarjos and their everlasting problems. Tired of talking to the priest. She wished he would go.

But he was not finished. "I would be better satisfied if you had found it possible to give them more understanding and less material gain. Do you really feel no pity for them?" His eyes searched her face and found only the hard, enigmatic mask of the Gypsy.

"Pity? Why should I? Do they understand or pity me?"

"You have little need of either, Tarifa. You are strong and you are fearless. The strong must shoulder the burdens of the weak, or we shall all perish."

"My strength is for myself," she said harshly, "and for Lasho's memory. Let the others stand or fall, I do not care."

Padre Cazon got slowly to his feet. Though she puzzled

him often with her strange, bold, primitive reasoning, he
had tried to accept her on her own terms. Yet he could not
help but wonder at her lack of feeling. Only for Ygnacio
and Lasho and the palominos had she ever shown any outward mark of affection. Like an animal, she lived only in
the present, her emotions stirred only by what she desired,
what she had determined to make hers. He wondered that
she had not once asked after Bart Kinkaid. Did she really
care so little for human life? If Kinkaid died, would she
still feel no remorse, no guilt for her action?

When he reached the door, the priest said, "Don't you
want to know how Capitán Kinkaid is?"

"Why should I?"

She had gone back to the window and the breeze blew
her loose hair about her shoulders. She still wore her
Gypsy costume, and there was an aloof barbaric beauty
about her, compounded, Cazon thought, of the imp and the
Devil.

"It is your fault he is near death."

"It is his own fault. He was trying to kill me."

Loud voices in the patio drew their attention from each
other. Padre Cazon opened the door and found Zenobio
with his hand raised to knock. Behind him stood a red-
faced, broad-chested Americano dressed in seaman's garb.
There was a sharp anxiety in his blue eyes.

"Padre," said Zenobio, "I have brought the mate from
Capitán Kinkaid's ship. Señor Banner."

Banner took off his cap and shook hands awkwardly with
the priest. He felt out of place here in this fine house, and
his halting Spanish deserted him. He missed half of what
they said, and had only a bare understanding of the rest.
He only wanted to get to Kinkaid as swiftly as possible.

"I must see Captain Kinkaid at once, Padre. How is he?"

"He still lives," the priest said, "thanks to a Gypsy
woman here who is skilled in medicine."

Banner's face paled. "The one who knifed him?" Over
the Padre's shoulder he could see the dark sultry woman
standing at the window. There she stood, bold as brass, the
cursed harlot.

"No," Cazon was saying. "Another—a maid here. Come
I will take you to the Capitán."

"No," Tarifa said from behind them, "I will take him to

the cabaña." She came swiftly across the room and faced
Banner. "He came here to kill me. See the marks on my
throat where he was choking me? I knifed him because I
was not willing to let a *gorgio* take my life."

Banner stared at her. He could see the livid finger marks
on her throat. But he knew she must be lying. He could
not believe it of Bart. Only a fit of madness could have
made him do such a thing to a woman.

Tarifa stepped by the priest and touched Banner's arm.

"Come."

He followed her up the trail to the hilltop and entered
the small house built on the narrow level space overlooking
the valley.

Penti rose from her chair by the cot and Banner saw
Bart. He lay with his eyes closed, his chest bared except for
the wide bandages crisscrossing it.

Tarifa examined his pale face dispassionately.

"How is he?" Banner asked in a low, unsteady voice. He
was shocked at Bart's appearance, and mistrustful of everyone on the place. But at least they had made some effort to
keep him alive. He was grateful for that.

"He is going to die," Tarifa said.

Fear and anger washed over Banner's weatherbeaten
face. He strode over and jerked the Gypsy away from the
cot as if her words alone could cause the wounded man's
instant death.

"Ye devil, ye damned Gypsy devil incarnate! Stay away
from him. If he dies, by God, I'll finish the job he started!"

Tarifa did not understand a word he said, but the old
sailor's tone and gestures were unmistakable. She stared at
him with cold contempt.

"Jake—"

A mere sliver of sound, and yet it jerked Banner around
as if he had been garroted. He sank to his knees beside the
cot and took one of Kinkaid's hands in his horny palm.

"Bart, my boy—I'm here, I'm here."

Kinkaid's eyes were open but he could only make out
the mate's face dimly, and speech cost him an effort that
whitened his lips and brought out sweat on his face like
glistening oil.

"Tarifa . . ."

"The lady's here, sir."

Memory came in a flash then. He had reached for the gun when she failed to pull the trigger, and she had struck him with it. There had been a crash of pain behind his ear and then blackness. He had no idea how long he had lain here or who had sent for Jake Banner, but he was grateful to whoever had been responsible for it. He had forgotten the ship and his duties as a captain, as once before he had forgotten them, because of a woman. Now he could redeem himself at least in part by turning the *Lorelei* over to Banner.

"The—ship," he said painfully. "You'll—sail her—back."

Banner thought he was out of his head and so humored him. "Yes, yes, sir. Don't worry about a thing. Ye'll be right as rain, soon, sir. Just lie there and rest. I'll see to the *Lorelei* till you're well again, sir."

Kinkaid shook his head. There was no breath in him. No strength. He felt as empty as air. But he must make Banner understand that he was in command of the *Lorelei,* and that he must sail her safely back to Boston at the end of her tour. Kinkaid knew he would never again stand upon her decks.

"Jake?"

"Yes, sir?"

Kinkaid tried to moisten his dry cracked lips, but his tongue felt like cotton. It didn't matter. Nothing would matter for long now. If he could make Jake understand, then he could sink back and forget everything but Dolores. He had seen her, smiling, beckoning to him in his dreams. There would be forgetfulness and peace if he could close his eyes, but first he had to make Jake understand.

"Dolores," he told the Mate, "she's dead."

"I know, sir," said Banner quietly. "Señor Sanchez told me. But she'd want ye to get well and go back to your ship."

Bart shook his head. "I won't—be going—back."

"Sir, ye can't give in like this! I'll not sail the *Lorelei* back without ye. Ye've got to fight, lad, fight."

"Can't, Jake—no strength. . . ."

"No! No, by God!"

Kinkaid's eyes closed even as he spoke and Banner reached out to shake him by the shoulders.

"Bart—Bart listen to me!"

When Banner raised his head, he found Tarifa staring at him with a mocking, infuriating smile on her face, and he realized suddenly why Kinkaid had wanted to kill her. It was all he could do to keep his own big clenched hands from leaping to her throat. In his heart he cursed them all. Every man, woman, and child on the place that had brought him to this sorry predicament, kneeling helplessly beside the one person in the world who meant anything to him. Forced to watch him die. Powerless to stop it.

Zenobio watched from the door, blaming himself over and over for what had happened, wondering what he could do to make things right again.

Tarifa spoke to Penti in Romany, and the old Gypsy shrugged her shoulders with an elaborate grimace, then turned to address the men in Spanish.

"Go now. Let him rest. I will call you if there is any change."

Banner was going to refuse point-blank to leave, but Zenobio touched his arm gently and said, "She is as good a doctor as I have seen, *amigo*. There is nothing you and I can do to help him. Come, have a glass of *aguardiente* and then we will return."

Unwillingly, Banner allowed himself to be led from the room. He was afraid. Mortally afraid. And he did not like it when Tarifa failed to follow them outside, but there was little he could do about it.

When the men had gone, Tarifa went to touch Kinkaid's forehead lightly, and then sat down in the chair beside the bed.

The women's voices came dimly to Kinkaid, like sound in the depths of the ocean, and he listened without opening his eyes.

"When will he die, Penti?"

"It is in the lap of the gods, *miri pen*. A pity in a way. He is big and strong like a lover I once had, as I told the Padre. You will not believe it, but once I was young and beautiful like you and I lay in my lover's arms under the wide sky and knew joy such as you have never known. The hot Romany blood does not run strong enough in your veins."

Tarifa was instantly aroused and angry, as she had

once been made furious by the taunts of the full-blooded
Gypsy children in the Sacro Monte.

"You lie, *chovihani!*"

"What do you know of men," Penti spat, "or love? You
have been brutally attacked by a young man who took you
by force, then married to a doting old man. What do you
know of the fire and passion of true love? That man lying
there, ready to die because of his love for a woman, knows
more about it than you will ever know. There is nothing
in you but an iron will to get what you want out of life, regardless of the consequences. You are incapable of love—
and I pity you."

"Ygnacio loved me!"

"Yes. But did you ever love him, except for what he
could give you? Did you ever love even Lasho?"

"*Premita Undebē!* I will not stay here and listen to the
ravings of a demented old witch!"

"Did you ever love him? Be honest with yourself. He
was something that belonged to you. Something that bolstered your pride—that you could use to prove your power.
Do I not speak the truth, *miri pen?*

"And because you have no heart, what memories will you
have when you are as old as I am? What memories except
for the things that gold has brought you? Will it be enough
for you to remember the vast herds of cattle and horses you
have raised? Of the land you own? What does a Gypsy
want with such things?

"The sun, the moon, the sky—these are the proper possessions of a *gitana.* We do not need to surround ourselves
with the things of the *gorgios* because we own everything
already. Has not the universe been put here for our use?
The joys that are your birthright you throw away with both
hands so that you can sit on this cursed piece of land like
a duck on an infertile egg. Give it up. Leave this place."

Tarifa glanced at her coldly. "I will never leave. It is
mine, and I am going to keep it—for Lasho. Is not my son
buried here?"

Penti's deriding laughter filled the room. "It is not for
Lasho's sake you keep it, *miri pen,* but for your own stubborn greed. Stay then, and waste your youth and beauty on
the brown grass and the silent oak trees, instead of on red-
blooded men. Hug the cold memory of your wealth and

power to your breast when you are old, instead of the children you might have borne in love and passion."

"Get out!"Tarifa shrieked. "Get out before I kill you!"

"Even that you do not do well." The old Gypsy cackled, nodding her head toward the man on the bed. "A full-blooded *gitana* would have sent the blade clearly through his heart."

"Get out!"

Penti took up a bucket and sauntered to the door while Tarifa glared at her retreating back.

"I will get some fresh water," said the old woman. "Stay with him until I get back."

Tarifa sat down by the bed, nursing her black anger at Penti, the sorrow and desolation driven from her heart momentarily. Alone with her thoughts, she began to weigh Penti's words. She had never been aware of the lack of feeling in herself. She was sure her emotions ran as quick and strong as any Gypsy's, in spite of what the miserable lying old witch had said.

She had loved Ygnacio and Lasho, but in her own way, not in the undignified, frenzied way of a caravan *gitana*. She had loved in the proud, contained way worthy of her Moorish ancestry. She had once heard Bandonna say that the Moor shutters his face as he does his house, and so it was with her. But that did not mean that her emotions ran any the less strong.

She wanted Loma de Oro with a passion Penti could never fathom. But she had wanted it just as greatly for Lasho. At the thought of her dead son a dry sob rose in her throat and she covered her face with her hands, rocking back and forth in the chair. She felt the tears on her palms and pressed hard against her face to stop their flow. She would never weep again after this moment, she vowed. For as long as she lived she would never weep again. But she could not control the sobs that shook her now.

"Don't—"

Astonished at the sound, she peered out through her slatted fingers and found Kinkaid staring at her.

"Don't cry . . . beyond . . . tears . . . you and I?"

"I could not let you kill me," she said bitterly, "even though I wanted to be with Lasho. And so Penti says I did not love him."

"You—loved him."

Kinkaid had heard Penti's words. He looked at Tarifa now and saw her in a new light. A creature of indomitable will, able to control her destiny as he had been unable to control his.

He found that he could not longer hate her for what she had done to Dolores, anymore than one could hate a volcano for erupting. He realized now the fault had been his. He should have recognized the potential danger to Dolores in Tarifa's powerful drive to accomplish what she set out to do. In an odd remote way, he felt sorry for her. No matter what her faults and misdeeds, she was alone now. As was Dolores' baby. He had not remembered it until this moment. He had a sudden desire to see the child, this one bit of his beloved that was left upon earth. He wondered if Tarifa would grant his last wish.

"Dolores' baby—could I—see it?"

Tarifa was startled. But on second thought it seemed only natural that he should ask about the infant, be curious to see it.

"I have named her Dolores, for her mother," she told him. "She has been ill with the fever, like Lasho." She was aware of a sudden resentment that the other child still lived while her own son lay dead. "But perhaps I can bring her here for a few minutes."

He watched her leave the room and then closed his eyes again as a great weariness washed over him. He wanted to drift off into space, to be done with the struggle to breathe. But his mind would not let go. The thought of the baby Dolores had borne in such sorrow and loneliness would not leave him. It disturbed him to think of the child, left in Tarifa's ruthless, unpredictable hands. If only he could have provided for the infant—if Tarifa would let Jake take her back to Boston—but that was madness. He could no longer think clearly.

"Bart."

With a superhuman effort he dragged his eyes open. Tarifa was bending toward him holding out an infant wrapped in a blanket. Only the tiny face was visible.

Dolores' face.

Hair, eyes, mouth, chin. It was astonishing, as if some supreme sculptor had copied in delicate detail the face of his beloved.

Tarifa uncovered a tiny hand and Bart touched it and

felt the fingers close around his own. The gossamer touch of life stirred him as nothing had since he had held Dolores in his arms and kissed her soft mouth. For an instant the blood surged in his veins with a new strength, then faded away.

Tarifa, herself was aware of a new interest in the child that surprised her. She had felt no personal attachment to Dolores' baby, until this moment. Now she found herself hoping the little girl would not die of the fever as Lasho had. She was tired of death, tired of burying people. Death was an enemy to be fought and beaten back wherever she met it.

Her eyes rested on Bart Kinkaid's face as he lay watching the baby. In that split second she made up her mind he was not going to die. She would give death no more easy victories with which to taunt her. She did not care personally whether Kinkaid lived or not but she was determined he would not die under her roof.

"Take her," he murmured. "Look—after her?"

"No," Tarifa said in an odd flat tone. "She is going to die anyway, like you and Lasho. I will leave her here."

His eyes widened in disbelief at her callousness.

"You can't—leave her!" He fought for the strength to shout, but there was no strength in him. "Call—Penti!"

"There is nothing she can do." She laid the child deliberately on the chair near the bed and started for the door.

"Wait!" He dragged himself upright in spite of the pain that clutched him like a giant hand, leaving him weak and dizzy. "Are you—inhuman? Come—back!"

But she was gone.

He cursed her, feeling the hot anger rise in him despite his weakness. Damn her! Damn her filthy, lying, Gypsy soul! She was inhuman. Penti had been right. She had no more feeling than a piece of granite.

He struggled on the bed aware of the blood spurting afresh from his wound, and managed at last to get his feet on the floor.

The baby was crying in a faint, fretful fashion. Dear God, what was he going to do with it? His hands shook as he reached to grasp the blanket and drew the child toward him slowly. If he dropped it—but he did not. Somehow he got the blanket-wrapped bundle onto the bed and, soaked with sweat, laid it beside him. He touched the baby's petal-thin cheek. It was warm, but not burning hot. Damn her, the child was not dying! She would survive if she were given the proper attention, not left here alone with a dying man. And with the despairing feeling of having been trapped, he knew that he did not dare die until he had given Dolores' baby into safer hands than Tarifa's. Somehow he had to reach Jake Banner, or Padre Cazon. But how? He was not even sure when or if Penti would return. Perhaps Tarifa would forbid her to come back until it was too late.

His eyes wandered feverishly around the small room. Table, chairs, cot, bookcase, writing desk. Above the desk there was an old-fashioned musket hung on the wall. There was only a bare chance that it was loaded, or that it would fire even if it were, but if he could reach and fire it, they were bound to hear it down at the hacienda.

He glanced at the baby and found that she had stopped crying and was sucking her fingers. He took a deep breath and slid off the bed to the floor. Crawling on all fours he inched his way toward the desk. It seemed an interminable distance. When he paused for breath every few seconds, he lowered his burning head to the tiles for an instant to cool it, but he knew that he would never make it. The weakness was creeping over him like a lava flow.

He forced himself to move another few inches, shaking his head to clear his sight, gasping breath into his lungs, and his hand touched wood.

The desk.

Giddy with relief, he closed his eyes. Behind him the baby began to whimper again. He put out his hands and felt them slip on the wooden legs of the desk. There was no response in his arms or legs. After an age he managed to drag himself erect and brace himself with his hands on the desk top. Blood had soaked through the bandage on his chest, cold sweat ran into his eyes, his nose, and left a bitter salty taste in the corners of his mouh.

He reached for the gun with one hand, holding onto the desk with the other. There wasn't time to make sure if the weapon was loaded. His sight was swimming out of focus, his knees would give way in a second. He got the gun to his shoulder clumsily, found the trigger, and aimed out the window beside the desk.

He was aware of a brief rumble like a distant thunderclap, of a jolt against his shoulder, and then he felt the rifle slide from his nerveless fingers and he went with it. Falling, falling, down into a bottomless pit. For an instant he still struggled to stay out of it, but in the end it enveloped him like a shroud. Smothered him in thick blackness. While behind him Dolores' child cried weakly, alone and helpless, with a dead man. . . .

They heard the shot when they were halfway up the hill, Penti, Zenobio, and Banner, who was carrying Penti's bucket of fresh water.

Jake Banner tossed aside the bucket and ran with desperate agility to the cabaña.

He swore mightily when he saw Bart sprawled beside the desk, the rifle under his slack hand. He turned him on his back, and incredulously at the same moment, became aware of a baby crying from the bed.

Penti exclaimed when she saw the child and instantly gave it to Zenobio to return to the nursery. Then she bent briefly over Kinkaid's body.

"I don't understand anything about this hellish place," Banner shouted. "He got out of bed to fire that rifle. Why, in God's name? You said he was dying. I knew I shouldn't have believed you on a stack of Bibles!"

An odd look crossed the old Gypsy's face. What Banner had said was true. She could not credit her own senses with what had happened. She knew that only Tarifa could have brought the child here, for what purpose she could not yet fathom. But it was plain something of a powerful nature had happened to stir Kinkaid out of his lethargy. For despite his evident exertions and the new loss of blood, his pulse was stronger, his color better than when she had left him. It seemed incredible. But she did not waste time asking herself foolish questions. Instead she redressed Kinkaid's wound and drew the blankets up to his chin.

"Damn it, woman, why don't you answer me!" Banner demanded. "How is he?"

She glanced up at him sharply. "My people do not question fate, señor. He is better."

A great weight seemed to slide from Banner's shoulders. "He will live?" he asked slowly.

"Perhaps." She shrugged. "One hour ago, he was dying.

He had given up. Now—if he does not take the fever in his weakened condition—perhaps he may live."

Banner slumped into the nearest chair, as if his legs could no longer be trusted to support him. He felt very old. But he would sit here in this room, day and night, until Bart was better and not the Devil himself would be able to budge him from the spot again.

He glanced at Bart's quiet face and felt a rush of affection for the younger man that made his eyes water, unbecoming as it might be to an old sea dog who had spent some forty years rough 'n tumble before the mast. He was beyond embarrassment, even in front of Penti. He was only aware of a humble gratitude that his captain might live to sail the seas with him again.

The badly needed rains continued intermittently for the next three weeks, and the grass turned from russet to a dull olive green. Water ran again in the creeks of the Santa Teresa, Loma de Oro, and Bolsa Coyotes. With the change in the weather the pestilence and fever abated, too, and little Dolores recovered.

Kinkaid's convalescence took longer, but from the time his fears for Dolores' child had roused him, there had been little question that he would survive.

Kinkaid was never satisfied until he had seen the child each day. He had never mentioned what had taken place in the cabaña on the night Penti left him alone with Tarifa, nor had Tarifa spoken of it or returned to the place since that time. But both shared a deep interest in little Dolores' welfare that puzzled Penti. Like all self-willed men who are unaccustomed to illness, Bart was an irritable patient once he had started to mend, and the combined efforts of Banner and Penti would not have been enough to have kept him so long at Loma de Oro if it were not for his interest in the child. His only peace and contentment seemed to come when he held her in his lap and stroked her fair hair, or watched her tiny fingers curl around his own.

He had not forgiven Tarifa for her callous treatment of the infant, when she had deliberately left it alone with him, as he thought, to die. And he was determined not to leave the child behind when he left the rancho. He thought of broaching the subject first to Padre Cazon, but in the end it was Santos who shared his first confidence in the matter.

The mayordomo had ridden up late one afternoon to inquire after Kinkaid's health, and found him sitting in a
chair on the veranda smoking a cigar. Kinkaid offered him
one and Santos squatted down on his heels, leaning his
back against the door.

He thought with satisfaction that the capitán looked a
good deal better than when he had last seen him. Then the
high cheekbones had seemed ready to pierce through the
skin, and his eyes had been sunken in his head like those
of a death mask. Now there was a returning color and
strength in his face.

"I am glad to see that you are better, Capitán."

"Thanks to Penti. I will be leaving soon." He blew
smoke toward the valley and stretched out his hand.
"Once, Santos, I thought of quitting the sea and settling
down here."

"Many Americanos come every year to stay, señor."

"But it is too late for me now."

"Too late?" It was only polite interest that made him
say the words; he knew full well what Kinkaid meant and
was certain that the capitán realized it.

"For Dona Dolores, I would have stayed because this
was her home and I knew how much she loved it. Now
it is too late for both of us, but perhaps I can ensure the
future of her little one?"

"I do not think I understand, Capitán," Santos said
uneasily. "Will she not be well-cared-for in her mother's
old home? And did you not know that Bolsa Coyotes will
be hers someday?"

Kinkaid seemed not to hear him.

"Tell me, Santos, who has charge of the child, Tía Isabella?"

Santos shook his head. "Dona Tarifa has charge of her;
so she had it put in the paper that she made Don Julio
sign when he left Bolsa Coyotes."

"Don Julio is dead?"

Santos looked uncomfortable. He knew that this was
not a matter he should be discussing with the capitán.
"No, señor."

"Then I don't understand how Tarifa—"

Santos raised his eyes to Kinkaid's puzzled face. He

had no right to break a confidence, to repeat what had happened at Bolsa Coyotes on that terrible night, especially to an outsider, a foreigner. Don Ygnacio had hated Americanos. Distrusted them. He had once forbidden this very man to step foot again on his rancho. Santos' loyalty was a deep and sacred thing to him. His love for the Alvarjos had always been a symbol to him. But since Don Ygnacio's death his loyalties had been torn in many different directions: Toward Loma de Oro as the trust Don Ygnacio had left him; toward Tarifa for her efforts to keep it intact; toward Dona Isabella, as the one remaining link to older days; and to each of the children with their conflicting personal problems. Santos did not always agree with Tarifa's methods, but he recognized, as he knew Dona Isabella did, that in her lay the only hope of saving Loma de Oro. To complicate his feelings, Santos had developed in these last weeks an admiration for Bart Kinkaid, for his strength and the strength of the love he had had for Señorita Dolores.

Now, without pausing to weigh his thoughts, the Indian broke in on Kinkaid's words. "If you will not repeat what I am about to say, señor, I will tell you what happened on the day little Dolores was born."

Kinkaid bent forward in his chair, his hands locked in front of him, listening to the mayordomo's quiet voice. Incredulity, and then shock crossed his features. It wasn't possible that any woman, even Tarifa, could have acted so brutally. Could have exacted so sadistic a revenge with her own two hands. And yet, even as he rejected Santos' words with his mind, with every ounce of his male ego, he knew with a sickening feeling that it was true. The cold, primitive, animal emotions that ruled Tarifa made acceptance inescapable.

But why? Why this cruel retribution? He himself could have shot Julio down with no more feeling than if he had been a mad dog. He could have killed him with his bare hands. But he would never have been able to stand and cut him to ribbons dispassionately with a whip, tear out his eye, leave him forever a whimpering wreck of his manhood. It was too monstrous to credit, and yet he knew that every word Santos had told him was true.

Now more than ever, Kinkaid realized that he could not leave Dolores' child in such remorseless hands.

"Santos," he said slowly, "do you think Tarifa would let me adopt little Dolores, take her back to my own people, and raise her?"

It was the Indian's turn to show amazement.

"Take her away, Capitán? But she is to be mistress of Bolsa Coyotes someday. Dona Tarifa would never let her go."

"Tarifa can keep Bolsa Coyotes," he said shortly. "I will see that Dolores wants for nothing. It is the rancho Tarifa is concerned about, not the child."

"You are a mind reader, too, Capitán? You should tell fortunes from the tarot cards like Penti." Tarifa, dressed in her riding clothes, stood watching them from the corner of the house, her face dark and bitter as she beat a nervous tattoo against one thigh with her riding crop.

Kinkaid got to his feet. He was still shaky, but he was thankful that he could stand to face her now. Glad that she had come at this moment, and that he could have the matter out with her.

"Leave us," Tarifa told Santos curtly.

When they were alone she sauntered over to a bench near the door and sat down, removing her sombrero and pulling off the black silk kerchief underneath that bound her hair. It fell like a cloud around her slender shoulders giving her the appearance of a sultry woodland nymph. She was restless under his gaze, and when he failed to speak she said impatiently, "You are never slow in your judgment of others, are you, Capitán Kinkaid?"

"I'm glad that you overheard part of the conversation," he said simply. "It will make it easier to repeat the part that you missed."

"I have no wish to hear any of it. I cannot see that what we do here on Loma de Oro concerns you at all."

He was aware of the rush of heat to his face but he forced himself to answer her calmly. "I am only interested in the welfare of Dolores' child."

"And you presume I am not?"

"Are you?" His eyes raked hers.

She turned away from him, staring down at the valley below, shimmering in the heat haze like something underwater.

"Of course I am. Didn't I provide for her future when her mother died?"

Anger crackled through his voice in spite of his effort to keep it calm. "I know you crippled her father and used her mother's death as an excuse to get your hands on Bolsa Coyotes."

A Romany oath escaped her lips and she was on her feet and across the veranda to his side with the swiftness of a cat.

"I avenged Dolores' death because my husband was not alive to do it, and none of her brothers was capable of doing it. I got Bolsa Coyotes for her because it was hers, and I have kept it separate from Loma de Oro, because one day it will belong exclusively to her. Until that time I intend to act as her guardian and administrator of her property."

"And if Don Julio reconsiders and comes back, or takes you to court over the matter?"

"He will not come back!"

"Let's be honest with each other, Tarifa. You don't want Dolores for herself. I do. I loved her mother and I love the child. Let me take her and raise her as my own. Keep Bolsa Coyotes, she will have no further use for it. I can provide for her."

Her grim smile mocked him. "And are your motives for wanting to take the child so pure, so much less selfish than mine? Is it not the mother you see when you look at her, and not the child? You want to take her with you not for herself, but because by having her near you, you hope to revive your own lost love. Well, it will not work. You lost Dolores long before her child was born. You lost her when she made up her mind to marry Julio."

"You lie! She would have waited for me if you hadn't used some devil's trick to force her to marry him!" he shouted. It was no use, you couldn't talk to Tarifa. Everything in him wanted to strike out at her. No matter what he did she took the upper hand. What she had said about his feelings for the child were not true of course—she twisted and tainted everything to her own advantage—but she would make the others believe her and without her consent his cause was lost. Nevertheless he made one last attempt to move her. "There must be something you value more than the child? If not Bolsa Coyotes, then money. Don Zenobio says you never found Don Ygnacio's gold."

"Zenobio talks too much!" flashed Tarifa. She turned

away from him because she could not bear the brutally speculative look in his eyes, as if she were an odd species of bug he was studying. For an instant something deeper than anger stirred in her and then quickly disappeared. She was not pleased at experiencing new emotions, emotions that she was unfamiliar with and could not be sure of controlling.

"Since you have not been above bargaining for human beings in the past," he said, with a cold merciless edge to his voice, "why not bargain for the child? How much will you take, in gold, to sell her to me? Or would you prefer trade goods?"

She struck him across the face with her crop, as Ygnacio had struck him years before. But it was not the suddenness or the pain of the blow that made his eyes widen in astonishment. It was the surprising sight of scalding tears blurring the wide black pupils of her own eyes, the wetness on her cheeks, before she flung away the crop and raced away from him around the side of the house.

He did not know why he followed, or what he expected to find.

She stood with both arms thrown tightly around Guindilla's neck, her face buried against his golden hide, frightening the stallion by the sudden violence of her sobs.

Kinkaid reached for the bit chains and halted him as the horse tried to rear back. He swept Tarifa away from the stamping feet and against his own body for protection. She seemed not to notice. He stood holding her lightly until the terrible paroxysm of grief had passed and she leaned weakly against him, her face hidden from him in her hands.

"I'm sorry for the things I said," he told her quietly when he knew that she could hear him. "I had no right to say them. I did not know all the circumstances of Dolores' death when I came charging up here that night. I did not know until I talked to Santos today. You should have told me everything that day on the beach when I first returned.

"But it doesn't matter now," he went on, resignation in his voice. "I am going. I know that you will take care of little Dolores as well or better than I could. Perhaps you are right and I did want her for purely selfish reasons. I'm not certain of anything anymore. Will you—let me see her sometime, if I ever come back to California?"

She moved away from him and wiped her face roughly on her sleeve like a small boy. There was the faintest trace of a smile on her face.

"Come when you like," she told him.

It was the nearest thing to a concession that he had ever heard her make, perhaps the only sort she was capable of making.

They stood looking at each other, neither one of them completely satisfied with their awkward truce, yet neither of them able to say more.

Kinkaid said, "I would like to leave tonight. If Santos can ride as far as San Diego with me and bring back the horses I would be grateful."

She nodded, wondering why she found speech so difficult, why she felt suddenly embarrassed in front of his searching gray eyes. Was it because this man had seen her weep, a thing she considered a mark of weakness and disgrace, not once but twice in the past few weeks? She only knew that another human being was making her acutely uncomfortable for the first time in her life, and she wondered that the old anger and resentment did not rise up in her as it always had in the past at the threat of anyone witnessing the inner core of her emotions.

Perhaps it was because the entire outburst had taken them both so completely by surprise. She was sharply aware also, as he had held her lightly against him, that only a short time before they had stood locked in combat above the dead body of her child, bent on killing each other. She longed for him to be gone from Loma de Oro and out of her life. And yet she found herself lingering to hear him finish speaking.

He was saying, "If you wouldn't mind, I would like to send back some things for the child from the ship. Santos can bring them."

"Yes. That will be very nice." I sound just like Rufina or Soledad, she thought with disgust, and added in a crisper tone, "If you would care to see little Dolores before you leave, stop at the hacienda and I will have her brought to you in the *sala*."

His eyes warmed with gratitude. "Thank you."

There was nothing more to be said. She turned and mounted the still nervous Guindilla, quieting him with a firm hand on his neck.

"I will have Santos bring your horse up here, Capitán. *Adiós.*"

In an instant she was galloping heedlessly down the hill, her blue-black hair streaming out behind like an Indian's.

After supper Kinkaid rode down to the hacienda with Santos. Only Tía Isabella was in the *sala* when he entered. She gave him a quick uncertain smile. When he told her his errand, she picked up her basket of colored threads and her embroidery hoop and rose at once. He noted that she seemed ill-at-ease. She had not been to see him during his enforced stay at Loma de Oro. In truth, she did not know how one was supposed to receive a man in a house in which a short time before one of the family had tried to kill him.

"Don't go," he begged her.

"But I always go into the chapel at this hour to say my rosary," Isabella said, wondering at the glib way in which she could lie to the Americano. "I'll tell them to bring the child. Please be seated, Capitán. I will send Hilaria to you with a glass of wine."

He was amused by her flustered withdrawal. When she had left he wondered when, if ever, he would enter this house again. Once it had held all that was important to him on the face of the earth; now it was just another house.

He heard footsteps on the veranda tiles and looked up to see not the maid he had expected, but Tarifa herself carrying the baby in her arms.

She wore a simple short-sleeved, low-necked green silk gown, with a string of pink pearls at her throat. The same throat, he recalled with a pang of remorse, that he had held between his hands and bruised so terribly on that mad night in the cabaña. There were green velvet slippers on her small feet, and her black hair had been done up simply, parted in the center and coiled under a high ivory comb. The sort, he reflected, that had sold for six hundred dollars apiece a few years back aboard the *Arabella*. Like the one he had given Dolores. His first and only gift to his beloved.

Tarifa brought the baby to him in its silken shawl and placed it in his arms. He sat down with the child in his lap and played with her for a moment, marveling again how closely she resembled her dead mother.

A moment later when he stood up to go and handed little Dolores back to Tarifa, he was surprised at the high color in her cheeks. I've embarrassed her enough, he thought. She can't wait to get rid of me and the memory of all I stand for.

He stood for a moment looking at the woman and the child—the one so dark and intense, the other so fair and helpless. And he found himself hoping that life would be kinder to them both in the future than it had been in the past.

Tarifa walked with him to the door.

"Take care of her," he said, touching the baby's cheek.

She nodded. She wanted to tell him things suddenly that she wished he knew. That she had not deliberately meant to harm Dolores when she made her marry Julio. That she was glad now that her own knife had not killed him that night on Loma de Oro. But it was in her to explain, to seek justification for her actions. Perhaps she might have explained to Ygnacio, but not to this steady-eyed, watchful man with the set jaw and unconscious air of command. There was no ground on which they could meet as equals. Neither could take the inferior position. Even after he had apologized to her earlier that day, she had been aware of the hard core of unbending Yankee reserve in him.

He parted the shawl with his fingers and bent to kiss the child gently on the forehead. Raising his head, he found Tarifa's fathomless black eyes fastened on his face. Suddenly, without conscious intent, he bent and kissed her on the mouth. Done so swiftly, it was merely a brush of his lips against hers, a kiss as impersonal and undemanding as he had given the infant in her arms. But she drew back, too stunned to speak. The next moment he was gone, galloping out of the yard with Santos beside him.

Now that she was alone, Tarifa was aware of conflicting emotions swirling around in her brain. Hot resentment, anger, embarrassment, and then a wry and helpless sense of futility. It was the first time in her life a man had kissed her in friendship, gently and without passion.

On her way back from the chapel where she had gone to say her rosary in order that her words to Capitán Kinkaid might not be entirely a lie, Tía Isabella heard Tarifa's dry laughter and wondered at this change from her black moodiness of the past weeks.

As she watched Tarifa come out of the *sala* to return the baby to the nursery, she realized that for the first time since Lasho died she was wearing a dress. Perhaps she would not go mad after all and leave them, as Isabella had feared these last nightmarish weeks. Perhaps she would stay to keep Loma de Oro from falling into ruin. Isabella moved into the *sala* with a lighter step and called with some of her old asperity for Candelaria.

Rufina and Nazario's second child, born in the late fall, was also a girl, and was named Isabella Rufina, for her great-aunt and her mother.

Nazario hid his disappointment in not having a son, and gave a large christening party on Bolsa Coyotes. The child was baptized at Mission San Diego, which was closer to the rancho than San Luis Rey, and because it appealed more to Rufina to have her daughter baptized at a pueblo rather than a mere mission.

But the church at San Diego had fared even more poorly than San Luis Rey. And as the christening party passed the presidio on its rise above the town, they could see the ruinous state it, too, was in, on all but the side which housed the commandante. Of the two cannons in sight, one had no carriage while the other was spiked and useless. Francisco joined them at the presidio gate to accompany them to the church. He looked ragged and half-starved, and he told Tarifa ruefully that there was no powder for a musket in the garrison.

The cluster of brown mud houses strung below the presidio, with the square plastered ones of the *gente de razón* in the plaza, that formed the town of San Diego, also wore a crumpled, abandoned look.

When they crossed the small river to reach the Mission, Tarifa felt a pang of uneasy remembrance. She had sworn never to come here again, where she had been held a prisoner so long ago, and danced half-naked in the sweltering *monjeria* before the startled eyes of three strange men and a priest. She had not been ashamed then.

Only now, when she recalled how Bart Kinkaid's startled gaze had changed to one of wry amusement as he watched her, his eyes as steady and gray as a winter's sea, did she feel a quick shift in her emotions.

She did not relish the thought now that he had seen her like that. She was not quite sure why it disturbed her so deeply, unless it was because he continued to be an enigma to her. The one person her swift Gypsy intuition could not pierce.

In her mind she tried to examine her knowledge of him. She knew that he had a strength and determination equal to her own, but she was also aware of his weaknesses and these she looked upon with scorn. No male worthy of his manhood would fall prey to the spineless sentimentality he had shown for Dolores and her child. Strength, as she understood and admired it, was the strength of force, or might—of cruelty even, if need be. Yet even when Bart Kinkaid had hated her enough to feel the need to kill her, he had not been able to do it. And she could feel nothing but contempt for that.

But Bart Kinkaid was gone, and Francisco, riding beside her, was asking her something. She turned her attention to him; he was the reason she was here.

Tarifa had come only because Isabella had urged her to, and because Padre Cazon had added his plea to hers.

Isabella had said, "You are the head of the family, Tarifa, and since the child is an Alvarjo, you will be expected to attend the baptism." *

"I am busy with the barley crop," Tarifa had replied. "Let Luis go in my place. Anyway, you are going."

Isabella had stood twisting her rosary beads in her long, aristocratic hands.

"There is something else?" Tarifa asked impatiently. "Some other reason you want me to go? In heaven's name, woman, can't you say it!"

Isabella brought her chin up. Her sharp-featured face was pale but proud.

"It is Francisco. Padre Cazon is here, if you will let him speak with you—?"

Tarifa made a motion of exasperated assent with her pen. Curse the old woman and the whole family. Could they never leave her alone a moment without saddling her with their idiotic problems? They were worse than chil-

dren, more helpless than babes in arms. Lately, she was
forced to make every decision for them. Had they no
idea how tired she was of it? How could they expect her
to salvage the rancho, if she was constantly interrupted
in order to straighten out their muddled personal affairs?

Padre Cazon, sitting across from her in his patched
gray robe, told her of Franicsco's interest in the Indian
girl Lisita, once of San Luis Rey and now a maid for the
Canejo family in San Diego. He told her of Francisco's
frequent visits to the *rancheria* at Temecula with the
Picos whenever he returned to San Luis Rey with messages for the mayordomo.

Tarifa heard him out then said with a bitter twist to
her lips, "What am I supposed to do, Padre? Unfortunately the commandante will not put Francisco in prison
for admiring the charms of an Indian girl. That, as you
know, has become all too common these days. As for the
rancheria, it is well known, so Santos tells me, that most
of the young men go there."

The blood darkened Cazon's cheeks. "It is little better
than a seraglio!" he burst out. "Yet we are helpless. We
no longer control the Indians. And what is the result?
There is disease, rape, drunkenness, perversion, everywhere
you look. Yet no one will try to stop it. The authorities
least of all. They use the Indians as they wish and then
abandon them."

"But all this is not Francisco's fault, Padre."

"No. But he is not like the others; he is worth saving,
and I believe he will listen to you. He is an Alvarjo; certainly you do not want this disgrace brought upon the
family if you can prevent it?"

Tarifa's laugh was devoid of humor. "What do I care
about the Alvarjo reputation now? My son is dead. My
only interest is in preserving the rancho."

"But are they not a part of it? You guard and protect
Don Ygnacio's palominos; surely you will do as much for
his sons and daughters?"

"Why should I? There is nothing admirable about them.
They are weak, lazy, grasping, and they despise me. The
only holds I have over them are my whip and their own
greed."

"Then you must use them," said the priest firmly, "to protect them against themselves."

Tarifa stared at him in amazement. "You want me to make them hate and fear me even more than they already do?"

His face was inflexible. "If that is the only way."

And so she had come to San Diego to see the child of one of her stepsons baptized, and to rescue another from the bonds of his own passion, by force if necessary.

Inside the church they found an older, frailer Padre Martin lighting candles on the baptismal altar in his surplice and stole, with the aid of an aged Indian acolyte.

He was tearfully glad to see them, and did not even seem to recall Tarifa's face when he pressed her hand and called her his dear Señora Alvarjo, widow of his beloved *amigo* Don Ygnacio.

The baptism of little Isabella Rufina proceeded without incident. Afterward as they stood outside in the courtyard drinking a glass of inferior Mission wine with Padre Martin, who told them regretfully that he could not go on to Bolsa Coyotes for the celebration to follow, Francisco also made his excuses. He was on duty that afternoon at the presidio, he explained, but if time permitted he would ride out to the rancho later in the evening.

Tarifa watched his thin sharp face, noting the deep-set eyes that now had a narrowed, sly look about them, like the eyes of a lynx. He doesn't deserve any better than an Indian whore, she thought. Padre Cazon is wrong. He is not worth saving. Yet he had Ygnacio's blood in his veins, the same as Lasho had had. They would have been half-brothers. And as Padre Cazon had pointed out, he was a part of Loma de Oro, still under her jurisdiction as head of the family. Was she going to let the *gente de razón* laugh and say that she was not capable of managing her husband's property, or the family entrusted by him to her care? She tightened her hand on the whip she held and spoke briefly to Luis.

"Go back with the others, I have something to take care of in San Diego before I return."

Tarifa rode Guindilla into town at a leisurely pace. It was a crisp cold day and the outlines of the slate blue hills in the distance were as sharply etched as steel saws against the gray sky.

Macario Canejo was coming out of his mother's house in San Diego, as she rode into the square.

"*Buenos días,* Don Macario." She was amused at the startled look that crossed his weakly handsome face at sight of her. Actually, he made a very entrancing picture as he stood there in his short close-fitting jacket; red trousers slashed from the thigh down jingling with small carved silver conchos; snow white trousers ending in stamped and embroidered boots. Around his waist he wore a heavy green silk sash, with a gay woolen serape draped gracefully over one shoulder, and in one hand he carried a pair of silver spurs with enormous gilt rowels.

"Surely you remember me, Señor Canejo?" Tarifa's eyes held a wicked light. "We first met at the Mission, I was dancing in the *monjeria*—"

His face flamed and the words tumbled from his lips.

"Ah, Señora Alvarjo. It gives me great pelasure to welcome you again to San Diego."

"*Gracias,* Don Macario. I trust that your mother is well?"

"My—yes, yes she is very well, thank you. May I ask what brings you to San Diego, señora?"

"A stepgrandchild of mine was just baptized at the Mission. I have just come from there."

"Of course. My congratulations, señora." He seemed vastly relieved and even smiled at her.

She smiled back sweetly. "But that is not the only reason I am in San Diego. It was my intention to call upon your mother, to ask her if I may see a maid of hers, an Indian girl recently of Mission San Luis Rey."

"A—maid, señora?"

"Yes. Her name, I think, is Lisita. Do you know her?"

"But there are so many in the household." His eyes shifted away from hers, then inspiration came and he blurted out, "In any case, Mother is not at home."

"When will she return?"

"I am not sure, Dona Tarifa."

"Then you will not mind taking me to Lisita yourself, Don Macario? One of the other servants can point her out to you, if you do not know her?"

Macario's face had grown very pale.

"I—I have an appointment, señora. I am on my way to San Juan."

"I won't detain you long," Tarifa told him smoothly. "However, if you really prefer that I wait for your mother—"

"No! I will show you to the girl."

Tarifa followed him into the house and studied the interior with frank curiosity. It was a large square adobe. The walls had been papered, and the *sala* furnished with a profusion of heavy mahogany pieces, glass-fronted bookcases which contained hair-wreaths and art objects rather than books, sacred prints in heavy gold frames, and a collection of inferior clouded mirrors. Enveloping everything in the room like a miasma was the sour odor of dampness and recently served *olla podrida* and frijoles. In the adjacent dining room, a maid was just clearing the table. Macario went to speak to her in a low, hurried tone, then came to sit opposite Tarifa in the *sala*. The charcoal brazier in the corner gave off very little heat, and Macario spread his serape around his shoulders.

"She will be here presently," he said.

Tarifa watched his sulky face and then got to her feet and stood toying with the heavy crop hanging from her wrist. It had belonged to Ygnacio.

"I believe I would prefer to go back to the servant's quarters to see her," she said easily.

"But that is impossible!"

Her brows rose. "Why? In my hacienda, I visit the servant's quarters whenever I choose. I afford my guests the same coutresy. Surely you can have no objection?"

He gaped at her in silence as she strode onto the patio. What could he say? She was a guest, no matter how unwelcome, and he had already sent a warning to the girl. If she had no more sense than to ignore it he could not be held responsible. Unpleasant as the whole affair might be, at least his mother was not in the house, thank God! He got up and followed Tarifa.

She snapped a question at the first surprised servant she met, received a startled answer, and marched quickly to the long wing behind the kitchen where the servants all slept.

The windows and doors of the little cells were all open save the last one, which was ajar barely a quarter of an inch. With the toe of her boot, Tarifa kicked it inward. Like an accusing finger, a shaft of pale sunlight sped across the dirt floor and the sound of the door crashing against the inner wall parted the two figures lying on the low rawhide cot.

The girl, heavy-eyed and sullen, dragged a serape closer around her naked shoulders, while Francisco stared up at the intruders owlishly as if they, and not he, had been caught in a distasteful situation.

Tarifa stood with her legs braced, the crop between her palms.

"You are on duty, Francisco, as I see? So the tales I have heard about you are true? You stoop to wallowing in filth with a savage behind your family's back?"

Francisco tugged on his shirt awkwardly and glared at her.

"What I do is my affair!"

"Not while you are under my jurisdiction."

"I am a soldier! Only my officers have jurisdiction over me!"

"Get up and put on your clothes."

"I am not going anywhere with you!"

In two strides she was over to the cot. She raised the crop and brought it down across his shoulders.

Francisco yelped with pain, and the frightened Indian girl scrambled wildly out of the bed, crawling into a corner of the tiny room with a whimper of terror.

The heavy crop rose and fell with a vicious regularity that made Macario, watching from the door, wince and wring his hands in dismay. God in Heaven! She would cut Francisco to ribbons. But he was afraid to do anything to stop her.

Francisco cursed her amid his cries, and his fingers clutched the rawhide strips of the cot in agony. He could not escape her; the heavy crop beat everywhere about his body like a thing sent from Hell to torment him. When at last he lay spent and panting like a cornered animal, he heard her voice, as deliberately dispassionate as a judge's, commanding him to get dressed.

He groaned in pain, cursing her to hell under his breath.

He had every intention of refusing to budge, of killing her as soon as he could get a weapon in his hands, but her remorseless voice beat against his eardrums in spite of his determination not to listen.

"I stand in your father's place as head of the Alvarjo family, Francisco, and I will not allow you to bring disgrace upon his name. You will dress and return to Loma de Oro with me, and from now on you will work there as your brothers and sisters have done. I believe your commandante will gladly allow me to buy you out of the service to which you have been nothing but a disgrace."

"I will not go with you, damn you!" He was trembling and spoke through clenched teeth.

"Then," Tarifa replied stonily, "I will launch a complaint against this woman, naming her a public prostitute and wanton, and you may watch her sweep the streets when she is not in the stocks, and see her stand outside the church during Mass with her head shaved. And I will see that there is not a man, woman, or child in California who does not know that Francisco Alvarjo is to blame for it. Is this what you want to brand your father's name with? Do you intend to make this foolish Indian girl pay for your own carnal desires and stubborn stupidity? Answer me!"

Francisco writhed on the bed. He would rather have had her lash him again with his father's crop than with her merciless biting tongue. "No!" he shouted at last, covering his ears with his balled fists. "I won't listen to anymore! I'll come, I'll come—but get out of here now and leave me alone. For the love of God, get out and leave me alone!"

Tarifa waited in the patio till he joined her. Macario had long since disappeared, and she had seen the girl Lisita slink away, to hide somewhere in the servant's quarters, no doubt.

At the presidio, while Francisco waited sullenly for her this time, Tarifa found the commandante more than pleased to accept a full purse in exchange for Francisco's release from military duty. He was delighted, he explained, to do the charming widow of his old friend Don Ygnacio the favor of returning her stepson to her when she had such dire need of his help to run the rancho.

CHAPTER 19

During the long months that the *Lorelei* traded up and down the coast, Kinkaid spent most of his time in the northern ports. He had struck up a warm friendship with the Vallejos and the Argellos, in Sonoma and San Francisco, as well as several of the Russians at Fort Ross, and he often left the ship for days at a time to join them in hunting or fishing.

Kinkaid was vaguely aware that he had come through his own private hell altered but not broken. He knew that he was not as he had been before. Everything in his temperament seemed to have been heightened, given more impetus. When he worked now, he worked at a desperate driving speed. When he withdrew into himself, it was into a new armor-plated sanctuary that not even Jake Banner could penetrate. Even his anger now was not the hot accusation and swift reprisal it had been in the past. It moved slowly, with the coldness of an iceberg, only partially visible to the observer but twice as deadly.

It was some time before Jake Banner realized the antipathy, even the dread, Kinkaid had for turning his ship toward the southern ports.

Their sojourn in San Francisco gave the captain more than one valid excuse for delay. Soon after their arrival the rainy season began, and for weeks it rained every day without ceasing, making trade impossible.

The collecting of hides in San Francisco was handled differently than in any other port in California. The Mis-

sion at San Francisco had no hides to trade at all, being
built at the edge of the pueblo and having no stock or vaqueros. Only the Missions lying inland twenty to fifty
miles, Mission Santa Clara and Mission San José, had any
commerce to offer, and it was necessary to send the hides
down the creeks and rivers to the bay on large boats pad-
dled by the Indians.

Usually a sailor or two from the ship's crew went along
on these inland trips to oversee the loading, and when they
returned two or three days later with their sodden cargo,
it was necessary to spread the wet hides to dry, until the
ship was a mass of drying hides from top to bottom, from
larboard to starboard.

On a wet, gusty morning, Kinkaid called Banner to his
cabin and told him that he had decided to go into the interior with the Mission boat that waited alongside. Banner
was silent, although he worried now whenever Bart was
gone from the ship for any length of time.

Kinkaid, wearing thick-soled boots and his sou'wester,
dropped into the small boat and Banner watched from the
rail as it moved off in the murky morning light.

Bart welcomed the silence that settled in around them,
save for the slapping of the oars, as they headed up the
bay. Intervals of complete solitude had become a necessity to him since Dolores' death.

It bothered him not the slightest that the rain ran down
his collar and filled the bottom of the little boat, soaking
his feet. When the rain stopped at last the air grew notice-
ably colder and as the boat threaded closer to shore, he
could see white frost on the ground.

In the clearer light the land appeared rolling and green,
with parklike clusters of giant oaks and red-barked toyons.
Cold blue mountains hulked at the end of the valley as if
to put a shoulder to the recent storm. The weather was still
clear and cold when they disembarked at San José. Kinkaid
was able to get a horse at the landing and rode on to the
Missions of Santa Clara and San José to complete arrangements for shipping the hides.

The pueblo of San José, situated in the center of a wide
fertile plain, boasted a cluster of adobe houses with a road
running between them. Shortly after he had left the town,
Kinkaid drew up at the hacienda of an old friend, John

Mabrey, an Englishman who had been a passenger on the first ship Kinkaid had sailed on to California.

Mabrey was something of a mystery, close-mouthed about his past, but a bluff hearty man in his early forties, now married to one of the young Castro girls and father of a tribe of handsome, healthy children. Kinkaid knew that he was a good deal better educated than he pretended to be, remembering a case of books that had been unloaded with his belongings when he landed in California. Since that time he had personally delivered to him many volumes on special order from London or Boston. He had hoped, in coming, to be able to borrow a few of these from his old friend.

The Mabrey *casa* was set in the midst of several thousand acres of oak-studded pastureland, where Mabrey grazed the cattle and horses his wife had brought him as a dowry.

When Kinkaid rode up, Mabrey was seated on the veranda wrapped in a black cape with a scrambling assortment of children and stray dogs, of which he was inordinately fond, milling about his chair.

At sight of his guest, Mabrey rose, shaking himself free of the mild chaos and shouted:

"Bart! By the Lord Harry, is it really you, man? Come in, *amigo mío*. Lupe, I say, look who's here!"

The Mabreys made Bart welcome in their fond, noisy fashion.

Finally John Mabrey, a tall big-shouldered man with a shock of unruly graying hair, and sharp blue eyes under deceptively lazy hooded lids, dragged Bart into his private study at the back of the house. He asked without preamble, "What the devil's happened to you, Bart?"

Kinkaid accepted a glass of brandy and said with his curt New England reserve, "I don't know what you mean, John."

Mabrey cocked a shaggy eyebrow. "Come off it, my lad. You haven't traveled this far in our worst weather to tell me all about it only to come all-over stiff-necked Yankee on me, have you?"

Kinkaid was about to ignore the whole matter, shaming his host into dropping the subject, when he suddenly realized with a shock that he had come here to do just that. Not merely to borrow a book, the excuse he had been offering himself all the way here, but to discuss his affairs with a man of his own kind, a man of Mabrey's caliber and understanding. He had not even been aware that he wanted or needed to talk about Dolores with anyone else ever again. Certainly it should have been enough that Padre Cazon, Jake Banner, and Zenobio Sanchez knew of his emptiness and desolation. Why should he feel the need to torture himself with further revelations to John Mabrey? It made no sense.

He was only aware of a compulsion to unburden himself to John Mabrey. It puzzled him because, though they were old and good friends, they were not of the same nationality and nothing alike in temperament.

Mabrey was hearty, outspoken at times to the point of rudeness; Kinkaid was withdrawn and coolly reserved, and of late even unapproachable. He would have thought it impossible that he would want Mabrey to have even an inkling of his ill-fated romance with Dolores Alvarjo, and its subsequent results. The idea would have appalled him at any other time, but he found himself telling Mabrey every detail.

Mabrey sat slumped in a chair across from him, his glass resting between the palms of his large hands. He did not break the silence for some time after Bart had stopped speaking and there was an odd expression on his face and in his heavy-lidded blue eyes.

"We are not as isolated here as you might think, Bart," he said kindly. "Gossip travels faster in California than a brush fire, my boy. Lupe heard most of the story from her relatives in the south. But, knowing you, we could not believe it was true. Dona Tarifa Alvarjo sounds an incredible creature. I should like to meet her."

Kinkaid was angry that tongues should have wagged all over California concerning his most intimate affairs, and he blamed Tarifa for not having stifled the gossip.

Mabrey said, "I'm sorry for what happened, my boy. But I cannot help feeling that you are fortunate in not finding yourself allied to the Alvarjo family. I knew old Don Ygnacio, a fine gentleman of the old school. He has not one son, I understand, who can measure up to him? Times are changing rapidly in California, as I'm sure you must realize, and the old families must change with them.

People like the Alvarjos will find change impossible, I'm afraid.

"Secularizing the Missions is only the first of the mistakes this government is bound to make. You saw the condition of San José and Santa Clara? When the Padres pull out for good, what is going to become of law and order as we have known it?"

Bart studied his friend's face. "Frankly, I don't give a damn what becomes of the land, John. Once I wanted to settle here, raise a family as you've done. Now all I want is to get away from here as soon as possible and never come back. I have only one regret, that I am forced to leave Dolores' child behind."

"Surely you can come back to see her when you wish?"

"What good would it do? I can't take her from her people anymore than I could have taken Dolores. She belongs here; I realize that now. So why should I return to renew my—memories?"

"But if the child means so much to you—"

"That's just it, John. I'm not sure whether it's the child herself I want to keep near me, or the memory of Dolores. Tarifa accused me of that. I'm not sure anymore. It will be better for me to get away and stay away. I no longer feel that I have a stake in California's future."

Mabrey rose and came across the room on his long legs to replenish Kinkaid's glass from a heavy cut-glass decanter. The Spanish costume which most American and foreigners adopted when they became residents of California, would have been becoming, Bart thought, to his tall spare figure. But Mabrey wore, as he had always worn, impeccable British clothes. Dark coat and trousers, pleated linen shirt, gray foulard tie, and neat handmade black boots.

When he sat down again the Englishman said quietly, "Do you mind if I tell you a story, since we are discussing intimate matters?"

"No, of course not," said Kinkaid guardedly. He was beginning to regret his personal revelations to Mabrey, fond as he was of him.

"I like you, Bart," said Mabrey. "You're a lot like I once was, odd as it may seem to you now, knowing me in my present state. And I think it's time you knew a little of the truth about me. If we're to help each other, and I think we can, the truth will have to be the first stepping-stone. Don't you agree?"

Kinkaid was silent, and Mabrey resumed his speech. "I wanted to study medicine, but the family wouldn't hear of it. I was destined for the clergy as the second Mabrey son always has been for God knows how many generations. Square pegs or round, the family fitted you in, hammered you in if you didn't fit according to your place on the family tree. My poor brother Colin didn't fare much better than I did. He was to go into Parliament, and had about as much ability for it as I would have in your top rigging.

"We both fell in love with the same girl, Clarissa Noles. Again the family decided which of us should have our love, and which should sacrifice his for the good of the clan."

"And the young lady?" asked Kinkaid, interested in spite of himself.

Mabrey's lips twisted in a wry grin. "She had more spirit than the rest of us. She asked me to run away with her."

"And you didn't?"

"Do you know what it's like to be raised from infancy to obey every parental command without question?" asked Mabrey harshly. "No, of course you don't. I've sensed the independence in you ever since I first saw you, and envied it. Oh, I'm independent enough now. I've learned to be. But it is only since I came to California that I have been this way. Too late to save the life of the one I loved better than anything else on earth."

Kinkaid watched the drawn face of the big Englishman and realized that he had never known John Mabrey at all. How many others had he failed to evaluate justly? How many other masks had he taken at face value, without even attempting to delve beneath?

"No, I refused Clarissa's offer," continued Mabrey, "and to cover my own pain and frustration, I pretended indifference. She and Colin were married and because I had not been well, because I had obediently given up Clarissa, my father agreed to let me enter the University at Edinburgh as a medical student.

"He did not expect me to stick it out, of course. But I had found my niche, what I thought was my purpose in life. I suppose I would have been happy as the years rolled on. I had begun to do some fairly clever work in surgery, even gotten some notice in the medical journals. Then one day I got a letter from Clarissa.

"After the first novelty of marriage had worn off, Colin had begun to treat her abominably, leaving her alone in the country while he entertained and amused himself lavishly in London. They had no children, but now she was expecting her first child, and she had hopes that the baby would bring Colin to his senses. She begged me to return to England to consult with her physician, as she was not too strong.

"I went to England at once and found that she was suffering from a severe lung infection, which had been aggravated by her pregnancy. In the end, it was necessary to take the child by Caesarean section. I used every skill I had learned, but it was no use. She died under my hands and the child with her. Colin went out of his head when he learned that the infant had been a boy. He claimed I had killed them both on purpose in order to leave him without an heir.

"For the first time I stood up on my hind legs and told the whole family what I thought of them. The next day I returned to Scotland. I packed up my things and sailed for America. For a time I sailed out of New York and Boston, as ship's doctor on passenger ships going to South America or Africa. I heard of California's opportunities from a trader in Rio, and decided to come and see it for myself. You know the rest. What you didn't know is what I owe to California, what this land has done for me."

Mabrey leaned forward and clasped his hands between his knees. "I came here to hide. I was beaten, cynical, uncaring. I found here a simple joy in living, a genuine warmth and hospitality that I have encountered nowhere else on earth. These people gave me not only their possessions—their homes, their lands—but their hearts as well. Lupe has given me love and understanding far beyond my worth, far more I am sure than Clarissa ever could have, and I feel I do neither of them wrong by having loved the other."

"I'm glad you've found contentment here, John," said Bart, and meant it.

Mabrey waved his hands impatiently. "I've gone on and on and you've missed the whole point of my story!"

Kinkaid glanced at him in surprise. "If you think I don't like California and the Californians, you're mistaken. But I have no roots here, not even the prospect of any now."

"No roots," shouted Mabrey. "Have you no eyes, man? Don't you realize what's happening right in front of you, and you an independent, patriotic American?"

Kinkaid stared at him as if he had lost his reason. He had come here merely to tell Mabrey of his loss, of his personal anguish, and now the Englishman was talking in riddles.

"Look, Bart. Every Englishman in California, and every thinking American, I'll wager, can see the handwriting on the wall. The Mexican government is not going to be able to hold California. There is not a primary nation in Europe that does not have its eye on this rich plum. The native Californians are not strong enough to keep California for themselves, even if they were able to agree long enough to sufficiently organize themselves into a governing body.

"This is my country now, Bart, and I love it as I love no other spot on this earth. I love its newness, its unspoiled freshness, its perseverance against great odds. But the very things I love and cherish most in it—it's vastness, richness, daring youth, its hospitable, easygoing people—make me afraid for it."

He turned to face Bart and there was sadness on his face. Kinkaid was disturbed in spite of himself. "What has all this got to do with me, John?" he asked quietly.

It was a moment before Mabrey answered. When he did, he spoke softly and Bart knew he would remember the words for a long time.

"We are alike, you and I, as I told you," John said. "We have both loved someone and lost her. Now I have found something else to love—a land. And I think you may have, too."

Mabrey got up and held out his hand. "I believe there's an old seaman's saying, 'A ship sails through many winds before she comes to snug harbor.' I'll pray for a fair wind to see you through, Bart."

When the hide boats, loaded to the gunwales with the hides and horns gathered from San José and San Carlos, headed downstream, Bart Kinkaid discovered that a new worry had settled on his shoulders. A genuine fear for the future of this rolling golden land, with its long girdle of blue water and its vulnerability to its enemies both by land and sea. And because he knew that Dolores would always remain a part of it in his memory, he felt a fierce new protectiveness for it that filled him with uneasiness.

CHAPTER 20

Tarifa grew impatient and angry with Padre Cazon when she realized he was growing shabbier and thinner each year, and whatever shse gave him for his own use seemed always to end up in the hands of the Indians.

When, infrequently, he came to the Loma de Oro and Isabella and Candelaria filled a huge basket for him to take back to the Mission, he would disgust Tarifa by saying, "I have no right to eat such food when others are in such dire need."

"Will it be better if you starve and die and are no longer here to help and advise them?" asked his benefactress.

"No. But I am so helpless. Able to do so little to relieve their plight."

Tarifa stared down the length of the table at him, past the bent heads of the family and interjected hotly, "No one can relieve anything! All they can do is stand on their own two feet as long as possible. That is what we are doing at Loma de Oro. And that is what everyone else in California with any sense should be doing."

"Everyone is not as strong and courageous as you are, my daughter, or blessed with so many willing hands to help them," said Cazon.

The smile curved Tarifa's thin lips as sharp as a scimitar.

Willing! There was not a willing person on the rancho, except Santos, Tomas, and Pablo. Everyone else considered her a witch and a tyrant, and still she drove them in spite of themselves. She forced them to work to clothe and feed themselves, to add to the small hoard of gold now buried deeply in a spot known only to herself, to stand together in unity no matter how much they rebelled, to form a bulwark against disaster. Padre Cazon often pointed out also, as a solace, that by her firm leadership she was also helping them to save their own weak souls. Nothing could have pleased her less. She was not in the least interested in the salvation of their foolish souls. What could a strong God want with the souls of people who had to be led or driven or frightened into even their own salvation?

Surrounded as she was by dissatisfaction, rebellion, and hatred, there was no warm spot left in her heart except for little Dolores.

Ever since Bart Kinkaid had asked to take her away, Tarifa's interest in the infant had grown until now, though she would not admit it even to herself, the child had come as close to taking the dead Lasho's place as anyone ever could.

Penti now cared for Dolores exclusively, and she and Tarifa kept her jealously to themselves. If Isabella and the rest of the family complained, the two Gypsies burst out in their wild Romany way and dispersed them like frightened chickens under the threatening claws of a pair of hawks.

Drawing Padre Cazon aside in the patio, Isabella voiced her fears for the child's welfare.

"Dolores is still an infant, Padre, but she is not being reared as a true Catholic or as an Alvarjo should be. Heaven only knows what those pagan women teach her. We are powerless here against them. Tarifa rules Loma de Oro, as you know. But perhaps you can make her see reason and return the child to our care?"

Padre Cazon sat down on a bench wearily. He had just inspected the baby when Penti carried her along the veranda to the dining room to feed her and he had found no evidence of ill treatment. On the contrary the delicate pale little creature had blossomed into a sturdy rosy child. smiling and unafraid, who clung wih trust and affection to Penti's shoulder.

"If it is true that the child's religious training is being

neglected, I do not think that it will do much harm for a few years yet, my dear Isabella. I realize your natural anxiety, but is it not also important that little Dolores grow strong in body and mind now, and be surrounded by love and affection?"

Indignant, Isabella fanned herself vigorously with a black lace fan. She had worn no color but black since the death of her brother and niece, as was only proper, and never would no matter what his pagan widow did.

"Surely, Padre, the child's family are the ones from whom she must get love and affection?"

"Why?"

"Why? But surely—we are her own flesh and blood!"

"But is Tarifa not acting as the child's guardian? Do you think that Gypsies are incapable of feeling love and affection, or of showing it?"

"They feel nothing—but avarice and greed! There is not a speck of warmth in those women, Padre."

"Yet Tarifa wept for those who died and were dear to her."

"For her child, perhaps, not for my brother. She was like a stone woman. She cared not one iota for him."

"But how do you know of the sorrow that was not shown outwardly, my daughter? Sorrow, like love, shows itself in different ways."

Isabella turned her flintlike profile away. "I only know what I have seen, Padre. And from the moment she came here this woman has ruined our lives." She pressed a handkerchief to her lips when they began to tremble and she felt Cazon's comforting hand on her shoulder.

"You must not dwell on such thoughts, Isabella," he said softly. "We have each a cross to bear in life, some heavier than others according to our strength. Bear yours in his name and you will find the courage to carry on.

"I will go and speak to Tarifa about sharing the child with the rest of you. Have faith; we must all have that or we perish."

Walking along the sunlit veranda toward the kitchen, Padre Cazon caught the unmistakable staccato of Candelaria's imperious tones.

"What have you done now, eh? You have spit on my floor again. You are a dirty, ill-bred old man! You should be fed outside in the yard like the dogs. Get out! *Váyate!*"

Pablo exited abruptly with a thick twig broom bran-
dished over his bare head. The little saddlemaker was muttering darkly to himself but he did not pause to return her
insults until he had reached the shelter of his own shop
across the square, when he spied Padre Cazon.

"I am looking for Dona Tarifa," said Cazon. "Have you
seen her?"

"She is in the study, Padre."

Tarifa admitted him when he knocked on the study door,
then threw herself wearily into an armchair, asking, "What
is wrong, Padre? Sit down and tell me."

He glanced down at her and smiled.

"It would be easier to answer what is not the matter, my
child. I suppose there are times, and perhaps rightly so,
when all of us see what we have built up with such toil and
struggle upon this earth scattered to the four winds, beyond
hope of recall. The difficulty is resigning oneself to it."

"And why is that so admirable or necessary?" asked
Tarifa impatiently. "Anyone with any sense would simply
start to build again. Keep on building."

"That sort of spirit is very rare, Tarifa. The human mind
can only absorb so much defeat without giving up. It is
human to err. We do not have supreme strength of ourselves."

"Then if your God is so great why does He not give
you supreme strength when you need it?" Her lip curled
and she looked with her wild mane of hair framing her
dark narrow face, like an Egyptian carving of a high
priestess.

Padre Cazon rubbed his forehead as if to rub away the
useless and disturbing thought. It was odd that he found
more understanding and more comfort in the presence of
this strange wild pagan creature, who he knew did not
believe in his God, than in the company of his own
brethren. Perhaps it was because of her bold defiance of
adversity, her complete reliance upon her human self. Was
not Tarifa correct? If God gave man a mind and a will of
his own, surely He expected him to use them?

"You are troubled, Padre," Tarifa said, searching his

face. "Let us not quarrel." She pressed a glass of wine into his hand. "I, too, am weary. But I will tell you, Padre, I will not give up Loma de Oro, and I will not sit down and let defeat wash over me."

"The Alvarjos are very fortunate." The priest smiled. "Everywhere I see the signs of disintegration, of failure and despair. But not here, niña. You have done well. And you are right. It is far easier to be a pebble upon the beach dependent upon the whims of the tides that stir and lift it according to their will, than to dig in one's own feet and refuse to give an inch."

"Bravo, Padre! At last we agree upon something. We must drink to that. *Bueno gusto.*"

Tarifa eyed him in amusement over the rim of her glass. As usual when she studied his firm-jawed, disciplined face, she wondered what sort of a soldier he had been. A killer of bodies then, rather than a saver of souls. She had known the lust to kill, the sweet taste of vengeance meted out with her own two hands. And yet when it was all over the feeling did not last. It swept away like a tide receding from a beach leaving the sand, with only the tracing of its tumultuous progress but none of its seething power.

"I have been thinking, Padre, it is time we came to an end of all pretense between us. We can help each other, you and I. We need each other. You know that I do not trust in your God, or believe in the symbols of your church. Yet I have faith in you as a man. I trust you. What wrongs I do I shall answer for myself if need be, but I shall not be held a prisoner on this earth for my deeds because of fear. I fear no man, and no God."

She stood up and the muscles rippled along her thighs under the tight-fitting velvet trousers slashed nearly to the knee above her doeskin boots and filled with silver braid over lace. As always she reminded Cazon of an animal, a beautifully made and wickedly dangerous panther with claws now sheathed but ready to tear at an instant's notice. He felt sad because of her lack of faith, the materialistic one-sidedness of her existence, but he could not help but envy her raw courage and stark intrepidity. All tyrants had a touch of it, he reflected. Just as all hatred, worldly malice, and fanatical intolerance were based upon it.

Turned in the right direction even such attributes might

serve a worthy instead of a base purpose. But how did you go about turning them in the right direction?

Cazon sighed and put down his glass. "I will not argue with you, *niña*. In spite of many of my holy and devoted brethren, I do not believe that you can drive faith in God into the skull or spirit with the mallet of piety or the wedge of devotion alone. We are all given a chance, I believe, at least once in this life to recognize God and to accept or reject Him. The choice is ours."

"And you think, like Isabella, that I have lost my chance?" Tarifa grinned wickedly.

"I did not say that. It is a matter between God and yourself, señora."

"But I told you I did not believe. I will never believe."

"I should be sorry, of course, if that were the case," he said, watching her face, "but if my teachings have failed I know that the blame can only lie in the manner of my teaching, not in the God I have told you about."

"Come, Padre. Let's not be so solemn. There are enough long faces in this house, and in all of California, for that matter. I want to tell you of my plans for Bolsa Coyotes."

The priest sat down and folded his arms across his chest. Despite Tarifa's bold confession that he had failed hopelessly to convert her to the True Faith, which should only have added to his burdens of defeat in this land he had come—fruitlessly, it now seemed—to save, his spirit was lighter than it had been in many days.

The *Lorelei* hove to in San Diego harbor on a Sunday and, in spite of a brisk wind and the sabbath, began to unload the green hides collected in the north, which would be left in San Diego so that the ship could be loaded with dry, cured hides to be taken on the return trip to Boston.

Jake Banner, directing operations from the quarterdeck, noticed unhappily that the captain had returned to his cabin and closed the door the moment the anchor was down. His brief bitter glance at the shoreline and the rigid set of his jaw told only too plainly of his feelings. In this place life had begun and ended for him, and he had no intention of setting foot on it again.

In spite of the miserable choppy waters and the men's general unwillingness to work on a Sunday, the transpor-

tation of the hides went well and at two o'clock Banner
gave them a breather and went himself to the captain's
cabin to report their progress.

He found Kinkaid standing before an open porthole
staring at the farthest point of land, a glass of brandy in
his lean brown hand. His straight back had a braced and
painful look but his face when he turned was calm and
steady-eyed.

"Yes, Mr. Banner?"

"We've made a good day of it, sir; we're about through.
The men are plagey tired and it's Sunday, sir. I was wondering if they could take a bit of leave for the rest of the
day, sir—"

"It's not your place to give commands on this ship, Mr.
Banner, nor to wonder," snapped Kinkaid.

"No, sir."

"I intend to sail from here as quickly as possible."

"Yes, sir."

"But you may tell the men they can have this one afternoon off. After that we'll work from sunup to sundown
round the clock till we are loaded for Boston."

"Aye, sir. And thanky, sir—for the men."

When the mate had left Kinkaid lifted the glass to his
lips, then flung it violently out of the open porthole. Memories of Dolores crowded upon him here in suffocating
confusion until he could scarcely breathe. If he remained
cooped up in his cabin another moment he would go mad.

He bawled out the door for Banner and to the mate's
astonishment ordered out the longboat, with a black scowl
that forestalled any questioning from Jake.

The crew, attuned to the mood and temper of the skipper, noted uneasily that he sat straight-backed and silent
in the stern with his eyes steadily focused on the distant
hills, not the shoreline.

Once on land Kinkaid struck off on foot over the sand
toward town at a swift pace. He had no desire to see
anyone and yet he could not bear to be alone. His thoughts
were too powerful and disturbing. Would this endless
whirlpool of despair, remorse, and bittersweet memory
never leave his brain? Was he fated to carry the burden
of his loss for the rest of his life? He had heard of men
going crazy from just such brooding memories and he
was beginning to think that he might be one of them.

Nothing was powerful enough to banish the tormenting thoughts from his brain. And lately whenever Dolores' face flashed before him there was another, darker one behind it. Tarifa's scimitar-eyed face, like an evil omen ready to rob him of his beloved again, this time even of her memory. He clenched his fists and felt the nails bite into his palms.

He scrambled up the slope on the outskirts of the town and, looking neither to left or right, made his way to Domingo Chavira's wine shop. There were scores of his sailors in the musty smoke-filled little room, but their faces swam before him like so many disembodied spirits as they touched their caps respectfully when he passed.

Chavira was not behind the bar, but a squat Indian-looking bartender gave him a bottle of *aguardiente* and a glass and stood watching as the Americano leaned there on his elbows and poured liquor with one hand and drank with the other in a horrifying sort of legerdemain.

After the third drink Kinkaid felt the sweat in his eyes and pushed back his cap and unbuttoned his coat. He glanced about the room and felt a pair of eyes on his face. A tall man was leaning against the wall at the back of the room, a cigar between his thin smiling lips. He straightened when he saw Kinkaid's eyes on him and came slowly toward the bar.

Kinkaid watched Titus Judah approach him like a stalking puma, his red hair shining in the afternoon light that came from the open door. There was a newly prosperous look about him and a slyly satisfied expression on his face, as if he had feasted well on forbidden fruit.

"Good afternoon, Captain Kinkaid. No hard feelings since our last meeting, I assure you. That stuff you're drinking goes to my head at times. Let me buy you a civilized brandy."

"No, thank you, Captain Judah, have one with me."

"*Muy gracias,* as they say in this place."

"I didn't notice the *Vulcan* in port."

"She's anchored at San Juan. I rode down—on private business. You're sailing for Boston soon?"

"As soon as we load," Kinkaid said shortly. The man annoyed him. He had no desire to talk to him, or to anyone else for that matter.

"A pity," Judah said. "You know, Kinkaid, there's a

great deal more to be gotten out of California than hides
and tallow."

"The Endecott Company isn't interested in anything
else."

"How about Captain Kinkaid?" Judah lifted his glass
in a mock salute.

"What do you mean?"

"Have you ever thought of the women of California,
Captain?"

Kinkaid's eyes smoldered dangerously. Was the man
alluding to Dolores? But he couldn't know the Alvarjos.
He wasn't the sort who would have had entrée to Loma
de Oro. Perhaps, like John Mabrey, he had heard gossip,
but he had no way of proving whether or not it was true.

"I don't believe we are interested in the same cargoes,
Captain," Kinkaid said flatly.

Judah laughed. "Not cargoes. Investments."

"Investments?"

Judah leaned on the bar and lowered his voice. It was
useless precaution if he wanted privacy, for no one in the
room except the rowdy disinterested sailors at the opposite end understood a word of English.

"These girls are lively as sin and downright pretty, some
of them. Did you ever stop to think of the lands and
herds their padres are ready to hand over when they
marry? Or the widows who own leagues and cattle of their
own? A man would be a fool not to see the ready-made
opportunity here."

"You're married?" Kinkaid asked disinterestedly.

"Hell, no! But I'm planning to be as soon as the Padres
pour a little water over me and label me a Catholic, so
I can hold land. I am going to own a piece of the finest
rancho in these parts."

Kinkaid drained his glass and prepared to move off.
He was sick of the man and his sly boasting innuendo,
but he asked carelessly in parting, "You're giving up the
sea, Captain?"

"No. I'll ship my own hides on the *Vulcan*, and I'll
wager I'll get better prices in Boston than you will! They
don't grow finer cattle than on Loma de Oro and Bolsa
Coyotes."

Kinkaid halted in midturn, his face like a cold white
mask. His voice was as taut as a halyard.

"May I ask the lady's name?"

"Señorita Soledad Alvarjo," replied Judah with a smile that sent the blood rushing to Kinkaid's head and almost blinded him in his anger and disbelief.

"You're lying!"

"On my honor, she's promised to marry me."

"You have her family's consent?" The words were thick as silt between his lips.

The lids dropped a fraction over Judah's light eyes but he said, "Of course," with a conviction it was hard to discount.

"Of her stepmother Tarifa?"

Judah smiled but refrained from speaking.

Kinkaid turned on his heel and left the room. Behind him he heard Judah laugh and order brandy for the assembled company.

It was unthinkable, monstrous, that Soledad, a mere child, should be allied to a man like Titus Judah. Tarifa, better than anyone else, should remember the violence of the man. She had sold Dolores into bondage to safeguard Loma de Oro. Could it be that she was doing the same with Soledad? What her purpose could be this time he could not imagine, but he had no intention of allowing her to carry out her ugly scheme.

He thought of going to the Padres first but that would probably do little good in the end. It was Tarifa he would have to deal with. The plaza was nearly deserted in the late afternoon light but two or three vaqueros were arguing the fine points of their mounts and rigging on one corner. Kinkaid hired the fastest looking stallion and turned him northeast toward Loma de Oro, spurring him recklessly into a powerful gallop.

CHAPTER 21

Soledad's admiration for Rufina had increased during her brief visits to Bolsa Coyotes. When Rufina received permission from Tía Isabella and Tarifa for the younger girl to spend the summer on Bolsa Coyotes, Soledad was beside herself with joy.

Bolsa Coyotes was a much gayer household than Loma de Oro these days. Rufina refused to do any of her own work and even had a mestizo housekeeper to instruct the other servants. Rufina spent her days as a Spanish lady of quality should. She enjoyed a late breakfast, sunned herself in the patio, went driving about the countryside or even to San Diego in her carriage—one of the few in California—to visit friends. And she entertained with dinner and dancing almost every night. It was delightful at Bolsa Coyotes, and Rufina, glad of feminine companionship, took pleasure in dressing up her young sister-in-law and instructing her in the finer arts of love, courtship, and marriage.

Soledad was an apt and eager pupil. Always pleasure-loving, herself, she gave no thought to the future or foresaw the web that Rufina would so cleverly weave for her.

Nazario, on his part, was completely ignorant of what was going on in his own household. Day and night he was occupied running Bolsa Coyotes to meet Tarifa's exacting requirements. He had developed into an excellent cattle-man and mayordomo, but one word of criticism or dissatisfaction from Tarifa on her frequent and impatient tours of inspection could throw him into a childish funk and wipe out all his newborn confidence. Francisco, since Tarifa had taken him out of the army, had also come with her permission to make his home on Bolsa Coyotes and the two brothers were often at loggerheads. Francisco was an indifferent ranchero; he, who had taken orders and carried them out unquestioningly all his army life, now resented the slightest command from Nazario. Still more did he resent those given him by Tarifa.

No matter how hard he tried everything seemed to be slipping away from Nazario, and he grew testy and morose. At night he found a bottle of brandy in his study preferable to the twittering noisy crowd his wife gathered around her for pleasure. They were not the old friends and neighbors of his youth. Most of them were strangers to him, visiting foreigners from San Diego, even some Americanos whom his father would not have admitted under his roof at Loma de Oro. He had nothing in common with them. Yet when he showed himself a sullen host and criticized Rufina, she turned from him with flashing eye and curling lip like a flower turning from the setting sun.

Anguished after a night spent alone in his study, he would creep up to bed and attempt to take her in his arms to apologize in whispers and try to recapture the fire of their first union. But it was useless. Rufina, her mind elsewhere, would tolerate him or openly and coldly repulse him, even going so far one night as to sleep on the floor like a serving maid. He was humiliated and angered. He thought of going to the Padres, even of writing to the Father Prefecto himself, but the Alvarjo pride was a hot sword in his vitals. He could not bring himself to run crying to the Church because he was not man enough to master his own wife. Nor could he go to Tarifa because he had failed to command his own household.

In the beginninng he had been pleased that his sister Soledad had come to join them. She was pretty and gay, and he could be sure that Rufina had a suitable escort on her unorthodox ramblings over the countryside. But of late their almost daily jaunts had been further afield than ever and their return to the hacienda grew later and more uncertain.

On the surface Rufina seemed gayer and more beautiful than ever before, but then so did Soledad. It was hard for him to realize that she had blossomed into a woman. Young men swarmed about the patio, strumming their guitars or haughtily showing off their horsemanship for the edification of the two enchanting women. And if tongues wagged about their conduct in the counryside, there was little that anyone could actually criticize the two Alvarjo women for in specific detail.

The young Dona Rufina Alvarjo was perhaps a trifle too gay and extravagant, but did she not go everywhere accompanied by her well-bred sister-in-law? Was not all of her entertaining done in her own home, with her husband present? If she chose to invite strangers and foreigners to her home, well, Barbareno women were notoriously independent—especially the Corlonas.

One evening, when Nazario caught his wife alone dressing for the evening's festivities before he had been at the brandy bottle, he attempted to discuss their problems with her. She was more beauiful than he remembered, her breasts and arms more gently rounded, her lips fuller and more sensuous. He desired her more than ever. But he felt crushed from the moment he opened his lips. She seemed as cold and remote as the highest peak in the Sierra Nevadas.

"Rufina?"

"*Si*, Nazario?"

"Will you sit down and listen to me for a moment? I have been wanting to talk to you—about us."

"I haven't time to sit down. I am dressing. Our guests will arrive any moment. I can hear you just as well standing. What is the matter now?"

"What do you mean?"

"You always find something the matter with me these days." She sighed, hooking up her bouffant red dancing dress with slim nervous fingers because she had just dismissed the maid in a fit of temper.

He attempted to put his arms around her but she wiggled away from him, her hands busy behind her back like small scrabbling crabs.

"It is not you, *querida*, it is both of us. We do not seem to be the same anymore."

"Is that my fault? I do the best I can. I run this house,

though it is not really mine. I see to your comforts, I look after your sister and brother, and I have borne you two children. What more can you ask? I have lived up to my vows. If I invite a few people here now and then to help fill in the monotony of this desolate place while you are engrossed with the business of the rancho, is that a sin?"

"No, my darling, I want you to enjoy yourself—and show Soledad a good time."

Rufina's eyes snapped. "Then what are you complaining about?"

Nazario's mouth hardened and he took a deep breath.

"It has been weeks since you slept with me. I think it is time we had a son."

Rufina stared at him with black hatred in her eyes.

"Do you think I want a husband coming up to me drunk every night? Do you think I take pleasure wallowing in bed with an insensate animal? Did you marry me for a wife or for a brood mare, Nazario!"

Stung, he fell back, his hands slack at his sides. In spite of his effort to keep it calm his voice quavered like a schoolboy's when he replied.

"I married you because I loved you and I thought you loved me. I still love you, Rufina. Whatever is the matter between us we must find it out and end it. We will go and see Padre Cazon or Padre Martin."

"No! I've had enough of the Church meddling in my affairs."

"We can't go on like this!"

Rufina lowered her eyes and twisted the pink pearl ring Nazario had given her on their betrothal. "It will all straighten out, Nazario. Give it time. We have both been tired and under a strain these past months. It's Tarifa. She drives you too hard. She expects too much from both of us."

This was a new thought to Nazario, and it made some sense to him. He knew his stepmother made him nervous and uncertain; why should she not have the same effect on Rufina? A great weight seemed to slip from his shoulders. He had not lost Rufina's love as he had begun to suspect; he had only misplaced it due to Tarifa's consuming dominance over their lives.

He reached for her and brought her into his arms and

kissed her gently on the forehead and lips, and then with burning passion. There was a new response and fire in her he had not known before and his pulses leaped. But he put her quietly from him and said, "I understand now, *querida mía*. I will wait and be patient. And I will join your friends tonight and every night if you wish. No more *aguardiente* or brandy. We are husband and wife and we will greet and entertain our guests together."

Rufina, her lashes still lowered, said, "*Gracias*, Nazario."

He went from the room and Rufina dashed to examine her face in the mirror. She would have to let him sleep with her tonight. It was high time. But she might as well let him think it was a hard-won victory. No, nothing showed in her face. It was as pretty as ever with only a trace of puffiness under the eyes and along the chin line.

Thinking back, she could remember the moment she first set foot upon the deck of the *Vulcan* and saw the tall, light-eyed, red-haired captain standing on the quarterdeck with his big powerful hands resting on the rail.

His glance had gone through her like a bolt of lightning and left her giddy and quivering inside. She had come to San Diego on a routine shopping jaunt, and when a friend had mentioned there was a new trading ship in the harbor she had gone aboard purely out of curiosity.

Only that morning she had found out that she was not pregnant again, a fear she had carried like a lead weight for some weeks, and now with the onslaught of this Americano's bold and challenging eyes she had known the sudden joy and relief of her freedom like a live bird taking wing within her.

Captain Judah came down to greet her and introduce himself, and it was he who showed her around the fascinating crowded storeroom, ignoring the services of the supercargo.

In the end she bought nothing because she had little money with her, and she knew Nazario would not approve of her being aboard ship unaccompanied. Besides he would object to her signing a credit chit for hides or tallow. But Titus Judah was a man not only of astute perception but of long-range strategy as well. He would not hear of her leaving the ship empty-handed.

He sent a sailor aft to fetch a small keg of his own personal rum, a gift to Don Nazario, he explained, and presented Rufina with a Manilla scarf for herself and china-headed dolls for the two children.

"It is only my way of advertising my wares, señora," he told her glibly when she protested. "So that you and your husband will pass the word and come together to shop here. Last week I gave Don Santos Coronel gifts for every member of his family and he has twenty children."

"You are most kind, Capitán."

"It is my great pleasure to be of service to my California customers. Are you in town often, señora?"

Rufina glanced up at him warily. He was a foreigner and she recalled her father-in-law's hatred and mistrust of all Americanos.

"I come when I am able, señor."

"I wonder if on your next visit you would do me a great personal favor?" It was his turn to seem embarrassed. He smoothed his red moustache with a blunt forefinger.

"I would be most happy to assist you in any way I can, Capitán," Rufina murmured politely. A flag of color had appeared on each cheek. True, she did not know the ways of these big Americanos, but she intuitively knew the ways of men and it was clear that Titus Judah had every intention of seeing her again.

He smiled down at her and made a sweeping gesture with one of his large freckled hands. Rufina could see how the hairs stood up on the backs and over the wide knuckles like stiff red wires. Nazario's hands were lean and slim as a woman's and olive-hued. They would be no match against the smashing brute strength of hands such as these.

"Out there is a whole new world I haven't explored yet," he said. "A poor sailor-man doesn't have much chance to explore. He touches at a port, takes on or puts off cargo, and is on his way again. When I was a boy I used to like to take a tramp in the country, study the trees and the hills, enjoy a picnic under a tree. You've no notion how homesick a sailor can get for the sight and smell of a tree, señora. You've some mighty pretty ones out there back yonder apiece. Oak trees, eh? I'd like to

see a few of them close up. Would it be asking too much
for you to show me around a bit some afternoon when
you're in town? Provided, of course, your husband doesn't
disagree? I expect to be in port for a few weeks, trading
and unloading hides."

Rufina was at a loss for words. It was unthinkable to
accept his suggestion; indeed, she didn't dare. San Diego
was too small and gossipy a place to be seen alone with
a foreigner or, for that matter, with any unmarried man.
She would have to find someone they could trust to accompany them, someone innocent.

As if the problem had lain already solved in her brain
all along, she thought of Soledad. The silly little goose
would follow her blindly anywhere in her steadfast admiration. She could invite Soledad to come with her to show
the lonely and generous Capitán Judah the surrounding
countryside. Nazario would be contented with the arrangement, and after all what could be more respectable than
a staid young matron graciously chaperoning her innocent
sister-in-law and the reptuable captain of a foreign trading
ship on a sight-seeing tour of the countryside?

"I will bring my sister-in-law Soledad with me next
time I come to San Diego, Capitán Judah," Rufina said
demurely. "Then perhaps we can both show you the countryside?"

She was pleased that a shadow of irritation passed over
his face before he bowed and told her in his warmest
tones, "That will be a double pleasure. I shall look forward
to it, Señora Alvarjo."

Soledad took to the frequent sojourns to the harbor
with exuberant delight. She was as attracted to the tall
red-haired captain of the *Vulcan* as Rufina, and in her
case, much to Rufina's annoyance, there was no reason to
hide it. Because she wanted Soledad's attention occupied
by something other than Captain Judah, Rufina included
Macario Canejo in their little party.

Macario did not come at all unwillingly. Soledad had
grown into a most beautiful and seductive young woman,
and she had mastered all the wiles that Rufina had been
at such pains to teach her.

Often the couples would take a picnic and, mounted on
Canejo horses, separate to enjoy their lunch in some secluded spot.

Rufina was amused, then alarmed that her old tricks of coquetry failed to have the same effect on Judah as they had always had on the other men of her acquaintance. The Americano's objectives were as clear as the glass in Rufina's gilt-edged mirror. Though she often found him crude, sometimes even debasing, she never found him unexciting.

As they lay in the shade of a giant oak on the gentle swell of a slope in one of the small hidden valleys far from the prying eyes of the Mission or the town, Rufina found herself recklessly abandoning all her old precautions and scruples.

When he kissed her carelessly, even roughly, she pretended to herself that he loved her, even though the mockery in his light eyes and a warning bell in her own heart told her that this was not true. In the end it made no difference to her. His harshness, his virile strength, had become necessities to her like meat and drink. Even when she saw him casually studying Soledad's fresh young charm in sardonic speculation she could feel no jealousy, no anger.

Frequently in the reckless extreme of her passion she had even pretended to Nazario to spend the night in San Diego with friends, and gone instead aboard the *Vulcan*. There, after being secretly rowed out by Judah himself, she shared the narrow bunk in his cabin. Feeling the gentle roll of the ship beneath her as they lay in each other's arms, she wondered at her own shamelessness.

It was on such a night that she first told Judah about the child. He jerked away from her as if he had been stung.

"Judas priest!"

"Why do you swear, Titus?"

"Why the hell wouldn't I! Do you know what this can do to me? What it can cost me?"

He leaped up from the bunk and began pacing the cabin in giant strides, his big hands locked behind his long bare back.

"I trade along this coast, and I intend to go on trading here for a long time to come!"

"Do I mean nothing to you?" Rufina murmured in wonderment.

Judah gave her a satirical glance from his light eyes under the slanting red brows.

He is a devil, she thought, a cruel pitiless demon without heart or feeling, ready to devour everything in his path to feed his own appetites.

She secretly feared the cold ruthlessness in him, much as it had attracted her to him in the beginning. He had been an unknown quantity then. Now she knew him very well indeed, his ugly as well as his expansive moods. He would certainly not stand by her in her hour of need. But she had already taken that into consideration. All along she had meant to throw him Soledad like a bone to a surly dog, when the time came to make her own escape. As for herself and the child, Nazario would provide a safe haven for them. Only one thing worried her—if the child had bright red hair. But that, she considered, with her own dark coloring, was a remote possibility. In any case, if it were a boy Nazario would be more than easy to convince that it was his own. It was a sore point of masculine pride with him that he had so far produced no male offspring.

Rufina cuddled deeper into the covers and contemplated her scowling lover with a cool detachment that she would have thought impossible just weeks ago.

"If the prospect of an illegitimate child upsets you, how would you welcome the prospect of having a young landrich wife, Titus?"

He turned to stare at her and his lip curled in derision. "What hairbrained scheme have you got in your devious mind now?"

"One that will please and profit you, no doubt." She studied him from her thick-lashed, somnolent dark eyes, noting with satisfaction the open cupidity on his face. A good deal of his cynicism had rubbed off on her but, unlike Judah, she found nothing to regret in her present predicament. She had had her throw of the dice. It pleased her now to see him tense and discomfited.

He came to sit on the edge of the bunk, his big hands flat on his muscular thighs. What a lot of red hair he had on his chest, Rufina thought idly. In the past it had intrigued her when it tickled her breasts as they made love, for Nazario's thin dark chest was smooth. Now she could view it as she did him—dispassionately.

She knew that she was as finished with the affair as he was, but for a different reason. His was greed, hers was self-preservation, and since her reason was the more primitive, more powerful, she knew she held the winning cards. Rufina was prepared to gamble anything to save herself.

"I don't know what the hell you're talking about," he told her darkly.

"It's quite simple, Titus, a logical problem to be solved in a logical manner. You wish to remain in California? So do I."

"And what do we do about the brat?"

"Nazario accepts it as his own, of course. I am not very far along."

Judah laughed harshly.

"No man is that big a fool. What if it has red hair and light eyes?"

"There are ruddy men and light-eyed ones among my own ancestors," she answered smoothly.

"By God, Rufina, you're as sly a bitch as I've ever come across!" He laughed in reluctant admiration. "I wouldn't have believed it of you. What was that mention of a well-born, landed wife? Another of your tricks?"

"Far from it. I was referring, of course, to Soledad."

"Soledad!"

"Don't act so surprised, Titus. I've seen you eyeing her these past weeks. A purebred young Castilian virgin, that is what you have been thinking. Blood finer and purer than mine. A real prize, and a virgin as well."

"Damn you, Rufina," laughed Judah, "you're cursed with the devilish insight of that black Gypsy mother-in-law of yours! And what will she say to all this?"

"Nothing," said Rufina smugly. "She will accept it because she has to. She has developed a great sense of family pride and responsibility since her husband's death. No breath of scandal must ever touch the hallowed name of Alvarjo again."

Judah pursed his thin lips. He found himself liking the idea more and more. "There may be some truth in what you say, Rufina. Tarifa has gone out of her way time and time again to protect the family honor—why not now?"

Rufina was not fool enough to count completely upon Tarifa's reactions, even if it directly involved Loma de

Oro and Bolsa Coyotes. Her mother-in law was too violent and unpredictable for that, but she did count on Tarifa's reluctance to involve the Alvarjo name in a further scandal. And there was Tía Isabella, who would tip the scales in her direction for honor's sake.

Tarifa was suffering from a summer cold, her eyes and nose ran and she was completely miserable. The sunny days had alternated with foggy cold ones, and she had been out in all weather trying to safeguard the stock.

She had long discarded Penti's remedies, and now depended solely on her own strong constitution coupled with generous draughts of *aguardiente* or brandy. In the last months she had become more man than woman.

Circumstances demanded it of her. Not only was there a large and helpless family to provide for, but a host of dependent servants as well. Where before, vaqueros and servants had left the ranchos in droves emboldened by their new freedom, now they flocked back in pitiful numbers, ill, disillusioned, begging for a crust of bread, a place to lay their weary heads.

Most of the ranchos were too depleted and poor themselves by this time to support even their former neophytes, but Loma de Oro and Bolsa Coyotes still had herds and food. So the hapless Indians came daily to fill the kitchen square or huddle discontentedly along the roadside leading to the hacienda till it looked like a beggars' road.

Tarifa got to her feet and crossed to the front window to stare out. Something in the sudden stiffness of her pose made the visiting Padre Cazon inquire, "What is it, *niña?*"

Tarifa knew without question now who rode toward her door and with every fiber of her being she wished she could reach out, turn both horse and rider around and send them off in the opposite direction.

She remembered her last meeting with Kinkaid only too well and she had no wish to have him near her again. She sensed with her Gypsy intuition that this man spelled danger for her and yet she was powerless to stop his coming.

"It is Capitán Kinkaid."

With an exclamation of pleasure the priest hurried to join her at the window.

Kinkaid leaped from his sweaty blowing horse, tossed

the reins to one of the little Indian boys who always hovered at the end of the veranda near the tethered horses hitched there for daily use.

Tarifa went onto the veranda followed by Padre Cazon, just as Kinkaid turned from his horse.

"*Buenos días,* Capitán." There was bare civility in her tone.

"Tarifa—I must speak to you. At once and alone."

He caught sight of Padre Cazon and rushed forward past Tarifa to press the priest's hand.

"Thank heaven you're here too, Padre. It will save us time."

"Time, *amigo?* What is it in this land that so presses for time? That is the one thing unchanged in this unhappy place."

Tarifa had been studying the American, her black brows drawn together in the sullen way he best remembered her. There was no hint of the softness and womanliness he had seen for a moment in her the last time as she had stood garbed in the soft green dress, with the pink pearls at her dusky throat, and the blonde child Dolores cradled in her arms.

Now she seemed fine drawn but as lean and hard as rawhide, and her coppery-colored skin and sharp aloof profile reminded him of a statue cast in bronze of an Algonquin Indian he had once seen in a museum in Boston.

"Perhaps we had better go into the study?" Padre Cazon suggested.

Tarifa merely turned abruptly on her heel and led them toward the room without a word or a backward glance.

"Sit down," she invited as Kinkaid closed the door. He had caught a glimpse of Tía Isabella and another young woman at the far end of the patio sewing. No one else had been in sight, nor was there a sound from any quarter of the rambling house. He hoped Soledad was not far off. He sat down across from the Padre while Tarifa perched on a rawhide stool near the fireplace.

"You bring us news of some kind, my son?" Cazon was overjoyed to see that the American seemed recovered from his remorse over Dolores' death.

Kinkaid turned directly to Tarifa. Their eyes met and clashed as they had done so often in the past, and Kinkaid felt the same rising tide of anger and dismay, yet he forced himself to go on.

"Where is Señorita Soledad?" he asked bluntly.

The surprise of his request made Tarifa's eyes fly wide open. She had expected anything but a bald request for Soledad.

"She is not here. She is away visiting."

"Where?"

"Is that any business of yours, Capitán?"

"Yes, dammit, it is! And it should be yours. Where is she?"

Padre Cazon held up his hand as he saw the dark color rising in Tarifa's cheeks.

"Please, Capitán, *por favor*, if you know something the Señora should know tell us at once."

Kinkaid turned to the priest. "Did you know that Soledad has promised to marry Captain Titus Judah?"

Father Cazon gave an exclamation of dismay and Tarifa leaped to her feet.

"You lie! You have come here to cause more trouble. You have never come to this house without bringing trouble with you!"

Kinkaid clamped his jaws and spoke through his teeth, the anger seething in him like a waterspout. He got to his feet because he could no longer sit there under her accusing eyes.

"I'm telling you the truth. Judah is going to become a Catholic and marry her. He told me so himself. I just left him."

"Santa Maria," sighed Padre Cazon, crossing himself.

"Now, will you tell me where she is?" Kinkaid asked in a tight hard voice, "or do you look after the Alvarjo girls so well you don't even know—or care—what kind of men they consort with?"

It was a cruel, useless thing to say, and he could have bitten off his tongue the moment it was said as he watched the naked helplessness and disbelief that crossed Tarifa's face.

She turned away from him. "She has spent the summer with her brother Nazario, and Rufina, at Bolsa Coyotes."

"I'm sorry," Kinkaid said awkwardly. "If something has happened you would have no way of knowing?"

She whirled to face him, her eyes blazing.

"I have visited Bolsa Coyotes at least once a week ever since I sent Nazario there as mayordomo! I am supposed to know everything that goes on there. Everything!"

"But surely you will not permit Soledad to marry that man?"

"I will handle the affairs of my family, Capitán Kinkaid, as I alone handle the affairs of Loma de Oro and Bolsa Coyotes."

Kinkaid stood with head lowered and his feet apart and braced as if he were riding out a nor'wester.

"I can't leave it at that."

"What do you mean?"

"I have a stake in this family too. Soledad is Dolores' sister. I must have your word that you will stop this marriage, for the girl's sake."

Tarifa drew herself up as slim and taut and deadly as a rapier.

"How dare you enter my house and tell me what to do!"

"Please!" Padre Cazon stood between them, his arms outstretched like an unsteady cross. "There is no need for recriminations. Tarifa has taken care of Don Ygnacio's children in a manner both efficient and commendable in every respect. And you, Capitán, doubtless came here with only the best of intentions for Soledad's welfare. Can we not sit down and work together to ensure what is best for the poor child?"

Kinkaid sat down and bit the end off a cigar with savage fury and spat it on the floor.

"I want that man out of here," cried Tarifa, "at once!"

"Wait, I beg of you, for the *niña's* sake? Let us hear what he has to say."

Tarifa turned her back on the two men and stood in a black and sullen silence.

"Now," said Padre Cazon in what he prayed was a reassuring and conciliatory tone, "tell us everything you know, Capitán Kinkaid, *por favor?*"

Kinkaid told his story in short terse sentences, in a voice that had absolutely no inflection. He kept his eyes studiously on the toes of his boots to avoid any stray glance in Tarifa's direction.

When Kinkaid had finished, the Padre rose and went to put his hand on Tarifa's arm.

"You have heard, *niña*. It seems that all is not well at

Bolsa Coyotes. And now that I think of it, the last time
Padre Martin wrote to me he mentioned that Dona Rufina and Señoria Soledad had been in San Diego frequently
of late, unaccompanied by Don Nazario."

"Nazario!" cried Tarifa bitterly. "Why can't he run his
own household as a man should? I trusted him, I put him
in charge, and I find that he has no more sense than little
Antonio. Must I be in every place, at every moment, looking after these wretched Alvarjos!"

"My child, my child—"

But Tarifa had whirled to face Kinkaid and he saw at
once that her black anger had been replaced by something
else. He had questioned her stewardship and that had
flicked her on the raw; now she was in complete control
of herself again. But it was clear that she meant to handle
this thing alone, and this Kinkaid knew he could not permit her to do.

"I will take care of the matter in my own way, Capitán.
You need have no fear, no Americano shall marry or attempt to marry an Alvarjo again. I would appreciate it if
you would leave my house—now."

Kinkaid watched her expressionless face for a moment
and then stood up, the cigar between his strong white
teeth. She seemed small when he was standing at full
height, almost as small as Dolores, but formidable and
deadly. Like a delicate asp ready to strike at any sign of
movement.

"I suppose, as you say," he told her shortly, "this is not
precisely my affair. But I'm sailing for Boston soon and
I can't go without knowing how this matter is going to
turn out. I imagine you'll be riding to Bolsa Coyotes to
investigate for yourself. All I ask is to go along with you
and hear the facts for myself. Judah is a man I understand
and can handle—as you may remember?"

Tarifa's face darkened and she clenched her fists but
said nothing.

"You may need help with the captain, señora."

"Not from you!" The words, spat with the velocity of
grapeshot, held him silent for a moment.

"Tarifa!" It was Cazon's voice, the voice he had once
used on the battlefield in command of troops, the voice he
believed he had laid aside forever.

Tarifa glanced at him in astonishment, and there was respect mingled with her surprise.

"Soledad is the important thing at this time. Capitán Kinkaid can no doubt be of use to you, in advice concerning the Americano if nothing else. He asks only to go with you and learn the facts. I must tell you that this is an ecclesiastical matter as well as a temporal one. The church must also be appraised of all the facts. Since I am the first religious to learn of the affair, and since I myself am unable to go and ascertain matters for myself before reporting them to the Father Prefecto, I appoint Capitán Kinkaid to go in my place, at once, and report back to me at the Mission. Will you do so, Capitán?"

A slow smile curled Kinkaid's lips. He took the cigar from his mouth and said, "Gladly, Padre, gladly."

Tarifa shot him a baleful glance and left the room. When Kinkaid would have followed, Cazon detained him with a hand on his arm.

"Wait, my son. All will be well. We can wait for her on the veranda. She will not leave without you now. I know her tempers and her moods."

"I wish to heaven I did!" exclaimed Kinkaid under his breath as he followed the priest from the room.

Soledad was sitting before the dressing table in her bedroom at Bolsa Coyotes while a young Indian maid, Tica, brushed and braided her thick dark hair, weaving pink and blue ribbons in between the strands.

She was very pleased with what she saw in the mirror. The white skin like her dear *madrecita*'s was the creamy texture of a magnolia petal. The narrow-browed, rather wide-jawed face was also reminiscent of her mother's plumply pretty one. The brows were straight and thick and glossy as raven wings. The eyes large and sleepy but of a beautiful deep brown and were her best feature. Under Rufina's tutelage she had learned to use them to great advantage over the edge of a lace fan, or lowered demurely under her thick lashes while talking with a caballero.

Today she wore a new blue-sprigged muslin gown, scooped low at the neck, with short lace-trimmed sleeves that ended well above her dimpled elbows. There were pink velvet slippers on her tiny feet tied with pink satin ribbons, and a wide pink satin sash around her narrow waist.

Rufina had made her a present of the gown several weeks ago, when it was apparent that her newest pregnancy would make it impossible for her to wear it herself.

With Rufina's indisposition keeping her in her bed late in the mornings when she seemed to feel the worst, Soledad found herself virtually mistress of Bolsa Coyotes.

At first she had enjoyed ordering the servants about in the haughty manner Rufina always used. But they were all so docile and obedient that this soon palled. She thought of inventing slight misdemeanors to report to Nazario, and thus have the amusement of watching them reprimanded or even put in the stocks for a day, but in the end she found that she had no stomach for such things and a guilty conscience would be too high a price to pay for such trivial amusement.

She knew that she would not lack for amusement today, however. Her fiancé was coming. He had sent word that morning, a note delivered by a hired pueblo vaquero written in his poor, almost undecipherable Spanish, with the one English word that Soledad could recognize—"Love"—and his scrawled but bold signature—"Titus."

The heat that rushed to Soledad's face at the thought of him made her lower her eyes, lest the Indian maid read their message and gossip about it later in the servants' quarters.

When she had dismissed the maid, Soledad dabbed scent behind her earlobes from a bottle Titus had given her on his last visit. She could not quite recall all the details of the whirlwind courtship that had ended with her promise to marry Captain Judah. And she had a fearful and guilty feeling because so far only Rufina knew of her betrothal.

At first Titus had seemed more taken with Rufina than herself, Soledad reflected. But that hadn't been true, he had convinced her later, since Rufina was a married woman. No, it was only that from the first he had admired his little Soledad so intensely that he was afraid one glance of his would mar her spotless reputation. His love for her was so great that he wanted to make her his wife as quickly as possible, but only after he had complied with all the rules of her church and state.

Rufina had given them her blessing and gone with them

to ask Padre Martin to baptize Judah, which he agreed to do after giving the captain a brief series of instructions which he was now completing. Because of Tarifa's aversion to Americans, both Titus and Rufina convinced Soledad that it was best to wait until Titus was baptized and therefore eligible to marry, before telling her stepmother. And for the same reason, Rufina pointed out, it was best not to tell Nazario either. He might go at once to his stepmother and upset their plans.

Soledad knew that Nazario did not like Titus Judah. At first she had been afraid of Titus herself. He was not at all like the young men she was used to flirting with and then casting aside. At times he had the iron authority of her father that had always cowed her. At others, she sensed that he was trying to be patient and kind, to keep a strict control over what she imagined were his passions for her. Soledad did not have the deep intelligent sensitivity her sister Dolores had had, or the swift perception of Tarifa, but she had been gently reared and protected all her life, and her horizons, both mental and worldly, were limited.

The only time in her life she had been thoroughly frightened had been on the night she had accepted Titus.

For weeks the American had been telling her of his great love for her and urging her to marry him. Rufina had added her plea to his case.

"So many California girls have married Americans," she had said, and added with a knowing smile, "and not one of them with regrets. They say they are wonderful lovers."

Soledad had turned scarlet and hidden her face behind her fan.

"You mustn't say such things to me, Rufina."

"Why not? It's time you young girls knew a few things. The Indian girls at the Missions and *rancherías* know them well enough and not from their Indian husbands and lovers alone, either."

"Rufina! What would Tía Isabella say?"

"This is my house," Rufina said with spirit. "I say what I like here. I tell you Capitán Judah will make you a splendid husband. Why, every girl for miles around will envy you."

Soledad's eyes lost some of their shock and began to

shine with a more familiar and greedy light. Rufina noted it with satisfaction. She could not waste much more time arranging this marriage. The little dolt was stubborn and spoiled. Judah would have to do something on his own and she meant to tell him so if he didn't bring matters to a satisfactory head tonight.

In the end it hadn't been necessary to speak to Judah, for that same night he had been accepted.

Nazario and Francisco had ridden over to the Martinez rancho on business and planned to stay the night. Only Rufina was left to chaperone Soledad when Captain Judah called to pay his respects.

It was a beautiful moonlit night and the three of them sat in the patio until a wind rose and Rufina, pleading her indisposition and a sudden headache, left them to go to bed.

"I know you'll see Capitán Judah has everything he needs, *querida*," she told Soledad, who stared at her with pleading eyes which her sister-in-law studiously ignored.

Rufina added lightly, "I'll send Tica back to sit near the door when I am through with her. We must be proper at all costs, isn't that so, Capitán Judah?"

"Of course."

"And I can trust you alone with my little sister-in-law these few moments?"

"Like she was my sister, señora."

"Ah, of course. *Buenos noches*. Soledad, why don't you show Capitán Judah the prayer closet Don Julio's father built? Quite an oddity in our house, Capitán."

"I should be most interested, Señora Alvarjo."

When Rufina and the maid had gone, Judah stood at a respectful distance looking down at her. Soledad, suddenly afraid, turned and led him quickly into the study.

After she had opened the prayer closet in which Judah showed a sincere and lively interest, Soledad told him all she knew of its history, which unfortunately fell quite short of its juicier points. To Judah, however, who was an observant as well as a shrewdly imaginative man, fuller explanations were not necessary.

He stepped inside the closet and began to study the little altar, touching the wood and bringing his eyes close to it as he lowered his head. He was so intent that Soledad stepped in behind him, and when he turned abruptly she was nearly in the circle of his arms, as Dolores had been in Kinkaid's.

One of Judah's arms went around her waist, and with the silent, powerful pressure of a boa constrictor he drew her closer, while his other hand slid under the low-necked white muslin blouse she wore and cupped one breast in his palm.

Panic filled Soledad like a suffocating wave, but she could no more have cried out than a dying sparrow in the ruthless talons of a hawk. The faint pressure and release above her fluttering heart were filling her with nausea. In her ears drummed a terrible and silent thunder. The pressure of his body bent her head back and for a moment she gazed into the inflexible naked desire of his gleaming agate-hard eyes, then she dropped her own eyelids and felt his breath, then his mouth, on her thick-feeling lips.

She did not know how long they stood locked in this awkward embrace. She was dimly conscious only of his movement, his hands and his lips, and sometimes faintly, as from a great distance, of his voice.

She knew when her knees began to buckle and he picked her up and carried her to the sofa in the study and pressed a glass of wine to her numb and trembling lips.

She heard his voice and his apologies while he sat holding her hands but it was only when he changed his tone and the ring of command and something sharper, even more menacing, crept into his voice that her benumbed brain began to untangle itself and she found her voice responding.

"I think it would be better all around if you agreed to marry me, Soledad, after tonight."

Soledad nodded her head like an obedient puppet. The shame of what he had done almost made her faint. She darted a glance toward the open study door, but the Indian girl had not come back yet. Had it all taken place in such an incredibly short time? Her life irrevocably tied to this big Americano who had frightened her so by his bold uncouth actions? She shivered and a deathly fear ran through her. What if Tarifa found out? She had only heard gossip of what Tarifa had done to Don Julio when Dolores died in this very house. Would her ungovernable

Gypsy temper not turn on Soledad as well as Judah if she
found out what had happened here? No, it was better to
marry Judah, as he was carefully pointing out to her. He
bent and kissed her again, his lips lingering and then falling to her throat, her neck. And this time she found a
thrill of pleasure mingled with her fear.

When the Indian girl's rough leather sandals could be
heard coming down the hall and she took her place in the
chair by the door, Titus and Soledad sat at opposite ends
of the sofa discussing Don Julio's father's books.

A moment before Soledad had consented to marry the
Americano capitán, and in spite of her shocking experience she found that she did not regret it.

Now, hearing horses in the yard, Soledad rose eagerly
from the dressing table and went to glance out the window. The blue-coated figure must be Titus. She was about
to call a gay greeting from the window when she caught
sight of the second rider, half-hidden in the shadows cast
by the veranda.

The breath stopped in her lungs and she felt a wave of
dizziness that left her clinging to the window frame.

Tarifa! And the other one was not Titus, it was Capitán Kinkaid.

Soledad fled from her room down the *galleria* and in
upon a reclining and startled Rufina.

"Santa Margarita! What is the matter with you, Soledad? Can't you greet your lover without this childish show
of exuberance? He's a man, not a calf-eyed boy."

"Rufina! What are we going to do? I'm afraid. Afraid!"

Rufina sat up. She was fully clothed but not wearing her
slippers, which lay in a little heap of black silk and ribbons at the foot of the bed.

"Get hold of yourself. What are you afraid of, you
little goose?"

"Tarifa! Tarifa and Capitán Kinkaid! They just rode up.
They know about Titus and me, I'm sure they know! She
will kill us. Kill us!"

A flash of fear, quickly suppressed, crossed Rufina's face;
then she was on her feet taking her sister-in-law's arm.

"Come, we must go to meet them."

"No!"

"Come, I say!"

"You haven't your shoes."

"Never mind. Do exactly as I tell you, Soledad. Say nothing if they question you. Let me do all the talking, do you understand?"

Soledad nodded miserably and dabbed at her eyes with a lace-edged handkerchief.

Tarifa, followed by Kinkaid, had just stepped into the *sala* when Rufina and Soledad came in from the *galleria.*

"Buenos dias," said Rufina politely. "We are very happy to have you in our house again, Dona Tarifa. And you are welcome to our home, Capitán Kinkaid. Won't you sit down and make yourselves comfortable while I send for refreshments? Will you take tea, Dona Tarifa?"

Tarifa measured her stepdaughter-in-law and found her face a mask of polite impassivity. She had never liked Rufina nor trusted her, and she secretly blamed her for Nazario's occasional failure to do his work well. Nevertheless she could detect no visible sign of nervousness or guilt about the girl. She plainly showed her pregnancy now and at such times women were notoriously prey to upsets and nerves. If Rufina had been shielding a guilty secret she would have betrayed it by some sign. But there was nothing.

Soledad was another matter. Her face was as white as eggshell and her eyes as wide in her head as those of a bolting horse. Was it possible that this silly child had affianced herself to a man like Judah all on her own?

Tarifa said, "We'll go to the study. Tell them to bring a bottle of brandy and two glasses."

"Of course," Rufina murmured, signaling the little maid hovering at her elbow. "I'm afraid Nazario isn't here, Dona Tarifa. He spends most of his time in the saddle these days. It's shocking how many cattle the freed Indians are killing and stealing for their hides."

"If he and Francisco spent more time looking after them, perhaps we wouldn't be losing so many," Tarifa snapped. "Well, are we going to the study or are you and Soledad rooted to the floor?"

Soledad stumbled and almost fell in her haste to get out of the way.

Tarifa gave her a sharp and withering glance as she passed, and Kinkaid thought that the girl had the look of a stricken rabbit. For himself he was only relieved to find out that she had not run off to meet Judah.

In the study Tarifa, still wearing her sombrero and spurs with a plaited quirt dangling from one wrist, poured brandy into two glasses and handed one to Kinkaid.

Rufina and Soledad sat side by side on the sofa, staring at her like a pair of birds held in horrible fascination by a sleek cat.

"Nazario is not here, you say? Perhaps he takes his duties over the stock too seriously. He fails to report fully to me as ordered."

"No," murmured Rufina. "I am sure he reports everything to you, Dona Tarifa."

"When I put Nazario in charge of this rancho, I meant him to be responsible for all of it, including this house, and to report to me everything that happens in it."

Rufina's chin shot up.

"This is our home while we are living in it. We are entitled to some family privacy, are we not?"

"The privacy of your boudoir and no more," said Tarifa, putting her glass down with smashing hardness on the table.

Soledad started and pressed her handkerchief to her lips.

"And what is the matter with you?" her stepmother asked smoothly. "Every time I have inquired you have told me you enjoy this hosuehold so much you do not wish to leave. I have been lax with you. I have allowed you to stay and amuse yourself, instead of keeping you at Loma de Oro where you would have to do your chores like the rest and soil your pretty hands. And how have you been enjoying yourself? Tell me!"

Soledad burst out crying and Rufina put her arms around her.

"You cannot bully her in my own study," cried Rufina.

"It is little Dolores' study," said Tarifa flatly. "I will say anything I please in this house, at any time while I am in charge of it, and if you open your mouth again I will send you and Nazario and all your brood packing at daybreak!"

Rufina bit her lower lip but was silent.

"Soledad!" The command burned like lava across the room.

The girl's head jerked up in alarm.

"Is it true that you have affianced yourself, without my knowledge or consent, to Capitán Titus Judah of the *Vulcan?* Answer me!"

"Por favor!"

"Answer me!"

Soledad nodded her head and immediately covered her face with her hands.

"Did you know about this?" Tarifa thundered at Rufina.

"Why—no. I can't believe it."

Soledad dropped her hands to stare at her sister-in-law in stricken disbelief.

"So many young mén have been calling upon Soledad, which is only natural. But both Nazario and I always insisted that she be properly escorted and supervised, even here at the hacienda. Just as she would be at Loma de Oro. Why, when she went out, I always went with her myself— you can ask anyone in the countryside or in San Diego. In spite of my condition I have never permitted her to go out alone. I cannot understand this!"

Soledad lowered her head. She had not believed Rufina capable of such treachery, but even with her limited perception she began to recognize the deadly enormity of the trap she had fallen into and with such blind stupidity.

"Capitán Judah called upon Soledad here?" Tarifa's voice rang hard above Rufina's head.

"Yes."

"With Nazario's knowledge and consent?"

"Certainly. Nazario is the master of this house. I am only his wife."

"Someone had to invite Judah here."

"He came with some of our other friends—Macario Canejo, I think."

Steps sounded in the hallway. Nazario stood on the threshold looking at the little tableau in blank surprise.

"Come in, *querido*," called his wife. "We have guests."

Nazario hesitated a moment, his eyes riveted to Tarifa's face, and then he came forward slowly. He sensed a disagreement of some sort and was reluctant to enter into it, but Rufina's eyes had pleaded with him, and he did not want her upset when she might be carrying the son he so longed for.

He greeted his guests with a grave politeness, and sent a servant for tea for the ladies and another glass for himself.

"I have some very old imported brandy," he told his stepmother, "far superior to this. A gift from Capitán Judah of the *Vulcan*."

"Sit down, Nazario," said Tarifa.

"Yes, but—"

"Sit down!"

"*Sí*." He sat next to his wife and Soledad and took Rufina's trembling hand in his.

"Did you know that your sister has affianced herself to Capitán Judah of the *Vulcan*?"

Nazario shot a startled glance at Soledad's bent head, but he hesitated to speak out when he felt the sudden warning pressure from Rufina's fingers.

"*Premita Undebē!* Answer me!"

"I—he came here, like many others. I knew that," he answered lamely.

"You allowed scum like that into your home, something your father would never have permitted, and allowed Soledad to become involved with him to the point of promising to marry him—and you knew nothing about it?"

"No—I did not." He could not lie to her. She would find out and it would go harder for all of them.

"And your wife knew nothing about it, though she's watched over Soledad so carefully?"

"Of course she knew nothing about it! She took Soledad everywhere with her. They were never apart. Lately she has been unwell, as you know. When we have guests here it is impossible to watch each individual every minute."

"I told her we knew nothing about it," murmured Rufina.

"I will speak to Capitán Judah. Explain. He will understand," said Nazario.

"It is not your place to conduct the affairs of this family. You have proven yourself incapable of even running your own household."

Nazario flushed and the line of his mouth grew sullen and hard.

She drives them too hard, thought Kinkaid. She is surrounded by enemies and she doesn't even realize or care about the danger. Someday they will join and attack her and pull her to pieces. Oddly, he found that he did not like the thought. Much as she annoyed and angered him he found that he admired her audacity, her fearless raw courage.

Tarifa turned to him and said, "You left Capitán Judah in the pueblo?"

"Yes. At Chavira's wine shop."

She nodded and told Nazario, "You will ride with us. Get Capitán Kinkaid one of the palominos."

"*Sí*." Nazario rose after exchanging a long look with Rufina, and went out of the room, his footsteps ringing hollowly on the tiled *galleria*.

"You will take the carriage," Tarifa told Rufina, "and return Soledad to Tía Isabella's care at Loma de Oro."

Rufina nodded. She didn't know whether Tarifa believed her story, but she meant to play her part as long as it was expedient. She doubted that Judah would betray her, if only to ensure his own safety and reputation. No, he would not tell them that they had been lovers and that she now carried his child. He would not dare. She was safe.

Soledad continued to weep into her handkerchief, praying to all the saints she could remember that this ghastly interview would end and she could hide herself away in her own room. She thought with passionate longing of some peaceful secluded place far from Tarifa, Rufina—everyone. Especially Titus Judah. Perhaps she could go into a convent? Tarifa could not reach her there. But what convent would want a girl besmirched and ruined, who had lain as she had lain in the prayer closet in Judah's avid embrace? The hopelessness of her thoughts brought forth a fresh wail of anguish followed by a sharp reprimand from Tarifa.

"Stop your foolish crying! You brought all this on yourself."

Outside the wind had increased, blowing the horses' manes and tails and billowing out the shirts of the Indian boys who held them.

Kinkaid mounted a tall, well-muscled palomino, and was pleased at the smoothness of his gait as they galloped out of the ranch yard.

Nazario watched them as he mounted his horse. He had been shocked to learn of Soledad's involvement with Judah. He did not like the man. Once he had even seen him eyeing Rufina in a manner he did not approve of. But Macario Canejo had brought the fellow to Bolsa Coyotes, and one could not insult a guest in one's own home. His father had ever drummed into them the sacred rules of hospitality.

Nevertheless Nazario was keenly aware of his own failure to protect his sister properly from the man. In this one instance he could agree with Tarifa's wrath, though his dislike for her was as strong as ever. Of late he had begun to think that it would be better if he took Rufina and the children and left Bolsa Coyotes. But where would they go? They had no money, and all their friends were in worse straits than the Alvarjos. At least Tarifa had managed to keep the ranchos running despite the persistent droughts of the past few years and the lack of adequate help. He had to give her credit for that.

They had ridden halfway to San Diego without seeing more than two or three *carretas* laden with green hides, when Nazario saw a horseman approaching, walking his horse in a leisurely manner. It could be no Californian. Then with a start he recognized Judah's red hair and blue cap.

At the same moment Tarifa reined up Guindilla sharply, signaling for them to halt in the shade of giant live-oak. Tarifa dismounted and the two men got down also and stood watching the approaching rider.

Kinkaid glanced at Tarifa. She stood with her feet apart watching Judah through narrowed eyes. He had no hope that Tarifa would allow him to speak to Judah first, but he was determined that no harm would come to either of the Alvarjos. On the other hand, dislike him as he might, Judah and he were countrymen and he could not stand by and see him killed in cold blood. He meant to make Judah see that he had lost the game and that clearing out was his only alternative.

Nazario felt only a cold loathing for the approaching American and a grim determination to give him a beating if nothing more for his audacity. How this was to be accomplished when Judah could easily have broken him in two, he did not stop to consider.

There was a half-smile on Judah's face as he rode up and reined his horse to a halt.

"A windy morning for a ride, *amigos?* I was just on my way to Bolsa Coyotes."

"We would like a word with you, Judah," said Kinkaid.

Judah's gaze locked with Kinkaid's and the smile disappeared from his face.

"I—see. You ran with my little tale to Dona Tarifa? Well, no matter. What can you do about it now—any of you?"

"Get down!"

Judah's face hardened and his hand brushed against his coat, disclosing a pistol tucked into his waistband. "Don't use that quarterdeck tone with me, Captain Kinkaid."

"I'll use any tone I damn please, Captain Judah. These people want to talk to you, and by heaven I'll see that they do."

Judah smiled faintly and spat over the horse's rump. He dismounted with slow deliberation and stood holding the reins in one hand, the other hand on his hip over the gun.

"You wanted to speak to me, señora? I am at your disposal, but not due to the request of Captain Kinkaid."

Tarifa stared at him, contempt and hatred naked on her face.

The fury of her gaze made his own glance flatter and brought a dull red glow over his cheekbones. Curse the damn witch. She had the eye of a demon. For a moment he felt something deeper and more ancient than fear brush him and he was glad that he was not alone with her. Nevertheless he addressed her again with a show of bravado.

"You wanted to speak to me, señora? Here I am."

"I will not waste words on you, Capitán Judah," said Tarifa. "If my husband were alive he would kill you where you stand."

"And what am I supposed to have done that warrants murder, señora?"

"Don't amuse yourself with me, Capitán Judah! Capitán Kinkaid has told me of your brazen abuse of Nazario's negligent hospitality, of your secretly affiancing yourself to a silly heedless child. And Soledad has admitted it."

One of Judah's red eyebrows climbed higher above his agate-hard eyes.

"Is there anything wrong with telling a lady of my tender feelings for her?"

"In this land it is customary to speak to the parents or guardian of a young girl before speaking to her, Capitán Judah, as I believe you are well aware. In any case, you have no more affection for Soledad than you have for that horse you ride so badly."

Judah flushed and his jaw hardened.

"I had only the most honorable intentions toward Soledad," he told her, clipping off the words. "I hoped to make her my wife, and still intend to. You don't own the girl body and soul."

"She is under my care and not of age. I would refuse to let her marry you if her life depended on it. She is a vain, silly, unthinking child, but only a child and she is an Alvarjo."

Judah laughed. "Is that supposed to put some special brand upon her, like sterling on silver? She's a common enough wench, if you only knew it. I'll be honest with you. She's pretty enough, but she bores me a little. I intend to make her my wife, however, in spite of you and all the Alvarjos."

"For what reason, Capitán?" Tarifa purred. "So that you can claim her share of Loma de Oro?"

She stared into his eyes, a long withering look that made him want to leap at her throat and throttle her. He would not back down. He would have the best of her in spite of Kinkaid and all the Alvarjos in California. She wouldn't be able to refuse him the land once they were married. He would find some way to smuggle Soledad aboard his ship. Once they had lain together, there was nothing Tarifa could do but recognize the marriage. But he knew he must be careful. If Tarifa had any inkling of his intentions she would have him killed by one of her vaqueros. He wouldn't put it past her to do it herself.

"My reasons are my own," he told her smoothly.

"I give you fair warning, Capitán," said Tarifa. "If you set foot on either Loma de Oro or Bolsa Coyotes, or link Soledad's name with yours in any way publicly, you will be killed."

"Then we understand each other at last, señora? I have told you my intentions. I still intend to carry them out."

Tarifa took a step forward, the quirt clutched in both hands. Kinkaid expected to see her fly at Judah and lash him across the face, but at the last moment she held herself in check.

Judah waited a moment and then mounted his horse. Nazario leaped on his own horse and with lightning speed uncoiled his *reata*.

"You will do as Dona Tarifa says, Capitán," he warned, "and ride back from where you came. My vaqueros will have orders to kill you on sight if you attempt to come to Bolsa Coyotes again. Make no mistake, señor, with this *reata* I could take your pistol from you before you could fire."

"You have heard our ultimatum," said Tarifa.

Judah touched a finger to the visor of his cap and wheeled his horse obediently toward San Diego. He turned to Kinkaid before he put heels to the horse's sides and said, "A sudden squall means lightened canvas, eh, Captain, if you want to bring her to anchor in snug harbor?"

The three under the tree watched the long-backed, blue-clad figure until it was out of sight.

"What did he mean?" asked Tarifa.

"That he doesn't intend to give up."

"He knows the consequences."

"A man as determined and slippery as Judah won't give up at the first threat."

"Then we will have to kill him," said Tarifa matter-of-factly.

Kinkaid glanced at her with a mixture of amusement and dismay.

"Civilized lands don't countenance cold-blooded murder, Tarifa, even for daring to court an Alvarjo without permission."

Tarifa said, "Our ways are not yours, Capitán; it would be better if you remembered that. I have warned Capitán Judah of what I will do, and make no mistake about it, I will do it."

Kinkaid sighed as he put his foot in his stirrup. He hadn't the slightest doubt in the world that she would indeed do exactly as she had threatened. The whip hand of authority was a thing he understood only too well. As captain of a ship, he reigned in supreme command, with the power of life and death if he chose to use it. Judah was also a ship's master, and a ruthless one, if all Banner had told him was true. Tarifa did not understand what she was up against, and unless she were warned and heeded the warning, she might well be outmaneuvered.

"I'll go and speak to Judah in a manner he'll understand," he told her.

"No. You have done enough." She mounted and turned Guindilla toward Nazario's horse. "This is an Alvarjo affair. I can handle Capitán Judah when the time comes."

"Then if there's nothing further I can do," said Kinkaid, "I'll be getting back to San Diego. I sail for Boston in a few days."

"You'll be back?"

"Perhaps. But I wish you'd take a word of warning about Judah. He's tricky and he's dangerous. If he's determined to marry Soledad he will never give up short of death, and I'd hate to see his blood on your hands."

"It would not bother me, Capitán," said Tarifa coolly. Her hair blew in a tangle about her narrow bronzed face under the wide black sombrero fastened tightly under her pointed chin. For a moment, in spite of her words, he saw a primitive childishness and defenselessness in her. Given a softer upbringing, a less demanding and harsh maturity, might she not have been simply a wild, gay, entrancing creature? With the fluid warmth of her nature, stripped of its destructive claws, would she not have been able to intrigue and delight men? As unpredictable as the winds off Cape Horn, she offered him the challenge—to ride out the variable storms of her nature just as he would bend himself to sail his ship through a perilous passage.

To still his own thoughts Kinkaid rubbed the neck of the magnificent palomino he rode and asked, "What is his name? He's a handsome fellow."

"His name is Jilguero, señor," said Nazario. "Goldfinch."

"Goldfinch. An apt name. He flies like the wind and he's as golden as ripe wheat."

"You ride him well," Tarifa said unexpectedly. "Keep him as a gift from the Alvarjos, for your assistance today."

"I would like nothing better," smiled Kinkaid, "but I am leaving soon."

"Ride him until you leave then, and he will be waiting for you when you return."

"*Gracias,* señora."

They exchanged a long look. Until that moment Kinkaid had had every intention of never returning to California. Now he knew that he would.

The stallion sprang into a full gallop like a powerful engine under him at the first pressure of his knees, but Kinkaid reined him in a few yards down the road and whirled to wave a last farewell.

Tarifa and Nazario were still halted under the tree, their horses pointed to face his. For a moment Kinkaid allowed the scene to fill his eyes and mind as if he were filing it away for future contemplation.

The rolling dun landscape with whirling dust devils in the distance, under the blue cloud-flecked sky. The wind-swept oak, its leaves rippling like green water, and underneath, as motionless as painted statues, the pair of golden horses, their silver accoutrements winking in the sunlight. And the two colorful riders so gay and brave in their bright sashes and wide sombreros, looking so sure in their arrogance, and so doomed, he felt, to failure in the end.

As he turned Jilguero again toward the pueblo, he wondered about the Alvarjos and this hospitable, indolent, helpless land. How would they bring order out of the chaos they had brought upon themselves?

Though Kinkaid rode to San Juan the next day seeking Judah and the *Vulcan,* he found that the ship had slipped out the night before for an unknown destination. Kinkaid cursed his luck but there was little he could do. His ship would be ready to sail in a few days and he would not delay his departure.

CHAPTER 22

Soledad's return to Loma de Oro brought tears, prayers, and recriminations from Tía Isabella. Had her dear Encarnacion been alive nothing like this would ever have happened. Between her visits to the chapel to say innumerable rosaries and novenas to beg intercession for the soul of the disobedient, misbeguided girl, she resolved to keep Soledad constantly at her side day and night, and insisted Soledad move her things into her own large front bedroom. Tarifa, of course, had been negligent in her duty to let the girl stay so long at Bolsa Coyotes, with only the young and irresponsible Rufina to supervise her. Tía Isabella did not acknowledge the thought that she also had agreed to Soledad's sojourn to the other rancho, thinking to spare her from the household chores and Tarifa's uneven temper.

Isabella felt herself growing older and more helpless each day, and she missed the warm companionship of her sister-in-law far more than she had ever missed her brother. She was like someone cast up on a strange, desolate island. Nothing was the same at Loma de Oro since Tarifa's coming. The children were scattered, or cowed and sullen. The servants lacked the willing spontaneity they had had under Encarnacion's gentle undemanding hand, and Tarifa's whiplike temper dominated everything and everyone who crossed the threshold of Loma de Oro.

Soledad found to her dismay that she had returned home to a life of imprisonment. If she so much as stuck her nose out the door, Tarifa or Tía Isabella or one of her brothers appeared as if by magic and ordered her inside. She was so sick of pacing the *galleria* and circling the patio that she could not see straight. Her life had become a horror of suspicion and restraint. Anything would be better than this, even Titus Judah's exploring hands and untender embrace, she admitted guiltily to herself. She knew that she should despise Judah for his coarse treatment of her, yet she found with surprise that she did not despise him. He had taken vulgar liberties with her, besmirched her name, and brought her to the brink of ruin, yet she had a wild desire to see him again. By comparison the young caballeros like Macario Canejo, whom she had once thought handsome and entertaining, seemed insipid and weak. The same dominant ruthlessness that had first appealed to Rufina also attracted Soledad; but where Rufina had always seen Judah in his true light, Soledad only knew that he brought forth in her a titillating passion and a devastating weakness that made her willing to succumb to it.

It was Macario after all who was unwittingly responsible for bringing about her release. He came early one morning and, plainly smitten with Soledad's charms, asked Tía Isabella if he might take Soledad and herself for a ride in the family carriage.

Tarifa, with the annual tallies of hides and tallow to go over, urged them to go, thankful for a respite from their constant wrangling and complaints. She approved of Macario's attentions to Soledad following her recent disgrace. He came of a good family and though Tarifa knew he was weak and ineffectual, and she harbored no affection for his mother, she realized that Soledad was better married to a socially acceptable Californian than talked about and in trouble with men like Titus Judah.

Dressed in their best afternoon gowns and *rebozos*, with their silk parasols shading their faces from the afternoon sun, the two women got into the carriage, reprieved for the moment from their incarcerations.

Macario and Soledad sat in front on the driver's seat while Tía Isabella spread herself in solitary grandeur in the back of the carriage and admired the perfection of the day, the cloudless blue sky, the ocher and olive green of the valley, with the mauve-shadowed sierras in the distance and the sweet heady smell of tarweed. Feeding stock dotted the landscape or stood heads down resting under the shade of the oak trees. In the distance a group of vaqueros rode with swift and reckless abandon, their *reatas* swinging above their heads as they hazed a band of mesteños over a hill toward the Mission.

Macario drove slowly in deference to Tía Isabella, while he conversed in sly but polite asides with Soledad. Soledad liked Macario and at the moment was deeply grateful to him for taking her away from Loma de Oro, so she was putting herself out to be cordial to him.

None of the three occupants of the carriage was aware of the mounted man halted in the shadows of an immense oak until he stepped directly into their path and leveled a gun at Macario's head.

His hair was bound vaquero-fashion, in a black silk kerchief under his low-pulled sombrero, and there was a second black kerchief bound across his face up to his slitted eyes like a mask.

He did not speak but he motioned impatiently with the gun for Macario to get down.

Tía Isabella screamed, *"Bandito!"* and dropped her parasol in her fright, and Soledad moaned in terror. Mexican bandits were becoming more and more prevalent throughout California since the government had begun sending released criminals to her northern territory as a safer repository than the mother country.

A shot cracked over their heads to spur Macario on and he scrambled crablike from the carriage.

The bandit rode closer, reached down to feel in Macario's sash till he found his money pouch, and then with sudden viciousness brought the barrel of his gun down behind Macario's right ear, felling him in his tracks like a steer.

Isabella screamed and crumpled in the seat in a dead faint, and Soledad shoved her fist in her mouth and bit down on it to still her chattering teeth. Where were her brothers? Where were all the vaqueros on Loma de Oro while this dreadful nightmare was happening?

"Soledad."

The sound of her name brought her up with a start. The bandit was untying the mask from his face, and under the black dyed brows she recognized Titus Judah's agate eyes. He was grinning at her.

"Titus! You did this dreadful thing!"

"Only for you. They can't keep us apart, eh? I told you I was going to make you my wife and I'm a man of my word. I've come to take you aboard the *Vulcan*. They can't get at you there. I've got her stashed away below Capistrano. Come get up behind me; we'll have to ride double."

"But—I can't. Tarifa—"

"Hang Tarifa! Get aboard, wench, we've a long ride before us."

Soledad knew that it was madness, yet she had little choice really. If she refused she knew he would take her anyway by force, and there was no one to dispute his actions.

As they rode, Titus told her how he had audaciously planned the whole thing. Macario had unknowingly been his dupe.

"I met him in town yesterday at Chavira's," he told her, "and when he said he was coming to your place to pay his respects to you, I suggested, all cozylike, that he should offer to take you for a drive in the carriage. I pointed out the advantages to be got by being alone with a girl in a carriage. He agreed. I rigged myself up like a highwayman, painted my brows with some of the ship's tar—by the way, I'll probably be black-browed for some time to come, *muchacha*—and set myself to watch the house. When I saw which way he was heading I circled 'round and picked my spot. Easy as eating duff. When they come to neither Macario nor the old woman will know who robbed them and stole away their bonny companion. They'll be looking for a black-browed bandit who will have disappeared without a trace, not for Captain Judah of the *Vulcan*, I'll be bound! And what do you think of that, *chiquita mía?*"

"You don't know my brothers, and Santos, our mayordomo—and Tarifa. They will find us, and when they do—"

"We'll be miles at sea, and who's to find us then?"

Soledad was sobered by the thought. Where was this unpredictable ruthless man taking her? And what were his plans?

"I'm afraid," she shivered. "Please—let me go, Titus. There will be nothing but trouble if you take me. I cannot run away with you like this."

He laughed and she felt the hard muscles of his chest

through her bare arms as she clutched him for support.

"You're not running away, *muchacha*. I'm taking you against your will, if you want to put it that way. In a few hours you'll be Mrs. Titus Judah, and then I'd like to see 'em interfere with us!"

"But—there have been no banns, and we have no Padre to perform the service."

"We'll see to those details all in good time, my poppet."

"I—I have nothing, no clothes."

"Haven't I a ship filled with more clothes and gewgaws than a queen could ask for? Stop your worrying; Captain Judah'll look after you now."

Soledad was silent for a long time and her eyes wandered slowly over the golden, inviting California landscape, with its gently rolling brown-clad hills dotted with live-oak, here and there a tall eucalyptus or wide-spreading sycamore with rippling leaves of greenish-gold, and she knew a terrible desire to free herself from this man and take cover in the underbrush like a frightened rabbit. But he would never let her go. He would hunt her down, drag her with him, whether she willed it or not. She bowed her head, aware of the wetness on her cheeks and also for the first time in her life of the empty futility of tears. It was the first time since her parents' deaths that she had wept in genuine sorrow. Often she had wept in vexation, in anger, even in fear as at Bolsa Coyotes, and her tears had always accomplished their purpose or brought at least a measure of relief. This time there was no such blessed respite. From this moment on, she realized, tears would be useless.

At dusk Judah rode the horse out onto a high bluff overlooking the sea. Below them the sharp abutment of rocks fell straight to the narrow lip of pebble-strewn gray sand. Beyond the swells and surf line, Soledad could make out the lines of the *Vulcan*. Judah dismounted and helped her down and taking out his pistol fired it into the air. In a moment there was an answering shot from the ship.

Judah grinned at her and spread his jacket on the ground for her to sit upon.

"We'll have to wait a spell till my bully boys row out to get us."

"But—we can't go down there?" Soledad glanced fearfully at the high rocky bluff.

"Just you leave it to Captain Judah, my girl."

In what seemed to Soledad an interminable time, voices halooed from below. Actually it had been only minutes since Judah fired his shot. He had already stripped the horse of saddle and bridle, and shooed it off with a slap on its rump.

Something like a striking snake came swishing through the air and landed with a metallic clink near Soledad, causing her to cry out in alarm.

"Just our ladder," Judah explained. He held up a section of strong rope with a deep-bitted iron hook at one end. He wedged the hook deep into a crevice of rock, tested its holding power with his own weight, and dropped the free end over the side of the cliff.

Soledad watched the disappearing rope with horrified fascination. Judah was unwinding a length of short line from around his waist.

"Time to go aboard ship," he told her.

"No! I can't. I won't climb down that thing!" She was near hysteria.

"You'll just hang on to me," he soothed. "I'll do the climbing for us both. Here, let me tie you to me 'round the waist, then put your arms around my neck and hold on tight, understand?"

Soledad nodded dumbly. She was stiff with terror, but when he took hold of the rope with both hands she obediently locked her arms around his neck and closed her eyes.

For a moment they swung out into space and began to revolve giddily till Judah got his feet braced against the rock wall and began a steady hand-over-hand descent.

As in a dreadful nightmare, Soledad clung piteously to the only solid thing around her. She could feel the powerful muscles of Judah's shoulders working under his shirt as they went. And then incredibly there were other hands on her body, steadying her descent, and she felt something uneven but solid under her feet. The roar of the surf was deafening in this spot, but when she opened her eyes she found to her amazed relief that they were standing on the shore and that a small boat was beached on the tiny strip of sand perilously close to the incoming tide.

Two men in sailor's garb were helping Judah unwind the length of rope that had bound Soledad to him in their descent.

Judah waited till they had the boat in the water, then carried Soledad out to it, installing her amidships, and leaped in beside her. The men ran the boat out into the surf till they stood over waist-high, then leaped in themselves and began rowing toward the distant *Vulcan*.

The rocking of the little boat made Soledad's stomach queasy and she shut her eyes to shut out the last lines of darkening shore and the bulky *Vulcan* waiting like a monstrous bird of prey to carry her off.

At the ship, Judah had them let down a bosun's chair to take her aboard in safety and comparative comfort, and once aboard he took her straight to his cabin. Its proportions were generous and it was exceedingly well-appointed and comfortable.

Judah went back on deck after telling the cabin boy, a gentle-faced little Kanaka called Hilo, to bring her whatever she wanted. She could hear Titus giving blunt orders to the mate to get under way at once, and to report to him the moment his orders were carried out. The rasp of his voice in command made her shudder.

Hilo had brought her a glass of water at her request and she was sipping it when Judah came back into the cabin. He stood with his big hairy hands on his hips grinning down at her, and Soledad felt a pulse start to beat thickly in her throat. What madness or dreadful sin had brought her to this place? She burst suddenly into tears and covered her face with her hands.

Judah's grin was replaced by a scowl. The little dunderhead was going to be a thorn in his side, but he did not mean to give her up. She still represented an eighth interest in Loma de Oro when the vast lands and herds were divided up according to Don Ygnacio's will, as Rufina had been at pains to find out for him from Nazario, and Judah meant to hold and control that land.

He went and put his hand on her head and when she glanced up through wet lashes, he drew her to her feet and circled her shoulders with his arms.

"Look, my poppet, this is no time for tears. This is to be our wedding night, a time for celebration. I'll even break out some grog for the crew, and the old *Vulcan* will ring with gaiety. Come now, what would you like for a wedding gown? White, pink, blue? I'll send you below with the supercargo and you shall have your choice of everything in the storeroom. And a ring, you must have a ring."

He left her drying her tears, for the prospect of finery had ever been able to drive every other thought from Soledad's scatterbrained head, and unlocked an iron-bound sea chest resting against one wall of the cabin.

Outside she could hear the running feet, the creak of ropes and rigging, and the shouts of the men as they got the ship under way but she heard it all dimly, as if in a trance. In here it was warm and quiet and orderly. Life perhaps would not be too bad aboard ship after all. And Titus was generous, even if he was crude. To be turned loose in the rich storeroom of a trade ship such as this was to Soledad like a child's wildest Christmas dreams come true.

Titus was standing at her elbow holding out an open velvet-lined box containing rings of all sorts and sizes. Everything from wide gold wedding bands to huge emeralds, rubies, and diamonds winking and sparkling in the light of the swaying whale-oil lamp like so many imprisoned fireflies.

"Oh! How lovely. May I touch them?" She smiled for the first time and Judah heaved a sigh of relief.

"Play with them if you like till Mr. Pincer, the supercargo, comes to take you below. Here, sit at my desk and spread them all out. You'll need one of these first." He selected several of the wedding bands and tried them on her finger till he found one that fit and threw the rest back in the box. "But you can take your choice of these others, for your wedding present from me."

Soledad's eyes were shining. "You are kind and generous, Titus! I've never had a ring before with a real jewel in it. These *are* real?"

He laughed. "Very real."

"What a pity I can't wear it to the governor's ball, as Tarifa wore the jewels Padre gave her."

"You may just do that one day," said Judah, "but right now I've got to go and see about this wedding."

The *Vulcan,* buffeted by a rising wind, was having some difficulty making headway when the mate, a dark-skinned, cold-eyed young man with a small triangular scar below

his left eye that puckered the cheek and gave him a perpetually sneering look, came into the cabin, touching his
cap to Judah as he did so.

His eyes slid over the winking display of gems on the
desk before they riveted themselves respectfully to the
captain's face.

"Mr. Frye?"

"The ship's under weigh, sir."

"Very well, Mr. Frye. You know our course."

"Yes, sir."

"In an hour return to my cabin; I will need you and
Mr. Pincer as witnesses to my marriage."

"Very well, sir. And may I offer my congratulations?"

Frye's perpetual sneer lifted in a lopsided smile. Jem
Frye was a Cornishman. He had been convicted of smuggling by a British court and stripped of his mate's papers
eight years before, but managed to escape from Newcastle
Prison and stow away on an American merchant ship sailing from Bristol for Norfolk. From wharf gossip in Norfolk he learned that the *Vulcan*'s master was more interested in a man's seamanship and lack of scruples than in
his papers, and with little difficulty he got himself the
berth of mate on the newly refitted *Vulcan*. From the beginning there had seldom been friction between Frye and
Judah. Each had an eye for the main chance and a cold-
blooded willingness to trample underfoot anything that
stood in their way. Both were excellent seamen, and they
knew that they had a sound ship but only a scrub crew
with which to sail her. Consequently, each felt it necessary
to drive the men like dogs, and life aboard the *Vulcan*
was not an enviable thing for the hands luckless enough
to ship aboard her under such a captain and mate.

Judah grunted at Frye's words of felicitation. He realized with what lack of sincerity they were parroted. There
was no love lost between the captain and his sneering
mate, but there was a grudging respect and the need to
present a united front of command to the surly and unhappy crew.

"Is there anything else, sir?" asked Frye.

"Yes. Ask Mr. Pincer to report to my cabin at once."

"Aye, sir."

Frye left the cabin after saluting smartly and allowing

his eyes to wash once more over the jewels spread out on the desk.

The ship was beginning to roll and pitch with a will when Mr. Pincer, the supercargo, led Soledad into the trading room. Pincer was a man of entirely different caliber than Mr. Frye. A stooped, gentle-voiced man of uncertain years, with wispy light hair and thick square spectacles, he looked more like a clerk than a seaman, which was indeed what he had always been. Talbot Pincer came of a good but impoverished Virginia family, and had been apprenticed to his Uncle Carswell's dry-goods store in Norfolk. Unfortunately he enjoyed the fleshpots of Norfolk too well, and had little money from the mere pittance his uncle allowed him with which to indulge his fancies. It was inevitable that he should begin selling trade goods to the sailing ships that frequented the port and were not too interested in manifests or bills of lading. The *Vulcan* had been one of his customers, and when his uncle discovered his perfidy and threatened arrest unless full restitution was made at once, Pincer took refuge on the *Vulcan,* which was sailing that night for Africa.

Judah was glad to have him, for Pincer knew the value of goods and could drive a hard bargain. He was aware that Pincer stole from him and pocketed the profit from time to time, but he wrote this off to running expenses and, except in rare instances, never questioned the clerk's actions. The books he kept himself, insuring that the amount Pincer was able to pocket was small.

Pincer had a southern courtliness about him that reminded Soledad more of her own people, and that seemed relaxing after the hard-driving energy of Judah.

He showed her gowns of every fashion and color, fingering the materials with the same interest and pleasure that she did.

"You must select a whole trousseau," he told her conspiratorily, "while the captain is in such a generous mood. Morning and afternoon dresses as well as a wedding gown. The wedding gown, of course, should be white satin for such a young and, if I may say so, lovely bride?"

Soledad did not reply. She thought it impolite to tell him that in California brides seldom wore white. Color was the thing for weddings. White always reminded her

of corpses and funerals, and she did not want to be reminded of death tonight.

In the end, and over his gentle remonstrances, she chose
rose watered silk with full skirt and deep cleft neckline
and sleeves coming just below the elbow and trimmed with
plum colored velvet bows. Pincer produced a magnificent
white silk Chinese shawl, a mantilla of imported Manila
lace, a carved ivory comb set with mother-of-pearl, silk
stockings, and slippers of rose satin with rosettes of white
satin on the toe.

He also brought out a small carved sandalwood chest
and packed daintily in it the other items of clothing she
had selected.

It was Judah coming to a halt at the foot of the companionway, a cigar between his teeth and a brandy glow
on his freshly shaven cheeks, who finally brought the
shopping spree to a close.

"Are you going to stay down here all night?"

"Titus! Oh Titus, you can't imagine the lovely things
Mr. Pincer has helped me pick out. I'd be the envy of
every girl in California if they could only see me in them."

"And a devilish penny they must have run me up if I
know Mr. Pincer." He flashed a withering look at the supercargo, who flushed and busied himself replacing the
boxes and merchandise in the lockers.

Judah bawled up the companionway for a hand to carry
Soledad's chest, and helped her up the narrow treads to
the deck above. His powerful arm steadied her against the
driving wind till they reached the refuge of the cabin.

Soledad saw that a supper had been laid out for two
under covered dishes and that Hilo hovered in a corner,
his soft brown eyes alert to Judah's every expression.

"Get dressed in your wedding finery," Judah told her.
"I'll be back with our witnesses in a short while."

"But—who is going to marry us?" asked Soledad.

"I am."

"You?"

"A captain can marry anyone—even himself."

"But—no Padre? I will not even be married in the eyes
of my family or the church."

"You'll be married, all right," said Judah grimly. "And
have papers signed and sealed to prove it, as legal as the
Constitution."

"But not in California," murmured Soledad. "If I am not married by a priest—"

"You will be, dammit," cried Judah impatiently. "Later, when we reach our destination."

"Our destination?"

"Chile. I know a Padre there; he'll marry us again. You'll be married in the church and out of it, and have the papers to prove it. Now get ready, and don't be all night about it. Hilo will get you what you need."

He went out and slammed the door, and Soledad asked Hilo to bring her hot water in which to wash, and a comb and brush.

When Judah returned to his cabin half an hour later he was far from displeased at the sight of his bride-to-be. Rose brought out an answering color in her rounded cheeks and full lips, and there was a demure sparkle in her large brown eyes as she flirted with him over the top of a white lace fan. He had never seen her with her hair done up as the married women wore it under the high comb, and covered with the fine and expensive lace mantilla Pincer had been at great pains to select for her.

He was amused to see that for her wedding jewel she had selected a huge yellow diamond, merely because it was the largest in the case. There were many finer, more valuable stones there but it was useless to point it out to her. Like a greedy child, size and flashiness meant more to her than value.

"How do I look, Titus?"

"Beautiful." And he meant it. She was beautiful in her rounded, fresh-skinned innocence. Like a newly ripe peach ready for the plucking.

He had drawn up the papers, and when Frye and Pincer appeared, he took a Bible from the desk drawer and read the marriage ceremony in a suitably solemn voice. He slipped the wedding band on Soledad's trembling finger while she stood white-faced at his side, and ended the ceremony with a decorous kiss on her brow.

When the two witnesses had signed the papers Judah locked them in his chest and poured them each a glass of brandy.

Frye carefully wished them happiness before he left, and Pincer's eyes were frankly misty behind his thick spectacles when he pressed Soledad's hand in parting.

"Such a touching ceremony," he told her, "and such a beautiful bride. It reminds me of when my sister Clara Lou was married."

Left alone, Judah took Soledad in his arms and kissed her hotly. It had all been so easy, almost ludicrously so. What unsuspecting easy marks these Californians were. Living in a land of milk and honey, they were too lazy or indifferent to realize what they had.

Soledad felt dazed. She could not believe that she was married to this big red-haired American, and guiltily she felt that she would be punished for marrying without the consent of the church and the presence and blessings of the Padres.

But Judah gave her no time to think. There was nothing to stop him now; a wife could not demur against her husband and part of his plan was to get her with child as soon as possible so as to have tangible proof of the necessity of their marriage.

Later in the night, with the thin moonlight filtering through the portholes, and in the new and grave enormity of what being married really meant, Soledad asked timidly, "Do you love me, Titus?"

And his sleepy reply was affirmative. Somehow it did not reassure her.

CHAPTER 23

Tarifa was still seated at her desk in the study wrestling with the account book with Luis drawn up in a chair beside her, when she heard the commotion in the front yard.

"That sounds like Tía Isabella!" Luis cried, leaping up. "They must have had an accident."

Tarifa followed his running figure from the room and into the *sala* where a gasping and tearful Isabella and a dazed Macario poured out their tale of assault and robbery.

"And Soledad," wept Isabella, "the demon has taken Soledad as hostage! You must send for help at once, Tarifa. And for Padre Cazon."

"It was one of those *cholo bandidos*," Macario insisted with parrotlike monotony. "He hit me across the head after he shot and missed me. He stole my money pouch and took Soledad with him!"

"What did he look like?" Tarifa insisted.

Neither of them could give her a clear description of the *bandido*. He was tall and thin; he was squat and bull-necked. He was black-browed, great thick menacing brows, only on this one point did they agree emphatically.

"But why would he take Soledad?" Tarifa asked. "She would only slow him up and he would be in a hurry to get away. Unless he released her somewhere nearby after—"

Tía Isabella buried her face in her hands. "Santa Maria, protect her!" she moaned.

Tarifa, glancing down at the old woman's long thin hands in scowling concentration, saw the rings on her fingers. A large amethyst surrounded by seed pearls and a cumbersomely set diamond that had been in the Alvarjo family for centuries, an heirloom, Don Ygnacio had once told her, presented to Isabella as a child by their grandmother. Isabella also wore a pearl-and-ruby brooch at the neck of her black gown. Odd that a bandit would steal only a paltry few pesos, which was all Macario claimed he had been carrying, and pass up gems such as these. The only other thing he had been at pains to steal was Soledad. Tarifa questioned the two victims again more closely and came to her own conclusions.

Judah had vowed to get the girl and undoubtedly he had succeeded. Whether he himself committed the robbery and took Soledad, she could not be sure, but she doubted it. More likely he had paid some pueblo hanger-on or unscrupulous cholo to do the job for him, with orders to deliver Soledad to him at his ship wherever that might now be.

She spoke quietly to Luis. "Bring the horses and all the vaqueros and tell Santos I want him."

Under the immense oak that Macario had described to Tarifa, they got down and studied the still fresh markings of the carriage wheels and the horses' hooves. Here was where Macario must have stood and fallen as he was struck down. The prints of his bootheels were in the leaf-strewn dust, but no footprint of Soledad's.

"He took her directly from the carriage, Dona Tarifa," said Santos. "They went west and north, riding double."

"To San Juan?"

"Perhaps. Or they may have cut back inland."

"Not if the man was carrying Soledad to Judah. It is useless for us to go after them. We will ride after Luis to San Diego, and see if anyone there has word of the *Vulcan*."

"*Sí*, Patróna."

Tarifa and Santos cut inland before heading for the coast and San Diego, stopping to inquire at the various ranchos and cabañas along the way for information of any stranger matching the *bandido*'s description. No one had seen such a rider, much less Señorita Soledad.

Tarifa knew in her heart that Judah must have secreted Soledad aboard his ship and put out to sea. And that there was little that she or anyone else could do. She thought of their last meeting so short a time ago beyond Bolsa Coyotes, and of Judah's boast that he did not intend to give Soledad up. She wondered also why she had dealt with him so leniently. It was not in her nature to let a wrong go unpunished. And she was aware that if Kinkaid had not been present, she would have exacted payment from Titus Judah regardless of the consequences.

She was puzzled and irritated by Kinkaid's effect on her. Whether she liked it or not, like Padre Cazon, he had a compelling steadying influence upon her. She might rage and storm inwardly against its constricting influence, but it was like an unyielding rock wall against which her own violent nature clashed itself. And she was uncomfortable in Kinkaid's presence because of it.

As they rode over the last rise separating the land from the San Diego shoreline, Tarifa felt a sudden thrill of excitement. Judah had not escaped after all! Surely that was the black-hulled *Vulcan* riding at anchor? How could the man have had the nerve to put in here, unless he had the girl hidden and meant to lie about it? Even so, how could he hope to brave out such a lie?

Tarifa felt her pulse quicken as they urged the weary horses across the sand.

Two men came to the open door of the nearest hide house and Tarifa pointed toward the ship asking, "Can we hire someone to row us out to the *Vulcan*? I must speak to Captain Judah."

The larger of the two men, who knew Tarifa, shook his head.

"No use, Señora Alvarjo. She ain't the *Vulcan*. That be the *Lorelei*, Captain Kinkaid's ship."

"But he was to have sailed days ago?"

"That's right, señora, but they had a might of trouble stowing the hides in the fo'rd hold. She's right as rain now though, be sailing on the morning tide."

"I would like to go aboard," she told him thoughtfully. "Can you get me a boat?"

"Certainly. Me an' Jake here'd be pleasured to row you out ourselves. Jest been sittin' here amusin' ourselves with a game of cribbage."

A youthful member of the starboard watch poked his head over the side when the warehousemen asked permission to come aboard from their bouncing little boat.

In a matter of minutes Jake Banner was at the rail seeing to the lowering of the bosun's chair, and a few seconds later was helping Tarifa to step onto the deck. Just to touch the woman made his fingers burn with distaste. And in his superstitious way he was unhappy to have her aboard the *Lorelei*, since he was convinced she had brought misfortune upon his master's first ship, the *Arabella*, as certainly as she had nearly caused Bart's death. The woman was a sorceress, with an evil spell-binding eye, and he couldn't imagine what devil's business she had come upon this time.

"I want to speak to Capitán Kinkaid," she told him tersely.

No maybe or please about the Devil's spawn, thought Banner. She speaks like she ruled the universe, dresses like a man, and looks like the black-hearted witch she is. He was glad that his Spanish was too limited to hold more than a scant conversation with her.

"If you'll wait a moment," Banner told her. But there was no need for further delay, for Bart came that second from his cabin and exclaimed in surprise at sight of her.

"Tarifa! Has something happened? Is it Soledad?"

She nodded, scowling at Banner and the crew members who were still clustered round the deck within earshot.

"Come into my cabin," said Kinkaid.

When they were seated and Tarifa had removed her sombrero and run her hands wearily through her tangled hair, she accepted a glass of brandy and told him of the false robbery and Soledad's disappearance.

Kinkaid took a cigar from a box on his desk and began to pace the cabin, moving the unlighted cigar between his lips.

"If I sailed at once I might track him down somehow, but the wind's against us, and even if I sighted him he could easily show us his heels in the *Vulcan*. We're loaded to the gunwales with hides, we've nearly sprung our decks with the load we're carrying and I expect to wallow like a sea cow all the way to Boston." He turned to face her. "Are you sure he's got Soledad?"

"He must have. He either used one of his own men or hired someone to kidnap her and bring her to him somewhere."

"Or did the job himself," Kinkaid said bitterly.

"Where could he have hidden the *Vulcan* to have taken her aboard so quickly?"

"A dozen places, if you had Judah's nerve and knowhow. He's spent his life slipping in and out of forbidden ports."

"You think he put directly to sea?"

"He'd be a fool if he didn't."

"Then there's nothing we can do," said Tarifa simply. She put down her glass and got up. There was a resignation and weariness about her that was new to him; never before had he seen her accept fate without a violent personal struggle.

"I'm sorry this happened," he told her sincerely, "but I'll find him somehow, someday, and pay him back, I promise you. I feel that I am to blame for this," he added slowly. "That day we met him near Bolsa Coyotes, I knew he needed killing but I didn't want his blood on your hands. I see now it should have been on mine, and it will be, whenever we meet again."

She stood looking up at him, measuring the unequivocal sincerity of his words, and his cool gray gaze held hers captive for an instant in a powerful stillness that made her step away from him with the feeling that he had penetrated a secret hidden recess of her spirit that even she had been unaware she possessed. It was at moments such as these that she felt a flashing hatred for him, as if he threatened something violent and powerful within her that was vital to her own existence.

Kinkaid turned away from her to light his cigar and was amazed that his own hands trembled. It was madness to think of Tarifa as a woman. She was a houri, a siren, a tempestuous sorceress, who lived only to lure and entice her unsuspecting victims to their own destruction. She had no heart, and for all he knew, no soul. There was no warmth or affection in her, only a withering core of passion and fire that consumed everything in its path; yet she had held a strange and compelling fascination for him ever since the night they had struggled in each other's arms in the cabaña atop Loma de Oro, trying to kill each other. Oddly too, since that night, he had felt a form of pity and compassion for her. Even though he realized she would have laughed him to scorn at the suggestion, he sensed her isolation, her vulnerability. Her strength was the charging, heedless strength of a lioness, with eyes only for the prey of the moment. She would always remain arrogantly unconscious of the dangers lurking in the underbush. He knew also that to rob her of this sense of omnipotence was to destroy her entirely. In his mixed feelings for her, he only knew that at the moment he merely wanted to stand as friend and ally to her if she would let him.

As if she sensed his desire and was somehow relieved, she smiled and said, "I know that you will do what you can, Capitán."

He looked at her, wondering what it was in that thin pointed face, with its scimitar eyes blazing as hotly as coals under the tangle of black hair, that attracted and repelled him at the same time.

The gentle, protective love he had felt for Dolores had contained none of the violent emotion he felt when he was with Tarifa. He didn't know himself what he really felt for her. Pity, admiration for her strength of spirit, as well as body, for her courage and tenacity. But what more did he feel, if anything? That she could easily bring out the worst in him he was aware. They had the power to destroy each other. And Kinkaid was a man who was not afraid, dispassionately, to parade and study his own failings. Due more to his sense of decorum as a ship's captain than to his rigid New England upbringing and outwardly reserved nature, he had usually managed to keep a tight rein on his emotions and actions. But he was no saint. He had enjoyed his share of Manila cribs and Canton singsong houses. He had lain drunk for a week in a Melbourne hotel, while his ship waited and Banner hunted from street to street for him like a worried bird dog. He had had his share of slugfests on the decks of ships and on the wharves of the world. He had killed men and nearly been killed by them, but he had never killed without justification.

Tarifa was still smiling at him and he thought what a rarity it was to see her smile, and how it softened and changed her.

"You are very pretty when you smile," he said simply. "You should do it more often."

The smile vanished quickly but she seemed pleased and touchingly confused at the same time.

"I have little to smile about these days."

It was the stark truth, he realized. She was like a small vital flame flickering in every vagrant wind, but burning bravely nonetheless. Someday he knew a hurricane would come along and put out the flame forever.

"You need a friend, Tarifa. Someone you can go to, call on, when the going gets too rough. Someone to write to if necessary. Will you let me be that friend? Will you write to me? I'll give you the Endecott address in Boston where they hold my mail."

She weighed his words, watching him silently, and for a while he thought she was not going to reply. Then she said, "Yes, I would like that, Capitán."

"Bart." He smiled. "You used to call me Bart."

She nodded and returned his smile. "Bart."

He poured them each a glass of brandy and touched the rim of his glass to hers. "To our newly launched friendship. May it have a long, successful, and happy voyage."

Tarifa sipped her brandy sitting on one corner of the desk, one booted and spurred foot dangling over the edge. In spite of the litheness of her figure, her thighs were well-muscled and softly rounded from her hours of dancing and days spent in the saddle.

"I will find Soledad and bring her back," Kinkaid promised.

"They have all gone since Ygnacio's death," she sighed. "Perhaps it is true, I have been a curse upon the Alvarjos. Penti says my mother foretold it when Santiago brought me here." She told him then about Bandonna, and her stormy childhood in the Sacro Monte, and the other days in the Triana of Seville.

"Do you want to go back?" he asked her gently.

She put down her glass with a trace of her old annoyance and stood up.

"No. This is my land now. I will stay and build Loma de Oro into a monument to my son Lasho, in spite of all of them or anything they can do to try and stop me. Ygnacio left it in my hands and so I shall keep it!"

"You don't intend to give it to his children eventually, as he planned?"

She gave him a withering glance. "Which one of them is capable of running even a piece of it? They would all starve to death in a month's time if it weren't for me."

He knew that she spoke the truth. Only Tarifa's superb management and dauntless spirit had kept Loma de Oro successful and prosperous when half the other ranchos in California were succumbing to debt and ruin.

"You will write and let me know how matters stand at Loma de Oro?" he asked.

"Yes."

He went to the desk and wrote out his address on the edge of a bill of lading and handed it to her. Then he took it back and bent to scrawl something else on it.

"This is a name of a very good friend of mine in San José—Dr. Mabrey. He's married to one of the Castro girls. He's intelligent and trustworthy. He has considerable influence in northern California. If you need his advice

or help, don't hesitate to call upon him, and tell him I
sent you."

"*Gracias*, Bart."

He watched her tuck the paper carefully into her sash
and pick up her sombrero.

"I must go. Santos is waiting for me. And do not worry,"
she added with a smile, "I will take good care of little
Dolores and see that Penti does not turn her into a
Gypsy."

He went on deck with her and stood at the rail till she
was safely lowered into the boat. She glanced up at him
once before the oarsmen rowed her away.

It was a look, he thought, that he would long remember. A sharp, inquiring, and somehow challenging look
from hot Gypsy eyes and it left him wondering if it would
be possible after all to be a friend to this strange, contra-
dictory creature.

On a cold February midnight, Nazario rode to Loma
de Oro to fetch Penti to deliver Rufina's child. Tarifa
decided to go with them on the spur of the moment and
sent a servant to have Guindilla saddled while she dressed.

When she returned she found Nazario in the dining
room with his brothers, who were toasting him in wine
and wagering that this time it would be twin girls in place
of a boy.

"It is a boy," said Nazario stoutly. "I am certain of it."

"Come then," said Tarifa, from the doorway, "or he
will have arrived before we get there."

At Bolsa Coyotes Tarifa sat in the *sala* with Nazario,
while he paced the room, making frequent forays to the
bottles on the dining room sideboard.

He was in the dining room when Penti sidled into the
sala and beckoned Tarifa imperiously with her head. When
Tarifa reached her, the old Gypsy drew her into the *galleria* and hurried her toward Rufina's bedroom.

"What is it?" whispered Tarifa. "Has something gone
wrong?"

"That depends upon how you look at it," answered
Penti.

Rufina lay asleep in her bed, her face pale but beautiful between the thick dark braids of hair.

In a cradle nearby a shawl-wrapped bundle moved and cried lustily.

Penti bent and pulled back the shawl and Tarifa, who had been leaning down to examine the infant, drew back in shocked astonishment.

The cap of bright red hair covering the baby's head, the large square fists, and flat broad shoulders had never graced the frame of a delicate, aristocratic Alvarjo. It was as if every feature of the child's face had been stamped in miniature from Titus Judah's.

"A boy?" asked Tarifa incredulously.

Penti nodded. "As strong as an ox. He gave her a very hard time. You know it is not Nazario's?"

"Yes. It is undoubtedly the child of Capitán Titus Judah. She must have lain with him in secret while she and Soledad were cavorting about the countryside last summer. Then to save herself she interested Judah in Soledad, and convinced Nazario the child was his."

"What will you tell him? Shall I dispose of the child and say that it died at birth?"

Tarifa glared at her. "The child is born. It has a right to live. Are we murderers? I will tell Nazario the truth."

"He will kill it and the mother."

"Bring the child into the next room and fetch Nazario," Tarifa said tersely. "Do as I say."

The old Gypsy shrugged and gathered the baby into her arms, carrying it to the bed in the adjoining room. Tarifa bent and studied him while waiting for Nazario. He had wanted a son and now he had one, but he could take no pride in it. Tarifa cursed Rufina for the deceitful, scheming wanton she was, and knew that this time she could not spare the Alvarjos the searing scandal that would envelop them all.

Nazario bounded into the room, his eyes alight with joy.

"She says it is a boy! I told you, I told all of you. Let me see him!"

Tarifa stepped aside and watched him stop as she had done while incredulous disbelief washed over his thin dark face.

"*Dios!* It—can't be!"

"Take hold of yourself, Nazario. We must talk."

"But—I don't believe it! It can't be—she wouldn't—"

"You must face up to your trouble like a man, Nazario. As your father would have done."

"Judah—it is Judah's! I will kill him, as God is my witness; I will hunt him down and draw and quarter him!"

"Judah is miles away, and this problem is the one we must solve at the moment. I know how you feel, and I regret this thing as much as you do."

"Rufina—and that Americano!" he groaned.

The baby began to cry, waving its wide hands above its head, and Nazario gave it a look of murderous hatred.

"What are you going to do?" asked Tarifa.

"I don't know. What can I do? I must go to the Padres, I suppose. She must be punished. I will have no more to do with her."

"She is your wife."

"No more! Never again."

"Do you want me to have Penti take the child to Loma de Oro?"

"Yes! Get it out of my sight, and Rufina too!" he choked.

"She can't be moved yet, but I will send Luis to stay with you, and Francisco is here. I will tell the others; it is best they know the truth."

He nodded and left the room without a backward glance at Tarifa or the infant on the bed.

The Padres and the Father Prefecto were not as astonished at word of Rufina's infidelity as they were amazed that a woman of her breeding and position would stop to flagrant adultery with a man like Captain Judah. It went without saying, of course, that the woman must be publicly chastised and openly punished, as were all other wantons and adulteresses.

It had long been the practice in California to shave the heads of wantons and imprison them in the *cuartel* with Indians and women criminals. Putting them into the stocks for any infraction of the rules, making them sweep the public streets with twig brooms, and forcing them to stand each morning during Mass in front of the church where passersby vilified and spat upon them.

The alcalde, relishing the thought that an aristocratic Alvarjo was involved in such a shocking scandal, or at least the wife of one of them, and coming himself from a rather dubious background, was at pains to point out that no distinction could be made in the carrying out of the punishment in this case. Dona Rufina must share her guilt with the other women of ill-repute.

Rufina herself had lain in a stupor of fear ever since Tarifa had told her coldly what lay in store for her. Nazario had never come into her room, nor had any other members of the family, and Rufina was afraid to leave the security of her boudoir to face them. They had even taken the child away, but she was not sorry for that. She hoped never to see him again, after her first glance at his hair and face so like Judah's, who had brought her to this sorry plight. What a monstrous fool she had been! What moments of pleasure had the great oaf ever given her that could make up for this degradation and suffering, this utter humiliation? She had lost everything because of him.

The alcalde had persuaded the Father Prefecto that it would be more expedient if Rufina fulfilled her sentence of punishment at San Diego, the pueblo and Mission nearest to her place of residence. Also, he added with gusto, it was probably the scene of her faithlessness with the Americano, and would remind her of it more vividly.

On a bright cold Sunday morning, Tarifa and Santos delivered her to the women's jail in San Diego, not far from the presidio. Here Rufina's long dark hair was shorn, she was forced to put on a shapeless garment of coarse wool, and marched with the other adulteresses to the Mission, where she stood among them barefooted in the cold wind while the townspeople jeered and spat upon her as they entered the church.

She stood with her head bowed, the tears washing down her face, her sobs shaking her from head to foot. She prayed wildly that she would die. Here, right on the spot, in the face of their cruelty.

Tarifa sat at a little distance on Guindilla, watching her in disgust. The little fool couldn't even do this right. Even in such a predicament, why didn't she stand proud and erect as an Alvarjo should, and spit back at them when they spat upon her? In a towering rage at the perfidious girl, she put spurs to Guindilla and whirled him toward Loma de Oro.

* * *

It was some days later that Rufina's father, Don Carlos Corlona, arrived at Loma de Oro from Santa Barbara. He had stopped at San Diego first to see his poor suffering daughter, and he was distraught to the point of collapse.

Tía Isabella and Tarifa plied him with brandy and forced him to take a little food, but it was impossible to stop his childish weeping. He was a small-boned, delicately built man of seventy, with a white square beard and his hair plaited and tied in the beribboned old-fashioned queue. He clung also to the short velvet knee breeches of an earlier era, with white stockings bound around the leg with fancy garters from which dangled satin rosettes. On his small feet he wore soft buckskin shoes, low-heeled and turned up at the toe with a fancy carved leather ornament.

Because he was elderly and a *gente de razón*, Don Carlos wore only black these days, but the Californian's love of ornamentation had not been suppressed in him entirely. Around his neck, over the fine ruffled linen shirt, he wore several heavy gold chains, and on his hands an assortment of large, ostentatious rings—an emerald, a diamond, an opal, and a huge sapphire that dwarfed his small thin fingers.

When he had wiped away his latest tears and blown his long thin nose on an immense silk handkerchief, he said brokenly, "When she is released, Dona Tarifa, when this terrible thing is over, what is to become of her?"

"Nazario has not told me what he intends to do, Don Carlos," said Tarifa. "She has deceived and dishonored him in the worst way a woman can injure her husband."

"True, true," sighed Don Carlos. "But I am sure it was the influence of that terrible Americano. *Dios!* How I would like to get him between my hands!"

The ludicrousness of such a proposal brought a faint smile to Tarifa's lips.

"Would you permit me to take Rufina home to Santa Barbara?" the old man asked. "If there is no place for her here—?"

"You must ask Nazario. She is still his wife, at least according to law and the Church."

"I have spoken with the Father Prefecto," Corlona murmured. "He has explained the same thing. But what is to be done? Nazario will not take her back. It is only possi-

ble for her to return to her own people. And I will take
the child, too." He straightened his small thin shoulders
with a pride that Tarifa admired. "The Corlonas do not
shirk their responsibilities."

"The child is here," said Tarifa. "Do you want to see
him?"

He hesitated for only an instant and then nodded.

When Penti brought the baby he examined it carefully,
but Tarifa could detect no malice or rancor in his glance.

For all his frailty and weaknesses, Corlona held to his
pride and his principles and that, thought Tarifa, was the
terror of all well-born Californians.

When the child had been taken away Tarifa told him,
not unkindly, "Don Carlos, the Alvarjos also live up to
their duties and responsibilities. The child will stay here,
and be raised with little Dolores. The child himself shall
not suffer because we despise the father and abhor the
actions of the mother."

"You are a kind and generous woman, Dona Tarifa."
Don Carlos lifted his ring-heavy hand and wiped his eyes
with the kerchief again. "Have you named and christened
the poor *niño*?"

"Padre Cazon did that some weeks ago. He named him
José, in honor of St. Joseph, in the hope that the good
saint will take the place, spiritually, of the father he will
never have on earth."

"*Bueno*. It is well. And now I must ride to Bolsa Coyotes to see Nazario."

"No," said Tarifa, rising. "You are weary, Don Carlos.
I will send Antonio to ask him to come here."

"But," stammered the old man, "in this case, at such
a time, it is my duty to go to him."

Tarifa raised her chin a trifle higher. "In this household I am still ruler," she said harshly. "He will do as
I say."

In the festering misery and humiliation of his agony,
Nazario had first thought of killing himself. He could
dash himself and Hidalgo off a high cliff into the sea, as
they ran off the superfluous mesteños in time of drought.
Or he could hang himself with his *reata*. Plunge a knife
into his heart. There was even the old dueling pistol of

Don Julio's father's, still on the wall of the study. But in the end he found that he dared not make use of any of these methods. Not because of his fear of dying, but because he could not bring himself to face eternal damnation for his deed. The Church had taught him only too well that to take his own life meant Hell's fire for all eternity. Life had been given him and only God had the right to take it from him.

Frustrated and despairing, Nazario was in no mood to obey Tarifa's command to come to Loma de Oro to converse with his father-in-law. Anything to do with Rufina or the Corlonas sickened him. What did they think he was? As great as a saint, able to magnanimously forgive any wrong? Even the wicked, monstrous wrong Rufina had inflicted upon him?

Luis, who had been staying with Nazario these past weeks, said kindly, "It will be better to see him and have it over, *muchacho*. Shall we come with you?"

Nazario nodded miserably. His dependence upon Luis, with whom he had always been close, had increased enormously in these past weeks. He hoped that Tarifa would let him remain at Bolsa Coyotes with him and Francisco.

The interview was not so painful after all. Don Carlos offered his apologies, his deepest sympathies, and again offered to take Rufina to Santa Barbara when she had fulfilled her public penance.

Nazario was delighted and vastly relieved at his suggestion, but Tarifa persuaded him to stay the night and sleep on it before giving his final decision.

Padre Cazon appeared at the dinner table when Nazario and his brothers returned from a hunt in the sierras, and Nazario glanced at him suspiciously, wondering whether Tarifa or Tía Isabella had sent for him, urging the priest to speak further with him concerning Rufina's fate. He was tired of talking to the Padres. It was futile their pointing out that Rufina was still his wife, that he could rightfully put her away from him, but that while she lived he could never marry again. What did he care about such things now? He only knew that he hated the thought of her, that at all costs he had to be rid of her. Surely Don Carlos had offered him the perfect solution, the only solution?

As he had suspected, Padre Cazon drew him aside after

dinner and asked him to walk with him in the patio. Both wore hats and capes, for the weather was still harsh. The great bare grapevine clattered against the house and the rail at the top of the *galleria* like a ghostly skeleton. The hanging flowerpots that had been his mother's pride and joy swung back and forth on their rawhide supports, empty of blooms, as his heart was empty now of everything but bitterness. The little bird cages had long been taken to a warmer part of the house by Tía Isabella and Candelaria. The patio, Nazario thought unhappily, looked like his present life, dead and lifeless and forlorn.

"My son," Padre Cazon began, "Tarifa has told me of Don Carlos' proposal concerning Rufina. May I ask what you are going to do?"

"Let her go, of course," Nazario said shortly.

"You have thought this over?"

"There is nothing to think over. I can't stand the sight of her!"

"Have you thought of your two little daughters?"

Truthfully, Nazario had not thought of them. He had been too immersed in his own troubles, and he felt a stab of remorse, for he was a good and considerate father.

"They will be taken care of," he said. "Tía Isabella, or Candelaria—someone will come to look after them."

"Do they not need their mother?"

"Their mother! That . . . She will never lay eyes on them again!"

"You could not bring yourself to ask God's help and take her back into your home, for your children's sake?"

Cazon watched Nazario's face harden and the new lines deepen around his thin mouth.

"Never! Not if my soul depended upon it!"

"Perhaps it does. Did you ever stop to think God might have sent you this trial to enable you to earn the grace your soul needs for salvation?"

Nazario tried to close his ears to the calm, logical voice telling him truths he had known all his life. He was determined not to be swayed. At the moment he cared very little about his soul. Yet because of the fear of losing it forever, he had been dissuaded from killing himself. He was not going to take Rufina back because of it, however, no matter what Padre Cazon said.

The Padre's voice went on. "Jesus forgave an adulteress once, and invited those free from sin themselves to cast the first stone at her. None were thrown. And she became a saint. Perhaps God has given into your hands not only your own soul's salvation, but also that of Rufina?"

"I will not listen to anymore!"

Nazario turned abruptly on his heel and left the priest, walking in giant strides toward the kitchen. Perhaps with Pablo or Santos he could find some peace. Behind him he could hear Padre Cazon's deep sigh and the rattle of his beads as he took them in his hands. Let him pray. Let them all prate and pray! It would not change his decision. He was going to be rid of her once and for all.

In the kitchen yard he happened to glance up and saw the light in his father's old cabaña atop Loma de Oro. Tarifa must be there. He decided to go at once and tell her of his decision and have it done with.

He found her seated at the desk, writing a letter. She was dressed in the old Gypsy clothes she had first worn at Loma de Oro, with bracelets on her bare arms and large hoops of gold in her ears.

"Nazario?" She was surprised to see him.

"I have decided. Rufina is to go with Don Carlos," he stated abruptly.

"Sit down. Pour yourself a glass of *aguardiente,* and bring me one, too."

Nazario came to hand her the glass and stretched out in a deep rawhide chair that had been a favorite of his father's.

Tarifa said nothing while they drank. For the first time since his arrival that afternoon, Nazario began to relax. There was an aura of his father still here that gave him a sense of assurance and confidence.

"What do you do up here?" he asked curiously. "I have often wondered."

"I read and write. Sometimes I dance. Here I can get away from them all and forget my troubles."

"We cause you a great deal of trouble, don't we?" he asked, looking into the depths of his glass.

She shrugged. "Everyone causes trouble."

"Do they?" He looked up and realized that for the first time they were talking easily and naturally, as equals. His father must have talked to her like this. He had never realized that Tarifa had this softer, easier side to her nature. Stripped of her air of haughty command, she could be a woman of warmth and depth.

"Trouble is what you make of it," said Tarifa, reaching to refill his glass, "not what it makes of you."

"I don't understand."

"You can always turn trouble to your own advantage if you want to."

"Not my trouble," sighed Nazario.

"Yours as well as any other."

"You speak in riddles, Tarifa."

"What is it you always wanted from Rufina and never got? A docile wife? Sons?"

Nazario nodded wonderingly.

"They are still your right. And now you are in a position not only to desire, but to command them. Don't you think that Rufina would jump at the chance to return to her own home and children, after this fiasco, if you so graciously permitted it? And would she not spend the rest of her life groveling at your feet, turning herself into an exemplary wife and mother to make it up to you? What a fine revenge you would have then!" Tarifa's eyes sparkled. "If I were in your place, Nazario, I would not only take her back, I would drive her back. And I would see that she bore me a son for every year of her remaining childbearing years."

A ridge of hot color had risen above Nazario's cheekbones just below his eyes. She was speaking the truth. Rufina would feel who was master this time! Revenge was what he needed. What he must have. Tarifa was right. For that reason and that reason alone, not for the salvation of souls, he was suddenly ready and eager to take her back. He looked at his stepmother and a thin, cruel smile curled his lips.

"You are right. It is the only way to deal with her. Everyone will say that I am magnanimous, won't they?" He laughed. "But you and I, and Rufina, will know the truth."

Tarifa smiled at him. "I told you all troubles can be turned to your own advantage, *muchacho*."

"I won't forget," he said slowly. "You are very clever, Tarifa, devilishly clever."

And though he heard her chuckle in warm amusement,

he felt a chill run up his spine. Satan looked out at him through her black mocking eyes. And he felt the brush of something that left him shaken and strangely fearful.

Due to the unusual severity of the latest drought, which had withered the grass and dried up the creeks and springs throughout southern California, Tarifa decided to direct the roundup and running off of the scrub mesteños in order to save the other stock.

With a shortage of gunpowder and the impossibility of destroying so many animals with lances, there remained but one solution, to drive them over a high cliff into the sea. To Tarifa's animal-loving heart, it was a difficult thing to do. She remembered only too well the first mesteño hunt she had witnessed—the day Ygnacio had fallen—and the horror she had felt then. But she fully realized the alternative—death by starvation of her beloved palominos and the cattle necessary to the family's very existence.

Because Guindilla had recently injured a knee from a fall, Tarifa rode Calabaza today, and she missed the quicker, more fiery response of Guindilla underneath her.

Crossing a small hill as they neared the coast, Tarifa was surprised to note a group of men encamped on the edge of her property.

A fire was smoldering between two large boulders with several men squatting around it. One, standing at a little distance, was grooming a handsome strong-chested black stallion.

Tarifa spoke to Luis, telling him to come with her and whirled Calabaza toward the strangers camped below.

"Who are they?" Luis asked, wiping his sweating face with his sleeve.

"We will soon find out."

"You had better be careful; there are many *bandidos* about these days."

Tarifa did not reply, but urged Calabaza faster with the big rowels of her spurs. He seemed as clumsy as an elephant after Guindilla.

The man grooming the stallion glanced up at their approach. He was bareheaded and naked save for a pair of worn brown trousers, and the sun had beaten his body to the hardness and color of brass. His hair was thick and curling and had been deepened in blackness by the almond oil. He stood and faced them, frowning and haughty as a caliph.

Tarifa pulled Calabaza up a few feet from him, noting out of the corner of her eye that the other men around the fire were not so prepossessing, and that the herd and her own riders had moved on without waiting for her and Luis. She fingered the whip in her hand and asked the stranger curtly, "Who are you, and what are you doing camped on my land?"

He raised his brows over his wide, intelligent dark eyes.

"This is your land, señorita? A thousand pardons. I am Agapito Larios, at your service." He made a sweeping bow with the horse brush he held in his hand, and teeth flashed whitely in his dark handsome face. Surprisingly, he spoke in good Castilian.

"I am Dona Tarifa Alvarjo," she replied, scowling at him. "You and your companions will remove yourselves from my property at once. I do not allow trespassers."

"A pity," he said, shaking his head, "we had heard so much of Californian hospitality. We are horse traders from Mexico, señora, but we are weary and our animals have had little grass and water."

"I have scarcely enough for my own herds," said Tarifa. "That is why we drive the mesteños to slaughter."

"If I had known," he said quickly, with an admiring glance at the two palominos, "perhaps I could have taken some of them off your hands."

"They are culls, unbroken and worthless."

"Yet you have enough of them here in California to drive them off of cliffs? It is hard to believe. I have never seen it. I would like to watch such a thing—with your kind permission? And I give you my word we will be away from here in an hour's time."

Tarifa shrugged indifferently and turned her horse away from him, as he reached for a heavy saddle resplendent with silver and colored thread. The saddle and magnificent black stallion did not match the ragged, ill-clad, and poorly mounted group around the fire. Tarifa saw Luis staring at one of the men with startled preoccupation, a thick-shouldered black-bearded ruffian with a pistol and knife tucked into his sash.

As they rode up the hill together he said, "Did you see that big hombre by the fire?"

"Yes, I saw him."

"I am certain it is Francisco Badillo, one of the criminals banished from San Blas after the Revolution. He was sentenced to ten years in chains when he came to the *frontera*, a companion of Vicente Gomez 'El Capador,' the fiend who tortured all the Spaniards he could lay hands on in Mexico before the Revolution. A thief, a murderer, a despoiler of women. We must notify the alcalde that Badillo is here."

"And the other one that calls himself Agapito Larios?"

"I do not know anything about him," frowned Luis, "but he must be a renegade also."

A flash of black beside her cut short any reply she might have made, and Tarifa turned to find Larios riding at her elbow on his black stallion, the animal fitness of the man matching that of the horse.

Larios was still as naked to the waist as one of the wild gentile Indians, but he wore a cream-colored sombrero heavy with gold lace jerked tight by the braided strap under his strong chin. His eyes boldly admired Tarifa's easy assurance in the saddle, and the dexterity with which she handled a stallion as powerful and mettlesome as his own.

"You do not object that I ride with you, señora, to witness the end of the drive? It is not far, I think?"

Tarifa did not wish to give him an open invitation, but neither could she find it in her heart to refuse him. His interest in the operation was quite open and unmistakably honest.

She was aware of Luis' frowning disapproval. As much to show him that the decision was hers to make and not his, as to please Larios, she nodded a haughty permission to the stranger.

His smile flashed wide and white, and he touched his knee to the stallion's silky shoulder and was off like an arrow shot from a bow.

Calabaza could not accept this affront, and neither could Tarifa. She did nothing to stop him when Calabaza gave a great piercing challenge and bolted after the other horse. Golden stallion after black, they raced across the hogback of the ocher hills like moving clouds. They were fast gain-ing on the herd of wild mesteños, who were restive and frightened now that they smelled the sea and sensed disaster.

Larios pulled up the black first and Calabaza shot by, ears flat to his head, still eager to best his enemy. Tarifa used the spade bit ruthlessly to bring him around, something she had never found necessary to do to Guindilla. When she looked up she found Larios lighting a *cigarrillo* and grinning at her.

"*Magnífico*, Dona Tarifa. I have never seen a woman ride like that before. Are you Californian?"

"I was born in Granada," she said stiffly, irritated by the tolerant amusement she found in his eyes. Her tone and curtness seemed to have no effect whatever upon him. He seemed to weigh her words and recognize the truth or falsity of them, no matter how she addressed him. There was a relaxed freedom and carelessness about him that was very unlike Bart Kinkaid's iron reserved calm. But so far he had been the only man who had come close to understanding her, and she sensed that Larios, too, comprehended the duality of her nature.

A ragged pounding of hooves cut into her thoughts, and she saw that the men had started the ill-fated mesteños running toward the distant high cliffs in the last mile of their journey to the sea.

She put spurs to Calabaza and with Larios and Luis beside her, galloped the rest of the way until they were at the tail of the onrushing herd.

No one heard the tattoo of other hooves behind them, until two glossy golden comets shot by them, and were instantly engulfed in the milling, swirling herd.

"*Sangre de Dios!*" shouted Luis. "It's Guindilla and El Capitán!"

Tarifa's heart seemed to stop in her breast. She could not think or breathe. She was only conscious of Guindilla's magnificent proud head disappearing in that welter of doomed horseflesh heading for the cliffs. There was no explaining how they had gotten there. She had seen them safely fastened in the small breaking corral back of the hacienda when she left.

"What is it, señora?" Larios asked quickly. "Are the golden ones yours?"

"Yes," Tarifa strangled on the word. "They were locked up; I don't know how they got here."

At the head of the herd Santos had also seen what was happening, and he already had Marca galloping down the side of the herd, his *reata larga* swinging in a great loop above his head.

Larios unwound his own *reata,* and built a wide loop with swift dexterity. He glanced at Tarifa's ashen strained face and asked, "If I can only reach one, which shall it be?"

Silently she pointed to Guindilla's bobbing head. But she knew it was impossible. He was being pushed further and further from the edge of the herd, into the vortex of the thrashing, maddened horses. If he fell he would be trampled and what loop could reach him there?

Larios was off like smoke, drifting dangerously into the edge of the running horses, his arm straight and high above his head to give the *reata larga* maximum throwing range; his eyes darting like lightning from horse to horse, for the best moment to make his throw. He rose up in the saddle, standing on his toes, knees braced against the mochila, and cast his loop with the adroitness and skill of a consummate *reatero.*

For an instant Guindilla seemed to falter and stumble to one knee, his head all but disappearing in the rushing sea of horseflesh, and then he pulled erect and was held like a boulder as the others rushed on in their mad frenzied marathon.

The black stallion stood braced, at his master's command and Larios, his dark face grimy with dust and sweat, played Guindilla like a great fish on the end of a line, until in the thinning ranks of the mesteños he was able to pull him slowly to the side of the maelstrom.

Tarifa flung herself from Calabaza and raced to take the head of the frightened, battered, blowing stallion in her arms. Her eyes rose to Larios where he sat on the black, holding the end of the *reata* in his burned, blistered hands. He was smiling at her in complete sympathy and understanding.

"He is your own mount?" he asked softly.

"Yes. A gift from my dead husband. He is all I have left. I cannot thank you—"

"Please, I do not want thanks, Dona Alvarjo. It is

enough that a magnificent piece of horseflesh has been spared the fate of these others."

"You must come to the hacienda and let my maid dress your hands, Señor Larios. She is very skilled with medicines," said Tarifa.

"It is nothing," he said lightly.

"But I insist. And you must at least have some refreshments for your trouble."

"You are most kind, señora. I accept with pleasure."

Santos rode up, anguish and frustration clearly mirrored on his face.

"I missed him, Dona Tarifa. I tried for El Capitán, and missed him! Another second and Marca and I would have gone over, too. What wretched devil allowed them to get loose?"

But for the moment Tarifa could only stroke her trembling pet, and thank her own secret gods that Larios had rescued him in time.

At the cliff's edge the vaqueros were driving the luckless mesteños grimly over the precipice into the sea, and the sound of their piercing screams and thudding bodies so sickened Tarifa that she mounted Calabaza and told Luis and Santos that she would start back. Larios, too, seemed to have lost interest in watching the end of the ghastly drive, and leading Guindilla, sore and limping at the end of his *reata*, he followed Tarifa at a leisurely walk holding the reins gingerly in his torn, blistered hands.

"Have you any idea what horses such as yours would bring in Taos or Sonora?" he asked as they rode.

"No. We have never sold or bought horses. We have always bred our own. My husband Don Ygnacio brought his stud horse, Khalid, from Spain."

"They are magnificent, these two. Have you others?"

"Yes. Many of them."

"I envy you. Fine horses have always been my greatest joy."

"I have admired the one you ride, Señor Larios. Is he a New Mexican horse?"

"No. From Sonora, where I was born. My father raised fine horses and cattle—before he died."

"I am sorry to hear of his death. But you have other people?"

"No. No one."

"And your father's rancho?"

"I no longer have it," he said briefly.

Tarifa felt that she had asked enough personal questions. No matter who he was, or with what caliber of men he traveled, he had saved for her the one creature she loved most, and for that she would reward him to the best of her ability.

"You are most fortunate, señora. To have a rancho like this, a man would go to any lengths." His bare torso gleamed in the hot afternoon sunlight and his eyes on her face were brooding and speculative.

"It will remain in my hands during my lifetime, if I choose," she said, "and then it is to go to the Alvarjo children."

"Your children?"

"I have no children. My only son lies buried in the graveyard there below. These are my husband's children."

"And there is something about leaving it to them that you do not like?" he said, with that uncanny perception he seemed to have of her thoughts.

"I do not trust them. They do not desire the rancho for itself, for its memories, or for what it might become in the future. The dream of unity their father had for it. They want to divide it. Scatter and dissipate its potenial, to fulfill their idle dreams and lazy, selfish interests. Only I stand in their way. But they are cowards and afraid of me. And so I hold them in check."

He laughed with delight. "And do you know I do the same thing with my men? The scum who follow and serve me, because I have a better brain and a stronger arm than they have. I knew we had something in common the moment I saw you astride that magnificent golden *caballo*."

With his flashing eyes and teeth, his arrogant self-assurance and relaxed tawny body, he reminded Tarifa of the young *gitano* men she had known in the Sacro Monte and the Triana. A memory dim, but insistent now, came to her of just such a man who had moved through Bandonna's dim cave when she was a child, and watched her with catlike insolence when he passed her. She saw the same quick recognition in Penti's eyes as the old Gypsy bent to dress his hands.

"There is something about me you disapprove of, señora?" he asked.

"It is just that you remind me of someone—in Spain. It is nothing. A childhood memory. I was born in Granada," she said. "My mother Bandonna was Queen of the Gypsies. She had many who shared her cave. He was one of them, the man you are like."

"I am sorry I remind you of something unpleasant."

She stood up and stretched her arms above her head like a cat, and he could see the sharp outline of her small pointed breasts under the linen open-necked shirt. She still wore the tight-fitting black velvet trousers and scarlet sash of her riding costume, but she had kicked off her *botas* and stood barefooted and he noted the delicate shapeliness of each foot and how the sun was bathing them in deep golden hues.

"I am not sure that he was unpleasant," she said lazily, "only that I believed him to be at the time."

Larios stood up beside her and she saw that he was nearly as tall as Bart, her chin coming just a little above his throat. His eyes looking down into hers were pools of blackness, deep and fathomless. She barely felt his hands on her shoulders or his breath on her face, before his lips closed over hers.

CHAPTER 24

It was Francisco, Tarifa found, who had inadvertently released El Capitán and Guindilla from the corral. Returning drunk from the *ranchería,* he had learned from the Bolsa Coyotes vaqueros that he was wanted at Loma de Oro, and had ridden off posthaste. Arriving there to find everyone gone, he had decided to put his saddled mount in the corral with the other two palominos while he took a short nap behind the hide shed. He had failed to latch the gate properly, and Guindilla by some twist of equine perverseness had led El Capitán after the herd and other riders.

Tarifa vented her anger on Francisco by recalling him from Bolsa Coyotes and installing him in the least desirable room at Loma de Oro with strict orders to report to her morning and night. She gave him the most unpleasant chores to oversee, despite Tía Isabella's pleading, and turned a deaf ear to Santos' warning that she might be driving him too far. Letting the palominos out had been an accident. But Tarifa could only see her pet struggling in the sea of wild horses, and brave El Capitán being swept to his death because of the stupidity and laziness of one man.

She did not insist on Larios and his men leaving Loma de Oro at once, although all the Alvarjos and even Padre Cazon urged her to do so.

What she felt for Pito, as he told her his friends called him, was a strange mixture of all she had felt for the few men in her life who had pleased her. The hot, wild elation she had felt for Hobarra, the friendship and security she had shared with Ygnacio, and the more recent self-knowledge and depth of understanding Bart Kinkaid had given her. She could relax with Pito; there was no need to be on guard to protect herself from him. Their attraction for each other was as elemental as rain falling upon parched ground. Whether riding or lying stretched in the shade of a giant oak in the pastures, or in the moonlit silence atop Loma de Oro, there was a natural oneness about them that made speech superfluous and left only desire to be given full rein. Now Tarifa understood what Penti had meant when she claimed Tarifa had never lain with a man in his prime while in the full tide of her own passion.

Almost but not quite, she could lose herself in Pito's embrace these days, and forget about Loma de Oro entirely. Once she asked him idly, "Is it true that one of your men is the criminal Francisco Badillo?"

He laughed. "Yes. But we are all men with a price on our heads, *querida*. My parents were of Spanish blood, and after the Revolution when those of Spanish birth were banished from Mexico, my father's lands were confiscated. He was seized and shot on a trumped-up charge of treason. My mother and I went into hiding, but she couldn't stand the hardships and died a few months later. Badillo was witch-hunting with the rest, routing out and killing Spaniards. But I had been born in Sonora, and in his eyes was not exactly a Spaniard. And I had once done him an important favor. Before he was seized and sentenced to the chains for ten years, he had formed this little band of cutthroats, and he asked me to act as their capitán until he could rejoin us. We came here, as a matter of fact, to pick him up." Pito smiled. "We have not done too badly in New Mexico these past years."

"Stealing horses and cattle?"

"If you like."

"And now you intend to do the same thing in California?"

"You have so many unbranded horses and cattle, why not, *querida?*"

Tarifa lifted her head from his shoulder and sat up.

"If you ever take a head of stock from my rancho, I will see that you and your men pay for it with your blood."

He laughed up at her, looking like a fit and lazy panther. "I believe you would, my little *gata.*"

Though the passion she felt for him was all-consuming, while it lasted, there were other moments when Tarifa did not quite trust him. She sensed that he could be as completely dedicated and as ruthless as she. She was aware, also, even if he was not, that there could be no lasting alliance between them.

When he broached the subject of marriage, she laughed and shook her head. "We could never work in harness, you and I, Pito. We are too much alike, too used to traveling alone. Besides, I do not like marriage. Here one gets married and is married forever, not like the Gypsies where a man and woman stay together only as long as they please each other. I shall never marry again."

"Come with me, then. You are a Gypsy. You should enjoy the freedom of my life. You care nothing about these Alvarjos. Why should you stay and work your heart out so that in the end you can hand the profits over to them?"

"I must stay," she told him. "It is my rancho now. Until

I decide to hand it over to someone else, I will see that it remains mine. Besides I have the child Dolores and Bolsa Coyotes to care for."

He looked at her sharply. "You mean to keep all the land for yourself. None of them will ever own an inch of it." He got up and pulled her gently to her feet beside him. "Am I right?"

"Perhaps. I don't know."

"You are an oddity, Tarifa. A Gypsy who is so besotted over a piece of land that she is willing to give up her birthright to guard and possess it. I only hope you won't live to regret it."

She pulled free of his arm. "Now you sound like Penti."

"She knows the danger as well as I do," he said somberly. "They do not like you, these Alvarjos. They will do all they can to pull you down and make you suffer. You stand alone here, save for Penti and Santos and the Padre you speak of. You have nothing and no one to fill your empty life. Nothing but the horse Guindilla and surely you will outlive him? What is to become of you when you grow older and have no one you can trust, no one to turn to with your problems?"

"I have a friend—an Americano." She told him about Bart Kinkaid, and was surprised at the look of loathing that came over his face.

"You cannot trust Americanos. It is they as much as the foolish Mexican government who are ruining California."

"You do not know him," Tarifa replied. "In a way he is like you. I can trust him."

Larios smiled and took her hands in his. "For your sake, querida, I hope you can trust him. You must know you can also depend upon me?" Then: "Since there is no future for us, I have decided to be off in the morning."

Tarifa looked up in surprise. She was not happy to see him go, and yet she had been expecting it. Had he wanted to stay, rather than pursue his own wild, free life, she would have thought the less of him. Pito had been restless for days, had probably only stayed to please her.

He drew her to him and kissed her softly on the lips.

"Where will you go?" she asked.

"North, I think, before we cut back to New Mexico. We

should have gathered a few fine horses by that time, eh?"
He winked at her in elaborate seriousness.

"You mean you should have stolen enough by then to make your trip worthwhile."

"What an unkind thing to say, *querida*. *Borrowed*, that is the kinder word, not *stolen*. I will ride back this way from time to time; our paths will cross again." He took a small carved gold ring from his sash and pressed it into her palm, closing her fingers over it. "This was my mother's. I would like you to have it. I believe there is wisdom in your words, Tarifa. People like us should never marry. It stifles the freedom in our souls. So I shall have no need for this. Look at it now and then, and think of me?"

She nodded, and watched him gather up the serape and fasten it behind his saddle. A moment later he was astride his black stallion, his sombrero held aloft in one hand as he waved farewell.

She watched horse and rider until they were mere specks on the distant brown hillside. Then she slipped the little gold ring on one finger and mounted Guindilla, wheeling him toward Loma de Oro, already hearing Penti's cackling derision when the old woman learned her choice: servitude to the rancho in place of the freedom and passion that might have been hers had she gone with Pito Larios.

Now that she was alone in the gathering dusk, Tarifa analyzed her own secret reasons for refusing Pito's offer: Larios was not a man she could give herself to unequivocally, completely. They shared much in common. Their fearlessness, their strength of purpose, their swift abandonment to their emotions, but Tarifa knew that she would never be able to accept his complete mastery over her, even temporarily, as Bandonna had accepted the mastery, however fleeting, of her lovers. And for a Gypsy to lack this feeling of complete domination by the lover could lead only to disaster. Tarifa admitted wryly to herself that there was too much of her father in her to allow such a liberty to any man. She was, after all, only half-Gypsy. And the fiercely proud and independent Moorish traits had always been far stronger in her nature than the Gypsy ones. Love and affection and passion she had shared willingly with Pito, but his domination she could not accept.

Zenobio Sanchez called a few days later, to complain

that Larios and his men had stolen some of his best horses. They had been seen by some vaqueros from Santa Margarita *ranchería*. Such things did not happen in the old days. But when Tarifa offered him some of her own horses to replace his loss, Zenobio refused. He seemed to have lost interest in his rancho.

"Perhaps I am growing too old to care," he told her as he nursed his glass of *aguardiente* in her study, "but there is no sense in anything anymore. Look at this family, broken and scattered like chaff, and brought to disgrace in spite of all you could do to prevent it. And look at these idiotic young Paisanos, who have grown too big for their breeches, wanting to take over the government and declare us independent of Mexico. Do they intend to fight off Mexico and every other nation who charges up to our shores with spiked cannon and a few musket balls! *Ay de mi,* what are we coming to, Tarifa?"

"Who can say? I only know one thing, no one shall take Loma de Oro from me."

"I would not be surprised if all our lands were stripped from us by the same idiots who are despoiling the Missions," he said darkly. "And for the same reason—greed! They want to own all of California, these Paisanos, and without lifting a finger to deserve it. In my day young men did not presume to so much power overnight." He paused, studying her face as he said, "Did you know that Francisco meets with them regularly? Perhaps the boy does not know what he is doing, but there is madness and danger in this business."

Tarifa did not know. And she was angry. There was a slyness and deviousness in Francisco of late that made her distrust his most innocent remark. Had it all begun with her dragging him from the bed of the Indian girl in the servants' quarters of the Canejo hacienda that day in San Diego? In any case, Don Zenobio was undoubtedly telling the truth. The Paisanos were a danger to everything that had stood for the old California of Don Ygnacio. Tarifa felt only a faint concern for her own holdings, but she meant to make it quite clear to these young men that to interfere with Loma de Oro or Bolsa Coyotes was to court disaster. She still had many faithful vaqueros, and could call up more from the neighboring ranchos if necessary.

"Tell me, Don Zenobio," she said, "would you like me to send you a few extra vaqueros to see you through this bad time?"

He shook his head, his eyes old and weary above his bearded cheeks. "What cattle I have that are not stolen by *bandidos* or butchered by thieving Indians wander into the sierras and arroyos where I can dig them out with a few vaqueros when I need them. They are probably safer there than wandering loose in my pastures. I manage to sell enough hides and tallow to exist and that is all I ask."

Zenobio roused himself with a grunt, and limped to the door with his battered sombrero on the back of his head.

"You must warn Francisco. Those men will bring him nothing but trouble."

"I will speak to him, and thank you, Don Zenobio. If you need anything, do not hesitate to call upon me. I would like to feel you will come to me as if I were Ygnacio?"

He stood leaning against the door, looking at her from under his fierce shaggy brows.

"I do not deserve your friendship, Dona Tarifa. I once sent a man here to kill you."

"That was a long time ago, Zenobio. In any case, I almost killed him."

"I am to blame for that also. And Kinkaid is my friend."

Tarifa fingered a paper on her desk. "He is also mine, now. I have received two letters from him. He met the brig, *Nancy Lee*, in Rio, and sent them by her on his way to Boston."

"Is that possible? You and he—I would never have thought it. Has he any word of Soledad, poor *niña?*"

"No, nothing. He thought the *Vulcan* had sailed for South America, but now says perhaps he was wrong. He could find no report of her."

"Kinkaid is a good man," Sanchez said. "He has strength tempered with compassion. You do not often find that combination in a truly strong character. You do not have it, *muchacha,* and neither have I. Nor did Ygnacio have it, heaven rest his soul. I am glad you have made a friend of Kinkaid. *Adiós,* Tarifa."

"*Adiós,* Zenobio."

Tarifa sat at her desk for a moment after he had gone,

and stared at the letter Bart Kinkaid had sent to her. It was written on thick white paper in a bold but clear hand.

Looking at just the written words, and without the challenge of his personality to confront her, Tarifa found that she could think warmly of his friendship. When they were together there would always be a barrier between them, but in letters she had discovered that she could confide in him as she had never been able to do with another individual. She was grateful that Padre Cazon had taught her to write so well. And though these were the first letters she had ever written or received, she found that her delight in writing and reading them did not diminish with time. Often she read them over to herself in the cabaña atop Loma de Oro, and composed and wrote countless answers, epistles of many pages which she eventually tore up and burned in the fireplace before one suited her well enough to send off by the next trade ship leaving port.

Besides getting for himself the ex-Mission lands of the Santa Margarita y Las Flores, which had belonged originally to San Luis Rey, Pio Pico owned Rancho Paso de Bartolo, nine thousand acres on the Gabriel River, which he named El Ranchito, and on which he built for his bride, a sister of Governor Alvarado, a two-story, thirty-three-room hacienda. Built around a brick-paved patio filled with rare plants, it had a red-tiled roof, and a kitchen that opened onto the wide patio where guests flocked to enjoy the hacienda's hospitality. Always lavish, Pico had not spared himself on El Ranchito. Though most of the rooms were small and dark, the bedrooms, *sala,* and ballroom were resplendent with red-and-white flowered paper, and two great doors led into the chapel beyond. The dining-room walls were painted pink and white in a Mexican floral design, and on the upper floor were other bedrooms and a ballroom plus a study, though the eaves were so low it was barely possible to stand upright. Outside, near the well, a huge fig tree shaded the patio yard and verandas.

The hacienda at El Ranchito had been lavishly furnished with massive mahogany tables, sofas, chairs, with huge French mirrors in gilt frames between the windows and doors. Brussels carpets with great glaring patterns had been laid without thought of matching the design, and a twelve-thousand-dollar piano graced one corner of the overpowering *sala*.

Pico also claimed Jamul Rancho and Temecula, which he had always desired; so far he had been unable to get a clear grant to the property.

Francisco Alvarjo found in Pico a figure much to be admired, and Pico was pleased to have one of the well-born Alvarjos in his retinue. He and Santiago had always been friends, and if Francisco was less sharp mentally, he was at least a willing follower. Francisco realized that Pico's political star was rising, and he had hopes of joining him in his climb to power.

Together with his two brothers, Don José Antonio and Don Andres, both capable soldiers and politicians, Pio had begun to make a name for himself as a political leader with a flair for flamboyant oratory and a certain cunning opportunism.

With his brother-in-law, Juan Batista Alvarado, ruling as governor *ad interim* following the ousting of Governor Nicolas Gutierrez in 1836, Pico stood in a good position to further his own career.

So far California had been successful in her armed protest against the centralism and disdain of Mexico. She had ousted her Mexican ruler, and for the first time a Paisano Californiano sat in the governor's house. What he lacked in experience he more than made up for in zeal. He was a young man of ability and good character, better qualified than many to rule. It was heady wine he was tasting though, this sudden overthrow of the hated Mexican government, and his wild acclaim by all classes. Even the Americans had flocked to his banner, marching with him when he seized Monterey, in a battle that was more bombast than bloodshed.

But the disputes between North and South still burned. Rumors ran like wildfire to fan the flames. The northerners were bound to put on airs and grab the lion's share for themselves. The *abajerros* of the south would leave California defenseless to the rapacious foreigners pouring into Los Angeles, and deliver her into the hands of the United States.

In the end it was clear that the south would declare her independence despite the heated protest of older, wiser men, who tried desperately but fruitlessly to hold north and south togther. And watching from the sidelines were men like Pio Pico, waiting for the ripe moment to seize power for themselves.

Francisco Alvarjo found himself caught up in the exciting vortex of a rising revolution. He had not served as a soldier for nothing, he told the others; he wanted to take an active part.

There was no one in California with the exception of Tarifa, he thought, who did not have an interest in its outcome. Tarifa merely listened in silence to the young men talk at the dinner table, and she was hardly more receptive to the warnings and fears of Padre Cazon or Zenobio Sanchez.

Let the south split from the north, what difference did it make to her? Loma de Oro was hers no matter who sat in the governor's *palacio*. As long as the family did not become involved in the wrangle she need not concern herself about it. But she knew that Francisco managed to sneak out to meet with Pico and the others, and though she had warned him to stay away she had begun to wonder if he had already committed himself in some foolish way. Did he not see that such a senseless wrangle could only end in defeat for all of California, an open invitation, as Zenebio so often predicted now, for a foreign power to step in? This was one thing that did worry her. She had no desire to see California fall into foreign hands. But there was little she could do at the moment to prevent it, other than keep Ygnacio's sons safely at her side until it was all over. She found herself wishing that Bart were here. There was not a man on the rancho, she thought bitterly, whom she could rely on for anything. Save old Santos.

Rufina had not been able to credit her senses when her father paused again at the jail on his way back to Santa Barbara, and told her tearfully that Nazario, in the extreme generosity and goodness of his heart, was willing to take her back into his home.

"You must pray and do penance for the rest of your days," Don Carlos warned gravely, "for the great and grievous wrong you have done God, your husband, and your family. And you must thank Him for having granted this miracle of forgiveness in your hour of need."

When the period of her chastisement and public penance was over, Nazario came to San Diego accompanied by Luis to get her.

He had brought her own clothes, and a maid to help her dress and bind her shaven head in a black silk scarf under her mantilla.

It was a subdued, hollow-eyed young woman, with the lines of her anguish and suffering etched on her face, who stepped outside the jail door that morning to confront her wronged husband.

Nazario was sitting stiffly erect on Hidalgo's back when she lifted her eyes to his. He had changed also, she noted with a pang. Surely the deep lines around his mouth and eyes had not been there before? She had been the cause of them. In the long days that she had lain praying for death in the fetid, rat-infested jail, she had come to know many things about herself that she had never known before, the most startling of which was the intensity and depth of her love for her children and for Nazario.

She had never dared to hope for this generosity but she was determined to see that he never lived to regret it. She would be a model wife and mother, and from this moment on exist only for her husband and family.

But watching his thin dark face in the one moment she allowed herself before she lowered her lashes, she could read no sign of emotion there—nothing but a searching coldness as he stared at her. And a powerful and stunning thought struck her and made her stumble as she walked toward the carriage.

Perhaps he was only giving her shelter for the sake of the children, and to save the Alvarjo name? Perhaps he meant never to speak to her again? She had once known such an estranged couple, and the silent thunder of their presence had been unendurable. Like a broken reed, Rufina sank back in the carriage seat and closed her eyes. Prayer and penance would indeed be her only solace in the days to come, if what she imagined was correct.

She watched as Nazario and Luis rode swiftly ahead of the carriage and out of sight. It must have been painful for Nazario, coming to get her, and yet he had come himself when he could as easily have sent others in his place. How in the name of all that was holy could she ever have compared him disparagingly with that animal Titus Judah?

A burning anger filled her breast at the thought of the
Americano: Not only had he cost her Nazario's love, her
reputation, the agony and humiliation of public disgrace,
but he had made her responsible for the loss of Soledad
as well, and she was sorry for what she had done to her
little sister-in-law. She must find some way to make Nazario understand that.

It felt odd coming back to Bolsa Coyotes. While she was
away something had changed; the rancho had grown more
beautiful and desirable in her eyes—perhaps because she
had never expected to see it again.

Nazario and Luis were in the dining room when she
entered the house. She could hear them but she did not
attempt to go to them there. Instead she hurried to the children's room, and scooped the two little girls into her arms.
The hot tears felt good on her cheeks, like a benediction
after her ordeal of suffering, and when at last she broke
away from her children's embrace and went to her own
room she felt a heady joy of repossession, as if her soul
had just re-entered her body after a sojourn in Purgatory.

The room was just as she had left it, all her garments
in the chests and great armoire against the wall. It had
been freshly cleaned and there were fresh flowers on the
dressing table. Could it be that everything was going to be
as it was before? Her heart gave a wild lurch of rapture,
but she extinguished it instantly. No, nothing could ever
be the same. Nazario had given her sanctuary, and had
given her back to her children, but only for their sakes,
not for his own or hers.

Rufina sat on the edge of the bed, one arm around the
elaborately carved mahogany post at the foot, listening.
Someone was walking down the *galleria* toward the bedrooms. Her heartbeats quickened when the footsteps halted
outside her door. She could barely get breath enough into
her lungs to answer the knock that came a moment later.

But it was Luis who walked into the room. Not Nazario, as she had hoped.

He stood looking at her a moment, then quietly closed
the door. In his glance she had read condemnation and a
tightly leashed anger.

"My brother has asked me to speak to you on his behalf," he said shortly.

"Why does he not speak to me himself?"

"Because he does not choose to do so. You must understand you are in this house by sufferance. I cannot agree with what he has done—what he is doing. There can be no forgiveness for what you have done. Nazario is younger than I am. I have tried to dissuade him from this useless foolishness. But he will not listen.

"He asks me to tell you that you are still mistress of this house. The servants will do your bidding, and the children are at your disposal to rear. You will not leave here, however, nor will you receive guests."

Rufina stood up with a touch of color in both cheeks, but she could not raise her eyes to face his hotly accusing ones. She could not blame Luis. He loved his brother and he could see in her only a further threat to his happiness and honor.

"I will do as Nazario says," she answered softly. "And will you tell him, please, how—grateful I am for what he has done for me?"

The door closing sharply was her only reply.

It was well past midnight when Rufina was awakened by a muffled sound in the bedroom. She thought at once of the roving bands of bandits and marauding white renegades that infested the countryside lately, and quickly suppressed a cry. Whoever it was, perhaps they only wanted money and jewelry. Her jewel case was on the dressing table in plain sight, and the little gold madonna that had belonged to her mother was in the niche in the wall near the door.

For the moment, there was no further sound and she crouched, clutching the bedclothes to her breast, afraid to move lest she make a sound herself and let the intruder know she was awake.

Then a hand closed over her shoulder. She screamed, but the hand did not go away, and no one stirred in the household.

It was like a diabolical nightmare, crouching in the darkness while screams tore at her throat, and the hands kept moving downward and no one seemed to hear or care.

She felt the bedclothes torn from her nerveless fingers as she was thrown violently back on the bed.

"Be still!"

Just two words whispered above her ear, but they caused the breath to fill her deflated lungs so sharply that it felt as if a knife had pierced her breast above her heart.

"Nazario!"

He did not speak to her again.

When he finally left her worn and exhausted in the early hours before dawn, she lay on her face weeping bitterly into the pillows.

She knew now what her role was to be. For as long as she lived, Nazario would use her for only one purpose—and she was helpless to do anything but fulfill that role, hateful and degrading as it might be.

CHAPTER 25

Luis had argued in vain with his brothers about joining the hot-blooded movement to sever the south from northern California rule.

With Francisco particularly and with Nazario to some extent, his cautioning and pleas fell on deaf ears.

"Where is your pride in the your homeland?" Francisco sneered. "Would you see the arrogants of the north take all the rich plums for themselves and trample us in the dust? Is not the south the cradle of California, the first to be settled?"

"Zenobio Sanchez is right," Luis replied calmly. "It is California we must think of first, not the rights of north or south."

"Don Zenobio is an old fool. What does he know of our problems? He is a relic of Anza's time!"

"So was our father," said Luis soberly.

Francisco flushed and bit his lower lip. "Even so, what do they understand about the insults heaped upon us? Father was a fighting man, so were all our ancestors—men who fought the Moors and drove them out of Spain. Are we too spineless to drive a group of mangy dogs from our doorstep?"

"Well spoken, *hermano*," Nazario said, his eyes shining with excitement.

They were seated in the *sala* of the tiny cabaña hidden in a far section of the Canejo property near the southern *frontera*. Macario had built it to house the half-breed paramour he had taken after Soledad's disappearance.

Outside, thunder crackled like bullwhips across the bare brown backs of the low hills. So far there had been no rain but undoubtedly, thought Nazario, it would come before nightfall.

In the tiny bedroom beyond, he could hear the soft laughter and murmur of voices where Macario was being entertained by the girl Rosa. He thought grimly that tonight he would not go into his own bedroom in the dead of night to share with his wife the only thing he ever shared with her these days. She would have one night's respite. He often wondered what she thought, for she had never attempted to speak to him since that first night when her voice in his ear had poured out the passionate story of her remorse.

His only answer had been the savagery of his attack, followed by utter silence. He had never varied the formula. And yet after the first few nights he had found his victory bitter and empty. He would have his sons, he was certain of that, but that was all. Perhaps he was foolish not to take a lusty half-breed like Macario's. Francisco, too, seemed to find joy in the Indian women. But Nazario knew that his pride would spoil any pleasure he might try to find there. It was as if all warmth, all affection, save for his children, had been burned out of him. Perhaps that was why he thirsted for the action and danger joining the Paisanos would bring.

Both he and Francisco had been with Pio Pico on his two abortive marches to meet the enemy, first on the way to San Fernando when Alvarado had taken Los Angeles, and again on the way to Buenaventura when they had met

Castaneda's fleeing stragglers. In both cases, much to the Alvarjos' disgust, they had come up too late to take part in any of the fighting. Now, with Don Carlos Carillo's troops under Captain Juan Tobar, perhaps things would be different.

As members of the company, all the young men had been armed with pistols and lances, and the more accomplished marksmen with ancient muskets. For himself, Nazario intended to rely mainly on his own *reata.*

Luis was present merely as a spectator, and in the hope of somehow turning his brothers from what he considered their useless destruction.

Macario came out of the bedroom tucking in the end of his red sash, looking like a cat who had enjoyed a dish of cream. His weakly handsome features wore a heavy sleepy look.

"*Cristo!* Listen to that rain? It's coming in the window onto the bed."

Francisco laughed. "*Bueno!* It has done something we could not then, and brought you to your senses, at least temporarily."

Macario grunted and bawled into the tiny kitchen for the old Indian woman who served as Rosa's maid and companion.

"*Vino, muy pronto, mujer. Ándale, ándale!*"

The old woman, wrapped to the eyes in a heavy black *rebozo,* hobbled into the room with two bottles of wine and a collection of battered tin mugs.

Macario sent her into the bedroom to join her mistress, and standing at the crude oak-plank table, poured wine into the mugs.

He turned, holding his own cup above his head. "*Compadres, Viva* Don Carlos!"

"*Viva!*" echoed the others loyally.

Macario frowned at his empty wine mug, "And we will all have a wet ride tonight, *amigos.*"

"Francisco and Luis have been at Bolsa Coyotes helping me brand calves this past week," replied Nazario.

"And Dona Tarifa will not check up on you?"

"The child Dolores has been ailing for the past few weeks. Tarifa has not bothered to come to Bolsa Coyotes. She has merely sent Santos with her messages, and they are many, I can tell you!"

"What would become of Bolsa Coyotes if the child died?" Macario asked. He was surprised when Nazario's face grew dark with anger.

"I do not know or care! The child must live, that is the important thing. She is all that is left of my beloved sister. Did you think we had any wish to keep the property for ourselves?"

Macario saw at once that he had gone too far and was about to apologize, when they were interrupted by the sound of horses in the yard.

"We haven't much time, *amigos,*" he said. "Regardless of the weather, you will find when we join Tobar's army that he is a real military leader. This time we shall not fail *compadres,* I guarantee you that."

Luis, who had been sitting quietly in a corner of the room, stood up and faced his brothers. "You will be defying everything that Father believed in if you join this rebellion to split California," he told them.

"We are only protecting what is ours by right." Francisco's face worked with the intensity of his feeling.

Nazario came to his brother's support. "We, at least, are backing the only legal ruler of the territory, Don Carlos."

"Are you sure?"

"Hasn't Don Carlos a paper from Mexico to prove it?"

"I don't know," said Luis. "Have any of you seen it?"

"You question the integrity of our national representative to Congress, José Antonio Carillo, who obtained the appointment for Don Carlos?" Nazario asked in amazement.

Luis' eyes moved to Nazario's face, as calm and unflinching as his father's had once been. "I don't trust any man until I have the proof of his honesty."

"You sound like Tarifa," Francisco spat in disgust.

"Perhaps. I have found that she has a certain common sense that you and I lack. She questions first and acts afterward. You would do well, in this case, to copy her."

"If you think so much of her, why don't you go back to her?" Nazario sneered, his eyes hot and dark in his head. "What are you doing here if you do not believe in our cause?"

Luis searched his young brother's face and found only anger and stubborn determination written there. Like all

young things, he reflected sadly, he would have to meet
hurt and defeat in his own way before he could accept the
wisdom of his elders.

"I am going with you," Luis said simply. "It doesn't matter that I do not believe in your cause. I am an Alvarjo,
and I shall stand or fall beside you."

Luis gave him a quick smile. "Besides, *muchacho,* where
but in the front lines does a horse or a son bred by Don
Ygnacio Alvarjo belong?"

The one hundred men that made up the army of Don
Carlos Carillo, under Capitán Juan Tobar, had passed San
Luis Rey and nearly reached Las Flores when a scout re-
turned with word that Governor Alvarado and General
Castro, with over two hundred men, were marching south
from Los Angeles to intercept them.

Tobar, a tall, hawk-nosed veteran of fifty, elected to
make his stand on Las Flores rancho. He mounted three
cannons facing south in the direction he hoped the enemy
would come, and sat down to map out his military plans.

The Alvarjos and Macario Canejo huddled in a corner
of the crowded adobe with the other *gente de razón* members of the little army. The rest clustered outside, standing
about the small fires they had built in the yard.

The rain, which had just ceased as the Alvarjos arrived,
had made the adobe as clammy and damp as a tomb. Mois-
ture still dripped from the tulle roof overhead, and the
fireplace inside did little to dispel the bone-chilling cold.

Nazario and Luis stood facing each other in the barren
room, chewing on unlighted *cigarrillos.* Like the others,
each had been provided with a pistol on his arrival, though
neither was familiar with guns since Don Ygnacio had
never allowed them to shoot his weapons. And though
neither would admit it even to himself, both felt a gnawing uncertainty as the moment for the attack approached.

Luis was convinced that they had no right here, while
for Nazario the challenge had lain in flaunting Tarifa's
wishes. Now, there was no time to reconsider, for Tobar
was already issuing commands.

"The two of you," he said to Nazario and Luis, "scout
along that ridge yonder, and report back what you see.

You"—his eyes swept Macario and Francisco—"circle off to the right and left beyond them."

When Nazario and Luis neared the ridge beyond the adobe, they could hear rifle fire to their left where Francisco had ridden, but there seemed to be no real purpose or deadliness in the reports. It was more like the aimless shooting over the heads of stock to scare them off.

Nazario held his pistol in one hand, primed and ready. As they rode cautiously over the little rise that separated them from a shallow saucer-shaped pasture below, they could see Alvarado's men grouped and waiting, their muskets and lances in their hands as if awaiting the word to attack.

The Alvarjos sat their horses, half-concealed by a growth of greasewood and chaparral. Neither of them saw the man rising to his feet behind a boulder halfway up the little hillside to their right. He stood, a long, lanky figure, dressed in buckskins and bearded to the eyes, with a practiced swing to the Kentucky rifle he was fitting to his shoulder.

Hidalgo pricked his small ears forward and gave the muffled, questioning little whinny Nazario had learned to expect when they sighted grizzlies in the sierras.

"*Donde está*, Hidalgo?" he asked gently. Then, glancing up, he and Luis saw the stranger in the same instant.

"Quinteras?" asked Luis in surprise. This did not look like one of Alvarado's army.

"I do not know who he is," Nazario replied grimly, "but he has a musket aimed at us and I am taking no chances." He leveled the pistol he held, and saw the buckskin-clad figure stiffen against the boulder.

Luis was between Nazario and the man with the rifle, and Nazario spurred Hidalgo forward a little so that he faced the man.

The stranger shouted something to them in English that they did not understand. Almost at the same moment, Luis' Amarillo bounded forward. In the suddenness of the movement, Nazario's finger pressed the trigger. The ball singed Amarillo's forelock before it buried itself harmlessly in the ground a few yards beyond.

A second, louder shot followed Nazario's, and he saw

Amarillo rear in panic as Luis slumped in the saddle, then slipped to the ground.

In an instant, Nazario was off Hidalgo's back and on his knees beside his brother. There was blood on Luis' sleeve and jacket front, but he still could not believe that he had been shot.

Nazario did not even hear the man come up behind him and stand with his rifle leveled carefully at his own back.

When he did turn and see him, it made little difference that he stood in danger himself. He could think only of Luis, and that his brother might be dying while he wasted time on this hide-covered barbarian.

The other, seeing that Nazario showed no more concern for his presence than if he had been an oak stump, squatted down beside the fallen man and examined the wound. It did not look good. The young Spaniard was breathing heavily, and the ball seemed to have shattered his left arm below the shoulder, ricocheting off the bone and entering his chest.

Thad Tatum was not a man who wasted powder and shot or who often missed his mark. He had been frankly puzzled by the two young Californians. Neither had replied to his demand to put down their weapons and advance slowly, as he had been ordered by Alvarado to request any strangers to do. When he had seen Nazario leveling a pistol at his head, at the same instant that the other horseman had darted forward as if drawing his own weapon for attack, Tatum had fired. He had actually been aiming for Nazario's arm, but Amarillo rocketing forward had brought Luis in front of his sight just as he fired. Tatum realized now the whole thing had been a tragic mistake. The one lying on the ground had not even drawn his pistol, he saw glumly; it was still in his sash.

Tatum felt a wave of anger at himself. These were no ordinary vaqueros. They were probably sons of some rich padrone and it looked as if he'd shot one of them up real bad.

He opened the beaded sac-a-feu at his belt, and took out a cotton handkerchief and the polished tip of a buckthorn. He made a tourniquet for the young man's arm, using the horn as a lever to twist it tight.

"Is *mal heiro?*" Nazario asked anxiously, watching his brother's white face and closed eyes.

"I sure don't know what you're sayin', señor," said Tatum quietly, "but if it's what I think it is, yep, he's pretty bad hurt, looks like. And I'm almighty sorry I done it. Didn't mean to more'n disarm ye. Thought you was both aimin' to ride me down. Thet General Castro hombre told me to stop all comers—that's all I was tryin' to do. Savvy?"

Nazario shook his head impatiently. The only word he could be sure of was Castro's name, and he repeated it with emphasis.

"Castro, señor, *donde está, por favor?*"

"I don't understand—no savvy," said Tatum unhappily. Then he pointed to the men below them and said, "Castro. Down there."

At the sounds of the shots on the hillside, three men had detached themselves from the group below, and now came loping up the crest of the rise. As they slid to a halt beside the fallen Luis, Nazario noted with surprise that one of them carried a white flag on his lance. The other two he recognized as Juan Alvarado and José Castro. Under their questioning, Tatum explained what had happened. Alvarado dismounted to examine Luis' wound himself.

"You are one of the Alvarjos, aren't you?" he asked Nazario. "How do you happen to be here?"

Haltingly, Nazario explained, adding that his brothers and himself were here unknown to their stepmother, and completely against her wishes. He could not bring himself to lie about that.

"I did not think that the Alvarjos would join in a dispute of this kind," said the governor. "Tell me, Don Nazario, do you think it was worth it to get your brother killed?"

Nazario's eyes widened in alarm. *"Por Dios,* Excellency, he will not die? I am the one who should be lying here. Luis did not believe in the cause; he did not want to come here. It was only on my account that he came. Take me prisoner, Excellency, but send him back to the rancho or to the Mission where he can be cared for, *por favor?"*

Alvarado stood regarding him in silence for a moment. The governor was a delicately built young man, but erect and with an unmistakable air of command about him.

"This is what happens when kinsman fights kinsman, countryman against countryman, Don Nazario," he said sternly. "You have tasted the bitter futility of war. I have no wish to punish you more. My *compadres* and I go with a flag of truce, to see if words, not bullets, will put an end to this senseless discord before all California lies as your poor brother there, broken and bleeding, for no other reason than that they are willing to follow any leader blindly like sheep to the slaughter.

"Take your brother home, *muchacho*. We will help you tie him in the saddle. I am afraid that we can provide no other conveyance."

Luis opened his eyes as they were lifting him and asked vaguely, *"Qué sucedio, Nazario?"*

"What'd he say, Governor?" Tatum asked as he hoisted Luis into the deep saddle and fastened the *reata* loop over the wide horn, passing it around Luis' waist and handing it under the stallion's belly to Nazario on the other side.

"He asks what happened, señor," Alvarado replied.

"I'm almighty sorry I done this, Governor," said Tatum. "I hope you'll make 'em understand that? I tried, but they don't savvy Americano."

"I will explain it to them, señor."

"Think I oughta ride along with 'em, help with this here wounded hombre?"

Alvarado shook his head. "That will not be necessary, Señor Tatum. These gentlemen are from Rancho Loma de Oro, nearby. They also have relatives in the camp of Don Carlos just below. But I will convey the goodness of your offer to Don Nazario."

When the governor had finished translating the American's words to Nazario, who had bowed and murmured his thanks, Tatum turned away and spat over his shoulder in embarrassment. He was still deeply angry with himself. They were a pair of polite, fine-looking young men, and shooting one of them down had been about as risky and unrewarding as clubbing a fool hen over the head with the butt of his rifle.

The child Dolores had lain ill and listless with a low fever for some weeks, and Penti had been unable to concoct a cure for the malady. She had tried her various Romany remedies, even made use of some of the suggestions of the Indian women in the kitchen yard, but nothing had helped. The child still languished, her small face growing thinner and more peaked, her eyes only lighting up when Tarifa was in the room.

Tarifa had grown fond of Dolores' child. Perhaps because little Dolores filled the gap in her affections after Lasho's death. Now she was aware of a sudden foreboding that this little one also would be snatched from her by death, and she drove Penti relentlessly to find a cure for the child.

Tarifa had wandered into the *sala* after making sure that Dolores and Rufina's bastard son José were taking their naps. It was the siesta hour, and she was surprised to find Tía Isabella still up. She was writing a letter on the small portable wooden case she held across her knees for such purposes. She had aged since Soledad's disappearance.

"*Buenos días,* Tarifa."

"*Buenos días,* Tía Isabella."

They seldom had much to say to one another when they were alone, which was not often, and their elaborate politeness on such occasions was like a stilted and complicated minuet.

"The little ones, they sleep?" Isabella asked.

"Yes, Tía Isabella."

"A blessing. I shall add that to my letter to Joaquin, if you agree?"

"You have written him about Soledad?"

A shadow crossed the old woman's lined face.

"No. Working among the gentiles as he does on that wild *frontera* in New Mexico, he has enough of God's sorrows to bear. You agree?"

Tarifa shrugged her shoulders. She was bored with Isabella. She went to touch the keys of the piano Ygnacio had bought for her so long ago in Monterey. No one played it anymore now that the girls were gone, and she found that despite the trouble they had caused her she missed their warmth and gaiety about the hacienda.

Tarifa wore a figured muslin skirt and low-cut lace blouse, and for the first time in weeks her thick black hair was piled high under the ivory comb Ygnacio had given her.

She had been restless since Pito Larios left. She wondered as she fingered the gold ring he had given her, whether she would have been more sensible to ride away with him and leave Loma de Oro and its ceaseless worries and cares behind her. Would Pito and she ever have had anything besides their passions to sustain them? It did not seem probable, and yet. . . .

The thought was torn from her mind by the sound of horses and loud voices in the ranch yard.

She went to throw the door open and felt Tía Isabella at her elbow. Nazario and Francisco had dismounted and were standing with their arms raised, supporting a figure slumped low in the saddle on the back of a fretful golden stallion. Another man appeared from behind the riderless horses and Tarifa was surprised to recognize Padre Cazon.

He came quickly across to the two women, explaining tersely what had happened at Las Flores.

Tarifa listened with her face as hard as flint. She watched while they lifted Luis down gently and carried him past her into the hacienda. Blood still dripped from his sleeve, and at the sight Tía Isabella cried out in anguish and covered her face with her hands.

"They came to the Mission," said Padre Cazon, "but I saw at once we could not give him the care he needed there. I fear he is very badly injured. That is why I came with them, to give him Extreme Unction if it becomes necessary."

Tarifa stared at him coldly. "They disobey my commands, they dishonor their dead father's name, taking part in a rabble-rousing that could only lead to disaster, and you bring them back for me to care for as if they were merely children who had played in a forbidden fishpond!"

"This is their home, Dona Tarifa."

"Only because of me! Because I have kept it, protected it, in spite of their efforts to bring ruin and disgrace upon it ever since Ygnacio's death. I will not permit them to involve Loma de Oro in a political war. I will throw them all out first!"

The priest's voice had grown cool and distant. "And that boy who may lie dying, in spite of the fact that Nazario assures me he alone did not wish to disobey you, will you throw him out too?"

Tarifa said nothing, but her expression was as inflexible as granite.

Cazon said sharply, "He has lost a great deal of blood. Will you let him die without lifting a finger? Is he not still your responsibility as much as Loma de Oro, according to the promise you made Ygnacio?"

"Premita Undebē!" Tarifa shouted. "I am sick of hearing of the Alvarjos, sick of hearing you talk of my responsibilities. I did not promise Ygnacio to wet-nurse them forever!"

But she went with the priest to Luis' bedroom. Her lips thinned as she watched the others standing helplessly around the white-faced man on the bed, while Penti bent over him holding a towel and a basin of stained water.

"Get out. All of you."

Tarifa's voice surprised them; their heads jerked up like a row of puppets on a string, but they obeyed her in silence.

When they had filed out Padre Cazon shut the door and went with Tarifa to stand at the bedside.

Penti had loosened the tourniquet Tatum had applied and blood gushed afresh from the wound.

"Well?" Tarifa demanded.

"He is unconscious from loss of blood," said Penti, "though he would be dead if it were not for the tourniquet someone had sense enough to apply. The bone is shattered. I believe the arm will have to come off if we are to save his life."

"Santa Maria," whispered Padre Cazon.

Tarifa did not speak. She stood looking down at Luis' pale face, noting the thickness of the lashes that rested on his cheek. Since he had learned to buckle down to the work of the rancho she had come to admire him the most of Ygnacio's sons. She liked his quiet level-headedness, his sense of honor. In him she recognized the makings of the heir Don Ygnacio had deserved and dreamed of having. And she knew that no matter what he had done against her wishes, she could not let him die now.

She spoke to the old Gypsy in rapid Romanes: "Must you take off his arm?"

"Yes, or he will die, *miri pen*, of that I am certain."

"He must not die."

Their eyes met and held for an instant, then Penti murmured, "I will do my best, *miri pen*."

Padre Cazon stood watching their faces anxiously.

"What is it?" he asked Tarifa.

"She is certain she must remove the arm or he will die. I must go and get Santos and Tomas to help her. Will you stay here?"

"Yes," replied the priest, "and I will add my own poor assistance, for whatever it is worth."

When Tarifa had sent the servants to join Penti, she went to stroll in the patio. The smell of jasmine and roses was heavy and muffled under the afternoon heat.

How often, she thought bitterly, had she sat or walked in this same spot when someone lay ill or dying? She thought of Lasho and Ygnacio, of Dolores and Soledad. Was Soledad dead now too? All of them gone since her coming to Loma de Oro, as had Joaquin and Santiago. Truly she had brought a curse upon this family, yet had she not paid dearly for it also? Had she not sacrificed everything her people held sacred? Her freedom, independence, the right to wander the world with the lover of her choice.

She wondered if Penti could be right. Had she given up her birthright, only to reap hatred and disloyalty on all sides? Loma de Oro was not something that could be hugged to your breast. It was merely something that could be used, added to, and then left in the end to another's care. She felt hollow, drained, as empty as a well that has at last gone dry.

Even the desire to dance had been stilled in her these last weeks since the child Dolores had become ill. She knew that it was a bad thing when the spirit of the dance could no longer console her. An evil omen. But she could no more have danced than have flown over the peaks of the sierras into the waiting desert beyond. With the thought, a great heaviness came over her limbs and forced her to sink down wearily on the nearest bench.

Padre Cazon came out of the sickroom wiping his perspiring face on the sleeve of his habit.

"It is done," he told her. "God protect and preserve the poor boy. It is a sad thing."

"It would be sadder if he were dead," Tarifa answered with a flash of her old spirit.

"*Sí*. We must all pray for his recovery." He sat down on the bench beside her. "These are evil days, Tarifa. It seems that prayer is all that is left for us to turn to."

"I do not believe in prayer," she said.

He glanced at her at first in surprise and then with compassion. "Have you ever really prayed, Tarifa?"

"Yes. Once I prayed for rain, in the first bad drought after Ygnacio died."

"And did it rain?"

"Yes."

"And yet you do not believe—"

"And then I prayed for Lasho to get well. And he died. It is an evil God who says yes to the small thing, and no to the great thing that you ask!"

"How do we poor mortals know which is the great thing, and which the small, in God's eyes."

Tarifa shook her head impatiently, but there was a whiteness about her lips. "Don't let us waste time talking about it further, Padre."

He said gently, "Won't you come into the chapel with me and say one prayer for Luis?"

"No." She fingered the amulet that she always carried now tucked into the bodice of her dress. "I have no prayers for him. But I will help him in my own way."

The priest sighed as he rose and moved off toward the chapel, his sandals slapping on the patio tiles. He was thinking that he must make another novena to the Blessed Virgin that Tarifa might recognize God as her friend and not her enemy. Poor child, she had much to bear in this household and he prayed that her load might be lightened, her cross of woes made more bearable. It never occurred to him to ask a like favor for himself, or for his long-suffering brethren in the Order of St. Francis.

In the cool of evening, Tarifa went again into the sick-room. Penti still crouched in a chair near the head of the bed, her small glittering eyes watching the face of the man resting there, like an alert and anxious monkey.

"How is he?" Tarifa asked in Romany.

"He sleeps. Soon he will awaken. You will tell him about his arm?"

"Someone must tell him," Tarifa sighed. Even this painful duty fell upon her shoulders, not the Alvarjos'.

"Perhaps the Padre, or one of his brothers, *miri pen?*" Penti suggested. She studied Tarifa's strained face and taut lips.

She saw the younger woman straighten her shoulders and was proud that Romany blood could produce such strength and fearlessness.

"No. It is better that I do it. If he must hate the moment he wakens, let him hate me. I am used to being hated in this house."

When she glanced up from the wounded man a moment later, Nazario was standing in the doorway, his own face as ashen as Luis'.

"I can't stand it any longer," he choked. "I must know how he is."

"He still lives, but no thanks to you," Tarifa said coldly.

Nazario twisted his hands together. "I know. It is my fault. My fault entirely that this happened. I can never forgive myself for going to Las Flores, or allowing him to go."

Tarifa glanced at him in cool distaste. "I could have told you something like this would happen. I warned you to take no part in these foolish political disputes. But you would not listen. You are all alike. You smash everything you touch, then bring me the broken pieces to put back together again. I am sick to my guts of your heedlessness and incompetence!"

Her voice had risen and Nazario, pinioned by its force, stood helplessly in the doorway unable to move away.

He would gladly have given his life to be lying on the bed in place of Luis. Everything Tarifa was saying he had already said over and over to himself, like a morbid rosary. Luis was more to him than a brother. He had been his prop and mainstay all through childhood. The one person in whom he had confided all his boyish hopes and dreams, the one he had looked up to, believed in. If he should lose him now . . . The unfinished thought brought a dry sob to his throat. Not even when he had learned of Rufina's faithlessness had he felt so bereft.

"Go into the chapel and add your worthless prayers to Padre Cazon's," Tarifa said in disgust. "There is nothing else you can do to him—or for him."

"Please," Nazario murmured, "let me stay? I just want to be near him. I will not make a sound."

Tarifa shrugged and turned her back on him.

Penti said something under her breath as she leaned over

the bed. Tarifa saw that Luis had opened his eyes and his lips moved faintly.

"Penti?" The word was a wisp of sound.

"*Sí*. You must be quiet, Don Luis. Do not try to talk, but you can listen. Tarifa is here beside you to tell you what has happened. Don Nazario is here also."

At the mention of Nazario's name, recollections came swift and powerful into his eyes.

Tarifa sat down lightly on the edge of the bed. She told him without preamble, "You were shot by one of Alvarado's men at Las Flores." Then calmly but briefly, she explained what had happened afterward.

Luis did not speak. But when she told him about his arm his eyes widened until they seemed enormous in his head.

It was Nazario who cried out as if in mortal pain at the words, and he came to bury his face in the bedclothes.

"My fault," he sobbed. "It was all my fault, *hermano mío!*"

"Your tears and lamentations will not bring back his arm," Tarifa said coldly.

She had watched Luis' face smooth itself out carefully after he had absorbed the first shock of her words and she was proud of him. With only one arm, he was still more of a man than the rest of the Alvarjos.

"Go now," Penti said. "He must rest."

Nazario, still wiping his eyes with his handkerchief, rose to follow Tarifa reluctantly from the room.

When they were outside she said tartly, "Go home to your wife; perhaps you can find a shoulder to cry on there."

"But I cannot leave until I am sure Luis will be all right."

"You are a ranchero," Tarifa snapped. "Go home and attend to your chores. I will send you word how he is."

Padre Cazon, coming out of the chapel, overheard the sharp words and felt a pang of sympathy for Nazario. Tarifa in this mood could be relentlessly cruel.

In the days that followed, the family spoke in whispers as they walked down the *galleria* or crossed the patio on silent feet to the chapel.

Penti had done her work well. She had removed the
arm just below the shoulder where the ball had shattered
the bone so badly, and she had removed the lead pellet
from Luis' side where it had been stopped by a rib. The
severe loss of blood and danger of infection were the
main things to worry about, but fortunately Luis had always lived an active outdoor life, and he was young and
vigorous.

When Tarifa paused to see him on her way to or from
the pastures, he seemed quiet and thoughtful but not
morose.

"When do you start the spring roundup?" he asked her
one morning.

"In a few weeks, when Pablo is through repairing saddles. Nazario has already begun on Bolsa Coyotes."

"I won't be much of a *reatero*," he mused, "with only
one arm."

"A good *reatero* only needs one arm."

"You have an answer for everything, don't you? Do you
ever admit defeat, Tarifa?"

"I do not believe in defeat. Sometimes it is necessary to
achieve your purpose by seeking it in a different direction,
to raise or lower your sights, but to admit defeat, no, that
is never necessary. I do not believe that human beings were
meant to admit defeat. They were made to stand up to
adversity, to fight and win." Her voice grew quieter and
there was a look of proud command in her long eyes. "To
win it is only essential that you keep fighting for a long
enough time."

"I wish I could be like you," Luis said. He spoke with
genuine warmth and respect.

Tarifa was forced to lower her own eyes in embarrassment. It had been so long since she had been offered
friendship and warmth that she felt at a loss to cope with
it. She got to her feet and made a great show of studying
the landscape. The window, on the upper floor of the hacienda, commanded a view of the undulating pastureland
stretching like an olive-hued oak-dotted carpet toward the
sea.

"Would you like to know the outcome of the meetings
at Las Flores?" she asked.

"Yes. What was accomplished?"

"What is always accomplished by these silly little men, with their fanfare and bluster and flowery oratory? Nothing. Alvarado and Carillo disputed each other's title, but signed an agreement to meet at San Fernando. Carillo flourished his paper from Mexico which made him governor, but it turned out it was merely a paper signed by the Minister of the Interior, Pena y Pena, and not by the President himself, and so far no official word has come confirming it.

"The government met in Los Angeles and accused Don Carlos of blunders and advised that he side with the north until official word arrived. Pio Pico and the others would not accept this, and now Alvarado has put them all under arrest and carried them to Santa Barbara."

Luis smiled. "You were right. They are like children playing at charades."

"Dangerous charades," Tarifa said, turning to face him. "While they squabble like dogs over who has the right to the bone, some watchful cur will steal it from behind their backs. They would do well to join in making the government as unified and strong as possible. If they had any sense they would return to their ranchos and herds before they also are taken from them."

When she had left him, Luis shut his eyes against the pain in his side and the fever he could feel mounting in him. It would be ironic if he died, now that he knew with certainty what he wanted to do. To serve both Loma de Oro and California.

He wanted to go into politics.

How Tarifa would laugh at that.

In the warm, scented days of spring that followed, Luis lay more dead than alive while Penti, Candelaria, and Tía Isabella hovered over him.

Tarifa would not allow him to be bled as Tía Isabella suggested.

"He has lost too much blood as it is," she said.

"But it will help to bring down the fever."

"You will not take anymore blood from him!"

Santos suggested that they might try the roots his mother had taught him to prepare as a boy. When Tarifa gave her consent he brought a long yellowish root to Luis' room, and made him chew on one piece of it, then swallow the juice, while he boiled the rest and bathed his body in the liquid.

The women were amazed at the results. The fever slowly abated, leaving Luis as sunken-eyed and thin as a death's head, but lucid and free from pain.

While Isabella and Candelaria rushed to the chapel to make a prayer of thanksgiving for his recovery, Tarifa silently slipped her amulet from under his pillow, where she had put it when the fever first came upon him.

The excitement of the spring roundup and the attendant stripping and dressing down of the hides was over before Luis could sit in a chair by his window and gaze down at the green countryside.

He wondered if he would ever ride again over the vast acres of Loma de Oro. Tarifa had not laughed when he told her of his determination to go into politics.

"Not like these others," he said. "I want to study the basic points of politics. I've never been much of a scholar, but perhaps with Padre Cazon's help, I could learn? I think it's time some Californians learned how to govern themselves."

"I agree," said Tarifa. She smiled at him and added, "And you will not gallop off chasing rainbows of glory like these others?"

She brought him all the books she could find in the house that had to do with the subject, which were painfully few, but Padre Cazon happily augmented the little library with volumes from the Mission. And he stopped in whenever he was passing to discuss their contents with Luis.

Sometimes Tarifa perched on the *galleria* railing to listen to them talk. She herself had no interest in politics, but she was pleased to see Luis take an interest in something again. He was still pale and weak and far too thin, but there was a hard core of intense determination in him now that he had never had before.

Rufina sat in the patio in a pool of warm sunlight while her children played around her. Under the kerchief she wore waking and sleeping, her hair was beginning to grow longer. She was expecting a child. She prayed that this would be the son she should have given Nazario when she had borne Judah's child.

In her long hours of silence and isolation she had grown to know herself very well, and she was constantly amazed at the depths to which the human spirit could sink and still survive.

For the first time she had found real solace in prayer, and the sure knowledge that, no matter how great her suffering, she did not stand unheard and alone in the world. Due to her own unhappiness she could feel a new sympathy for the trials of others.

The servants were the first to note the change in her. She no longer ordered them about in a voice of haughty, cold command. She went to the kitchen now to supervise the cooking, and often she labored along with a servant at some household task. She praised and commended where compliments were due, and when any of them were ill she went to the servants' quarters to tend them.

The household took on an air of order and serenity that it had never known before. Rufina, with the best seamstresses among the Indian girls, made new drapes for the *sala* and dining-room windows and crocheted doilies for the arms and backs of the furniture. She kept the house filled with flowers which the children helped her pick each morning, and there was a new affectionate warmth and gaiety between them.

When she dined alone with Nazario, he never spoke and she kept her eyes on her plate. But when his brothers were present she answered them courteously in a quiet voice. She had never spoken to Nazario since that first night after her return from San Diego, except to tell him about the child. He had nodded curtly and walked out the *sala* door to mount Hidalgo without a backward glance.

Rufina had heard through the servants of Luis' injury. One of them secretly carried a letter which she had written to her father, and gave it to the captain of the first ship sailing for Santa Barbara. In it, Rufina had asked Don Carlos to forward any books he had on law or government to Luis at Loma de Oro.

She was touched and surprised a month later when Luis wrote her a note of thanks, sending it to her by Santos.

She asked the old mayordomo into the patio and insisted that he drink a glass of wine. It might not be the proper thing to do, she thought, but at least it was kind and she found herself thinking a great deal of kindness these days. Besides, her loneliness was like a live thing within her breast, filling her every waking moment.

"How is Don Luis now?" she asked.

"He is much improved, Dona Rufina, since the fever left him."

"I am very glad. Are the others well at Loma de Oro?"

"Quite well, thank you, Dona Rufina."

The old Indian studied her drawn face, more arresting now in its controlled dignity than it had been before, and he wondered what it was she wanted of him. He had heard rumors, of course, that all was not well at Bolsa Coyotes since Rufina's return to her husband. That Nazario never spoke to her, yet was seen coming from the bedroom they had once shared each dawn. It was sad to see two young people living in such a world of sorrow and scorn that they had ceased to exist for each other.

"Is there anything else, Dona Rufina?" he asked as he rose to go.

"No—thank you, Santos. I mustn't keep you. I know you have much to do."

He bowed politely and as low as his saddle-stiff knees would permit and turned toward the kitchen, sombrero in hand, to go out through the servants' wing.

Suddenly Rufina burst into tears. When he turned in astonishment, she was rocking back and forth in her chair as if in agony, her hands covering her face.

"Dona Rufina! What is the matter? What have I done?"

He stood awkwardly beside her chair, not knowing what else to do or say.

At last, to his great relief, her sobs lessened and she wiped her cheeks and swollen eyelids with a handkerchief.

"I'm sorry, Santos. It's just that I am so lonely for someone to talk to. It seems so long since I have spoken to anyone except the servants. You must forgive me."

He sat down on the edge of a chair and regarded her gravely. He knew the great sin she had committed and he could see that the guilt of it would never leave her in peace. Anymore than his own guilt at having killed Bruno

Cacho with Don Ygnacio would leave his soul. The punishment of his own conscience.

"It is wrong that you should suffer like this," he said. "How can I help you, señora?"

"Talk to me," she whispered, "just talk."

He began haltingly, telling her the most mundane and minute news about the family and Loma de Oro, recalling for her bits of gossip Candelaria had told him and she seemed to drink it in as a thirsty flower absorbs rain.

When he was finished and stood up to go she was smiling at him radiantly, a new glow of color in her cheeks and a sparkle in her brown eyes.

"Thank you, Santos, thank you! Will you come and speak to me again sometime?"

"If you wish it, Dona Rufina."

She walked with him out to the kitchen and watched him mount Marca. When he turned northeast toward Loma de Oro and glanced back, she was still standing in the open doorway of the kitchen watching him.

"She is sad, that little one," he told Marca. "And even though she is a sinner like you and me, *amigo,* it is not right for the young to live in sadness. Unhappiness overtakes us all in time, but youth should be spared the chill of its coming so soon."

CHAPTER 26

On a cold, sparkling September morning, Luis rode Amarillo into Los Angeles to call upon his old friend Don Tiburcio Novàto. Since his recovery from his injury, Luis had been in a fever to learn all he could about jurisprudence and the law, as a stepping-stone to his next dream, a political career. It was Zenobio who had reminded him of Don Tiburcio, who had served with Don Ygnacio and himself in the same company at San Diego in the old days.

Don Tiburcio was a Catalán who had once studied law before entering the military service, and he was reported to be practicing in a small way now that he was retired and living alone in his tiny house on the outskirts of Los Angeles.

Novato was delighted to welcome the son of his old companion into his modest home to read law with him.

"Come whenever you like," he told Luis, his twinkling gray eyes gazing out like a porcupine's from under peaked white brows. He was a very old man, much older than Zenobio, short and fat, clinging to the knee breeches and white stockings of his own era, as did Don Carlos Corlona, with his hair tied in a queue by a variety of silk ribbons. Around his neck he always wore a large silken scarf delicately trimmed with lace, the folds cascading over his chest.

As he rode through the pueblo today, Luis had noted with distaste that the place seemed more crowded and squalid than usual, with a teamster's long line of bellied mules and several wagons drawn up in the plaza outside a wine shop. Indians in every stage of drunkenness or despair hovered over the scene like a blight, and his heart contracted when he recognized an old woman who had once worked in his mother's kitchen, now toothless and in rags, holding up one clawlike hand to beg alms from the uncaring passersby.

Santa Maria! he thought. What have we done to these poor savages? If the sins of the fathers are visited upon the sons, what have we to answer for now?

He reined in Amarillo and spoke a few kind words to her in Tamancus, before pressing a coin into her palm.

"Don Luis," she murmured wonderingly as if he belonged on another planet, not here in her chaotic, befuddled present existence. *"Gracias, gracias."*

"Por nada, Teresa."

"Vaya con Dios, Don Luis."

In a moment he was out of her sight and out of her thoughts as well, he imagined.

Always conspicuous, Luis noted that his palomino stallion now drew envious stares from the American and halfbreed New Mexican horse traders who lounged against the walls of the buildings smoking their evil-smelling pipes.

One black-bearded giant, bolder than the rest, called out in a jeering voice, "How much you take for the yaller hoss, sonny?"

Luis glanced at him coldly, looking like a young rajah in his silver-trimmed suit of dark blue velvet on his richly caparisoned horse. He might dislike the man on sight but he had been raised to answer anyone who addressed him with courtesy.

"Un momento, señor."

He did not understand English. Carefully, he looked about for a countryman who might understand both English and Spanish. But the Californians had learned not to frequent this part of town where the American teamsters and horse traders held sway.

"You deaf?" the horse trader bellowed, moving belligerently into the street with his grimy thumbs hooked into his belt near a brace of pistols. "I asked what ya wanted fer that nag!"

Luis, completely ignorant of what the man was saying, was still searching the crowd for an interpreter. Others had surrounded the pair until there was only a small space in the center of the dusty street.

The Californian was completely taken by surprise when a pair of powerful arms lifted him bodily from the horse's back and deposited him on the ground with a jolt.

"Now we'll talk, señor," said the stranger. "Me, I'm the friendly sort. Name's Alf Grimes, of St. Looie. Been hoss tradin' outa New Mexico this past year. I like the looks of your stallion there. I'll pay a fair price or trade you another nag or two for him. What say?"

Luis stood stiffly erect in dignified silence, his arm over Amarillo's rump and his hand resting lightly on the new coiled blacksnake whip Pablo had just made for him. Because the loss of his arm had made his balance slightly awkward, he had asked the saddlemaker to weight this whip with a lead handle. Ever since he had been able to be up and about, he had practiced with it daily and with his *reata,* until he had satisfied both himself and Santos that he had mastered their use again.

Grimes spat into the dust. "Dammit, you tryin' to high-hat me, you spik bastard?"

The tone, if not the words, were unmistakable to Luis.

His face grew white and his dark eyes glazed with anger. He moved back a step from Grimes nearer his horse, and the American laughed.

"I scared him, boys, right outa them fancy pants he's wearin'. Don't aim to let him run far, though. Reckon I'll knock them fancy duds right off his back, startin' with that there sombrero."

As he spoke, Grimes pulled a gun from his waistband and leveled it at Luis' head.

At the same instant, Luis' hand came away from the saddle trailing a dark ribbon, like a writhing asp. It cracked over the heads of the startled onlookers, and plucked the pistol from Grimes' fist as neatly as if a knife had done it.

Grimes cursed in surprise and pain, then clawed at the second gun in his belt. It went off a fraction of a second before the whip lashed around his throat, burying itself in the thick flesh of his bull-like neck.

Luis had felt the shot graze his temple, knocking him temporarily off-center, but he had recovered quickly. He had every intention of choking his opponent to death. It would be very simple, he thought savagely, to drag him down the street by the neck behind Amarillo until he was dead.

A black madness had come over Luis, making him oblivious to everyone and everything, save the man at the end of his whip, clawing with popping eyes and strangling breath at the ever-tightening rawhide.

He did not know when he first became aware of the hand resting lightly on his arm, or of the quiet voice addressing him in Spanish.

"I know he deserves killing, señor. I saw the whole thing. But do you think this is the best way?"

He glanced up. A girl was standing beside him. Her eyes were as level and blue-gray as his sister Dolores' had been. She had blonde hair with reddish lights in it, like winter wheat in the sunset, plaited and tied in braids down her back. She was wearing buckskin trousers and a man's shirt like the American traders wore, and there was a bridge of freckles over her short nose and across her pale forehead.

He had never seen an American woman before, and the very novelty of her appearance held him speechless.

"Do you have an alcalde, señor, or someone in authority to whom you can take this man? You must make a report"—she nodded toward the struggling Grimes—"then let the authorities see that he is jailed and punished. That is the proper thing to do. Can you understand me, señor?"

He managed to nod his head. She was right, of course. He must take the man to the alcalde and see him put safely in the stocks, if nothing more. He undid his *reata*, and with the girl's help, bound Grimes with it and loosened the whip from the trader's swollen throat. Grimes stood gulping air like a bullfrog, while Luis mounted Amarillo and took a dally with his *reata* about the wide horn. He put spurs to the stallion, and led his prisoner at a brisk walk down the middle of the dusty, rutted street to the office of the alcalde, as if he had been leading a winded balky grizzly from the sierras.

The alcalde was nervous about detaining an Americano, but neither could he afford to offend one of the wealthy and powerful Alvarjos. In a stupor of incredulity, Grimes felt his legs being fitted into the heavy oak stocks, his captor watching dispassionately as the lock was snapped in place.

Afterward, Luis looked about the square for the American girl to thank her for her help, but she was nowhere in sight and his lack of English prevented him from asking her whereabouts from the staring Americano traders. They had not interfered on behalf of their countryman, but it was plain that they did not like what Luis had done.

Don Tiburcio's patio was a tiny square of greenery and fragrant blossoms, made cool and shady by a large pepper tree in the center, under which he now sat entertaining his guests. There were wine decanters, glasses, and a huge basket of fresh fruit on a table under the tree. Tiburcio was passing a cedarwood chest of his best cigars to a tall, large-boned American, who appeared to be somewhere in his fifties. His iron gray hair was neatly trimmed as was his military moustache and he was freshly shaven. Across from the two men, on a small straight reed-bottomed chair, sat the girl Luis had met in the plaza.

"Luis!" cried Tiburcio delightedly.

"Señorita, señor, may I have the pleasure of presenting to you Don Luis Alvarjo, the son of my very old friend and *compadre,* the late Don Ygnacio, owner of Rancho Loma de Oro."

"Luis, may I present the Señorita Elena Havelock, and her Uncle Don Patricio, of Santa Fe. They are here to purchase land for their herd, which is being driven overland from the southern *frontera.*"

"I believe I once met your father in Loreto, when I was a young man," said Havelock. Like his niece, Luis noted, he spoke excellent Spanish.

"My father was in Loreto before his marriage," Luis said politely. "I regret that he is unable to greet an old friend upon his arrival in California, señor." He wished that the girl Elena would not stare at him so boldly.

"Did you arrange to have the man jailed?" she asked him a moment later, then in answer to the questions of the older men went on to explain the story of Luis' clash with Grimes in the plaza.

Havelock glanced sharply at his niece. "But you could have acted as interpreter and stopped the whole thing."

A dimple appeared in Elena's cheek as she smiled back at Luis. "I knew my words would only prolong things, not prevent them, Uncle Patrick. Grimes is a natural bully. He was spoiling for a fight. Besides, I believed that Don Luis could take care of himself and I was right."

Luis flushed and lowered his eyes. He could not get used to the lightness of her skin. His mother and sister Dolores had been fair, but their complexions had had nothing like the milk-whiteness of this señorita's. He wished that, like the other young girls he knew, she would simper or play the coquette. It was unsettling to have her stare back at him in that level, quizzical manner that left him feeling both helpless and confused, like a calf at the branding fire.

"Loma de Oro is the finest rancho in California," Don Tiburcio was saying, "at least it is the finest in the southern district, Don Patricio."

"I would very much like to see it," Havelock replied.

Confronted by such a request, in the home of a friend, Luis could do nothing less than issue an invitation to Señor Havelock and his niece to visit Loma do Oro.

"Oh, Uncle Patrick, let's go tomorrow," cried Ellen Havelock impulsively.

Luis and even Tiburcio were taken by surprise at the bold suddenness of her acceptance. It was all very well to issue a cordial invitation to call, but one had the right to expect a certain decorous delay before being called upon to entertain the recipients.

"Why not?" said Havelock with the same bold abruptness of his unusual niece. "We have our own horses. You must tell us how to get there, Don Luis."

Luis managed to stammer out the directions, adding a word of pleasure at the honor of enjoying their company so soon in his father's house.

When they had enjoyed Don Tiburcio's excellent Manzanilla, Luis arose to go. The Havelocks, he had learned, were staying the night with Tiburcio.

As they were parting, Havelock asked Luis, "Is there any chance that your family might sell me some pasture for grazing, Don Luis?"

"I do not know, señor. You would have to discuss the matter with my stepmother, Dona Tarifa."

"I understand. I shall do so at my first opportunity."

When Tiburcio saw him to the door, Luis whispered, "Who are these Americanos, Don Tiburcio?"

"Don Patricio and his brother ran a trading post at Santa Fe. But the younger one, Juan, and his wife died in a cholera epidemic some years ago and Don Patricio was left to raise his small niece. He spent his youth as a trader in Sonora and Mazatlan, and to my knowledge he has always been a most honorable and trustworthy man."

"The Señorita, I do not like her bold ways," Luis said darkly.

The old man laughed. "That is because you are too young to appreciate such a one, *muchacho*. For myself, I find her charming. She is a young lady of spirit and decision. And I think she has an eye for your handsome face, *niño*?"

Luis gave him a black look as he stepped out of the house and swung gracefully into the saddle. Behind him he could still hear Tiburcio laughing. Truly the old fool was losing all his senses!

❖　❖　❖

In the end, Luis did not have to explain to Tarifa his meeting with the Havelocks, or the fact that they would soon arrive at Loma de Oro at his invitation.

Nazario's first son was born that night, two months prematurely. He was to be named Ygnacio Nazario, in honor of his dead grandfather and his father. All the Alvarjo women, including Tarifa, left the hacienda at dawn to visit the newcomer and see for themselves that this time the infant was indeed an Alvarjo. Luis found himself quite alone in the hacienda after his brothers had ridden off to see to the work of the rancho.

He hoped that the Havelocks would forget to come. If they did arrive, he was determined to have their visit over before Tarifa returned to the rancho. They arrived just before luncheon, and he went to the veranda to greet them. He had to admit with a grudging admiration that they rode their bay mounts well. And Ellen Havelock did not look quite so strange today, wearing a full-sleeved cotton blouse softly open at the throat, and a divided skirt. Her red-gold braids were wrapped around her small neat head like a glowing crown.

Luis politely showed them over the rancho and was both pleased and surprised when they displayed such flattering and intelligent interest in it.

"I am most anxious to speak with Dona Tarifa," Havelock told Luis as they left the dining room following the noon meal.

Luis explained why she was at Bolsa Coyotes and not likely to return for several days.

"Then we must come back another time, Uncle," said Ellen quickly. "That is if Don Luis will invite us?"

"Our house is yours, señorita, señor, at any time that you choose to visit it," Luis replied with a courtly bow. As an Alvarjo, it was impossible for him to say anything else, but his lips were stiff against his teeth as he smiled.

Francisco came in at that moment and, after being introduced to the Havelocks, invited Don Patricio into the study for a glass of *aguardiente* and a discussion of the horse market in Santa Fe.

Luis felt panic rising in him. It was unthinkable to be left alone with an unchaperoned girl as young as Elena Havelock. He could not suggest she come into the study to drink with the men. Damn Francisco and his thoughtless, careless ways!

"Don Luis?" She was staring at him in that level, disturbing way again, showing a dimple in one cheek.

"Yes, señorita?"

"Would you show me those marvelous palominos again?"

"Of course." He was relieved. Anything was better than sitting here in the *sala* alone with her.

"Someday," Ellen said, a few minutes later, as they stood looking at the palominos, "I will raise fine like horses like yours."

His brows rose. "A señorita like you? You want no hacienda—no family of your own?"

Then, to change the subject, he said, "I have a young mare my father gave me, I call her Rapaza. That one in the far corner. If you would accept her as a gift, I would be most pleased."

"I couldn't accept a gift like that, Don Luis." Ellen Havelock said, "These exquisite animals must be worth a small fortune."

"We have many, señorita." Luis replied gallantly, although he was already regretting his generous offer. He was fond of Rapaza. But he added firmly, "It would please me if you would accept the mare, since you are kind enough to admire our horses."

"Admire!" She stepped down from the fence and stood beside him. "They are perfection itself. But I couldn't accept one as a gift."

"It is nothing in California to give a fine horse as a gift, señorita."

"But—such a horse? You are most kind, Don Luis, but it is impossible for me to accept." She thought wildly, why did I say that, when I want the mare more than anything else on the face of the earth, not just because she is one of these magnificent palominos, but because she is his. And she wondered in detached amazement what madness had come over her that she could carry on a polite conversation with him while thinking these wild thoughts.

She felt like a young maiden alone with a man for the first time in her life, which was absurd, for she was more accustomed to male companionship than feminine. She had grown up with the rough-and-tumble, harum-scarum boys of the frontier, and she had never been at a loss to give them as good as they sent. It was true that they had been of an entirely different type from Luis Alvarjo. It was Luis' kindness and gentleness and his unmistakable personal integrity that drew her to him, not just his dark good looks.

Luis was troubled. Now that he had made the offer of a gift, he could not permit his guest to depart without accepting it. A new note of firmness came into his voice.

"Señorita Elena, I do not wish to seem insistent, but for my own sake you must take the mare."

Ellen raised her fair brows. "For your sake?"

He plunged on, "I mean, señorita, that it would dishonor my household if you should refuse to accept a gift from Loma de Oro."

"That is a most charming way of making certain I accept something that I have no right to take, Don Luis."

His eyes brightened. "Then you will accept Rapaza?"

She studied him for a moment, wondering if she was doing the right thing. "If it is the only thing that will please you and save you from dishonor, Don Luis, how can I refuse?"

Suddenly he was smiling back at her, the flash of white teeth transforming his whole appearance, and she realized that it was the first time she had seen joy on his face since they met. It was a face that had been meant for joy, too, she thought. There was a natural warmth and gaiety in the dark eyes, but there was a reserve also, as if they were wary of showing pleasure or happiness. Could it be just the loss of an arm, or was there some deeper reason for his brooding?

"I really couldn't refuse the horse, Uncle Patrick," Ellen said as they rode across the gently curving hills that pastured herds of sleek horses and cattle.

"We will make some proper excuse for refusing it when the time comes," said Havelock easily. Ellen had always been an impulsive girl, but she had taken care never to show her naked feelings for a man until now. Havelock was shocked and displeased at the frank admiration in her eyes when she looked at Luis Alvarjo. Granted the fellow was handsome and courtly; certainly his stepmother appeared wealthy and landed, but he was still a Spaniard and a Catholic, and the Protestant New Englander in Havelock rebelled at the thought of Luis Alvarjo as a suitor for his niece. He went on, avoiding her eyes. "One of the traders who came through Santa Fe last year told me that he had collected fifty horses, well-broken prime mounts, as gifts from his California hosts as he passed through. But it is out of the question, of course, for you to accept Don Luis' gift."

She turned in the saddle to face him, "They are wonderful people, aren't they, Uncle? So warm-hearted and gentle and gay—and so marvelous-looking? Did you ever see such hair and eyes and teeth?"

"You seem to have been very impressed, my dear," Havelock said shortly.

Ellen flushed. Had her admiration really been so obvious? She must have embarrassed Luis and all of them.

"Don Luis is different from anyone I've ever met before," she said in quick defense.

On the following Monday, Tarifa was seated in the study writing a letter to Bart Kinkaid. The day had turned dark before noon, and now there was a flurry of raindrops at the windows and on the tiled roof of the hacienda. The mustiness and dampness that filled the house had forced Tarifa to order all the fireplaces and braziers in the adobe lighted and the outer shutters closed.

She had discovered a certain emotional release in writing to Bart Kinkaid, even if his responses were long in coming. When he was not with her, she found that she could lay bare every thought in her mind or heart on paper. She wrote him candidly about Pito Larios, telling him at great length how much she missed the bandit, but adding that she did not regret her decision not to follow him and leave Loma de Oro, no matter what Penti said. She told him also of Nazario's new son; she hoped, as the first legitimate Alvarjo grandson, he would take after Don Ygnacio.

She was interrupted by a tap at the closed door. It was Antonio, looking slightly rumpled from the siesta he had been taking in the *sala* following luncheon. Because of the

threatening storm, Tarifa had called off the regular outdoor chores, and put most of the men to helping Pablo
cut and stretch the strips of rawhide to be used in the
next roundup for *reatas,* reins, and stirrup lacings.

"An Americano, Don Patricio Havelock, and his niece
have called to see you," Antonio said uneasily. "He is
a trader and ranchero from Santa Fe, a friend of Don
Tiburcio Novato's. They were here once before, the day
you went to see Nazario's son."

"Why do they call upon me? Were they friends of your
father's?"

"It is possible. I believe Señor Havelock wants to buy
land here to pasture his cattle."

Tarifa rose and closed her writing folio over the unfinished letter. She was wearing a severely cut gown of
plain black bombazine, high at the neck, and relieved only
by a small pearl brooch at the throat. Her hair was pulled
back smoothly under a tortoiseshell comb and she covered
it now with the short lace mantilla that had been draped
about her shoulders. She looked surprisingly like a well-
born Castilian woman.

She walked briskly from the study, down the rain-spat-
tered veranda, and entered the *sala.*

Patrick Havelock stood with his hands behind his back
in front of the small fire. His niece, with the odd white
skin and bold blue eyes, was sitting upright on the sofa in
her damp riding costume.

Tarifa did not bother to give them the conventional
courtly welcome of the Californian *gente de razón.* Antonio had not followed her into the *sala,* and since it was
the siesta hour of a cold rainy afternoon, no one else was
likely to overhear their words. She said simply:

"I am Dona Tarifa Alvarjo. My stepson Antonio said
that you asked to see me?"

Havelock controlled his surprise at her youth, but he
could not dismiss as easily the disturbing quality in her
bearing.

"Yes, señora," he said, "I am sorry we've arrived at
this awkward hour. The storm held us up."

Ellen Havelock added, "Don Luis invited us."

Tarifa frowned at the girl. She recalled now that Luis
had been in Los Angeles while she and the other women

had gone to Bolsa Coyotes to see Nazario's new son. But Luis would never invite Americanos to his house, knowing how his father had felt about such people. Or would he? Because she was curious now about the Havelocks, she decided to play the role of hostess.

"Please sit down, Don Patricio," she invited, taking a chair herself directly across from the girl. Havelock sat down beside Ellen on the sofa, and began, in the straight-forward tactless way of Americans, to state his business immediately.

"Señora, I have a herd of cattle due to arrive here in a short time, and it is my desire to settle in California and raise them for market."

"There is no market here except for the hides, tallow, and horns, Don Patricio," Tarifa said quietly.

"I am aware of that, and it would take a large operation such as your splendid Rancho Loma de Oro to make such a market profitable. But it is my belief that some of the beef can be marketed south across the border, and other meat in the form of jerky can be sold to the northern trading posts as well as the ships.

"It would be more convenient for me, if I could establish myself in this locality. Don Tiburcio has already told me—and indeed your stepson Don Luis has shown me—that you have the largest and most desirable rancho around here."

Tarifa raised her brows. So Luis had shown them Loma de Oro without telling her or asking her permission. A dark suspicion crossed her mind, but she swept it aside as preposterous. It was impossible that this white-skinned creature sitting so boldly upright on the sofa could have addled Luis' wits. No, Luis had never cared much for female companionship, not even for the pretty, fawning girls of his own acquaintance, and Tarifa was convinced that he was still a virgin. There must be some other explanation for all this.

"I am gratified that you like my rancho, señor," she told Havelock politely.

The American continued with difficulty, for her polite noncommittal replies left him with no proper opening. "I have been wondering, Dona Tarifa, with so much land at your disposal, if you would consider selling me a portion of it? I am prepared to pay you whatever you ask for it, in gold."

Tarifa stared at him without comment, until he continued lamely, "Surely a few hundred acres of land would not be missed from such a vast rancho, señora, and you could no doubt use the gold? I understand that many Californian rancheros are financially embarrassed these days?"

He realized that he had made a mistake the moment the words were out of his mouth.

"Here on Loma de Oro, we are not in need of gold," Tarifa said in a voice like flint.

"I did not mean—"

"Señor Havelock, Loma de Oro was left to me as a trust by my husband. It was his wish that his children, coming of age, should settle here on their various portions and run the rancho as a single unit."

"A most commendable idea, señora," said Havelock, smoothing his moustache, "but one that does not always work out. Even relatives do not always see eye to eye."

"The Alvarjos will do as their father wished!"

Havelock recognized the iron-clad determination in her words, and he did not envy the Alvarjos or any other luckless individual who crossed wills with her. Too late, he saw his mistake in trying to bargain with her. But he had had no warning. She was something beyond his ken, a woman of inimical intransigence. A woman with the face and figure of a Fury and the flashing, unwinking eyes of a sorceress.

"Don Luis."

Ellen's voice tossed the two words across the room like a caress, in spite of her effort to disguise the joy in her tone.

Luis, who had just come in from the saddle shop, stood transfixed in the doorway, his mouth slightly agape in his surprise.

Ellen had been startled at Tarifa's appearance. She even felt a flick of jealousy for the woman who could only be a few years older than she was herself—certainly still young enough to attract Luis? Tarifa was only his stepmother, and she was a widow. Stranger things than an alliance between stepmother and stepson had happened. Then, at the sight of Luis standing in the doorway, she had abandoned all her unwholesome thoughts. Just the sight of his face had the power to banish every other thought from her mind. She was horrified to hear herself calling out his name with the unmistakable girlish abandon. It was ridiculous. She had sounded sixteen.

"Luis, please come in." It was Tarifa's voice, as clear and hard as a diamond. "These are some friends of your, I believe?"

Luis found his wits and his tongue at the same time.

"Sí. I had the pleasure of making their acquaintance at Don Tiburcio's recently." He greeted each of the Havelocks with a low, courtly bow.

"They have been telling me how much they enjoyed their visit to Loma de Oro," Tarifa went on relentlessly.

A bright color had risen in Ellen's cheeks. She could have killed Dona Tarifa Alvarjo. Luis looked like a child caught in a truant act.

"It was very kind of Don Luis to invite us to the rancho," she said quickly, "when Uncle Patrick was so anxious to speak to you about buying land, Dona Tarifa." Instantly she knew that she had only made it worse for Luis by defending him.

Tarifa's eyes narrowed. "You knew that the Havelocks wanted to buy land and you suggested that they speak to me, Luis?"

"No—I did not suggest it. When they asked about land I explained that they would have to take the matter up with you."

"Then you are to blame for causing these people to make not one, but two futile trips here. You knew that under the terms of your father's will; I could not sell or divide the land."

"I was not sure," he said unhappily, his eyes never leaving Tarifa's face.

He might be a pet dog, thought Ellen angrily, standing meekly by for a whipping even though he has no knowledge of why he has earned it. The woman was a demon. No wonder Luis' face wore such a solemn, perpetually sad expression.

Tarifa had not missed the tone of Ellen's voice when she spoke Luis' name, or the expression in her eyes when they rested on his face. The pale hussy, she was besotted with Luis! And Tarifa sensed that, unlike the docile Californian girls, she would not be so easily controlled. Tarifa had never cared for other women, she found little in them to admire, and she despised this one more than any other she had ever met. Instinctively, she always sought out any weakness in an enemy, and it was poignantly clear that Ellen Havelock's most vulnerable spot was her infatuation for Luis.

Tarifa would not admit to herself that it could be anything more than infatuation. She would not allow herself to face the possibility that such a woman could love Luis, even in her mind. Luis belonged to Loma de Oro. He was part of the legacy Ygnacio had left her, and if he must have a wife he would marry a California girl, as Nazario had done, and settle down with her here on the rancho. But she was determined that he would not fall into the clutches of this American woman.

There was more to her reasoning than mere dislike for Ellen Havelock, though she would not have recognized or admitted the pang of jealousy in her own breast. Since his accident and the loss of his arm, she had come to believe that Luis would never marry, and in their newfound closeness and understanding she had hoped that he would remain beside her at Loma de Oro.

The only bright spot in her present disillusionment was the realization that Luis seemed to be not in the slightest aware of Ellen's feelings toward him.

"You must understand, Tarifa," he was saying more firmly, "I only acted as my father would have done if he had been alive."

Tarifa gave him a brief smile, like a basking anaconda. She had decided to discuss the matter with him later in private, away from the prying eyes of the Havelocks, whom she had determined to get rid of as quickly as possible. There was no telling when other members of the family might drift in and prolong the leave-taking of her unwelcome guests.

"I regret that you and your niece have been inconvenienced by these long and profitless trips to Loma de Oro, Señor Havelock," she told the American politely.

Havelock answered grimly, but with the same façade of politeness, "It was a delight to ride over your great rancho, Dona Tarifa." He realized now that it was hopeless, but he meant to play out the game with her for his own satisfaction.

"No doubt you and your niece will find land for sale elsewhere. But I know of none available in this district, señor."

Havelock had not meant to pursue the subject with her, but the woman's caustic superiority enraged him. His voice took on a tiger-purr softness, "That is odd, señora. Only yesterday I learned that some of the Mission lands would soon be for sale."

Tarifa's face went white.

Luis blurted out, "Surely, señor, you would not commit the sacrilege of taking Church lands?"

"Not take, my boy," said Havelock easily. "Buy, with good solid gold."

Luis' chin came up. "These men who talk of selling Mission land, they are miscreants, renegades!"

"I'm sure that Uncle Patrick doesn't understand all the circumstances," Ellen said swiftly. She had seen the disbelief and horror on Luis' face.

"Get out of this house!" cried Tarifa in the high keening Gypsy voice that every *gitano* and *gorgio* in Spain knew meant trouble. *"Premita Undebé!* Get out! You are the kind of people who come to suck the blood of California and pay for its pulsing life with dead gold! We want no part of you here!"

Roused by the words shouted in spitting Romany, Penti had come to the door. She stood watching with her small lizard-black eyes riveted to the strangers, her arms folded across her breast.

"What is the trouble, *miri pen?*" she asked in Romany.

"Go away," Tarifa snapped. "I can handle this."

Penti moved from the threshold and Luis said in a tight voice, "This is a disgraceful thing you do in my father's house, Tarifa. These people are our guests while they are under our roof, no matter what you may think of them otherwise. No Alvarjo has ever spoken to a guest in this manner, and I cannot permit it!" He turned swiftly to the Havelocks and said, "I apologize for what has happened here, señorita, Don Patricio."

Ellen felt a glow of pride as she watched his straight back and determined chin.

"You will not permit!" Tarifa roared. She was standing

in the center of the room. "This is my house now. I am
the mistress of Loma de Oro. I shall say who goes and
comes here, and I shall speak any way I please to whom-
ever is present; I repeat, Señor Havelock, you will leave
my house!"

Havelock watched her coldly with a mixture of anger
and speculation. She had been furious at his mention of
the Mission lands, but he had also recognized her fear of
the truth of his words. There was hope yet of buying land
if he played his cards right. At first he had thought it
but a rumor; now he knew that it had been more than
that. And perhaps this spectacle had served to bring Ellen
to her senses over the charm of the Alvarjos.

He bowed to Tarifa stiffly and nodded his head to Ellen. She started to follow her uncle and then turned back,
speaking directly to Luis, whose face was convulsed with
anger and humiliation.

"Please don't think that we judge you and your family
by your stepmother, Don Luis. We appreciate all that you
have tried to do for us. When we are settled I hope that
you will call upon us?"

He could only give her a quick miserable glance before
he lowered his eyes and bowed.

Tarifa turned on Luis when the Havelocks had ridden
off, demanding, "Why did you sneak such people in here
behind my back?"

Luis drew himself up proudly. "I had no need to sneak
them in. This is still my home, the house my father built.
When they asked to see Loma de Oro, I had no alternative but to invite them."

Tarifa was faintly mollified. "You should have had them
wait until I was at home, and you should have told me."

"I did not want you to know about them because I
knew something like this would happen," he said simply.
He felt a great weariness coming over him. He was not
really strong yet, and with his weariness some of his anger
and humiliation evaporated. He found to his astonishment that he was relieved to be rid of the Havelocks by
whatever methods involved. Tarifa could anger him to his
soul, but he understood her better now, and he told himself she had not been enraged so much at the Havelocks
and himself as she had been at Havelock's unhappy mention of the Mission lands.

"Sit down," said Tarifa crossly. "Surely you can see that these people do not belong on Loma de Oro, or in California for that matter?"

Luis sank down in a chair and put his head back wearily. "I only know that it is wrong to be impolite to them in our own home."

"I am not concerned with such things," Tarifa snapped. "If a jackal enters your cave you throw him out. This—señorita, what have you had to do with her?"

Luis opened his eyes, which had fallen closed. "Nothing. She came with her father and rode with us over the rancho."

"And you like her?"

"I haven't thought of her one way or another," he lied, feeling her eyes sharp and hot on his face. "But now that you mention it—no, I don't much care for her forward ways. Why?"

Tarifa decided to refrain from mentioning how she had seen the girl look at him. If he was ignorant of Ellen Havelock's infatuation for him, so much the better. Tarifa felt suddenly pleased. Luis was hers again.

She went to stand behind his chair and began to stroke his forehead with her strong fingertips. She felt him stiffen under her touch and then relax as the gentle rhythm soothed the pounding ache in his head.

"I was afraid you might be attracted to this Elena Havelock," she said softly. "Men are not always wise about such things. And I have a responsibility for you—all of you, for your father's sake."

He smiled faintly but kept his eyes closed. When she was like this no one could ask for a better companion. She had a softer side that others saw all too seldom. He found that he could not even recall Ellen Havelock's face as Tarifa's voice murmured warmly in his ear.

"Is the old pain there?"

"Yes. A little. It is nothing, it will go away."

"I will have Penti give you something for it. You must go and lie down and rest. Shall I get you a glass of brandy?"

"If you will have one with me." He opened his eyes and stared into hers directly above. How hot and blackly deep they were. He felt that he was sinking, sinking helplessly into their depths. She came from behind the chair and took his face between her hands, bending to touch his forehead with her lips, then his mouth. It began as the light impersonal caress one might give a child, then the pressure of her lips increased, hot and searing as branding irons, and Luis grasped her around the waist with his good arm and drew her against him like a sea drawing its waves back into itself from the shore. A mushroomy blackness descended upon him, with only a hot pulsing red center that was alive and that he knew to be her mouth. He was lost in the vastness of his passion, like a ship lost in a giant blinding fog. He was not even aware, when he came to his senses, that she was no longer kissing him but sat on his lap pressing his head to her pulsing breasts.

He drew back and stared at her as if both of them were disembodied spirits and he had already lost his soul in Hell.

"Tarifa—"

"Don't talk, *kushto*. You understand now why you cannot leave me?"

"But I must go!" he gasped. "What have I done!"

"Hush, *querido*. It is what I have done as well. Are you ashamed to have kissed me?"

"No, no." But he was ashamed, he was devastated to his very core. It was unthinkable what he had done! It was like taking his father's wife in front of him. He shuddered and Tarifa asked, "Are you ill, Luis? You must go to bed. We must get you well, *querido*."

She rose from his lap and he got up instantly, wondering if the sign of his guilt was written on his face for all the others to see. *Dios!* He must leave this house.

He said thickly, "I think I will retire, if you don't mind. I am very tired."

"Of course," she smiled. "And I will send Penti to you with something to ease your pain."

But as he walked off, moving like a man in a drunken stupor, he knew that nothing short of complete escape from her would ever ease the pain of his guilt. And perhaps not even death would release him from the pangs of his tortured conscience.

In the morning he had Amarillo saddled and rode away from Loma de Oro at a furious gallop. At breakfast he had told the family that he was riding to Bolsa Coyotes to see his new nephew. But he had no intention of going to Nazario's. In his saddlebags were some extra clothing and all the money he possessed, which was little enough, but might buy him passage from Loreto or San Blas to Valparaiso or perhaps Rio.

He did not intend to leave California without a word, however. He was going first to his father's old friend Don Zenobio to explain at least part of the reason for his leaving.

Don Zenobio, always a late riser, surprised Luis by being out in the yard already, with a young vaquero at his side. Luis rode Amarillo from a full gallop to a stop that could have been measured in inches, and heard Zenobio chuckle approvingly, *"Muy bueno, muchacho mío!* I couldn't have done better myself, when I was your age."

Luis dismounted and, turning to face Zenobio with a smile, felt consternation fill his heart instead. It was not a young vaquero who stood beside Zenobio, but Ellen Havelock, looking at him with a puzzled frown between her blue eyes.

Luis stammered a greeting and explained to Zenobio that he had only stopped by on his way to the Mission.

Zenobio listened and said nothing. He knew the Alvarjos, and Luis in particular, well enough to know when he was telling a deliberate lie.

"Come into the house, *muchacho*," he invited.

"No, Don Zenobio, I do not have the time."

"After coming all the way up my drive you don't have time to sit down long enough for a glass of *vino?* "Santo Domingo!" Zenobio bellowed. "What is the younger generation coming to? Begging your pardon, señorita?"

Ellen looked clean and fresh and poised in her neat white shirt and leather trousers. She sensed that Luis might still be embarrassed after Tarifa's actions of the day before, and put his rush to get away down to that.

"But I have some important matters to attend to," he told them desperately.

"Un momento, hijo," said Zenobio. He turned to Ellen. "Do you mind if I have a word in private with this young caballero, señorita? You can wait for us in the hacienda, if you will be so kind?"

"Certainly, Don Zenobio."

"You did not expect to find the Señorita here?" Zenobio gave Luis a shrewd glance. "I know what happened at Loma de Oro. Do not worry; they do not blame you. And if the gold of Señor Havelock is too uncouth for Tarifa to touch, it is not too obnoxious for Zenobio Sanchez."

Luis' eyes widened.

"You did not agree to sell land to Señor Havelock?"

"I agreed to sell him my northern pastures for ten thousand dollars in gold. You will never find another hacendado in the district who has got that many pieces of gold to rub together, *muchacho*."

"But—to sell your land to Americanos—"

"Why not? Do they not already own land all around us? Their money is as good as any others and I grow old and poor, *hijo*. And I have no children to inherit from me."

"If you had gone to Tarifa she would have bought your land from you," Luis said slowly.

"With what? She has land and cattle as I do, but not ten thousand dollars in gold. And I do not want to be beholden to Tarifa. No, I have done what I must do, and the Havelocks are good people. Now in the name of heaven, why is it that the Alvarjos who come to ask my advice must always have their little *contradanza* first? You are just like your father. What in the name of Christ is the matter?"

Luis felt a weight slip from his shoulders, much as his father had when he had come to Zenobio's on the day Dona Encarnacion was killed. The grizzled old warrior laid a gnarled hand on his arm.

"Come, tell Tío Zenobio, *niño*."

Luis found himself telling his story of disgrace and corruption in a steady flat voice that belied the emotion tearing at his breast. When he had finished, Zenobio gave him a searching, startled look.

He said, "Yes, I can see how it would happen. She is a vixen, that woman. She will stop at nothing to get her own way, or to protect what is hers. But you must stop blaming yourself, *muchacho*. There is no sin or guilt attached to what happened between you, except for herself, and I do not believe she has a soul."

Luis did not believe that he bore no guilt. Zenobio went

on, "You cannot run away like a jackrabbit just because she has embraced you. Think of the others at the hacienda, your aunt and brothers. Too many have been driven from Loma de Oro because of that woman; you must not be one of them."

"I am going, Zenobio; will you lend me some money?"

"No! I will not help you to run away!"

"I am going anyway," Luis said unhappily, "with or without your help."

"*Sangre de Dios!* You are as stubborn as a Catalán donkey. Very well, come inside."

"No! I will wait here for you."

"Are you afraid of the Señorita Havelock also, *por Dios?*"

"Since yesterday—I do not wish to speak to her."

"You act like an idiot schoolboy," Zenobio mumbled in disgust as he trudged away.

Luis stroked Amarillo's nose and tightened the saddle girth to pass the time until Zenobio returned. He was gratified to see Ellen come out of the house with the old man, mount her horse, and gallop off toward the south. At least he would be spared any further conversation with her.

Zenobio put a leather pouch of coins into one of the decorated pockets on Luis' saddle.

"If you need more you can write to me," he said unhappily. "But it is a wrong thing you do. I would not have expected it of you, Luis, running away."

"I can't do anything else! She is like a volcano, I tell you. She erupts and swallows up everything in her path."

"And how do you feel about her?" Zenobio asked. "Inside, I mean?"

Luis shook his head. "I don't know. I haven't stopped to think. I only know I am helpless when I am with her. That I must get away from her!"

Zenobio was too wise to ask whether Luis was really afraid of Tarifa or of himself. He watched the young man swing up into the saddle with the graceful perfection of all the Alvarjos, and his heart was heavy within him.

Luis rode south of the Mission, then turned west at a place where he was sure he would avoid casual riders or Indian work parties.

He was more annoyed than startled when a horse and
rider moved swiftly out of the shadows cast by a large
boulder, and caused Amarillo to shy.

"I had to speak to you, Luis, to tell you that what happened yesterday meant nothing to Uncle Patrick and me,"
said Ellen Havelock, reining in her horse next to his.

"Señorita, I did not expect to see you in this lonely
spot." He didn't actually know what to say to her. He
only knew that he must end the conversation and get away.

"I'm afraid I waited and then followed you from Don
Zenobio's," Ellen blushed, "and then lost my nerve until
now, about speaking to you. Do you mind very much?"

"No, of course not." But he did.

"I hope you realize that we did not wish to make trouble for you?"

"It is not important, señorita. I am only sorry that you
and your uncle were subjected to an inhospitable act in
my father's house."

Would he never stop talking in his polite clichés and
treat her like a human being?

"I don't like her," Ellen said suddenly in a flat voice,
and she saw his dark brows raise a fraction of an inch.
The only thing to do was to startle him into realizing that
he couldn't treat her like the other women of his acquaintance, with stiff-armed, meaningless courtesy.

"You mean Tarifa? I admit she acted badly, señorita,
but—"

"She is a devil incarnate! Anyone can see that, and she
has made your life a hell, hasn't she?"

Luis looked away from her. Caught between Tarifa and
Ellen Havelock, it seemed as if he could never make his
escape.

"Answer me," Ellen demanded. "Isn't it true?"

"Not exactly. She has done her best for us—all of us,
since my father died. She was his wife—"

"A wife younger than some of his children? A woman
who wants to keep the reins of power in her own hands
and intends to rule all of you until the day she dies! Luis,
are you afraid to stand up to her and declare yourself
free?"

He looked at her softly rounded pale face with the
brush of color over the low cheekbones, the full, pink

tremulous lips, and something began to stir in him. *Madre de Dios!* Had he lost his wits entirely? First succumbing to Tarifa's embrace, and now falling under the spell of this strange-acting Americana who not only puzzled but frightened him fully as much as Tarifa did.

"When I saw you stand up to Grimes in the street in Los Angeles and beat him with only one arm, I didn't think you could be afraid of anything," Ellen said. "Why are you afraid of that woman?"

"I'm not sure." It was true. He did not know precisely what it was he feared in Tarifa. He was filled with shame at the memory of their embrace, and yet he had not fought it, he had even kissed her back, lost in a surge of emotions that engulfed him like a tide. He was not afraid of the things in her that his brothers feared, her violent temper, her caustic tongue, her unrelenting drive against their passive easygoing natures. What Luis feared, he realized now, was the loss of his own strength and willpower when she was near him. The touch of her was like Hell's fire, and yet when he held her he would gladly have thrown himself into the everlasting pit of it.

"You do not have to be afraid of her," Ellen cried.

"I am going away."

"Away? Because of her? It is because of her, isn't it?" A wild fear clutched at Ellen's heart. Now that she had found him she couldn't lose him. She couldn't.

"It is better if I leave California."

"No. You mustn't go, Luis."

He glanced at her strained face and she reached across and touched his arm impulsively.

"Please listen to me. You mustn't let her drive you away. Go back and face up to her. You will never be able to live with yourself if you don't. She will haunt you wherever you go. You are too good, too fine, to let her ruin your life."

"Señorita—"

"Ellen, please call me Ellen? I want to be your friend, Luis, to help if I can."

"Elena—you are very kind, but you do not understand the circumstances."

She watched his face, and she knew a suffocating frustration. She could never tell him how she felt, he would be shocked. And if he rode out of her life, he would never know even her friendship. She could at least give him that, was determined to give it to him, if that was all she was to be allowed. She leaned back in her saddle and clasped her hands on the horn and spoke in a deliberately cold voice.

"I think I know exactly why you are going away, and what happened after we left Loma de Oro last night. She made love to you, didn't she?"

Luis stared at her blankly and then slowly his face suffused with color.

"I know as well as I'm sitting here that she forced you to make love to her. And now you feel guilty and so you run away?"

"Elena—"

"I suppose you want to tell me it is none of my business? But it is. I want to be your friend, and I will not see her ruin your life. I won't see you sacrifice what is yours to her. If you don't want to live under the same roof with her, come and help Uncle Patrick run his new rancho."

Luis saw that she meant what she said and he was touched, but he could no more have gone to the Havelocks than he could return to Loma de Oro.

"I appreciate your offer, Elena, but I cannot accept. I have a brother Santiago. I would like to find him. I believe he is somewhere in Mexico or South America, and with the money Don Zenobio has lent me I will be able to join him. To stay in California, as you wish, would not bring an end to my troubles because they are within my own spirit."

Ellen felt tears of anger and humiliation filling her eyes and she didn't care if he saw them or not. Once she would have died of shame to admit that a man could do this to her; now it seemed of no consequence.

Damn her, oh damn her! Ellen thought. He'll go and I'll never see him again.

She could barely see him now through the blur of tears. Suddenly she put spurs to her horse and galloped off, heedless of direction or the roughness of the terrain. The horse stumbled over a rocky wash, recovered himself, and leaped clumsily at a wide ditch. He missed it and came down heavily on his right side. Ellen was thrown over his head and landed in a sprawling heap on the opposite bank. She did not move.

Luis sank his spurs in Amarillo's sides. The stallion sailed effortlessly over the ditch the other horse had missed, and he threw himself out of the saddle before Amarillo had stopped running, and knelt to gather Ellen to his chest with his arm. There were scratches on her white cheeks and a swelling, already turning purple, over her right eye.

"Elena, Elena!"

She opened her eyes and stared straight into his anxious dark ones. She felt his chest expand as he sighed with relief.

"You shouldn't have tried to run your horse at the ditch without giving him time to judge the distance," he said mildly. "Can you get up?"

She had no desire to move. With his arm tight about her and her head resting against his chest, she was in the one spot she would have chosen above all others in the world, but she made an effort and he helped her to her feet.

Luis glanced at her pale face anxiously. "Are you sure you are all right, señorita?"

"Yes, quite all right, thank you. It was my own fault. How is my horse?"

Luis glanced at the animal who was cropping grass on the other side of the ditch. "I think he is a little lame, but it is nothing serious. Can you ride?"

She smiled at him. "Of course."

They crossed the ditch and Luis helped her into the saddle and mounted his own horse.

"I will ride back with you to the main road," he told her with quiet firmness. "This is not a safe place for a señorita to ride in alone."

"I am not afraid. I won't detain you any longer."

"But you are unhappy with me," he said shyly, "and perhaps if I talk to you a little, you will understand the reasons why I must go?"

Ellen said nothing. The sharp misery she'd felt before her outburst had given way to a strange lethargy.

Luis kept the horses at a walk, searching for the right

way to begin his explanation. Pride would not permit him to tell her the whole truth.

"You must not think that I am leaving California because of Tarifa entirely," he said. "I would have left eventually anyway. I am sure of that now. Since my— accident, I am no good as a ranchero any longer."

She turned to face him, "But even with one arm you are as good with a *reata* and whip as anyone I have ever seen!"

Luis waved his hand with the plaited reins in the lean fingers. "I can still throw a *reata larga,* but there are too many things that I cannot do. You must understand it is hard for me to watch from the sidelines when I cannot take part. I have a desire to become a lawyer and eventually enter politics. It is something I feel I can still do. But it will be better if I can attend the university in Mexico for a time. I need a great deal of study. I did not have the educational opportunities of my older brothers Joaquin and Santiago."

"But you could study here. I will help you, and Uncle Patrick attended Harvard. I know he'll do everything he can to assist you."

Luis smiled at her, then shook his head. "No, Elena. It is very generous of you and your uncle, but this is something I must do for myself."

"Halt! *Den el dinero! Pronto!*"

The harsh command rang out across the quiet countryside like the crack of a whip.

Both Ellen and Luis were struggling to control their startled horses, but they had glimpsed the man standing in the shadows of a toyon tree, leveling two pistols at their heads.

As swiftly as he could, Luis reached into his boot for the knife he always carried there, but the man under the tree saw the movement and leaped to crack the barrel of one of his pistols against Luis' wrist and tear the knife from his nerveless fingers.

The bandit was a squat Mexican, a cholo with a dark matted beard and beady avaricious eyes.

Luis drew himself up straight in the saddle. "Who are you?" he demanded. "What do you want?"

"Ah, the fine caballero has decided to honor me with

his conversation? I am Juan Isidro Jesus Solar, Excellency. And I want to relieve you of the gold I hear clinking so prettily in your saddlebags. I will use it for charity, you understand, and to help the poor. Is not that a worthy ambition, Excellency? You and the Señorita could not object to that? And I will relieve you also of your fine horse and fancy saddle, *amigo*. Then you and the Señorita can ride home double on her horse—if my *compadres* and I decide to let you go."

In the bracken back of the tree a horse stamped and a bit chain rattled in the still air.

"*Compadres!*" called Solar. "*Ven acá!*"

Two men moved out of the brush. One was a tall Mexican, with a long eager face and a strangely dreamy manner, holding a rifle. The other was a white man, black-bearded and powerfully built, with two pistols stuck in his waistband. At sight of Ellen and Luis he let out an oath.

"Carnsarn! If it ain't my friend Señor Alvarjo, who gave me such a nice ride up the main street of the pueblo the other day." The heavy sarcasm was not lost upon Luis or the girl.

Ellen translated Grimes' words for Luis as the big man spoke them.

"That was a real big favor you done me, señor, puttin' me in them stocks for the day. That's where I met up with these here interestin' hombres, an' we been doin' a right peart trade of relievin' travelers of their excess baggage. Why me an' you'll have us a real ol' gabfest before this is over."

"This is the hombre who put you in the jail?" asked Solar in wretched English.

"Yep, *amigo*, he sure enough is. And I reckon it's only fair I pay him back for the favor."

"*Sí, compadre!*"

The tall Mexican asked a question in Spanish, and on being informed of the facts by Solar, disassociated himself from the others and retired into some dreamworld of his own.

"Get down, both of you!" Solar ordered, brandishing his pistol.

There was nothing to do but comply. Ellen and Luis

stood beside each other in the grass while Solar and the tall Mexican went through the saddle pockets and chortled with glee on finding the gold on Amarillo.

Solar filled one hand with gold coins.

"They will kill you if you do anything to us," Ellen told Grimes in English.

"I don't know about that, ma'am. They let me loose from the jail, an' I tol' everybody I was headin' back for Santa Fe. Far as that alcalde know, Alf Grimes has left the country. And I mean to settle my little score with your fancy hombre yonder."

Ellen was unused to pleading, but she found herself doing it now.

"Please. You know he can't understand English. That was the trouble that day in Los Angeles. He was looking for an interpreter. He did not mean to be impolite to you. It was really my fault. I was standing there; I saw the whole thing and did nothing to stop it. I should have offered you both my services as an interpreter."

Grimes' small pig eyes gleamed like flecks of blue steel in his bearded face.

"Mebbe you should've, girlie. But the damage has been done. Alf Grimes is a man who always pays off his debts."

"But he has only one arm!"

"That's all he needed to down me once. He oughta be able to defend himself now."

"You've got to give him a fair chance!"

"Nothin' but. Tell him we're goin' to use knives, him an' me, to settle our little differences. I'll have Solar tie one of my hands behind my back so's we'll be equal. Now don't that sound fair to you?"

Fear beat like a live thing in Ellen's throat, threatening to suffocate her, but she translated Grimes' message in a level voice and watched Luis lift his head and nod to the big American in proud agreement.

Grimes cleared a small space on the ground by kicking away some of the grass with his heavy boots, then he went to hold a whispered conversation with Solar.

The American returned with his left hand bound behind his back by a scarf fastened to his wide leather belt. Solar came forward and handed a knife to each man.

"You caballeros are pretty good with these things," said

Grimes. He moved up a pace, a glint of malicious anticipation in his eyes. "But so's an old trader like me, who's mixed it up with Blackfeet braves around the campfire."

Luis did not speak or move. He stood straight and still, his arm at his side, the knife held point downward in his hand.

Grimes crouched forward and began to circle him warily, waiting for the right moment to attack. He knew better than to jump the Spaniard first off, and get his belly ripped open. He had seen these spiks fight before. And Luis did not look as though he would panic and charge him. He would have to chance an in-stroke and force the Spaniard into action.

Grimes' arm shot out, the knife barely missing Luis' shoulder, and Luis' hand moved swiftly upward, ripping the fabric of the American's sleeve but leaving the flesh untouched.

Luis stepped forward a pace and Grimes backed away, leading him into rougher ground. In spite of his own awkwardness at having his arm tied behind his back, Grimes realized that Alvarjo was even less well-balanced on his spurred boots. If he could cause the younger man to stumble, it would all be over in an instant.

Luis was fully aware of his disadvantage, but he could not refuse to attack. He knew also that he was probably the more skilled with a knife. Santos had seen to that, just as he had taught him to rope and ride. But Grimes was more powerful, and unless he could attack quickly and get in under the other's guard, he would not be able to beat him. He knew, too, that he couldn't chance a long-drawn-out struggle with the American. He was still weak and the sweat had already broken out on his forehead and was dropping into his eyes. He rubbed his face briefly with the back of his sleeve.

"Come on, caballero!" Grimes taunted. Whirling suddenly he now had Luis walking backward away from him. This was exactly as he had planned it, and he pressed his advantage by moving steadily forward like a huge crouching bear.

Wary and alert, Luis stepped backward over the uneven ground with its cover of dry grass and weeds. When his foot slipped he recovered himself quickly, but Grimes, watching like a cat at a mousehole, had been waiting for just that moment. He moved in, charging, his head lowered and his guard up. His sheer weight threw Luis to the ground, and they rolled in the short brown grass like bound logs of wood.

Luis freed his hand and drove his knife at Grimes' chest, but his arm had not been completely free and there was not enough power behind the blow to do more than nick the big man's chest.

First blood. Grimes cursed under his breath, and pressed Luis flat to the ground in a jarring attack that drove the breath from his lungs. He fought desperately to hold Grimes' arm, but felt it rising in spite of his efforts. For a moment the knife in the Americano's fist glinted in the sunlight, and Luis could see the flash of the big man's teeth between his bearded lips, and the little beads of sweat like oily dewdrops on his forehead.

As if she were living through a nightmare, Ellen saw the American's knife rise and fall in the tick of a second and bury itself in Luis' chest just above his heart. She screamed, but it was as if she were listening to the voice of a stranger, while she watched the ghastly tableau. Grimes held onto the knife for a moment, twisting it with sadistic satisfaction, and then he felt Luis go slack under him.

She ran to Luis' side and cradled his head in her arms. There was no thought, no feeling in her. Nothing but an engulfing deadness.

At first she was not even aware of the shots when they rang out sharply from the hillside above her head. Then, dimly, she heard Solar cursing and the sound of gunfire around her. A moment later a horse bounded out of the brush and disappeared with a man clinging to the saddle like a burr.

She was only faintly surprised when she glanced up and found Zenobio Sanchez and three Indian vaqueros standing behind her.

"It is a good thing my men and I were driving some mares to the Mission and heard your screams, señorita," said Zenobio. He knelt down beside her and gently released Luis from her grasp.

He withdrew the knife with a swift deft movement, and

instantly made a pad of his scarf and bound it tightly over
the wound with his sash. He squinted at Luis' white face,
laid a finger over his nostrils, and bent to bring one cheek
close to his lips.

"He is not dead, *muchacha*," he told her in a relieved
tone, "but we must move him from here quickly."

He spoke in brisk command to his vaqueros, directing
them to make a litter of their *reatas* and serapes between
two of the horses.

Ellen had been aware of nothing that followed Zenobio's
words, "he is not dead."

She had been so certain Luis was lost to her forever that
her mind had sealed itself off from every other thought.
Now, a great surge of blood seemed to fill her veins, her
heart, bringing life again to her body.

She bent to touch his face and forehead softly with her
fingertips, and she saw her tears on his cheek but she did
not know that she was crying.

"We must take him now, señorita," Zenobio said quietly
a moment later.

"Where?"

"To Loma de Oro."

"No! Take him to your rancho, Don Zenobio—please?"

He looked at her sadly.

"We are closer to Loma de Oro, señorita. And there is
a maid there who is skilled in medicine. She saved his life
once before, when it was necessary to remove his arm."

Ellen raised her chin sharply. "I will not let you take
him back to that woman! He was running away from her.
That is why he was leaving California."

"I know, señorita. But if you want him to live, we must
take him to Loma de Oro. Wait at my hacienda. I will
bring you word of him."

CHAPTER 27

Penti stood looking out of Tarifa's bedroom window when she muttered, "What is this? It looks like one of Don Zenobio's men has been injured. They are bringing him in."

As Tarifa reached the *sala*, Zenobio entered from the front door followed by three of his vaqueros carrying a fourth man between them.

Tarifa could not see the injured man's face and she asked Zenobio, "What has happened?"

He stepped aside without speaking and she saw Luis. For an instant her face blanched and her lips grew taut. Then she heard Zenobio's voice as from a distance.

"Luis was attacked by *bandidos* in the arroyo south of the Mission." He thought it better not to mention Ellen Havelock for the moment. "Fortunately my vaqueros and I were driving some mares to the Mission and we came upon him in time. We managed to kill two of the *bandidos;* a third got away. The two we killed were cholos."

Tarifa went to glance at Luis' face.

"Is he badly hurt?"

"He has been knifed. That is why we brought him here."

Tarifa nodded and directed the vaqueros to follow her to Luis' bedroom. Penti met them in the *galleria,* her bundle of medicines on her arm, and followed them into the room.

When the men had gone, Penti stripped off Luis' stained jacket and shirt and probed the ugly wound speculatively with her finger.

Across the bed Tarifa cried, "Well?"

"It is a deep wound, but not so deep as the one you gave Capitán Kinkaid, *miri pen*. I have seen worse in the Sacro Monte. I think he will live. It is only a pity that he has not more strength. His other illness sapped his vitality."

As she began to cleanse and bandage the wound the old Gypsy knew a dark unhappiness, for she was fond of Luis. She decided to move her things into his room in order to be with him day and night during this new crisis.

While Penti dressed the wound Tarifa paced the floor restless as a tiger, prey to her own churning feelings. What she now felt for Luis was not what she had felt for Pito Larios. There was a protective gentleness in her emotion for Luis. Yet it was a strong ruling passion that filled her whenever she looked at him or touched him. In a way she felt that he now belonged to her as Guindilla did, or as Lasho had. Her concern for his welfare was the comingled fear of a mother and a lover. She regretted that he lay injured and suffering again, yet at the same time she knew a warm pleasure; once again he needed her.

Luis opened his eyes and stared for an instant uncomprehendingly at the familiar walls of his own room and at Penti's and Tarifa's faces hovering over him.

"Zenobio rescued you from the *bandidos* and brought you here," Tarifa told him, taking his hand in both of hers. "He killed two of the renegades; the third got away. You will be all right. Penti will look after you, but now you must rest, *kushto*."

A spasm of pain crossed Luis' face as he struggled to his elbow despite the entreaties of the two women to lie still.

"Elena," he gasped. "The Señorita Havelock—what has happened to her?"

Tarifa thought him merely befuddled. Gently but firmly she eased him back onto the pillow.

"You must rest, *kushto*. You have not much strength."

"You do not understand," he moaned. "She was with me when I fought the Americano. I must know what has happened to her!"

Tarifa frowned. This was the first she had heard of an Americano, or of Ellen Havelock's presence during the skirmish. But she had no intention of discussing the matter with Luis.

Before leaving she drew Penti aside and said, "Give him something to make him sleep."

The old Gypsy nodded in silent agreement.

Tarifa found Zenobio in the *sala* regaling Tía Isabella with the lurid details of Luis' rescue. He was not pleased when Tarifa carried him off to her study for a private conversation and told him bluntly, "Now you can explain why you failed to mention that Señorita Havelock was with Luis when you found him."

Zenobio sat stroking his beard while he eyed a bottle of *aguardiente* with shameless longing.

"Take a drink," she said impatiently, "and answer my question."

"*Gracias.*"

Zenobio was maddeningly slow in pouring his drink, a large one, and in resuming his chair.

"I did not tell you because I did not believe it was any of your business, and because I knew it would upset you—which it has."

He tested his drink and sighed with satisfaction.

Tarifa glared at him. "You are an unspeakable old liar, Zenobio."

"Perhaps. But I am an observant and realistic one also. Two things which you are not upon occasion, *muchacha.*"

While she stood staring angrily at him he told her all he knew, adding that he had sold part of his property to Patrick Havelock, information that made Tarifa's face tighten into grimmer lines. He also explained why Luis had decided to leave California, and why he had lent him the money to do so.

"You had no right to help him run away from home," she cried. "Ygnacio's children belong here, on the land that their father left to them."

Zenobio asked resolutely, "What are you trying to do to the boy, Tarifa?"

Her head came up as she met his challenge.

"I love him—is that a crime?"

"Love? You never loved anything. You don't know what the word means. You want to keep him, entrap him, so that he will be no use to anyone else, not even himself. And the unholy part of it is that you can do it. He made his bid for freedom, and fate put him right back in your hands." He took a swallow of his drink and added sourly, "You may as well know the truth. Elena Havelock is in love with him. It is a real, honest love. She did not want me to bring him here. But when I told her that his life depended upon it, she put her own feelings aside at once. Would you have done that for him—handed him over to her? I can answer for you. You would have spit in her eye, and hauled him off dead or alive to keep her from touching him."

Tarifa moved away from him, but she could not escape the sound of his voice.

"If it is any comfort to you," he said, "I do not think that Luis is in love with her yet, but I think he could be if you would let him alone."

Tarifa whirled to face him, hands clenched, teeth bared, her eyes blazing with fury and hatred. "He is an Alvarjo, I will decide what is best for him! He will have nothing more to do with the Americana!"

Zenobio tossed off his drink and sat holding the empty glass, turning it 'round and 'round in his stubby fingers. "Yes, he wears your brand, like the rest of the Alvarjos and everything else on Loma de Oro. In all fairness, I cannot accuse you of not having done good, as well as evil, with everything Ygnacio entrusted to you. I agree with Padre Cazon. Without you, Loma de Oro would have gone to ruin. But that does not give you the right to exercise the power you do over the lives and hearts of these people."

"You think I have no feelings. That I am like an animal, with only the surface sensations of hunger, cold, pain? You will not believe me when I tell you that I love Luis, will you?"

He answered more kindly. "I believe that you think you love him as a woman should love a man who is all of life to her. But it is not true. Yours is not the kind of love he needs—or that you need, for that matter. Luis is not strong enough for you. You will devour him, crush him, and in the end he will despise you and himself, because he can no more give you what you want than you can give it to him."

"You lie!"

"I speak the plain truth. He is filled with angiush and guilt over merely embracing you in his father's house. In his mind you are still his father's wife."

"But Ygnacio is dead."

"Does a son ever truly feel that his father is dead, especially such a father as Ygnacio was? Do you intend to crucify Luis because you are too jealous or selfish to allow him to seek solace with another woman?"

"I will not listen to you. You are an evil-minded old man, Zenobio. I should have you thrown off the rancho."

He grinned. "We are both evil; that is why we understand each other. I am concerned for Luis, not our mutual regard for each other. He lies in his room injured not only in body, but in mind and spirit. Yet you and Elena Havelock are ready to pull him apart like two dogs with a rabbit. I will not see him hurt more because of you. There is a goodness, a generosity of soul in Luis, that must not be sacrificed. There are too few like him in this wretched world. I happen to love him also, as if he were my own son. You shall not make demands upon him while I have the strength to prevent it."

Tarifa stood across the room from him, drumming angrily with her fingers on a tabletop. "And if you are wrong and he loves me in spite of everything you have said?"

Zenobio shrugged. "That is something he must decide for himself. But I intend to see that he does decide it for himself."

"I am not afraid to let him make his own decision concerning me, Zenobio." There was a thin smile on her lips as she turned to face him, glancing at him from hooded eyes. So might a cobra have gathered itself before striking, he thought. He had no real hope that she would abide by her easy promise to let Luis decide matters for himself, but he had done the best he could for the boy at least for now.

"I would like to look in on him again before I leave," he said, getting to his feet.

"He will be sleeping," she said shortly.

"No matter. I will make no noise."

Tarifa followed him from the room, frowning at his

retreating back. He was nothing but a miserable stubborn old fool, but his words had managed to disturb her. She had no intention of allowing Luis to stray from her side. no matter what she had said. What made her uneasy was the knowledge that Zenobio also was aware of Elena Havelock's love for Luis.

Tarifa had never known real jealousy over a man before, and she fought against the choking rage that blinded her senses and muddled her thinking.

Zenobio entered the sickroom quietly, putting a finger to his lips and shaking his head when Penti would have waved him out again. He went to stand beside the bed, looking down at Luis' face. He lay turned slightly to one side, pale as a communion wafer save for the black lines of brows and lashes. Why was it, the old soldier mused, that the best ones were so often penalized by fate, as if a jealous God demanded payment for their virtue?

As he watched Luis' shallow breathing, Zenobio felt a pang of uneasiness and glanced questioningly at Penti. As if she had read his mind, she whispered, "It is only the draught I have given him, *rya*; he will be all right."

When they stood outside on the *galleria* again, Zenobio studied Tarifa's face for some sign of what he could tell Elena Havelock when he reached the Santa Teresa. But Tarifa's features were as impassive as a statue's.

"I will come tomorrow to see how he is," he told her.

"There will be no need. I will send you word, Don Zenobio."

He grunted, dissatisfied but unable to think of a suitable argument. She was in command again and there was little he could do to dispute her authority.

Padre Cazon came to Loma de Oro as soon as word reached him of Luis' illness. He was shocked to find the young man too weak to even take communion. The Padre administered Extreme Unction as a precatuion in case the boy died, and added his own heartfelt prayer that through the sacrament God might see fit to strengthen and heal his body.

Zenobio had come to the Mission to inform Cazon of Luis' injury, and he had spared no detail of the story in the telling, including his final conversation with Tarifa.

"Padre, you must see that she does not destroy him," Zenobio said as he paced the priest's narrow cell.

"I will try, Don Zenobio."

Now, finding himself alone at last with Tarifa, Padre Cazon told her, "There is no purpose in mincing words. Don Zenobio has explained everything concerning yourself and Luis."

She whirled to face him, "Zenobio is a lying, meddlesome old fool! He mixes in matters that are none of his concern. What right has he to go babbling to you of what happens at Loma de Oro?"

"The right of a Christian and a friend."

"If you and Don Zenobio are worried about Luis' welfare, you have no further cause for alarm. I will look after him from now on."

"That is precisely what both Zenobio and I are afraid of."

Her head came up like a startled horse.

"What do you mean?"

"Luis is ill and weak. Worse still, he is badly disturbed over what took place between you. He must have time to sort these things out in his own mind. And that is something you will never allow."

Her face flushed as she replied angrily, "Yes, you are exactly like Zenobio, Padre. You think I am a monster. That there is no good in me. That I cannot honestly care for anyone or anything."

He watched her steadily, noting the pulse beating at the base of her throat, the dark wine color seeping under the bronze skin of her face and neck.

He said slowly, "I believe that you do not have the courage to deny your ambitions and desires, even for a short time. Even for someone you profess to love."

"Why should I deny my desires? If I take what I want, it is because I have the strength to do it."

"And what you destroy in the wake of your desires means nothing to you? It is the Señorita Havelock who has genuine strength and courage in denying her own wishes, for Luis' sake."

At mention of the American girl, Tarifa exploded like gunpowder that had been touched with a match.

"*Primita Undebé!* You talk to me of that *mujercilla*

who is not ashamed to boldly flaunt her feelings for a man she has just met, for all the world to see? You speak of that hussy, who would make Ygnacio turn in his grave if he knew she had been under his roof, let alone ogling his son. A woman who would not only ruin Luis, but everything the Alvarjos stand for. A creature whose uncle is shameless and greedy enough to buy Mission lands. You would have me give Luis his choice of such a woman? Never! I love Luis, and I intend to make him happy."

Cazon shook his head. "There will be no happiness for Luis, or for you, my child, unless you set him free to choose his own life. Does Luis love you—can you honestly say that he does?"

"Of course he does!"

"Then you have nothing to lose by letting him decide matters for himself."

Tarifa's glance slid away from his and the flat, age-old mask of Gypsy secrecy settled over her face.

"If you love Luis," Padre Cazon went on, ignoring her obvious desire to mount the golden horse that now stood pawing the earth in front of the hitching rail, "you will want to marry him, yes? But, alas, I could not sanction such a marriage. You no longer believe in the Church, and Luis will not marry outside it."

"*She* is not a Catholic!"

"No, but the Señorita Havelock could become one as you did, if she so desired."

Her black eyes moved across his face in bitter rebellion, then suddenly she smiled.

"Marriage is unimportant to me. I will live with him according to the rites of my people if we cannot be married in the Church."

The wicked impudence of her words shocked him.

"You were baptized a Catholic. God's mark is upon you. Would you make a mockery of the sacraments of baptism and matrimony, and add these to your sins? Luis will have nothing to do with you in that case."

"He will do as I wish!"

Tarifa stood scowling at him with her head lowered like a belligerent bull. He had no way of knowing whether she had fully understood what he said, or if she had, whether she would pay the slightest heed to it.

He watched in uncertainty and distress as she mounted Guindilla and turned him away from the hacienda. Padre Cazon sent his prayers after her, but there was a momentary weakness in his own faith as he stared at her rigid unrelenting back.

"Luis," he prayed aloud, "Heavenly Father, you must save Luis, even if it means taking him to Yourself to keep him from this woman."

Tarifa had given no thought to what it would be like to be married to Luis. Actually, until Padre Cazon mentioned it, she had never considered it. Now suddenly it appealed strongly to her, the solution to all her troubles.

No longer would she suffer loneliness at Loma de Oro. It would be like having a younger, gayer Ygnacio to champion her and defend her against the rest of the family. She would have love and warmth and companionship again. And there might be children. She longed now to have a child of her own again, an Alvarjo, and yet a part of herself to follow in her own footsteps. She was convinced that Luis loved her, and that it was his undeclared passion for her that was upsetting him. How blind and foolish both the Padre and Zenobio were. . . .

She arrived at Bolsa Coyotes in a warm and expansive mood and went immediately to join Rufina in her bedroom where she lavishly admired little Ygnacio in his cradle.

There was no question that this child was an Alvarjo.

The thin elongated face, coin-sharp features, and delicate long-fingered hands were as different from the first son Rufina had borne as a wild mesteño from a Loma de Oro palomino.

Rufina was shyly proud of her new son, and Nazario was ecstatic. His old aloofness for Rufina had not changed. But he now came to the room many times a day to inquire of the maid how his son was progressing, or to stand silently admiring him with a faint smile of satisfaction on his lips.

Ellen found Zenobio, booted and spurred, sipping a cup of tea in front of the fire.

His small eyes looked conspiratorial under his shaggy brows. "Señorita, we will take a ride this morning, you and I," he told her jovially. "So do not dawdle over your breakfast! I have something of interest to show you, *muchacha*."

When they had left the ranch yard and were headed southeast, she asked, more to be polite than out of real interest, "Where are we going?"

"To see Luis."

"Luis? But they would never let me in?"

"By 'they' you mean Tarifa? I will not disagree with you, *muchacha*. She would bar the door and perhaps knife you on sight, and me also for bringing you to Loma de Oro. And poor Padre Cazon for suggesting it. But do not worry, she is not there."

The deep gratitude mirrored in her eyes made Zenobio tug harshly at his beard in embarrassment. All Californians were born romantics, but playing Cupid was really an asinine thing for a man of his age to do. Yet he had to admit to himself that he found it oddly rewarding.

Loma de Oro lay white and still in the morning sunlight. The pungent odor of tarweed came strongly from the browning hills around the rancho.

Padre Cazon stood at the open window of Luis' room and made a pretense of saying his beads. At Tía Isabella's invitation he had stayed the night. As soon as he learned that Tarifa planned to be away for the day, he had sent word to Zenobio to bring the girl Elena to Loma de Oro as they had planned. Now, following early Mass and the departure of Tarifa and the males of the family, he was endeavoring to persuade Penti to let him relieve her after a night spent watching over Luis.

"I will sleep later," she told him. "My pallet is here as you see; if Luis calls I will hear him."

The priest turned from the window. "But you will rest better in your own room. I will watch over him, never fear. If you are needed I will call you."

She studied his face with faint suspicion, but could find nothing there to make her doubt his words. She was bone-weary this morning after her long vigil, and Luis seemed to be resting quietly. There would be little harm in returning to her own room for an hour or so and leaving the Padre in charge. Besides, Tarifa was not on the rancho to learn of her slight dereliction from duty.

Padre Cazon felt guilty at the ease with which his little plot was succeeding. The Gypsy even drank a cup of chocolate with him, unaware of the drug which the Padre had, with some misgivings, slipped into her cup a moment before as she bent over Luis. A harmless enough concoction which would ensure her sleep for several hours.

When she had gone, the Padre had sat quietly in a chair near the bed saying his beads and asking forgiveness for his mild subterfuge. And when he heard the unmistakable ring of Zenobio's spurs mounting the stairs of the *galleria,* he sprang to open the door.

"*Buenos días,* Padre," Zenobio greeted him, with hushed solemnity, followed by an elaborate wink.

Padre Cazon chose to ignore the wink. He replied with formal politeness, "*Buenos días,* Don Zenobio. *Buenos días,* señorita. I am surprised to see you out so early."

Chastened by the priest's lofty manner, Zenobio introduced Ellen.

"Good morning, Padre."

Ellen stepped into the room with the eerie sense of not having moved at all. There was a high burning color in her cheeks, yet her lips looked bloodless.

Cazon was pleased with the clean wholesome lines of her face and figure. She would be good for the boy. But he was thankful that Tarifa was not at the hacienda to see the naked emotion on her face and in her clear blue eyes.

"If you would be kind enough, señorita," he suggested, "to sit here for a moment with poor Don Luis while I speak to Don Zenobio out on the *galleria,* I would be most grateful."

Ellen nodded without looking at him.

She was beyond words. Beyond thinking. She could only sense the miracle that had brought her to this room to be alone with her beloved.

She found herself kneeling by the bed, staring in wordless happiness at Luis' face.

He lay pale and still, a thick bandage visible under the open neck of his nightshirt. He looked, she thought, like a young god toppled by some capricious fate from his column, lying broken but still heartbreakingly beautiful where he had fallen.

After a time she spoke his name, because she could no longer refrain from doing so.

In spite of the softness with which she had spoken, she saw his eyes open at the sound and fill with a quick recognition and pleasure.

"Elena."

She smiled at him. "I don't think it is good for you to talk, so I will be brief. Don Zenobio brought me to the rancho. I had to see for myself how you were, and Dona Tarifa—"

"I know," he said.

"Are you feeling better? I was so afraid they had killed you."

Without being aware of it, she had grasped his hand and now his fingers had closed involuntarily around hers.

"It was kind of you to come, señorita. I am much better."

He was so pale, so infinitely fine-drawn and weary-looking. She longed to hold him in her arms, to give him all of her own strength and fortitude.

"If I hadn't followed you," she said savagely, "this never would have happened! You would have gotten away from here as you planned." She couldn't stop the tears that rushed to her eyes and fell on his sleeve and over their entwined fingers.

Gently he freed his hand and brushed the tears from her cheeks with his fingertips. "You must not cry, Elena. It makes me hurt inside to know I have caused you to cry over me. I am not worth it." He smiled at her. "Besides, you wanted me to stay."

"But not like this!"

He glanced at her with a hurt, puzzled expression in his eyes.

Ellen bit her lip. It was all so hopeless. She couldn't tell him how she felt, throw herself at him. He would hate her for it if she did. And even in the extremity of her emotion, she still had her pride as a woman. She was no Tarifa to sweep him off his feet, and force him to do her bidding against his own will. There was nothing she could do but watch and wait, and love him with every fiber of her being, in silence.

Her voice was controlled when she told him, "I didn't want you to stay if it was really against your wishes,

Luis, or if it meant your being hurt—by anything. I never wanted you to have to come back to this house, to her."

He turned his head away and she saw the faint color in his cheeks, and the pressure of his lips against his teeth.

Suddenly, without giving herself time to consider the wisdom of her words, she said, "Luis, I have no right to ask, but I must know—do you love her?"

He turned to face her and their eyes met, hers mirroring pain and doubt, his dark with the sudden turmoil of his thoughts.

Ellen covered her face with her hands. She had read the incredible answer in his eyes, and found it more unbearable than a spoken confirmation would have been.

He did nót know!

"Elena—"

Remorse washed over her at the sound of anguish in his voice. She had come here to comfort him and all she had succeeded in doing was to bring him more pain and suffering. In her selfish desire to make her own existence more bearable, she had only added to his own burdens.

"Forgive me, Luis. I had no right to ask that question. I must go and let you rest."

"No, wait." He took her hand again and his fingers trembled. "You are so good, Elena, so kind. You remind me of my sister Dolores, and my mother. But you must not worry about me."

She bent her head as if it were too heavy to hold erect. There was no point in her staying. There was nothing more for her to discuss with him. He must know as well as she did that he could not escape Tarifa now. Only his hand grasping hers left them with a frail last link that she could not bring herself to break.

"Elena." His voice was low and gentle. "You must not care too much about all this."

She looked at him then and found sadness and an inexpressible compassion in his dark eyes. Like a young Christ with the crown of thorns already about his head. You could not fight another's battles for him, no matter how great your desire to do so. And it was plain that Luis had already accepted his cross and lain upon it.

"You will come to see me again?" he asked.

Elena shook her head and withdrew her hand from his.
"I'm sorry, I can't."

She bent and kissed him softly on the lips, then rose
and left the room as if she were merely a stranger who
had strayed there by mistake and paused to give what
comfort she could.

After she had gone Luis lay perfectly still for a time
with his eyes closed. He could still feel the touch of her
lips. Gentle, undemanding, yet oddly stirring in their
yielding generosity. He had felt himself responding to
them like a thirsty plant to warm rainfall. Unlike Tarifa's
devouring embrace, Elena's kiss had not plunged him into
a bottomless abyss. It had left him moved, refreshed, yet
feeling free of any claim she might have upon him.

In his new realization of his attraction to her, he found
that he no longer resented what he had once considered
her abrupt American ways. Her pale skin and red-gold
hair now seemed marks of special beauty to him. But he
knew that he could never accept the gifts she offered him
so freely. She must know as well as he did that it was
impossible for them to share anything as long as Tarifa
stood between them.

Presently, when Padre Cazon returned to ask him how
he was, Luis responded irritably and sent the priest from
the room again to order a meal which he had no intention of eating.

He merely wanted to be alone with his thoughts for a
little longer. How seldom people were willing to leave you
alone in quiet repose unless you were outwardly engaged
in doing something.

Sunlight filtered through the iron grillwork of his windows, making a measured pattern on the counterpane like
the bars of a prison.

It was very fitting, he thought. He was imprisoned. As
completely as if he lay in the Bastille or the Tower of
London. And Tarifa was the jailer as well as the monarch of his realm, ruling with an iron hand, and a heart
that knew passion and desire but not mercy.

Slowly, Luis became aware of the weight at the back
of his head, as if a quantity of hot lead had gathered at
the base of his skull, and he smiled grimly to himself. It
was the thing Penti had been inquiring about anxiously

each day. The thing she feared most, he knew. The beginning of the dread fever.

He lay still and let it wash over him.

Padre Cazon and Tía Isabella glanced up from the foot of the bed where they knelt praying. Penti, crouching like a troll over Luis, raised her head as if in startled guilt.

Penti felt not only guilt, but a naked fear at what Tarifa would do when she learned of her having left Luis alone in the Padre's care. When she had awakened, still groggy from the drug, it was to find Padre Cazon and Candelaria struggling to restrain the fever-stricken Luis, while he moaned and thrashed on the bed.

"You promised to wake me!" Penti accused the priest.

"Heaven knows I tried," he said helplessly, "but you would not waken." The burden of guilt at the unhappy outcome of his little plot made his own heart heavy. "Tell me, what can we give him? What can we do for him?"

"Nothing," she answered blackly. "Leave him to me. You have done enough."

Her glance full of angry suspicion held the priest silent. The responsibility for what he had done weighed heavily upon him. And yet he had not realized that matters would take the turn they had taken, or that Luis was so weak and ill.

When he had returned to the sickroom with a maid carrying the food Luis had asked him to fetch, he was disturbed to see the young man's high color and the wide unblinking glitter of the fever in his eyes.

Luis' face burned to his touch. At once he instructed the terrified maid to help him wring out cloths in cool water. But as fast as they applied them Luis flung them off, cursing them both between his teeth.

"Run and waken Penti!" the priest told the weeping girl. *"Vaya!"*

But Penti had been unable to do much more for her patient when she finally stumbled into the room. Luis continued to moan and toss until he was exhausted. Ellen Havelock's name was often on his lips, mingled with curses and rambling phrases that made no sense.

Tarifa strode across the room to the bed and glanced down at Luis.

She did not like the rigidity of his face and jaw. His eyes, slightly open, glittered like obsidian. He looked as Lasho had looked before he died.

A wave of violent, towering rage swept over her.

Savagely, like an eagle poised to swoop down on its prey, ready for the first luckless creature to cross its path, her flashing eyes swept the faces present. Only Penti's eyes wavered and were unable to meet her gaze.

"What is it that you hide from me, you devil's spawn of a witch?" she cried in Romany.

"Nothing, *miri pen*. I swear to you!"

"You lie! You hag of the devil, were you with him when the fever started?"

"I have been expecting it for days, *miri pen*, watching to ward it off," babbled Penti, her Gypsy eyes canting to left and right in their effort to avoid Tarifa's lynx-eyed stare.

"Were you with him!"

"I—you must believe me, *miri pen*. It was not my fault. The Padre insisted I lie down in my room. I had watched over Don Luis all night. He promised to wake me if Don Luis grew worse. I am not to blame. It was the weakness of my age, my old bones, that made me fall asleep so soundly—"

"A weakness you will pay for with your life," hissed Tarifa between clenched teeth, "if he dies!"

"I must speak to you for a moment, Tarifa," said Padre Cazon. "If we could step outside?"

"Not now, Padre."

"It is important."

She frowned at him, but followed him out onto the *galleria*.

Haltingly, he tried to explain what he had done and why. He saw the white ring of fury around her mouth, and the bleak anger mirrored in her eyes. Yet, though he stood accused in his own mind, she did not speak. Instead she turned on her heel and went back into the sick-room, closing the door firmly behind her.

All through the night, she sat beside the bed with Penti. Santos had been sent for and instructed by Tarifa to brew more of his yellowish root mixture, but this time it seemed powerless to halt the fever.

Tarifa's lips grew grim whenever Luis, in his ramblings, called out for Ellen Havelock as if she were his one hold on life.

Despite her cold rebuff, Padre Cazon returned quietly to the room just before dawn. And when he could stand Luis' weakened cries no longer he said, "Send for the young woman, Tarifa, in the name of charity. She might ease his last moments."

"No. He has no need of her. I will look after him."

"But surely you see that he is dying?"

"That is not true!"

She bent and took Luis' hand, now so dry and flaccid, and held it to her lips.

"*Kushto*, you must hear me and get well."

At her touch, the man on the bed seemed to brighten. He opened his lips and murmured, "Elena? Do not leave me, Elena. . . ."

Tarifa sat for a moment as if turned to stone, then she released his hand slowly and stood up.

"If the Señorita will ease his last moments," began the priest again, "surely—"

Without glancing at him, Tarifa called sharply:

"Santos."

"*Sí*, Dona Tarifa."

"Ride to Don Zenobio's, and bring his guest, Señorita Elena Havelock to Loma de Oro. *Vaya, muy pronto!*"

"*Sí!*"

Tarifa left the room walking stiffly, but with her head erect. She would come back when Santos returned with Ellen Havelock, she vowed, but for the moment all she wanted was to be alone in the cabaña on top of Loma de Oro.

Ellen entered the room first, followed by her uncle and Zenobio.

Her eyes met Tarifa's full on where she stood silently at the foot of the bed, and there was humble gratitude and a quiet joy she could not hide in her glance.

"He has been calling your name," Tarifa said without inflection. "We thought perhaps you could quiet him."

Before she went to the bed and knelt down to take Luis' hand in her own, Ellen said, "My uncle knows something about medicine. Perhaps he can help Don Luis, if you don't mind?"

"I have some quinine," said Havelock. "If we can just get some of it down him, it might help."

Penti glared at him in rebellious suspicion, but at Tarifa's nod she fetched some water and helped him raise Luis' head while the American spooned the liquid into the injured man's mouth a little at a time.

A little later, when Luis roused and called out her name again, Ellen answered firmly, "Yes, I am here, Luis."

His eyes opened at the sound of her voice, and there seemed to be a glimmer of recognition in their depths.

"Don't—go," he whispered. "Don't leave me."

"I won't. I promise. Now try to rest."

Tarifa stood for a moment looking at the fair head bent over the dark one on the pillow, then left the room abruptly and as silently as a cat.

Padre Cazon slipped out of the room also and followed her down to the patio.

Dawn was streaking the sky with pearl gray and stippling it with rose in the east, outlining the black jaws of the sierras.

He spoke awkwardly because of the nature of their last conversation. "That was a fine and a generous thing you just did," he said softly.

He watched the bitterness in her face deepen.

"I have no use for a man who finds comfort in a creature like that."

"I told you Luis was not the man for you. He never could have been. If he lives, will you permit him to lead his own life, to marry Señorita Havelock if he wishes?"

"He can do as he pleases," she told the priest shortly. "All the Alvarjos have a weakness in them. I do not need such people."

"No," he said, "but they need you. I told you once before, the strong must look after the weak or we all perish. You have done this fine thing; do not spoil it now by showing weakness yourself and running away."

She stared at him as if he had lost his senses.

"I do not run away!"

"I merely thought, because you were hurt and disappointed—"

Her head came up proudly.

"I do not need these people," she repeated in a voice like stone, "but I will not leave Loma de Oro in their foolish hands. This land is mine. I have made it what it is. I shall keep it, have no fear."

Tarifa spent the next several days alone in the cabaña on Loma de Oro. With the Havelocks still in the house, it was the only way to avoid seeing them. She had made an odd discovery, however, on going to the cabaña after speaking to the priest that night in the patio.

She could dance again.

The wondrous feeling of languor and passion that had the power to fill her body and mind and make her blind to all else had returned.

Stripped naked, she had danced through the early dawn hours, until she lay at last in an exhausted stupor on the floor, empty of all sensation but a languorous gratitude.

It was not until Penti roused her in the midmorning with a jug of chocolate and loaf of bread that she learned Luis' fever had broken. If he could hold on through the days that followed he would recover.

Tarifa said nothing as she dressed. She was glad Luis had not died, but her desire for him seemed to have evaporated in the violence of her dance. She was aware of only a cool indifference, as if she had put him into a cupboard and locked the door, intending never to look inside again. There was a strange exhilaration in her this morning, a sense of freedom and well-being that she had not known in months.

She drank the chocolate and ate the bread with Penti, and it was like the old days of their breakfasting together in Gaspar Escobar's little house in San Diego.

"You are in good spirits, *miri pen*," chuckled Penti.

"Why shouldn't I be?"

"No reason. You had an eye for Don Luis these past months. I could see. But I could also have told you the cards said you would find no happiness with him."

Tarifa scowled at her. She did not believe in the cards but they had always had the power to make her uncomfortable. "I do not like fortune-telling!"

"Little sister," Penti chortled, "fortune-telling is deceiving, yet what the lines say I can read. Let me see your palm."

Reluctantly Tarifa gave the old Gypsy her palm.

Penti chuckled and hummed to herself and sucked on her thumb before tracing out the lines.

"I see the cards were right, *miri pen*. The young one, he was not for you. But there is a death in your hand."

"You lie!"

"No, not yours, another's—a man's. But you are connected with it. And there is a great happiness for you, if only you have the wisdom and courage to grasp it. If you do not, it will never come again."

Tarifa thought at once of Pito Larios.

"A man has to do with this happiness?"

"*Si*," said Penti. "A strong man. As strong as you are yourself, but he brings trouble and danger with him also."

Tarifa drew back her hand angrily. "You make all this up to bewilder me. I do not believe a word of it!"

"The lines of your hand and the cards do not lie," said Penti solemnly.

Tarifa rode that morning toward the *arroyo seco* and the cabaña where she had lived with Penti where Santiago had attacked her on that night so long ago, before Don Ygnacio had married her.

There was no one living at the cabaña now. She could not spare vaqueros these days to man the farther ranch outposts.

The land still had the ability to entrance and charm her. All of her nature-worshipping Gypsy soul expanded at the sights and sounds spread out around her in the clear morning light.

Beyond the swelling breasts of the sweeping sienna-colored hills, the chaparral matted and twined amid the feathery greasewood, varied as tortoiseshell in its shadings of greens and blacks. Above the broken jutting sandstone walls of the arroyo, draped with moss and vines, she could see the majestic oaks and sycamores standing like sentinels around the brink. The air was balmy and seductive, as if distilled from strong perfume, a mixture of warm earth and the heady pungent aroma of tarweed and chaparral. Here and there were clumps of alder, white sage, and wild lilac.

The sounds of birds and small animals scurrying and scratching in the undergrowth was a faint but steady movement that made the bushes move as if with a life of their own.

High overhead a hawk wheeled and then swooped to earth to gather up its prey.

Guindilla's hooves moved quietly through the ankle-high grass and the aroma of leather and warm horseflesh, mingled with the pleasant tinkle of spurs and bit chains, lulled Tarifa into a deep relaxation that was not unlike sleep.

She was not aware of the man on horseback sitting on the brow of the little hill in front of her, until Guindilla gave the first warning with his questioning whinny.

Tarifa's head jerked up and she saw the man sitting bulkily in his saddle, his sombrero pulled low over his eyes so that all but the bottom of his face was in shadow.

"Buenos días," she said tentatively, displeased to have her ride interrupted and to find a stranger on her land.

"Buenos días, Tarifa."

She glanced at him sharply as she drew nearer, finding nothing recognizable in the lumpish ill-dressed vaquero.

Then as she reined in her horse a yard away from him, the man suddenly swept off his sombrero and she saw the black patch he wore over one eye.

"Julio."

"Sí."

"What are you doing here?"

"I have come to get what is mine." She saw that he was holding a pistol in one hand. "What you robbed me of by force. My rancho and my daughter."

"They no longer belong to you," she said in a flat voice.

"It will be simple to prove they were taken from me under duress."

He had grown heavier, she thought, and there was a determined ugliness about him.

"I have been a long time in returning to claim what is mine," he said. "But I was ailing, thanks to your savage attack. And then I had to raise the money for my return and for my lawsuit."

"I told you I would kill you if you came back to California," Tarifa said boldly.

"Ah, but I hold the winning cards this time." He grinned. "I could shoot you right where you sit, and I would have no qualms about it, I assure you. But I prefer to have my land legally cleared first. If you make trouble for me, however, I shall use whatever means necessary to rid myself of you."

"This is my rancho. You have no right here," Tarifa said between her teeth. If only she had a knife or a gun, but she had neither, nothing but her quirt and her *reata*, and at this distance she could not hope to build a loop before he fired the pistol. She clenched her teeth in helpless rage.

"We will go to the cabaña and talk," Julio said motioning toward the abandoned adobe.

"I have nothing to say to you."

"Ride!" He waved the gun. "If you don't, I'll shoot the horse from under you. I know you prize him." The pistol centered on Guindilla's forehead.

Tarifa turned him toward the cabaña.

Inside the adobe Julio made a small fire against the chill of the long-closed cabin, and motioned her to a seat.

He had brought in a writing case from his saddlebags, and placed it on the table by the window.

"I have a paper here, drawn up by a lawyer. It will assure everyone concerned that you are declaring null and void the agreement we made previously concerning my land and daughter. It further states that you give and bequeath back to me all the stock and equipment on Bolsa Coyotes at this time."

Tarifa stared at him in contempt.

"I will not sign such a paper. I will give you nothing. Bolsa Coyotes belongs to Dolores, and she will stay at Loma de Oro until she is old enough to claim it."

He cursed at her, his hand trembling on the gun and his good eye blazing with hatred.

"You will sign it or I will kill the stallion out there! You will not get away with thievery again!"

Tarifa said nothing, but when he went to the door and thrust it open, the pistol leveled at Guindilla's startled head, she leaped at him, clawing and biting, jabbing her spurs into his legs until they both fell rolling and gasping to the floor.

She could not hold out for long against his strength, but while she could, she fought him like a tigress, without thought for her own safety, taking his blows as if they were nothing but wind, hating him to the core of her being. Her fingers sought his throat and his damaged eye, but he rolled and twisted away from her, and lashed her across the face with the barrel of the pistol. She felt the blood gushing from her nose and relaxed her grip. In an instant he was on his feet again, leveling the gun out the open door at the luckless stallion.

Tarifa dragged herself to her feet. A great terror filled her breast. She heard the crack of the pistol followed by Guindilla's sharp cry. At the same moment Julio seemed to leave the doorway as if he had suddenly taken to the air like a bird in flight.

Tarifa moved on clumsy leaden feet to the door and saw Guindilla, still on his feet but with a deep groove of red furrowing one shoulder. On the brow of the little hill a horseman was riding very fast, dragging something like a log of wood furiously behind him.

She went to the stallion and held his muzzle, whispering to him as she staunched the blood with her sash. It was a flesh wound, no bones were broken; he would be all right, she kept telling herself.

The horseman had turned on the hill and came back walking his mount slowly. She recognized Marca and Santos. The mayordomo dismounted and went to kneel by the thing at the end of his *reata*.

"How did you know he was here?" she asked wonderingly.

He pushed back his sombrero with his thumb and continued to stare at Julio Marcos' swollen, mottled face.

"I saw smoke from the chimney, and I knew no one was supposed to be here. When I got close I saw Guindilla and heard Don Julio's voice threatening you. I'm afraid his neck is broken. They will kill me when they find out, even though I did it in defense of you, Patróna."

Tarifa hunched down beside him and laid her hand on his shoulder.

"This is my crime, not yours, Santos. I would have killed him if I could. If anyone needs to know that he was killed, let them know that I killed him. But if we bury him who will need to know?"

"The people he has spoken with since his return. They will ask questions."

"And if they come to me, I will tell them I killed him when he threatened and attacked me on my own land."

Santos nodded. "But I must confess it to Padre Cazon. I killed once before, but it was not a man like Don Julio— only a half-breed Indian who was responsible for my mistress's death. But I had to confess the sin, all the same."

"You do not have to confess the name of the man, do you?"

Santos considered, his lined, leathery face twisted in concentration. "No, I do not think that will be necessary, but I must confess the sin and do penance for it."

"You saved my life," said Tarifa, "and Guindilla's. I am grateful to you, Santos."

"I could not do otherwise," he said in simple gravity. And he knew the truth in his words. Sin or not, he had been ordained to protect those of Loma de Oro, whom he still served and loved.

They made a grave together deep in the bottom of the canyon, and buried Don Julio's pistol and saddle and bridle along with him, and shooed his horse away. But Tarifa kept his writing case and the legal paper he had insisted she sign, to destroy later at Loma de Oro.

CHAPTER 28

Soledad and Titus Judah were married in Valparaiso by a priest, a friend of the captain. Judah himself had no qualms about not having a church ceremony, but he knew that his marriage would not be recognized in California without written proof that they had been married by a priest.

Now he had such documented proof.

Soledad was already two months with child.

Judah was taking a northeasterly route, planning to visit the Caribbean before sailing to New England. He had no wish to run into the various ships' masters from California who might be watching for sight of the *Vulcan*. In Barbados he had the ship repainted and renamed the *Heron*.

In the constant misery of her first pregnancy, Soledad had only two bright spots to console her. The fact that a priest had finally blessed her marriage, and the friendly thoughtfulness of the Kanaka cabin boy Hilo. He was seldom away from her side these days, and his large mournful eyes seemed to reflect her own fear and misery. She had learned that the fancy baubles and jewels that had taken her attention at first were poor solace when her heart ached for her homeland and her own people. Titus paid little attention to her now and she was left to amuse herself for days at a time.

Most often she stood at the rail staring over the stern toward where she imagined California lay.

She conversed with Hilo in the halting Spanish he knew, or the little English she was picking up from Judah and the crew.

Hilo told her that he had many brothers and sisters in the Sandwich Islands, a place of deep sunlight and flower-filled beauty where one never had to work, but only to gather up the bounties of nature.

"I think it must be like California," Soledad said with a sigh.

"Yes, something like, missus."

Soledad's child was born on a blowing windy night off Jamaica. A boy, small and dark, but with the unmistakable mark of Judah in his form and features. Hilo delivered the child and made mother and infant as comfortable as possible aboard the pitching vessel.

Soledad found that the child was a blessing because it commanded so much of her time. She and Hilo fashioned infant garments from the materials supplied by the supercargo, and Soledad secretly baptized and named the child for St. Sebastian, though Judah called the boy William, after his father. He seemed pleased with the boy, after his fashion, and he told her now she must learn to speak English properly so that she could talk to his son in his own language when he grew older.

"No son of mine's going to prattle nothing but Spanish," he said.

When they reached New England, Judah established his wife and child with Hilo and a maidservant in a small house in Salem, Massachusetts. He had chosen Salem because it was less apt to draw the prying eyes of the skippers in the California trade, most of whom shipped out of Boston, New Bedford, or Portsmouth.

Once Soledad was established, Judah secured the services of Miss Dora Fynchly, an acid-faced spinster, who agreed to tutor Mrs. Judah in English, reading, and penmanship.

Soledad's hours with Miss Fynchly were torture. She could not keep her lonely distracted mind on the lessons, and Miss Fynchly would sit glaring at her in frozen disapproval. She did not care for the featherbrained, dark-skinned little creature from wherever Titus Judah had brought her, and she saw nothing but a waste of time trying to teach her anything. Nevertheless, Judah was paying her handsomely to tutor his wife, and Miss Fynchly struggled on.

Judah left his family and sailed for the South Seas two months later, and despite Soledad's pleas that he take them back to California on his return, she could get no promise from him.

In the months that followed, Soledad suffered the pangs of her isolation and homesickness in a dull silence. The bare, ugly little house with no sunny patio or fragrant hanging flower baskets, or birds in gay cages, appalled her. The harsh severity of the climate congealed the very marrow in her bones, and nowhere did she hear the soft lilting words of her people, except from Hilo when they conversed in whispers out of Miss Fynchly's earshot.

Every night Soledad prayed to the Holy Mother for deliverance from this evil land. She lost weight. The sparkle and bloom were soon gone from her eyes and cheeks.

When Judah returned in the spring, she was almost pitifully glad to see him. While his ship was being refitted and provisioned, he took her about a little in the quiet countryside or to the smaller shops, and she was filled with a quick gratitude. To her pleas that he take her back to California, though, he turned a deaf ear.

"All in good time," he would say easily. "I'm a sailor and I have to go where my cargoes take me. I've a chance to make money on a trip to the Spice Islands."

"Then take me with you? I can't stand it here."

"Why not? Aren't you comfortable? You have a house, servants, a tutor for female companionship, what more do you want?"

Useless to tell him of her passionate longing for sunshine and blue skies, for the scent of roses and jasmine outside her windows, the murmur of the gentle voices of the Indian servants, of her brothers and Tía Isabella.

"When I come back, we'll see," he said. But when he returned it was only long enough to get her with child again, and he told her, "A ship is no place for a pregnant woman. You'll stay here and have your child."

For four intolerable years it was the same thing. Each time he returned she got another child, and it was useless to ask him to take her away. She had the boy William and two girls Leila and Jennifer, all quiet, delicate children, with their mother's tragic dark eyes. Only one of them, Jennifer, had her father's red hair and abrupt manner, and she was by far his favorite.

Judah had done what he set out to do. With a passel of children, and the paper from the Padre in Valparaiso, there could be no question of the validity of his claim to Soledad's portion of Loma de Oro. He had only to return to California and demand it.

Soledad had given up hope of seeing her home again, and resigned herself to her fate. She was like a ghostly somnambulist, docile and gentle, but uncomprehending of most of what went on around her. Thin and transparent as paper, Soledad sat at her window and moved her chair to whatever spot of sunshine she could find, like a wild flower seeking pitifully to sustain its weak life. Only the image in her mind, the thought of her beloved California, kept the will to live feebly aglow in her.

In the four years since he had been to California, Kinkaid had made a trip to Europe for his uncle, and one to the South Seas. He had asked everywhere, but could get no word of the *Vulcan* or of Captain Judah. It was as if the sea had swallowed them up.

Both were gone from sight. In the letters he exchanged with Tarifa, Bart had told her of his fruitless but continuing search, and had in turn learned the latest news of Loma de Oro.

Oddly enough, her frank mention of her affair with Larios and her brief word of her decision to marry Luis had left him in a towering rage. Luis was no match for her, he knew. But that she could have given herself so freely to a man of Larios' evident nature and reputation made anger erupt inside him like a waterspout.

He felt like a cheated husband. Yet Tarifa meant nothing to him. Could never mean anything to him. He thought of their last moments alone on the night she had come aboard the *Lorelei* searching for Soledad and Judah, and he wondered at the odd mixture of emotions he had felt then and unexpectedly felt now.

They were as far apart as the poles, with nothing in common, and yet she could affect him as few women ever had. Even Dolores had been different. He had loved her with his whole being, adored her, and the tragedy of her loss had never left him. The gentle goodness of her he could still worship in his lonely nights on the quarterdeck. But she had become something dear but distant. Like a childhood memory, warming, but no longer essential.

When he found himself thinking of Tarifa lately, he was surprised and disquieted to feel a flick of fire in his loins. He called himself every kind of a fool, and determined to get himself a woman in the next port he struck.

But he did not. He paced the streets instead for hours, and ended by going back to his cabin at dawn to write Tarifa that he was sailing for California as soon as he reached Boston and could refit his ship.

Jake Banner had an aged aunt living in Salem, and while the *Lorelei* was outfitting and loading cargo in Boston, he went to pay her a visit, persuading Kinkaid to accompany him.

Restless, Bart agreed. Salem was a quiet, sleepy little place, and Miss Jessie Banner lived in a cottage outside the town with her maid, an apple-cheeked Irish girl named Molly, and her seventeen cats.

She was delighted that Jake had brought his captain

along, and pleased to have two males to dance attendance on her ninety-two years.

"I lived right here in this same house all through the Revolution," she told Kinkaid over tea. "General Washington often passed this way."

Jake was standing by the window listening idly, when he bent forward with an exclamation of surprise.

"What is it?" asked Kinkaid from his seat by the old woman.

"That Kanaka, sir, passing by with those children. I'd swear he was aboard the *Vulcan* at San Diego."

"Where?" Kinkaid was across the room in a giant stride, his heart hammering against his ribs.

"Went around the corner, sir."

"Come on!"

"Wait, what is it, Jake?" the old lady called.

"Be back in a minute, Auntie. We've seen an old shipmate," Banner answered.

"Oh, your tea will get cold. Never mind, boy. Bring your friend back to tea?"

Kinkaid whirled down the road like a nor'easter tearing at the top gallants.

As they turned the corner the Kanaka was nowhere in sight, but the children Jake had seen were playing in a small square of fenced yard in front of a cottage.

"Those the children?"

Banner nodded.

Kinkaid waved the startled children aside and sprang up on the small porch to pound on the door with his fist.

A tall, dour-faced New England woman opened the door a crack and stared at him stonily.

"Yes?"

"Whose residence is this?" demanded Kinkaid.

"What business is that of yours? Who are you?"

"Captain Bart Kinkaid. Whose house is this?"

Miss Fynchly was somewhat mollified. A sea captain might well have legitimate business with another captain, and she had no wish to jeopardize her soft berth by angering Titus Judah.

"It is Captain Judah's house," she told him primly.

Kinkaid's heart leaped.

"I'd like to see him—or Mrs. Judah."

"The captain's at sea, and Mrs. Judah is not well and does not receive guests," came the simpering reply.

"By God, I'll bet she doesn't! Stand aside."

"You can't force your way in here, whoever you are—"

"Get out of my way!" He shouldered past her and strode into the cramped living room.

Soledad sat hunched in a chair, her face as close to the cold sunlight as she could get it. There was a vacant look in her sunken eyes when she glanced up at him, but no flicker of recognition.

This could not be Soledad Alvarjo, he thought wildly. Where was the plump prettiness he remembered, the sparkling coquettish eyes, the air of inner merriment? In God's name what had Judah done to her, damn his stinking soul!

He went to take her hands gently in his own, while Miss Fynchly whined and fumed behind him.

"Soledad. It's Bart Kinkaid. Don't you remember me? We met in California."

The dark eyes lifted and her whole being seemed to cling to the word *California* like a drowning man reaching for a piece of driftwood.

"Yes, California! You came to see Dolores at Loma de Oro," she said haltingly, wonderingly.

He spoke to her in Spanish and she seemed to rally and grow stronger under his eyes as her lips formed the old familiar words.

"I've come to take you back to California," he told her, quietly. "Home to Loma de Oro."

Her face lighted up and then a sudden cold fear washed over it. "My husband—he would never permit it! And the children—"

"You and the children are going back to California on my ship," he said firmly.

"But—Titus—"

"When he catches up to us," said Kinkaid, trying to keep the grim fury out of his voice, "he'll have to answer to me."

Hilo came in from the rear yard where he had been chopping wood, and Kinkaid put him to packing Soledad's and the children's things. He sent Banner to hire a suitable rig to transport them all to Boston.

Hilo, he promised, could go with them, but he paid off
and dismissed the maid and an obdurate and horrified
Miss Fynchly.

"When Judah returns," he told her, "you can say Captain Kinkaid of the *Lorelei* took his wife and children back
where they belong."

"A wife's place is with her husband," said Miss Fynchly
with haughty propriety.

"Not the wife of a bilge rat like Titus Judah!" thundered Kinkaid, and had the pleasure of seeing her blanch
and scurry from the house like a frightened weasel.

Soledad did not grow stronger during the voyage, in
spite of Bart's constant efforts to get her to take nourish-
ment and fresh air. But as the end of the voyage neared
she seemed to become more alert and excited. Her eyes
ever scanned the horizon for sight of land, and when at
last California hove in sight, she was like one possessed
in a delirium of complete joy.

Kinkaid did not even pause to declare his cargo at Monterey, but sailed directly down the coast to San Diego.

He was alarmed at the crumbling forlorn condition of
the presidio and the Mission, when he went there to hire a
conveyance to carry Soledad and her children to Loma de
Oro.

The only thing he could find was an ancient *carreta*
which would take days to reach their destination, so he
hired horses instead, taking Soledad in front of him and
ordering Banner and Hilo to carry the three children.

It was a warm rose-scented night when they rode up to
Loma de Oro. Antonio opened the door, and let out an
exclamation of disbelief when he saw Kinkaid and Soledad.

He came to lift her gently down from the horse and
asked wonderingly, *"Por Dios!* How did you find her,
Capitán?"

"By accident. She has been very ill; take care of her."

"Sí! And the *niños?"*

"Her children, by Judah."

"Santa Maria! They were married?"

"She says so—by Judah, and then by a priest in Valparaiso. Take her to your aunt."

"Sí! Come, *querida mía."*

Later, when Soledad had finished wandering through the house, touching the walls and furniture with little moans of delight and disbelief, Kinkaid sat with Antonio and his brothers in the study and told them everything he knew of Soledad's experience.

"Poor *niña*," Antonio murmured, "if that animal ever comes this way—"

"He will cross my path before he does yours, I hope," Kinkaid said grimly. He wondered why Tarifa did not appear, and Antonio explained that she was at Nazario's, where Rufina had just given birth to another son.

Kinkaid asked tentatively after Luis, and Antonio informed him that Luis had married an American girl, Elena Havelock, and lived now on a portion of Don Zenobio's rancho that the girl's uncle, Don Patricio, had bought and renamed the Rincon de Norte. Luis was also studying law, said Antonio, with Tiburcio Novato, and helping him with his law practice in Los Angeles.

Kinkaid felt an odd restlessness and disappointment that Tarifa was not at home. He had wanted to see her when he returned with Soledad, to find out once and for all if there was any truth to his mixed feelings for her, in his strange desire to be with her again.

At last he excused himself, though Antonio had begged him repeatedly to spend the night, and rode for Zenobio Sanchez's.

He found the old soldier still up playing monte with his servant for piles of beans.

"I am rich now, *amigo*," he said joyfully, "so I no longer have the desire to play for real *dinero*. I might lose it!"

Seated with the *aguardiente* bottle between them, Zenobio told him all the news that Tarifa had not written him in the past years.

"Tarifa has changed since Luis married. Maybe she did love him after all, and Padre Cazon and I were wrong? She is not a woman one can judge accurately. I tell you, *amigo*, she did a courageous thing in giving him up as she did, if she was in love with him."

Kinkaid watched the flames in the little fireplace and there was a brooding distant look in his gray eyes that made them seem almost black in the dim room.

Before breakfast Kinkaid mounted and rode southeast

toward Bolsa Coyotes. He still wondered at the impatience in him, but he no longer fought it. He had never done anything by halves, and because he had learned to be brutally honest with himself he knew that he could accept whatever he now found within his own heart.

He saw her coming when she was still a great distance away. No one else rode like that. Madly, fearlessly, and yet with the easy grace of a hawk flying through the air.

As she drew nearer he saw her hesitate and then come on, her long black hair flying out from under her sombrero. She wore a red velvet jacket and trousers trimmed with black braid, and a black sash wound about her slender waist. Something about her reminded him of a small brave flame, and he felt the surge in his own blood.

She reined Guindilla to a halt, and he could see a patch of white on the stallion's shoulder where an old scar had healed. Tarifa sat watching him with surprise and pleasure.

"I did not expect you so soon," she said.

"I found Soledad," he told her, "and brought her to Loma de Oro last night."

She glanced at him in grateful amazement, and listened attentively while he told her all he knew of the girl's story.

"She has children, you say?" Her eyes were hard as agate.

"Three of them, a boy and two girls. She herself is very frail; the experience has broken her, I'm afraid."

Tarifa said nothing and he cursed himself for all the things he wanted to say and now found that he could not. When they were actually together the old barriers rose up again. Neither of them could yield, so there was no point at which to start.

He watched her face and realized that he had been hungry for the sight of it. There was no real beauty, no softness, no affection there. Yet it stirred him as no other face in the world.

Was it really possible, he thought, that he had felt this tugging attraction to her from the first? Even when it seemed that he had hated her, even while he knew himself in love with the gentle Dolores? It couldn't be, and yet he had the conviction that it was true. The knowledge shook

him to the core. It meant he could no longer trust even
his own senses where she was concerned. And how would
Tarifa repay him if she knew the truth of his feelings for
her? There was a savage, cruel streak in her that could
throw a man's love for her back in his teeth while her lips
and eyes mocked his weakness. And he would never dare
to show her even a trace of weakness.

Determination, ruthlessness, mastery, these were the
things she understood in a man. He wondered, in savage
self-castigation, if she had really loved the bandit Pito
Larios, or Luis Alvarjo—or Don Ygnacio for that matter?

Tarifa said, "You must come to the rancho so that we
can thank you properly for returning Soledad."

"I must declare my cargo at Monterey," he said.
Then: "Come with me? It will do you good. I'll only be
gone a few weeks."

She glanced at him and smiled. She sensed something
different in him and wondered idly what it was.

"It would be nice, Bart, but the rancho—"

"Let Santos worry about it for a few weeks," he said
brashly. "Come with me? It's all the repayment I ask."

She patted Guindilla's shoulder absently and seemed to
consider it for a moment. "There are some things I could
do in Monterey," she mused, "but I would have to take
Penti along, or Tía Isabella would be shocked."

"Take her then!" laughed Kinkaid, giddy with his easy
victory.

It was a calm sailing, and on their first night Tarifa and
Kinkaid dined alone in his cabin.

She wore a white gown and comb and carved ivory earrings that cast long shadows on her slender cheeks in the
lamplight. Her dusky Gypsy beauty had never shown to
better advantage. Kinkaid was content just to watch her
and listen to her voice.

When he could pry her mind away from the affairs of
the rancho, she discussed with him the ports he had visited,
the politics that were shaping the destiny of his country
and might lead to a war with Mexico, and the uncertain
future of California.

He bit off the end of a cigar, lighted it, and leaned back
in his chair. Tarifa could see the hard muscular span of his

chest under his unbuttoned coat where it drew tight about the shoulders. All night she had seen his gray eyes watching her in a new way that she was at a loss to explain, and that she did not like exactly.

"What will you do if the price of hides goes on dropping as it has been this past year?" he asked suddenly.

"I will sell for the best price I can get," she answered promptly, "and I will dry and ship beef as Señor Havelock does, to New Mexico, if necessary."

"I fear the end is in sight for the hide and tallow business, Tarifa. If war breaks out with Mexico, our ships will be needed there to run supplies and to blockade. They will bypass California. Have you ever thought what you would do when the rancho no longer is able to pay for itself?"

Her lips hardened. "I will find some way to run it. I will not lose Loma de Oro!"

"Perhaps you won't have to." His face was impassive through the smoke of his cigar. "Have you ever thought of—taking out insurance?"

"Insurance?" She eyed him suspiciously.

"Exactly. Have you ever thought of marrying to protect Loma de Oro?"

"Marriage? To Luis, you mean?" She sounded frankly puzzled.

He controlled the hot stab of jealousy and said, "No, not marriage to a gentle weakling like Luis, or to a ruthless renegade like Pito Larios. Marriage to a man with enough means and strength to ensure Loma de Oro's future against catastrophe, no matter what happens."

She frowned at him. "I don't understand you when you talk like this."

"I mean marriage to a man like me." He watched her face and realized that for the first time he had really astounded her.

"You!" Her black eyes widened in disbelief; the look deepened into dislike.

"Why not? I'm fond of Loma de Oro, too. It holds— memories for me. And we understand each other, you and I? What would you have to lose? I could guarantee the rancho's future, and you could provide me with something solid to build upon. Something to take up my interest. Since Dolores' death I've been restless, too restless."

Tarifa turned away from his watchful eyes and clamped her lower lip between her sharp white teeth.

"I could never marry an Americano," she said slowly.

"Why not? I assure you we are just like any other men. With the same faults, same tastes, same desires—"

"No!"

"Are you afraid of me?" His eyes bored into hers.

"I'm not afraid of anyone." She threw the words at him scornfully. She stood up with her arms straight at her sides.

"Then it is Ygnacio and his dislike of Americans that speaks, and not you? I would not have thought it of you, Tarifa. Did Ygnacio hold that much sway over your opinions?"

"Perhaps," she said coldly. "I don't know. I only know it would not work for you and me."

He got up and came to stand behind her. She could smell the smoke from his cigar as he put it down on the table and placed his hands lightly on her shoulders to turn her to face him.

"Listen to me. We have been friends, at least by letter these past years. Do you honestly dislike me, Tarifa?"

"No. But you must realize the truth of what the others say of me. There is no softness, no affection in me. I must be my own master, free and independent."

"I do not believe there is no affection in you," he said slowly. "And I want you to be free. Understand, I will make no demands that you are unable or unwilling to fulfill. I wouldn't want you any other way. You would be worse than useless to me unless you came of your own free will. I will place no ties upon you."

She stared up at him, watchful and alert as a wild creature, tense under his firm hands, and he fought down the desire that swept over him to pull her into his arms and put his mouth to hers.

"Why do you want to marry me?" she asked, genuinely puzzled.

"I told you." He kept his voice light. "Because I am fond of Loma de Oro, and fond of you as well. I want to provide for you both. I also want to be near the child Dolores."

This she accepted as fact.

"And you would ask nothing in return?"

"Only what you wanted to give me," he said evenly.

There was a slyness now in her curved eyes that put him on guard, but he continued to hold her.

"You would not often be at Loma de Oro?"

"Not often."

"And you understand that I will not leave it? Ever?"

"Yes. I understand."

She lowered her eyes and then quickly glanced up at him again from under her straight lashes. He felt the blood pound in his throat and temples, but even her next words did not make him lose control. He meant to have her in any way he could, on her terms or his. It didn't matter which.

"Since Ygnacio died I have found that marriage is not a desirable thing for a Gypsy. I am through with the physical ties of marriage. I must be free, as my people are free, to take love where I choose. And what else is left for a husband's rights if he cannot share his wife's bed?"

Kinkaid's cheeks felt as if they were blazing, but his voice in his own ears was as calm and cool as polar ice. He even managed a faint laugh.

"I can have all the bed wenches I want from here to Zanzibar, and I have had them, if you're interested. It's something different I want from you. Partnership. Loma de Oro is a good business proposition, if it is handled right. And I want companionship. There is no reason we can't be friends, is there? And a sailor likes a feeling of belonging somewhere, even if he is a poor hearthside dweller."

Tarifa watched him and was still not satisfied, although she had been intrigued. She was often lonely these days, she did need companionship, and she already valued his friendship. She was convinced that he was sincere about Loma de Oro, and that she could trust him, something she had never been able to do since Ygnacio died. And there was that odd dual feeling for him in her, of attraction to his strength, and wariness at his air of command. She knew that she could never allow him to dominate her. She might have allowed Pito Larios, on occasion, to dominate her physically, but she had always remained in control of her own mind and spirit. She might never be in danger of physical domination from Kinkaid, unless she chose it, but his very presence frightened her. It was a suffocating feeling, as if her very soul were being swallowed up, devoured by another creature whom she did not understand or want to understand.

She stepped away from him. He let her go instantly, dropping his hands to his sides.

He said softly, with a twinkle in his eyes that deepened the crow's-feet above his tanned cheeks, "You don't have to be afraid I won't keep my word, Tarifa. I swear to you that you can be my wife on your terms, not mine, for as long as you like. Forever, if you choose."

"Then why can't we just be partners? I will sell you Lasho's interest in Loma de Oro."

He shook his head and yawned elaborately before picking up his dead cigar.

"No, I want to know you are my wife, in whatever capacity you choose to fulfill the role. We should make a success of our marriage. We are alike. We each have a streak of ruthlessness and determination. And, if you'll pardon my saying it, a touch of Yankee—or Gypsy—ingenuity? When I want to feel sure of the tie that binds, an anchor to windward, I'll have you. And when you need support, whether monetary or mental, you can call upon me. Do we up anchor on that bargain?"

Tarifa stood watching his face. He felt the conflict within her scheming, suspicious Gypsy brain, and the deathly stillness inside himself as he waited. It was done. He had been honest with her, perhaps too honest. But he had not let her know the depth of his true feeling for her. And that had not been completely avoidable. He was not even certain himself of his feeling for her.

He knew that she angered and entertained him more than any woman he had ever met, and he desired her more than he had ever desired any other female, with a hot need that would not leave him. And yet he could stand back and dispassionately decry any physical demand upon her and mean it. He loved her with a passion more complete than he had ever thought it possible to give to one woman. Far more than the tender flood of warmth and desire he felt for Dolores.

This was a tumult, a mountainous tide that lifted him

up and flung him helpless into the seething depths, and yet he was aware that it might never be released. That he might never be able to even tell her about it. It was like watching yourself dashed to pieces on a cruel coral reef, without being able to lift a finger to save yourself, or even desiring to do so.

She said slowly, "They may not like it at Loma de Oro."

His eyes were amused, but his heart lifted.

"Have you ever been concerned about the opinion of others, especially the Alvarjos?"

She laughed. "No."

"Neither have I."

"You want to marry me now?" she asked, watching his face with shadowed eyes.

"As soon as it can be arranged. But I will not marry you by reading the services myself, aboard ship, as Judah did Soledad. I want it legal and binding, according to the laws of the land."

He turned back to the desk to relight his cigar. "We'll make a pair of pretty poor Catholics? But if that's what we have to do to make our marriage valid, we'll do it. When we come back from Monterey, I'll take instructions from Padre Cazon, and let him baptize me. Then he can marry us. Is that satisfactory?"

Tarifa shrugged. "For me it is not necessary to be married by the Padres." She was not sure Padre Cazon would consent to marry her, though she could probably convince him of her return to the faith.

"It is for me," Kinkaid said sharply. "No one is going to say that ours is not a real marriage, even if they happen to be correct in one respect."

Tarifa glanced away from him. Her face was dark in the lamplight, enigmatic as a panther's.

"Another thing," he said, "before we drop the subject. For the remainder of our married lives when you feel the need to fulfill your physical desires—do so in secret and well away from Loma de Oro."

"As you will do?" She smiled mockingly. The malicious, venomous smile that he hated, that made the blood thicken in his veins. But he kept his voice calm.

"Exactly."

She laughed.

"You do not need to worry on that score. I have the

same desire to protect the name of Loma de Oro as you have."

He forced the tension out of his limbs by sheer will-power, and smiled back at her.

"Let's drink a toast then, to our mutual regard for the welfare of Loma de Oro? That at least we can share on an equal basis."

She came to pour the wine herself and touched the rim of her glass to his with vigor.

"To Loma de Oro, Bart."

"Loma de Oro," he said. "Hill of gold, in my language. I wonder why Alvarjo named it that?"

"For the nob of hill where the cabaña stands," she said. "In the spring it is covered with wild mustard and poppies, like a vast sea of gold."

Her face had taken on a softer, more dreamy look than he had ever seen there. He had not fully realized before how much the rancho meant to her. If Loma de Oro was to be his real rival rather than some other man, he was more pleased than jealous. Let her pour her heart and soul and energy into the rancho, and he would back her every inch of the way.

"Do we also seal the bargain with a kiss?" he asked lightly, expecting her to refuse. But she surprised him by stepping into his arms and putting her own around his neck.

"Why not—this once?"

But the instant their lips met they both knew that her words were not true.

This was not the gentle kiss he had given her at Loma de Oro, when she stood with Dolores' child in her arms, and he had wanted merely to take them both to his heart to envelop them in tenderness and protectiveness.

This had the supercharged electrical violence of a thunderbolt wrapping around them like a streak of lightning, making them quiver with the intensity of its blinding flash.

Tarifa pushed away from him and her face was ashen under its coppery glow, as if a dull fire burned within her.

"Never kiss me again," she said with an effort. "Never come near me again!" Her hands clutched the folds of her gown like talons.

He had been as shaken as she, but he moved toward her a step, one hand thrust out as if to beg her pardon. He wanted to make her understand that he had not done it deliberately, that he was as startled in his own way as she had been.

"Tarifa—"

"Keep away from me!" Her eyes blazed with fury.

He said in a low voice, "I wouldn't hurt you, you know that."

"There is something wrong between us," she cried. "I have known it from the first. We do not belong together!"

With an effort he got a grip on himself and said, "I told you I want nothing from you that you are not willing to give."

She stepped away from him warily.

"I cannot be tied to you in any way!"

His tone changed suddenly to one of gentle mockery.

"Because you are afraid it wouldn't be safe?" He forced himself to laugh. "I assure you nothing could be further from the truth. I might desire you, as I'd desire any red-blooded woman who attracted me momentarily, but I would never go to the trouble of seducing you against your will. The husband who can only satisfy his sense of possession and mastery in bed is no husband at all. And as I have told you, a sailor can get all the female companionship he wants, in any size, shape, or color."

Tarifa flushed and a look of black anger crossed her face.

"I have told you I am not afraid of you. I do not always understand you, and I despise you at times, but I am never afraid of you!"

"Good," Kinkaid said gallantly. "It is always helpful to know how a future bride really evaluates her groom. If you are not afraid of me—and if a moment such as we have just had never occurs again—are we still agreed upon our connubial pact?"

Tarifa scowled at him. He had forced her into an untenable position. She had declared her lack of fear of him as a man, and offered a toast to their wedding. If she backed out now, on whatever pretext, he would laugh at her and he would no doubt believe in his own heart that she had fallen prey to an emotion for him which she would never admit to herself even if it were true. Which it was not.

She drew herself up proudly and he admired the straightness of her shoulders, and the high-pointed line of her breasts. She looked like the delicately cut figurehead of a Javanese brig he had once seen in the Dutch East Indies.

"If you still wish to live up to the letter of our pact, Captain Kinkaid," she said, "I will live up to mine. *I* have nothing to lose."

"And much to gain—materially?" He laughed, trying not to show his relief. "I've put aside a good bit of money —something from every voyage since I first sailed before the mast—more than enough to ensure the future of Loma de Oro. What else shall we do with it?"

In this generous, open frame of mind, she could almost enjoy his company. The avid Gypsy in her exulted at the thought of his wealth—while the Arab in her plotted and planned how best to use the power it would also bring her.

Ygnacio had left her land and stock, and with it a certain authority and influence. But it had been limited to what the Alvarjo name and legacy controlled. Now she could extend her sovereignty if she chose, and reach out to grasp an empire, to start a dynasty, if it pleased her. She could rule like a caliph. What did it matter that she did so bearing the strangely harsh American name of Señora Kinkaid, not the aristocratic one of Dona Tarifa Alvarjo?

"We must buy more land," she told Kinkaid breathlessly, "and enlarge Loma de Oro."

"But I thought you had barely enough vaqueros now to run the rancho and Bolsa Coyotes?"

"I will get more! What does it matter anyway, whether we use all the land or not? It will always be ours—they cannot take it away."

Kinkaid nodded his head at her sagacity, for he had always felt much the same way himself. The land could not be despoiled, no matter how often the provisional government changed its governors or policies.

"Very well. Start buying. I will back you to the limit of my pocketbook, which I must assure you is by no means limitless. But it will no doubt buy several thousand leagues. Make sure that you get proper deeds to the land, however, and that they are properly recorded."

"Of course. I will have Luis and Tiburcio Novato handle it."

Her black eyes shone and now she reminded him of a bold precocious child who has gotten her own way, and is searching for a way to please her benefactor, if only temporarily.

"Would you like me to dance for you?"

"Because you dance when you are happy?"

"Yes—or when I am upset, or sad."

"No, thank you."

"But why not?" She was clearly hurt annd puzzled by his lack of interest.

He gave her a level look and went back to his chair and sat down.

"Because I would never know which emotion you were feeling while you were dancing for me."

"But that is foolishness!"

"To you perhaps—not to me. I value my emotions too highly to play loose and fast with them. You may do your dancing as you will do your—other recreations. Privately."

She gave him a superior, knowing smile, but he saw it vanish to be replaced by a scowl at his next words:

"Never think that the sight of your dancing alone would raise erotic emotions in me. I have seen dancers who could put you to shame. Nautch girls, Egyptian belly dancers, Africans, Sandwich Islanders, and Samoans, who know more of eroticism and of sheer passion than you will ever know. But I have never felt that I had to participate in their gyrations, either before or afterward, when I had seen them dance."

"You lie! There are no better dancers than I am. I am the daughter of Bandonna, the *faraóna*, and she taught me herself!"

"I congratulate you. But you have never seen the others dance, and I have, so how can you judge?"

She flounced away from him and sat down as far from his chair, as she could, watching him with murderous hatred while he took up a fresh cigar and calmly lighted it. When he had finished he said, "Let's not quarrel on the night of our betrothal, Tarifa. Shall we make a list of the subjects that are tabu in our conversations, and stick to the rest, however meager, my dear?"

She shrugged elaborately but he knew he had scored a point. His victory made him feel magnanimous.

"In honor of our wedding, I would like you to select new furnishings for Loma de Oro. Send the old things to Bolsa Coyotes, if you like."

He could see by the softening of her lips that the prospect pleased her, but she was too proud—or still too cross with him—to accept his proposal at once.

"The furnishings at Loma de Oro are of the best."

"But one can always improve a house by new furnishings? Though I only expect to be there at rare intervals, I would like to feel that it was furnished in the best fashion we are able to afford."

"Well—I have no objections in that case," said Tarifa graciously.

"After I've declared the cargo at Monterey, you may select what you want for Loma de Oro before I begin to trade."

He was amused at the look of carefully concealed greed as she lowered her lashes to watch him covertly out of the corner of her scimitar-shaped eyes.

She was a vixen, a hellion, a witch, whatever you wanted to call her, he thought, and she would never change. He would always have to be on his guard against her to protect himself, and yet he found her so damned stimulating and intriguing with her devious corkscrew mind, her incomplete emotions, and her startlingly primitive brutal physical reactions, that he knew he would never regret his bargain. Let her strip him mentally, physically, and spiritually, if she could. The experience would be cheap at the price.

They were married a month after the *Lorelei* returned from Monterey, at Mission San Luis Rey, by Padre Cazon. It was a hot, windless summer day, with only the members of the Alvarjo family and the crew of the groom's ship in attendance, each group uncomfortable and awkward in the other's presence.

Afterward they held a small celebration in the patio at the newly redecorated Loma de Oro, and Bart Kinkaid toasted his bride with imported champagne and danced with her gaily while the bemused and secretly shocked Alvarjos looked on. They had no objections to Tarifa's marrying an Americano, if that was her wish, but that she should presume to bring him to Loma de Oro and make it clear that both of them would consider the rancho their home was unthinkable.

Only Luis dared broach the subject to Tarifa in the name of his disgruntled relations.

"I am still the legal executor of your father's estate," Tarifa snapped, as they sat in her study. "I have married only in the hope of safeguarding Loma de Oro, and providing for the Alvarjos' future—as I promised your father to do."

Luis stared at her in disbelief. "You married the Americano for this reason only? You have no love for him?"

"There are other reasons than love for marrying." She turned away from him. "He understands. We are going to enlarge the rancho, improve it. You have seen what he has already done about the furnishings? Never fear, when the time comes you will each get your share of the estate."

Luis lowered his eyes, a hot flush on his face. He had never quite forgotten that this woman had professed to love him, and given him up voluntarily. He had no way of knowing that she had then dismissed him as a weak, useless creature, more to be pitied than desired. But his own marital happiness, in the face of her newest stark sacrifice for the family, filled him with guilt. His strong sense of fairness made him also pity Captain Kinkaid.

"What does he get out of it—the capitán?" he asked softly.

"What he wanted—a stake in a good business proposition and in the future of California," Tarifa answered firmly.

"We could have taken him in on a partnership basis," said Luis, avoiding her gaze by staring at his hand resting on the arm of the chair. "It was not necessary to marry him, Tarifa."

"He would not have it any other way. Stop worrying. Instead, find out for me which ranchos in the area can be bought. And how cheaply."

"I will do my best. But Tarifa—"

"Yes?"

"Will this sort of marriage be enough for you? Will you be happy?" He forced his eyes to meet hers and was shocked to find a glint of mischief mirrored there.

"Happiness! How long can happiness last for anyone? I shall be more than satisfied to have a rich husband who is seldom home, and demands nothing of me when he is."

"You are a cruel woman sometimes, Tarifa."

"I am an honest one. If that bothers your proud but gentle Alvarjo soul, I am sorry. I assure you it does not bother the New England conscience nor wound the spirit of my husband."

Padre Cazon had voiced much the same doubts after the wedding to Kinkaid, when he found to his consternation the type of marirage they planned.

"But it is sacrilegious! A marriage that is never to be consummated is not recognized by the Church as a marriage at all! Why didn't you tell me?"

Kinkaid smiled at him in amusement. "Precisely because we knew you would voice the objections you are now shouting to high heaven. The Church recognizes that we fulfilled all the requirements and were married properly by a priest, doesn't it?"

"Of course."

"Then the marriage is legal and cannot be considered invalid?"

"No, but—"

"If we then choose to live out our lives in each other's company without consummating our vows, does it mean that we do not have the right to declare ourselves married?"

"No. But as husband and wife—"

"We will be husband and wife in every way that the world can see. In every way but in one."

"But this is preposterous!" the priest exclaimed. "A mockery of the sacrament of God."

"No, it is not," Kinkaid said in a hard voice. "I married Tarifa in good faith, because I love her and because this was the only way to do it and make her happy. I put her happiness before any other, but I do not mock God or the church I have joined, in doing it my own way. I did

not have to tell you this, but I wanted you to know, because I like and respect you. I count you as my friend,
and I want to count on you to look after Tarifa when
I am gone. I must ask you to say nothing of our conversation to anyone else."

"But I do not understand," said the bewildered Padre.
"If you love her—does she know?"

"No." Kinkaid looked uncomfortable. He had not
counted on the priest's shrewdness. "And you must give
me your promise that she never will."

"You must tell her yourself. It will make all the difference—"

"Your promise?" Kinkaid said harshly.

"You have it. But you cannot—"

"My married life must be my own affair from now
on, Padre."

Cazon looked unhappy. "I am sorry for you, my son.
You do not know how cruel she can be, even to those
of whom she is most fond. It is as if there were a demon
in her that takes enjoyment in the suffering of others."

"I understand her, Padre," Kinkaid replied. "She will
not injure me. I know she does not love me, and most
likely never will. It is not important. We will make a
success of our marriage. I shall demand nothing of her
that she is not willing to give, and I'll see that she does
no further harm to others."

The priest turned away. He could not face the bold
confidence written on the American's face. It was a form
of brave but impossible hope. If the captain loved Tarifa
as deeply as Cazon suspected he did, she had already
scored a crippling victory over him. And he did not wish
to see the cruel but inevitable end of his friend's act of
hopeless folly.

Kinkaid was as good as his word. He was seldom at
Loma de Oro in the weeks that followed, and when he
was, he spent his time riding over the rancho on the horse
Tarifa had given him when he had last left California.
Often he took little Dolores up in front of him and galloped over the countryside for hours, to her delight. In
the evenings he went over the books with Tarifa in her
study, or discussed the new lands they were acquiring.

When they were finished they went arm in arm through
the patio, and up the stairs to the two adjoining bedrooms
that had belonged to Joaquin and Santiago, that they now
used as their own. Tarifa put up her cheek indifferently
for his kiss. And he gave it carefully, dutifully, without
lingering and turned at once to his own door.

If the family were puzzled by the lack of passion in
the union, they refrained from discussing it even among
themselves.

Only Penti was not as considerate, or reticent.

"What is this madness you do now?" she asked Tarifa
one morning when they were alone in her bedroom.

"I don't know what you are talking about," Tarifa re
plied as she brushed her hair with hard vigorous strokes
that made the blue-black strands leap with electricity in
the sunlight.

"This unnatural marriage to the Americano, that is
what I mean."

"It is none of your affair."

"*Ai!* If it is not my affair, whose is it? Am I not of
your blood? Did not Bandonna send me with you to
protect you?"

Tarifa put up her hair with swift savage strokes.

"You are a meddling old fool. Go back to the nursery
where you belong."

"Not until I know what devilment is in your mind now.
Long ago I told you the capitán was a strong man; what
have you done to talk him into this foolishness? This marriage that is no marriage?"

"He requested it himself."

"I do not believe you."

Tarifa turned on her angrily. "And I do not care what
you believe! It is my affair. We have made an agreement
that is satisfactory to us both. Now, go!"

Penti's lips curled over her broken blackened tooth-
line. "When you speak like that you are not sure of yourself. Take care, *miri pen*, that the snare does not catch
your own feet. I have read the cards, and there is trouble
ahead for you both. The man has been a fool, as well
as you, and he will pay for it, but it is your own safety
I worry about."

"You prattle nonsense as always. What do I care for

your idiotic tarot?" Nevertheless she felt a whiff of primitive fear. In the Triana she had seen men sicken and die after an evil turn of the cards. What had the old witch found out now? She decided to make a clean breast of it and tell Penti everything that lay between Bart and herself. When she had finished she felt better, and she noted an odd light of satisfaction in Penti's eyes.

"It is as I thought, even as the cards said. You should not have married him. A Gypsy does not have to marry, but when she does, she is bound by her vows. To make a mockery of them is to revile the gods."

"You speak nonsense! It was his idea, I tell you. He would not have it any other way."

Penti gave her a long searching look and left the room. But her words had upset Tarifa.

When she came downstairs, Bart was in the patio drinking early chocolate with Tía Isabella and Soledad. Soledad's eyes, far too large for her pale face now, followed him worshipfully like a faithful dog adoring its master from a distance.

Bart glanced up at Tarifa with that quick speculative look she had come to expect from him, and rose to offer her his chair.

"No, I haven't time," she said, pulling on her gloves. "I am riding to Zenobio's. Luis says he is willing to sell the portion of the Santa Teresa that adjoins Loma de Oro."

"Then I will go with you," Bart said. He knew that she did not want him along but there was very little she could do to stop him in the presence of the two Alvarjo women. It gave him an inner satisfaction to get the best of her. In her black riding clothes and sombrero, she looked far more regal and aristocratic than the two pale women staring up at her with faint dislike on their faces.

When they were mounted and riding toward Zenobio's, Kinkaid said, "Why didn't you want me to come? I assure you I won't interfere with your plans."

"I didn't know you wanted to come," Tarifa answered impatiently. She had no way of telling him that at times his mere presence irritated and disturbed her. She had hoped for a few hours of quiet conversation with Luis. She could still find a certain peace and contentment in his quiet gentle manner. She recognized his weakness; married to him she would no doubt have grown irritated and impatient with him before now, but he would have been a restful person to live with. Undemanding and mild. With Kinkaid she could never relax, and she detested the cold speculative way he had of watching her lately, as if she were an insect that he was examining under a glass. But he could always secure her attention by discussing the rancho or the property they were buying, as he was doing now.

"If we buy Zenobio's land, will that satisfy you then?" he asked. He saw her shoulders straighten and a look of pleased satisfaction come into her eyes.

"Yes! We will then own as far as the Mission lands on the north, with the exception of the Havelock property."

"And the Havelocks do not wish to sell?"

"No." Tarifa frowned. She still had no friendship for either Ellen or Patrick Havelock, and she considered it a breach of neighborliness for Zenobio to have sold them any part of his land.

"Never mind," Bart said quickly. "I had a talk in the pueblo the other day with Don Martinez. He may be willing to sell us the strip of land that fronts on Bolsa Coyotes and the southern boundary of Loma de Oro."

She turned to him joyfully. "He has said so?"

It was incredible the animation that anything to do with the rancho could spark in her.

"He hinted as much. I thought we might go to call upon him before I leave." He was overdue to start the trading up and down the coast that would take him the better part of a year, and yet he was reluctant to go. He wished Tarifa would sail with him, but he knew better than to ask her. He was determined to fulfill his part of their bargain.

He did not know what he expected in the long run, certainly no miracle of change in her. But he had hoped that patience and friendship might cause her to respond. She did not hate him, he knew that, but there was still a barrier between them when they were alone together. It was as if she were reluctant to accept anything from him for herself, only for Loma de Oro, as they had agreed.

Zenobio greeted them joyfully and rode out with them to where his property adjoined the Havelocks'.

"We should have had the whole piece," Tarifa fumed,

reining Guindilla around a boulder and staring down the hillside with distaste at the newly whitewashed adobe Havelock had built.

"You have land enough," Zenobio chided. "And at the time, if you recall, Dona Tarifa, you had no money with which to buy my land?"

Tarifa flushed and her hand closed angrily on her quirt.

Kinkaid stepped into the breach, saying quietly to Zenobio, "If you will let us know how many leagues you will sell, Zenobio, I will bring the money to you tomorrow."

"I am growing rich." Zenobio chuckled, and tugged at his beard with a grimy fist. "You know, I may go as far as Monterey with you, Capitán, and buy myself a fine house near the best wine shop."

Ellen and Luis came to the door of the hacienda to greet them, and Kinkaid was pleased at the wife Luis had taken for himself. He had met her briefly at the wedding and had been impressed then with her air of quiet dignity. Now he sensed her inner strength and warmth as he saw her exchange a look of affectionate understanding with her husband. He has someone worthwhile to lean upon now, the American thought; they compliment each other and there will never be any misunderstanding between them because they can both give and take without fear of losing their individuality. He glanced at Tarifa; her eyes were carefully averted from the happy faces of the young couple.

Bart said, "I will be leaving in a week; we will have a small fiesta next Sunday. I hope you will all come?"

"Will you be going, too, Dona Tarifa?" Havelock asked.

"No. My place is here on the rancho."

"But if your husband—"

"My husband understands and agrees," Tarifa said in a cold voice.

Havelock turned away and methodically refilled his glass. He raised it to Kinkaid.

"To the day when you can retire to Loma de Oro, Captain."

"Thank you, sir."

Kinkaid's fiesta was a great success. Because of the hard times, no one had given a really gala celebration in a long while, and everyone in the countryside accepted his invitation with spontaneous delight.

Bart insisted that the thing be done right. He personally supervised the hanging of paper lanterns and colored streamers in the patio, rehearsed the Mission orchestra in the tunes he wanted played, and sent Santos and Tomas aboard the *Lorelei* to fetch a *carreta* load of food and the ship's cook to instruct Candelaria in baking American pies and cakes.

At Antonio's insistence, Bart donned the clothes appropriate to a California hacendado, and found much to his amusement that he looked well in the black velvet trousers and short braid-trimmed jacket, with the wide red sash about his lean waist.

When he entered her room to show her his costume, Tarifa thought he seemed taller and at the same time more withdrawn than in his seaman's garb.

She herself wore a red satin gown, the full skirt decorated with huge exotic birds made of yellow and green bugle beads, and a soft yellow lace mantilla on her black hair.

He stood behind her chair at the dressing table, looking into the glass at their twin images.

"Don Bartolomeo and Dona Tarifa Kinkaid"—he pronounced it *Keenkhaid* as the Californians did—"Quite a sumptuous couple, don't you think?"

"I think you are acting childish," she said crossly.

"You mean you don't like me in this costume?"

"It is very becoming."

She had lowered her eyes to the bracelet she was fastening around her wrist, but they flashed upward swiftly when she felt his strong hands on her bare shoulders.

His eyes gazing back at her in the mirror were as cold and black as the Atlantic in midwinter.

"When I am gone will you remember that you are Señora Kinkaid? Or will it be easy to forget it?"

"How could I forget it?"

"You will act the part, even if you do not live it. Is that clear?"

"It will not be difficult."

The violence with which he jerked her from the chair to her feet made her gasp with surprise and anger. He stood holding her off from him, searching her face as if he hoped to find insincerity there as an excuse to strike her.

Her own voice was as cold as his had been.

"What is the meaning of this? You have no call upon me, remember? I am your wife and I will not dishonor your name publicly—more than that I did not agree upon, and I will not promise! Now take your hands off me."

He let her go and stepped back as if a bad dream had passed, and he had wakened to the safety of normality still bemused by the nightmare.

"I'm sorry, Tarifa. I have no right to ask more than you have agreed to give. I want no more. I'm better away from this place. But for the sake of the others, today we must put on a fair show. Do you agree?"

Tarifa shrugged. "If you like."

From the time the first riders, *carretas*, and carriages began to arrive, Bart could find no fault with Tarifa's bearing. She stood beside him on the veranda welcoming their guests regally, and the visitors seemed agreeably surprised at her air of open hospitality. No doubt, they thought, being married to the *Yanqui* capitán was improving her nature, if that was possible.

As soon as the first guests had arrived, including a reluctant Jake Banner and as many of the crew of the *Lorelei* as could be spared, the feasting and games began. The hardier souls rode whooping off to the sierras to try and rope a grizzly for the bearbaiting later in the afternoon, and the others began the favorite games.

The younger boys descended upon the racetrack Don Ygnacio had built, and proceeded to back their fastest horses with money, cattle, land, or anything else that might be suggested as a bet.

Kinkaid was amused to see his men from the *Lorelei* stand back in abashed silence watching these outlandish antics, disapproval written all over their staid New England faces. But as the infectious hilarity and horseplay continued throughout the afternoon, they were drawn into the celebration in spite of themselves. And despite the language barrier, the warm-hearted Californians managed to win over the diffident Yankees.

Bart watched Tarifa dance tirelessly with one man after

another, and was proud of her amazing grace and agility. He wanted to have her dance for him alone, the way he had first seen her, half-naked at the Mission *monjeria* in San Diego, but he could never risk it. He knew now he could keep his bargain only if he kept his distance from her. It was only common sense that he was leaving now, that they would be separated for the next few months. Perhaps then he could come back for an interval without either of them feeling the strain. For he knew that in spite of her indifference Tarifa was uncomfortable in his presence.

Ellen Havelock Alvarjo surprised him by demanding that he ask her to dance. As he whirled her into the waltz, she said, "I really wanted you to ask me to dance so that I could talk to you." She was smiling up at him.

"What can I do for you, Dona Elena?"

She laughed, the dimple showing in her cheek. "That name sounds so incongruous, doesn't it? Between two Americans?"

"Not any more so than Don Bartolomeo."

Ellen grinned up at him. "Would it be awfully impolite if I spoke to you alone for a moment?"

He was surprised. Ellen wasn't the sort of girl to be coy or play at games. He had a feeling that whatever she said or did would be done in dead earnest.

"Come into the study," he offered.

She refused a chair. And when he closed the door she stood facing him, looking small and trim in her simple white gown with a string of pearls at her throat.

"Captain Kinkaid, since we have both married into the same family, I feel that I may speak to you frankly."

"Of course," he said, puzzled by her air of tense urgency.

"I don't like your wife, Captain. I never have. I don't understand her, I suppose. And then I was jealous of her once—because of Luis." She lowered her eyes and her hands gripped her white fan tightly. "I know the things she can do. Ruthlessly, without a qualm. Forgive me if I'm upsetting you?"

"I'm not upset. I happen to know my wife quite well," he answered dryly. "Please go on."

She glanced up at him searching his face for something

she did not seem to find there. "Do you know her, Captain? Are you quite sure?"

"I'm afraid you will have to be more explicit with me, Dona—"

"Ellen, please?"

"—Ellen. I don't quite know what you're driving at."

"I'm afraid I have a selfish purpose. You see, I love my husband very much. Anything that touches him also touches me. I can't have him upset—or unhappy."

"And how does that concern my wife?"

"Luis feels that you should never have married. He is convinced, you see, that he is responsible for it. Tarifa was—in love with him. She wanted to marry him. Instead, she gave him up when she found that he was in love with me."

"Then she can't be all bad?" Bart asked gently.

Ellen shook her head. "You don't understand. She has married you for a reason Luis considers infamous and unfair to you both. She has married you to further the welfare of Loma de Oro. I'm sorry to tell you this, but I'm also selfish enough to consider Luis' well-being above anyone else's."

"A very commendable and rare thing to find in a wife," said Kinkaid. He studied her troubled face and found that he was not even annoyed that she and Luis suspected the truth. In their own way they were trying to save him, as well as Tarifa.

He said quietly, "Ellen, listen to me. I have not been duped, I assure you. I knew exactly what I was doing and how Tarifa felt before I married her. We came to a satisfactory agreement."

"Satisfactory agreement!" Ellen gasped. "But I've never heard of anything so cold-blooded! I can see what she gets out of it—money, more power. But what do you get?"

He took a cigar from his pocket, glanced inquiringly at her, and at her nod of permission lighted it.

"Ellen, everyone knows the things he wants out of life, his own desires and what price he is willing to pay to realize them. You ask what I get out of our—arrangement? An interest in Loma de Oro, and the satisfaction of knowing that no matter in what fashion she has agreed to it, Tarifa is my wife."

"And that is enough for you?"

"It has to be," he said flatly.

"But—it's so unfair. You deserve so much more. If you know her as you claim, then you know how heartless and cruel she can be."

He smiled at her through the spiraling cigar smoke, and he saw her eyes widen in sudden alarm.

"You—love her, like that?"

He had not thought her so perceptive. The smile left his face and he turned away momentarily.

"Then Luis was right. It is monstrous and wicked. She won't change, you know. She will never change."

Kinkaid tossed his cigar into the fireplace and turned to face her. There was a grim line about his mouth.

"This is entirely my business and Tarifa's," he said. "Besides Padre Cazon, I had no intention that anyone else should ever know the truth of how I feel about Tarifa. Can I trust you to keep this to yourself, not even to tell Luis?"

Her chin came up. "Of course, Captain. But I am sorry, so very sorry."

"Don't be. I am satisfied, I tell you."

"Does—she know?"

"No. And she never will, if I can count upon you."

Ellen lowered her head. She had not meant their conversation to end like this. She had not meant to guess his secret or share its burden, but she knew that she would now, till death if necessary, and her anger, her dislike for Tarifa rose stiflingly in her throat. Next to Luis, she liked and admired Kinkaid more than any other man she had ever known. Now Tarifa had touched them both, played cat-and-mouse with their emotions, their very lives. It was unbearable.

She was surprised to feel the tears on her cheeks, and then the handkerchief that Kinkaid was pressing into her hand.

"Don't weep for me, Ellen," he said softly. "Tarifa has done nothing to me that I have not let her do. That I am not willing to let her do."

His hand was on her shoulder, his head bent over hers, when the door opened.

Both Ellen and Kinkaid stepped back, startled by the intrusion.

Tarifa stood in the doorway, her eyes narrowed and a faint smile on her lips.

"Luis is looking for you, Elena."

"I'll—go at once. Thank you, Tarifa."

Tarifa stood aside to let her pass.

"Our guests are ready to leave," she told Bart indifferently. "Are you coming?"

"Of course." He made no attempt to explain why he and Ellen had been alone in the study, but he wondered how much she had heard before she opened the door. There was a sly self-satisfied expression on her face. It made him uneasy.

CHAPTER 29

Jake Banner was a man who seldom discussed his personal feelings with anyone. From the day when he had first put to sea as a young hand before the mast, he had learned to be completely self-reliant. Only in the matter of his affection for Bart Kinkaid was he at all vulnerable.

He could not believe at first that the captain meant to go through with his marriage to Tarifa. It was not until he stood in dumb horror inside the adobe Mission, and heard the priest pray over the couple in undecipherable Latin, and then pronounce them man and wife, that he had been forced to accept the inevitable.

The night before the wedding, as they shared a glass of brandy in the captain's cabin, Banner had forgotten himself long enough to ask:

"Why, sir, beggin' your pardon? Why should ye want

to marry her, sir? A woman as tried to kill ye once and almost did!"

Kinkaid had glanced up at him and smiled.

"Don't worry your head, Jake. I know what I'm doing."

Banner sighed and turned his glass around in his thick fingers.

"The other young lady, sir, the one as died, God rest her, she was a gentle sweet lady. But this one, sir—"

"Jake, I told you I know what I'm doing. She'll be my wife for my own reasons. Let that be an end to it."

"Aye, sir."

Now, with Kinkaid safely back aboard, it was almost as if the creature who was now his wife did not exist. Banner, ever watchful of Bart's mood, was relieved to find no repetition of the black desolation that had enveloped him when Dolores died. Whatever this woman meant to him, she did not have the power to bring him to the brink of self-destruction as Dolores had done.

But there was a strange, quiet waiting about Kinkaid now, like the lull before a violent storm, that bothered the mate.

When he watched the captain standing on deck, a cigar clamped between his strong white teeth, his eyes quietly scanning the horizon, he seemed exactly as he had always been—alert, watchful, competent. But there were times, in unguarded moments, when Banner thought he caught a look of haunted introspection in Kinkaid's eyes.

On his way up the coast after leaving San Diego, Kinkaid had seen the evidence of the ruin and destruction of the Missions that followed secularization, and it was with a new dread in his heart that he sailed into the magnificent bay at San Francisco. Fog swirled around the mountaintops, but the sea and shoreline were crystal clear, bathed in sharp fall sunlight.

Besides the *Lorelei*, there was a Peruvian brig, an American whaler, and a Russian hide ship in the harbor.

San Francisco, with its population of fifty including sixteen foreigners, was not a prepossessing sight, and yet Kinkaid was pleased to see William Richardson's abode that had replaced his earlier board shanty. Richardson, granted his lot in 1836, collected produce from points around the bay to make up cargoes for trading ships, aided by his Indian crews and the two or three launches belonging to him. Another trader, the American, Jacob Leese, had built a larger frame store near Richardson's. When he went ashore, Kinkaid was glad to see the road to the Mission had been widened and graded, no doubt by the ambitious Americans.

The trader, Richardson, alone at his store, was delighted to see Kinkaid.

"Ah"—Richardson wagged his big head as he poured brandy into his guest's glass—"it is a pity the way these politicians are strangling the life out of this beautiful land. You should hear Dr. Mabrey on the subject. San José has been a hotbed of revolt."

"Mabrey has been here?" asked Kinkaid.

"Yes. This morning. Came up to treat one of the Mission Indians. He'll be back along shortly."

Kinkaid was shocked at the big Englishman's appearance. He was thin and drawn and there was an ugly light in his heavy-lidded eyes. This was not the happy husband and father he had left only a few years back, the lover of all that was Californian, the hospitable hacendado who had given up medicine as he had turned his back on the bitterness of his past life. Then Bart had been the one in need of succor. Now it was his friend.

Mabrey slung his bag onto the nearest table and demanded whiskey. He downed two glasses and then sank into a chair as if his legs had collapsed under him.

He no longer wore Spanish clothes, but the dark somber suit in which Kinkaid first remembered seeing him.

"I'm glad you're here, Bart," he murmured. "I'm happy to see you looking better than when I last saw you."

"And you look like the devil," Kinkaid said. "What's the matter, John?"

Mabrey's mouth lifted wryly at the corners. "You might better ask what isn't. I once lost what I loved most. Somehow, I lived through it, as I'm glad to see you have done. But I've found out one thing, Bart—a man can't take the same blow twice."

"Lupe?"

"Dead. Two years ago." He poured himself a drink. "I told you I was through with medicine when I came to this land of bounty and beauty. I meant it. I wanted nothing to remind me of my old life.

"Then the bad drought came, followed by the fever. I started through the countryside doing what I could. It was little enough, God knows, but I tried. When I returned home I found Lupe and all the children down with it. I —wasn't able to save a one of them." His voice dropped away like a vanished breeze.

Kinkaid broke the spell by asking, "Will you sail with me when I leave here, John? I have a young sister-in-law I'm worried about. She seems to have gone into a danger-ous decline."

"Sister-in-law! Don't tell me you're married, boy?"

Kinkaid told him of Tarifa, of Soledad, and the other Alvarjos. And he found that in the telling he had aroused the Englishman's interest and taken his mind temporarily away from his own troubles.

"Married to the Gypsy wench I've heard so much about? I can't believe it! Are you happy, lad?"

Kinkaid lowered his head to light his cigar.

"Yes, very."

"A ranchero—a hacendado no less? I'm glad to hear it, my boy."

"Will you go south with me, John?" Kinkaid asked.

"Perhaps—I don't know. Give me time to think it over?"

"I'll be here for a couple of months, is that long enough?"

"Quite." For the first time there was a real smile on the doctor's worn face. "And now I'll take that whiskey—to salute the happily married couple."

In February when he returned to San Diego, Kinkaid brought John Mabrey to Loma de Oro as his guest.

Tarifa greeted her husband with a mixture of pleasure and annoyance, for she had been in the midst of leaving for Los Angeles to go over some land grants with Tiburcio Novato and Luis.

"I believe your trip can wait," Kinkaid said steadily when they were alone. "I want you to be particularly nice to our guest."

He watched her where she stood with her back to the study window, her sullen Gypsy beauty more exciting than he had remembered it. Unlike the Spanish California women he had met, her beauty did not fade but seemed to grow more mysterious and voluptuous with time. She wore a green corded silk gown, made after the fashion of Ellen Havelock's dresses, high at the neck with long fitted sleeves. She had pushed the black *rebozo* from her head and wore it now like a shawl about her shoulders. Long jet earrings hung from her ears and a wide band of jet circled her wrist.

"Why did you bring a doctor here?" she asked crossly. "We have Penti, we have no need of doctors."

"You haven't, my pet, I can see that," he said dryly. "I brought him because he is my friend. I believe this house is partly mine, as long as we share it together?"

She turned the bracelet on her wrist impatiently.

"Of course."

"Then all I ask is that you play the part of my wife, at least in public, and make yourself a suitable hostess to Mabrey."

Kinkaid sat down in front of the fire and stretched out his legs to the blaze.

"How long will he be here?"

"Does it matter? I thought time was one element that did not exist in California."

"You know what I mean! I was on my way to Los Angeles."

"With Luis?"

"Yes."

"And I told you your business could wait. How much more land are you thinking of buying anyway?"

"As much as I can!"

She came to stand by the fire and he reached out and caught her wrist and pulled her to his lap.

She sat as stiff as an iced mainsail.

"Is this against the rules?" he asked with a wry smile.

She said nothing, neither did she relax, but she made no attempt to rise.

"Have you never heard of being land-poor, Tarifa?" How black her hair was against the coppery smoothness of her skin, blue-black with molten highlights that seemed to quiver and give it a life of its own.

"I don't know what you're talking about."

"People who sink all they have into land have nothing

left with which to improve it. And unimproved, unproductive land is a constant drain on other resources."

She turned to face him and he saw that she was smiling at him lazily, almost tauntingly, like a satisfied cat. He felt the blood quicken in his veins and his clasp tightened around her wrist.

"I will raise cattle on all of it—in time," she said.

"You haven't enough vaqueros."

"I will get more! Those I have will work harder, longer!" He shook his head.

"Even you can only drive men just so far, Tarifa. You should see the condition this country is in up north. Mabrey can tell you. Ranchos are going to ruin right and left for want of laborers."

"I am not like these lax northern rancheros," she cried. "Loma de Oro will never fall into ruin. Never!"

He glanced at her speculatively.

"I think you believe that, and I admire you for it. But you are not God, Tarifa. You cannot order the elements or foresee the future."

"Premita Undebē! Who said I was? And what do I care about seeing into the future? But as long as I live I will take care of the future of Loma de Oro!"

She loosened her wrist from his grasp and stood up with the springing grace of a lioness.

"You told me I could buy land, improve the rancho."

"And so you have. But I also told you my pocketbook was not inexhaustible. I think it is time to stop and consolidate what you now own."

Her lip curled over her small white teeth, like the teeth of a marmot ready to bite.

"Your generosity is not very long-lived."

"Nor is your promise to make a home for me when I am at Loma de Oro," he answered steadily. His eyes stayed on hers and he had the satisfaction of seeing her long straight lashes sweep downward over her angry glance.

"I will go and make your guest—"

"Our guest," he corrected sharply.

"—our guest, comfortable. I will tell Candelaria to prepare something special for his dinner. Is there anything else?"

"Yes. I want Mabrey to see Soledad."

"Soledad?" Tarifa's eyes fastened on his face in surprise. "Why should he want to see Soledad? Penti is taking care of her. She is in her room, of course. She grows no worse and no better."

"Take Mabrey to her."

"But Penti—"

"Now!"

Tarifa stared at him for a moment and then left the room, swishing her green skirt angrily as she went through the door.

Mabrey, whom she had mistrusted on sight as she mistrusted most foreigners, was in the *sala* deep in conversation with Antonio. She noted that Luis had just ridden up and was handing his horse's reins to a peon.

When he came through the door, his sombrero in his hand, he asked quickly, "What is it, Tarifa? What is wrong?"

He always understood her moods. He was so kind, so gentle. She smiled at him and drew him outside again to a corner of the veranda. She told him of Bart's return and of Mabrey's presence.

"Then you cannot go to Los Angeles? Do you want me to look at the grants for you?"

"No. It will have to wait. Bart would have to come back right now and bring that ugly giant of an Englishman with him!"

"But Don Bartolemeo is your husband?" Luis reminded her, his eyes warm with sympathy. "He asks little enough from you, yes?"

Tarifa glanced at him sharply. It was impossible that he knew how little Kinkaid actually demanded. How could he know? No one did, save Penti. And being a Gypsy she would rather have cut out her tongue than betray the secrets of a tribeswoman to *gorgios*.

Luis spoke with the gentle courtliness of his father, and something about him soothed and reassured Tarifa just as Ygnacio had been able to do. Weak Luis might be, but she found herself longing once more for his comforting sympathy and understanding.

Luis seemed to become aware of her feelings, for he said suddenly, "If you do not need me further I will go. There is much to do on the rancho, and I must set out for Los Angeles tonight. You will make my excuses to the others?"

Tarifa watched him ride away with a dull sense of frustration. She wanted him and did not want him at the same time, but she resented his leaving her.

She found that Mabrey spoke excellent Spanish, far better than Bart, and that he knew Spain well and had visited the Triana as well as the Sacro Monte.

"You say that your Gypsy countrywoman has been treating the young Señora?" Mabrey asked as they went to Soledad's room.

"Yes."

"I have seen remarkable cures wrought by native medicine," the doctor said. "What seems to be the matter with the patient?"

Tarifa shrugged. "She is languid and listless and coughs a good deal. The climate in the United States did not agree with her, but I do not see what you can do."

"I can try to help her, Dona Tarifa," Mabrey said simply.

Soledad, lying pale and thin on her bed, showed little surprise or interest in the big gaunt gray-haired man who bent over to examine her and then crossed the room to hold a whispered conversation with the scowling Penti.

"How long has she been like this?" he asked.

"Ever since Capitán Kinkaid brought her back a year ago. But she has only taken to her bed in the last few weeks," said the Gypsy.

Penti grudgingly told him what she had done for Soledad, dosing her three times a day with a mixture made of herbs—Mouselar, liferoot, licorice root, goldenseal, marshmallow root, Iceland moss, and linseed boiled in a quart of water with two tablespoons of honey added to make it palatable.

The remedy was not unknown to Mabrey. He had visited in the Gypsy camps in England and Scotland and seen the remedy used, often successfully, for coughs and chest conditions.

"Continue to give her the medicine," he said and Penti, somewhat mollified, asked what he intended to do.

"We must get her to eat," he said. "If we can keep her alive until spring, then we must get her out into the sunshine. She is young, thank God, that is in her favor. If you don't mind, I'll come to see her from time to time."

Penti nodded and when he left her eyes followed his large lumbering figure with a curious speculation.

Mabrey set up his dispensary in the now abandoned shop that had once housed Pio Pico's store and wine shop. With the help of an Indian, Umberto, whom he had rescued from pneumonia, and an elderly sailor, Ben Grover, who had been left on the beach with a bad leg by a callous whaling captain, he fashioned leather-thonged cots, crude tables, and chairs, built bookshelves and cupboards to house his meager medical library, drug dispensary, and instruments.

Mabrey was tireless. He worked from sunup till sundown to the continual astonishment of the indolent San Diegans, and wherever he went a trail of grateful adoring Indian patients followed like the tail of a kite.

Faithfully once a week he rode to Loma de Oro to visit Soledad and to spend the night. While Kinkaid was still in port, they often rode out from San Diego together.

Mabrey, as acutely aware of any change in his friends personality as Jake Banner was, soon realized that things were not as they should have been between Kinkaid and his attractive but decidedly strange wife. Mabrey knew something of Gypsies, knew the depth and violence of their passions, the careless abandon of their love once it was given, and he realized that Tarifa had no such passion for Bart Kinkaid.

An Englishman, and reticent about questioning another's personal affairs, he could not bring himself to ask Bart the real reason for the marriage—and quite obviously there was no normal marital tie involved. In San Francisco Bart had stated that he was happy, but Mabrey now felt that he had deliberately lied. Unless the American was a complete fool or a misfit—and Mabrey was convinced he was not—surely he could find no real satisfaction in such a union?

After Kinkaid's first unfortunate experience, Mabrey had hoped that he would find happiness and contentment as he had found with Lupe. But he was convinced of what he had said, that a man could not accept a deeply wounding experience twice with the same equanimity. He was frankly

worried about Kinkaid. The more since he seemed determined to keep it all to himself. Yet there was little that
Mabrey could do to help him.

Soledad hung on, as frail as porcelain, her eyes enormous
in her small peaked face, but she seemed to look forward
to Mabrey's and Bart's visits. On these occasions she could
be coaxed to eat a little more just to please them.

Mabrey read to her from his English books, translating
them for her, or regaled her with stories of his rancho in
the north. These seemed to interest her the most, though
he never discussed his lost wife and children.

On sunny days he would have Penti bundle her up warmly and go outside to pace the patio for a short time, holding her gently in his big arms.

He seemed to Soledad to combine her father's gentle
authority and Bart Kinkaid's steadfast strength. When he
was near she felt safe. Only from the terror of her almost
nightly dreams of Judah was he powerless to protect her.

One evening young Antonio returned in great excitement
from a trip to San Fernando Mission where he had gone
with Tomas to sell some horses for Tarifa.

He took a leather bag from his sash and poured a few
yellow pebbles into Tarifa's palm.

"The mayordomo of the Mission, Francisco Lopez,
found them in San Francisco canyon! He was resting under
a tree and reached down with his knife to dig up some
wild onions and found these."

"What are they?" Tarifa asked, puzzled.

"Gold nuggets!"

"This is gold?"

"Yes!"

The others crowded around to examine the little pieces
of metal and Bart took one between his fingers and scruti-
nized it with care.

"Yes, it is gold."

"He says there is more," Antonio laughed, "a good deal
of it! I am going to help him mine it. Why should we work
for gold when we can dig it out of the ground?"

"You will go nowhere," said Tarifa. "There is probably
little enough there for this good for-nothing lazy mayordomo."

"She is probably right, *muchacho*," said Kinkaid kindly.

* * *

Bart spent five more months collecting hides on the coast before returning to San Diego to process and load them and say farewell to what he now considered his family at Loma de Oro, before sailing for Boston. He was reluctant to leave and at the same time determined to prove to himself that he could. That he was still his own master.

It was a hot windless summer night, and a wide moon made the saffron landscape as bright as day, picking out the graceful olive-black trees and the smudged purple outlines of the sierras. Kinkaid had left San Diego late, riding in his shirt-sleeves because of the heat, and when he approached the hacienda at midnight it lay silent and stripped of color like a pale ghost house.

He dismounted softly so as not to disturb the sleeping peon curled like a dog on the veranda and slipped into the house.

No place in the world smelled like this one, he thought. Cool, fragrant, with the scent of roses and honeysuckle coming from the patio, and the heady aroma of the little jars of crushed rosepetals and cinnamon that Tía Isabella kept in the *sala*.

Bart had never had a home since his mother died. He had never felt the loss so acutely as at this moment. Suddenly he longed, with a passion that surprised him, for material things he had not believed himself capable of wanting. He longed to make this place really his home. To know, when he stood inside its walls, the pride and joy of true ownership, the warmth of belonging, of being needed. Only no one actually needed him here except little Dolores, or perhaps Soledad. He was indispensable to no one nor of concern to anyone, except Jake Banner and the crew of the *Lorelei*. Perhaps also to his uncle and brother, where it concerned the good of the Endecott Company.

He laughed suddenly under his breath. The moonlight had indeed made him moonstruck. In its brilliant glow he made his way into the dining room without a candle and poured himself a stiff drink of *aguardiente*.

Afterward, he never remembered how long he had stood there staring into the moonlit patio. He actually heard the small movement before he saw the shadow. A wraith moving swiftly, whitely, in the moonlight. He stumbled to the patio door, cursing the slight noise he made and stood looking out.

Tarifa moved in and out of the shadows around the fountain, her hair a black cloud obscuring her face. She wore a thin white petticoat and nothing else. Her throat and breasts looked gilded in the moonlight. Her bare feet moved soundlessly over the tiles in that intricate, wildly beautiful pattern he had seen her use in the cabaña the night Lasho died—the night they had stood locked in a deadly embrace trying to kill each other.

He grasped the doorframe to support his swaying body. She had not seen him. Her eyes were closed and there was a remote, distant look on her face, as if she were a somnambulist or under an hypnotic spell. He thought her lips moved, but he could not be sure. She turned so quickly, so rhythmically, it was hard for his drink-fogged eyes to follow her.

The feeling that rose up in him, and that he knew he was powerless now to stop, was like a gigantic mushrooming fog that obliterated his senses. It filled his mind with feverish longing, and sent a powerful tremor through his limbs.

He felt himself move out onto the *galleria* and cross the patio swiftly, surely. His hands found her waist as she turned toward him and he was aware of her quick gasp of surprise and her cry of anger. Her hands rose like talons but he swept her up in a powerful grasp, pressing her tight to his chest as if she were a child, and strode toward the stairs.

Tarifa struggled silently, fiercely. But he was like an avenging god, pitiless, indomitable. She could hear the loud beat of his heart where her head rested against his open-necked shirt. She could smell the *aguardiente* on his hot breath that stirred the crown of her hair, and though she had often seen him drink a good deal, she realized that she had never before seen him drunk. His arms were like iron bands, his chest hard and implacable under her cheek, his hands bit into the bare flesh of her thighs under the thin skirt where he held her.

As they surged up the stairs she felt the violence that was engulfing him, making his skin burn to the touch and

his eyes gleam hotly in his head. She knew a twinge of
fear but her glittering defiance wiped it away in an instant.
She could cry out but her pride would not allow her to
rouse the house. What would she say to them anyway? He
was her husband. He might have broken his word to her,
but they would not understand that either. As always, in
every crisis, she stood alone. The thought seemed to calm
her; she relaxed a little. She could certainly handle a
drunken man, even Bart Kinkaid.

He opened the door of her room and banged it shut
behind him. At the sound, two dogs in the kitchen yard
began to bark but soon fell silent under a vaquero's angry
quirt.

Kinkaid threw her onto the high mahogany bed and she
gathered herself up quickly, crouching on her haunches
like a cat, sitting as she had in the cabaña the night he had
found her there alone with her dead child.

She saw that his face was still flushed, but his eyes had
a cold hard glitter like polished granite. When he looked
at her she saw something powerful and inscrutable flicker
for a moment in their depths, something she had never
seen there before. Something she could not decipher. Pain,
anger, passion? A mixture of all these and something more,
though she did not recognize it. A driving cold-willed
determination that his crew would have recognized instantly, and that certain men who had crossed his path at an ill-
timed moment had learned to respect and dread.

He stood watching her, his hands balled into fists at
his sides, swaying unsteadily on his feet, and yet she sensed
that his brain was clearer now.

She scowled up at him in the old expression of haughty
defiance he knew so well and he laughed in harsh amusement.

"What are you doing here?" she asked evenly when she
could endure the silence and his burning gaze no longer.

"This is my home, isn't it? I came home to my wife and
hearthside. And my charming spouse was good enough to
come and greet me."

"You are out of your mind. I was hot—I went into the
patio—"

"In a most delectable state of undress. Do you do this
often, señora?"

"You are drunk and you have no right in my room."

His expression did not change but he uncurled his fingers and his eyes moved over her bare shoulders and breasts with a deliberate speculation that made her more furious than if he had assaulted her. His big, swaying form seemed like a curse hovering over her. He laughed, still keeping his eyes on her.

"Rights interest you very much, don't they, Señora Kinkaid? Land rights, water rights, the rights of the Alvarjos—"

"We made a bargain—" her voice rose angrily.

"Of course. And you are thinking I am being very ungentlemanly in not keeping my end of it? I assure you it won't matter after tonight—to either of us. I tried, God knows, but you wouldn't meet me halfway. I wanted to make this a home—for all of us. But you didn't want that, did you? Not my partnership, my companionship, or my presence here. You wanted Loma de Oro as you have always wanted it, to run and rule the way it pleased you. Alone. You don't know how to share or give, do you, Tarifa? And that's your misfortune. There's an old saying —you only keep what you give away. You will have very little to put safely in your bank of memories when you are an old woman, Tarifa."

"I will not listen to you."

"Oh yes, you will!" His voice rang with a note of command that made her own glance waver and fall. "You once said we were bad for each other. For the first time I agree."

She felt relief wash through her. If he felt like that . . .

"After tonight I'm clearing out. For good." He laughed at the look of alarm that came into her eyes. "Oh, you don't need to worry. I'll still send you the money for your precious Loma de Oro. The only thing you've ever cared for is this cursed rancho, isn't that right?"

Her chin came up and she met his black eyes squarely. "I promised Ygnacio—"

"Ygnacio be damned! All you ever wanted was to get your greedy scheming little hands on all the land you could beg, borrow, or steal, and keep every inch of it for yourself! Oh, I admire the cleverness with which you've managed it. A Vermont Yankee couldn't have done it better. But you've overlooked one thing in your little scheme of

mayhem and plunder—the human equation. And for that
reason, my dear, I very much fear that in the end you are
not going to be able to hold on to your spoils. You've built
your house of cards on Loma de Oro, and if you lose it—"

"I'll never lose it!" She sat up stiff and erect, defying
him with every molten curve of her body. The lips were
drawn back from her small white teeth and she looked as
if she would like to bite him.

"What happens to you or Loma de Oro will not concern
me after tonight," he said heavily. He knew it was not true
but he vowed she would never know it. A clean break was
the only sensible way to handle the situation he now found
himself in, the best way for all concerned, and he was
prepared to make it no matter what it cost him. But after
tonight.

He took a step toward the bed and saw her stiffen, her
eyes narrow. He had always admired her bravery in the
face of disaster, and now her Gypsy pride was superb.

The only light in the room other than the shaft of pale
moonlight filtering through the grated windows came from
a small candle guttering low on the nightstand. It suddenly
went out.

He heard the sharp intake of her breath and there was
venom in the shine of her long eyes as she raised her head
in the shaft of moonlight. A Cleopatra, vanquished, but
daring him to claim his empty victory against her insolent
defiance.

He sat on the edge of the bed and reached for her,
dragged her roughly into his arms. He bent his head and
kissed her with a savage violence that left them both trembling. She fought against him and yet he did not feel it,
did not know the precise moment when she ceased to
struggle and lay limp and lanquid in his embrace, her lips
trembling under his.

In a dizzying surge, ecstasy, enchantment, engulfing
surrender, they clung to each other, transported like ships
on a tempest-tossed sea.

The sudden primitive fire that blazed through Tarifa left
her giddy and helpless. Never before in her life had she felt
this stark helpless abandonment of her own strength and
will. She was enveloped, swept wildly along on a dark tide
that had no beginning and no end. On, on, into an eternity
of blackness, emptiness, and mad, fierce passion. . . .

CHAPTER 30

The Havelock rancho, Rincon de Norte, became a haven for Americans traveling the southern route.

Tarifa viewed the tide of Americans, now so close to her own boundaries, not only with distaste, but with alarm. She had Santos post armed guards along the property she had purchased from Zenobio Sanchez that adjoined the Rincon de Norte. She passionately wished the Havelocks were out of there and had offered to buy Don Patricio out at his own price. But he would not sell.

On a brilliant spring morning, she rode south across the lands of the Santa Teresa, not knowing why she took that route unless it was to be alone with her thoughts. There was no one on the Santa Teresa now. Zenobio had gone to stay in Monterey to enjoy his money, and Havelock and Tarifa had hired his vaqueros and bought what was left of his herds. Zenobio had not wanted to sell his house and surrounding pastures.

"I may be back," he chuckled, "if I lose all my *dinero* at monte, or drink up all the *aguardiente* in Monterey. You will keep your eye on my hacienda, *amigos?*"

The little house looked bare and deserted as she approached, and then she was startled to see a figure standing in the doorway. She was more surprised still to recognize Padre Cazon. He had a broom in his hand and his gray habit was tucked up to his calves under his rope cincture. She had not seen him in months but she knew that they had been very busy at the Mission since the governor had restored their property to them. There was a new light of eagerness and contentment on the priest's worn face.

"*Buenos días,* Tarifa."

"*Buenos días,* Padre." She dismounted and came to the veranda. "What are you doing here, Padre?"

"Don Zenobio told me I could use his house if I had need of it in his absence. You know the new governor is advocating schools?"

Tarifa nodded.

"I thought it would be well to start one here for the young emigrant children of the Americanos."

The corners of Tarifa's mouth turned down bitterly.

"Haven't you enough to do instructing the Indian children at the Mission?"

"*Sí.* But it will not be I who will teach here."

"Who then?"

"Elena has promised to teach them."

"I think it is a waste of time. They come and go all the time; what good is it to teach them for a day or two?"

"Nothing is a waste of time that is done in the name of charity, my child. And who knows what a little one may learn, even in one lesson?"

Tarifa stirred restlessly. She had learned not to dispute such things with him, but the thought of more Americanos nearly nettled her into doing so.

"What do you hear from Capitán Kinkaid?" the priest asked suddenly.

Tarifa looked startled. She had tried not to think of her husband since that night when he had carried her half-naked up to her bedroom, and remained to strip her of all her defenses. She had wanted to wipe every vestige of the memory of that night from her brain but she had not been able to do so. When she had awakened the morning after, he had been gone and she had had no word from him until Dr. Mabrey called a week later with an envelope containing a large sum of money and a brief scrawl: "I apologize for last night. Bart."

"He sailed the morning he gave me that," Mabrey said, watching her. Her nostrils were distended and her eyes flamed with anger. But he had no idea of what had transpired between them.

"Thank you, Doctor. And now if you will excuse me,

I have a great deal to do." Dismissed so abruptly, he could do nothing but leave.

She had avoided Mabrey ever since. On his visits she took care to be absent, or occupied somewhere else on the rancho.

For the same reason, she now realized, she had stayed away from Padre Cazon. Both men shared that uncanny perception that she had herself but dreaded in others.

"My husband will not be back for some time," she told the priest calmly.

"The sea is a lonely profession," said Cazon. "I hope that soon he will be able to settle down here on the lands he loves."

Tarifa could have laughed in his face. All the love Bart had for Loma de Oro could be measured in ounces. He had taken advantage of her, broken his promise in the rudest, most flagrant way, but he was not going to break his word to Loma de Oro. She would write to the Endecotts for money if he failed to continue to send it, and they would have to give it to her. She was his legal wife.

"Tell me," said Padre Cazon, putting down his broom, "aren't you lonely with your husband so far away?"

"I have Loma de Oro to look after," she muttered.

"But it is a woman's duty to cleave to her husband, have you forgotten that?"

"I made a promise to Ygnacio long before I made one to Bart," she said. "The way I run my life is my own affair. Why do you question me?"

The Padre studied her for a moment, and there came a sadness to his eyes.

"I am sorry you married Capitán Kinkaid. If I had known—"

"Known what?"

"How much you dislike him—that you were doing it only for Loma de Oro. Ah, my child, a piece of ground is not worth the hearts and souls of human beings. When will you learn that?"

She turned away from him impatiently.

"Loma de Oro is the future for all of us, Padre."

"You are wrong. Every man carries his future within his own heart. No one can change it or take it from him except himself."

"I prefer to build my future with my own two hands."

"Then I am sorry for you, for such a future will not bring you happiness or contentment."

Tarifa laughed. "I am perfectly happy and content. I want nothing more. I started with nothing; now I have everything."

"And how long do you think it will last?"

"As long as I want it to!" It was futile to talk to him. She was relieved to see Luis and Elena riding toward them across the meadow. Their two golden horses matched perfectly and they rode with equal grace. Elena seemed to satisfy Luis in every way and yet they had no children. Tarifa wondered about this; the Alvarjos always produced children.

Luis greeted her warmly, and Ellen smiled at her, though there was a new facet to her reserve when they met these days, ever since the evening of the fiesta when Tarifa had found her in the study with Bart bending so solicitously over her. Tarifa had wondered what they had been talking about, but she had not been curious enough to ask Bart, even if he would have told her.

Luis explained to Padre Cazon that he was sending over some carpenters to install tables and benches for the students.

Ellen stood on the veranda beside Tarifa, and asked politely after the other members of the family, then she said quite casually, "I had a letter from Capitán Kinkaid the other day."

Tarifa stared at her through narrowed eyes, not believing her.

"You knew, of course, he was on his way to China?"

Tarifa nodded, though she had known no such thing. So! He was on the other side of the world. Her dark anger at him mingled with a strange relief.

When Luis came out of the house he paused to put his arm around Ellen's trim waist and smile down at her. Her return glance was filled with a warm tenderness that filled Tarifa with a sudden blinding fury. The foolish woman had no more sense or shame than to go mooning after a man in public, looking like a dying calf, even if the man happened to be her husband.

She turned abruptly and went to mount Guindilla.

"But you'll come to the hacienda with Padre Cazon for luncheon?" protested Luis.

"No, I have to get back to Loma de Oro. Nazario is coming over to let me know when he can start branding calves."

She wheeled the stallion swiftly, then firmly put spurs to his gleaming flanks. Curse them, every one of them, she thought. All they could do was stand around and question her about Bart, when she wanted to forget about him, to forget she had ever met him, much less married him. Everytime she had married, it had ended in disaster. She should have been warned by Penti, by her senseless diabolical fortune-telling.

At the hacienda she found John Mabrey sitting in the sunny patio with Soledad and Tía Isabella.

Soledad had improved so much that she was now able to be up and about the house most of the day. She had gained some weight and the deathly pallor was gone from her cheeks, but as Mabrey cautioned the family, she was still far from strong.

She and Isabella were sewing, and Mabrey had been reading aloud to them from a book of Keats' poems.

He rose to give her his chair, bowing gallantly from the waist, and when she shook her head he requested a few words with her alone.

Tarifa poured him a glass of wine in the study and sat down on the arm of a chair, swinging one booted and spurred foot impatiently.

Mabrey watched her from his heavy-lidded eyes. "What do you know about Texas?" he asked suddenly.

"Texas?"

"It used to belong to the Mexican Republic until a group of Americans were killed to a man defending their independence at the Almo in 1836, and another group avenged them and captured Santa Ana in April of the same year. She's been an independent republic ever since."

"Why should this concern me?" asked Tarifa, puzzled by his sudden air of gravity.

"Because I've heard that Texas is going to be annexed to the United States, and there's a good chance of war when that happens."

Tarifa frowned and put down her glass. Bart had mentioned the possibility of war between Mexico and his own country; how shipping on the California coast would decline if this occurred.

"When will this happen?"

"I'm not positive that it will," said Mabrey, "but everything points to it. If it does, your hide and tallow business will die, and so will the ranchos of California."

"Not Loma de Oro!"

"My dear young woman, be sensible. Is Loma de Oro any different from the other ranchos in California? You must have a market for your commodity, which is cattle, and you will find no market for them in any great quantity outside of the Boston trading ships. The whole economy of California is based on the Boston traders, and they grow fewer by the year. How many of them will come here at all if there is a war?"

Tarifa got up and paced nervously in front of the empty fireplace. She knew the truth of Mabrey's words, and yet she could not accept them.

Bart had promised to be her ally, to protect Loma de Oro, but where was he now, when chaos threatened it? She had not heard from him since she had received the money and note. She could almost have forgiven him his vulgar use of her if he had safeguarded Loma de Oro as he had promised. But you could not trust the promises of Americanos. Ygnacio had been right. They were bold, conniving, unscrupulous. They would not hesitate to use anything or anyone to gain their objectives. A tremble of terrible fear smote at her heart. What if they were victorious in a war with Mexico? Would they then control California? The thought almost made her swoon with agony.

Mabrey got up and put his right hand in his pocket. He brought out an envelope and passed it to her.

"Bart sent me this money to give to you. He's on his way to China, and doesn't expect to be back for some time. But he told me to tell you you're not to worry—about money, I mean."

"Why doesn't he write and send it to me himself," she cried savagely, ripping open the envelope. There was money there, a good deal of it, and nothing else.

Damn, him damn him. He could write to Ellen and

Mabrey, and leave her the humiliation of being informed of his whereabouts by outsiders. He had no honor, no conscience. He had treated her with a callous contempt from the first. It did not occur to her that she had also treated him in the same manner.

"He's a fool," Tarifa muttered.

"Yes," Mabrey agreed sharply, "he is. But not the sort of fool you think."

"What?"

"Never mind, my dear, it's not important," he replied. "I must be getting back to San Diego."

"But you always stay the night!"

"Soledad is coming along nicely, and there's a poor young devil of a vaquero whose leg I set last night waiting for me in my dispensary. He will need me."

Tarifa forced herself to thank him politely for bringing her the money and word of Bart. She didn't care if her husband was at the bottom of the sea, but it was a relief to know he would continue to send her money. If what Mabrey told her was true, the rancheros of California were in for even harder times than they had ever known. She was determined that Loma de Oro at least would not go down in defeat.

Luis came to see Tarifa at Loma de Oro one day, and told her, "There is a chance that I may be made *juez de pas,* justice of the peace, of Los Angeles."

"But that is wonderful!" Tarifa cried, her eyes shining. "Then surely you can do something about this madness that surrounds us?"

"I don't know how much my poor efforts will amount to," he smiled, "but I will try my best to serve California and the district."

He was very handsome as he stood bareheaded in the center of the *sala,* in his snuff-colored velvet jacket and trousers heavily embossed with gold lace, and his fine linen shirt in startling white contrast to his dark, finely chiseled face. He wore a moustache now, small and black and neatly trimmed, that lent him an air of august dignity, and his empty sleeve was fastened to his breast with a golden pin depicting the Mexican eagle.

Tarifa felt a surge of her old passion for him, and because she had never in her life denied her emotions, she went swiftly to him and clasped her arms around his neck.

He looked startled and began to reach behind him to undo her hands when she rose on tiptoe and covered his mouth with her own.

It was not a kiss of heart-swelling, electrifying power, such as she had experienced with Bart, when her own identity had been overwhelmed, swept away, engulfed in a seething helpless passion. But there was an excitement and pleasure in Luis' lips, and she felt his arm go around her waist as he bent his head obediently, helplessly, to meet her demanding embrace.

When he finally freed himself, his face was white with agonized dismay.

"Tarifa—"

"I am lonely," she cried, clutching his sleeve. "Bart has treated me abominably. He has deserted me, left me to my own resources. You do not know the pain and suffering I have had to endure—alone. There is no one, no one! You must come to me, Luis, you must help me! Once I made a sacrifice for you."

"Querida," Luis murmured in his embarrassment and misery. Although he suffered an agony of self-recrimination for having allowed her to kiss him, he did not know how to extinguish the simmering, volcanic emotion he sensed in her, ready to burst forth and engulf them both.

"Luis, you have not lost all your old feeling for me?"

"I—Tarifa, we are both married!"

"Vows, words, what do they matter? We are both unhappy. My husband is a bleak-hearted barbarian who has deserted me, and you are tied to a cold statue of a woman who gives you no children."

Luis flushed and his hand tightened on a chairback.

"Tarifa, you must not say these things. I am happy with Elena, and you are Capitán Kinkaid's wife. He is now of our family, and he has saved Loma de Oro for us."

"I have saved Loma de Oro!"

"Yes, yes, but could you have done it these last years without his help? Have you no affection for him, no loyalty to him?"

"None! He is a beast, an animal, who takes what he wants and goes back on his word! I do not wish to discuss him."

Luis turned miserably to pick up his white sombrero.

"In God's name, Tarifa, do not make me sin again. I have too many offenses on my soul now. It is better for us both if I do not come here again."

"She stared at him in dismay. "You are going to desert me, too, when I need someone so badly?"

He came to touch her cheek gently with his finger. "You do not really need anyone, Tarifa. You are so strong, so self-sufficient. Perhaps Kinkaid realizes that, too. It is your blessing as well as your cross. The rest of us who are weak can only envy you. I cannot help you. I have nothing you need. And I need Elena. I know how much I owe you, how much we all owe you, and I am most humbly grateful. I admire you more than anyone I have ever known. I am proud that you are one of us, but I cannot help you now by doing as you wish. It is better that I do not come again," he repeated.

"No!" she cried. "You owe me something! You can't go."

"I owe you too much," he said sadly, "to repay it by causing you nothing but disgrace and dishonor."

In a flaming fury she watched him march outside and mount his horse with the quick, graceful swing he had learned to use. She saw him ride away swiftly. He did not once look back.

Nazario rode home from San Diego accompanied by Francisco and Macario Canejo.

"You have heard," Macario said, "of the governor's ruling? The officers of his battalion are to be quartered in private homes. We have never been forced to accept this disgrace before! My mother says she will lock up the house and throw away the key rather than see it shelter any of Micheltorena's cholos."

"They empty the jails of Jalisco and Mexico City and foist them on us as governmental troops!" said Nazario bitterly. "When will this disgrace end? Zenobio Sanchez sent word from Monterey that a group of cholos committed a beastly outrage upon an Indian woman in the very streets of the pueblo. José Castro's kitchen was entered and robbed, and the Frenchman Pierre Atillan was set upon, cut, and crippled for life because he refused to give the ruffians a supply of *aguardiente*. They say the government will be forced to give him a pension."

"Luis tells me," Francisco added, "that the cholos bait lines with corn and steal the chickens out of the very yards in Los Angeles. He saw one of them shot while trying to break into a store in the pueblo. And what does our precious Governor Micheltorena do about it? Nothing! He is afraid of his own troops. He orders severe punishments to appease the pueblos, and then fails to carry them out. He claims the troops only steal to cover their nakedness and fill their bellies!"

"We are fortunate that he has moved north with them," said Nazario. "We can only hope that they will not be back. I do not understand why Micheltorena does not shoot the worst offenders and ship the rest back to Mexico as everyone has begged him to do, or send them out to fight the Indians in the Tulares. *Dios!* We have lost enough horses and cattle since they came to restock the Mission!"

Francisco leaned back in his saddle and said with sneering sarcasm, "He has an answer for everything, that indolent one. He does not find it possible to shoot men for stealing food, when they are hungry and unpaid. And when has Mexico paid the soldiers in California, since the early days? He claims he has no right to send his soldiers out of the country without incurring the wrath of his superiors. The entire affair is a fiasco. Better Alvarado than this Mexican bombast in uniform!"

As they approached the hacienda, Nazario was surprised to hear guitar music and gay laughter coming from the patio.

Rufina did not receive guests unless he invited them, and there were no horses or carriages in front of the house. He dismounted hastily, threw his reins to an Indian and led his guest and his brother inside.

An elderly Indian was seated on a stool in a corner of the patio playing a *jota,* while Rufina beat time with her hands and a group of children danced gaily about her.

Nazario stood watching the little scene silently for a moment before Rufina saw him and quickly motioned the musician to stop playing.

Nazario had wanted sons and now he had them, all handsome, clear-eyed boys. The youngest, just two months old, gurgled in his crib on the veranda tended by a maid-servant.

"What is the meaning of this?" Nazario asked his wife, his eyes hot with disapproval.

Rufina's chin came up and there was a tinge of color in her cheeks. She had grown slightly buxom but it was becoming to her.

"It is Salvador's birthday; did you forget?"

Nazario glanced at one of his small sons, a plump three-year-old, and felt an unreasoning anger that she should not have reminded him privately, before making all this to-do about it. He could not bear it that his children should think him either cold or disinterested in their welfare.

"*Gracias* for my gift, Padre," Salvador lisped, coming to throw his arms about Nazario's knees. He held a painted iron horse in his hand, mounted by a gaily decked Zouave. It had obviously come from abroad.

Nazario bent to kiss him and pat his head, then rose to stare at his wife again with disfavor. He had no desire to converse with her, but he must know how she had obtained the gift she had given Salvador in his name. She did not leave the hacienda, of that he was certain, and she had no money.

"Go on with the party," he told the children, and Rufina nodded to the musician. At one side a table had been laid with cakes and fruit and cups of chocolate.

Francisco, aware of his brother's displeasure, drew the curious Macario into the study for a drink.

"I want to speak to you," Nazario told Rufina roughly.

She came obediently, pausing only to direct the maid to look after the children, and followed Nazario to her bedroom. She had not expected him to be so angry at the little celebration, but he was completely unpredictable these days.

He turned on her furiously.

"Where did you get Salvador's gift? And why did you lie to him and say it came from me?"

"Because I knew you were not likely to remember his birthday," she said calmly. "The rancho and politics seem to take up all of your interest these days."

Smarting under the truth of her words he shouted, "And the gift? I suppose that came from the good San Antonio when you prayed to him to find it for you?" His face flamed with anger.

"I gave Santos a pair of earrings my father had given me long ago. I asked him to trade them for something for Salvador's birthday. He brought me the little horse when he came by from San Diego last week."

"He had no right to be doing your bidding! I will speak to him. He had no right on this rancho without Tarifa's or my permission!"

In spite of the heat of their words they had not spoken so intimately in years, not since Nazario had allowed her to return to the hacienda as his wife.

"Are you going to spoil a child's party and make a scene by taking his gift away from him because you are angry with me?" Rufina asked.

He stared at her blackly. At the moment she seemed stronger than he, and there was a hint of her old taunting authority in her wide brown eyes. The flesh of her arms and throat and neck looked soft and creamy against the becoming green-sprigged muslin gown she wore, and there was a red rose fastened in front of the high comb in her dark hair.

Since the birth of her sons he had noted a gradual change in her, without being able to entirely decipher it. Now he knew it was the unshakable complacency of the true matron. His mother, for all her gentle ways, had shared the same unquestionable air of command and assurance after she had borne her sons.

"I decide what happens in this house," he told her crossly.

But he knew he had lost the battle even when she answered meekly, with her eyes downcast, "Of course, Nazario."

Curse the woman! She had escaped beyond his grasp, into a realm of her own. And the worst of it was, he could find no fault with her as a wife and mother. The hacienda was run even more smoothly than Loma de Oro, and her personal touch was evident everywhere, in the flowers she tended and cut, the rugs she hooked or braided, the curtains, crocheted bedspreads, and the attractive clothes she designed and sewed for the children. She was a meticulous and devoted mother. The children adored her, as did the servants. Even with him, she had fulfilled her wifely duties without complaint.

He thought how long and hard and bitter the years had been for him since she had betrayed him with Titus Judah. The emptiness of the life he had forced upon himself and her, and he tried to bring back into his heart the outrage that he had thought would never leave it. It was with a feeling of profound shock that he discovered all he could dredge up at the moment was a petty disappointment that she had remembered a child's birthday when he had forgotten it and a terrible pity for himself at all she had robbed him of. He wanted to weep. At the same time he wished she would leave him and not bother him with more words, more arguments. Arguments were useless between them now. They had even lost that. He would rather have argued with Tarifa in her scorching fury, than with Rufina in her present calm, dignified air of command. She defeated him by her very submissiveness, and for the first time he sensed that it was not submissiveness at all.

"Nazario," she said quietly, "do you want me to leave Bolsa Coyotes? My father has repeatedly offered me a place in his home, and you now have your sons. That is all you ever wanted of me these past years."

His head jerked up in surprise. "Leave? But what of the children, who would look after them?"

"The servants are well-trained. You could send for Tía Isabella."

"You would go off and leave your children?" A righteous fury filled him. She was the same. She had not changed. Could not. She was a born wanton.

Rufina glanced down at her hands and turned her gold wedding band thoughtfully.

"I would not leave them willingly or with any pleasure," she said, "but if it would be best for them, and for you—"

"I am the one to decide that!"

"Of course. But we do not speak these days, and I have been meaning to ask you. You have not been happy these past years, Nazario. I know you took me back only so that you could have your children. You now have them."

"Do you think I want to bring further disgrace upon my children by our separation?" thundered Nazario. "Have you no sense of propriety?"

"You want me to pay more for my sin, is that it? I

assure you, Nazario, nothing you could do from now on
would punish me more severely than I have already punished myself, than I shall continue to punish myself until
the day I die."

She raised her eyes and there were tears on the thick
lashes like luminous jewels.

He wanted to tell her to be silent, to turn on his heel
and leave the room, but he could not bring himself to
speak or move. A strange lethargy seemed to have washed
over him. Long ago he had desired her, loved her, with a
passion he had thought unquenchable. Now he felt only
this peculiar heaviness of his brain and limbs. It was as
if he stood at a distance outside himself and studied the
tableau they made, and could reach no conclusion concerning it.

"I know the life we lead is wrong," said Rufina. "The
children are not old enough to sense it yet, but they soon
will be. Isn't it better for them and for you if I go?"

He said nothing. He stood with his eyes on the distant
landscape visible through the open window, his arms
stiff at his sides and his slender hands clenched. The years
had wrought changes in him also. He could no longer hate
or love with the same burning degree of passion. Since
Luis' injury, he had held himself to blame for his brother's maiming. He knew what it was to feel powerless to
restore what he had been responsible for smashing. As
surely as Rufina had ruined their life together, he had
ruined Luis', by ignorance, selfishness, carelessness. At least
his wife had tried to make reparation for her sins, by bending to his will, by giving herself unstintingly to him and
to their children. But what had he been able to do to make
things up to Luis for the loss of his arm?

He remembered something Padre Peyri had told him
long ago when he was just a lad:

"God gives to everyone, at some time in his life, the
opportunity to accept grace for his soul, or to reject it.
The choice is always up to the individual. Sometimes we
fail to recognize the shape it takes in presenting itself to
us. But there is one test you can always apply, niño."

"What is that, Padre?"

"If the decision is difficult, even distasteful to you, if

it takes all your strength to accept it, and yet you shrink
from it even though you realize it is the right thing to do
—then you are faced with grace, my son. And the choice
is up to you. You can turn your back on it and go your
way, without a care perhaps, until the Day of Judgment.
Or, you can accept the weight of its burdens, offering it
up to God, and He will not tax you beyond your strength
even though it may seem at times that He does. And your
soul shall be magnified in Heaven for all eternity."

"I will save up all my sins," Nazario had replied smugly,
"and make a deathbed confession, receive the last rites,
and go straight to Heaven. Then I will be able to do as I
please on this earth."

Padre Peyri glanced at him sadly. "I knew a young
soldier who used those very words to me once in Spain.
He thought he had a long life before him. He would not
even accept baptism, he said, until his death, for he declared the Church was too strict for him to live up to on
this earth. He would ensure himself of Heaven and God's
pleasure by receiving everything at the end and going to
Heaven as white as the driven snow."

"Yes," said Nazario, thinking the young soldier very
wise, "that is what I will do."

"Six months after he spoke to me," the priest went on,
"a cannon exploded during artillery practice and he was
blown to bits. There was no priest present to give him the
last rites or to administer baptism. You cannot make bar-
gains with God, my son."

Nazario heard the rustle of Rufina's skirt.

"I—will go back to the children," she said quietly.

"No, wait!" He did not turn his head to face her; he
could not. The words caught in his throat as if to strangle
him, but he fought for breath to get them out.

"I want you—to forgive me."

"It is nothing. You had a right to be angry about the
little horse. I should have reminded you it was Salvador's
birthday."

"No. Not that—everything."

Suddenly he swung to face her and his eyes were burning in his thin, dark face.

"I want you to forgive me for the way I have treated
you since I brought you back from San Diego. For the life

I have made you lead. For the sins I have brought down on both our heads—children conceived and born in anger and hatred—"

"No, Nazario! I loved you all the time. I was wicked, mad, and I didn't understand until it was too late, but I loved you. Only you."

She was weeping now, not even attempting to touch her face or eyes, letting the tears flow as if they were a benediction, her hands clasped at her waist.

He thought that she was mad, that they both were. Love! How could she love him when he had degraded her fully as much as she had disgraced him?

He took one stumbling step forward and folded her in his arms. She trembled violently and then lay still, but her lips were warm and moist. They clung to his and there was the taste of salt on them from her tears.

"*Querido*," she murmured, "are you sure, can you forget what I did, forgive—"

He laid a finger over her lips.

"There will be no more words of forgiveness between us, *carita*. *Forgive* is a bad word, it should be shortened to *give*. If you give of yourself, surely that is the answer to everything? There is then no need of forgiveness, yes? We will start over, you and I, and we will make a good life for our children."

"Yes, yes! You are good Nazario, so very good. I do not deserve—"

"Hush! Let us not say anymore about it." But he was smiling, and for the first time in years he felt curiously lighthearted and free of cares. He had struggled for so long in the dark abyss of his own hatred and desire for revenge, that he was giddy now with the freedom acceptance and reconciliation had brought to him. It was not too difficult to do God's Will after all. He was amazed at the discovery. How much worse had been his long struggle in the darkness by himself? Now he found that he still had Rufina's love, indeed had never lost it. But more, he had restored the peace to his soul that he had been thirsting for without even realizing it.

"We will go to Santa Barbara," he told Rufina, "take the children, and tell your family that our difficulties are all over. Would you like that, *querida?*"

"Oh, yes, Nazario!"

"I will speak to Tarifa tomorrow and tell her we are going."

"You think she will approve?"

"What do I care whether she does or not?" Nazario laughed with his newfound strength of purpose. "I can take my family where I choose, can't I?"

They stood laughing together in each other's arms, and the sound of their merriment reached Macario and Francisco on the veranda where they sat smoking. The two young men exchanged startled glances. After all, it was an open secret that Don Nazario and Dona Rufina lived a private life of silent estrangement.

CHAPTER 31

Even under Governor Alvarado, loans of Mission cattle to private individuals had been made freely, with the understanding that the borrower would, in due time, return to the Mission the number of cattle borrowed. The governor claimed it was the only way of rewarding soldiers for their patriotism. But seldom, if ever, were any cattle repaid to the Missions. In the days of their great herds, this had made little or no difference, but now in their straightened circumstances the loss of any livestock was a blow to the Missions' survival.

The mayordomos who had come with the first secularization were more often than not stupid, incompetent men, inclined to let Mission affairs drift into chaos. A few were depraved and vicious as well as lazy, and would sell anything on the place, from cooking pots to tiles from the church roof in order to have money for gambling or *aguardiente*. Still others, like the Picos, were busy building their own fortunes, and thought nothing of stocking their newly acquired lands with "borrowed" or stolen Mission stock. As the soldiers had thrown dice for Christ's robe at the foot of the Cross, so the mayordomos divided the remainder of the Missions' goods among themselves.

The Indians, as the Padres had always known, were not ready yet for freedom in whatever capacity it was given them. Philanthropy, religion, common sense, and justice had not yet been mixed in the proper amounts in the crucible of time. Indian horse thieves had become very troublesome, and the Missions were prey to their depradations. Those among the rancheros who were able armed the vaqueros and kept guards posted over their best animals night and day.

Tarifa was all too aware of the temptation the Loma de Oro palominos represented. She tightened the fences that enclosed the prize stock, and saw to it that at least one of the Alvarjos was always on guard with the vaqueros.

Antonio was petulant about the arrangement. Grown now to slim young manhood, he was courting one of the Soto girls, Magdalena, and taking his turn at night duty outside the corrals after a long day in the saddle did not suit him.

When he mentioned the fact in Tarifa's hearing, she turned on him like a viper.

"Do you think you are better than the rest of us? That you cannot take your turn at night-riding? Do you want to lose the palominos? I will tell you this, all of you, if one palomino is lost whoever is in charge will answer to me!"

On a starless evening in early fall, Antonio was circling the far end of the mares' pasture, cursing the chill that had come up and caught him without his cape or serape, when he heard a small sound. It was a mere rustle of something, but he could tell by the nervous way in which Relampago tossed his head that it was a sound that was not familiar to him.

He quieted the stallion with a touch on his neck and drew him to a silent halt.

A small wind had risen but though it was cold it was not sufficiently strong to do more than move the tops of the greasewood bushes and bend the tall grass slightly. Antonio could see nothing; it was nearly pitch dark.

A faint rustling in the grass confirmed his suspicions that someone was there, watching him. His hand tightened on the pistol in his sash, and felt for the long knife in his boot top. He eased it out in his hand, deciding a silent kill would be better in case there were others who might be warned by a shot. Besides, he was not a very good shot, and he was extremely accurate with a throwing knife.

He slipped off Relampago's back and stood silently, listening. He reached down and removed his spurs, taking care to be quiet.

Another whisper of sound from his left. He crouched down and strained his eyes in the darkness. He knew that Tomas rode on the other side of the corral, but he dared not call out to him lest he warn his prey annd lose him altogether. Relampago gave a soft questioning nicker, and Antonio cursed him for it silently.

Feet sounded beyond him, moving swiftly on the hard-packed earth, and something flew by him and landed in the saddle on Relampago's back. The stallion reared and Antonio threw the knife at the faint bulk he saw on the horse's back. Then in a flash the horse whirled and galloped away and something struck Antonio a glancing blow on the back of the head. Dimly, he heard Tomas' questioning shout, "Don Antonio, *qué sucedio?*"

Then he felt himself falling deeper and deeper into the hard ground until oblivion wiped everything from his memory.

Tomas and two of the other night riders rode up a few seconds later on their winded horses, and found Antonio stretched face down in the grass.

"Sangre de Dios!" Tomas muttered as he knelt beside Antonio and gently turned him over. One of the vaqueros lighted a small lantern and they examined their fallen master. Though there was blood on the back of his head where the skin had been broken, he seemed to be breathing all right. They could find no sign of the marauder.

"Go and look for Relampago," said Tomas. "In the

excitement he must have run off. Dona Tarifa will have our hides, amigos. We must get Don Antonio back to the hacienda *muy pronto*."

Tarifa had been on the point of retiring when Tomas came to tell her what had happend and, with the help of another vaquero, went to bring Antonio into the house.

Penti came to his room to dress his wound. Though it had bled freely, it was not a deep cut. She bandaged it tightly and had the satisfaction of seeing Antonio stir and moan against the pain as she finished.

He opened his eyes to find Tarifa, hard-eyed and impatient, sitting in a chair beside his bed.

"You were in charge," she said in a tight voice. "What happened?"

"I'm not sure." He put up a hand to touch his aching, bandaged head and winced. "I heard something. But it was too dark to see. Someone attacked me from behind—"

"Relampago's gone," Tarifa broke in. "Were you thrown?"

"No. I got off to see if I could sneak up on whoever was making the noise. There must have been two of them."

"You should have stayed on your horse."

"I—someone got past me, took Relampago."

"Took him!"

"Rode away on him. It was all so dark—and then I was struck from behind. I threw my knife at whoever was on Relampago, but I think I missed him."

"So you left your horse for someone to steal—as easily as he pleased. And when they see the prize they have taken, they will be back for more!"

"I—couldn't help it!"

Tarifa whirled out of her chair and began to pace the room in her anger and frustration.

"You're all alike, you Alvarjos! Weak, spineless. You cannot follow the simplest orders without tangling them up like a novice with his first *reata*. You disgust me! And what am I to do now? Go out and spend a week scouring the countryside for these renegades, and kill them before they can tell of the rest of the horses waiting here to be taken—and all because of your stupidity?"

Antonio sulked against his pillow in raging silent fury.

He hated himself because she had this power over him, because he was afraid to defend himself against her. Yet he was powerless to speak.

Tarifa gave him one last bitter condemning look before she flounced out of his room, slamming the door after her.

Antonio took the pillow from behind his aching head and flung it with impotent rage at the closed door.

At dawn Tarifa rode out with Santos to the spot where Antonio had been attacked. Tarifa picked up Antonio's silver spurs where he had left them, and Santos knelt on one knee to study the ground.

"Two of them, Patróna," said the Indian. "One a gentile, I think. You can see the print of his bare foot, here and here."

Tarifa looked where he pointed and nodded her head. "And the other?"

"A white man. Look at the print of the leather heel."

"Are whites stealing our horses now?" Santos grunted.

"If so, they will not come here again," said Tarifa with decision.

"What will you do?" asked Santos.

"We will find Relampago," she said, swinging into the saddle, "and we will dispose of the thieves, whoever they are."

"Surely you do not intend to kill a white man?"

Tarifa sat on her horse as regally and proud as an Egyptian princess, and there was cold contempt in her eyes.

"I am going to get what is ours, and I shall punish whoever has taken it. Come."

At noon they paused in a fairly open place to rest the horses and eat the meager lunch they had carried in their saddlebags.

Tarifa was cross and displeased at the slowness of their progress, and only Santos' repeated assurances that they were on the right track kept her going without comment.

As they rode, she had become aware of a certain watchful quietness on Santos' part, a grim almost apprehensive look on his leathery face. At times it almost seemed as though he was reluctant to go on.

From a small defile they saw the smoke rising. It was
surrounded on three sides by grassy knolls, and opened
on the remaining side into a small boulder-strewn valley.
A huge oak sheltered the fire and men from view as the
riders paused atop the center bluff, but they could see
the three horses tethered in the grass nearby.

It was with something of a shock that Tarifa realized
that not one but two of the animals were palominos, Loma
de Oro horses—and one of them was El Canario.

Santos glanced at her sadly.

"You knew," she whispered fiercely.

"I was not certain, but I thought I recognized the hoof-
prints, though it has been a long time. And when I saw
the golden hair on the bushes, a lighter shade than Relampago's—"

"You should have told me."

They came down the little embankment swiftly, Tarifa
in the lead with her pistol ready in her right hand.

Just as they had started, a man rose and came out to
the edge of the tree's shadow to stretch and yawn, his
back to them. Now he turned and with an oath made a
grab at the saddles piled nearby.

Tarifa's pistol cracked and he jerked back into the shadows. She put spurs to Guindilla and charged after him,
limbering her whip as she went.

He stood holding his bloody wrist facing her at the
base of the tree, and Tarifa pulled Guindilla nearly to
his haunches with the abruptness of her halt.

Pito Larios grinned up at her, his face as bold and
handsome as ever.

"If it hadn't been for the shadows, you would have gotten me up here, Dona Tarifa," Larios said, touching his
heart. "I think you are not as good a shot as you are a
horsewoman, for which I am most grateful."

A half-naked Indian leaped from behind the wide trunk
of the tree, his knife leveled at Tarifa's breast.

"No, *amigo*," warned Larios. "We are old friends, Dona
Tarifa and I."

"What are you doing here?" Tarifa demanded harshly.
She was furious with him.

"I am here with my *amigo* on business, señora."

Tarifa frowned at the Indian, his body slim and hard

in the sunlight, his flat eyes filled with a bitter dislike of her. His face was somehow familiar.

"The business of stealing my horses? I know this Indian, wasn't he a neophyte at San Luis Rey?"

The Indian stood very still but Pito Larios merely shrugged as he bent to tie up his wrist with his handkerchief.

"We do not question each other's past, my *amigo* and I."

"You knew you were on Loma de Oro last night when you struck down my stepson and stole his horse!"

"You must forgive me, Dona Tarifa," Pito said with mock humility, "but it was necessary to get only the best horses for the difficult journey my friend and I have ahead of us."

"They shoot horse thieves in the pueblo now."

"How sad. But when a friend merely borrows a horse from another friend who has many others, surely that cannot be counted as stealing, señora?"

Tarifa turned and spoke quietly to Santos and he went to toss his *reata* over Relampago's head. At once all trace of amiability disappeared from Pito's face.

"Where did you get El Canario?" Tarifa asked flatly, her eyes never leaving his face.

"I did not steal him," snapped Larios. "If you like I will buy this other one from you, if it will satisfy your sense of ownership?"

"Relampago is not mine to sell. He belongs to my stepson Antonio whom one of you knocked in the head last night when you stole his horse. In any case you haven't money enough to buy one of my palominos."

She saw Pito's face harden; he was dangerous-looking and not so handsome when he failed to smile, when he dropped his pose of easygoing *caballero elegante*.

Tarifa dismounted and said to Santos, "Keep your gun on these two."

She walked over to El Canario and ran her hands over his head and body. He was thin and there were old scars on his legs that he had not had when Santiago had ridden him away from Loma de Oro. Something in Pito's story left her uneasy, dissatisfied. With her Gypsy intuition she was convinced that he had been telling the truth when he said he had not stolen El Canario. But how had he gotten him then? Had Santiago given him or sold him to someone else long since? She supposed that he had, but she had a feeling that Pito had himself been in contact with Santiago somewhere.

She went back to where he stood and he smiled in his old way and she was aware that he was thinking of the days and nights they had shared, and of the fact that she had been tempted to run away with him. As if this knowledge gave him a certain power over her, he said, "For old times sake, suppose you take back Antonio's horse, and let us leave as we came, on El Canario and the bay."

The bay was a small, unbranded Indian pony that favored one foreleg when he moved.

"Where did you come from, Pito?"

"From New Mexico. I told you I was horse trading there."

"Get Antonio's saddle and bridle and put them on Relampago," she told Santos. Then turning to Pito she said dispassionately, "I promised to kill whoever stole him."

She saw with inner satisfaction that he was not only taken by surprise, but that he believed her.

"I once saved your horse at the peril of my own," he said, watching her face carefully. "I do not bring it up because I think you owe me anything. But you can believe me when I tell you that I have every legal right to El Canario. We will be gone by evening and you will not see us on Loma de Oro again. I give you my word you shall never have to fear for your golden stallions, as far as Pito Larios and his men are concerned. Will you accept my word, or do you have to have blood to satisfy your honor?"

His grin was an added insult but she sensed that he was not as sure of her as he pretended to be. She frowned at him, and yet she would have trusted Pito Larios' word above that of some well-born hacendados she had known.

"You will be gone by evening and you will not be back?" she asked slowly.

"Not to Loma de Oro, señora. I must congratulate you. I have heard that you are remarried."

She glared at him in sullen silence.

"Unhappily? Ah, that is too bad. I would not have

made you unhappy, señora. But then neither could I have poured gold into the coffers of Loma de Oro. A pity, for we are suited to each other, you and I."

"Shut up"! Tarifa cried wildly. Of all men she would have least preferred him to know of her marriage to Bart Kinkaid. Larios was like a thorn in her own conscience, bringing back memories she did not wish to think about. She only wanted him out of her sight. Oddly enough, she believed he would keep his word and stay away from Loma de Oro and its herds.

It made her heart ache to let El Canario go, but he was not her property, and unless Pito had a mount he couldn't very well keep his end of the bargain and leave.

"Take El Canario and go," she told him. "And I hold you to your word that you will not be back."

"You have my word, señora." He gave her a long questioning look. "Will you be satisfied with that?"

"Yes."

"Thank you, Doña Tarifa."

He turned and spoke to the Indian, who began saddling the horses.

Revolution was brewing in California all during Micheltorena's reign, just under the surface, watched by the eager, waiting Paisano clique, the dissatisfied group of young Californians, among them Pio Pico and Macario Canejo, who had sought from the beginning to govern their country themselves, and use its revenues to further their own interests.

Now, with feeling running against the weak, bombastic governor and the marauding unchecked cholo troops he had brought from Mexico, the time was ripe to fan the flames of discontent against the Mexican government.

A group of young northern hotheads had taken the bull by the horns in November, driven off all the government horses they could find at Monterey, and ridden to San Juan Bautista, the stronghold of the Castros, where they seized arms and ammunition and roused the populace to back their act of selfless patriotism.

Micheltorena issued a sweeping proclamation intended to crush the rebellion, declaring that the "horse thieves" would be caught and stripped of all property, and that any foreigners joining in their disorders would be put to death.

But the Paisanos were on the march. Couriers summoned all loyal Californians to back the rebels, and most responded with men or arms. Only the south remained quiet and watchful as always, while Micheltorena and his battalion of cholos, one hundred fifty strong, marched northeast of San José and met the rebel forces, two hundred twenty strong, in the foothills of the Santa Teresa rancho, belonging to the Bernals—a rolling, beautiful rancho with a lake, where the two forces camped uncomfortably in the hills a few miles from each other in the cold November rain.

At once the usual pen-and-ink bombardment commenced from both sides; days later a treaty was signed whereby, in the familiar bloodless settlement of California revolutions, the governor agreed to retreat to Monterey and send away his cholo battalion, while the rebels would await fulfillment of the treaty at Mission San José.

Still playing his double game, Micheltorena issued a proclamation to the people in December, announcing that since he "preferred the voice of humanity to the horrible roar of cannon," he had listened to their pleas and restored peace and order. "This frankness will always be the guiding star of my proceedings," he wrote piously—while he sent two of his officers to Mexico to obtain aid, and instructed Andres Pico to form a troop to safeguard the government in the south.

Early in December the townspeople of Los Angeles assembled in the pueblo and gave their usual vote of fidelity to Mexico, but they protested rising to protect the territory without proof of foreign intervention or attack. The "patriots" could find no joy in serving in a campaign without pay, if the truth be known. And most were not yet sure which would come out on top; Micheltorena as the legal representative of the government, or the young Californianos de Norte.

Foreign interest in the rising revolution was divided. The staid early settlers with commercial interests wanted to keep peace and order: Micheltorena had always been lavish in his grants to foreigners, as had Alvarado.

In the north, foreigners newer to California found it to their advantage to aid the revolution in one way or another. The wily John Sutter offered the governor a contract ensuring the military support of his fort and men, armed and ready, in consideration for full payment of his rather considerable debts, and more California land to augment that which he already owned on the Sacramento.

Feeling ran high in all the pueblos, and though the action was mainly verbal, that contentious hotbed of southern revolt, San Diego, was no exception.

John Mabrey found that, as one of the few foreigners present, he was suspect. At first he was mildly amused and then he became angry. When a rather down-at-heel member of the San Diego *gente de razón* accused him of being like Sutter, of trying to plunge the country into a bloody civil war, when all the Californians were doing was trying to rid themselves of a band of cutthroat convicts, Mabrey reared up on his heels in Chavira's wine shop, cursing the Californian in a flood of four-letter Anglo-Saxon words.

The startled old gentleman understood none of the words which was perhaps fortunate, for he had two beady-eyed half-breed nephews at his side, but no one in the room could mistake the tone of the doctor's voice or the flashing anger in his heavy-lidded eyes.

Luis Alvarjo and Patrick Havelock, who had just come in the door, stood in abashed silence listening to him. Luis, with Ellen's help, had learned to speak English, and even Havelock, used to the bald language of the frontiers, knew that he had seldom heard a more proficient bawling-out even from a Taos mule skinner.

He came across the room to Mabrey's side, and put his arm around the Englishman's shoulders.

"What's the matter, John, they riding you like they are me, just for being a foreigner?"

"Yes, blast 'em! Called me a bloody scavenging traitor, like Sutter!"

"Sutter is an opportunist. Always has been. But he's clever. He has vowed to support Micheltorena and he's already raised a force of Indians and foreigners to do it."

"There are many absurd rumors," said Luis, fingering his glass. "Some claim Sutter hopes to take California for himself. And I tell you, señor, his arming the Indians, some two thousand of them, is a dastardly thing in the eyes of my countrymen who remember the Indian attacks of the early days. Others fear that the governor has promised the lands and cattle of the Californians to the foreign element, if they help him to possess the country.

"I do not know the truth of these things, but since I was appointed *juez de paz* last month, I have found bitterness and fear rising on all sides."

Luis looked thoughtful as he continued and Mabrey knew the young man was voicing his deepest fears. "I am very much afraid the young Californians here will use this as an excuse to take power into their own hands as they tried to do once before. I even rode with them, though I did not believe in what they were doing when they rode against Alvarado. I have this"—he indicated his empty sleeve—"to show for it. I would not like to see my brothers embroiled in such a fiasco again."

"You must speak to Dona Tarifa about it," said Mabrey. "She will see that they do not get into trouble."

Luis looked toward the door in an effort to avoid the doctor's eyes. It still seemed to him that everyone could read his guilt in having embraced Tarifa.

"She did not know of the affair before," he said, "until it was over."

What would his brothers do in the coming crisis? Luis was only too certain that he knew the answer.

As he came out of Tiburcio Novato's house one cold afternoon not long after his talk with Mabrey at Chavira's, he was surprised to see Francisco ride by. He hailed him with pleasure for he had not seen his brother in several months. He knew that Francisco had concocted a sly way of screening himself from Tarifa's observation. He now divided his time between Bolsa Coyotes and Loma de Oro, but whenever Tarifa wanted to know his whereabouts he always managed to be busy on the rancho that she was not inspecting. Even Tarifa seemed to have given up on him, and Luis surmised that she must have half-suspected that Nazario and Santos both lied on occasion to protect him.

"*Buenos días, juez de paz.*" Francisco made his brother a low mocking sweep with his battered sombrero.

Luis realized unhappily that he was drunk, and his clothes looked as if he had been sleeping in a pigsty, which might have been the literal truth if he had been sleeping with some Indian maiden in the hogans at Las Flores as rumor had it he often did these days.

"Come into Novato's and let him give you a cup of tea, before you fall off your horse," said Luis shortly.

"A drink of brandy, *hermano,* that is what I need," Francisco leered, clutching at his wide saddle horn. "I never fell off a horse in my life." He promptly sprawled in the dust and Luis went to help him up.

He said nothing as he led his brother into Novato's house. The old man was shocked at Francisco's condition but he dispatched the maid for tea, and at Francisco's surly insistence a small measure of brandy.

"Will you put him to bed for a little while, Don Tiburcio?" asked Luis. "I apologize for the inconvenience and his—condition, but I have no way of talking to him now, and I have business to do."

"Go, *muchacho,* of course I will look after him," said Novato. It was amazing, he thought, that a man of Don Ygnacio's birth and background could have produced two such dissimilar sons—one so gallant and fine, the other no better than a cholo.

When Luis returned to Novato's at dusk, he found Francisco sitting in a chair in his bedroom holding his head in both hands and groaning lustily.

"*Sangre de Cristo*—my head! A thousand savages are chopping it to pieces with bloody axes! Get me a drink, Luis, *por favor?*"

"No," Luis said firmly, sitting down on the edge of the bed across from his brother. He noted that Francisco's clothes had been cleaned and brushed, his shirt laundered, and someone had made at least an attempt to repair his battered sombrero.

"Where have you been?" Luis demanded. "Temecula? Las Flores?"

"In hell," groaned Francisco. "Las Flores—what does it matter? What does anything matter these cursed days?"

"If Tarifa found out she would whip you."

Francisco groaned and cursed her feebly.

"Why do you go there? What interest can you have in such places?" Luis asked in frank disgust.

Francisco raised his head and his small dark eyes

gleamed with malice. "You do not know, do you, Luis? You have never had much fun. You did not serve in the *escolta* as I did. You do not know the excitement of a red *mujer*'s thighs?" He straightened up. "I got sick of hearing Nazario prate of his wife and precious sons, and the new one they are expecting. Only the Americano does not produce Alvarjo progeny, eh Luis?"

Luis flushed darkly but held his temper.

"At least your brothers are leading a useful and honorable life," he said evenly. "Why must you be the one to bring nothing but disgrace upon the Alvarjo name?"

Francisco laughed.

"You will pardon me, *hermano*, but that is a very funny thing you have just said. I have done much more for the Alvarjo name than you have done, than any of you have done!"

Luis got up in disgust. "You speak nothing but nonsense. I will get you some food, then we will ride back to the Rincon de Norte."

"You do not believe what I say?" cried Francisco, his eyes red-rimmed in his dark face. "I already have eight children—eight! More *niños* than any of you fine caballeros of the *gente de razón* have been able to produce. Eight! Each by a different Indian mother. Eight little half-breed Alvarjos, to people the wilds of Temecula and Las Flores and San Juan. Eight to call you Tío Luis."

Luis struck him with all the strength of his full-swinging body and saw him fall in an untidy heap at the foot of the bed, his eyes open and glazed.

Looking down at him, Luis felt nothing. Not anger, not disgust, not pity or remorse. Just a void of feeling as if the man lying before him were indeed merely a fallen animal, whose death was more desirable than his life had been.

The decision of Governor Micheltorena to break the treaty he had signed, in which he agreed to remove and disperse his hated cholo troops, was backed by the knowledge that he now had the support of Sutter and his "army" of foreigners and Indians.

The fury of the Californians against the barbarous cholos was now raised to a fever pitch to include the governor himself.

As good as his word, Sutter marched on Alvarado and Castro. It was a mixed but rather impressive force that he brought south with him. But at San José, where Sutter had thought to meet up with Castro, they were disappointed to find their prey gone and the wine shops shut. Still they managed to get drunk on the wine and *aguardiente* available at the Mission, and pushed on to San Juan Bautista and the Salinas, where Micheltorena and his force of cholos joined them.

The Californians under Alvarado and Castro were enjoying the game of cat-and-mouse they were playing with Micheltorena's superior forces. Alvarado seemed to take on his old initiative and military sagacity.

Every inch of the terrain was familiar to them, while the Sutter-Micheltorena army was on alien ground. Everywhere the Californians had kinsmen and, if not active supporters, at least sympathizers. Moreover, Alvarado, familiar with the peculiar impetuosity of Americans, was convinced that any long-delayed campaign, especially one of continued inaction, would soon leave the foreign contingent bored and restless.

With another brilliant stroke of intuition, he determined to transfer his forces to the south, where bitter feeling against the cholos and the governor's failure to keep the terms of his treaty could be used to advantage by the young Californians to ensure the south's aid.

In Los Angeles Pio Pico had been ordered by the governor to raise a militia to defend the pueblo in Micheltorena's name, against the rebels. Pico was at San Juan Capistrano when word came that the rebels were already in Los Angeles, having attacked the small garrison and, after a brief skirmish, taken over the plaza.

Again, Alvarado's evaluation of the situation in the south had been correct. Sympathy for the young Californians was swift and effective. Even the Americans of the pueblo, hoping to safeguard their property, enlisted.

Don Pio Pico was forced to go with the tide.

And Pio Pico soon found himself legal governor of California ad interim.

With Micheltorena's defeat at the battle of Cahuenga and the treaty of Campo de San Fernando that sent the former governor back to Mexico, Alvarado became administrator of the Monterey customs house, and Castro established his military quarters there, while Pico as governor and the assembly made Los Angeles the undisputed capital.

Inevitably the stage was set for a renewal of the old north-south battle over sectional rights and advantages.

But at last Pio Pico found himself in the position he had always desired, with the fate of the Missions resting solely in his own hands. He had an added and legitimate advantage in the fact that Micheltorena had decreed that the Missions and their properties should be used to equip and arm California against invasion by the enemy. Micheltorena had never put his power to use, *but now it was already in Pico's hand* and he lost no time in taking full advantage of it. The abandoned Missions of San Rafael, Dolores, San Miguel, Soledad, Parisima, as well as the pueblos of San Juan Capistrano, San Luis Obispo, Carmelo, and San Juan Bautista—all went to the auction block.

All in all, Pio could congratulate himself that he and his relatives now controlled more than half a million acres of the best California land. He had come a long way from the poor, landless son of a Mission soldier. After all, there was no use in being governor if one could not do as he pleased.

CHAPTER 32

In April, Tarifa instructed Santos to prepare for the annual rodeo. It was a month earlier than she usually held it, but the cattle and hides were poor due to the lack of water, and she hoped by killing off the older, less desirable stock to save enough grass and water for the best of her herds.

Santos sat cross-legged on the ground outside Pablos's shop, waiting for the saddlemaker. He was surprised to see a stranger leading a heavily packed mule enter the kitchen yard as if he were completely familiar with his surroundings.

"*Buenos días,* mayordomo!" shouted the little man.

Crisogono Ayala was an old Andaluz ex-picador who had fought in the bullrings of Seville and Madrid before coming by way of Mexico to California to seek his fortune. He was a rough, simple old soul, habitually drunk, who made his living by selling *tirutas,* a type of Indian blanket made of black and white wool from the lower Colorado basin, much sought after by the hacendados of California.

"*Saludos, amigo!*" Santos rose to clap him warmly on the back.

At the sound of their voices, Pablo came out of his shop to greet his old friend also. Santos offered the traveler a glass of *vino,* concealing his amusement when the old picador glanced quickly toward the kitchen before accepting it. Crisogono and Candelaria shared a long and bitter enmity. It was Candelaria who had discovered him drunk one day behind the washtubs and ordered a vaquero to strip and scrub him with the horsebrushes. She had returned his comfortably filthy garments to him later, freshly laundered but hideously stiff and unfamiliar. Crisogono had feared and hated her ever since.

"Where is the Old One?" he whispered, nodding his head warily toward the open kitchen door across the yard.

Santos reassured him, "You do not have to worry, *compadre;* she is at the hacienda." Smiling, Crisogono squatted comfortably on his heels next to Santos in the shade of the wide veranda.

"Everywhere I go in this land, mayordomo, I see hard times. Poverty, destruction, suffering, except here on Loma de Oro and on the ranchos of the Americanos. But I hear an Americano now owns even Loma de Oro?"

"Then you heard a lie," said Santos. "There has never been any question who owns Loma de Oro. It belongs to

Don Ygnacio's heirs, but it is up to Dona Tarifa to administer it as she sees fit during her lifetime. She has done well, *amigo*. Don Ygnacio himself could have done no better in these bad times. As for Capitán Kinkaid, he does not own any part of Loma de Oro; yet with his money and by his agreement, Dona Tarifa has bought more lands and improved the rancho."

"This Americano surprises me," said Crisogono. "Who would not wish to run such a rancho as this for a lifetime?" He glanced about the bustling kitchen yard with envy. Here at least, faces were still round with health, the young Indian maids still ground mountains of yellow corn for tortillas, and others carried baskets of beans and red and green peppers into the fragrant kitchen, ready to be made into the delicious dishes Candelaria concocted.

"How are things on the Colorado and in Sonora?" Santos asked his friend, offering him a *cigarrillo*.

"Ah, things are not good in Mexico either, *amigo,* even though they have a new *presidente*. You have heard of the war with the United States?"

"We do not concern ourselves with such things here."

"I have it from the Indians—there are many Americanos coming into California overland, by oxteam. I have seen armed expeditions myself, from a safe distance. Does the governor think to defend California against them?"

"The governor is too busy carving up the Missions and dividing the spoils between his relatives and friends to worry about the Americanos," replied Santos with a wry smile.

"And too busy quarreling with General Castro," added Pablo from the open doorway of the saddleshop. "Like two *niños* calling names, they bluster and swagger and wag their tongues at each other when they should be watching what the Americanos are up to."

Crisogono nodded his head in agreement. "A trapper friend of mind in Taos has told me of an Americano called Fremont, a military leader, who is in California now at the head of a large party somewhere to the north."

"We have not heard of such a man," said Santos with a frown. "Perhaps it is just as well I tell Dona Tarifa about this. She has an interest in such matters these days."

* * *

Since coming south, John Mabrey was aware of a new restlessness in him. At first he could find no reason for it. Outwardly he was more content than he had been since the loss of his wife and children. He knew that he was alert, strong again in body and mind, useful in his community. And then one day as he rode leisurely toward Loma de Oro for his weekly visit, he realized to his chagrin and mortification that he was in love again.

He was not really an old man yet in years, and yet ever since Lupe's death he had considered himself old. He had felt old. He had wanted no further part in the mixed joys and sorrows of romance.

The worst of it was, he thought, that the thing had come upon him so gradually that he had not even been aware of it.

When he visited Loma de Oro, it had always been as a trusted friend. He neither asked for nor expected anything more. Yet for months he had been aware that he found his deepest contentment and pleasure there. He loved the small children who reminded him of his own, and basked in the relaxing intimate family atmosphere that filled the hacienda in spite of Tarifa's driving influence.

He had succeeded in bringing Soledad back to at least a semblance of her former health, a feat for which the family was deeply grateful, and Mabrey was satisfied that she would recover completely, given time and loving care.

He was touched by her warm gratitude, which he did not in the least want, and by her growing childlike dependence on him. When he was at the rancho Soledad was content to listen to him read, or walk slowly up and down the patio by his side in the warm afternoon sun. When he was detained or failed to make his weekly call, she grew nervous and distraught.

Mabrey was aware of the great fear that haunted her, that Titus Judah would return one day to claim his wife and children. Though they had never discussed the matter, it was a thing he was determined never to allow to come to pass.

Long before he had been able to admit it to himself, Mabrey now realized, he had loved Soledad, loved her from the first time he had seen her. Different from the love he had felt for Lupe, or for the woman who so long ago had chosen to marry his brother.

Soledad was at once both child and woman to him.

When she clung to him after waking from a nightmare during the first of her illness, she seemed as appealingly dependent as one of his own daughters might have been. And as she walked quietly beside him in the patio or along the shadowy veranda, turning up her face to listen so intently to his every word, she seemed a woman, mature and waiting.

He cursed himself for this newly discovered idiocy, and yet he could not bring himself to abandon her when she seemed to need him so sorely. He had no way of knowing how she felt about him, beyond her present need. He didn't want to know how she felt. The whole thing was an impossibility. She was married. In the eyes of her family and religion, she could never hope to be unmarried or to marry again, unless her husband died. And scoundrels like Judah lived forever. So John Mabrey bore his bittersweet love like a secret talisman.

Now, as Mabrey dismounted in the April sunlight in front of the hacienda, he found Soledad with her face pressed anxiously against the *sala* window as if she had been watching for him.

She was trembling and as white as paper when he entered the room a moment later.

"Soledad, what is it? What's the matter?"

She flung herself against him, and his long arms went automatically around her slight frame.

"You must tell me what it is," he said gently, "so that I can help you."

She stepped back from him to pull an envelope from her sash and handed it to him with a stifled sob.

It looked battered and travel-worn. It had come, Mabrey saw, from Boston. He knew with a certain heaviness of heart that it must be from Judah.

Because she stood watching his face so intently, he opened the letter calmly and read it with detached deliberation.

Dated a year before, it was a documnt of calculated brutality:

My dear wife and children,

I was completely shocked, not to say thrown into a

state of acute melancholia, when, upon returning to my happy home, I found it empty and deserted. It was not until I had searched for and found Miss Fynchly, who had removed herself from Salem to a teaching position in New York, that I was able to get some word of your whereabouts, my dear Soledad.

Since I realize that Captain Kinkaid undoubtedly forced you to abandon your happy home, after telling you I don't know what lies, and taking advantage of your frailty and ignorance, I cannot find it in my heart to put the full blame for this act upon you, my dear wife. But I do hold you accountable for not having tried to contact me since that time, so that we might have been reunited. For as your religion, if not your mother, must have taught you, a wife's place is at her husband's side.

I am forwarding this by a faster ship than my own, and by the time you receive my letter, I will be nearby. Take heart therefore that our little family will soon be reunited.

Since, my dear, you have shown some preference for life in California, I have decided to claim your share of your father's rancho, so that we can settle down together to raise our family.

Until the moment in the near future, when I can claim you once more as the wife of my bosom, I remain your loving but lonely husband,

Titus.

Soledad stood with her hands clasped in front of her waiting for him to speak.

"You must not be afraid," he told her firmly. "On no account are you ever to be afraid of this man again. Do you understand, Soledad? I will see to it that he does not harm you or your children."

A little color came into her face, but her voice still shook with her inner fear. "But he is my husband. He has the right to take me away. And I could not bear that—I could not bear it!" She covered her face with her hands. Mabrey put his arms around her shoulders and drew her gently to a seat beside him on the brocaded love seat.

"Soledad, listen to me. You must not upset yourself over this letter. Husband or not, what chance do you think

he will have of taking you from Loma de Oro against your
will, with Tarifa, your brothers, Santos, and me to stop
him?"

She gave him a fleeting smile, and he could see that she
was comforted. He quickly pressed his advantage. Words
were what she needed now. Reassuring words, whether
there was any truth in them or not. "And how far do you
think Captain Judah will get when he asks Tarifa to part
with a piece of Loma de Oro?"

The thought made her laugh softly. "She would not let
any of the boys have their shares when they asked her for
them. Of course she will refuse to give up mine. And that
is all he wants of me—the land. I know now it was all he
wanted from the beginning. I did not suspect then. I was
so young, so foolish."

Mabrey spoke cautiously. "You never loved him?"

"No. Never! At first I didn't understand him, his ways,
and then I grew—afraid."

"The man's a swine!" Mabrey swore, with more heat
than he had meant to put into the words.

But she seemed not to hear. "If he had ever been like
you," Soledad said, touching his sleeve, "perhaps I could
have grown used to life in the United States. If he had
been kind, considerate, but there is no use going on, is
there? He will come, and there will be more unpleasant-
ness for everyone, and if he takes me away with him again
—I will kill myself!"

"Hush. You must never speak those words again. You
must never think them. Promise me?"

She looked up into his eyes and found sadness and pain,
and quite unknown to him, the open secret of his undeclared love for her.

Soledad's eyes flew wide with astonishment, and a
strange joy at what she read there. It did not seem possible that in her hour of blackest despair, happiness could
envelop her. Yet she knew that it had happened. She could
look into his eyes and find the strength and hope and understanding she had longed for but never expected to find
upon earth.

She had never known true love, other than the love she
had felt for her parents, and now felt for her children.
Until this moment, she had not realized the heady mixture

of pleasure and pain that went to make up the real emotion. The free gift of self that was like an unending tide, flowing and receding between the lovers. She had been a silly, witless girl for most of her life. Even now, she knew that she could never be as wise and strong as Tía Isabella or Tarifa, but at least now she could recognize love and give it to another without thought of self. The thought filled her with a pride and quiet confidence she had never experienced before.

She no longer stood alone. Even if it could never be, even if John Mabrey never mentioned it to her, as she felt he never would, knowing the dear stubborn sense of honor he lived by, she would be content. Immeasurably richer than she had ever been. If only she could go on seeing him, speaking with him, touching him occasionally, it would be enough; she would ask nothing more of life.

If only Titus would not come.

"Have you shown this to Tarifa?" Mabrey asked, holding up the letter.

Soledad shook her head. "I—couldn't bear to show it to anyone but you."

"She must see it," he told her. "I will take it to her. and you are not to worry about it anymore, understand?"

"No. I won't worry anymore, now that you are here," she answered in a low voice.

Mabrey got up and crossed the room in long strides. Watching him, Soledad found that she was no longer afraid of Titus Judah, or of the threat implied in his letter. John Mabrey's love stood as a shield between her and whatever disaster Judah could bring upon her.

Mabrey found Tarifa in the study scowling down at a letter she had just received. It had come on the same ship that had brought Soledad's.

Mabrey flung himself down in the nearest chair holding Soledad's letter between his fingers. "Not bad news, I hope?"

"It concerns Bart," she answered. "It's from the Endecott firm in Boston." She paused for a moment, then went on more slowly. "They say that the *Lorelei* has been reported lost in a typhoon off the China coast, and it must be supposed that all hands went down with the ship."

"No!" Mabrey cried. "I can't believe it, not of Bart Kinkaid. He'll turn up again, you'll see."

Tarifa shrugged her shoulders. The knowledge of her loss seemed to sit lightly on her, Mabrey thought. Wearing a white shirt and black riding trousers, with her coarse black hair loose on her shoulders, she had the look of a lean, sardonic pirate.

"They tell me I will receive no more money, at least for the present," she said bitterly. She read aloud to him from the letter written in Ephraim Endecott's spidery old-fashioned script.

"—and so my dear niece-in-law, although my nephew, Bartholomew, wished you to have everything of which he died possessed, and though you are fully entitled to such by law, as his legal widow, I must inform you that all his ready cash has already been paid out to you. All funds which remain have been invested in the Endecott Shipping Firm, in which he owned certain stock. Needless to say, it will be impossible to liquidate same while our country is at war with Mexico. I can only enjoin you to be patient, until I am able to put your husband's affairs in the proper order. I deeply grieve for your loss and my own.' "

"I can't believe it," Mabrey repeated. "Of any other sailorman I might believe it, but not of Bart Kinkaid."

"Why not?" mused Tarifa. "Did he bear a charmed life?"

Mabrey glanced at her accusingly. "Yes. I think he does. There are certain individuals who have an aura of indestructibility about them. I think you must have noticed it in him also."

Tarifa felt a ripple of uneasiness pass over her, as if Bart and not the doctor sat across from her, watching her with his cold gray eyes and his knowing and faintly derisive smile.

"What is to become of Loma de Oro?" she said, rising from her chair in an effort to shake off the spell Mabrey had cast over her thoughts. "What is to happen to us, with Bart's money stopped? With a rapacious, greedy fool for a governor, the Missions gone, and this idiotic war with the United States? How many more vultures are going to gather to peck at the bones of California?"

Mabrey smiled wryly. "Here is another of your birds of prey." He handed her Soledad's letter, and watched her as she stood in the light of the window reading it in silence.

When she had finished he saw that her face was convulsed by fury. Her Gypsy eyes glinted like obsidian in the sunlight. In their depths he seemed to catch the flicker of red, like the smoldering coals in a fire.

"*Primita Undebē!* What does this *gorgio* want!"

Though Mabrey could not understand the torrent of Romany, the consuming fire and biting contempt of her rage was unmistakable. Words foamed from her mouth as, with a naked violence that reached Mabrey even across the room, she ripped the letter to pieces and flung it out the open window. He saw that she was panting like an animal, her face bathed in sweat, her eyes glazed and shining like a panther's.

Suddenly she shook her head and ran her fingers through her tangled hair as if to clear her brain.

Mabry got up, poured a glass of wine, and took it to her. He watched thoughtfully while she drained the contents and a bit of the angry color that had suffused her face receded. She sank down on a chair and for a fraction of a second her shoulders trembled.

"I am sorry about Bart—and about this," he told her quietly. "Anything that I have is yours to use for Loma de Oro, or for Soledad and her children, if it will help. I haven't much left. Like the other rancheros, my wealth was tied up in my property in the north. But I still get some revenue from my mayordomo, and I have what fees I am able to collect for my services as a doctor, plus a little ready cash of my own."

"*Gracias,*" Tarifa said stiffly, "but Loma de Oro must stand on its own feet. As for Judah"—she spat on the floor with the venom of an adder—"he will die by my own hand if he steps on my land again."

"And what will you do if the hide ships quit coming to California altogether?"

Her chin came up. "I will find a way for Loma de Oro and the Alvarjos to survive."

She might be British, thought Mabrey, for all her hard-headed stubbornness in the face of overwhelming odds. He had not meant to stay longer, but he sat down again, leaning back and steepling his big hands over his chest in a characteristic pose.

"You puzzle me, Dona Tarifa," he said. "You take your

husband's loss and Judah's threat in stride, you think only
of Loma do Oro, and yet I wonder—is it enough, this
stake for which you have sacrificed everything, this place
you are ready to defend to the death? Don't you want anything else out of life? Is Loma de Oro going to be enough
for you for a lifetime?"

"Loma de Oro is my life."

"And if circumstances made it necessary for you to give
it up?"

"I will never give it up!"

His eyes were speculative and compassionate. She stood
like a rock in the torrent swirling around her, but even a
rock can be worn away in time, and he sensed the loneliness in her. "Someday you may find that Loma do Oro
is not enough, señora. That you value something even more
than you now value this rancho. I hope for your sake that
the realization will not come too late."

She smiled back at him lazily, like a lioness willing to
purr like a kitten—for one moment.

"If that time ever comes, Mabrey, you will know that
I have ceased being a *gitana,* and forsaken the gods of my
people forever. And such a thing can never happen until
I am dead and have gone to join Lasho in his grave."

The fear of foreign invasion temporarily put a stop to
the fruitless quarrels between Pico and Castro, and between
the north and the south. Mexico had sent formal recognition of Pico, but to all appeals for military help her promises were as empty as ever.

When Castro reported that due to the threat from the
American, Fremont, in the north, he would take over the
defense of California as her military leader, the danger of
invasion was immediately lost sight of by the indignant
southerners who claimed that Castro had no right to take
charge without the consent of the governor and the entire
Assembly. Once again a bombardment of missives flew
from north to south, widening the breach in California's
solidarity.

But Castro had valid cause for alarm. The increase in
immigration in the past months, coupled with the presence
of so many armed Americans in the north, namely Fremont and his band, was an active threat to California.

Not only did Castro fear the Americanos, but he mistrusted Pico even more, and lived in lively suspicion of his wily colleague's next move. Ironically, it was because of Castro's fears of Pico that he played into the hands of the Americans.

Completely unaware of the rumors circulating among the Americans in the north to the effect that he had issued a proclamation ordering them out of California, and that he was even now marching north to drive them out of the country, burning and killing as he went, Castro rode north to Sonoma to secure horses from his old friend Mariano Vallejo, in order to mount more men and thus protect himself against Pico, should the governor ride against him from the south.

By temperament, especially since the annexation of Texas and the long expected war with Mexico, the northern settlers were disposed to look upon Mexican jurisdiction as invalid, and upon any man with Spanish blood in his veins as inferior. Moreover, a reckless, rootless element had grown up around Sutter, made up of adventurers, unprincipled traders, deserters from ships—men ready and eager for a fight, any fight, that would bring them benefit or excitement.

Each man had his private reasons for wanting to tangle with the proud Californians. Some had a patriotic motive —to free the downtrodden natives and raise the Stars and Stripes. Others sought political honors rather than military glory. The majority simply coveted the herds and wide ranchos to the south.

The appearance of Castro's aides, Alviso and Arce, at once gave credence to the rumor that Castro was attacking, and word quickly reached Fremont's camp. The Americans rode in hot pursuit, captured the Californians, and secured the surrender of Sonoma and Mariano Vallejo. The Bears, as they would henceforth be known, raised their own, hastily made flag in the Sonoma plaza amid shouts of glee as it fluttered bravely in the breeze from the bay.

Upon Fremont's arrival, July fourth, at the height of the celebration of America's Independence Day, he was immediately placed in charge of the successful "revolution," although he had taken no active part in the Bear Flag Revolt.

The prize in the war between the United States and

Mexico had always been California. The United States had never made any secret of her intention of having the Pacific Squadron, already in southern waters, seize the California ports whenever war should be officially declared.

On the first of July, Commodore Sloat arrived at Monterey aboard his flagship, *Savannah*, and, on July seventh, demanded the surrender of the port.

While General Castro pondered the right moment to make his dash south, the American flag rose over San Francisco, San Juan, and floated unopposed over the Missions and pueblos throughout northern California.

Commodore Sloat, in ill health, was presently replaced by Commodore Robert Stockton. Stockton, unlike Sloat, did not look askance upon a land engagement; he was quite willing to accept the military services of the Bears, or Osos, as the Californians called them.

Pio Pico issued a stirring call to his people to defend themselves against invasion. But even by the time Castro had joined him in Los Angeles, making at least a public show of unity, everything went wrong for the two California leaders.

As usual, Los Angeles could muster no real enthusiasm to fight. The foreigners were understandably if secretly in sympathy with the American invaders, and though many of the *gente de razón* were as bitter as Castro and Pico against the Yankees, they had little confidence in their own general or governor.

Recruits were gathered in painfully slow numbers. The hacendados only reluctantly supplied weapons and horses. In their unending struggle for personal supremacy, Pico and Castro had at last succeeded in cutting each other's throats and that of California as well. Each had worn out his popularity, as well as the resources and credit of the country in their ceaseless plots against one another, and neither could hope to come out the victor. Equal in their strivings to the last, both Castro and Pico had managed to muster one hundred men, and now, characteristically, neither could feed his troops, maintain their loyalty, nor think of an adequate means of using them in this, their country's critical hour.

* * *

Tiburcio Novato, as the leading lawyer, and Luis Alvarjo, as *juez de paz* of Los Angeles, could foresee only chaos ahead for California and particularly for their own southland, as the scene of military activity shifted south.

Stockton had raised the American flag at Santa Barbara, and was now encamped at San Pedro drilling his troops. Fremont, at the same time, had landed at San Diego, raised the flag without opposition and, after finding horses, started north once again.

Castro at once sent his emissaries, José Flores and Pablo de la Guerra, to enquire of Stockton his purpose in being at San Pedro, and to offer to confer on a settlement of the difficulties. All hostilities were to cease during the time of the negotiations.

Stockton had no wish to negotiate, even if the Californians would agree to voluntarily raise the Stars and Stripes. He had no intention of recognizing the present authorities, and promptly refused, unless California declared her independence under the protection of the United States.

This, Pico and Castro, as duly appointed Mexican authorities, could not promise to do. They had no power to declare California independent, and both considered it an insult to simply surrender without even a show of resistance. Spanish pride reared its head.

Castro's reply to terms "both humiliating and preemptory" took a strange turn, however. It was his decision to leave California at once in order to report the situation in person, to the Supreme Government in Mexico. He magnanimously invited Governor Pico to accompany him.

Pico realized, as Castro did, that adequate defense for the south was impossible. The only thing to be done to save what remained of their honor, not to mention their necks, was to dissolve the assembly and report the results of the hopeless fiasco to the authorities in Mexico. But Pico, still the opportunist, used what little time was left to him well, by hastily filling out land grants, bills of sale, and long-term leases at ridiculously low prices, on all of the desirable lands still left to be distributed; most went to his close relatives, friends, and neighbors.

Pico's farewell address, made with tear-filled eyes in the sunlit plaza, was a fitting monument to his self-styled devotion and loyalty to the country he was about to abandon.

"And so," mused Tiburcio Novato to Luis, "California is left without a government."

"And I say it is better off without such a one as it has had these past months, Don Tiburcio."

The two Californians stood glumly in the plaza and watched the combined armies of Stockton and Fremont march into the pueblo of Nuestro Señora de los Angeles, where the American flag was raised with ceremony and dispatch.

Many Angelanos had fled the pueblo at sight of the Americans, but by nightfall most had straggled back, encouraged by the friendly sounds of the brass band and word of the notices being posted in the plaza that no harm would come to them from their captors.

The days immediately following the taking of Los Angeles were not easy ones, especially for the proud *gente de razón*.

Luis confided to his wife bitterly, "Commodore Stockton signs his latest proclamations, 'Commodore-in-Chief and Governor of the territory of California.' By what right, I wonder? His own? He is no better than Pico. He promises protection of life and property to all who accept the new government, yet he occupies the ports and then blockades them so we cannot trade. It now takes a written permit for a Californian to be out before sunrise or after dark, or to carry a weapon. This is justice for our people?"

Ellen told him firmly with a woman's incontrovertible logic, "But it will all work out satisfactorily in the end. I know it will. And at least there has been no bloodshed. You must just be patient, darling."

Luis was far from convinced that matters would simply work out as his wife suggested, and as the days went by his dissatisfaction with the way in which local affairs were being handled by the Americans reached a pitch of open accusation and distrust.

Matters grew worse in September when Stockton left Los Angeles in charge of Captain Gillespie with a garrison of fifty men to keep order in the little pueblo, while Major Fremont and his men marched north toward the Sacramento.

The older citizens of Los Angeles were willing enough to comply with Gillespie's newest regulations, but the younger element, always hot-blooded, revolted at once against the stiff yoke of restriction put upon them by the new commander.

Unfortunately Gillespie had neither the patience nor the wisdom to take into account national pride.

Without having considered real rebellion, the townspeople found themselves labeled rebels for the least infraction. Thus a ripe hotbed of resentment was prepared for the use of ambitious Mexican officers who began to foment actual rebellion among the excited, unhappy Californians.

It was all so easy. With but a slight effort the land could be theirs again! All they had to do was rise and fight. Throw off the American yoke! Was not young Serbulo Varela already setting them an example with his defiance of Gillespie for an unjust arrest? Did he not even now boldly range the countryside as an outlaw against injustice, harassing Gillespie and his men? This was the way for men of action. Men of daring, of honor!

Yet Gillespie's tyranny increased. And by his very actions he drove others to join Varela and his little band of outlaws, among them Francisco Alvarjo. And it did not take such young hotbloods long to believe that they were capable of attacking Gillespie and freeing the southland once again.

In the middle of a hot September, Varela and his men attacked a detachment of Gillespie's soldiers at San Diego, and with their little victory the fat was in the fire.

California rippled with the news that war had broken out once more, and patriotism demanded that each citizen do his duty in the name of national honor. Castro's ex-officers, who had been disbanded and were under parole not to take up arms again, were quick to join Varela and his patriots. Capitán José Maria Flores, an able Mexican officer, was elected Commandante General, with José Antonio Carillo as his Major General, and Capitán Andres Pico as Commandante de Escuadrón.

The new patriots would postpone the fate of California even temporarily. Who could tell what help might come from Mexico if they only held on. The hour promised power and glory and the Spanish soul, fed for a lifetime on her power and glory of the past, could not resist opportunity to gain it in the present.

Tarifa was in the patio amusing little Dolores and Rufina's somber red-haired boy José, when Antonio ran out from the *sala* carrying a copy of the rebel's proclamation.

Antonio, his face flushed with excitement, sent the children away and pressed the paper into Tarifa's hands.

"Read it," he commanded. "California is on the march at last! These caballeros are not like that spineless pair of oafs Pico and Castro. Read what they have had the courage to say!"

Tarifa stood up under the shade of the pepper tree and read the document in silence. Then grim-lipped and tight-jawed, she returned it to him.

Ever since the Americans had landed in the south and marched boldly through the countryside, she had never mentioned them in the family's presence, although they had heard her discussing the situation quietly with Dr. Mabrey and Padre Cazon.

She told Antonio wrathfully, "This is idiotic!"

"But they are patriots—all California is now roused to action."

"They are fools, these men. Roused to what? Bloodshed and loss of all they possess?"

Antonio looked crestfallen. Because he was younger than the rest, a mere child when Tarifa had come to Loma de Oro, he had accepted her authority more readily than the other Alvarjos. In a way, he had come to regard Tarifa as a real parent, taking her word as law. But at the moment he was convinced that it was wrong for her to call the brave patriots fools.

"It says here that every male between the ages of fifteen and sixty must take up arms," he said slowly, "and the property of any who oppose this action will be confiscated."

Tarifa turned to face him, her eyes blazing. "What do I care for their ridiculous rules and regulations, anymore than I did for those of Echeandia, of Micheltorena, or the Americanos for that matter? Let them all hang or kill each other, what do I care? I care only about the welfare of Loma de Oro, and that they will touch at their peril!"

"Francisco has been with Varela from the start," defended Antonio. "José and Marco Martinez have joined him, and Macario Canejo and Nazario—"

"What is that you say about Nazario?"

"It is true. I saw him yesterday."

"You mean he has gone? The fool! Who has he left in charge at Bolsa Coyotes?"

"The mayordomo, but he has asked me to stay on the rancho also until he returns."

"Primita Undebē! Then why aren't you there now? How do you know what that imbecile of a mayordomo is up to? Where are they camped, these ridiculous rebels?"

"I do not know," Antonio lied. "But I want to join them."

"You will go to Bolsa Coyotes and stay there until I give you permission to leave!" she thundered. Her brows seemed to meet over her eyes like a threatening black band.

Antonio remained silent but his own lips were compressed and there was a dull red color over his high cheekbones. Antonio was slim and soft-spoken, like Luis, but in him reposed more of Don Ygnacio's cold stubbornness and tightly leashed temper. He had always been impulsive, a luxury his father had never allowed himself to indulge in, and for this reason the son was the more dangerous.

"How long do you think Loma de Oro will last if California falls entirely into the hands of the Americanos?" he demanded a moment later.

"That is not the question at the moment," Tarifa said bitterly. "How do you expect this handful of rebels to hold off all the Americanos?"

"Long enough, perhaps, for aid to come from Mexico. Pico is there by now, and Castro. When they have explained what is happening here—"

Her laugh sounded like the harsh flat ring of an anvil.

"And you put your trust and your hopes for the salvation of California in the hands of those two gallant administrators? They accomplished so much for California's welfare when they were in charge of her affairs."

Antonio turned to leave and felt her hand on his arm.

"You must promise me not to leave Bolsa Coyotes unprotected," she said quickly.

His answer was sullen. "I will see that the rancho is safe."

She did not release her hold on his sleeve, and he felt helplessly pinioned, like a calf on the end of a *reata larga*.

"You are to stay at Bolsa Coyotes until you hear from me, Antonio. Do you understand?"

He nodded, though he kept his eyes averted from hers, and because he had never lied to her before she let him go.

All through dinner there was an uneasiness in her mind, and she noted with displeasure the preoccupation on the faces of the other members of the family. It was as if they had withdrawn from her in a body, as if she were the outsider and they had made a pact between themselves to keep her from sharing their secret. After the uncomfortable meal, she ordered Santos to saddle his horse and her own, and rode thoughtfully toward the Havelock rancho.

It was a bright moonlit night but there was a crispness in the air. Tarifa wore a black cape drawn tightly under her chin, and Santos was wrapped in his brightly colored serape. Although the mayordomo did not mention it, Tarifa knew that his rheumatic pains were bothering him by the way he eased his feet in the stirrups and coiled the reins over the horn, controlling Marca by knee pressure alone.

"I suppose you think I am wrong," she told him shortly, "because I oppose the rebels just as I do the Americanos? Because I refuse to allow Antonio and the others to throw away their lives in a futile struggle that can only end in disaster?"

"No, Dona Tarifa," the old mayordomo replied quietly. "Though it is not for me to say, I do not think this thing of you. I do not believe you are against the *niños* or the thing they would fight to protect."

Tarifa turned impatiently in her saddle to face him.

"Well, what is it you do think of me?"

The Indian sat hunched in the saddle, his hands folded on the wide horn. He might have been seated in a rocking chair before a comfortable fire the movement of the horse disturbed him so little, was so much a part of him.

"I think, Señora, that like these horses we ride, blood and breeding run true."

"You speak in riddles."

"Forgive me, Dona Tarifa, I did not speak so to con-
fuse you." His eyes sought hers and she found them re-
flective and a trifle sad. "You must know the Alvarjos were
born of proud parentage and that their blood courses hotly
through their veins, even as it does in these palominos.
Neither could deny their heritage, even for you. You know
the weaknesses of the Alvarjos, just as I do, but I do not
think that you ever knew their strength? Yet I tell you it
is there, Dona Tarifa."

She was thoroughly annoyed with him. She had asked a
simple question that should have evoked a simple answer.
Instead he prattled on about the Alvarjo bloodlines. She
chose to ignore his remarks about the family completely.
"And what is your opinion of these daring rebels under
General Flores?"

He replied patiently, "I think, since you ask me, señora,
that they are foolish hombres to stand against the Americanos who have so many more ships and guns and men."

Tarifa seized upon his answer.

"You see, then," she said, "why we must all keep to
ourselves to preserve the rancho, as Don Ygnacio would
have wanted? That is why no Alvarjo must ride with the
rebels."

"What will you do about Don Francisco, and Don
Nazario then?" Santos asked, for every servant on the
rancho knew where they had gone.

"I will send you to bring them back, of course," Tarifa
said flatly.

He raised his eyes in surprise, "But they will not return
for me, Patróna."

"Don Luis shall ride with you. That is why we go now
to the Rincon de Norte."

Santos said nothing more, but he was not pleased. He
did not relish the prospect of riding into a hostile camp to
forcibly take away two valued soldiers. And he did not
believe that even Don Luis' presence could ensure the
success of Tarifa's plan.

Ellen opened the door of the hacienda herself. She kept
few servants, and even though there were some women in
the kitchen, the amazed stories ran that she did most of
the family washing and ironing, and had been seen on at

least one occasion scrubbing the *sala* floor on her hands and knees like an Indian serving girl.

She greeted Tarifa with her usual cool reserve, and suggested that Santos go around to the kitchen for refreshments and to warm himself by the kitchen fire.

As Ellen ushered in their guest, Luis and Patrick Havelock rose from a table near the *sala* fire where they had been going over some account books.

Tarifa explained her errand briefly, standing with her back to the fireplace.

"The Varela forces captured a party of Americans at Chino," Havelock said gravely, "and turned them over to Flores."

"Flores is demanding Gillespie's surrender," added Luis, "and it looks as if he may get it."

Tarifa was dumbfounded.

"You mean the Californians have already beaten the Americanos?"

Havelock's smile was grim. "Not beaten, but outmaneuvered them, at least temporarily. What will happen when the rest of the American forces return I cannot say, but Gillespie may consider it the better part of valor to retreat—for now."

His words made sense to Tarifa. She had no intention of backing down but she realized that it might be wiser, considering the surprising turn of events, to say nothing to Luis or Havelock about recalling Francisco and Nazario from the rebel band. Always an opportunist, she thought she saw the chance to benefit Loma de Oro by this unaccountable victory of the rebels. With her two stepsons already represented on the rebel rolls, surely Loma de Oro would remain safe from seizure by the new government?

Her voice was casual as she asked Havelock, "Have you considered that the rebels will feel privileged to take your cattle and horses for military use, just as the Americanos have done?"

Ellen answered before her uncle could open his lips. "Yes, we have just been discussing that. But there is little we can do to protect ourselves."

Tarifa gave her a derisive glance and spoke again to Patrick Havelock. "They will not dare touch Loma de Oro cattle, or the herds on Bolsa Coyotes, because of Francisco and Nazario. I will pasture whatever stock you wish to safeguard on one of my ranchos, at fifty cents per head."

Luis flushed in anger that an Alvarjo, a kinswoman, could demand payment for a plain deed of hospitality. But to his astonishment Havelock seemed merely amused and grateful for her suggestion.

"Done, Dona Tarifa! I'll have the mayordomo start driving them over in the morning."

Luis could not face his wife, but he gave Tarifa a look of wounded pride, and excused himself on the pretext that he must return to Los Angeles.

The unexpected capitulation of Gillespie, at the end of September, with his subsequent sailing from San Pedro, filled the southern Californians with wild elation.

Every active male in the southland now considered himself part of the bold revolution against the Yankees, though barely two hundred men could be equipped for fighting. Only inferior powder made at Mission San Gabriel was available to fill the few muskets and pistols provided by the people, or to fire the ancient four-pound cannon that had lain buried in Inocencia Reyes yard since Stockton's arrival. It had never been used for anything in the past except to fire salutes on festive occasions, but a cannon lent class to any military arsenal. Now it was proudly mounted on a pair of wagon wheels to accompany the victorious rebels in their next battle.

Ranchos and haciendas were ransacked for lances, swords, knives, any sort of weapon, and horses were commandeered to mount the troops. The new army did not have long to wait to try out its military skill.

Stockton returned to San Diego in early November, and found the pueblo under a state of seige by Varela and his band. They continued to drive off the stock, and harass the American contingent who still sought refuge in the city.

Skirmishes on the outskirts of the pueblo were a daily occurrence. The frightened *gente de razón* stayed close to their homes, watching helplessly while their horses and cattle were driven off by the rebels, and what stock remained was promptly taken over by the Americans in order to mount their troops for the proposed march on Los Angeles.

* * *

Francisco and Nazario had been with Capitán Andres Pico's party of rebels since he had come south in November at Flores' command and set up his headquarters at San Luis Rey. Pico had some eighty men under his command when word reached him that Gillespie had left San Diego, no doubt to gather stray horses and cattle for the San Diegan forces as he had done in the past. Since it was Pico's duty to keep supplies from reaching Stockton, he followed the American, without knowing that General Kearny had arrived in California or that Gillespie had gone to join him.

Andres Pico made camp at the Indian pueblo of San Pascual on December fifth, paying little attention to the garbled story from the Indians that a large American force was camped nearby. He was used to such groundless rumors, and ordered his horses pastured some distance from the camp where the feed was better. In the cold and continuing rain of the wettest season California had experienced in years, thought of enemy attack seemed preposterous.

Nazario, sheltering his head under a serape, was roused at midnight by the sound of a dog barking sharply in the distance. A moment later the sentry nearby cried out, *"Quién vive?"* but there was no reply, and after a moment of restlessness Nazario went back to sleep.

Early the next morning he was roused by Francisco.

"Nazario! Enemy scouts were here last night. They have found tracks, and a blanket one of them lost. It is Americano."

It seemed incredible to Andres Pico that Gillespie's few men would attempt to do battle with his own superior forces, but as a precaution he ordered his men to mount and make ready.

At that moment, Nazario looked up to see Antonio charging into the camp.

"Does Tarifa know you are here?" he asked, as his youngest brother reined to a halt before him.

"No," answered Antonio uncomfortably. "She was very angry when she learned you and Francisco had joined the rebels. She made me promise to stay at Bolsa Coyotes in your place. I gave her my word not to leave the rancho without her permission—but I could not keep it when I learned the others were coming to join you. Pico will need every man he can get."

"Amen to that," said Francisco, who had come up to join them. He carried a brace of pistols in his sash, and there was a tense readiness about him, as if he had been poised and waiting for this moment all his life. He should have stayed in military service, thought Nazario; a soldier's life seemed to suit him better than any other.

The short ten miles separating the two armies, between Santa Maria and San Pascual, was covered rapidly by the American forces in the early dawn. The Californians had barely mounted, lances in hand, when the first vanguard of the Americans came riding full tilt downhill toward them. Valor alone could not stand against the heavy loss of life in the brutal hand-to-hand scuffle, nor against the charge of Californians on their fleet horses. Still the Americans stood their ground, blood dripping from their wounds, grim-lipped as they swung rifle butts and sabers at the cruel sharply pointed lances.

When the Americans finally managed to bring up their two howitzers, the Californians again dispersed and galloped off, and in the excitement two mules drawing one of the howitzers took fright and galloped off after the enemy.

Taking advantage of what had happened, Francisco built a loop in his *reata* and charged after the racing mules, catching one of them neatly around the neck with his first throw.

The dark-bearded American soldier riding the second mule pulled a pistol from his belt and fired point-blank at Francisco's forehead. He saw a hole appear between the Californian's eyes like a large black insect that had suddenly alighted there, and then he saw the man in the saddle twist and fall sideways from his golden horse to lie sprawling on the muddy ground.

The soldier had no time to notice anything else. A lance pierced his back and threw him forward under the feet of the frightened mules.

Nazario and Antonio had watched Francisco's pursuit of the howitzer, and came racing to their brother's aid. Antonio had no weapon save his *reata*, which he quickly used to halt the nearest mule, while Nazario ran his lance through the dragoon before the man had time to turn his head.

With the mules secured, their great nostrils flaring with fright, the Alvarjos threw themselves off their horses beside Francisco's body.

Nazario turned his brother over gently, crying out at sight of the wound between his eyes.

"*Muerto*. He is—dead," whispered Antonio. He was badly shaken. Somehow he had not thought the day's action would end in such carnage and personal tragedy. Certainly, he had not allowed himself to think that an Alvarjo would lie dead at the end of it.

"He must have been killed instantly," said Nazario, noting his younger brother's pallor. He put one of Francisco's pistols in Antonio's sash, the other in his own, and stooped to gather his brother's body in his arms. "Come. Bring the horses," he told Antonio quietly.

The battle of San Pascual, the bloodiest in California's history, had ended.

The Americans were unable to give chase now, and both sides began to gather up their dead and wounded. Eighteen Americans had been killed, nineteen wounded, and three of these would soon die of their wounds. Some men had as many as ten lance thrusts in their bodies. Kearny himself had two wounds. Gillespie had three lance thrusts that had caused him to be left on the battlefield for dead. Under cover of night they buried their fallen comrades, side by side under a willow tree facing east and home, while Kearny sent messengers to San Diego reporting his condition, and requesting supplies, wagons for his wounded, and reinforcements.

Andres Pico, on his part, had lost no time in reporting his "victory" to Flores, and announced that he would await help, due any moment now from Hermosilla and Cota.

Later, in the eyes of those who took part in and those who watched the battle of San Pascual, it was impossible to say which side had emerged victorious.

Through the rain and fetlock-high mud, the Alvarjos led El Segundo, with Francisco's body bound across his saddle by the *reata* Pablo had made for him so many years ago.

It was dusk when they reached Loma de Oro and rode slowly up to the hacienda, wet to the skins and silent in their sorrow.

Tarifa was not present, only Tía Isabella and Soledad, when they brought Francisco's body inside, and they had become inured to horror.

"Who—is it?" Isabella asked presently, and her low, proud old voice scarcely trembled.

"Francisco, Tía Isabella."

She nodded. "You have all been fighting with the soldiers? There can be no other explanation for—this."

"*Sí.* We have been with the soldiers, Tía Isabella, God have mercy on us. Where is Tarifa?"

"She thought you had gone to join the rebels, as I did. She rode to Bolsa Coyotes this morning. She will be very angry with you, Antonio. You gave her your word to remain on the rancho, and now—this. Take Francisco to his own room, *por favor.*"

The women of the household had washed and laid Francisco out on his own bed, and Tía Isabella had lighted tapers at his head and feet and was just kneeling to begin the prayers for the dead, when Tarifa and Padre Cazon arrived. They had met on the driveway coming into the hacienda.

Tarifa stood by the door in silence, still wearing her wet cape and sombrero. She watched without comment as the priest went forward to perform his duties for her dead stepson.

For Francisco she felt nothing. He had disobeyed her, defied her. But she felt a pang of sympathy for the others. It was hard to lose something you loved, something that was part of you, as Lasho had been part of her. And in some strange fashion which she could not fathom, these Alvarjos seemed to go on loving one another no matter what they had done. In a flash of intuition she knew that she wanted to be loved like that. Above and beyond anything that she could do or say. For herself alone. And no one was ever likely to love her like that now.

Padre Cazon, looking very old and worn in his shabby robe, came to stand beside her.

"Come down to the study," said Tarifa wearily, "when you are finished."

In front of the small oak fire in the study, with the rain beating a tattoo on the deep-set windows, Tarifa sat with her trousered legs spread apart and her chin sunk on her chest. She had never smoked *tuvalo*, the harsh tobacco of the Gypsies that Penti and Bandonna had used, but now she held a small black *cigarrillo* between her fingers made from the patch of tobacco Penti had grown each year to supply her wants. A glass of brandy rested on a table near her hand.

"*Sarishan*, Padre," she murmured.

"*Sarishan*," he replied gravely, sitting down near her. "I am glad to see you."

"And I am glad to see you, Dona Tarifa. It is long since we have talked. You find a need for the old Romany words?"

She nodded.

He was aware of the strange deep element of Gypsy mysticism that ruled her people, often passing into morbid gloom. Nature, their true belief in life, seemed to ebb away and take on a darker meaning in the cold of winter. They were indeed creatures of the sun and open, these people. And he had not realized until now how supreme had been the sacrifice Tarifa had made in giving up her freedom to stay on at Loma de Oro.

"It is long since I have thought of my childhood," she mused in the soft hollow voice that was so unlike her. "Help yourself to the wine or brandy, Padre, and let me talk."

"I will be most interested—*miri pen*, that is what Penti calls you?"

"My sister—I beg your pardon. *Miri pen*, it means *my sister*.

"I have often wished I could speak a little Romany," the priest replied, sitting down in an armchair.

"I was teaching Ygnacio a few phrases when he died. I have been surrounded by death ever since I came to this land," she said suddenly. "I am weary and sick of it. It is such a waste."

"When are we not surrounded by death, my child, or by life either, for that matter? We choose only to look at whichever side of the mirror is nearest us at the moment and ignore the other."

Tarifa raised her head and drew smoke deeply into

her lungs. It soothed and at the same time stimulated her. Once, the dance had been all she needed or wanted, but recently it had lost its captivation for her.

"Do you know Granada, where I was born, Padre?"

"*Sí*. A most beautiful place. I remember the peace and loveliness of the Alhambra woods, the cypress trees, and the nightingales."

"And do you know of the Moors who built it? My father was a Moor."

"None surpassed the aristocratic race who planned such cities as Xauen and Granada. It is odd how the Moors built their gardens and forts together—as if the fierceness of their characters must relax in the mournful contemplation of nature.

"I have known many Moors," the priest went on, "proud, dignified men, solemn without a trace of a smile. Seemingly without tenderness or curiosity, yet fearless defenders of their noble race. The Moors are part Berber and part Arab, you know. A white race. And with their brutal warfare they also brought art, education, science, to Spain."

"You do not hate them then?" she asked curiously. "I thought all true Spanish subjects hated the Moors."

He smiled at her and put down his glass.

"You may hate what a man does, Tarifa, but not the man himself. It has taken me a very long time to find that out. Once, as a soldier, I hated all the enemies of Spain. Now I realize that what I fought against in them was the hatred and injustice I felt for myself. You cannot forgive and understand another person—or nation, my child, unless you first learn to know and forgive yourself. God was right when he said 'Love thy neighbor as thyself'— but first you must love yourself. And how many of us are wise enough, or have faith enough, to keep on doing that?"

Tarifa seemed impatient with his words. She waved her hand as if to brush them away.

"It is the small things of Granada that I remember," she said. "The gazpacho, the cold soup, thick with garlic and tomatoes. The fountains playing in the Generaliffe, where I used to hide and dance. The *Shasto* or feast days, with wine and music and stories.

"I recall the green forest below the snowy Sierra Nevada, the Inns squatting below near the marketplace, and the sounds of the peasants coming to town through the sharp cold air. There was the noise of the street players' *bandurrias*. And at night the *Martinete*, one of my mother's tribesmen would sing, stark and shrill with no accompaniment but the beat of a *kasté* on the stone floor of a cave in the Sacro Monte. He would sing of feuds, of those hanged for their crimes by the *gorgios*, of lovers leaping to their deaths from a mountainside rather than be parted."

She paused and straightened in her chair, and there was a pale luminosity on her face as if it had been lighted up from within.

"Best of all, I think, I remember going up the steep Calle de Gomeres, through the arched gate into the Alhambra woods. I needed no other amusement when I was a child. I could lose myself in it like a fairyland, listening to the running water, the birds, burying myself in the ferns and moss under the trees. And then I would take one of the paths going up to the Generaliffe or the Alhambra, and I used to sit and wonder what had really taken place that night in the court of the lions, when the Sultan's favorite maidens had been murdered and their blood left to stain the marble basin when Granada fell. Once a visiting Grenadino read me the inscription around the windows of the Lindaraja where the Sultanas had sat to admire the view, 'I have gathered here so many beauties that even the stars wish to take them from me and carry them to the palaces of the sky.' I used to sit and pretend that I was one of the Sultanas, and then I would lose myself in the dance until I fell exhausted on the marble floor."

"You have much that is good in your memories, Dona Tarifa," Padre Cazon said gently. "Do you wish to go back to Spain?"

She got up and stood facing him with her back to the fire, looking like a young Sultana, proud and aloof, her introspective mood wiped away as if it had never existed.

"No! I will never leave Loma de Oro!"

"It is good that you love this place," the priest said slowly, watching her guarded face, "but I worry that you love it too well, to the exclusion of all else. The Commandments have warned that we cannot worship false gods, and what is the love for a place or thing above all

else other than the worship of a false god in place of the
Almighty?

"You do not believe, I know that, but it is only by His
Grace that we are here at all, or remain to work out our
own salvations. Everything is here for us to use or mis-
use, is as He made it for us. But we were not made to
worship trees, or mountains, or the sun or moon. Admire
them, use them, wonder at their magnitude, but do not
fall down and worship what is only the shadow of God's
greatness. Lift up your mind and heart beyond the stars
and the sun and the moon, and you will discover real
glory, my child."

Tarifa stared back at him, looking like a graven image
herself, aloof, unmoved with only a trace of pity on her
face.

"I told you before, Padre, we do not see things in the
same light. The moon and the sun, wedded brother and
sister, are the gods my people believe in. Through them
nature is controlled, and the *gitanos* are the children of
nature."

The old priest rose and there was defeat on his face,
the stoop of failure in his shoulders.

"I am very weary, and I must say one last rosary in the
chapel for Francisco's soul. You will bury him in the
morning, after Mass?"

Tarifa nodded and watched him go slowly out the door,
his tonsured head bent, and she felt a helpless anger rise
up in her for the virile man he had been and the sham-
bling wreck he had become since the bad times, simply
because he insisted on giving up his own food for the
sake of the Indians. Not one of them deserved it or ap-
preciated it, she thought. He would kill himself in the foolish name of holy sacrifice, and she would lose another
friend. She who had had so few of them in life. What
frightened her the most was the discovery as she grew
older that she needed friendship from others, that she
found it harder and harder to stand alone. Even Penti's
sly railings she sometimes welcomed now, from her peculiar well of loneliness.

She turned and stood with her hands thrust out to the
fire, and her eyes caught the glint of her wedding band.
She wondered if she were indeed again a widow. Her

mind went back to the last night she had spent with Bart
Kinkaid. Anger and humiliation and something more
powerful than either of them, something she could not de-
fine, like a suffocating warmth, washed over her and she
cursed aloud to herself but softly because it was late:

"*Premita undebē!*"

But the memory of Bart Kinkaid refused to leave her
mind.

On January thirteenth, at Cahuenga, Andres Pico and
Colonel Fremont signed the treaty of capitulation drawn
up in Spanish and English. Its terms were generous, even
if bitter for the Californians to accept. All Californians
were pardoned for past hostilities, given the protection
and privileges of American citizens. It only remained for
the Californians to give up their few muskets, two cannons, and promise not to take up arms again. The war
was over for California, and an uneasy peace descended
on the land.

With Americans quartered at San Luis Rey Mission, and
temporal affairs in the hands of an American manager,
Padre Cazon had left for Pala to care for the Indians who
flocked to him like bewildered, frightened children.

There was no rest for anyone. Tarifa and every man on
the two ranchos who was capable of riding spent twelve
hours in the saddle daily. Rounding up stock, branding
and marking them to save the best animals from being stolen by thieves or claimed by small ranchers as strays. Killing, skinning, and burying the rest. No matter how hard
she drove herself or the men, it seemed to Tarifa that they
were never finished with their chores. Many of the vaqueros grew stubborn and surly, or slipped away, taking
a few Loma de Oro cattle and horses with them, or demanded cash for their wages, which was now the law and
which Tarifa could not pay.

At last she understood Bart's warning. She was land-
poor now. Land, the best land in California, went begging for a price. It was nothing for a ranchero to part
with thousands of acres for a few hundred dollars. And
land that you did not occupy or constantly patrol was liable
to fill up with foreign squatters who refused to move on.
Although settlement of such claims was promised as soon

as peace was restored, there was little the Californians could do to protect themselves or their property in the meantime. American troops were everywhere, but when they attempted to ride onto Loma de Oro or Bolsa Coyotes land, Tarifa met them with grim determination and armed vaqueros, and they withdrew rather than risk another bloody incident in the strife-torn south. Only Tarifa's constant vigilance over every inch of her property, and her reputation as a fiend in trousers, unafraid of man or devil, who would as soon cut your eyes out with her black-snake whip as look at you, or drag you to death with her *reata* behind her golden stallion, kept all but the more foolhardy souls from crossing the boundaries of Loma de Oro.

Because the family were all in rags and because she needed the money so desperately, Tarifa had sold a few of the palomino colts to a New Mexican horse trader in Los Angeles for one thousand dollars. The money had been a godsend. With it she had bought clothing, badly needed hardware for the ranchos, and had been able to pay the vaqueros at least a token wage with a promise of more later to delay their leaving.

"If the men leave," she told Santos, "we are done for. The herds will be rifled and disappear just as the Mission cattle have, and without the herds Loma de Oro will sink into ruin."

"Fools, ungrateful fools!" cursed the mayordomo. "Have they not lived and died on Loma de Oro? Have not Don Ygnacio, and now yourself, seen to their every need? I have no patience with them. *Borricos!* All of them."

Tarifa straightened her aching back. She had mounted at dawn and still sat her horse now at sundown. They had halted in the pasture to the right of Loma de Oro and stood facing the valley floor on a little table of land.

At a distance, a horseman could be seen galloping at a furious pace from the direction of the Mission.

"Who is that?" asked Tarifa. She leaned forward to examine the horse and rider but in the uncertain light could not make out who it was. "He is riding toward the hacienda," she said uneasily. For these days any swiftly approaching rider might bring news of a fresh disaster. Like a dog that has been conditioned to a whip, she had learned to brace herself against assault.

"I do not recognize him, Patróna," said Santos, "but we can cut him off from here if you like."

Tarifa nodded and the two put spurs to their weary horses and dashed over the rough grass-clad hills toward the valley floor.

It was Antonio who pulled to a sliding halt beside them a few minutes later in the road that led to Loma de Oro.

His face was transfixed with jubilation, and the words tumbled from his lips as from the lips of an excited child.

"Gold, Tarifa! The Americanos have found gold at Sutter's Mill! Gold, oceans of gold, rivers of gold, nuggets as big as your fist—"

"Where?"

"At a mill the Swiss, Sutter, built some forty miles above his fort in the Sacramento. Everyone is going! They say men become rich overnight. For a little work you can get all the gold you can carry. Think of it! I hear San Francisco is nearly empty of people; so are Monterey, Santa Barbara, San Diego. Soldiers have left their posts, sailors have deserted the ships in the harbor, stores are left open. Everything is deserted, abandoned. It is like a great fever that has demented everyone. We must go, too, Tarifa."

She listened to him, weighing his words, but not allowing herself to be influenced by them. As always, she thought first of how this new stroke of fate would affect Loma de Oro—provided it was as Antonio said.

"We must go," Antonio insisted. "We can get gold for the rancho. We can buy whatever we want. You would not believe the stories I have heard. Because everyone has rushed to the goldfields and left their belongings behind, every commodity sells at a premium to the gold seekers. Hundreds of dollars for a barrel of flour, for a pick or a shovel. Thousands for horses and mules, hundreds for a cow to eat!"

Tarifa's long eyes flickered with interest, but she spoke calmly, "I must speak of this with others first. Ride back to the rancho, Santos, and bring us fresh horses."

"Sí, Patróna, muy pronto!"

John Mabrey opened the door of his dispensary late that night to find Tarifa and Antonio standing wearily on the doorstep.

Mabrey turned up the lamp he carried and pulled his gray dressing gown more closely around him.

"Good God, Tarifa, you look like a ghost! Is something wrong? It isn't Soledad?"

"No. Nothing is wrong, Doctor. We have just come to talk with you."

"At this hour? Then it must be important, sit down. Here, drink this and I'll see about food. There's bread and cheese, I think, and some dried beef in the cupboard."

He busied himself laying out wine, and food on a collection of odd plates, while he watched Tarifa's white, strained face from the corner of his eye.

"Now," he said, busying himself with a big cigar while they ate, "what is all this about?"

"What do you know about gold?" Tarifa asked.

"The gold the Americanos found at Sutter's, in the Sacramento!" broke in Antonio.

"Ah! So that's it? Well, there's gold, all right. I've seen it myself, some of it."

"Seen it?" asked Tarifa. She was suspicious of the whole affair, but she trusted the Doctor.

He nodded. "Some Mormons came through carrying over a hundred pounds of gold taken in less than a month from a place they called Mormon Island. The populace has been leaving Los Angeles and San Diego ever since, as fast as ships, horses, or their own two feet could carry them."

Antonio waved his hands impatiently. "We mustn't waste any time. We must all go at once!"

"And leave everything we own to whatever thieves happen by?" Tarifa asked coldly. "Are you going, Doctor?"

He frowned. "I don't know. If I still had a use for money—my own needs are modest, as you can see. I cannot make a decision yet," he ended lamely.

Tarifa stared at him with her strangely intuitive eyes and he glanced away. She knew he was hiding something from her but she was not certain what it was.

"How is this going to affect the ranchos?" she asked presently.

"Loma de Oro, you mean?" he smiled indulgently. "Well, for the time at least, while the gold craze lasts, you will not have to worry much about cattle and horse thieves.

Everyone will be going north, and those passing through will not stop long enough to burden themselves with extra goods. On the other hand, hides and tallow will be worth nothing, and labor will become nonexistent. You may as well make up your mind that this fever will infect every man, woman, and child on your place."

"Then there is no use in ranching any longer," said Antonio. "We may as well go to the goldfields, too."

"Shut up!" Tarifa snapped. There was a sharp, bitter note of defeat in her voice that neither man had ever heard there before. "If I go to the goldfields, it will be for Loma de Oro, and for no other reason. And it will not be to root for gold like a grizzly for ground acorns."

"But why else should anyone go there?" Antonio asked, bewildered. Truly his stepmother was an enigma. He had made up his own mind to go with or without her consent, but he was not brave enough to tell her so to her face.

"You answered your own question when you first told me about the gold," she said. "They have need of everything in the goldfields. Cattle for meat, horses, mules, clothing, food. We shall take these things to them, and demand a high price in return. The gold seekers shall dig not only their own gold, but ours as well."

Mabrey glanced at her with admiration.

"You are a damned clever and resourceful woman, Tarifa," he laughed. "But you won't find it's quite the easy job you think it is to go alone into the diggings with valuable and scarce merchandise. I've heard of a man murdered for his overcoat, another for a pair of boots. If you take a large party, perhaps—"

"I will take no one but Antonio."

"But that is sheer madness. You will both be robbed if you are not murdered. And what of the rancho—the others?"

"You will keep an eye on them for me?"

"Yes, but—"

"I will leave Santos in charge. I have gold enough to pay some of the vaqueros to stay. Even if there is gold for the taking, many of them are too lazy to go."

"Then take them with you for protection," said Mabrey.

"No. I need them on the rancho. I am not afraid for myself or Antonio."

"You can't go alone; it is madness, I tell you."

"My mind is made up. We will take some horses and cattle, some of Pablo's leather goods, and a few barrels of flour I have at the rancho. We will go to the nearest gold camp and no further."

Antonio had a sullen, mutinous expression on his handsome face, but any opportunity that would take him to the goldfields was welcome. He would not tell Tarifa until he had to that he had no intention of returning with her until he had gotten his own share of the gold. He would be rich again, as his father had been, and everyone would bow as he rode by and call him Don Antonio and Patrón Generoso. And he would not be forced to leave the cantinas because he had no money to satisfy his thirst, and he could indulge to his heart's content his passion to play monte.

When she told them, the family had been excited at the prospect of riches, but divided in their opinion of Tarifa's plan to go to the goldfields herself.

"You must not think of it," said Tía Isabella firmly. "A woman alone in such surroundings!"

In the end, Tarifa took two young vaqueros who were eager to visit the gold camps, one to drive the rough supply wagon that Pablo and Tomas had built, and another to help her and Antonio drive the small herd of cattle and mesteños they had rounded up to sell. She was quite aware that the vaqueros would desert them the moment they arrived at the diggings. But it made little difference. She had no intention of returning burdened by anything but gold.

CHAPTER 33

From the beginning the Americans and foreigners in California were more beguiled by the vision of wealth to be dug out of the brown earth, or pried from the rocks of icy stream beds, than were the native Californians. Many hacendados ignored the whole thing as beneath their interest or dignity; others remembered the savage Indian tribes never conquered on the northern frontier, and thought the risk not worth taking.

A few, like Tarifa, were willing to go as far as the southernmost mining settlement which lay near the headwaters of the Tuolumne River.

Sonora, as it came to be known, named in honor of the Mexican miners from Sonora who had arrived first to work the placers, was the richest strike as well as the most southern yet made in the district. At once the Mexicans found themselves surrounded by a motley crowd of foreigners and Americans, as well as Indians and native Californians.

Since Sonora was the latest strike and the farthest camp from law and order—if it could be said that there was any law or order on the *frontera de norte* between Sutter's fort and San Francisco—it became a mecca for those who refused to sow but were determined to reap.'

Tarifa found Sonora extremely unprepossessing as she rode into the little settlement of brushwood huts looking like Indian wickiups, with here and there a crude but more substantial log dwelling. On the wall of one of these, an American had lettered a crude sign: STORE-SALOON, E. HARDISTY & SONS.

Tarifa signaled Antonio to halt in front of the building, and dismounted. She was aware of the interest the group of foreign loungers took in her person and in her horse, but she already knew that she was not the only woman in camp. As they rode in she had seen several Indian women working beside the men in the placers, and even several Mexican-Californian women, though not of the *gente de razón*. There were men, however, from some of the best families, many of them with their Indian retainers to do the digging.

"Why do you stop here?" Antonio asked uneasily. He would have preferred a quiet spot on the edge of town at least until they got their bearings, for he did not trust the vaqueros they had left with the herd and wagon some miles back to follow them in more slowly. And he could not read the American sign on the building.

"It is the logical place to stop for information," she told him briefly. "This place is a store-Americano."

"But I saw Don Camilio Valdez back there," he said, indicating the way they had come. "Why do you not ask him for information; why go to an Americano?"

"Because what I have to sell will probably bring a higher price from the Americanos. We came for gold, did we not?"

"*Sí.*" Antonio licked his lips. He would have thrown himself from his horse and dashed to inspect the nearest diggings if he dared, but something in Tarifa's eyes told him that she would not permit it.

"Stay here with the horses until I come back," she ordered.

He made no reply, but he obediently took Guindilla's reins and scowled haughtily at the watching gringos who made remarks, laughing and elbowing each other as Tarifa pushed by them to enter the log building.

After the hot brightness outside she had difficulty focusing her eyes. When she grew accustomed to the shadowy gloom inside, she found herself in a long, dirt-floored cabin, with a single ship's lantern nailed to the beam at the far end over a rough pine counter set up on flour barrels.

Behind the counter four Americans in shirt-sleeves were busy attending to the store's trade, two at one end selling trade goods, while the remaining two dispensed liquor at the other.

The narrow room was crowded to the walls with a motley crew of Mexicans from Sonora, Wallas Indians, Californians, and Anglo-American miners. Wherever a space was available, a monte bank or poker game had been set up atop a barrel head, and a cluster of intense, watchful players crowded around.

Tarifa's nostrils flared. The place had a stench and smell of its own, redolent of sweaty unwashed bodies, dust, moldy footstuffs, and sour liquor. Acrid choking smoke, like a benevolent dragon, wreathed in and out above the heads of the occupants and found a permanent resting place against the low hanging canvas under the brush-covered roof.

The men parted at Tarifa's approach. Women of any sort did not often step over the threshold of Hardisty's store in Sonora, and they were hard-pressed to place this one in the camp's social strata. High-born Spaniard. Rich, from her costume, thought the Americans. Of the *gente de razón*, thought the Californians and Mexicans, some with careless indifference, others with malice and jealousy. The newly arrived foreigners to California thought her merely a highly attractive and colorful addition to Hardisty's drab establishment.

As she approached the counter, Tarifa saw that the tallest and heaviest of the shirt-sleeved men behind it was a bearded, bald-headed man of sixty. He kept his small beady eyes on every transaction like a juggler watching the movement of each ball he tosses into the air.

The other three were younger, burlier editions of the big man, but with thick unkempt brown hair and beardless ruddy faces.

"Somethin' I can do for you, señora?" the bearded American asked in a rumbling bass voice.

Elias Hardisty had come down from Oregon with his three sons the year before, intending to buy land and cattle. But gold had taken him to Mokelumne instead, where the quick sale of his wagonload of personal goods had convinced him that the real pay dirt lay in catering to supply and demand. When the richest strikes appeared on the headwaters of the Tuolumne, he had gravitated with the miners to Sonora. Since he had no competition as a merchant he was well satisfied to stay on.

"You are the owner of this store?" she asked in Spanish. She had decided it might be to her advantage if none of them knew she understood, spoke, or read English. No Gypsy ever gave away more of his secret abilities than was absolutely necessary, especially in a strange environment.

Hardisty studied her with his small shrewd eyes. She came from money, he knew, even if she had none herself. Her clothes and bearing told him that. Yet there was a peculiar quality about her that he could not place, and was inclined to mistrust. Arrogance he had encountered in many a high-born Californian hacendado who had bellied up to his bar for a drink, but this women had more than arrogance in her expression. It was more like a mocking derision, as if the roomful of men were no more important to her than the dust under her daintily booted feet. Hardisty grew suddenly hot with anger at the thought of her insolence, but he came of Scots-English ancestry and he was not a man to lose business because of personal prejudice.

"Any of you boys understand the Señora?" he bawled at his sons.

"No, pa," answered Abel, the eldest, standing at his father's elbow. He thought the Spanish woman a beauty, and his large watery eyes stared boldly at her.

"One of you gents speak Spanish 'n English?" Hardisty yelled into the throng.

A young man dressed in rough miner's clothes glanced up from a poker game nearby and ambled over, his wide-brimmed hat on the back of his head.

"I reckon I do, Elias. Grew up in Santa Fe and Taos."

"Fine, Billy. Answer the lady's questions and find out what she wants."

Tarifa studied the newcomer. He was perhaps Luis' age, of medium height, muscular, with light brown hair and blunt but amiable features. His candid blue eyes were studying her as carefully as she studied him.

"My name's Billy Bacon," he told Tarifa in good Spanish. "This is Señor Hardisty's store. He asks what he can do for you, señora?"

"Tell him I am Dona Tarifa—" she hesitated and decided the name Alvarjo would hold more weight "—Alvarjo, of Rancho Loma de Oro, near San Diego. I have brought some cattle, horses, and trade goods to sell. I have need of a suitable place to transact my business, also a place to stay with my companions. Does Señor Hardisty know of such a place for rent?"

Billy Bacon stepped up to the bar and spoke rapidly in Hardisty's ear. Tarifa saw a look of studied caution come over the bearded man's face as he replied.

"Tell her to come around back to the tent where we can talk. You come along, Billy. There'll be somethin' in this for you, too."

Bacon nodded and repeated the gist of the message to Tarifa. She accepted with a nod. The old man was already worming his way from behind the plank counter.

Bacon and Hardisty led her outside the log building and around it to the rear where a cloth-covered shack, canvas nailed over a rude frame of poles, had been made into living quarters for the Hardisty family. Tarifa noted with distaste the crude furnishings. Pole and canvas-bottomed beds, barrel tables, and boxes or wooden blocks for chairs. Someone had tacked a broken sliver of mirror to a pole and hung his clothing on nails.

A huge battered leather trunk filled one corner of the tent house, and empty whiskey bottles with candles sprouting from them like twisted broken fingers were scattered on the barrels that served as tables. Where or how the men cooked or ate she could not determine.

Hardisty dusted off the largest box with a grimy blue polka dot hankerchief, and invited her to sit down. He watched with beaming satisfaction while she perched gracefully on the edge of it, then he sat down on a wooden block across from her and invited Bacon to do likewise.

"Now," said Hardisty with Yankee dispatch. "Find out what she's got to sell. How much she wants. And if she'd like me to handle the sale for her—on commission of course—as the leading merchant in Sonora."

Tarifa gave no inkling that she understood one word of the conversation, and listened politely while Bacon carefully interpreted it for her.

This was more luck than she had expected to encounter. She had no doubt of Hardisty's unscrupulousness, his greed, but those were the very characteristics Bandonna had taught her to use to her own advantage against the unsuspecting *gorgios,* so long ago in the Triana.

She explained to Bacon that she had a desire to sell her cattle and horses first, to the highest bidder at public auction, so as to be free of the trouble of grazing and guarding them. Then she desired to rent a tent for living quarters and to display and sell her other trade goods. However, since Señor Hardisty was the leading merchant, she would be glad to deal with him on a commission basis, after the animals were sold, for at least a part of her goods. As a trial, she would place with his establishment three of her barrels of flour and some saddles and bridles. Of course she would have to demand something from him in lieu of insurance for the items she would give him, until they were sold and the money paid over to her.

Hardisty listened to the proposition and his small eyes gleamed with pleasure.

"Now don't that beat all?" he whispered to Billy behind his sledgelike hand, "a plum fallen into my lap right from the tree. Just when we're low on meat? And flour will bring $500 a barrel in some quarters, I know. Tell her everything's goin' to be just as she wants it, bless her heart. Come here all the way from San Diego to sell her goods, eh? Well, we'll sell 'em for her, give her some dust 'n nuggets, and pack her back south again? Like as not she'll be pleased as a pouter pigeon in a corn bin. Why not? There's plenty for everybody. You too, Billy. Now let's see, if I take fifty percent of the sale, and give you ten—"

"Better make it twenty-five for me, Hardisty," the young man said in an even voice.

"Now—that ain't rightly fair, Billy." The older man gave him a sad look and shook his head. "It was me she come to deal with. I could've got fifteen interpreters if I'd waited till night when they're all in from the diggin's."

"But you asked me to interpret," the young American reminded him, "and now I know a bit too much. If I was to speak to the Señora—"

A slow smile crossed Hardisty's face, lifting the beard over his cheeks, and parting to show his stained, broken teeth.

"Now, now, Billy. You know I was only joshin'? 'Course

you get your twenty-five percent. And what the Señora don't know won't hurt any of us."

Bacon frowned. "She looks high-class; we better find out who's with her, and how many riders. Old Coronel brought thirty when he came. You wouldn't want to fight that many?"

"No. No, you're right, Billy. Got a sound head on your shoulders, and you so young, too. Bet your folks are proud of you. Wish one of my boys was quick-thinkin' like you."

"I ain't got no folks," Bacon said, coloring in spite of himself at the frank admiration in the older man's eyes.

"That so? A pity, a father would be proud of a son like you. On your own, then?"

"I been on my own since I was a button. Ma and Pa and my little brother Ned were killed in an Apache attack near Cinder Wells."

"A pity, a great tearin' pity, my boy. I hope you'll consider me and my boys your friends? Yes, sir, my boys need a friend like you, Billy, as an example to 'em. You're welcome to move in here with us anytime you like. Plenty of room for another bunk."

"Thanks," Billy said, touched by the offer, "but I got a brush shack near my claim. With the money I get from this deal I'll be able to set up permanent quarters and buy a winter grubstake and some equipment."

"Suit yourself," said Hardisty, "but you're welcome here anytime. Tell the little lady I got canvas for a hut for her and her company. Comes a bit high, but I can put it on account for her till we've settled things."

Bacon spoke quickly to Tarifa and saw her nod with grave concentration at his words.

"Done," said the young miner to Hardisty with a grin.

"Fine," the merchant said. "There'll be a drink waitin' at the bar for you later on. I'll have the boys load the canvas and poles on a wagon and follow you. Go with the Señora, and find out where she wants it set up. When she's settled come and let me know."

Billy nodded and got to his feet. When Hardisty had gone, he explained to Tarifa that he would accompany her to the spot she wished her camp set up, and suggested a clearing near his own place on the bank of a branch of the Stanislaus.

Tarifa seemed completely amenable to his suggestions, though she gave him no smile of thanks as an American woman would have done. Her exotic allure and cold reserve filled him with pleasure and annoyance at the same time. He felt no scruples at all in cheating her. She was undoubtedly the wife or kinswoman of some wealthy Californian, who had come to the mines to make a killing for herself or for her people. She would hold the price of her goods up so high that only Hardisty or the miners who were fortunate enough to have struck it rich could take advantage of it and devil take the rest of the poor struggling devils, like himself. They could starve and freeze through the winter or pull out for other diggings while they still had the strength to get there.

Tarifa approved of the site Bacon showed her on the banks of the rushing stream some four miles from the main camp. It had sufficient grazing for the cattle and horses, and he assured her a temporary brush barricade could be erected to contain the riding horses.

She left Antonio and Bacon to set up the camp with the help of Hardisty's laborers, and rode back alone to where the vaqueros were supposed to be waiting with the stock and wagon. To her relief they were still there, frightened into submissiveness, no doubt, by the strangeness of their new surroundings.

Soledad sat in the sun-drenched patio in the old chair her mother had loved, where she could lie back. She could feel her skin grow warm, then hot, as the blood raced underneath it. Her thoughts were pleasantly torpid and sluggish. It was odd how even when she was only half-thinking her mind was completely occupied with but one thought.

John Mabrey.

It was a strange-sounding and yet pleasant name. And it was delightful to think of his deep pleasant voice, his quiet strength, and the single thing that now meant more to her than anything in the world; the fact that he loved her.

She understood now how Dolores must have felt about Bart Kinkaid, though the two men were nothing alike. She knew also that Tarifa felt nothing like the same emotion for Bart that Dolores had, or that she felt for Mabrey, and it puzzled her. She did not understand. She would never understand Tarifa, and it made her sad. She was still deeply grateful to Bart for having rescued her and the children and brought them back to California. She hoped that he was not dead, lost at sea, as Tarifa believed. John Mabrey was his friend and he had not allowed himself to believe it. She hoped for John's sake also that Kinkaid was still alive.

At that moment, Penti and the children came from the hacienda and disturbed her meanderings.

"Dona Soledad, I will take the little ones for a walk in the hills while it is warm. The two infants are asleep."

Soledad noted that the children clustered eagerly about the old Gypsy's skirts, all carrying small baskets in which to put the roots, herbs, and berries that Penti would gather for her medicinal purposes.

"Shall I send for Rita or Candelaria to keep you company?" Penti asked.

"No," Soledad answered. She wanted to be alone.

"We won't be gone long," said Penti, her eyes already on the hills.

"Do not hurry on my account."

Soledad watched them walk across the patio toward the kitchen yard where they would emerge to climb the low pasture hills facing the sierras behind Loma de Oro.

She was not aware of the steps on the patio tiles until a shadow crossed before her drowsy eyelids.

She glanced up, a half-smile on her face for whichever of her brothers it might be who had returned early from the pastures, and found herself staring instead into the icy, dancing eyes of Titus Judah.

The morning after her arrival, Tarifa sent Antonio with Billy Bacon to inform the camp that she would hold an auction of her livestock that afternoon at the branch of the Stanislaus where she had set up her temporary dwelling.

The vaqueros rounded up the herd and held them in readiness and Tarifa borrowed a scale from the reluctant Hardisty. She was ready to do business.

Hardisty informed her that the auction would be much better if left in his experienced hands, but this generous offer Tarifa declined with grave thanks.

Under a pine tree on the bank of the stream, she set

up a barrel with her borrowed scales on top, and perched herself on a low rock outcropping behind it.

By one o'clock the little clearing, the stream bank, and the surrounding hillside were teeming with men of every description, race, and color. Miners down on their luck, as well as Chinese and Indians with no hope of bidding, came anyway out of curiosity. There was so little excitement of any kind, other than drunken brawls or fights over mining claims, that the men were drawn as much by the novelty of the event as in the hope of buying something desperately needed.

Tarifa sat watchful and impassive behind the barrel and weighed out the gold dust and nuggets of the highest bidder for the animal just auctioned.

Before nightfall she had disposed of all the cattle and horses save the two palominos and the extra riding horses which were kept in the brush corral, and she had collected enough gold to have made Penti's eyes drop out with envy.

"Where will you put it?" Antonio asked after supper. "Surely they will try to take it away from us? They say there are *bandidos* in the hills; they will not let a woman keep that much gold."

"There are two of us, aren't there?" Tarifa smiled and her teeth were like ice gleaming in the firelight. "They do not know that I am not just a woman, but a *gitana*. We came for gold, *muchacho*, and we will take it back with us. But we will not go until they have made our saddlebags a little heavier."

She tossed him two pokes of nuggets and dust. "This is for your expenses. The rest I will take care of. It is best that only one of us knows where it is. Go and listen to the gossip, but be careful while you are in Hardisty's."

She glanced up as Antonio stood holding a sack of gold in either hand, a broad grin on his lean dark face.

"Don't you find this better than digging for it, like Señor Bacon?"

"*Muy mejora!*" He laughed.

She watched him mount and ride in the direction of the town, a faint frown on her brow. Antonio was young and impulsive; she would have to guard against his spoiling her plans.

Of the two vaqueros they had brought from Loma de

Oro, one had disappeared the moment the auction was over
and she had paid them both the ounce of gold that she
had promised them. The other, a boy named Casim, who
was some distant relative of the Loma de Oro maid Rita,
had elected to stay in her employ, whether out of laziness
or fear of the gringos she did not know.

She had promised him an ounce of gold a week, unheard
of riches for a vaquero, as long as he remained faithful.

"Your job will be to guard the palominos and do the
cooking and washing," she told him. And Casim had answered eagerly, "*Sí,* Patróna." Now he lay asleep on his
serape near the corral where the horses stamped in the
darkness.

Tarifa had long ago made up her mind where she would
hide her gold and she went now to put it there. It was an
old Gypsy hiding place, and one she would bet her life
these *gorgios* would never think of.

In the morning she went to call upon Hardisty to see if
her barrels of flour and the three saddles and bridles she
had given him had been sold. Since it was early she found
only the Hardisty boys attending to the slack business in
the store, while Elias himself was washing his clothes outside the tent house in the rear.

Tarifa never failed to marvel that the Americanos would
stoop to the most menial tasks with willingness and good-
natured banter, regardless of their position or wealth.
Hardisty, by all accounts, must already be rich. Don
Ygnacio, she knew, would rather have starved to death
than to have soiled his hands with such loathsome toil.

She wondered about Bart Kinkaid. Would he have been
like this sly bearded old man who gaily sloshed his shirts
and red underdrawers in a tub of dirty soap water as if it
were some sort of lark? Would he have lent his hand to any
task that came along, regardless of the loss of dignity in
the chore? She had an uneasy feeling that he would have,
and that, moreover, he would have expected her to do likewise. She had not thought of Bart in a long time. If he
were dead, someday she would receive his stock in the
Endecott Company. It was something, if it did not come
too late to save Loma de Oro. She thought petulantly that
if he had not died, she would still be receiving his money,
and it would not have been necessary for her to leave the

rancho in other hands and come to this wretched gold camp on her own.

Hardisty, bare to the waist and embarrassed, was wringing out his clothes. He had powerful sloping shoulders, and ropy arms, thick with graying hair.

"Now, little lady," he said lightly, "I'll get us an interpreter and see what you want." He wiped his hands on a towel and pulled on a dry shirt.

"Billy," Tarifa called. Antonio and Billy Bacon rounded the tent and for a moment Hardisty looked startled.

"I believe she knew what I said," he murmured.

"Understood your tone, more'n likely," said Bacon. He bent from the wind to light a cigarette. "Neither of 'em understands a word of gringo."

"You're certain?"

"'Course I am," the younger man snorted. "I tried 'em on a lot of words, some that most greasers understand. They don't savvy none of it. You're safe to speak your mind, Hardisty."

Tarifa's eyes had grown hot and bright at the insulting term, *greaser*. She was beginning to understand that it applied to anyone of Latin blood. But she held her tongue. Antonio, in his ignorance, was smiling graciously at the two Americans.

"Find out what she wants," said the bearded man as he tucked in his shirttail.

"Mr. Hardisty would like to know what business you have with him, señora?" asked Bacon.

What a ripe *gorgio* he was, cool and smiling and confident, thought Tarifa with wicked elation. All ready to fleece the unsuspecting *gitana*, was he?

She explained solemnly that she wanted to know if Señor Hardisty had sold her goods and for how much.

"I ain't really sold 'em yet," said the storekeeper. "Waitin' for the mule train to come through with supplies. They're pretty low on goods when they get this far south. I'll be able to get a better price. But you tell the Señora I sold her goods, got the best amount I could. Saddles won't be much good till spring, of course, winter comin' on. Tell her I got five hundred in gold for her, over at the store."

Tarifa received the news with a grave face and asked that the money be sent to her at her camp.

When Antonio asked her about the transaction she shrugged it off as a bad deal and told him they would do better when they were more used to the ways of the camp.

"Why do we not stake out a gold claim and mine like the others?" Antonio asked.

"If you want to do so, go ahead," Tarifa told him. It would not take him long to tire of the manual labor, she knew. No Alvarjo had ever toiled with his hands before in any fashion, save as she had demanded on the rancho, and that had not been menial work.

In the end Antonio bought a share in Billy Bacon's claim nearby, and for a while his enthusiasm at seeing the actual gold he dug with his hands appear in the pan compensated for his blistered palms and aching muscles. But a day's backbreaking labor yielded no more than Antonio required for a night's gambling and drinking at Hardisty's, and there were easier ways to get pocket money than digging all day in the wet mud of a riverbank for it. He often wondered where Tarifa had hidden the gold she had gotten for their trade goods, but he did not ask her.

Tarifa took Guindilla and, against the advice of Antonio and Billy Bacon, explored the countryside. It was very different here from the southern part of California she was used to. Here the ground was rocky and bush-covered, thick with sumac and elderberry. The trees were not the spreading oaks she was accustomed to, but stood tall and straight—pine, cedar, birch—lifting their arms like sentinels along the backs and rims of the sierras.

Here water rushed in a torrent, foaming over silver-gray rock, or eddied leaf-strewn, under a red bank around the base of a speckled boulder as big as a hacienda.

The mountains enthralled her. The vast silence of their towering might, the sight of their black jagged jaws yawning against a starlit sky. A feeling of peacefulness came over her, of freedom, and deep joy. For the first time she experienced the complete oneness with nature that was her Gypsy heritage.

Here, if she could pitch the tent of her people, she could live in peace, she thought, among the wildlife and the grandeur of lofty nature that surrounded her. Once, she might have come to such a place to live a nomad's life with Pito Larios. But now it was too late. If she had never known Loma de Oro, Ygnacio, the golden palominos; if Lasho did not lie in the graveyard beyond the little chapel, if she had not crossed Padre Cazon's path, or Bart Kinkaid's.

Her thoughts were interrupted by a tinkling bell. For a moment it seemed to her Gypsy mind that in the quiet magic of the spot where she sat on Guindilla, a wood sprite had come to life.

Guindilla picked up his ears and his mistress laughed in relief when she saw a floppy-eared mule with a silver bell tied round his neck emerge on the trail below.

Behind the lead mule came a string of ten heavily packed animals, their hides as gray as smoke against the green-and-brown hillside. A man walked at the rear carrying a bullwhip coiled over one bent shoulder.

Tarifa put Guindilla to a gallop and plunged down the hillside, coming to a halt just in front of the startled bell-mule.

"What'n hell's-fire you tryin' to do, boy!" The mule skinner shouted. "Scare my mules off the trail? Don't s'pose you speak a word of American neither? *Vamos.* Savvy? *Vamos!*"

Tarifa sat on her horse blocking the trail and grinned at him. He was an old man, rawboned and stooped, but with fearless gray eyes and look of independence about him that Tarifa had come to associate with the better type Americans she had encountered in the diggings.

"I am sorry if I startled you and your mules, señor," she said in English. "I am Dona Tarifa Alvarjo, and I have business with you if you bring in the supplies to Sonora."

"Business with me?" He paused to scratch his grizzled hair under the wide-brimmed slouch hat he wore. He was glad she spoke American, but he was wary of a high-class señora who rode a big mettlesome stallion like the Devil himself. The hills were full of Mexican bandits. This might just be a ruse. One hand fell to his hip and inched toward the pistol holstered there.

Tarifa's voice was crisp but polite. "No, señor, do not try to draw the pistol."

He saw that she was holding a gun in her right hand, though where it had come from under her short velvet jacket, he could not imagine.

"You are taking these things to Mr. Hardisty at Sonora camp?"

"Yeah. He'll get some of 'em. I don't aim to sell out complete to no one camp. Got orders not to."

"You don't own these goods?" Tarifa asked. She was disappointed. She had been so sure the supply trains would be one-man operations.

"Mule train belongs to me, Jeb Stokes. Goods belong to Sam Barnard of Mokelumne Hill. He provides, I haul. We divvy up the take."

Tarifa stared at him uncomprehendingly. If this was English it was not the way Kinkaid had taught it to her, nor the way John Mabrey or Patrick Havelock spoke it.

"I do not understand you, señor," she said.

"Thought you savvied American?" He peered up at her and there was a twinkle in his eyes that infuriated her. Gringos were always amused at a stranger's misunderstanding of them.

"I understand English, but not the way you speak it, señor. What is this 'divvy up and take'?"

"Senora, that means to divide up the *dinero*. Half 'n half. Fair 'n square. See?" He held up his two hands, palms up like a pair of scales.

"Ah! *Sí*. You are partners then?"

"In a manner of speakin'."

"Then I do have business with you, Señor Stokes. You want gold for your goods?"

"That's the idea. I ain't in this business for my health."

She dismounted, tucked the gun into her sash, and walked over to stand beside him.

"You want *dinero*, *mucho dinero* for all your goods?"

"Yep, that's right." Jeb Stokes was suddenly enjoying himself very much. She was a right pert little piece, Mexican or no, and the trail had been long and lonely.

Tarifa pushed her sombrero back with her thumb and examined the hitch on one of the mule packs.

"How much do you want for all of it?"

"Now hold your hosses, señora. I just said I couldn't part with all of it. Not all in one place. Ain't good for business. Riles our customers in the other camps, savvy?"

Tarifa was scowling at him, concentrating on the odd way he phrased his English. Truly these Americanos were very strange people. Much stranger than she had ever imagined. There was no rule of thumb by which to judge them as one judged other *gorgios*. They were like quicksilver, changing before your very eyes.

"Señor Stokes, I have gold, much gold, and I have need of your trade goods. Can we not make a bargain with each other?"

Stokes rubbed his whiskery chin with a grimy forefinger. "Well, now, what makes you so all-fired—what makes you need so much goods, señora? You supplyin' one of them bandit groups in the hills?" His eyes were sly, mirroring a sharp suspicion.

"*Bandidos?*" she looked started. "No! I only wish to keep the goods from reaching Señor Hardisty's store."

"That so? Now why is that, señora? You got a grudge agin' Hardisty and his boys?"

"Grudge?"

"You no likee?" said Stokes, for he had just come from a Chinese camp on Big Bar. More heathens were swarming into the diggin's than there were fleas on a hound dog, and each one of them had to be talked to in a different way, it seemed.

"He has tried to cheat me," Tarifa answered. "I would like to teach him a lesson."

"Ho! So that's it? Well now, that's a hoss of a different color."

"A what?"

"Never mind!" Impatience threaded Jeb's voice. "Don't care much for the Hardisty's myself. What's that old buzzard been up to now?"

Tarifa told him the tale from beginning to end.

"Up to his old double-dealin' tricks I see?" said Stokes. "Wal, don't know as a good lesson might not do him some good. What's your plan?"

Tarifa told him and the old man chuckled. "You got a varmint's head on your own shoulders, young woman. Danged if you ain't. Reckon I'll go along with your little plan, up to a point. You can have what's on them first six mules, that's my choicest goods, providin' you got six thousand dollars in cash or gold. I figure each mule's carryin' a thousand dollars worth of stuff. This is the end of the season. Won't be another supply train in or outa here till spring. You'll have Hardisty right where you want him. What say?"

Tarifa had nowhere near the six thousand dollars he was asking. "What about the other goods?" she asked idly.

"That's lesser stuff, señora. Hardisty ain't goin' to believe I lost them first six mules and what's on 'em, unless I come in with somethin' to show. Besides, only havin' a general idea of what you plan to do with that stuff, I couldn't rightly leave these poor bastards at Sonora to starve outright this winter. Ain't Christian, that's what. An' I always been a good Christian, Bible-readin' man."

"I have part of the gold at my camp," she told him quickly. "If you could go there, unload the goods, get rid of the six mules somewhere, I will meet you at Hardisty's and give you the rest of the money."

He studied her for a moment. He didn't know as much about women as he'd like to know, and he knew nothing whatever about Mexican women. But he had once trapped with a Texan on the Missouri who had been married to a Mexican, and who swore up and down she was the only honest female he had ever known. If this one was lying and fixing to cheat him, well, his goods would still be at her camp. She couldn't move it without horses or mules, and there were darned few of either in Sonora. Besides, the whole camp would go and help him secure his stuff if need be, what with the long winter coming on.

"How much gold you got at your camp?" he asked.

"Enough to pay you a substantial down payment," she said quickly. "I told you I will give you the rest at Hardisty's."

"He holdin' money of yourn?"

"He is holding some goods of mine," she told him as she swung into the saddle. "We are partners . . . in a manner of speaking."

Antonio had spent the better part of the day working the claim with Billy Bacon. They had moved back from the water onto a rocky dry ledge where Billy claimed he had found signs of coarse gold, and were dry washing in the manner an old Sonoran gambusino had recently taught them.

They had spent the morning "coyoting," digging in the

hard ground to sink a square hole to bedrock and then burrowing from the bottom along the ledge, using small pointed crowbars. Next, each using big horn spoons, they scraped up the loose pay dirt. Billy pounded the dirt into dust, loaded it into a wooden bowl, and with great dexterity shook it repeatedly onto an outspread hide until the wind left little but coarse gold particles for them to gather up.

To Antonio it seemed a fruitless and laborious operation. When they finally quit, the noonday sun was broiling and they had a little less than a quarter of a poke of gold to divide between them. Not enough, thought Antonio, for an evening's entertainment at Hardisty's. And what other place was there to go to for entertainment in this bleak godforsaken spot? You could be as rich as Midas, and what good would it do you here, or for miles around? One stinking camp was the same as another. Gold was the cheapest thing in the diggings. What could it buy you? Watered liquor, or something the Americanos called "gritty," raw corn meal brandy and water mixed in a tin pan, and served hot at twenty dollars a serving. Gold could buy you into a game of poker or monte for fabulous stakes at which you were bound to be cheated by the professional cardsharps. It could buy you a wretched meal of fat pork, beans, and jerky, washed down by coffee that tasted like muddy water.

You had riches under your feet. You took up fifty dollars, one hundred dollars in an hour of work, but what vast bonanza lay ahead, just over the ridge perhaps? In the next valley, over the next rise? Who would be the lucky one to search until he found the Mother Lode, El Dorado, the source of all the gold? The enticing, enchanting, will-o'-the-wisp that drew men's feet and eyes ever onwards?

Antonio left Billy on the ledge still doggedly shaking dirt in the basin, and rode to his own camp. He spoke to the vaquero Casim, crouching in the shade of a tree before the tent, and went inside to pour himself a glass of brandy.

Cristo, it was poor stuff! He poured half of it onto the dirt floor. He washed in a tin basin set on a wooden box and inspected himself in Tarifa's mirror. He thought of

the comforts of Loma de Oro, of the good food and wine.
What in God's name was the son of Don Ygnacio Alvarjo
doing in this camp of barbarians? He no longer remembered that he had wanted to come, had intended never
to return to Loma de Oro until he was rich.

He slid into his jacket and shouted to Casim to bring
his horse. Tarifa was staying to get gold for Loma de
Oro. Well, they should have it, and once they did they
could return to the rancho. He had not spent his nights
at the gaming tables at Hardisty's for nothing. True, he
had invariably lost, but he had also learned a thing or
two. Antonio smiled to himself as he tucked the poke
of gold into his red sash and went out to mount his palomino.

Tarifa was right. A wise man did not need to dig for
gold himself; he had only to help himself to what others
brought, like votive offerings, to the gaming tables at
Hardisty's.

CHAPTER 34

John Mabrey rode to Loma de Oro in the carriage with
Tía Isabella, his horse tied behind. They had met that
afternoon at Bolsa Coyotes when he called to see how
one of Nazario's sons was doing following a severe throat
infection. They were all strong, healthy little beggars, but
this one, Raphael, had drunk water from a putrid spring
before the vaquero who was riding with him could stop
him. The boy, however, seemed to be doing well under
the treatment Mabrey had prescribed.

Isabella had surprised him by asking him to return to

Loma de Oro with her, to check Soledad's health once more.

As they neared the hacienda in the early dusk, Isabella let out a murmur of surprise.

"Why are there no lights? Can that foolish Soledad be mooning in the dark in the patio again? I do not know what has come over that girl. And where can Penti or Candelaria and the maids be?"

"It has been a warm day and it is still early," said Mabrey.

"Nothing is done on schedule if I'm not around," the old woman complained. "I don't know what Tarifa would say if she were here."

"Do you have any word of her, Dona Isabella?"

"No, nothing. How can word come from such a wild distant place? I fear sometimes both she and Antonio are dead. It was foolhardy going there alone with only two useless vaqueros to protect them. My brother would never have permitted such a thing. Nor would he have demeaned himself by going among such people!"

The Indian boy who drove the carriage stopped before the unlighted hacienda and Mabrey helped Isabella to the ground and bent to gather some baskets of fruit, oranges, and pomegranates that Rufina had given her.

"No. Leave them, Doctor. The boy will bring them. Do you see the front door is ajar? They must all have lost their wits while I was away!"

Mabrey followed her into the cool, fragrant *sala,* and stooped to light the oil lamp on the center table for her.

When he raised his eyes he saw that she was frowning at a sheet of paper she had picked up from the carpet where it had fallen or been blown by the faint wind coming in the open windows from the patio.

She bent with it in her hands and held it under the light. Without meaning to read it, Mabrey saw with surprise that the salutation was in English.

"I cannot make this out," she said irritably. "It is in English. Elena or Donn Patricio must have been here and found everyone away. Though why they would write in English, I cannot imagine. They know that except for Tarifa, we cannot read it here. Unless of course, Soledad—"

Mabrey reached powerfully for the paper, nearly tearing it out of her hands. His eyes ran over the words and she saw him tremble violently, as if he were a great tree in an earthquake.

"Por favor, Juan! What is it?"

"Soledad's husband has come back," he said in a hollow voice. "She has gone with him. It does not say where."

"Madre de Dios! No, I cannot believe it. My poor *niña.* Where is that wretched Candelaria, where is everyone?" Then: *"Santa Maria!* He has not harmed the little ones?"

Isabella fled and Mabrey followed behind her, but his mind and his legs felt like lead. Only the words of the letter stood out in his brain as if written in fire: "I have come to take back my wife who was stolen from me. She has gone with me willingly and shall not return.— Titus and Soledad Judah."

Seeing her name actually linked with her husband's was Mabrey's undoing. She *was* Judah's wife, legally, and in the eyes of the church whose tenets Mabrey had honored ever since he married Lupe and gave his word to uphold its beliefs. While Judah lived—but he drove the thought out of his mind. He knew he was no cold-blooded murderer, even if the killing was justified. As a doctor, he was powerfully aware of the miracle of life. His role had always been to protect it, not to destroy it. He was also an Englishman to whom law and order were a sacred code. A man does not change his basic beliefs easily, even under stress. He cursed himself for a fool, for he knew what Bart Kinkaid would have done under like circumstances. Find Judah and kill him, and take Soledad back to the bosom of her family as he had done once before. But he lacked the American's reckless disdain for ethics.

What was he to do for his beloved? How to free her from the thing she had feared more than anything else upon earth? He recalled her nightmares, the days when he had held her trembling body against him, vowing that he would protect her, that no harm should ever come to her again. And he ground his teeth in frustrated anguish. How was he ever to find out where that devil Judah had taken her?

Isabella came down the veranda from the nursery, her face white with strain.

She was about to speak when José ran across the patio from the kitchen, a small basket of herbs and flowers in his chubby hands. His red hair glinted in the lamplight from the *sala,* and Mabrey felt a flash of anger as he stared at the child, followed by revulsion at the unreasonableness of his emotion. The sins of the father were indeed visited upon the child. How often did Nazario look upon this bastard son of Judah's with contempt and hatred, and was Tarifa's sheltering of him true charity, or only another wish to protect the name of Alvarjo? Were human beings truly so complex, so filled with subtlety, that they had lost the ability to move with a simple purpose or design?

"José, where are the others? And Penti?" demanded Isabella, catching hold of his shoulder.

The boy looked shyly up at her. He had Judah's hated light eyes, but the candor and honesty and something of the Corlona pride.

"They are coming, Tía Isabella."

"*Bueno.* Go and tell Candelaria to come at once and light the lamps."

"*Sí.*" He scampered off, and a moment later a group of people converged on the patio from the kitchen.

Candelaria, holding the side of her face and hurrying before the others, Penti, the children, and the Alvarjo menfolk who had just ridden in from the pastures.

"I had the toothache," Candelaria sobbed when Isabella had told them what had happened. "I took some laudanum and tea and lay down. I must have dozed, Dona Isabella, but I thought that useless Rita was about."

"The harm is done," Isabella said sternly. "Go and light the lamps, and Dr. Mabrey will give you something for your tooth. Tell Rita and the others to prepare supper." To Penti she said, "You should have come home with the children before this."

The Gypsy stared at her with haughty disdain. "I am no servant in this house, only as I wish to serve *miri pen.* If I were not awaiting her return I would leave. Come," she told the children, "I will give you your supper and put you to bed."

"You see what she is like?" said Isabella angrily to Mabrey when the Gypsy had gone. "I can do nothing with her. And Padre Cazon urges me to show her charity!"

"Don't worry about Penti now," Mabrey told her gently. He led her to a chair and tried to calm her. "He cannot have taken her far. We will search along the coast. I will tell Santos to saddle the horses and get the vaqueros mounted. Do not worry, Dona Isabella, I will not leave her in that man's grasp a moment longer than necessary!"

The stars were low and bright over the black choppy water. Titus Judah, standing at the open porthole in the captain's cabin of the Russian whaler he had boarded with Soledad at sundown, where it waited for them off San Juan, felt a smug gratification at his coup. They were already several hours at sea and in a short time should reach San Clemente, where he had anchored the *Heron*, as he still called the renamed *Vulcan*.

His letter to Soledad sometime back had been a lie. He had known of Kinkaid's taking her and the children almost from the day she left Salem. Returning to Salem himself a few days after their departure, he had learned of it from Miss Fynchly's self-righteous and disapproving lips.

"Naturally when she went with him so willingly, I thought he was a friend of yours, Captain Judah. It was not my place to stop them," she had told him.

Judah had not followed his wife at once because he had had no desire to overtake her then. Like money in the bank, she would keep until he was ready to claim her. Soledad had never been anything to him but an investment in the future. As for his children, they were added pawns in the game he was playing. When he was ready he would ask for and receive his wife's share of Loma de Oro.

For the present, he had a lucrative offer to carry a cargo to the Gold Coast of Africa, and return with a still more profitable one—Negro slaves. It was not the first time he had made such a venture and he had never found it to his disadvantage. He wanted money to buy more ships, a small fleet of his own, and the styles in shipping were changing, growing more expensive.

Word of the discovery of gold, following the end of

the war, had reached him at Panama where he had gone
to obtain more goods, and had brought him speedily to
California. Gold for the taking, wild as the tales were,
was mighty enticing bait but so was the claiming of his
share of Loma de Orò. How did anyone know where gold
lay? It might lie under the floor of the Alvarjo hacienda,
for all he knew. His first move, he realized, must be to
reclaim Soledad and so protect his interests.

Soledad had surprised him. After the first shock of seeing him standing there in the patio, she had not fainted
as he had expected her to do. Instead she had risen to
face him, hands clasped firmly in front of her.

"Well, we meet again, my dear? Is this the best welcome you can offer your long absent husband?"

Soledad held her head high. Her voice was low and
firm.

"There should be no further pretense between us, Titus.
We both know why you married me, why you kept me
far from home so long. Refused to bring me back."

He watched her eyes. She *had* changed. There was a
new purposefulness about her, a firmness in her mouth
and chin that had not been there before.

"You surprise me, my dear. You have grown up."

She said nothing.

"We do, however, still have certain . . . obligations to
each other, no matter what our feelings? We have a valid
and legal marriage in the eyes of God and man. We have
children. And regardless of how I may feel toward you,
or you toward me, Soledad, I want what is legally mine,
is that clear?"

She clutched the paper in her hands. She wanted to
scream out, to bring others to her defense, but she could
not. This was her problem and she must solve it some
way, or live with it for the rest of her life if that was
what God demanded of her. A sudden new strength
seemed to surge through her.

Were the Padres right? she thought wildly. Did God
actually give you the strength to bear what you had not
thought possible?

"You want me to go with you?" she asked calmly, seeing the look of satisfied relief that came over his face.
She thought for one blind, awful moment of another face

—older, more worn, but infinitely dear—and then she put it resolutely out of her mind.

"Yes. And we must leave at once. I wouldn't want a family squabble over your going that would end in bloodshed." He did not disclose the hours he had waited until he had seen the others leave Loma de Oro, until he was reasonably sure she was alone.

She saw that he wore a pistol. He was not speaking idly. She knew that he would kill to take her with him. Isabella would not return before nightfall. Santos was nowhere near, neither were any of the vaqueros who were of any use. The women servants would be worse than useless. There was the half-grown peon boy in front who took care of the guests' horses, but he was probably asleep. It was the siesta hour. Luck and Judah's patience had rewarded him well.

Her eyes swept the beloved sunny patio, the peaceful somnolent hacienda beyond. Would she ever see it again? She knew now, as she had not known when she first left, how the heartsick longing for home could wrench at the breast, wither away the soul. But she was no longer the only one concerned. There were the children, and she had made up her mind he would not subject them to whatever horrors he was taking her to face. Thank God Penti had taken them with her.

"Where are the children?" he asked, and she raised her head in startled guilt, as if he had read her thoughts.

"They are away—with Penti, the Gypsy woman. They will not return until dark."

"We can't wait that long," he said. "We'll leave a note and send for them later. I have a ship waiting off San Juan, and two horses outside."

"I—must pack a few things."

"There's everything you need, aboard." He had gone to the table, taken up her pen and a piece of paper from the portfolio there, and was scribbling furiously.

He straightened up and put his hand around her arm. She felt revulsion at his touch, a deep nausea in the pit of her stomach, but she would not let her flesh shrink under his grasp. She tried once more, speaking quietly, desperately, but knowing as she spoke the words that it was useless.

"All you really want is my share of the rancho, Titus.

You can have it; my brothers will give it to you. One of them is a lawyer. Everything will be safe and legal. Leave me here—with the children?"

There was an odd light in his eyes, and a faint grin on his hard windburned face.

"All the legality in the world won't stand up against Tarifa, you know that, Soledad."

"But Tarifa will give it to you, I know she will!"

"Give away part of the land when California is sprouting gold like poppies? She's no fool."

"She will, I tell you, for my sake—when she comes back."

"She's away?" Satisfaction glinted in his eyes. He had been afraid she might be here if no one else was when he walked in. I should have known better, he thought. A Gypsy who would not leave family and hearth at the whisper of gold would not be worth her salt. "Come, we waste time, my dear wife."

They went across the sunlit patio, under the shadow of the *galleria,* and into the cool *sala,* where Judah paused to put his note on the table, propped against the lamp.

Soledad followed him out to the horses. She did not look back.

Shortly after Antonio had left their camp, Tarifa rode in with Jeb Stokes and his mule train. Casim helped Stokes unload the first six mules and store the goods inside the canvas and brush-covered cabin.

Tarifa poured the muleteer a heavy jolt of brandy and left the bottle where he could reach it.

"Make yourself at home, señor," she told him, "while I get your money. I won't be long. Later I will meet you at Hardisty's and give you the rest."

"All right, señora. Take ye time, take ye time. Them mules and me is tuckered anyways." He sat down on one of the beds and tested its comfort with his fingers. "Don't mind if I stretch out a spell?"

"No, señor. There is food on the shelf; please make yourself comfortable."

"Thanks, señora. I'll just do that."

"What shall we do about the mules we have unloaded? It is most important that no one sees them."

Stokes scratched his chin. "Tell you what, tell your

boy to take Myrtle—the bell mare—as far into the mountains as he can, the rest'll foller her."

"But how will you get your mules back? What if someone steals them?"

Stokes laughed. "No one can get nigh to Myrtle but me, and the rest'll scatter like jackrabbits unless Myrtle's there to lead 'em. They'll likely stay the night in the hills, then come trottin' into town lookin' for me and the other mules." He slapped his thigh in a secret mirth that amazed Tarifa. She could see nothing humorous in what he had said. "Ain't that good, señora? Me and the other mules! Reckon that's about right. I been with 'em so long I feel just like one of 'em."

Tarifa left the old man still cackling over his own crude humor, and went to find Casim.

He was not pleased when she told him the chore she had for him. She led him back some distance from the cabin and pointed to a slender cedar tree. "You will cut this tree down, Casim, here near the base. And do not make too much noise to attract attention."

"Sí, Patróna." He went about his work sulkily but with some spirit, and when the tree lay on the ground, Tarifa dismissed him.

It was an old Gypsy method of hiding valuables, and though she had never used it herself before, she had heard Penti say that the caravan tribes prized it highly. Since Nature is the Gypsy's house, city, world, he uses it as intimately as any inhabitant uses his domain.

What more sensible way, thought Tarifa, of hiding valuables than in the slit bark of a standing tree? How many raise their eyes to look up? How many would notice the delicate and widely separated cuts in thick bark? And how many would investigate if they did?

Using her *reata*, she had first climbed to the higher portion of the tree, cut the bark in flaps and prepared the shallow pockets in the trunk underneath, securing the bark again after it had been carefully refitted over her gold caches, with sharp but sturdy wooden pins. Now that the tree lay at her feet, she went about collecting the gold and dropping it in a canvas sack she had brought from the cabin.

When she weighed it out for Stokes a little later, he tried to hide his disappointment.

"Three thousand, señora?"

"You will get the rest, I promise you."

"Coulda got it by goin' straight to Hardisty," he said, weighing the canvas sack.

"He would not have paid you that much," Tarifa said shrewdly. "He is the only merchant here. And the men, if they could pay for it, could not store your wares in their flimsy houses for the coming winter. They will have to depend upon Hardisty to store it in his stout log building, and they have no choice but to pay him double for the privilege of living in Sonora for the winter."

Stokes grinned at her. "I said you had a varmint's head on your shoulders, señora. Danged if it ain't the gospel truth!"

"Go into town with the rest of the mules and tell Hardisty what I told you to. I will come in a few hours."

"You want me to set the stage, eh?" he chuckled. "I ain't never been a play-actor before, but I'm willin' to try. Wished I had Myrtle with me, though; she sorta gives me confidence, if you know what I mean?"

Hardisty's cavernlike building, with a thicker pall of smoke than usual wreathing the heads of the patrons, was jammed to the walls.

The lantern splaying light over the bar and the four shirt-sleeved Hardistys behind it had been augmented by candles in crude tin holders and reflectors nailed to the log walls at intervals above the heads of the cardplayers.

Antonio's fine resolve to make himself rich at the gaming tables had ended in a fiasco. He had lost everything but the clothes on his back, and enough dust to buy the bottle of raw brandy in which he was now drowning his frustration and anger.

He stood at the far end of the bar under the derisive eyes of Abel Hardisty.

Like many others in the diggings in the last few months, Abel had learned to look down upon "greasers" and to heartily despise anyone with a tinge of color to his skin.

It is easy to hate those we have injured, and the Americans who had wrested California from the native-born and Mexico felt a defiant contempt for the dark, foreign-seeming Californians. Animosity between the two races had started at first over rival mining claims, but as the

Anglo-Americans saw the dark-hued—and in many cases more experienced—miners swarming over the countryside to share in their golden harvest, rankling jealousy turned to bigotry and hatred.

This land was now American soil. The gold belonged to the citizens of the United States. It didn't matter that a native Californian's forebears had held land in the territory since the days of Anza or Portola. If he was lucky enough to have found a good claim he would be luckier still not to be ousted from it.

Those of the *gente de razón* with ranchos and lands to go back to, and no driving desire or necessity to toil like menials for gold, quietly folded their serapes and rode away.

The Mexicans from Sonora, far from home in a strange land, and the lower class Californians were not so fortunate. They could stay in camp, accepting the abuse and derision of the Anglo-Americans and white foreigners with quiet resignation, while working the less desirable places; or they could leave camp and wander the wild countryside getting by as best they could, hoping to live out the winter in some safer, more remote spot, or more friendly camp.

Many of the younger men had banded together for self-protection and began preying on lonely miners, remote camps, and supply trains for their living. It did not take the dissatisfied and lawless element long to discover and join these self-made groups of *bandidos*. And as winter approached, the southern placers were rife with widespread alarm over the increasing bands of "greaser" outlaws.

Sonora, like the other camps, had early organized a council of sorts to act for its self-protection, but gold mining left little time for lawmaking. It was easier to banish all foreigners or to levy a heavy monthly tax on the few who persisted in remaining.

As a result of the "law" thousands of foreigners would leave the goldfields before the next year was up, not even allowed to take their implements with them.

Sonora, thus far, had been too rich and too busy to enforce her law properly, but Abel Hardisty and his ilk were hoping that the enforced idleness of winter would bring the presence of foreigners to an end.

It could be said, in all fairness of Abel and the others that they had exactly the same feeling for the Chinese, the Kanakas, and the South Americans in the diggings. Chileans and Peruvians were ousted from the middle and northern camps as quickly as Mexicans and Californians were from the southern. Even Frenchmen were sometimes included in the enforced exodus. Native Californians found so little protection in their citizenship, provided for in the U.S. treaty, that they turned from the goldfields in disgust.

From the first, Abel had disapproved of his father's dealings with the Alvarjos, even if, as Elias claimed, there lay a pretty penny in it for them. Taking something from them outright was all right, in Abel's limited intelligence, but stooping to dicker with them, or pretending to, was degrading. It gave Mexicans status, made them put on airs. Like this dandified young spik swilling brandy in front of him at the bar, drinking alone as he usually did, as if he was too good for anyone else's company.

Abel had earlier watched him lose heavily to a gambler from Big Bar, and he was waiting until he had finished the bottle to order him out of the place. Hardisty had a rule: as long as a patron had liquor in front of him that he had paid for, and was not breaking the furniture or someone's head, he could not be ordered outside. But a second rule stated that only paying customers could take up legroom in the building. Space was scarce. And Abel knew that Antonio's last gold pouch was empty. Like a buzzard, he watched and waited to pounce on the young Californian.

A commotion at the front door attracted the attention of the roomful of miners.

"What's up?" Elias called in his blasting baritone.

Heads shook in ignorance and then word sifted back to the bar.

"Mule train."

"Ol' Jeb Stokes, I reckon."

"Brung supplies, Gawd bless 'im! Sonora ain't goin' to starve. I was afraid we'd be chewin' bark 'fore spring."

And then a murmur of something else as the old man

made his way through the throng, a look of grim determination on his weathered face.

Stokes came to a halt before Hardisty at the bar and said in a voice that carried to the street:

"I was robbed!"

If he was acting, he couldn't have asked for a better audience. He had the eye of every person in the house, and you could have heard a pinch of gold dust fall to the floor.

"Robbed!" Hardisty cried. "Where? Who by?"

"Some of them Mexican bandits jumped me, way back by Coral Crick, while I was waterin' the mules. I managed to shoo off four of 'em into the underbrush, but Myrtle wouldn't leave me and they got her and the six lead mules."

"Six!"

"Yep, they had guns on me the whole time. Took mine, as a matter of fact, threw it into the brush. They warned me not to so much as look around for ten minutes, then they lit out takin' Myrtle and the others with 'em." Warming to his work the old man added, "They was fierce lookin' varmints, faces black as niggers. One of 'em had a scar clean across his forehead."

"Anyone ever see a Mexican like that?" Hardisty roared.

The inmates of the crowded room only shook their heads.

"We got to go after 'em," one man said sharply. "Hardisty's ain't got supplies enough left to see us through two months, let alone all winter. Y'don't want to starve as well as freeze, do y'boys?"

"No!" The word exploded through the room, and Antonio glanced up dully. It was the first word of their jabbering he had clearly understood. He seemed to be the only Spanish-speaking person there. He had no way of knowing that the other Californians and Mexicans had retreated at the first sound of trouble.

The men had started for the door in a body, when Hardisty's voice stopped them.

"Wait! There aren't a handful of horses in camp. And how are you goin' to chase 'em if you don't know where they've gone? It's a big country, gents, and those greasers are on fast horses."

There was consternation and grumbling for a moment, and then the man who had spoken first, and who seemed to express his comrades's thoughts said, "They can't have gone too far leadin' them mules. By the time they reached Coral Crick they must've been tired out, eh, Stokes? The mules, I mean."

The mule skinner glanced at the grim faces surrounding him and nodded his head.

"Plumb tuckered, even Myrtle, I'm sure of it."

The miner's face brightened. "You see? We'll mount a posse on what hosses we got, take the best tracker in camp, and follow 'em. Starting at Coral Crick."

"Can't track in the dark," Stokes said solemnly. Blast it, where was that female? He'd set it all up for her like she'd asked, and now she wasn't here to see the fun. Besides, as riled as they were, he didn't know how long he could hold them here.

"I know one way you can find 'em, day or night." Abel Hardisty's voice was harsh with contained bitterness.

"How's that, Abel?"

"What you sayin', son?" Elias's voice rose a notch in surprise.

Abel was staring down at Antonio's bent head.

"Find out from one of their own kind where the bandits hide out!"

The nearest men surged forward a step, but Elias cried, "Don't make fools of yourselves. That's Antonio Alvarjo; he's a partner of Billy Bacon's. He don't know nothin' about bandits."

"How do you know?" Abel asked sharply. "They all stick together. You can't trust any of 'em! Look how they cut up old man Fenner on his claim a week ago, stole his gold, and dragged his body through the crick bed with their *reatas*."

A roar of anger went up from the miners in remembrance.

"Now wait a second, son," Elias said nervously. He was a merchant, not a rabble-rouser. It would be too bad to lose a night's business just so the camp could go on some fruitless foray into the mountains.

But Abel had the ear of the crowd.

"The Mexicans would like nothing better than to starve out this camp, and then take it over! They can do it now.

They've got your grub! Enough to keep 'em in warmth
and comfort all winter, while Sonora starves. Is this the
kind of treatment we fought for in Texas, in Mexico
and California?"

"No!" The shout rocked the canvas ceiling.

"You goin' to sit on your tails 'n do nothin', let 'em
drive you outa Sonora, away from the gold that's yourn
by right?"

"No!"

"Or are you goin' to string this greaser sittin' here
drinkin' like he owned the whole of Sonora camp up to
the nearest tree unless he tells you where them other
greasers have holed up with your supplies?"

"Yes! By Gawd!"

"String him up!"

"Anybody got a rope? Come on, boys!"

Stokes, who had belatedly recognized the name Alvarjo and moved forward to speak, was swept aside like
a jackstraw.

Poor devil, must be the Señora's husband, he thought.
But it was useless to argue anything with the infuriated
mob now.

Hardisty hoped to stop the trouble for his own reasons,
but he was ignored as completely as Stokes had been.

Like flowing lava, the men moved forward in an inexorable tide that swept everything before it until it
reached the bar.

A thick-shouldered miner put a powerful hand on Antonio's shoulder and spun him around.

Antonio stared at him, startled.

"You savvy American?" asked the miner.

Antonio recognized the words *savvy* and *American* and
shook his head. He had no idea what they wanted of him,
but even in his befuddled state he drew himself up and
held his head high.

"*Qué haces,* señor? *Qué sucedio?*"

"Don't bother talkin' to him, Jake," called a tipsy miner.
"String him up!"

Two other men stepped forward and seized Antonio's
arms, and one of them whipped out a length of cord
and bound his hands behind his back. Antonio, fully
alarmed now, struggled with them but it was useless. They

were twice as strong as he was and there were too many of them.

He felt himself jerked forward and an aisle opened up for the men who were dragging him toward the street.

They were surprised to see a figure blocking the entrance, a figure holding a pistol pointed unflinchingly at their bellies.

"A woman!" cried the big miner, Jake Latham.

"Greaser woman," snorted another. "Push her aside!"

"If you attempt to do that," Tarifa said coldly, speaking in English, "some of you will be dead before you reach this door, señor."

"Tarifa!" Antonio sobbed. "What is the matter; what are they trying to do?"

"Be still," she told him steadily. "I will handle this." To the miners she said, "Let him go, *pronto!*"

They stood for a moment watching her in sullen silence.

Tarifa stood with her feet braced and the pistol steady as rimrock in her hand. "Free him! *Inmediatamente!*"

Hands reluctantly fell from Antonio's arms and he stumbled forward.

"Wait outside," she told him curtly. "Casim is there. He will free your hands."

"*Sí!*"

Tarifa's voice moved like a whiplash over the heads of the crowd. "You would hang a man who does not understand either the reason for your actions or your words? *Basura!* All of you. *Cobardes!*"

"What's she sayin'?" mumbled one man.

"That you are nothing but filth, cowards!" answered Tarifa, with contempt blazing in her long eyes. "Where is Señor Hardisty?"

Elias came forward, pushing his way through the crowd.

"This was none of my doin', señora," he told her as he came up. "I tried to stop 'em. They was a might riled 'cause our supply train got robbed by Mexican bandits, and that's a mighty serious thing with winter comin' on. I don't rightly know what we'll do. They thought, mistakenly I'm sure, that the young gentleman could tell 'em somethin' about where the bandits took the stuff." He did not mention the fact that he had been startled nearly out of his wits to hear her speaking English. A sly one she was, pretending she didn't know a word he was saying, claiming she needed Billy Bacon as an interpreter. Hardisty's corkscrew mind sought desperately for a way to take advantage of his new knowledge. Obviously she wouldn't have let the cat out of the bag except to save Antonio.

"Antonio knows nothing about your supply train," she told them sharply, her eyes glowing redly in the candlelight. She looked like a black spitting panther, thought Hardisty, and he knew suddenly that she was just as deadly. The danger in her, that's what he had sensed the first time they met. She had an animallike fearlessness, a primitive disregard for personal safety. The men stood silent and awed in front of her.

"You and Billy Bacon made a substantial profit on the goods I left for you to sell for me," she told Hardisty in a ringing voice. "I kept you from knowing I understood English to see what kind of a man you were. I found out, señor. You are a lying, double-dealing, two-faced *gorgio!*"

"Now, profit's profit here in the diggin's," he told her with offended dignity. "A man's a right to look after himself. You couldn't have set up here without me, señora."

She spat on the ground at his feet.

"*Premita Undebē!* Do you think I ever had to depend upon you for anything? I could have sold my stock and traded my goods at any camp in the sierras and probably done better!

"You don't like Mexicans here, do you?" she went on, "or Californians, or South Americans, or Chinese? Well, I am none of these. I am a *gitana*—a Gypsy from the Triana in Spain, and the world is my home. The trees, the mountains, the plains—here, or wherever I choose to claim them. I spit upon your *gorgio* souls that can see only the dirt you walk upon as your own!

"You would hang an innocent boy because he is not of your race and does not understand your tongue, and because you are afraid you will starve this winter. I pray that you do! But *bandidos* did not take your supplies, hombres. I did!"

Voices rose from an astonished buzzing to a threatening roar.

"Get her!"

"She can't hold us all off with one little puny gun!"

"String her 'n the boy up too. She's a thief, ain't she?"

The blacksnake whip Tarifa carried in the other hand had remained unnoticed. Now, it wrapped itself around the speaker's throat and he yelped in agony as the whip threw him to the floor.

"If you make one move toward me," she said coldly to the others, "you will never see your supplies again. They will be destroyed!"

Sobered, the men fell silent.

"Señor Stokes, are you here?"

"Aye!" Stokes moved forward, a sheepish look on his leathery face.

"Tell them I have their supplies."

"That's right, boys," he said laconically.

"You give 'em to her?"

"We made a deal, fair 'n square," Stokes said defensively. "Little lady bought 'em. Had her reasons, I reckon, for havin' me tell you they was stole."

Hardisty stared hard at Tarifa.

"Is all this true?"

"Yes." Tarifa's eyes held faint amusement. "I also am now a merchant in Sonora. And I think you know which of us will do the most business this winter."

Hardisty's face went pale and he licked his lips.

"Mebbe we could make a deal, you 'n me, señora? I'm the only one can store them goods safe for the winter, you know that?"

"Perhaps it would be better if you sold me your store, and I could set up here for the winter."

"Sell? I don't want to sell!"

"You may find yourself out of business for as long as the supplies last, then. But these men will have to take the chance of its spoiling in my canvas house. Unless—"

"Sell 'er the store!" shouted one miner. "We don't aim to starve fer you or anyone else, Elias!"

"If we could make a deal—" Hardisty began.

Tarifa's eyebrows rose. "A deal—with you, señor? After you have cheated me once? And stood by while they tried to hang my stepson?"

"An honest deal," the merchant pleaded. "The boys can all hear what I got to say. I can't do no cheatin' in front of them."

"Pay 'er a fair price and call it square," cried Jake Latham. "She's got you over a barrel, Elias."

"I am not interested in a fair price, señors," said Tarifa. "You have no choice but to pay *my* price."

"Now look here," Hardisty bridled, "we ain't goin' to stand for no highway robbery from you!" There was sweat on his face and on the palms of his hands. He saw everything he had worked for about to slip away from him. Damn the blackhearted creature with her devil's eyes. He should have known what she was the minute he looked at her. Trouble. Danger and trouble. She was out to ruin him, and he was helpless to stop her.

"You have no choice but to do as I ask," Tarifa said evenly. "And I am afraid you will not have much time to make up your minds."

"What devilish scheme you got in your mind now?" cried Hardisty, chagrin and uncertainty making him forget his pose of peacemaker.

"I instructed my servant to ride back to camp and dump the supplies into the river if I have not returned safely by a certain hour. He is a most loyal and obedient servant."

A roar went up from the men.

Hardisty opened his mouth as if he were gasping for air and asked, "How much do you want for the supplies?"

"Ten thousand dollars in gold."

"Ten—but that's crazy! The stuff's not worth five!"

"I paid six for it myself," Tarifa said, unperturbed. "But against sure starvation its worth cannot adequately be measured. I think my price is extremely fair. You can take it or leave it, but you must decide quickly."

"Well," said Jake Latham, "what you aimin' to do, Hardisty? Don't see as we have much choice. Most of us have sent our gold out already, but if we all chip in we should be able to raise her ten thousand."

"But ten thousand dollars!" Hardisty groaned.

"Can we eat gold, man? The smallest pinch of flour in them supplies will be worth more than the biggest nugget in the diggin's 'fore winter's over."

Tarifa smiled at them thinly as they went to empty gold dust and nuggets onto Hardisty's scales. When Hardisty brought the gold to her later with a black scowl on his face, she spoke to Stokes.

"Take this back to camp for me, *amigo*, and I will give you what I owe you."

He nodded. "An' any of you gets to thinkin' of bushwhackin' me, just remember I'm your only link with civilization? Me an' my mules."

"In an hour," said Tarifa, "I will be gone, and you can come for your supplies. Until that time, my camp won't be safe for any of you."

Jake Latham laughed at the morose faces around him.

"How about drinks on the house, Elias, since she cleaned us plumb outa pay dirt? Y'know gents, this day's goin' down in the history of the diggin's. They'll be tellin' it from here to the Trinity how a Gypsy gal backed the camp to the wall and walked off with all the loose gold in Sonora!"

His laughter filled the dark, smoky room and slowly, as the outrageous humor of the situation came over them, the rest joined in, slapping each other on the backs, rolling in the dirt of the saloon floor, laughing until tears came to their eyes at their own misfortune. Listening to them, Tarifa felt again the impossibility of understanding Americans.

Sonora would mine more gold, but they would never forget the day the Gypsy from San Luis Rey made them buy back their own supplies to the tune of ten thousand in gold.

When she returned to camp, Tarifa told Antonio and Casim to get ready to leave.

"They will not make trouble for you?" she asked Stokes, who had arrived a short time before she had with the gold.

"Not me, señora. They need me. I'm the one carries out their gold and brings in the supplies. 'Sides I got to wait for Myrtle to come back. That was some show you put on." He grinned. "Them horny-handed galoots ain't goin' to forgit that in a coon's age. Sorry about the young gent here, but you got there in time."

Tarifa frowned at him. "It is lucky I did."

"You aimin' to carry all this gold by yourself?" he asked.

"Yes. There is no other way."

"I'll sell ye one of my mules if ye like?"

Tarifa considered this and then shook her head.

"We will travel faster with just the horses. We can divide the gold between us."

"Pretty dangerous goin' alone like that. There's plenty of bandits in the hills these days."

"It is a chance we will have to take," said Tarifa. "*Adiós, amigo, hasta luego.*"

He took her hand and pumped it awkwardly.

"*Adiós,* señora. I don't know them other words, but here's wishin' you good luck and godspeed."

"*Gràcias,* Señor Stokes."

Long before dawn Tarifa and the two men rode out of camp, circling the settlement of Sonora where the raucous shouts of the celebrants could still be heard coming from Hardisty's, and headed southwest.

It was nearly noon before Tarifa would let them make camp in a grove of willows near the Tuolumne. Even then she would not allow a fire to be made, and they ate a cold meal washed down with water.

Antonio was pale and silent after his experience at the hands of the miners. For the first time in his life he had known numbing, blind fear. Yet Tarifa had stood up to them when his own courage had failed. He gazed at her covertly now and then, feeling a strange mixture of awe and apprehension. What was she really? A witch, as Tía Isabella had once said? A blackhearted demon, as Joaquin had called her? A ruthless despot, as he knew his brothers often considered her—selfish, greedy, demanding? Or was she something else, a woman who loved Loma de Oro more than her own safety, more than the love of a husband? He wished that he knew, but he was just as aware that he never would. She would remain an enigma to him for as long as he lived.

Some days later they had crossed the Merced and camped on Bear Creek not far from the San Joaquin River, intending to cross the sierras and go down the

Pajaro valley to Monterey. From there they could take their time going south without fear of bandits.

The fall weather had turned cold and the rains had begun, coming down in a steady torrent from leaden skies. The earth was a sea of ocher mud, sucking at the horses' fetlocks and delaying their travel.

Around the small fire Casim had managed to make in the lee of a giant granite boulder, the three travelers huddled silently sipping tea that tasted like boiled straw.

All of them wore heavy ponchos over their clothing but they were soaked to the skin anyway, and Antonio had developed a hacking cough.

Tarifa was concerned about him but also annoyed at his malady. These Alvarjos, there was always something wrong with them! They had no stamina. Their blood might be blue, but it was as thin as water. They were as helpless, as undependable as babes-in-arms.

"You must drink some brandy in your tea or you will get a fever," she told him. "Then we will be delayed still more. There are no habitations here where you could be taken care of."

He coughed violently, covering his mouth with his hand. "I will be all right."

"Do as I say! Bring the brandy, Casim."

At her direction, the vaquero poured a good measure of brandy into Antonio's cup.

"Now drink it. All of it, *pronto*."

Antonio drank the liquid obediently and at once went into a paroxysm of coughing.

Tarifa watched him in helpless fury. If only Penti were here with her bundle of herbs and medicines. But Tarifa herself had never been interested enough to learn about Gypsy medications. She had always been robustly healthy herself, and she had scant sympathy for those who were not.

Her brooding thoughts were interrupted by a pistol shot. She glanced up to see a group of riders encircling the boulder where they sat.

Her hand fumbled at the long wet folds of the poncho, trying to grasp the pistol in her sash, but a fat man in the center of the group warned, "Stand still, *mujer*, or we shoot!"

He was a man of indeterminate middle-age, heavy-chested and fat-bellied. His accent was Sonoran. He wore a dripping ragged poncho, nothing on his muddy feet but a pair of rusted wrought-iron spurs tied to his heels with leather thongs, and a rather fine sombrero on the back of his large head.

His companions were a ragged, unkempt lot, most of them young and mounted on scrub horses, but each was armed. It was quite obvious what they were, cholos turned bandit for expediency and profit.

"What do you want?" Tarifa demanded.

"Ah, señora, that is something about which you will find us most undemanding. We will take anything. Is not that an agreeable state of mind?"

"Who are you?"

"*Por favor,* allow me to introduce myself. I am Jorge Camilo Ramirez. And these are my poor suffering *compadres.*"

"You are *bandidos.*"

An ugly light came into Ramirez's small eyes.

"We are loyal Californians who fought with Colonel Pico at San Pascual."

"I don't believe you. My stepson fought at San Pascual. Were these men with Andres Pico's forces, Antonio?"

"No. I am sure that they were not."

"If you are loyal Californians, what are you doing armed?" Tarifa asked. "The Americanos have a law that you must turn in your guns."

"We have not heard of this law," Ramirez said darkly. "In any case, we have just been hunting."

"In this wilderness, in the rain?" Her voice rose. "Hunting for what?"

Ramirez swung down from his horse and approached the Alvarjo horses standing nearby.

"For the gold we know is in these saddlebags," he answered, opening a saddle flap.

Tarifa felt the breath burn through her lungs.

"Leave that alone! I swear you will regret it if you touch one part of that saddle."

"Ho! The Señora thinks we will be sorry for making ourselves rich, *compadres.* Shall we put her mind to rest and tell her we are quite willing to take this grave risk?"

Their laughter made Tarifa livid with rage. What she would have given to put hands on a gun, a knife, a whip. The gold she had schemed so hard to get, the gold that was meant to save Loma de Oro, was being taken in front of her very eyes and she was helpless to stop it. But she had no conception of what was really in Ramirez's evil, wily mind.

"*Amigos,* I think it is a pity to go to the trouble of unloading all this heavy gold when it has been packed so nicely? And we cannot take from the Señora, without giving her a little something in return? Carlos, Juan, Titro, give your horses to the Señora and her companions, and mount yourselves on these fine palominos."

A great cry went up from Tarifa.

Guindilla!

She could never allow them to take Guindilla, not if they killed her on the spot.

She flew at the startled Ramirez, clawing, scratching, biting, and he tripped over his spurs and fell to his knees while she beat him over the head with her fists, shouting Romany curses.

For a moment no one moved and then Antonio went to her assistance, slipping his knife from his boot. As he lifted it one of the cholos fired and he felt it go spinning from his torn, bloody fingers.

Ramirez had gotten to his feet and he and Tarifa struggled in the wet sticky mud, looking like brown plaster statues.

Ramirez shook himself free with a mighty heave and landed a powerful blow to the side of Tarifa's head. She went down like a crab, falling to her hands and knees, her head sunk between her shoulders.

"*Hola!*" said a new voice. "Why don't you finish her off, Jorge?"

Tarifa looked up with blurred sight to see a stranger mounted on a fiery black horse, his eyes flint-hard and mocking under his fine white sombrero.

Her eyes wandered over his face and figure and she was disturbed by some familiarity in his bearing. He reminded her of someone, something. She wasn't sure, and then suddenly recognition came like a flash of lightning through her weary brain.

Santiago!

He was waiting for the expression of shock in her eyes and she heard him laugh softly.

"Yes, Tarifa. I am Santiago. We meet again after these long years? Once I thought I had left you for dead, but I heard you were alive and mistress of Loma de Oro. So I did you a favor? I am the one who has been as good as dead all these years. I should have known you can't kill a Gypsy."

Antonio had turned incredulously to face his brother.

"Santiago? I cannot believe it—*hermano*, don't you know me?"

Santiago frowned down at him, a tall gaunt figure wet to his boots, with his fingers dripping blood.

"*Sangre*, it can't be! Not little Antonio?"

"*Sí!*"

Santiago dismounted and threw his arms around his brother.

"When I was last in New Mexico I heard news of Loma de Oro, but not that you were a grown man, *muchacho*."

"You knew Father was dead?"

"*Sí.*"

"Then why did you not come back?"

"There was no place for me on Loma de Oro anymore," said Santiago bitterly, glancing at Tarifa where she stood, mud-stained but haughty in the rain.

"But what are you doing with these—*bandidos?*"

Santiago laughed. "I ride with them. We are *compadres*."

"You rob and steal?" Antonio fell back a pace and there was pain and disbelief on his face.

"What a child you still are in spite of your manhood, Tonito. If I have learned only one truth in life, it is that a man must do the best he can for himself. When I left California I had not a *real* in my sash. I knew how to ride a horse, use a *reata*, and little else. I have learned a number of useful things since, *muchacho*. How to shoot, how to organize and control a band such as this, and how to keep out of the reach of the soldiers when I have made a successful raid."

Antonio's lips were as stern with disapproval as he had remembered Ygnacio's, Santiago thought. Pride, that empty, barren thing that could neither feed nor clothe you, nor warm your cold breast, how he hated it!

"What do you intend to do with us?" Antonio asked coldly.

"I will have to discuss that with my partner when he arrives. Unfortunately that will not be for several days. He and some of our men have gone looking for horses. Until then we will keep you at our camp a few miles north of here."

Santiago's camp was a bleak spot at the foot of a mountain, but it had a shelter of sorts. A crumbling, brush-roofed adobe built by some small ranchero and abandoned long ago.

It was a fairly large three-roomed building, and warm after the cold rain. Fires burned in the tiny fireplaces in each room, giving a little direct heat where clothing could be dried and hands and feet warmed.

Santiago did not bother to lock them up, merely posting an armed guard at the only door to see that they did not escape.

"It was very thoughtful of you to bring us all this gold," he told Tarifa while they ate a meal of soggy corn tortillas, dried beans, and harsh red wine.

When she had recovered from her first shock at seeing him, Tarifa regained her usual aplomb and cold indifference. She had no intention of bandying words with her captors.

Santiago was amazed to find that her arrogance could still infuriate him. Hatred for her had ridden with him, his constant companion through the long years of his enforced exile from home, and yet now that they were face-to-face, he found that it had been superceded by another emotion. Admiration, the first feeling he had ever had for her, that day they met outside the bullring in Seville.

No matter what she suffered, no matter what one did to her, she remained the same, a fearless, indestructible little hellion. You could hate her, even kill her, but you would never conquer her indomitable spirit. Even now she ate her meal with scowling relish, plotting God-knew-what machinations against him in her cold, unscrupulous, devious brain. Bandonna's words had been prophetic. In bringing her to California he had condemned not only Tarifa and himself, but all the Alvarjos as well.

In the afternoon Santiago went to lie down in one of the bedrooms and invited Antonio to share his nap, but his brother was being as coolly aloof as Tarifa. Let them sit in a cold corner and look at each other then, thought Santiago angrily, and slammed the door on their accusing faces.

Ramirez and his five companions had taken possession of the second bedroom where they were playing monte on a rickety table amid much talk and laughter, with intermittent pulls at the bottle of *aguardiente* on the floor by Ramirez's chair.

Except for the man crouching outside the door with his rifle between his knees, Tarifa and Antonio had the front room to themselves.

"Where are the horses?" she whispered.

"Under the oak tree in the rear. It is no use; we cannot get away."

Tarifa glared at him. "Do as I tell you. Get the knives and spoons from the table. Be quiet, *por Dios!*"

He brought her two horn-handled knives and two pewter spoons much the worse for wear. "What are you going to do?"

"Be still, can't you? Sit here on the floor by me, keep your back to the door, and start digging."

"Digging?"

"*Premita Undebē!* You are like a donkey, all ears and no brains. The gold is there in the saddlebags in the corner isn't it?" She glanced at the wet saddles that had been carelessly heaped in one corner near the fireplace to dry. The gold-filled saddlebags were just visible underneath.

"We cannot take the gold from here?"

"We are going to bury it."

"Bury it! Here in the floor?"

"Yes. We will fill the ponchos with the dirt we take out. Hurry!"

She had spread a serape on the floor and they sat, backs to the door, near the fire as if they sought more warmth.

For the next two hours the guard glanced in casually now and then but he could see nothing unusual in two people sitting on a rug before the fire on a cold day. He only envied them their nearness to the heat.

Tarifa inched the saddlebags from under the saddles. It took but a short while to empty the gold into the hole they had dug in the broken dirt floor of the house, and to fill the pouches with loose dirt left from their digging. With the hole neatly covered and tamped down, it only remained for them to replace the saddlebags where they had been under the saddles.

Tarifa had bent to slide the bags under the pile of saddles when Ramirez poked his head out of the bedroom. He was on her with a roar. His knife glanced against her cheek and she fell back, feinting and twisting to get away from him.

His cry had brought the other cholos and they stood in a group near the bedroom door watching the struggle. Tarifa tripped over the serape she had thrown on the floor while they were digging, and instantly Ramirez was on top of her, flattening her to the ground with his bulk, his eyes glittering maliciously as he raised the knife to drive it into her breast.

"Jorge!"

Santiago stood in the doorway of his bedroom, a pistol leveled at Ramirez's head.

Ramirez glared up at him with hate-filled eyes.

"She was trying to steal our gold! I caught her at it!"

"Let her go!"

A cunning look came over Ramirez's fat glistening face. He had enough *aguardiente* in him to make him both brutal and reckless. "Maybe you plan to join your fine friends and relations here, and ride off with the gold, too, señor?"

"Shut up, Jorge!"

"How do we know, poor ignorant cholos, that we will get any of the gold? Eh, *amigos?*"

"I have always given you your share before," Santiago said coldly.

"Ah, but this is such a great deal of *dinero,* Capitán."

"Get up and let her go or I will blast a hole through you!" Santiago's eyes were unflinching, his face as hard as granite. *"Vamos!"*

Ramirez moved, slowly, carefully, raising his bulk by inches. There was a conciliatory grin on his face. When he got to his feet he slipped the knife into his sash. The hand came back up holding a pistol. He fired suddenly, holding the gun low and directly in front of him.

Santiago sagged against the doorframe, but he pulled

the trigger as he did so and Ramirez grunted with pain as the bullet slammed into his shoulder.

Antonio ran to support his brother and Ramirez tossed his knife, narrowly missing Antonio's head.

A commotion in the yard drew the men's attention momentarily from the struggle inside the house.

"Who is it?" Santiago whispered.

"I don't know. A group of men," Antonio said. "Do not try to look."

"The—rest of our band. Help me to stand."

"*Sí*. But it would be better to lie down. The blood—"

Ramirez came across the room, his pistol leveled at Santiago's chest.

"We will have a new leader of our little band," he sneered. "A cholo like the rest, who will think first of his men and not of other *gente de razón* like these! I thank you for the gold, Santiago."

Antonio released Santiago and threw himself at Ramirez as he fired. There was another shot from the door, Antonio thought, and then he went down under the heavier man's weight.

There were voices, shouts, feet pounding on the floor and then hands clawing at him, freeing him from the pinioning bulk of Ramirez.

"Antonio!" Tarifa cried. "Are you all right?"

"*Sí*, I think so." He glanced up to find Tarifa kneeling on one side of him, and Pito Larios in the other. Pito carried a pistol in one hand and there was a grim look on his face. He spoke over his shoulder to the armed men who had come with him.

"Tie these others up and leave them in the yard!"

"*Sí*, mi capitán!"

When the cholos in the house protested, Larios slashed at them with his words.

"You would stand by and see your capitán murdered, as well as his prisoners, by this lump of garbage here?" He kicked Ramirez's body with his boot. "We have no traitors or mutineers in this band. *Vamos!*"

He went to kneel by Santiago where he lay by the bedroom door. The shirt front under his jacket was red with blood.

"*Amigo*, we must get you to bed."

Santiago shook his head. "No, don't—move me. I will have—no further use for beds, *muchacho mío.*"

"If I had come a little sooner, *compadre!* I came to warn you the soldiers from Monterey are on their way. They followed us from the sierras."

"You—must go. You will see—Tarifa, and my brother —get safely back—to Loma de Oro?"

"Lo prometo, Santiago! You have my word."

Antonio knelt on the other side and took his brother's hand. Santiago saw that there were tears in his eyes.

"Santiago, you cannot die. You must come back with us to Loma de Oro!"

"No, *hermano mío,* it is—better I rest—here." He closed his eyes for a moment, wondering at how easy, how simple it was to die. He would have liked a priest to confess his sins to, but God knew all of them anyway. In the end everything was between God and yourself, and no one could intercede for you. "Where—is Tarifa?" he asked. There was so much to say and so little time in which to say it.

"Here, Santiago." He felt her slide his head to her lap, and looking up he found her long eyes, as dark and inscrutable as death itself.

"Forgive," he murmured. "You must forgive me. For— everything?" He found the words surprisingly easy to say, but his lips and tongue were growing unmanageable.

"I forgive you, Santiago."

With a supreme effort he smiled up at her and said with his last breath, "Pray—for—me."

His head lay still in her lap, the eyes closed, looking curiously peaceful and young like the boy who had walked down the Calle de las Sierpes with her that hot Sunday in Seville to buy her a gaudy dress and cheap shawl and a new tambourine.

She bent her head suddenly and wept, for all of the things people did to each other in their greed and passion, and for all the things they left undone until it was too late. She wept while she detested her own weakness and vulnerability.

Pito raised her gently to her feet.

"My men and I must go," he told her. "The soldiers are not far behind. The soldiers will pick up the renegados I

have left tied up so conveniently for them in the yard, and
they will see you safely to Monterey. I am afraid I must
take the gold and one of your horses. I will need a fast
mount to get away."

Tarifa pointed to the saddlebags on the floor.

"This?" He hefted one of the pouches, put it back un-
opened and smiled at her. "I regret this, *querida,* but a man
must look after himself, *sí?* The horse, which one—"

"Take Guindilla," she said without inflection.

"You would give me Guindilla?" His eyes softened and
he took a step toward her and then halted. "I am deeply
grateful, chiquita. But, no, I cannot take the horse you
love so much."

"Take mine," Antonio said at once. "Concho. He is a
good animal. Take him with my blessing and best wishes."

"Muchas gracias, Don Antonio. If it is possible I will
see that you get him back."

"Por nada," Antonio said graciously.

They stood in the doorway until the men mounted and
galloped out of the yard, Larios astride the palomino, with
the bags filled with dirt slung across his saddle.

If he died he would die defending nothing, thought
Tarifa wryly, nothing but dirt. How cheaply men sold
their lives for a momentary earthly satisfaction. Then went
to their eternal judgment with all paradise lost.

The soldiers were Americans from the presidio at Monterey. While a detachment went in pursuit of the bandits,
the lieutenant in charge, a young Virginian named Mont-
ford, detailed some men to bury Santiago near the large
oak tree in the rear of the adobe. Antonio knelt nearby to
say a few prayers over his brother's grave.

Tarifa did not join him. She stood silent and aloof, her
eyes on the far horizon. It had stopped raining and in the
watery sunshine a double rainbow had come out, arching
gracefully over the little house.

Before the soldiers had arrived, Antonio and Tarifa had
dug up the gold and replaced it in sacks that had once
contained the cholo's supplies.

Antonio had been incensed that they should do such a
thing while his brother lay dead.

"You have no heart, no feelings," he accused Tarifa
hotly.

"No. I am like Santiago and Pito, I love only a piece of dirt, for gold comes from dirt also? Only mine is the soil of Loma de Oro. That I shall die defending."

"You think only of the rancho at a time like this?"

"I set out to get gold for Loma de Oro," she answered grimly, "and nothing is going to stop me. When you start out to do a thing, *muchacho,* finish it! Regardless of the circumstances, stick with what you are doing and then you will get somewhere."

Monterey had changed. There was a new atmosphere in the air, a hustle and bustle, a dispatch in getting things done that it had never known before.

The plaza and the streets were alive with Americans in uniform, in buckskins, in sailors' garb.

Zenobio Sanchez was overjoyed to see them and would not hear of their leaving that night as they had planned.

"No, you must stay and rest, a week, two weeks, months!" insisted the old man, showing them into the *sala* of his spacious, tree-shaded house at the edge of town.

His hair and beard were completely white, but he was as gruff and talkative as ever.

His money had been put to good use. The house was comfortable and well-furnished, run by a Mexican couple, he told them, and his clothes were spotless and of good quality.

He still kept a bottle of *aguardiente* at his elbow while he talked, but he went to his meals on time and he had put on weight.

When they had told him all their news, he mentioned that he had a desire to return to his rancho for a little time.

"The pueblo is pleasant, *amigos,* but I would like to see my land again, and my friends. I hear that Padre Cazon is not well? I would like to see him before he dies, and burden him with my sins." He grinned wickedly.

A sudden fear had taken possession of Tarifa at his words. Padre Cazon and death had never been really connected in her mind somehow. The Padre was like a part of her. Her mentor, her conscience, her sounding board, her dear friend in spite of their quarrels. He could not leave her.

"Padre Cazon is at Pala," she said sharply. "I left orders

he was to be supplied with food—everything! He was not ill when we left."

"And do not all priests starve at their posts to feed the Indians these days, now that the Missions are no more?" asked Zenobio crossly, reaching for his glass.

"We must leave at once, Antonio. I must get back to Loma de Oro as quickly as possible," Tarifa said.

"Then you would do better to go by ship, as I intend to when I go," Zenobio suggested. "You will save time, and your gold will be safer."

"No, we will ride. I will not leave Guindilla."

A servant entered and murmured in the old soldier's ear.

"A guest," he apologized, getting to his feet. "You will excuse me?"

"Of course, Don Zenobio," said Antonio.

They heard voices murmuring briefly in the patio, followed by a muffled exclamation of surprise from Zenobio, and then silence.

When Zenobio returned to the *sala* he had an odd expression on his face, as if he had just suffered a terrific shock.

"Something is wrong?" cried Antonio, rushing to help him to his chair. "What is it, Don Zenobio?"

"It is only because I am old that I cannot take these things anymore," sobbed the old man. "*Sangre de Dios,* where is my handkerchief?" He was weeping like a child, mopping at his face and mumbling to himself.

He is senile, thought Tarifa. He has grown too old and has had too soft living here in Monterey among the Americanos.

She walked to the open door leading to the patio, and stepped outside looking for one of the servants to come and see his master to bed.

She heard a sound to her left and turned sharply on her quick dancer's feet.

Bart Kinkaid, his cap in his hand, was standing in the shadows of the veranda staring at her face with an expression of awed disbelief.

CHAPTER 35

Though he had never gone to sea, Ephraim Endecott knew as much about ships and sailing as any shipowner in New England, not excepting Elias Hasket Derby, "King Derby," who had laid the foundation for the maritime trade in Salem, or Captain Nathaniel West, or the six Crowninshield brothers who had each commanded ships before they were twenty-one.

No detail of shipbuilding was too small to attract Endecott's attention. From his window he could see the forest of masts in the harbor, and it filled him with pride to think of the white, tight sails on the lordly clippers that would sweep around the Horn like graceful birds of passage. His ancestors had thought nothing of crossing the Atlantic in forty-foot ketches; what would they think of these giants of clippers with their sleek black hulls, high-tiered skys'ls and wide-winged stuns'ls flying over the gray seas at speeds never yet dreamed of?

It had grown dusk and he got up to light the lamp on his desk. His clerk had long since gone and he was alone in the narrow two-story brick building that had always housed his offices and was now his living quarters as well.

Footsteps on the stairs made him turn his head in surprise. He did not usually receive callers after office hours, and he was piqued that he should be disturbed in what to him was the most enjoyable part of his profession, the contemplation of the plans for a new Endecott ship.

He turned the lamp up and stood with one hand on the

desk, waiting for the intruder to knock. Instead the door was flung wide and he saw a tall figure outlined in the frame.

"Good evening, Uncle Ephraim."

Endecott could see the flash of white teeth in a dark face underneath the peaked cap; he knew it was Bart. But the shock of his presence left him numb and speechless. He had been so sure that he was dead, and yet he had fought against admitting it to himself. It was only of late that he had finally accepted it, and now his old mind refused to be turned so quickly from its settled course.

"Don't you know me, Uncle?" He stepped into the warm room and shut the door.

"Bart?" His voice quavered like a badly played violin.

"Yes. But I didn't come back empty-handed this time. I brought the *Lorelei* with me, what's left of her."

"My boy—I can't believe—" Behind his half-moon glasses, Ephraim's eyes began to water. He tottered, leaning against the desk, and Bart ran to help him into his chair. He poured him a glass of brandy from the decanter on the sideboard.

"Better," murmured the old man, "much better, thanks. Sit down, sit down, my boy."

They sat in the dimly lit room with its crackling fire of pine logs, and its somber mahogany furniture, and talked far into the night.

Bart's story was simple enough, and certainly not unique among seafaring men. The *Lorelei* had run into a typhoon on her way to Canton, been blown well off her course, and driven onto a reef off a small uninhabited island. Many of the crew had been lost overboard. Others, including Jake Banner and himself, were injured and it had taken weeks before they were able to turn their attention to the ship. The only reason she hadn't been beaten to pieces in the meantime was that she rested in a natural breakwater created by the odd volcanic eruptions of former years.

When the weather cleared they sent the second mate and some men in the longboat rigged with a jury mast and sail, to see if they could reach the nearest inhabited spot, which they reckoned lay some three hundred miles away. The men never came back.

There was nothing the rest of them could do but wait, and try to do what they could to safeguard the *Lorelei*.

They had been there eight months when a few natives landed on the island, explaining that it was a favorite hunting spot which they visited once each season for land turtles and birds. For payment of some salvaged trade goods, the chief agreed to take two of the crew members to the nearest habitation. A month later an East Indiaman anchored offshore, and with her help they managed to float the *Lorelei* free, patch her hull, and limp into Manila.

"It took a long time to refit and make Canton," said Bart.

"You went on to Canton, with your ship in that condition?"

"I started out for Canton," Bart said, taking out his cigar case.

Ephraim shook his head: "We all thought you were dead—even your wife."

"Tarifa?" He frowned. It hadn't occurred to him that word had reached her. The thought disturbed him.

"When your money stopped coming to her, and your letters, I suppose, she wrote to me. I explained that you must be supposed to be lost, another ship had seen you briefly during the typhoon, and I told her that your remaining funds were tied up in the company. That as soon as you had been legally declared dead, and we could liquidate your interests, I would get in touch with her."

Bart leaped to his feet. He was as lean and swarthy as an Indian, no doubt from his long exposure in the tropics, thought Ephraim, with a savage restlessness about him that he had seen in other men who had been marooned.

"You could have sent her money and charged it against my account," Kinkaid said, pacing the narrow room like a caged leopard. "I gave her my word about the money. She needed it. How long ago did you stop sending it to her?"

Ephraim told him, and Bart swore under his breath.

"Have you heard from her since?"

"No. But with the gold strike, very few ships are coming back from California."

"I was in Manila when a California ship brought word of the gold," Bart said. "You never saw madness take hold of people so swiftly. In an hour the waterfront was cluttered by everyone who could scrape up the price for passage."

"You have seen what it is like in Boston?"

Kinkaid's face was grim. "I've seen. And by the looks of some of the leaky old scows they're hauling out of drydock, I'll wager half the passengers never get to California."

"Ah," said Endecott, "exactly my viewpoint. Criminal, I call it, sending people to sea in such worm-ridden baskets. But what can shipowners do, when passengers are willing to pay one thousand dollars for any sort of accommodations? Tell me, my boy, what are your plans? Will you stay here and help me with this madhouse I am running? I could use you. Or will you join Caleb in New York? He says, if anything, it is worse there."

"No," Bart said slowly. "I'm going to California. You need skippers far more than you need desk clerks, don't you?"

"Ah, that is true." Endecott paused. "But when you were last here you expressed a desire not to return to California."

Bart sat down and spread his hands between his knees.

"I know. I felt there was no place for me there any longer. But I was wrong. A man can do a lot of thinking in eight months on a deserted island."

"I haven't asked you before," Ephraim said, looking resolutely into the fire, "I've no right to ask you now, but if you will indulge an old man's garrulity, are you and your wife happy together?"

Bart's eyes followed his uncle's toward the leaping flames in the Adam fireplace. He wondered what Tarifa would have thought of Ephraim, and what Ephraim would have thought of Tarifa. Happy? There had never been any question of happiness between them. It was desire that had driven them together. His desire for her, and hers for Loma de Oro.

"No," he said quietly. "She doesn't love me and never did. She's a woman of resolve and purpose, not unlike you, Uncle Ephraim."

He nodded, not turning his head. "A cold woman. Unable to show her emotion perhaps, poor creature? I have been accused of that myself."

"No. Not cold. Blazing with emotion like the fire in that grate, but determined, and ruthless. With one purpose, and one purpose only, to save her rancho. It has become an obsession with her. You might say," he added wryly, "that ours is a marriage of convenience."

"My poor boy!"

Bart got to his feet annd went to lean against the fireplace, his long back to his uncle and his arms folded on the mantel between the brass beehive candlesticks that had belonged to his mother.

"Don't feel sorry for me," he said in a harsh tone. "She didn't take advantage of me, or come to me under false pretenses. I forced her to marry me, by promising her security for Loma de Oro. And agreeing to ask nothing in return. Like many men before me, I thought it would be enough. Marrying her was the main thing. I thought, perhaps foolishly, that with kindness and patience, the rest would follow. I couldn't have been more mistaken. I should have known Tarifa always means what she says. She is brutally honest. She only wanted what I had promised her: my money to protect Loma de Oro's future. And in the end I was the one who couldn't keep the bargain. I broke my word to her in one wild night of madness. There was nothing left to do but leave California and never return. I intended to see that she never wanted for anything, and at least keep that end of my bargain. Now I have failed even to do that!"

When he turned, Endecott's eyes met his in a moment of shocked disbelief. One thing he would have staked his life upon was Bart's sense of honor. He could not believe that he would break his word to a woman, no matter what the provocation. He felt suddenly as if he did not know his nephew at all, and yet he could not discount Bart's integrity.

"And now," the old man asked uncertainly, "you will go back to her?"

"I'd go back to her on my knees if she'd have me. But it's too late for that. Tarifa does not forgive. It is one of her strengths and odd charms.

"I ran from her because she was too much for me. I couldn't be around her any longer and not touch her. And then I couldn't face her after what I'd done. Because I had

lost our battle. I was wrong. I should have stayed. I'm
going back. To give her the money I promised her. After
that she can do as she pleases. I'll leave California with a
clean conscience then, and she can have her freedom.

"My share of company stock should sell without trouble,
in the present state of maritime speculation."

"Like a shot, if you wish to sell it," Ephraim said. "But
it will increase fabulously in the next year. I had hoped——"

"Cash me out," Bart said firmly. "And I want a ship, a
fast one."

"Come here," said Ephraim, "look at these designs
McKay just made for me. Clippers, that's the thing! How
would you like to reach California in less than a hundred
days?"

"They can do it?"

"As easily as a bird flies. These two—the *Royal Endeavor*
and the *Flying Horn* will .be off the stocks in a few
months."

"I can't wait that long," Bart said. "If you haven't got
a ship, make arrangements for me to go aboard someone
else's."

Ephraim hid his disappointment. "I've been dickering
to buy a clipper from Scott and Company," he said. "She
just made a return trip from Hong Kong in ninety-seven
days. The *Celestial Queen,* sixteen hundred tons."

"When does she sail?"

"Will your old crew sign on?"

"I'm sure of it. Banner will go as mate."

"Then you should be able to sail in two weeks' time."

At first sight of the *Celestial Queen*, Kinkaid had known
the soul-satisfying thrill of the craftsman who finds at long
last the precise tool to turn his labor into art.

She was a typical full-rigged clipper ship, long-armed,
with spreading yards, raking masts, mahogany deck fittings,
and gleaming brass.

Bart noted with delight that she carried three standing
skys'l yards above her royals, yards which were not hoisted
aloft when the sails were set as in the past, but remained
permanently in place. Indeed such ships could "fly,"
thought Kinkaid. Their like had never been seen before.

The *Celestial Queen* was as good as Kinkaid had

dreamed she would be. She swept across the gray seas with seabirds squalling in her wake, and awed both passengers and crew by her miraculous speed.

From the cold gusty North Atlantic to the tropical Torrid Zone, the calms of Capricorn and the frigid violent Antarctic off the Horn, the *Celestial Queen* met every challenge of weather without slackening sail.

Kinkaid drove her day and night 'round the Horn with rackings on to'ps'l halliards, and locks on the chainsheets so the frightened crew members couldn't tamper with the gear.

As they approached the Farallones, that graveyard of ships, shrouded in fog, Kinkaid slackened sail for the first time. Once inside the Golden Gate, the fog lifted as if a curtain had been raised on a dazzling scene of golden hills, blue bay, and sparkling water. On Telegraph Hill three semaphores rose to signal the ship's type and arrival, and when they finally anchored off Howison's Wharf, the hills and waterfront were black with people come to greet the clipper.

Kinkaid and Banner, standing on the quarterdeck, could not believe their eyes. Yerba Buena Cove, that wide expanse of seldom disturbed water, was now alive with dark hulks, towering masts, and the flags of many countries besides the United States. Most of the ships swung at anchor, abandoned, without even a guard mounted to protect them. A few still held their helpless captains and a mate or two, waiting patiently until the gold madness had passed and their weary crews might return. Many ships, Kinkaid found, had never even unloaded their cargoes. Labor was too scarce. The more obdurate skippers had opened their ships as stores and carried on the sale of their goods as merchants, between decks. Still others had been beached and turned into boardinghouses, restaurants, stores, or hotels.

The city had changed, too. Rising in a crescent above the cove, it was still mainly a city of tents, dominated by Telegraph Hill with houses melting away along the California Street ridge in the distance.

There were still the scattering of adobe and frame buildings near the waterfront, where Richardson had had his store, but large numbers of new dwellings stretched to the southwest shores under the Market Street ridge where they had water and were protected from the sharp west winds.

Kinkaid had no idea of losing his vessel or allowing his crew to jump ship. He posted armed guards on the decks, weighed anchor, and sailed for Monterey without having unloaded a piece of his cargo.

"The gold camp won't be quite so close or the temptation to leave quite as great in Monterey," he told Banner.

But the mate merely shook his head. "You'll have a time holding them in any case, sir," he said. "I've heard them talking. Even wise old hands speak of the gold as if it's there to be picked up by the handful."

"We'll double the guard then," said Kinkaid, "and I'll pay one thousand dollars for information leading to the recapture of any man who jumps ship."

"Aye, aye, sir."

Monterey was as changed as San Francisco had been. The streets were abustle with movement and life. There were numerous new buildings, and everywhere he looked Kinkaid could see the signs of Yankee ingenuity and ambition.

Bart found himself heading in the direction of Zenobio's house at the edge of town. He hadn't meant to go there at once. He had many matters to attend to, but he had to know about Tarifa, and he was certain Zenobio could tell him something.

To be back in California after his record one-hundred-and-six-day run from Boston on the *Celestial Queen* gave Kinkaid a strange exhilaration and at the same time filled him with an odd foreboding. Once before he had returned to a loved one, only to find her dead. He could not believe that Tarifa was dead, and yet the unfounded fear gripped him that he had returned once again too late to find his heart's desire.

He straightened his shoulders under the new blue coat he had bought in Boston, as he walked up to the door of Zenobio's large attractive adobe and knocked.

An elderly Mexican woman answered his summons and, after listening to him politely, showed him into the sunny patio while she called her master.

Kinkaid was standing in the shade of the *galleria,* near a vine bearing purple grapes that climbed toward the roof, when Zenobio appeared.

He's grown old, Kinkaid thought. Then he saw the instant shock followed by pleasure and felt the thud of
Zenobio's hands as the old soldier grasped his arms. No, he
thought, not old, just more full of years.

"Compadre! Compadre mío! Dios! I cannot credit my
senses. We had all given you up for dead. Come and sit
down and tell me what has happened, *amigo?"*

He led Kinkaid to a bench on the veranda sheltered by
the roof, and listened to his story with narrowed eyes and
his mouth half-open in concentration. When he had finished
Zenobio said, "All that matters is that you are back, *amigo.*
Ah, everything has changed here since you left. Since they
discovered the accursed gold. Even my old *compadres,* the
ones who can still hobble, have gone in search of it. It is
like a madness that devours men's souls."

Kinkaid asked half-fearfully about Loma de Oro and
Tarifa.

"Ah, Loma de Oro prospers in spite of bad times and
the shortage of vaqueros that has ruined so many of the
other ranchos. As for Tarifa, you must excuse me a moment
before I speak to you of her?" He rose and then an odd
tremulous smile came to his lips. "You will wait here,
amigo? I will be right back."

Puzzled, Kinkaid watched him hobble back into the
house. He would have to indulge the old gentleman. He
had grown rather childish in the past few years after all.

Kinkaid lighted a cigar and rose to stroll up and down
the tiled patio. He had stepped up under the *galleria* again
when a door opened and a woman stepped out into the
patio.

They recognized each other at the same moment.

Kinkaid's pulse quickened in a moment of disbelief and
wonderment at finding her here. Her name escaped his
lips like a sigh, a prayer. "Tarifa!"

He saw the quick contraction of her black brows, the
darkening of her cheeks, the flash of amazement in her
black eyes that shone in the sunlight like polished ebony.
She wore her riding costume and it looked much the worse
for wear. The planes of her face had grown sharper, more
mature, but nothing could change the fire and grace of her
movements.

Her voice when she spoke was high-pitched but noncommittal.

"I thought you were dead. Your uncle wrote to me and told me your ship had been lost."

He explained what had happened to him, and said, "I am sorry that Uncle Ephraim stopped sending you the money. I have cashed out my interests in the company, and I have come to give you the sum I obtained. I want you to use it for Loma de Oro—or however you see fit."

She answered with light contempt. "I have no need of your money. I have been to the mines, and I have money of my own now. I always told you I could look after Loma de Oro. Did you think that just because you stopped sending me money, I would go down in defeat?"

It was his turn to look surprised.

"You struck it rich in the diggings? You went there alone?"

"Antonio is with me, and a vaquero from Loma de Oro." She told him the story. His astonishment, then his amused admiration, increased as he listened to her. It was exactly what he would have expected of her, he realized.

"Do I upset you by coming back?" he asked her finally.

She shrugged her shoulders. "Why should you upset me?"

"I lied to you," he said steadily, his eyes fastening on her face. "I used the money, even the gold rush, as an excuse to come back. I wanted to apologize to you for leaving so abruptly—for what happened the last night I spent at Loma de Oro."

She looked away from him and turned as if to leave.

"Wait, Tarifa! I must talk to you. I had no intention of breaking my word to you that night, or ever. I don't know what came over me, whether it was the drink or some devil inside me that I'd never known before. Whatever it was, you must believe I never meant it to happen. I came back for only one reason, to tell you how sorry I am."

He wanted to go to her, to put his hands on her shoulders, turn her to face him and make her listen. But he stood still, his arms at his sides, waiting.

When she faced him he felt a jolt at the complete lack of emotion in her eyes or face. This was not the Tarifa he remembered. She had changed. There was an air of weariness, even resignation about her that he had never seen her display before.

"It is over," she told him dully. "I told you long ago that we were not good for each other. It is not your fault the money did not come, I understand that. Loma de Oro is safe in any case. I no longer have need of anything you have to offer."

He met her cold gaze, and the bitter realization of the truth in her words was like standing naked in the teeth of a nor'easter.

"What," he asked slowly, "of our marriage?"

Again that Gypsy shrug that said nothing and could mean anything.

"Outside—of that one night, have I made you unhappy?" he asked carefully.

"No."

"Do you want a divorce—your freedom?"

"It does not matter. I do not intend to marry again. I told you marriage was not good for Gypsies."

"Then I will give you your freedom, if that will make you happy."

She stared at him.

"Do you think I would not take my freedom when I wanted it as I have always done? You could not stop me. You can neither give nor take anything from me again."

He said nothing, watching her as she stood slim and proud, as haughty and dangerous as a falcon. He would like to have taken her between his hands to hold her long enough to make her understand what she meant to him, what he felt for her, even though she might scratch his eyes out afterward. But he knew that to do it would be to sacrifice what little respect she still had for him. With an effort he stifled his emotions. Pressed them down hard into a secret compartment of his heart that he meant never to open again. He was discovering that it was possible to live with a fox gnawing at one's vitals, as the Spartan boy had done in the story.

"Is there anything I can do to help you, or Loma de Oro?" he asked finally.

"Yes," she said unexpectedly, as if the idea had just occurred to her. "Take Antonio and me and the gold safely to San Diego. Can you carry the horses? I have Guindilla with me."

"Of course," he said, relieved that she would accept
something from him.

"And Zenobio may wish to go with us," said Tarifa.

"There is plenty of room."

The voyage south to San Diego was speedy and unevent-
ful. In spite of the season, they ran into little rough
weather, and Tarifa ceased worrying about Guindilla and
the other horses in the hold. She and Antonio found much
to admire and to interest them in the fine new clipper.

"It is like a live thing dancing over the waves," Tarifa
told Jake Banner enthusiastically as they stood on deck.

"Aye, she be a real queen, ma'am," he said stiffly.

"*Faraóna.*"

"I beg your pardon, ma'am?"

"Queen—as my people say it in Romany."

Banner looked disapproving. A fine Yankee ship being
called by that outlandish pagan name. For all he knew she
was putting some Gypsy curse upon it, and his superstitious sailor's heart quailed. He had known of cursed ships
before, and all of them had come to a bad end. Either lost
at sea with all their crews, or found wandering the oceans
with slack sails and not a soul left on board. Ghost ships
with no one left to tell the tale of their abandonment.

Though Tarifa and Antonio took their meals with him
in his cabin, Kinkaid found no opportunity to speak with
his wife alone. She was clever enough to retire at night
before the men did, and she never entered the cabin without
Antonio by her side. Kinkaid reflected ruefully that all
her precautions were unnecessary. He had no intention of
bothering her, and yet he could understand her wariness of
him after what had happened at Loma de Oro when they
last parted.

The worst of it was that his desire for her, his need for
her, did not diminish. Like a hunger that could never be
appeased, he knew that he would go on craving the sight,
the sound, the touch of her for the rest of his days. And
that it would all be in vain. Like the torment of Tantalus,
the bittersweet agony would rage inside him unfulfilled,
until the day he died.

Watching her face, he saw that she had a cold repugnance, an antipathy, for him now, that was worse than
hatred. He was no longer important enough to her for her to

hate him. He felt her cold endurance of his presence when-ever they chanced to be in each other's company. She had said nothing more about her freedom, nor had he. And now he found perversely, that he did not want to lose that one last link with their past, that one claim he might still lay upon her whether or not they ever met again.

The night before they landed in San Diego Antonio excused himself after he had been in the cabin a moment, to return to his own quarters. He was still coughing, and though Kinkaid had tried to dose him with laudanum mixed with honey, the potion had had little effect upon him.

Zenobio had seldom left his cabin since they embarked, declaring loudly that he was dying of *mal-de-mer,* and that only the *aguardiente* bottle that he clutched to his breast day and night gave him any solace.

Tarifa was seated erectly with her back straight against the carved mahogany panel of the chair, and her hands clasped upon the table in front of her. The cabin steward had served them plates of soup and poured a white wine into their goblets, a light sauterne that had come from Ephraim Endecott's own cellars in Salem.

Bart leaned back in his chair and tried to keep his tone casual. "When we land, would you mind if I rode with you to Loma de Oro? I would like to see the others before I leave. And I want to talk to Patrick Havelock."

He looked firm-jawed and competent, she thought, in his carefully tailored blue coat, immaculate linen, and neat black string tie. The fingers curling around his wineglass were bronzed and powerful-looking, and she remembered the night when they had closed about her throat. The night he had borne her from the patio to her bedroom at Loma de Oro.

"What you have to say to Patrick Havelock is your business," she told him. "But I think it will be better if you do not go to Loma de Oro."

"Why?" His eyes were bright and hard on hers. "Are you afraid to have me come and say good-bye to them?"

She flushed and there was anger in her glance now.

"I have never been afraid of you, Bart Kinkaid, or of anything you could do. I do not want them upset by seeing you again. Tía Isabella is old, Soledad is frail, there are the children—"

"Why don't you say what you are really thinking!" he

broke in violently. "You don't trust me at Loma de Oro, anymore than you trust me in this cabin. You don't trust yourself alone with me, in spite of the fact that I have given you my word that nothing will ever happen between us again."

"You lie! I have told you my reasons for not wanting you at Loma de Oro." Eyes blazing, lips parted, she leaned forward and he could feel the heat of her anger. She had the power of generating small waves of heat and cold; it was uncanny yet stimulating, like no other feeling he had ever experienced. What a starkly magnificent creature she was. In spite of her lack of sensitivity, her bold rash changes, and the equally brave stands against the adversity that often followed. What a wife she would have made if she could have let herself. If he had been lucky enough to have been the man of her choice. And there would be a man in time; he felt sure of that. If not Pito Larios, some-one else. Suddenly he knew an unreasoning anger and jealousy. By all rights she should have been his, if he had only been able to make her see it. They suited each other. Whether she agreed with him or not, he was certain of it. Could it be possible that he felt all this while she felt no part of it? Could one human being love another, blindly, completely, and give off no spark of warmth that the other could recognize?

"I have never lied to you intentionally," he told her more quietly. "I will never do so. If it is your wish that I stay away from Loma de Oro—for whatever reason—I will abide by your decision. I did not mean to quarrel with you on this our last night. But I will ask one favor."

She eyed him suspiciously. "What is it?"

"Since you are in no hurry to have your freedom, may I ask that you keep my name—at least for the present."

"Why?"

"It will give me something—a memory if nothing else—of California and Loma de Oro."

She glanced at him curiously from her long eyes.

"You are so fond of the rancho?"

He stared down at the tablecloth and drew a square de-sign in grave deliberation with his knife.

"Yes, it was to have been the only home I had known since my mother died. I wanted to watch it grow and prosper, with you and the others. But since I spoiled all that, I only want to know that you still bear my name, as my wife."

She shrugged. "It doesn't matter. The name I bear is not important." She changed the subject abruptly. "What of the lands purchased with your money?"

"Our money," he corrected. "Keep it, and when you divide the rancho, divide it all among the heirs. Or do you ever intend to give the land back to the Alvarjos, Tarifa?"

She looked mean and sulky and she would not meet his eyes, except to glance at him from the corners of them when she thought he was not watching her.

"Ygnacio left that to my discretion. When they are capable of running their shares, I will give it to them."

"I don't believe you. I don't think you will ever give it to them."

"Premita undebē! What do I care what you believe?"

"What the rest of the world thinks has never concerned you, has it, Tarifa? But the time is drawing near when you will no longer be able to isolate yourself in independent comfort on Loma de Oro. The world around you is changing swiftly. If you have not realized it yet, it is because you have been lucky enough to protect Loma de Oro from the inroads of the foreigners. You have a different flag and a different country in charge now, and unless I miss my guess, California will wind up a state in the Union. Do you know what that means?"

She shrugged. "A part of the United States—we are that now. Why should I care?"

"Because you will be a citizen, responsible in certain ways to the government. And Loma de Oro will be part of United States soil."

"Loma de Oro will belong to me—and to the Alvarjos!"

"If you are fortunate enough to have your claim verified and acknowledged. It's my hunch there's going to be holy hell over these California land claims before it's all settled, especially since the gold rush. And since Pio Pico handed out grants and sold Missions right and left before he fled to Mexico, without having any valid right to do so. By the way, Zenobio tells me both Pico and Alvarjo are back, and Pico was put under arrest by the U. S. Government officials at Los Angeles."

"Yes, I have heard this also. But it will be years, will it not, before such claims can be actively disputed?"

"Perhaps."

"And a royal grant signed by the King of Spain cannot be revoked?"

"I don't know. I should think not. You have such a grant?"

She nodded. "Ygnacio left it to me. I will have Luis and Tiburcio Novato look it over."

"You still don't understand," Kinkaid said patiently. "Even if your grant is cleared, you can't go on like a separate little world at Loma de Oro."

"We will go on as we have always gone on." Tarifa frowned. "Loma de Oro can look after itself. We ask nothing of anyone."

He smiled wryly.

"Why is it so hard for you to ask, Tarifa, to accept from others?" His voice was genuinely puzzled.

"I need nothing from anyone else."

"Then you're unique in the world, my dear. None of us stands completely alone. It took me a long time to find that out.

"The captain of a ship rules with undisputed authority at sea, with the lives of every man aboard ship under his control. It's easy for authority to become domination—for control to become ruthlessness. There are many masters afloat, who command hell-ships because they have not yet learned to govern themselves and because they cannot brook the slightest insubordination against their wishes.

"They live in grim little Hades of their own making. They can't stand land, because their authority ends there, and so they are driven from port to port, like the Flying Dutchman, never daring to go ashore and never daring to stop their ceaseless, restless wandering."

"Why are you telling me all this?" Tarifa asked impatiently.

He put out his hand impulsively and covered one of hers with it, feeling her fingers tensed under his palm. "Because I want something better for you than the empty isolation you seem bent on making for yourself," he said quickly. "You've got to have something, someone, besides Loma de Oro, Tarifa. I had hoped that it might be me. But if not, then you must have something else. Someone else." He forced himself to add the last.

"I need nothing else. I am content."

He took his hand away from hers reluctantly when Antonio entered. He was carrying a square bottle of Jamaican rum that Jake Banner had given him.

"The mate says for me to try this in some hot buttered tea tonight, for my cough," he said brightly. "I'm sorry if I was gone so long. Mr. Banner is a most interesting man, Tarifa. He was telling me about the Sargasso Sea, the grave-yard of lost ships."

CHAPTER 36

With the help of the Indian, Salvador, Padre Cazon rose and made ready for Mass in the rude little adobe church at Pala. It seemed now so long ago that he had come here, after the closing of San Luis Rey, to care for the remaining Indians.

The Padre was very weak, for he would eat hardly anything, even when the worried Indians forced it upon him, for fear one of them would not be fed. At times his mind wandered light-headedly, but it was not an unpleasant sensation and he had managed so far to say daily Mass and give the neophytes the sacraments.

He was very grateful to Salvador, and sometimes he quite forgot how Salvador had come to him, for he was not a Pala Indian. Proud, aloof, he seldom spoke to anyone but Padre Cazon.

Some white soldiers had come by months before, looking, the lieutenant told the Padre, for a renegade Indian they had followed to the vicinity after shooting down a band of horse thieves in the sierras.

Padre Cazon and some of the Indian boys out searching for berries and roots had discovered him in a small arroyo at the foot of Mount Palomar. He lay in a ball, one leg hideously swollen from snakebite, his lips drawn back from bared teeth.

"Leave me alone, gray robe!" he panted, his eyes glittering with hatred.

"My son, let us at least see what we can do for your wound?"

The priest untied the sack fastened to his long wooden staff and laid it on the ground. He searched among the pitifully few articles it now contained, and then with a nod of satisfaction took up two objects. A knife and a length of rawhide.

Salvador tried to wrestle with them, but the boys, strong for their years in spite of their scant diet, stretched him out on the ground. The priest made a ligature above the swelling, and with a swift sure stroke, punctured the wound. Salvador lay still, never uttering a sound. Then Padre Cazon took up a small white stone, the chalklike Xaclul that Salvador's grandmother had given him after her baptism so long ago. He soaked it in his mouth as the Indians did, and applied it repeatedly to the open wound.

When they were able to move him, they carried him back to Pala, and Padre Cazon put him on his own cot and dressed the leg each day with an ointment the Indian women prepared from the seeds of red peppers.

As Salvador grew stronger he took on some of the menial duties Padre Cazon had been performing. Hauling water, helping the women to grind the small amount of corn, and tending the few cows. No one asked him to stay, but he did not leave. Instead, he slept at the foot of Padre Cazon's cot, and as the priest grew weaker and feebler he tended him like a mother cares for her babe. It was Salvador who fed him the little food they were able to force between his lips, always pretending that there was some journey they must take to aid a distant and luckless neophyte.

"You must have strength for the trip, Padre. No one

else can baptize, and the poor hombre's soul will be lost."

"Ah, but not so much. Only a little bite, Salvador, there are so many children. You say it is not far?"

"It is a long way, and we must hurry. You must eat so that you are strong enough to do God's work."

"Yes, yes you are right, Salvador. How wise you are, niño. How lucky we are to have you here at Pala."

When food and blankets came from Loma de Oro, Salvador secreted himself until Santos or the other vaqueros had gone, and then took charge of the goods for the Padre, locking them in the cupboard in the priest's room. It was Salvador, more often than not these days, who must divide them and make the corn and meal go as far as possible.

He found no joy in his task and little sympathy for the luckless Indians who hovered half-naked around Padre Cazon, asking in bewilderment for hope and sustenance. Yet he could not leave the Padre alone.

On a fall morning after a heavy rain, he saw one of the golden horses approaching. His thin lips drew down into bitter lines. The still all-powerful Alvarjos, how he hated them! They had used the Indians and the Missions to their own advantage, and had seen both go down in degradation and ruin without lifting a finger. Did Dona Tarifa Alvarjo think her little sop of food and clothing to Pala made up for her indifference of the past?

He was almost pleased to note that it was Dona Tarifa herself who rode into the Mission yard on Guindilla, a worried expression on her face.

She threw the reins of the stallion to him and he left them to trail on the ground.

"Where is Padre Cazon?" she asked haughtily.

He took his time about answering her, enjoying her silent rage.

"He is in the church. He has just finished Mass."

Tarifa turned on her heel and hurried toward the chapel.

At the sound of other horsemen, Salvador glanced up and found Santos and Tomas leading several horses loaded with foodstuffs.

Santos glanced at him in surprise.

"What are you doing here, Salvador?"

"I am helping the Padre, Santos. He is old and ill."

"*Sí*. So we told Dona Tarifa when she returned last night and she was much upset. She came as quickly as she could this morning. I am glad that you are here, *amigo*. Where shall we put these things?"

Salvador showed them the storeroom and then stalked away, his back like a ramrod.

"What ails him?" asked Tomas, grunting under a sack of meal. "He could have offered to help us."

"He is proud, *amigo*. And he is upset that we have found him here. It is hard for a man when he finds that he must go in God's way, and not his own."

"I do not understand you," Tomas grumbled. "We all know what he has been—a runaway, a cattle and horse thief. A murderer."

"*Sí*, perhaps that is all true, still he is here now and the Padre and God, no doubt, have need of him? When I see a man who has been wicked, *compadre*, I say to myself, how much more or less wicked would you have been in his shoes?"

"*Sí*," said Tomas, "that is true. But it is hard to reward a man's faith by demanding twice as much of him. It would be easier to be an unbeliever."

"I used to think that myself, *compadre*. But it is not true. A man cannot pull his own *carreta* alone, or if he does it is done awkwardly, with difficulty. But when there is a double yoke, each bearing the burden equally, and he takes God as his partner, he no longer has to worry about the load being too much for his strength. So the man who believes does not walk alone—and loneliness is man's greatest curse and his deepest fear. If we must pay for the privilege of faith, is it not a small price to pay?"

Tomas watched Salvador's retreating back with contempt. "And you think this one ever had faith in anything except himself?"

"Perhaps, when Padre Peyri was here."

"All he ever wanted from the Mission was what it could give him."

"One day when I was a youth," said Santos slowly, "I heard Padre Peyri say that to accept something from another was the first act of faith."

Tomas said nothing, but there was a disapproving scowl on his wizened, leathery face. The Padres had not filled his brain full of such nonsense. He had always been a faithful Catholic, attending Mass and making his Easter duty; he had always given value for value received, asking no more and no less. But he knew in his heart it was men like Salvador, backsliding, indigent Indians who, in abandoning the Missions, had been responsible for their downfall; just as a bright angel had once defied God and opened up the pits of Hell for all of luckless mankind. Not even Santos could change his mind about that.

Tarifa found Padre Cazon kneeling at the altar with two small, ragged Indian boys on either side of him. He had either removed his vestments or he had worn none, and someone had already put out the two slender candles on the altar.

Tarifa shivered in the damp cold of the church. She was appalled at the difference in Padre Cazon since she had last seen him.

His face was thin and wan, the eyes sunken in his head, and his whole body was so emaciated that he looked like a walking skeleton.

She spoke his name softly and he turned his head, looking at her blankly for a moment before the film seemed to lift from his eyes and he recognized her.

"Tarifa! When did you come?" Even his voice had a wavering insubstantial quality.

"Just this moment, Padre. I have brought you food and blankets and clothing."

"Ah! We have much need of these things, my child. My poor neophytes, they starve and suffer, and there is no one left to care for them. Come, we must go someplace where we can talk."

Tarifa and the little boys helped him to rise, and he leaned heavily upon them as they left the church and entered his quarters.

Tarifa insisted that he lie on the cot in the corner and she sent one of the boys for tea and for a flask of brandy in her saddle pockets.

When she had made him drink half the steaming liquid and eat a piece of bread and cheese, she drew up a stool to the cot.

She told him of her journey to the goldfields and of her meeting with Kinkaid in Monterey.

"Heaven be praised, he is back safely!" the priest murmured. "He will look after you now; he is strong, just as you are strong, *niña.*"

"I have no need of help now," she said impatiently. "I have gold of my own. I will build up Pala, Padre. You will have food and clothing, as much as you need. You will have no more worries from now on."

"So good," he murmured, "you have been so good to these poor unfortunates."

She did not tell him that she cared not a fig for all the neophytes at Pala, that it was only his life she wanted to save, and that she knew he would take nothing for himself unless she gave it to all. What in heaven's name was the matter with them at Loma de Oro that they had allowed him to come to this? Why hadn't they come themselves to force him to eat, to see to his welfare, as she would have done. As she had ordered them to do.

"First," she told him gently, "you must come to Loma de Oro, to rest and grow well again. You need Candelaria's rich food and your old bed at the hacienda. Then when you are strong you can return to care for your neophytes."

He patted her hand but there was a strange determination on his hollow-cheeked face.

"I cannot leave my children. Even for a little while, *niña.* They would not understand. You see, they have been abandoned by everyone. Everything."

"I will make them understand!" Tarifa said grimly. "You cannot stay here to starve and work yourself to death—how will that help them?"

"Knowing I am here is enough for them. They know that all is not lost while I am among them. It was not the fall of the Missions and the taking away of their material comforts that was the greatest cruelty, Tarifa. It was the smashing of their dreams, their beliefs. Faith is the thing man cannot live without.

"I am trying to teach them that faith is not in God alone, but in each other, if they will only search for it, guard its tiny flame with their own trust and belief."

"Padre, what good are words to them?" cried Tarifa. "All they know or care about is that they are hungry and cold! What good is faith to a starving man—can he eat it?"

"No, but he can starve by it, if necessary, without fear."

Tarifa stared at him, and a wave of uncertainty, then anger, washed through her.

He thought more of the needs of the neophytes than he did of her own. He was going to starve here with them at Pala, in order to prove to them that faith was stronger than death. He would leave her and she would be alone, and there was nothing she could do about it. There were so many questions she had wanted to ask him, so many doubts she wanted to have stilled. And now there was no time. No time at all.

"You must come with me," she said furiously. "You must! We will go at once. I will call Santos."

"No, Tarifa." The old strength was in his voice for an instant.

"Padre, I cannot leave you here in this place. You think the Indians need you—but I need you, too!"

"My child, I have always known of your need, and so has God. He will not abandon you."

"But I need you! I am alone—I am afraid."

She threw herself to her knees and buried her face against the wooden cot.

His hand rested on the tangle of her hair as if she had indeed been a child.

"God did not mean you to be afraid," he told her gently. "He made you strong, so that others might lean upon you. Like a bright staff of life, you have supported them in their hours of need. Even I have leaned upon you at times, is it not true?"

Tarifa raised her head and gazed into his sunken eyes. They were soft with tenderness and compassion.

"I will stay here with you then."

"No. Your place is at Loma de Oro. God has given us each our work to do. Many depend upon you there; many depend upon me here. But do not think when I die, as these other poor ignorant ones will think, that I have abandoned you to go your way alone. Do not think, because of these robes and the life I have chosen, that I am anything more than just a poor mortal man who has been striving to save his own soul. If I have known God more intimately, and believed in Him more strongly than you have, it is because I have actively sought Him out. God will not seek you out, my child, you must seek Him.

"I can only leave you what I have learned to live by. I believe in God because I have seen the wonderment of His creations upon this earth. You might say that so do the gentile Indians appreciate His wonders of nature, and you would be right. But I also see His spiritual wonderment. The life that everywhere abounds and perishes and yet never dies. The constant ebb and flow, the beginning and ending of life all around us, under us, over us, and the measure of eternity that keeps it moving. If this is only a portion of God's greatness, then how magnificent must be the whole of it? Can I believe all this and not keep my belief, my trust in Him and in His Divine Wisdom?

"Tarifa, if you do not believe, then faith will not be necessary. But if you believe, faith, like the dove of peace, will light on your shoulder and never leave you. If you have one, the other will surely come to you. It cannot be otherwise."

He closed his eyes and she saw the weariness etched on his gray face.

Penti! She must send for Penti to nurse him. Why hadn't she thought of that before?

She went to the door and called Tomas. She had Santos build up the fire in the small fireplace, and piled blankets upon the priest's cot. When he murmured that she should not be there she ignored his words. At noon an Indian woman brought a thick savory stew prepared from the food Tarifa had brought, and between them Salvador and Tarifa managed to get a few spoonfuls down the priest's throat.

At two o'clock he said weakly, "I would like to go back to the church."

"No," said Tarifa. "It is too cold and damp there."

But Salvador gave the priest a long searching look and then gathered him up in his arms. To the Indian he seemed to have no weight at all. It was like carrying a blanket wrapped around a few brittle branches.

He put the priest down in front of the altar and when he got to his knees, knelt to support him with his arms.

Tarifa had followed, a strange cold emptiness in her stomach. She knelt on the other side of the priest and put her arms around him.

Padre Cazon was saying his beads, an expression of beatific joy and peace on his worn face.

Tarifa stared at the altar as if she would crumble it with her eyes, but it still stood bleak and crude and wooden with only the gold monstrance like a winking eye, the one altar ornament that Padre Cazon had brought with him from San Luis Rey, to save the bare altar from complete nakedness.

"You will look after the monstrance?" Padre Cazon murmured to Salvador.

"*Sí, mi Padre.*"

"Tarifa?"

"Yes."

"You and Salvador will say the Act of Contrition with me?"

They mumbled the words, Tarifa stumbling over the half-forgotten phrases, but Padre Cazon's voice went on strongly to the end.

With the amen, she felt him sag against her arm and the beads drop from his lax fingers.

"*Dios!*" breathed Salvador as he lowered him gently to the altar steps.

Tarifa glanced at the priest's face and found it peaceful and content. Her own heart contracted with a terrible ache, as if something live had been torn out of it. So she had felt when she lost Lasho.

Mechanically she found herself repeating the words of the prayer they had just said, and strangely a modicum of peace settled over her. His words that had seemed so much gibberish to her when he was saying them, and when she was trying to persuade him to leave Pala, now came back to her and she felt herself wondering about the truth of them.

Her eyes wandered to the glittering monstrance on the drab altar, that winking all-seeing eye that the Padres claimed contained the body and blood of Christ, and she rose and went toward it, staring at the white heart of it. The white wafer that Padre Cazon's hand must have consecrated that morning at Mass.

"You must not touch it!" Salvador warned. "Only the Padres can do that. I must find another Padre and bring him here to take it."

But Tarifa was not listening. Long ago Padre Cazon had told her the story of Christ's first appearance to the apostles after His resurrection, and of how one of them, Thomas,

doubted and would not believe until he had touched the
wounds with his own finger to make sure they were real.

She stretched out her hand toward the monstrance and
her finger rested lightly on the glass covering the thin wafer
of bread.

Behind her, Salvador gasped and covered his face with
his hands, but Tarifa stood with her hands at her sides and
a deep amazement in her. She had expected crashes of
thunder, cymbals, bolts of lightning, a tumult to frighten
heaven and earth alike at her audacity. But what happened
was more starkly fantastic than any of those things.

Somewhere, starting at a very small corner of her being,
a great and mounting peace had taken possession of her.
All the restlessness, the driving need to accomplish, the
desire to dominate, to rule, was swept away and in its place
she found a strange contentment.

She was aware that she was wrought up over Padre
Cazon's death, that her Gypsy superstition and imagination
were capable of conjuring up an aura of romantic mysticism here in the lonely church with the monstrance displayed. But even when she went back to where Salvador
crouched over Padre Cazon's body, the feeling did not
leave her.

"We must take him to his room," she told the Indian
quietly.

"We will bury him under the altar, as was his wish,"
the Indian said, picking him up. There were tears on his
cheeks but no sign of sorrow on his face.

"What will you do?" asked Tarifa.

"I will stay here to look after the people as I promised
him. I am not a priest, but I can help them plant some
crops, and keep the church in repair. I can lead them in
morning and evening prayers."

"I will see that you get food and clothing each month,"
said Tarifa.

"*Gracias,* Dona Tarifa."

"You rode with Pito Larios?"

"*Sí.* He escaped to New Mexico."

"I am glad of that."

They buried Padre Cazon beside the altar, and because
there was no priest, Salvador read the prayers for the dead
and the entire congregation said the rosary, raising their

voices in the Aves and Pater Nosters like obedient but stricken children.

Tarifa and Santos gathered fragrant sumac branches for the altar. She found herself watching the thin legs and emaciated faces of the uncomplaining children. This was why Padre Cazon had not been able to eat. Their faces would haunt her at her own dinner table from now on. What if that had been Lasho standing there with sharpened bones and lackluster eyes? For the first time in her life Tarifa felt unselfish compassion for another human being, and a righteous indignation that was not brought about by some infringement on her own personal rights.

"Bring them some more corn," she told Santos, "and some cattle to butcher."

"*Sí*, Patróna."

They met Tomas and Penti just as they were leaving camp.

"I am sorry to hear he is dead," said the old Gypsy. "And Capitán Kinkaid will be sorry to hear it; too. He and Don Zenobio are on their way here."

Tarifa was upset. She did not want them at Pala. She had not seen Kinkaid since they parted at San Diego. He had promised that he would not come to Loma de Oro. Had he somehow received word of the Padre's illness? Or had he found out about Soledad?

When she had returned to Loma de Oro from the mines, it had been to find the rancho in a state of uproar following Titus Judah's visit and the kidnapping of his wife. She could not have gone willingly. And Kinkaid was a friend of Mabrey's, and still her husband. He would undoubtedly consider it his duty, if he knew, to go in search of Judah and Soledad.

Tarifa did not want him to do any such thing. She had every intention of handling Judah by herself. If Soledad was foolish enough to go with him, or to allow herself to be taken by him, which was practically the same thing, then she deserved what she was getting. But Tarifa had no intention of allowing Titus Judah to get away twice with taking Soledad by force from under her own protection.

Zenobio and Bart met them when they were halfway back to the house.

"So he is gone." Zenobio shook his head unhappily.

"And I did not even get to confess my sins to him."

"You mean you did not get to use him to demand absolution for your own sinful soul!" thundered Tarifa.

"You are hard, Tarifa. You have no heart, the old man complained. "He was a priest, it was his duty to hear the sins of the penitent and comfort them in their hour of need."

"And so he did, until the sins of the world must have been coming out of both ears! Did you never think of him as a man as well as a priest? Did you ever wonder what *his* sins were, his worries, his weaknesses?"

"You blaspheme, *muchacha!*"

Kinkaid's eyes met hers and there was a new respect and admiration in their gray depths.

"She means, Don Zenobio, that life holds a mirror up in front of us, and if we do not like what we see, we have only to remember that it is our own reflection unadorned."

Tarifa gave him a look of surprised gratitude. She had not known he was so perceptive.

"I've never heard such idiotic drivel," Zenobio said, jerking his horse around. "I think the Padre's death must have robbed you both of your senses."

They galloped back to the rancho in silence, through the cold wind that had arisen and Zenobio rode gruffly on alone when Kinkaid tarried at Loma de Oro.

"Will you come in?" Tarifa asked.

"I promised you that I would not bother you and I intend to keep my word."

She shrugged. It was bitter cold in the wind, and there was a coldness inside her that she knew even brandy could not melt. She would have to tell Tía Isabella and the others that Padre Cazon was dead. It was not a task that she relished.

"Come in with me while I tell them," she said impulsively, and she saw a look of faint pleasure warm his eyes for a moment.

He followed her into the *sala* and stood quietly at her side while she told the family her news. They were all assembled there, except Soledad and Penti, but Kinkaid, his eyes riveted on Tarifa, did not notice.

Tía Isabella cried out and then bent double in her chair, as if the pain were too acute to bear.

The others stood like statues, as mute as dolls.

"You let him starve himself to death while I was at the mines!" Tarifa cried fiercely. "I told you to look after him. You made me a promise."

"I sent food and clothing," Isabella said miserably.

"And did you ever go to Pala yourself to see how he was using it?" Tarifa cried, smashing the tabletop with her whip. "Did you ever sit by his side and see that he ate a decent meal, or put a cloak around him when he dug in the open fields in the wind? No!"

"Please," Tía Isabella said. "You know what Padre Cazon meant to us all, Tarifa. We would have done anything for him. It is sinful to quarrel now that he is gone."

"You make me sick, the lot of you!" spat Tarifa, her eyes blazing. "Your words are very touching, and as hollow and useless as your family pride. You would 'do anything,' but what *did* you do, beyond ordering a vaquero to carry some supplies to Pala?"

Even Tía Isabella glanced away from her accusing eyes, and shied back from the biting contempt in her voice.

"You are worthless, all of you! You stay here and take my browbeating because you are afraid to go anywhere else. You want what I have built, but you do not like working for it. Once I thought that you could become something, all the things your father wanted you to be, by toil, by effort. By believing in yourselves and Loma de Oro. Not by believing only in the empty glories of the past. But you would not listen to me. Always you wanted the easy way out. And when you found out that it did not come, you lost heart.

"You would not learn to fight, to keep on fighting. Especially you would not stand shoulder to shoulder with me, because I am a Gypsy. Because you despised me. Well, I tell you this—I despise you! I despise everything you stand for, all the hollow mockery of your past, all the lazy indolence of your present, and the emptiness of your future! Stay, with your useless dreams of the past, until the walls of the hacienda cave in about your ears, and the herds are gone, and Loma de Oro, like Padre Cazon, can no longer serve you!"

"Tarifa." Bart's hand on her shoulder drew her to face him. "Come with me a moment?"

She scowled at him, and then marched from the room leaving the Alvarjos stunned and silent behind her.

She went into the study and he followed her, shutting the door behind them. Tarifa stood in front of the empty fireplace and turned to face him. The room was damp and cold. It was like the family to have forgotten to light a fire in the room because she was not there to order it done.

"What good are words now," she said wearily. "I have used them all up."

"The wrong ones. But there are others."

He came to stand beside her and he knew that something in her had changed. Padre Cazon's death must have affected her profoundly.

"Words of love are always more powerful than those of hate. I loved the Padre, too. He was one of the few people I have ever known who dared to be honest with himself. He was like you in that respect, Tarifa."

"Like me?" For an instant she seemed pleased.

"Yes. You have always been honest, brutally honest with others, and even more so with yourself."

He paused to light a cigar, and blew the smoke toward the empty grate.

"Did you ever wonder why I married you?" he asked.

She glanced up at his face and found it neither amused nor passionate, merely watchful.

"Because you wanted a part of Loma de Oro," she said finally in an impatient tone.

"I could have bought all the land I wanted elsewhere. In spite of what you think, Loma de Oro is not the finest land in California."

Her eyes narrowed.

"Near San Luis Obispo the grass is better and so is the water. Monterey has a better terrain."

"That is not true!"

"I assure you that it is. And if you are as honest as I'm convinced you are, you will admit it."

She said nothing, but her hands were clenched at her sides. Small, hard hands. He wanted to take them in his own but knew that he would not.

He tossed the cigar, less than half-smoked, into the grate and put both hands lightly on her shoulders. She started to twist away from him but he held her still with a steady gentle pressure.

"Padre Cazon knew a secret of mine, a secret I made him vow never to reveal to you. He went to his grave with it still locked between his lips, and I realize now that I did him an injustice, and you, too. He knew the real reason I married you. Ellen Havelock guessed it, and so did Uncle Ephraim. Even Zenobio knew, but you never suspected, did you?"

She looked at him wildly. "I don't know what you're talking about!"

"But I want you to know. I ran away once. I was prepared to leave again now without telling you, because I thought you would be happier. But I have realized today how closely life and death are linked. The future is in God's hands, but this moment is in mine.

"Look at me, Tarifa! I married you for one reason, and one reason only. Because I loved you. I must have loved you from the very beginning, when I first saw you half-naked in the women's quarters at Mission San Diego. I must have loved you all the time I thought I loved Dolores and wanted her, even on that night I came to Loma de Oro to kill you. I have never stopped loving you.

"But I knew that I could never tell you of my love if I hoped to keep you. You would have thrown it back in my face, as you have thrown aside the feelings of every person who has come your way. You have always despised every gentle emotion. I knew that you had no love for me. But now, when we have come to the end of everything, I wanted you to know the truth."

Her eyes, fastened on his, were as black with intensity as an animal's, and as devoid of feeling. Lively, hard, inscrutable—there was nothing for him there, yet he ached to take her in his arms, hold her close to him for one last moment. But it would solve nothing. Serve no useful purpose, except to open old wounds.

"I am not mistaken," he asked slowly. "You do not love me? You never could?"

She glanced away from him and the line of her lashes made a curving half-moon on her bronze cheek.

"You said I was honest. I have not lied to you before."

"No, I don't believe you have," he said.

"I am grateful to you, Bart, but I do not love you."

His eyes moved over her face and there was a sharp disappointment and violent naked hunger in their depths for a moment, and then it was gone, replaced by the amused twinkle that had at first so infuriated her when she felt it directed toward her. Now she could smile back at him as if they shared some secret joke.

"The fortunes of war," he said easily. "I gladly dip my colors to you; it has been an honor and a privilege to love a woman like you. A pity, though," he sighed. "We would have made an unbeatable team."

She stepped forward, put her arms about his neck, and kissed him warmly on the motuh.

He bent closer and she could feel his heartbeat. But when she drew back he let her go without protest.

"You said we were no good for each other," he asked. "Do you still believe that?"

"Padre Cazon answered that for me, Bart. He said that he had his work, and I had mine. It is the same with you and me. You belong to the sea, and I belong to Loma de Oro."

"But if I were willing to give up the sea?" There was gentle raillery in his tone.

"You couldn't. I saw the way you looked at your new ship, the beautiful clipper, as if she were a desirable woman. The way I have looked at Guindilla and the palominos. You cannot give up what is in your blood. A wife should be ready to follow her husband—"

"I do not ask that—"

"But she should be willing to do so. It is the belief of my people, and my own. If I were more Romany than Moor, I would have been able to go away with Pito Larios when he asked me. I would be able to go with you now. But part of me loves the land and the animals, part of me wants to build and create."

"And you could not do that with a husband to help you—a family of your own?"

She shook her head impatiently. "It is too late for that. The things I love are not the things a husband would want his wife to love best. What husband would give his wife first place always, and what would she think of him if he did? No, for many reasons it is impossible. I did not pretend to love you, Bart."

"I did not ask it, or expect it," he replied solemnly. "I only wanted to love you, but that you would not permit."

"I am not sure I understand love," she said slowly. She turned to sit down on the arm of a chair and there was a pink color in her dark cheeks that he found entrancing. "The Gypsies rave of love, they sing and dance of it, but what they really mean is passion. When they are tired of one another they are quick enough to go their own ways. Pito Larios' idea of love was like that. As long as there is an attraction between two people they are raised to the heights of ecstasy. But such things do not last. It is why I thought little of the love I saw in the caves of the Sacro Monte.

"Ygnacio's idea of love was to treat me as a child, his most privileged child. He gave me everything I asked for, and though I loved him in gratitude, as a child will love an indulgent parent, I was not satisfied.

"Penti says that I have never felt the fires of true passion. She is wrong. Passion is an emotion that we start feeling from the moment we first suckle at our mother's breast. Every animal is capable of feeling it, to a greater or lesser degree. But is it enough to satisfy man, if he is more than an animal—as Padre Cazon claimed?"

"No," Kinkaid answered, "it is not. I never thought that it would be enough for you, anymore than it is enough for me. But love is not just a passion, Tarifa."

"How do you know what love is? To every individual it must mean a different thing. Padre Cazon's love was a blind faith in something he could neither see nor touch, and yet there was passion in it."

"Yes. And something more, perhaps the secret core of it all. To love is to give. Not an easy thing for selfish human beings. And the degree to which you can give yourself to another is the degree in which you can love and be loved."

Tarifa said, "We should have talked like this years ago. We have never tried to understand each other."

"We have tried, I think, but we have been like ships each sailing a different direction." He put his hand over hers where it rested on the chair back. "Is it really too late for us, Tarifa?"

"Padre Cazon knew that I did not love you when he married us?" she asked wonderingly.

"Right afterward. I told him so."

"And he thought the marriage good?"

"No. He was shocked. He wanted me to tell you how I felt, but I couldn't. I was afraid I would lose you entirely if you knew. Was I right?"

She nodded but there was a faint smile on her lips. "I would have left you because we had made a business bargain, and I would not have trusted you then to keep it."

"And now?"

"Now, I would know that you could keep your word no matter what you felt."

"In spite of what happened that night?"

"Because of it. You Americanos are funny people; you will do something wrong and then spend the rest of your lives making up for it. This is foolishness. Make your amends and then forget about it. Even the Church does not demand that you spend your life in sackcloth and ashes after you have confessed a mortal sin. You do your penance and go on."

"And how do you feel about the Church Padre Cazon and Don Ygnacio believed in so strongly?" he asked curiously. He saw her frown in concentration.

"I do not believe that Padre Cazon could have died with such peace and contentment unless he knew that God was there on that altar. And I cannot believe that Salvador, a horse thief and a murderer, would have come back unafraid to serve a God he was not convinced was more powerful than his own desires.

"I believe that Padre Cazon's God is there on the altar. If He will let me, I will make my peace with Him. I no longer blame Him for Lasho's death, and I believe that my son is in Heaven and I will see him one day if I made amends for my past sins. I will help Salvador with the Indians at Pala, as Padre Cazon wanted. I will deed them some grazing land, give them some animals, and help them put in a crop."

"You have changed," said Bart, raising her hand to his lips. "You were a temperamental child, and then a willful girl."

"And now?" She smiled at him.

"You are a woman—a magnificent woman. And I am proud of you."

She got up from the chair and went to throw wood violently into the empty grate.

"This place is like a tomb! Unless I am here to get things done, they do nothing."

He bent to light the shavings for her but she took the taper from him and stooped to do it herself.

If I could only learn, he thought, if I could only learn to let her be the kind of woman she must be. Coldly contemptuous or wildly passionate—mercurial, independent, unpredictable, but always fascinating. Always Tarifa.

He thought that he would never be able to erase the memory of her dark brooding face above the flames as she stared into their fiery depths like some young witch waiting to begin an incantation.

He was surprised at the softness in her voice when she spoke.

"Just because I believe in God, do not think that I am going to become a saint. Spend my time saying silly beads, or crouching like a statue in front of an altar or die in rags catering to the wants of a bunch of indigent Indians!"

He laughed.

"I would never have suspected any such thing of you. And I'm sure God in His Wisdom does not."

"You're laughing at me?"

"Not at you, my dear, with you. I suppose for your own generous act of faith you shall expect something in return?"

"Yes. I shall expect that for my good works, my faith shall not be taken from me—as it once was." She explained about the rain and Lasho's death. "I could not bear to lose my belief again."

"You will not lose it, Tarifa. Padre Cazon would have been very pleased with you."

He came to pull her gently to her feet. One finger lifted her chin and he gazed into her long inscrutable eyes.

In the endless watches of the night on deck he would remember them. Not with the joy and warmth he had once hoped to see in their depths for himself, but as they really were; speculative, wary, intense. Every feature of her proud, haughty face was carved upon his mind. Her golden skin seemed to have faded a shade paler, her nostrils were dilated, he could feel the warmth of her flesh through his hands, and her body quivered but he did not kiss her. Instead he said, "Your heart will tell you if what you are doing is right."

She seemed disappointed. "You would trust a human heart? I would not."

"I would trust yours," he said, and took her in his arms and, in spite of his resolution not to, kissed her.

She did not struggle, yet neither was she passive. He knew she fought him in some mysterious silent way that he did not understand, but when he released her she left him to walk quietly to the other end of the room.

"There is nothing more to say."

He knew then the full truth of her words.

It was over. If there had ever been anything between them to be over. He had possessed her in degree, her lips, her mind, her body, her interest in a mutual project—the safeguarding of Loma de Oro. She had been his wife, in name at least, and once he had possessed her body by force. But he had never possessed the only part of her he had ever wanted, her heart. Perhaps it was as she said, cold and empty and incapable of affection? Perhaps other emotions drove her too hard to permit love to enter it. Whatever the reason, he had lost. He would never have her love, nor more than likely would any other man, he now realized. It was small consolation. He would almost rather have had her go to another man than know she was incapable of love at all.

Someone knocked at the door and Bart felt relieved at the interruption.

"Come in," said Tarifa.

John Mabrey stood in the doorway, and Bart saw with surprise that a heavy pistol was strapped to his thigh. His fact was drawn and white and there was a hushed intensity about him like a lion waiting to spring.

Behind him stood Luis and Patrick Havelock.

Mabrey embraced Kinkaid, but like a man in a dream to whom nothing, no matter how startling, is quite real.

"Bart! I knew you were alive, I knew it! I told Tarifa so. It is good to have you back, so very good."

Luis said, "I must talk to you, Tarifa. Tiburcio and I have received a communication from an American lawyer at Monterey, who says that he represents Capitán Titus

Judah. He demands Soledad's property under penalty of federal lawsuit."

"Judah!" cried Bart. "He's here?"

They told him then, each adding his own interpretation of why Judah had dared return, and what he hoped to do with the property.

Tarifa asked, "He can do this, Luis? He can claim a share of Loma de Oro?"

"Yes."

"But under your father's will the property was not to be divided until I agreed it was right to do so?"

"Under the American law," said Luis, "the property left to heirs becomes theirs when they are legally of age, twenty-one years, or when they marry. Judah can claim Soledad's share. There is no doubt of it."

Mabrey said, "You could offer to buy him out, if the swine can be dealt with at all."

"I will never give him a penny or an inch of Loma de Oro," Tarifa spat. "I will kill him first."

"The only thing I'm interested in at the moment," said the doctor, "is getting Soledad back safely."

"Get her back?" Kinkaid asked in a hollow voice. "You mean she isn't here?"

Mabrey's face was white to the bone. "He took her—or she went with him, to save the children."

"Took her! And what have you done?"

"It was while Tarifa was gone. We sent out mounted parties, scoured the countryside, sent word north and south."

"He went by sea, of course. Didn't you think of that?"

"Yes. We tried to get information of every ship in port or on the coast. But there were so many, and none of them answered the description of Judah's ship."

Kinkaid shook his head impatiently. "His own, if he hasn't already gotten a new one, was probably stashed away behind a channel island. He must have used a smaller boat to reach it."

"We must get her back," Mabrey said. "He is a devil, and she is afraid of him."

Kinkaid's face was like stone. He could still remember her sitting in the little house in Salem, with her face pressed close to the cold glass to catch the pale rays of the sun.

"His lawyer is coming here?" Tarifa asked.

"We are to meet him in San Diego tomorrow. You must come with us, and Tiburcio will meet us there," Luis said.

"May I speak to you alone?" Mabrey asked Kinkaid.

"Of course. Come into the patio, John."

The two men walked down the veranda under the whispering grapevines. The wind had died but there was still a chill in the air.

"I cannot tell you what knowing you are alive has done for me, Bart," said the doctor wearily. "I had about given you up, given up my belief in the mastery of life over death, of good over evil."

"You believe that now, John?"

"Every doctor must believe it, in his secret heart, if he is to practice his calling. You think it is strange that I could think that after losing Lupe and all my children? And now Soledad?"

"No. I think it is brave and sane."

"You see, Bart," Mabrey went on, "I love Soledad. I tried to love her as one would a sick child at first, as I would have loved one of my own daughters. But I knew from the beginning that the love I felt for her was the love of a man for a woman. I knew it was hopeless—I'm sure she did too, but it would not die.

"When I found that devil had taken her—I'm going to get him, Bart. At first I didn't think that I could go out and kill a man in cold blood, but now I am going to do just that."

"No," Bart said gently, "you're not. This isn't your sort of tea party, John. I'll find him, and I'll deal with him. And I'll send Soledad back to you safely, never fear."

"I can't let you do my job, Bart. I'm sorry."

"You don't even know where to look."

"He will be in San Diego tomorrow to meet Tarifa, if she goes."

Kinkaid said nothing, but his eyes moved over Mabrey's determined face with a feeling of frustration. The doctor would be killed, of course. It was like sending a pigeon out to fight a hawk. Finally, he said, "Let me help you find him at least? I know his ways and his haunts better than you do. I regret to say, Titus Judah and I have a great deal in common."

"Heaven forbid! You're nothing like that animal Judah!"

"Only because I haven't wanted the same things badly and been willing to pay his price to get them. It's all a matter of values, I suppose, and conscience. Judah has strength without conscience. He's free to go his own way without a qualm."

"Not for long," said Mabrey grimly.

Kinkaid looked up sharply. "What are you going to do?"

"Take him if I can, and turn him over to the civil authorities. Kill him if I must. In any case I will save Soledad."

"The knight in shining armor?"

Mabrey flushed. "This is no boyish dream, I assure you."

"Then why not be realistic about it? On what charges will you turn Judah over to the authorities?"

"For taking Soledad against her will."

"She is his legal wife. She might even say, for many reasons, that she went with him of her own free will. Judah would laugh you to shame."

Mabrey looked at him uncertainly. "Then there is only one thing to be done."

"Let me do it for you, John. I made a promise to Tarifa long ago to deal with him."

"No," said Mabrey stubbornly, "it is my personal affair now. He turned to go but Penti stood in the patio doorway staring at Kinkaid.

"You must not go, *rya*," she said in the flat Gypsy monotone he remembered so well.

"I must go, Penti." Their eyes met across the room, and he found hers somber and brooding.

She shook her head. "I know why you go, you and the doctor. It is a very bad time. I have looked at the cards. Especially it is bad for you, Capitán Kinkaid. I have seen your name surrounded by darkness and blood, much blood!"

"Penti, I appreciate your interest," Kinkaid said, "but I must go with Dr. Mabrey. You will tell Tarifa good-bye for me?"

"There will be no need. She will know you are never coming back, just as I do."

"What is this gloomy foreboding?" Mabrey asked irritably.

"When the cards and the stars are in a certain way,

nothing can change them," said Penti, "or the course of events they foretell."

"Nonsense! Don't listen to her, Bart. She must have drunk one of her own witches' brews. Come along!"

Kinkaid stood for a moment looking at Penti, wondering at her look of fierce concentration. Suddenly she ripped something from her neck and came to press it into his hand.

"Take this, *rya!* It will protect you—it is my amulet. Take it—wear it! It cannot save you if the gods are against us. But if you wear it, there is a chance—a chance! Here, inside your shirt, that is where you must always carry it." Her fingers fumbled with the buttons of his shirt and in an instant she had transferred the grimy leather bag containing the amulet from his hand to a place between his skin and his shirt.

Kinkaid, scarlet to the temples, watched her go with mingled feelings of amusement and chagrin. He would never understand these Gypsies. Perhaps that was the answer: Never to try to understand them, just accept them as they are—unpredictable, and somehow wonderful to behold.

He was thoughtful as he followed Mabrey from the hacienda. Penti was right. He would never return to this house. He knew it as clearly as he had once known he would command a ship. He had known happiness here, and unhappiness, joy and despair, pain and ecstasy. The things that most houses meant to you if you had shared them with people you loved. Once he had hoped it would be his real home, but, even then, he supposed he had known it could never be. Even Tarifa must feel at times that this house belonged evclusively to the Alvarjos. Don Ygnacio had built it for his bride, for the sons and daughters who would come to him. Every tile, every tree and shrub, was a monument to Don Ygnacio and Dona Encarnacion Alvarjo. What a man built up could not be swept away so quickly after all, could not be taken over by someone else as if he had never existed.

Kinkaid thought of his own black future, of the ships he would command, bigger and faster clippers to sweep the trade of the world into American ports. And the emptiness that would be in his heart.

When he was too old to go to sea any longer he would be wealthy, no doubt, and beached and crochety as an old whale, like so many old salts landlocked in Salem and Gloucester and New Bedford. He could tell the young sailors then of his trips to California that had once taken a year to make, and of the hides and tallow he had traded for, the color and excitement that had been the beginning of the Golden State, for it would be a state in the Union, he was sure of that. And they would laugh, with tolerant amusement, at the slow old ways, while their minds and energies were taken up with newfangled things. Steam probably. For in time steam would sweep the sails from the seas. Even he knew that machines were always more efficient than men. But machines had no mind, no soul, and so they could only grow at the rate man's mind and ingenuity expanded. But whatever came, the power of the seas and the winds would remain the same. It was a comforting thought. You could meddle, you could experiment, you could discover the secrets of the universe and all that was in it, but you could never change Nature herself.

In San Diego, Mabrey hunted feverishly among the ships in the harbor questioning every seaman he could lay hands on about the *Vulcan,* or *Heron,* as she might now be known. No one had seen such a ship, let alone a red-headed captain and a young señora of Soledad's description.

"But he *must* be nearby," Mabrey cried, "if he is to meet with his lawyer and Tarifa tomorrow."

"Go aboard my ship and get a good night's rest," said Kinkaid. "Let me scout around a little?"

"I'll come with you."

"You're worn out, John. Go to Jake Banner and tell him to meet me at Chavira's wine shop. Go to bed on the *Celestial Queen.* I promise I'll be aboard at dawn, and I won't do a thing till I talk to you. Fair enough?"

Mabrey's eyes searched the younger man's and found only level truth there. The doctor groaned with his own weariness and inadequacy. All his life he had just missed serving those he loved. He could not fail this time.

"I will return to my own place after I see Banner," he said. "Send me word in the morning if you have any news?"

Chavira's was crowded with Americans, Mexicans, California *gente de razón,* and a motley collection of other nationalities who had drifted to the southern port in the holds and among the crews of foreign ships on their way to or from San Francisco.

Chavira had prospered from the days when Tarifa had danced in his dirt-floored cantina.

The building had been enlarged, and a magnificent bar of mahogany and teakwood installed along one side with an immense plate-glass mirror behind it.

The floor was now tiled and the tables covered with green baize. At one end, a full Mexican orchestra played. And the six dark-skinned bartenders all wore green velvet jackets trimmed with gold braid, and bright red ties.

Kinkaid ordered whiskey and went to the far corner of the bar out of the way of the milling crowd, to await Jake Banner.

Macario Canejo rose from a table nearby and came to join him.

"Hace mucho tiempo que no te veo, Capitán Kinkaid?"

"Indeed, a very long time since we met, Don Macario." He was thinking that Macario had outgrown his innocuous good looks, and was now merely a bitter, dried-up wisp of a man with a faint contempt in his eyes as he glanced at the Americans grouped around the room.

"You find many changes, Capitán Kinkaid?"

"Many. California's gold has changed the world."

Macario frowned.

"The gold? Ah, yes. But it was of other things of which I was speaking. You know the Alvarjos and I rode with Andres Pico at San Pascual?"

"I had heard, yes."

"A glorious battle. An honor to our superior California horses and riders."

"So they have told me."

"You knew our brave Francisco lost his life? He died a hero's death, I can tell you, señor."

"I am sure you all fought bravely," Kinkaid said uncomfortably. He could see that Canejo was one of the few rebel fanatics left among the Californians, and he had no time or desire to hear the details of the Californians' victories, and their complaints against the Americans.

"Governor Pico had a right to deed the properties of the Missions to his friends before he was forced to flee," said Macario belligerently. "Would you not have done the same if an outside force had been entering your country, driving you out?"

Kinkaid said nothing.

"Now your American government is saying such grants were illegal. Everything must be according to American law. We had no such law before, why is it suddenly the only law that is right?"

"I don't know much about any law but moral law," said Kinkaid. "It is wrong to give away what does not belong to you. The Missions were still church property, weren't they?"

Macario waved his hand impatiently. "If it is necessary to get a lawyer or have a paper for everything, half of California will pass into other hands. Is that fair—is that American justice?"

"They will undoubtedly set up a land commission to look into all property claims," Kinkaid said. "If you will be patient—"

"Patient! I notice the Americanos with claims to settle are not patient! They rush to the nearest lawyer. Even your precious wife is not immune, for all her 'legal arrangements' before Don Ygnacio died!"

Kinkaid's hand closed over the Californian's jacket, drawing him forward as if he were a sack of grain.

"What are you talking about, Canejo?"

"The—the lawsuit Capitán Judah is bringing against her to claim Soledad's share of Loma de Oro."

Kinkaid's eyes widened in surprise. It was not what he had expected.

"What do you know about Captain Judah and Soledad?"

"What—everyone knows," Macario gasped. "She has returned to him as his wife, and he will claim her land from Tarifa—legally."

"You believe Soledad went back to him of her own free will?" There was scorn in Kinkaid's tone.

"Why not?" Macario's voice was bitter. "Her husband is one of the exalted Americanos, isn't he? And he has a fine new ship, he can give her everything, more than any poor Paisano Californiano can give his wife and children."

"You have seen Soledad and Judah?"

Macario straightened himself as Kinkaid set him free.

"I am their friend; have I not known the capitán since he first came to California?"

Kinkaid failed to mention that Macario had also professed to be Nazario's friend, and had once pretended anger at Judah's treatment of the Alvarjo women. Hard times and political defeat had no doubt changed his viewpoint.

"Is Captain Judah in San Diego?" Kinkaid asked. "I have to see him."

"I have no idea where he is now," Macario said carefully. "I saw him two days ago."

"On his ship—here?"

"On his ship, but not here, señor. And I am not at liberty to tell you where I saw him. I have given him my word, and Dona Soledad also, that I would tell no one. The word of a Canejo is sacred, señor."

Kinkaid's lips twisted wryly. "I'm sure of it, Don Macario. I only crave to know one thing, the ship's name and her rig."

"No, señor, you will not get such information from me."

Kinkaid could see Jake Banner moving toward them across the room, parting the crowd before him like the prow of a man-o'-war.

"You sent for me, sir?"

"Yes, Mr. Banner. This gentleman, you may remember, is Don Macario Canejo?"

Macario bowed stiffly from the waist, and Banner touched his cap.

"Yes, sir."

"*Buenos nockes,* señor."

"*Buenos noches,*" Banner replied stiffly.

"Señor Canejo doesn't understand much American lingo," Kinkaid said quietly to his mate. "He knows Titus' ship and where he is, I believe."

"He won't talk, sir?"

"No. A point of honor."

"Leave him to me, sir." Banner's blue eyes took on a glow of determination.

"No. I'll leave alone, as if I'm going back to the ship. You stay here, make a night of it, and follow him when he leaves. I think he'll try to get word to Judah that I want to see him. I only want to know where Judah is. If you find out, report to me aboard the *Celestial Queen*."

"Aye, sir."

Kinkaid turned to Macario and ordered drinks for the three of them.

"I must be getting back to my ship," he said, "but I would like to offer a last toast to California. I'm sure you will drink to that, Don Macario?"

"With pleasure, Capitán Kinkaid."

"To California then—her past and her future."

"Saludos, amigos."

"Down the hatch," Banner growled, and swallowed his neat whiskey in one gulp, wiping his mouth with the back of his broad hand.

Kinkaid laid some gold pieces on the bar and shook hands gravely with Canejo.

"Adiós, Don Macario. Hasta luego."

"Adiós, Capitán. Vaya con Dios."

When Kinkaid had gone Banner bowed stiffly to Macario, and moved off to join a rowdy group of sailors from the brig *Comet*. For the next hour he laughed with the American seamen, as they ordered round after round, though he downed few of them himself, and kept Macario in focus out of the corner of his eye.

When Macario finally paid his bill from a thin purse, Banner let him have a good minute before he followed, moving swiftly for his years and girth. Surprised roisterers swung out of his way at the pressure of his bulk, and held their anger at the sight of the grim determination on his craggy face.

Once outside in the brisk night wind, he put a drunken roll into his walk, and staggered off in the direction in which he remembered the Canejo house lay.

There were too many drunken American seamen on the dimly lit streets to make Banner conspicuous. And his luck held. Macario was standing by a horse in front of his house while a serape-draped peon tightened the cinches of his ornate saddle.

Banner looked along the street wildly. If Canejo was going to ride somewhere he would have to follow, and by the looks of Macario's horse he would have to have a fast mount.

In the dark all the horses, tethered head down, looked alike. Then he saw one rear its head at a sound coming from the cantina opposite. A short but deep-chested blue roan, with a wide intelligent forehead and an American-made saddle.

Banner raced across the street, put his head inside the low smoke-filled room and bawled, "I'm Jake Banner, mate of the *Celestial Queen* in the harbor. Fifty dollars gold to hire the blue roan in front!"

"Sold!" laughed an American voice. A tall man in buckskins detached himself from the bar and came to the open door. "Luke Pettie, of Santa Fe." His eyes measured Banner with satisfaction, and his handshake found a matching iron in the sailor's grasp.

"In a hurry," said Banner, passing gold into his free hand.

"He's a good horse. Broke him myself. Return him here anytime. You don't want company?"

"No, thankee. A little private matter."

Pettie winked, and Banner went scarlet when he suggested, *"Bonita señorita?"* But he didn't wait to deny it.

The horse was all that his owner had claimed he would be, well-broken and dependable. Macario had just galloped out of town when Banner mounted the roan and headed south after him.

CHAPTER 37

Macario continued to travel due south for several hours, and Banner, whose rear end was torturing him and whose mouth felt as dry as picked oakum, had resigned himself that he was headed straight for Mexico.

Then, just as a pearl gray dawn was fingering the east above the black-ribbed mountains, Canejo turned inland for a mile or so. Presently he forded a brisk creek and Banner could see an adobe cabin up ahead, a small building with a sagging tulle roof. Behind it an outdoor oven, shaped like a mud-covered wasp's nest turned upside down, had been built a few yards from the rear door. Smoke came from a small chimney at the corner of the house as well as from the oven, and several horses grazed nearby.

Banner dismounted from the roan in stiff-kneed agony, tied the horse to a scrawny oak half-hidden by greasewood and sumac, and crept close to the cabin.

Macario had dismounted and gone directly into the house, but no one had come to take his horse. The animal still stood there saddled and bridled, so perhaps Canejo did not expect to stay here long.

Banner worked himself to a side position where he could keep watch of both front and rear. He saw an elderly woman thickly wrapped in shawls come out the back door and peer into the oven. She shook her head as if dissatisfied. At the same moment a comely young girl, Mexican or half-breed from what he could tell at a distance, came to the open door and stretched luxuriously like a cat. Her touseled black hair glinted like jet under water in the early-morning rays of the sun.

Macario appeared and ran his hand and arm around the young woman's waist, tipping back her head to kiss her.

Banner felt a sudden bitter disappointment, followed by billowing anger. Was this what he had had his long tortuous ride for? Nothing. A mere assignation?

For some time he wasn't aware of the face looking out of a window toward where he lay hidden behind a prickly thicket of yuccas. Then a white hand moved slowly and his eye caught the movement and followed it as it touched first the forehead then the breast, then either shoulder.

The familiar sign of the Cross as he had watched her make it a thousand times after they left Boston. It was Dona Soledad beyond a doubt.

He realized she could not see him, better if she didn't at the moment. It was enough for him that he had found her. In a little while her hand moved again, making the sign of the Cross, and he saw her turn from the window.

Banner hesitated. All his life he had taken orders, obeyed them without question. He knew that it would be enough if he went back now and reported to Kinkaid where Soledad was. But he wanted to be able to tell his master, also, where Judah and his ship were. It stood to reason that they could not be far away. Judah would not leave his prize unprotected for long.

On a hunch, Banner edged back to his horse, mounted, and with his pocket compass headed the animal due west. If Soledad was being kept at the cabin, Judah could not be anchored far off. A captain, especially one of Judah's class, would not be away from his ship in these waters.

When he sighted the coastline after a rugged overland trip, Banner headed south. A thick mist obscured the water. He walked the roan slowly along the low-lying cliffs, keeping away from anything that resembled a trail.

He stopped on a promontory as the sun grew warmer, and breakfasted on some jerky and a flask of fiery brandy he had found in the saddlebags. While he ate, he loosened the saddle and allowed the horse to graze on the long, damp grass.

Mounted again, he held his course due south. He could be wrong, he thought uneasily; Judah might have secreted the girl and sailed someplace else, meaning to return for her later. The stretch of blue was slowly widening between sea and sky. When the mist finally lifted, he calculated he had traveled some eight miles west and south of the cabin.

As he climbed a steep little bluff, his keen seaman's eyes saw the tips of the ship's masts before he could make out her hull. His heart quickened with elation. She was hove to in a U-shaped cove, a nasty place to be caught in on the southern California coast at this season of the year.

Banner climbed stiffly from the saddle, and led the horse behind a sheltering cliff shoulder.

She was a brig, fairly new by the look of her. With his land glass, Banner could make out the members of the crew on watch, and her name, *Venus,* above her gilt-and-scarlet figurehead. A fine clean ship, too fine and good for the likes of Titus Judah, he thought wrathfully.

As he watched, a red-haired man came out of the captain's quarters, put on his cap, and paused to speak over his shoulder to a dark buxom woman clad in a white wrapper who had followed him onto the deck.

At the sight, Banner's lips went tight as a hawser in a gale. He cursed aloud at his distance from the scene, and at his enforced anonymity. Ship's captain or not, it would have given him keen satisfaction to spreadeagle such a swine and personally give him two hundred lashes of the cat, or keelhaul him until he cried for mercy or drowned. Banner was not by nature a sadistic or revengeful man, but he had been reared in a hard school, and he believed in payment in full for all transgressions.

Banner saw that Judah was talking to the mate, and the longboat was being swung smartly from her davits and fitted with a jury sail.

So that was his game. He would leave the brig *Venus* here and sail to San Diego in the longboat without arousing suspicion from his enemies. His plan was precarious in these mists and in the uncertain weather along the coast, but daring. In the longboat he could land anywhere he chose unnoticed, and go into the pueblo to transact his business.

While he was watching the crew prepare the longboat, two riders galloped along the strip of sandy beach below the cliff, and Banner realized with a sudden shock that one of them was Macario Canejo; the other was Soledad.

Were they planning to leave Soledad here aboard the *Venus?* If so, in which direction, Banner wondered, did his present duty lie? To report back to Kinkaid at once? Or remain and try to free Soledad from the ship when Judah had left—a risky course, probably impossible. The crew of the *Venus* were not likely to release Soledad without a fight, even if he claimed to come from Judah.

But the decision was taken out of his hands, for both the girl and Macario were taken into the longboat with Judah, and rowed out to the headland where the wind could catch their sail.

Before they were out of sight, Banner was mounted on the roan, headed back for San Diego at the fastest gallop he was able to maintain and still keep his seat in the saddle.

*   *   *

Tarifa glanced with distaste at the little room that had once been a part of the presidio at San Diego, but was now rented out by the Canejos to anyone who needed the dubious shelter provided by a crumbling roof and four walls.

The Canejos had bought, or been given by Pico, a portion of the presidio and Mission lands at San Diego. They had done nothing to repair the buildings, which lay crumbling into ruins on every side, but they still pastured their horses and cattle on the land.

Waiting with her in the damp little room were Luis, Patrick Havelock, and Tiburcio Novato. Santos had come also, ostensibly to tend the horses, but in reality to make sure that no harm came to the Patróna at the hands of this wicked hombre she went to meet, Capitán Judah.

In his heart, Santos hated this man as he had once hated Bruno Cacho, with a smoldering brain-consuming hatred. Inside his breast it was like a fire that blazed from his head to his feet, yet left him cold and trembling.

Crouched in the alcove of a ruined wall, over a small mesquite fire, the Indian brooded and watched the entrance of the old presidio where once he had greeted such proud soldiers as Don Ygnacio Alvarjo, Capitán Ruiz, and Zenobio Sanchez.

Time was indeed a monster that devoured all before it. The buildings that the white men had so boldly erected when his father was young, now crumbled and fell; the fields they had planted and watered with such diligence disappeared once more into wild brown grass. It was as if a slate were wiped clean once an era had passed, and a new picture began to take form. Now, other white men came, with bigger ships, more soldiers, a different tongue and beliefs. Their buildings grew upon the ruins of the old ones. Would they last any longer? Would his people, who lived in such misery now, be raised up again by this new regime, only to become the pawns of fate once more when the fortunes of these new white men also waned?

Santos found that his mind, like his stiffened limbs, was growing obstinate and rebellious. He knew that he had been more fortunate than his brothers, first at the hands of Padre Payri and Padre Cazon, and then with Don Ygnacio and the Alvarjos. He could no longer think of himself as merely an Indian. He was Santos, mayordomo of Loma de Oro, and so he would die, he determined grimly. It would be well if he could die performing some last service for his beloved family. Such as ridding them of this *renegado parásito,* Capitán Judah. Or, if the fates were against him and he were killed by the Americano, it would be well to die a martyr to his belief in the Alvarjos and all they stood for.

Late in the morning which had at last turned sunny and windless, three horsemen galloped into the presidio yard and dismounted a few paces from where Santos stood.

He saw the lean, red-haired, red-moustached capitán, a strange Americano dressed in dark clothes and carrying a leather pouch over one shoulder, and Don Macario Canejo. So the worm had turned his belly up to be warmed by the other side, thought Santos bitterly. His hand closed over his knife.

But just then Don Luis flung back the door of the little room. The Indian saw Dona Tarifa standing in the opening, her head thrust high like Marca's when he first scented a grizzly and was too proud to show fear. Her eyes seemed to glitter with suppressed anger.

Judah stood with a half-smile on his lips, staring insolently at her flushed face.

"It is a long time since our paths crossed, Dona Tarifa." She said nothing and his own color rose.

"This is my lawyer, Samuel Trumble, of Monterey. Samuel, may I present Dona Tarifa—Kinkaid? You are still Mrs. Kinkaid?"

Tarifa glared at him, while the lawyer, a grave middle-aged man, hastened to make her a nervous bow. He was new to California and he did not trust the tempers of these high-born hacendados and their wives.

"You know Don Macario, of course," Judah went on.

Tarifa transferred her burning gaze to Macario, who seemed to shrink before the eyes of the onlookers.

"Come, Macario," Judah laughed, "you don't believe she can put a Gypsy curse on you merely by looking at you?"

Macario moistened his lips and glanced away from Tarifa nervously.

"I can put a curse on him—and you, Capitán," thundered Tarifa. "I am a *chovihani*, the daughter of a great *chovihani!*"

"I wouldn't care, madam, if you were the Devil's own daughter, which I don't doubt in the least that you are," Judah grinned. "I've never given a damn for the Devil's curses, so why should I cringe from yours? Suppose, for the sake of expediency, we postpone further discussion of one another's more appealing attributes, until we have transacted our business?"

Tarifa stood scowling at him, but she allowed Luis to take her arm and draw her back into the room. The others followed them inside, closing the door in Santos' brooding face.

The room had been provided by the Canejos for this occasion, with a deal table, several rough benches, and two worn armchairs with cracked leather seats.

Judah immediately seated himself in one of the chairs, and lighted a cigar. "You may as well state our business, Samuel," he said to Trumble before the others were fairly seated.

The lawyer, who surprised the Californians by addressing them in excellent Spanish, explained Judah's marital status, and his valid claim to the portion of Loma de Oro which his wife's father, Don Ygnacio Alvarjo, had left to her in his will. As proof of their claim, the lawyer exhibited the certificate of marriage from the priest who had married the Judahs in Valparaiso, and the birth certificates of the Judah children.

"You can see," smiled Judah, biting down on his cigar, "that I only ask for what is legally mine—and my wife's."

Tarifa rose from her armchair in one bound, like a leopard springing from a rock. "Nothing is legally yours! You kidnapped a child, forced her into a marriage that was loveless and not of her choice, used her as you saw fit, and abandoned her in a strange land! She would have died there if it were not for my husband. Don Ygnacio would see you dead before he let you step again on Loma de Oro soil, much less possess an inch of it!"

"Your passion does you full justice, Dona Tarifa, as a dedicated stepmother," assented Judah, adding with sly malice, "except for the fact that we both know that you don't care a tinker's damn about the fate of the Alvarjos, and never have. It is only Loma de Oro, any part of it, that you cannot bear the prospect of losing, isn't it?"

"You have no right to address such words to Dona Tarifa, Capitán," Luis said in a deadly calm voice.

"So you would rise to defend her, my one-armed caballero?" Judah squinted up through the smoke from his cigar. "You know her so well? And she has done so much for you and Loma de Oro?"

"Yes! She has done much for all of us at Loma de Oro, señor, and she was once my father's wife."

"The Alvarjo pride. Touching, isn't it, Tarifa, that it should rise to defend you, after the stranglehold you have kept upon Loma de Oro and its occupants all these years?"

"You will never get an inch of Loma de Oro!"

Judah's eyes were as hard as polished agate. "Any court in the land will uphold my claim. If necessary, Soledad will make the appeal herself."

"Where is my sister?" demanded Luis hotly. "What have you done with her?"

"Absolutely nothing, my dear brother-in-law. She is perfectly safe and quite content."

"That is a lie!"

"On the contrary. She went with me quite willingly. In due time we will return to live on our portion of the rancho, as a part of the family."

"Primita Undebē!" Tarifa flamed, her dark face livid with hate. "I will kill you myself if you so much as step foot on Loma de Oro!"

His eyes seemed to grow opaque and green as seaweed, but he glanced coolly at her flaring nostrils and taloned fingers. "I believe you. But the act would cost you all of Loma de Oro; the United States Government would not permit even such an influential murderess as yourself to get off scot free. Your own common sense will tell you that it is better to lose a small piece of your prized rancho than to risk losing all of it."

Tiburcio Novato stepped forward and laid his hand on Tarifa's rigid arm. "Permit Señor Trumble and me to speak together for a moment, Dona Tarifa?"

She shrugged, then turned her back on Judah's mocking eyes. Her black hatred for him ground like a knife against her ribs, and yet she knew that her fury was impotent. He was right. She could not risk losing Loma de Oro, even if it meant giving up the pleasure of killing him, or of having others do the job for her. Santos had killed for her once and gotten away with it, but with these cursed gringos all over the place, what would his fate be now?

There had been a time when she would not have hesitated to sacrifice any individual for the good of Loma de Oro. But since the death of Padre Cazon, she had found it increasingly difficult to think only of the rancho or herself. And there was Soledad. What would Bart say if she refused to even make an attempt to save her? Behind her, Tarifa could hear the lawyers arguing in an undertone, yet when Novato came to press her arm again she started as if she had been struck.

"Forgive me, I did not mean to startle you, Dona Tarifa," said the old man.

"It is nothing. What have you decided?"

Novato wiped his lips with a silk handkerchief and his eyes were sad.

"We think, Luis and I, that it will be better for all concerned if you deed to Capitán Judah the piece of property that was to have been Soledad's."

"Never! I will give that pig nothing, do you hear?"

The old man's voice was conciliatory. "It is only a small portion when taken from such a great rancho. And he promises to return Soledad to her home to live. Think of the poor girl, and her helpless little ones. We must help them in some way. And what harm can Capitán Judah do to Loma de Oro, owning such a small portion? Moreover, I greatly fear that if we refuse, he can claim the property legally anyway. Under the law, his claim is a valid one. His wife has a right to her inheritance, and he has documented, legal proof of their marriage."

Luis and Patrick Havelock joined them, and the other two men added their pressure to Novato's plea.

"No!" she told them bitterly. "You are all against me. I will not listen to you."

Hearing her words, Judah got to his feet.

"If that is your final decision, Dona Tarifa, I shall present my case to the officials at Monterey," he said.

Luis took Tarifa's hand in his and told her gently, "I know my father would never have sacrificed one of his children just to keep the rancho intact. Proud as he was of Loma de Oro, he loved his children more. We must think of Soledad first. She has suffered much because of this man already. I do not think that she is strong enough to bear much more. And there are her children. There is Alvarjo blood in them as well as Judah's, and the Alvarjos have always taken care of their own. I know how this tears your heart; I know of the promise you made my father, but all the rest of Loma de Oro will still be in your hands to manage, as you have done so magnificently all the years since my father died. You know what I think of this animal, Judah, how easily I, or any of my brothers, could kill him without a qualm. But surely the welfare of our sister is more important than the death of one miscreant?"

Tarifa said nothing for a moment. She knew that Luis had echoed her own thoughts, thoughts that she had tried to force out of her mind ever since she had returned to Loma de Oro to find Soledad gone. There could be nothing but acrimony and despair in acceptance. Bowing down to a man like Judah would be the hardest thing she had ever done, like seeing her own spirit crushed between iron jaws.

She turned to face Novato and Trumble and her voice was harsh with defeat.

"You will draw up the papers and bring them to me tonight at Loma de Oro."

Trumble's face brightened with relief. He had been so sure she would refuse.

Judah laughed quietly to himself, but Tarifa refused to look at him. She spoke sharply to Luis. "We will ride home; I am tired."

"*Muy pronto.*" His eyes were speculative as they met hers, but in their depths were reflected gratitude and admiration.

She thought disdainfully, he is proud of me, the fool, and I have failed. Feeling an unreasoning anger for herself as much as Luis, she passed him with a firm step, hoping to find Santos and the horses ready to leave.

* * *

Soledad did not like the Canejo house where Judah had left her after they disembarked at San Diego from the longboat. She did not care for old Señora Canejo, who had no real notion of what was going on under her roof, but was persistent in her efforts to pry into the affairs of the Alvarjos.

Due to her own pride, Soledad would tell her nothing.

"It is a miracle that you and your husband are united after such a long time, Soledad."

"*Sí*, señora."

Señora Canejo knew all the details of Rufina's disgrace at Judah's hands, and she was looking forward with relish to the opportunity of discussing the matter first-hand with his present wife. But Soledad gave her no satisfaction. Her replies were brief to the point of rudeness, and unenlightening. In a moment the stubborn girl excused herself, pleading a headache, and returned to the room she had been given. She was followed, of course, by the Indian maid her husband had instructed to watch over her while she was in the house and see that she remained on the premises until his return. The maid sat across from her now, watching her in stolid silence. At least the stupid creature did not ask questions. Soledad lay on the bed and closed her eyes wearily. It was painful to know that John Mabrey was here in San Diego, that his office was not a stone's throw away in the plaza. She tried to think of ways to reach him, or let him know that she was here. But the Indian girl looked strong and determined—obviously she would do as Judah and Don Macario had bidden her—and before he left the house Macario had given the girl a knife. Soledad was at a loss to understand Macario's part in all this. The only explanation that made any sense was that Macario, like all the other *gente de razón* in California, needed money. Judah must have promised him a good deal for his services and the use of his houses. Poor Macario, of course, had no way of knowing that Titus Judah never kept his promises.

Soledad fell into an uneasy sleep and when she wakened it was as if she had opened her eyes upon some fantastic dream.

Men were struggling in the room with the screaming Indian girl, and Soledad could hear Señora Canejo's scandalized shrieks from the *sala*.

One of the men bent hastily over the bed and picked her up. Soledad found herself staring into the face of John Mabrey. It was streaked with sweat and grime but he was beaming at her.

"Juan!"

"Yes, my darling. You're safe now, thanks to Bart Kinkaid and his mate here. I'm taking you to my place. Later on we'll get you home to Loma de Oro. But we intend to leave word with Señora Canejo that you've been taken aboard Kinkaid's ship in the harbor."

"But why? I don't understand. What about Titus?"

"It's because of him we must do it. A little trap Bart's laying for him, the bastard. I'll leave you at my place, *querida*, then go to join Bart on the ship. We'll deal with Captain Judah there."

"But you might be hurt! Titus is a violent man, Juan. And if he thinks you have taken me—"

Mabrey's gaze made her blush with confusion and pleasure.

"I pray he learns it the moment he steps over the threshold. I long to get my own two hands on him. Nothing can hurt me now, *querida mía*." He took her hands in his, staring down at her tenderly. "I'm in love with you, Soledad. I know it's ridiculous for a man of my age to feel the way I do, but I can't help it. And by all that's holy, I'll find some way to make you my wife—if you'll have me, that is?"

Soledad's arms went about his neck and her lips whispered against his cheek. "Yes, Juan, yes, yes, yes!"

He bent his head to kiss her, knowing as he did it that his fate was sealed forever, and that he couldn't have cared less about the odds of his living to enjoy it. Something more primitive, more powerful than logic ruled him today, and he knew that he would kill without an instant's hesitation to keep the girl he held so tightly against his heart.

Macario and Judah returned to the house an hour later, to find Señora Canejo dissolved in tears and outrage over the brutal treatment she insisted the entire household had been subjected to by Dr. Mabrey and some Americano sailors who claimed to be from the ship *Celestial Queen*. They had taken Soledad by force, and were carrying her aboard the ship, for what dastardly purpose only Santa Maria knew.

Judah's face went calm and still. "Have you got some men on the place?" he asked Macario.

"Only a few Indians who help with the household chores."

"Arm them and bring them along."

"Along?"

"Aboard the *Celestial Queen*. Kinkaid has taken my wife there. I intend to get her back. There isn't time for me to send for my own crew. Be quick about it."

Señora Canejo wept afresh when she learned where her son was going. She did not like or trust Capitán Judah, and had only allowed him the use of her home because her beloved Macario had begged it of her.

"You will be killed, *nino*. I forbid you to go!"

"I'm afraid he has no choice, señora." Judah's cold level tone brought her head up with a jerk. To her amazement she saw that he was holding a pistol in one hand.

"You dare to threaten me, Capitán! In my own house?"

"Only if you try to keep your son from obeying me."

She said nothing as Macario hurried from the room.

The little party left for the beach a moment later, riding at full gallop on the best Canejo horses. Macario, with the assistance of his neighbors, had succeeded in gathering ten Indian vaqueros of varying ages, most of them elderly. They were armed with knives, a few pistols, and one rifle—all the arms Macario or his friends had been able to supply.

A disgusting crew with which to board an American ship, thought Judah, but they were all he had. They would have to do.

Kinkaid had welcomed Banner back aboard ship that morning, and received the news of Soledad's whereabouts with deep satisfaction.

"So Canejo has thrown in with him? I thought someone among the local gentry must be helping him. When do you calculate they'll reach San Diego?"

"The wind was favorable; within an hour, I should say, sir."

"Judah won't risk taking Soledad to the meeting with

Tarifa," the captain mused. "He'll have to leave her someplace where she'll be safe and yet arouse no suspicions. At Canejo's house, unless I miss my guess. Do you agree?"

Banner nodded. "Yes, sir, that would seem logical, for a man whose jib is cut the way of Captain Judah's."

"Let's hope we're right. Go ashore and tell Dr. Mabrey what's happened. Go to Canejo's, and when the women are alone, take Soledad to Mabrey's place for safekeeping. Be sure that whoever is at the house guarding Soledad thinks you are bringing her here to me aboard the *Celestial Queen*. Understand?"

"Aye, sir. A little trap for Captain Judah?"

"Right, Mr. Banner. A trap with the right bait to catch a shark."

Banner grinned. "He'll come, sir, no mistaking that. But there's still a good many of the crew ashore on leave, sir. I don't like leaving you so shorthanded, sir, in case Captain Judah comes aboard before I can get back."

Kinkaid laughed and clapped the burly mate on the back. "Don't worry about me, Jake. I've been waiting for this moment for a lifetime. I suppose you might say it's an epitaph of sorts, the last real service I can perform for my wife. Oddly enough, it will comfort me to know I at least have her gratitude if I can have nothing more. Take a couple of men and go now, and don't worry about me or the *Celestial Queen*."

He stood at the rail a moment later and watched Banner and the two sailors he had selected row shoreward in the longboat. He had armed them with pistols from the magazine. There were only a handful of men on board, just a skeleton crew, for he had ordered Banner to give most of the men leave the day before.

Kinkaid returned to his cabin, after instructing the second mate to show any visitors directly to him. He sat down at his desk and examined the pistol he had armed himself with to make sure it was properly loaded and primed. It seemed to be in perfect working order. He poured himself a drink, and then thoughtfully returned it to the decanter untouched. He could use this time to write Tarifa a letter, in case he was killed, but he knew that words were no longer of any use between them. What he hadn't been able to demonstrate or make her understand at their last meeting, he could never explain to her in a letter.

He wondered if she could be right, if they were bad for each other. Her Gypsy intuition might have been shrewder, more farseeing than his own blind passion for her. He understood her so much better now, and himself so much less. He knew now that, for him, his own love for Tarifa was enough. But he could see that for her, that same love was a threat to independence and freedom. And it was true that when you loved someone, wanted someone as much as he did Tarifa, the depth of your own emotion couldn't help but demand something in return. She must have realized this in the beginning and known that she would never be able to give him anything of herself in return. He had only himself to blame and yet, given the opportunity to relive these last few years, he would have married her again.

He glanced idly at the amulet Penti had given him the last time he was at Loma de Oro. It lay before him on the desk where he had placed it when he removed it from his pocket that night after his return from the rancho. It was amazing the variety of forms people put their faith into. Penti's was firmly ensconced in this greasy sack containing God-knew-what. Padre Cazon had put his trust in the sacraments and teachings of his Church. Tarifa's belief lay solely in Loma de Oro; it was her fetish, her talisman. It sustained her through all adversity.

And his own belief? He was no longer sure. Once he had placed his faith in the sea and his ship, in his own strength and judgment. Now it seemed to have deserted him, been stripped from him, worn away in the crucible of his love for Tarifa. And it seemed as if he would go naked and bereft forever, with nothing to take its place.

Yet in spite of his emptiness he was looking forward to the meeting with Judah with a sharp anticipation, almost elation. The part of him that had always laughed in the face of danger exulted in the coming clash. He was surprised to discover that it mattered little to him, even if it cost him his life, as long as he succeeded in bringing Judah down with him. Still, as he sat toying with the amulet, he became aware of a nagging notion that there was something he had forgotten. Some important point he had overlooked.

The door burst open on his thoughts as the second mate, Mr. Middleton, stumbled into the cabin followed by Titus Judah and Macario Canejo, both with pistols in their hands. Behind them Kinkaid could hear a struggle taking place on deck, and the sudden sound of firearms.

He knew now what he had failed to take into account. The possibility that Judah might not come alone.

Mabrey seated Soledad gently in his best chair, sent the Indian boy who served him to make her some tea, and began to load his pistol while Soledad watched him with a pale strained face.

"Must you go to the ship, Juan? Bart has men there to help him, sailors—"

"I must go to him," he said gently. "He is my friend. I owe him more than I shall ever be able to repay. He has done all this to give you back to me. You have cause to remember as well as I have his kindness and generosity." He sighed. "I only wish he might have known more happiness himself."

Soledad watched him tuck the pistol into his belt and felt a wave of fear that he would never return.

"But if you should be killed, I would die too, Juan. I could not bear it!"

He sat down on the arm of her chair and drew her to him. "You are not to worry, my dearest. I have a feeling it is Captain Judah who is going to die." His voice was grim and Soledad shivered in his arms.

"How can you be sure? You don't know him as I do. How diabolically clever he is, how hard and ruthless."

"He will never touch you again, my darling, I promise you that. Wait here for me, and be patient? I promise I will return for you." He bent and kissed her cheeks, her brow, her lips, and she felt her fears fading under his touch. His confidence was contagious, and though she still mistrusted Judah, she needed so badly to believe in Mabrey's safety, that she forced herself to think of nothing but his words of encouragement and devotion.

It was Banner, entering the room like a tornado, who finally broke the serenity of her thoughts.

"That bastard Canejo, beggin' your pardon ma'am, has taken ten men and gone with Captain Judah to board the *Celestial Queen!*"

"What? Are you sure?" Mabrey reached for his coat and hat. Behind him he heard Soledad moan softly.

"I saw it with my own eyes, sir. Ten mounted men, all armed," said Banner.

"We must board the ship at once," Mabrey said. "Bart will need us."

"Juan!"

"You'll be safe here, my dear. No one knows where you are. Tomorrow I'll take you back to Loma de Oro. Have you a boat for us, Banner?"

"Aye, that I have, sir. Three of 'em, two from the hide-houses and our own longboat. And I've rounded up all our lads I could find in the pueblo. We'll be a match for Judah and his Californians!"

"Amen to that," said Mabrey quickly, but he was wondering if even now they would reach the *Celestial Queen* in time.

He turned briefly to embrace Soledad, gently loosening her fingers when she would not release him. "I'll be back, never fear." He instructed the Indian servant to watch over her.

"*Sí,* Señor Medico."

CHAPTER 38

Titus Judah leaned back on his heels and smiled at Kinkaid, who had not risen from his seat at the desk. Judah held his pistol aimed casually at Bart's chest. There was another tucked into the waistband of his trousers, Kinkaid noted.

"It seems we've both come up in the world, Captain." Judah drawled the words, but underneath his voice was as taut as a halliard. "You do yourself very well indeed. And I must congratulate you on your new command. The *Celestial Queen*'s as spanking a clipper as I've set eyes on. Too bad piracy is out of date; I might relieve you of her."

"Piracy still flourishes as far as you're concerned, Judah," Kinkaid replied evenly. "So do kidnapping, and rape."

Judah's face lengthened and his easy smile of superiority disappeared.

"Kidnapping, Captain? I understand that you seized my wife at Señor Canejo's house, and brought her here against her will. I want her, Kinkaid. Where is she?"

"Where you'll never lay a hand on her again!"

A look of blank surprise came over Judah's face. Then he laughed shortly. "You're bluffing, of course." Over his shoulder he ordered, "Search the ship!"

The scuffle on deck had ceased some time ago, and now one of the vaqueros put his head inside the door, grinning with pride.

"We have locked the sailors in the hold, Don Macario."

"*Bueno*. Go and search the ship for Señora Judah, *pronto!*"

"*Sí*, Patrón."

Bart had made no attempt to draw his own weapon. It still lay tucked in his waistband where he had placed it after he finished checking it, hidden by the folds of his unbuttoned coat. Judah had not bothered to search him, evidently thinking that he had taken him completely by surprise.

Kinkaid casually took a cigar from a box on the desk and proceeded to light it with precision and care. He sat toying with Penti's amulet when he had finished.

"You're wasting your time, Titus. I told you she's not aboard."

"You're lying!"

"I'm telling you the absolute truth. But I've been expecting you." He knew now that his mistake had been in not taking the crew into his confidence to warn them of a surprise attack, but it was too late to worry about that now. "I told the people who rescued Soledad from Canejo's house to spread the rumor that they were bringing her here. I counted on your following."

Judah's breath came through pinched nostrils; his eyes were ugly with rage and disappointment.

"Where is she, Kinkaid? Answer me, or by God I'll kill you here and now!"

Kinkaid blew smoke toward the open porthole. "If you kill me you'll never find out where she is."

Judah's long face paled with fury.

"Get on your feet, damn you!"

Kinkaid rose with a calm deliberation that masked his inner tension. There was something about Judah, an element of evil that emanated from him like a live thing.

"Get outside! You're going to take me to her, wherever she is."

Kinkaid obeyed because it suited his own purposes better to be on deck. As he went through the narrow bulkhead, he turned suddenly and lunged at Macario, grabbing the pistol from his hand, and dragged the startled Californian in front of him.

"*Por Dios!*" Macario wailed. "Do not shoot, Capitán Judah!"

The sound of the gun, followed by Macario's agonized sigh, cut short whatever else he might have added to his plea.

Kinkaid felt the weight of the body as it sagged in his arms, and decided not to risk a shot in his present position. He dragged his burden with him onto the deck where the startled vaqueros stood like statues, watching him in awed silence.

"Santa Maria!" cried one old man crossing himself hastily.

"It is the Patrón!" whispered another, but no man raised his weapon or tried to stop Kinkaid.

"Shoot, you damned fools!" Judah shouted from the companionway. He bounded onto the deck and his voice lashed out at the Californians. "Don't you see he's just killed your master?"

"He lies," said Kinkaid. "He killed Don Macario, even while he was begging for mercy. He pretended to be your master's friend and he killed him in cold blood. This is a matter that concerns only Capitán Judah and myself, amigos. Turn my crew loose and return Don Macario's body to San Diego, and I promise none of you will get into trouble with the authorities."

"Don't listen to him!" commanded Judah. "You know I was Don Macario's trusted friend. I was a guest in his house. Wasn't that same household violated and my own wife stolen from it by this very man?"

Judah cursed under his breath and snapped a shot at Kinkaid's head that missed. Kinkaid saw him jerk another pistol from the hand of a vaquero standing next to him.

Before he could fire again, Kinkaid dropped Macario's body, grabbed a belaying pin, and hurled it with all his force at Judah. He saw him wince with pain as the heavy wood cracked against his knee and his leg gave way beneath him.

One of the younger vaqueros stepped forward as if uncertain what to do. He held a pistol in his hand and his eyes swung questioningly between the two Americans. Kinkaid could have dropped the Californian with a shot at such close range, but he did not believe the man would shoot. He looked merely bewildered.

"Shoot, damn you!" Judah shouted. "Didn't I come here with you and your Patrón? I'm trying to avenge his death. Are you going to let his murderer get away?"

Without a moment's hesitation the young man raised his pistol and fired it point-blank at Kinkaid's chest.

A look of astonishment, then fear came over the vaquero's face as he saw the Americano still standing there by the rail, smiling grimly back at him. With a cry of alarm, the Californian dropped the pistol and fled.

At the same moment, Kinkaid turned by the rail and leaped into the shrouds. He began climbing swiftly hand over hand, hoping he could make the to'gallant yard before his breath gave out. The vaquero's bullet had not missed; it had found its mark somewhere inside his chest. He could feel the hot seep of blood down his side, but it hadn't weakened him appreciably yet. Judah would have to follow him aloft if he wanted him; that's what he was counting on. Aloft, out of the reach of help from below, it would be a personal, more equal duel, Kinkaid slowed by his wound, and Judah by his crippled leg. He had no doubt that Judah would come after him. It was no secret to either of them now that they would have followed each other into Hell to settle their account.

With an oath at the wrench to his knee, Judah had made his way painfully to the rail, crawled into the shrouds, and begun to follow Kinkaid.

Two captains, he thought savagely, running up the mainmast like a pair of deckhands. He cursed the slowness of his progress. His leg was all but useless. He had climbed laboriously some distance before he noticed the blood on the ropes. So the vaquero hadn't missed? Kinkaid was crippled too. The thought gave him added energy as he pulled himself aloft.

Kinkaid, panting with the exertion of his efforts, had reached the to'gallant yard and braced himself with his back to the mast. He could see Judah hoisting himself with painful slowness far below, coming on steadily. It would be some time before he was within pistol range. Kinkaid examined Macario's unfired pistol which he still carried in one hand. It seemed to be in good order. His own gun still lay tucked in his waistband under his coat. For the moment there was nothing to do but wait.

Not since his days as a hand before the mast, had he been aloft. He had forgotten the exhilaration of being above decks, above everything but the blue sky, with the gentle roll of the vessel far below.

In a moment Judah would be within range, then whichever man had the luck, or the steadiest hand, would go below again to the world of men. Or perhaps neither of them would ever reach deck alive. For this brief moment, though, Kinkaid's thoughts could go freely to Tarifa. He glanced northeast, in the direction of Loma de Oro. Even if he never saw it again every detail of the place would remain etched in his memory, the softly rolling hills gently rounded as a woman's breasts, dun-colored at this time of the year. The live-oaks dotting the pasturelands like wide-armed sentinels, that at this hour would be providing shelter for the scattered herds of cattle and horses. The pleasant irregularity of the clustered white buildings that made up the hacienda. And as always when he thought of the rancho, he could see Tarifa mounted on Guindilla, racing across the hills, her black hair streaming behind her. He had given much to Loma de Oro since first he rode there with Zenobio Sanchez, but the rancho had given him much in return. If he felt regrets for the way it had all ended, he felt none for the part Loma de Oro or its people had played in his life. He could see now that the ending, this ending, had been inevitable from the beginning.

Glancing seaward, he was vaguely aware of three small boats approaching the ship, but before he had time to study the occupants, Judah called from just below him:

"I know you're hit, Kinkaid. I saw the blood on my way up. Tell me where Soledad is. If you don't, I'll find her anyway, and I promise you she'll pay for your stubbornness."

"You'll never reach her to harm her again," said Bart, pressing the trigger of Macario's pistol. The jolt jarred him back against the mast, and the gun bounced from his nerveless fingers and fell to the deck.

Below, he could see the look of incredulity on Judah's face as the bullet smashed into his shoulder, making him lose his grip. He slipped a few feet and then saved himself, clinging to the swaying ropes. It was astonishing that he still grasped his gun, and that he began climbing again. Moving more slowly and cautiously, but climbing steadily upward toward the to'gallant yard.

Kinkaid had faced hate before in many guises, but he had never seen it so naked and malevolent on a human face as it now appeared on Judah's.

"Sit there and wait, damn you," he panted, "and I'll get you anyway. You can't kill me, Kinkaid, you don't have enough guts. You're a cripple, Kinkaid, a moral cripple. You've got a streak of weakness in you. It will betray you in the end." He laughed softly. "You're a damned fool, Kinkaid."

A wave of weakness passed over Kinkaid and he leaned back more heavily against the mast. It was uncanny that they could be so alone up here on the mast of the clipper, poised between Heaven and Hell.

Judah inched his way up. His left hand was slick with the blood seeping from under his coat sleeve, the arm nearly useless. The two men were almost close enough to touch each other but Kinkaid made no move.

"Your Puritan conscience won't allow you to take the advantage even now, will it?" Judah taunted.

"I have no conscience where you are concerned, Titus." Kinkaid inched his own gun out of his waistband and held it half-hidden in his palm under his open coat.

With a sweeping motion as swift as a striking harpoon, Judah brought up his pistol and fired at Kinkaid's head. Kinkaid felt the stunning impact of the ball as it pierced his left collarbone, shattering the wood behind him as it buried itself in the mast.

Through the mist that swam before his eyes, he could see Judah grinning up at him in triumph. He was standing braced against the ropes, like a jackal waiting to claim the wounded lion's kill, when Kinkaid pulled the trigger of his own gun.

The shot struck Judah squarely in the center of the throat, stilling the scream on his lips, as a widening flange of crimson appeared on his neck. He clapped both hands to the awful wound and fell suddenly backward. His body arched and plummeted like a falling star, striking the ship's rail, then dropping into the sea.

Kinkaid closed his eyes for an instant. When he opened them he could make out the telltale fins of a school of sharks veering toward the hull of the *Celestial Queen.*

There were shouts from below, from the three approaching boats, and he could recognize Jake Banner and John Mabrey gazing anxiously aloft.

Suddenly, in spite of his pain and weakness, he was galvanised into activity. By instinct more than skill, he made it back down to the deck. With barely a glance at the vaqueros huddled mutely now around Macario's body, he went to release the crew. He ordered the second mate to take the vaqueros into custody, and report to him in his cabin immediately.

In his own quarters, Kinkaid tore off his coat and shirt. He washed his wounds, wondering at the pain when he moved his left arm. He was trying clumsily to bandage himself when the mate entered.

"You're hurt, sir!"

"It's nothing. Here, help me fasten this, as tight as you

can! Get me a clean shirt, there in the top drawer of the locker, and my other coat. Get rid of these things."

"Aye, sir."

"One thing more, Mr. Middleton."

"Yes, sir?"

"Not a word of this to Mr. Banner or to Dr. Mabrey when they come aboard, understand?"

Middleton nodded as he helped the captain into his best coat. No matter what idiotic thing the master of a sailing ship did, it was not the place of any member of his crew to question his actions.

"Now get out, Mr. Middleton. And send Banner to me as soon as he boards ship."

"Very good, sir."

Middleton left the cabin, taking the captain's blood-stained garments with him.

Kinkaid sat down behind his desk and poured himself a whiskey with trembling hands. The liquor helped to clear his sight. He knew that if he could just get through the next few minutes without arousing Banner or Mabrey's suspicions, then order the *Celestial Queen* to put to sea, everything would work out as he had planned. But first, he must get Mabrey off the ship.

He lighted a cigar and then found that he hadn't breath enough to smoke it. He would have to be careful about that. Speak as few words as possible, and yet appear fully himself. He carefully wiped the dank sweat from his forehead and lips with a clean handkerchief.

Banner was the first aboard ship from the longboat. He glanced sharply at the second mate. Middleton returned his gaze steadily but there was something guarded about his look that made Banner ask sharply, "Is the captain all right, Mr. Middleton?"

"Yes, sir. He's in his cabin. He requests that you report to him at once, Mr. Banner."

"Thank'ee, Mr. Middleton."

Mabrey scrambled over the side, glancing in surprise at Macario's body.

"Dead?"

"Aye, sir," said Banner as he rose from examining it. "If ye'll come this way, sir, I believe the captain would like a word with us."

"Yes. Thank God it's over! That was Judah we saw fall from the mast?"

"Yes, sir."

Kinkaid did not rise when the two men entered his cabin, but his grin was reassuring. The sharp-planed face seemed pale, but his gray eyes were steady with a light of satisfaction in their depths.

At sight of him Banner felt some of the tension ease in his chest. He had been afraid. There had been more than one shot fired from aloft, but there was not a scratch on him, thank God. The movement of the vessel had probably saved him from Judah's point-blank range, but they had been bad moments for Banner, helpless and so far away.

Mabrey was wringing Kinkaid's hand, grinning like a schoolboy.

"We came as soon as we could, Bart. We didn't know until the last minute that Macario and his men had come with Judah."

"They did little harm." He paused carefully and went on, "Soledad won't have to worry anymore, John."

"No," Mabrey replied soberly, "and I for one will never forget what we owe you, my boy. If you'd been killed—injured, I'd never have been able to forgive myself. You aren't hurt, are you?"

"Not a scratch. Do I look as if I were ailing? I'm afraid I'm not going to give you any business, Doctor."

The long speech made him cough. He reached for his handkerchief and covered the bloody spittle before the others could notice it.

Mabrey was saying with relief, "I am eternally thankful that you're safe. I was worried about you. Judah was a madman, a devil incarnate. There was a kind of diabolical indestructibility about him." The doctor chuckled. "You know, Bart, I once said that about you—to Tarifa."

"What?"

"That you were indestructible."

Kinkaid grinned. "And now you see you were right? Why don't you go to Soledad—tell her the good news?"

"Yes, yes, I will. But you must come with me? We'll have a celebration befitting the occasion."

"I can't accept, John. We're sailing." He turned to the mate and told him, "Get under weigh, Mr. Banner."

"Aye, sir."

Banner touched his cap smartly and left the cabin.

"Well," Mabrey said as he got to his feet, "I wish you would reconsider and stay a little longer. I was hoping you would be best man at my wedding."

"I'm afraid I can't do that for you, John," Kinkaid said quietly. "But you know I wish you and Soledad every happiness? You both deserve it."

He coughed again into his handkerchief, and for an instant Mabrey looked at him speculatively. Why in heaven's name, thought Bart, didn't the man leave? He wasn't going to be able to hold out much longer. A debilitating weakness was beginning to envelop him, as fog closes in around a becalmed vessel.

"Are you all right?" Mabrey asked sharply.

Bart sat up with an effort. Carefully he put the handkerchief back in his pocket, then smiled reassuringly at the doctor.

"Of course. Just a cold I've picked up. I—don't like to rush you, John. But if we don't sail within the hour we'll miss the tide."

"I understand." Mabrey reached forward to offer his hand. "Our profound thanks again, Bart, Soledad's and mine. Shall I say good-bye to Tarifa for you?"

"No," Bart said slowly. "I've said that already."

"Then there's nothing left but to say bon voyage? I wish, oh hell, I wish things could have ended differently for you and Tarifa!"

"So do I, John. But I realize now—this was the only way it could ever have ended."

"Blasted shame!" Mabrey growled, and marched out of the cabin without a backward look, jamming his hat at the back of his head.

Banner stood by the rail waiting for him.

Below, the vaqueros and Macario's body, now shrouded in new canvas, had already been loaded into the small boats belonging to the hide houses.

"I'll turn Canejo's men over to the authorities when we get ashore," Mabrey said, "though Don Macario was responsible for their actions, I'm sure."

"Yes, sir. And thank'ee."

"You're a good man, Banner. I appreciate all you've done for Dona Soledad and for me."

Banner colored to the roots of his grizzled hair. "It was nothing, sir. Just carryin' out the cap'n's orders." When he was flustered the old Yankee vernacular returned to shorten and slur his speech.

Mabrey glanced aft for an instant. "Look after him, won't you, Banner? If he were my own flesh and blood he couldn't mean more to me. He seemed tired when I left him. It's been a trying time for all of us."

"Aye, sir. And you needn't worry, I'll look after the captain, sir."

Mabrey offered the mate his hand, then drew it back with an exclamation of surprise. There was a bright smear of blood on the back of his hand near the cuff.

"Must have scratched myself climbing aboard." He wiped the blood away with his handkerchief and saw that there was no mark on the skin. His eyes came up swiftly to meet Banner's in a sudden powerful realization.

Banner spoke first, echoing Mabrey's thoughts.

"The captain, sir?"

"I just shook hands with him. He was hit! He must have been lying to us."

"Come on, sir!"

The two men raced across the deck to the wonderment of the hands who were readying the ship to sail. Banner reached powerfully to fling open the door to the captain's cabin.

Kinkaid was slumped over the desk, his head on his arms.

"Cap'n Kinkaid!"

"Bart!"

Banner pulled him gently erect and Mabrey saw with relief that Kinkaid had opened his eyes.

"I'm all right, John. No need for you—to stay."

Mabrey was feverishly opening Kinkaid's coat, undoing his shirt. He drew in his breath sharply when he saw the blood-soaked bandages.

"Why in God's name didn't you tell me, Bart? You shouldn't have lost all that blood. Help me get him onto the bunk," he told Banner curtly.

The two men struggled to get him onto the bed. Mabrey's eyes narrowed as he watched Kinkaid fight for breath. Undoubtedly the ball had entered the lung.

They stretched him out and Banner helped Mabrey remove the injured man's coat, shirt, and tie. Mabrey himself carefully undid the bandages and critically examined the wounds. The left collarbone had been shattered, but the wound in the chest worried him more.

Kinkaid's face was pale, beaded with perspiration. His pulse, when Mabrey took hold of his wrist, was weak and thready.

"Get the ship's medicine chest," the doctor ordered. "Hurry, man!"

"Yes, sir. It's in the locker here."

He went to get a key from a drawer in Kinkaid's desk and opened a locked standing cupboard. The medicine chest was a weighty wooden box with a clasp and brass lock.

"I don't need you here, John," Bart protested between his teeth, as the doctor probed gently at the edge of the wounds with an experimental finger. "Banner can—look after me. We're sailing soon."

"You're not sailing any place," Mabrey told him flatly. "If I could, I'd take you ashore, but you can't be moved. Mr. Banner—send a man ashore to my place, and have him bring me my bag of surgical instruments. Quickly! Go, man!"

Banner stood looking in bewilderment from the captain's face to the doctor's.

Kinkaid said, using all the strength and force left in him, "I'm still captain of this ship. Put to sea, Mr. Banner!"

"If you do," Mabrey replied shortly, "you'll bury your captain there."

Banner had never disobeyed a captain's orders in his life. He would rather have cut off his own arm than have disobeyed Kinkaid. But his jaw hardened when he saw the pallor and lines of strain on Bart's sweating face, and the inexorable truth written on Mabrey's.

"I'll send a man for your things at once, Doctor," he said stonily.

"I'll have you—in irons—for insubordination!" gasped Kinkaid.

"Aye, sir," said Banner unhappily. "And I'll go to 'em with a will, sir. Ye can keelhaul me as well, if ye like, but I can't be responsible for your losin' your life, sir."

Kinkaid lay and cursed him weakly under his breath and closed his eyes. When they were alone he said to Mabrey, "You're—wasting your time, John."

"Don't talk; it's bad for that lung."

"Got to—while I can."

Mabrey was scarcely listening. His mind was leaping from one possibility to another. He had no way of knowing just where the ball lay in the lung, yet he was sure it was there. It had not emerged. He could take a chance and leave it there, hoping that it would not move or strike some other vital organ. Or he could risk removing it, providing Bart could withstand the operation in his present condition. It would be a dangerous business at best, especially on a ship. Yet if he did it at all, he knew that it would have to be done right here on the *Celestial Queen*, and at once.

Kinkaid muttered, "Promise me—one thing. You won't tell—Tarifa—about this. I—want your—word."

Mabrey hesitated. "Don't you think she should know?"

"No!" The violence of the exclamation started Kinkaid coughing, and Mabrey was alarmed at the sight of the blood on his lips. "We've—said our—good-byes," Bart gasped. "You can't—bring her—here—"

"All right, I promise. But for the love of heaven don't talk anymore!"

Kinkaid studied his face for a moment, seemed satisfied with what he read there, and closed his eyes again.

When Banner returned to the cabin the doctor was cleansing the wounds. He had the mate help him while he reset and bandaged the broken collarbone tightly in place.

Bart lay with his eyes shut, his lips parted a little, breathing in short uneven gasps.

When they had finished and moved a little away from the injured man, Banner whispered anxiously, "He's goin' to be all right, Doctor?"

Mabrey shook his head. "I'm not sure. I don't know where that ball is lying in his lung, and he's lost a lot of blood, more than he should have."

"But you're a doctor, sir; you can do something?"

Mabrey stood with a frown on his face, rubbing his chin.

"I don't know," he said finally. "I just don't know,

Banner. The gun was fired at close range. Why it failed to go clean through him I can't figure out. It's still lodged somewhere in the right lung. I'm certain of that."

Banner asked cautiously, "And you think there's a chance you could get it out, sir?"

"I could try. I'm no miracle worker, but I used to be a pretty fair surgeon. Still, is it worth taking the chance against such heavy odds? If only he hadn't sat there talking to us while he bled half to death!"

Banner glanced at Kinkaid's face and suddenly a look of acute pain crossed his own.

"He's all I have, sir," the mate said. "If he dies, I'll die too—in here." He touched the breast of his blue coat with a rope-scarred finger as blunt as the end of a marlinespike. "I love him, sir," he ended simply.

Mabrey laid a sympathetic hand on his shoulder. "So do I."

"Beggin' pardon, sir, but I'm a great believer in Providence," continued the old sailor. "What I mean is, your happenin' to be aboard ship just when he needs you so bad. Your discoverin' he was hurt, sir, before you left, when it would have been too late for any of us. It seems as if it was meant to be."

"You think I should try to take the bullet out?"

"Yes, sir. I do."

Mabrey glanced at his patient, then around the smallish cabin. He made up his mind swiftly, as he had always done on the important occasions in his life.

"Very well, Mr. Banner. He may clap us both in irons for it, if he lives, but we'll try our best."

There was relief and a deep gratitude in Banner's eyes as he said smartly, "Aye, sir!"

"I'll need help," the doctor said briskly. "Have the cook boil all the water he can. Get me some clean towels. And three strong men besides yourself, to hold him."

"Yes, sir."

"There's not much you can do about the roll of the ship I suppose?" the doctor asked ruefully.

"We can throw out some extra sea anchors, sir."

"Splendid. Now, I must have a steady base on which to perform the operation. That desk is fastened down?"

"Yes, sir."

"And a clean cover for the top?"

"A length of new canvas, sir?"

"That will do excellently. Now let's see what we've got in this medicine chest."

Mabrey went to the chest where it still lay open on the desk, and began to go through the contents with a practiced eye. Like most ships where the master had to double as doctor and dispenser of first aid, the medicine chest of the *Celestial Queen* contained a good supply of the more common drugs. Quinine, aloes, calomel, laudanum, turpentine, as well as a supply of lint and bandages and a few crude surgical tools.

The laudanum mixed with whiskey would have to do as an anaesthetic. In his own surgical bag Mabrey had catgut, scalpels, and probes, but it was going to be touch-and-go.

"Get me all the light you can," he told Banner.

"Yes, sir. There's lanterns a-plenty. You won't have to worry on that score."

But Mabrey was worried. In such a delicate operation, even if he could perform it satisfactorily and Kinkaid managed to survive the shock, the steadiness of the surgeon's hand was imperative. And how in the blue blazes was he going to control his reflexes on a rolling ship? Only the sight of Banner's trusting face, and the faint moan that escaped Bart's clamped lips, kept the doctor from refusing to go on.

He returned to his patient and laid the backs of his fingers against his cheeks and temples. He felt his pulse once again, and cursed at the enforced delay.

Bart opened his eyes and said, "Go, John. Leave—it alone."

Mabrey stood looking down at him steadily.

"I can't do that, Bart. I'm your friend, but before that I'm a doctor. The oath I took demands that I try to save your life."

Bart groaned as the ship rolled deeply, and blood appeared at the corner of his mouth.

Mabrey wiped it away gently. He was afraid, mortally afraid that whatever he did now would be done too late. Yet he had no choice but to try.

Banner had left the cabin to carry out the doctor's

orders. In seconds, it seemed, seamen brought in lanterns and hung them on the walls over and around the desk. Others unrolled a new length of white canvas on the desk top, tacking it down with swift, sure strokes of their hammers. They kept their eyes averted from their stricken captain's face.

"What are you doing?" Bart asked faintly.

"Fixing a place where I can operate," replied Mabrey. "Lie still and don't talk."

"No—use." The captain's eyes had a sunken, glazed look that worried Mabrey. Suddenly, to his surprise, he realized he was praying, had been praying to himself for the past few minutes. He can't die, he told himself stubbornly. I can't let him die.

Mabrey had no way of knowing that in the highly superstitious minds of the crew Bart's death was a foregone conclusion, depite the alacrity with which they had performed their chores. Deaths always came in threes, and already that day Captain Judah and Macario Canejo had died aboard ship. The captain would inevitably be the third.

Banner, coming upon them discussing the matter in the fo'c'sle smashed his fist into the nearest man's face, and roared like an angry bull at the rest of the hands:

"Ye bastards! Lay odds on the cap'n's death, will ye? I'll have ye all spread-eagled and give ye a taste o' the cat myself, that'll tear yer backs to shreds if he dies!"

Chastened, the crew went back to their chores.

It seemed an eternity to Mabrey before they were ready. Working quickly now, he mixed laudanum with some whiskey and forced it between Kinkaid's stiff lips. His color wasn't good and his pulse was weak, but to delay now, Mabrey felt, would be as fatal as to go ahead.

Three stalwart sailors came in with buckets of boiling water and arranged them on a stationary table near the desk, then stood by awaiting the doctor's orders.

"Now lads, get him onto the desk," said Mabrey. "Easy as you can."

The seamen moved Kinkaid's big frame as effortlessly as if they had been carrying a pack of hides.

The ship had settled to a steady roll and the three sailors, two near Kinkaid's feet, another and Banner at his head, held him firmly on the canvas-covered desk top.

Mabrey removed his own coat and rolled his sleeves up above his elbows. With all the lanterns lit, a circle of light played over the area where Bart lay. He noted with misgiving that the move had brought a trace of blood to the patient's lips again.

Mabrey wasted no time. Though it was not an age when antisepsis was practiced by the medical profession, he had always washed his hands and his instruments as a matter of course, before beginning an operation. When his hands were clean, he washed his instruments and laid them on a fresh towel near his hand. He removed the bandages from Kinkaid's chest and bared the wound. Holding a long slender probe, he felt delicately inside the wound, and then with a strange disbelief, felt the tip of it grate on something. Could the bullet be still imbedded at the very end of the wound? It seemed too good a piece of luck to be true. He withdrew the probe, and felt Kinkaid shudder as he clamped his teeth against a groan of pain.

Mabrey glanced at his face quickly. It was tinged with gray. Fear that he might be too late even now made him reckless. He reached for a scalpel and made an incision with a deep sharp stroke that made the man on the table tremble and draw in his breath with a rush.

"Hold him steady!" Mabrey warned, tying off blood vessels as he went, aware of the press of time, of eternity yawning at his elbow. The ship rolled heavily, and he held his hand with scalpel poised, until it righted herself again and he could continue.

There was sweat on his own face now, running down from his shaggy eyebrows into his eyes. Timing himself against the roll of the ship, barely aware of Bart's white agonized face or the faces of the other men bracing themselves around the table, he worked on.

Now! If he was lucky.

He could see the tip of the gray mishapen slug where it lay in Bart's chest.

The probe touched it and it moved sideways. Working like a madman, he pursued it.

Got it.

Lost it.

Then with the sweat streaming into his eyes and his own

breath failing him, he forced it up and out of the cavity. It fell with a dull clatter among his instruments on the towel.

He couldn't stop to breathe a sigh of relief. Bart's body had gone rigid under his hands. His eyes were open a mere crack and were black with agony. Suddenly he gave a short sigh and his head fell to one side.

"The Cap'n's dead!" cried one of the younger sailors, his eyes and mouth wide with terror.

"Avast, ye lubber!" Banner thundered. There was an unmistakable tremor in his voice.

Mabrey felt Bart's wrist, then bent his ear swiftly to his chest. He couldn't be sure whether it was Bart's or his own faint heartbeats he heard. There was no time to make sure.

He sutured and closed the wound, wincing himself at the raw solution of turpentine he had used in lieu of a better medicament, as it made the tissues shrink.

He bandaged the patient's chest and ordered him moved back to the bunk. When he was wrapped in blankets, Mabrey lifted his wrist in his own still-bloody hand. Behind him the white-covered desk looked like a butcher's block.

Had it all been for nothing? Had he been too late, or too slow? Mabrey controlled the trembling of his own fingers and forced them to probe the wrist of the injured man for a pulse. At last he found it, willing it to be there, it seemed, with his own soul. A mere tick of movement, but it made him giddy with relief.

Banner's face, close to his, was like a granite mask.

Mabrey nodded his head, his lips feeling too weak to form words. But he forced them out for the other man's sake.

"Alive—at least for now."

"Thank God, sir." Breath sighed from Banner's lungs as if from a huge bellows and he stepped away from the bunk.

Mabrey lifted Bart's eyelids gently and peered at his eyeballs.

He said tersely, "If you can pray, Banner, I suggest you start now."

"I been prayin', sir, ever since we found that blood on your hand by the rail," the mate said quietly.

When he turned around again, Mabrey discovered that the sailors had left, taking with them the stained buckets and canvas. He tottered to a chair and sank into it, accepting gratefully the large whiskey Banner handed him.

"I know I shouldn't bother you with it now, sir," the old sailor said uncomfortably, "but I have to know."

Banner's eyes wore a haunted look under their bushy brows.

Mabrey felt the heat of the whiskey beginning to relax the taut muscles of his stomach. He glanced at his patient's pallid face. His eyes were still closed. He hadn't moved a muscle since they put him there, poor devil, and perhaps he never would.

"I'll be frank with you, Banner," the doctor said. "I don't know myself. He nearly died there on the table. I don't know why he didn't. The shock to his system must have been tremendous. I can only say he's a strong man, and a fairly young one. Nature is on our side. There's a chance. How big a chance I don't know, and I won't hazard a guess. He could take a turn for the worse at any moment and be gone like a candle blowing out. He's weak. He's lost a lot of blood, too much to suit me." The doctor's voice was husky with emotion. "I think it was his wish—his intention—to die today."

"No!" Banner stepped back a pace as if he would separate himself from the implication of the words.

"If you recall," said Mabrey, "it was only by the merest accident that we discovered he had been injured. Another few hours and he would have been dead. He tried to make it end that way. He wanted to get rid of me; he even asked me to leave and he ordered you to put to sea at once, if you remember?"

The full impact of the doctor's speech was just beginning to show on the mate's craggy face. It looked as gray as a jellyfish in the swaying lamplight.

"I can't—believe it, sir."

"Even when I was working on him he asked me to leave."

"He's no coward, sir," Banner said stoutly. "He wouldn't have—"

"Killed himself? No. He's one of the bravest men I have ever known. He would never have killed himself deliberately. But fate played into his hands. I can't be sure, but I think he planned all along that he and Judah would kill each other."

Banner's eyes were wide. "But why? In God's name, why? I've known him all his life. I've never known him to back away from the blows fate dealt him."

The doctor sat watching him, a look of helpless compassion on his face.

Suddenly memory flooded back to Banner with the stunning force of a riptide. His last words were untrue. Once before he had seen Bart struck down, by the Gypsy's knife thrust. He had welcomed death then. Bart had gone to Loma de Oro to kill her, Banner knew. But might he not also have gone there hoping to die himself, because he could no longer bear life without Dolores?

But he had gotten over all that, Banner thought wildly. He had even married another woman. Surely that proved he had put his unhappy love behind him? Banner was convinced Bart could not really love the wild, heathen Gypsy woman he had married. But there was a strong bond between them, and he was grateful that she had given him a new interest in life. No, none of the doctor's suggestions made sense. Yet Banner was worried.

Watching him, Mabrey said, "You understand something of what I've been talking about. I can see it on your face."

Banner told him about Dolores, about the knifing, and Bart's strange apathy during his other illness.

"But that was because the young lady had been lost so tragically," said Banner. "It was a great shock to him to come back and discover what had happened to her. But I can see no reason now, sir, for him to want to die."

Mabrey's eyes fastened for a moment on the injured man's stark profile and he sighed unhappily. "Didn't you know? He loves his wife far more than he ever loved Dolores Alvarjo. The tragedy is that he knows she will never love him. He intended to sail today and never return. But fate offered him a better, a more permanent escape. He can't be blamed for taking it? The last request he made of me was to promise him I would not let his wife know of his injury. Now I do not feel that I can break that promise."

Banner's face was flame red, like a lobster shell just plucked from a cauldron of boiling water.

"No, sir, I can't believe it. Not any of it. I know him. He told me why he married Dona Tarifa—to safeguard the rancho, and because of his memories of Dolores, and to provide for her little one."

"You don't know him at all," Mabrey said sadly. "We go through life and so seldom know the innermost thoughts of those closest to us. Padre Cazon knew. So did Zenobio Sanchez, and Ellen Havelock."

Banner sat down on the edge of a chair and put a large hand up to shade his eyes.

"I—didn't know, sir. Didn't even guess. But why didn't he trust me—why didn't he tell me? During the other time he—"

"He couldn't have," said the doctor kindly. "He was trying to fight it all the time. I think it finally engulfed him and he couldn't fight it any longer. Even the strongest swimmer's strength gives out in time."

Banner's voice sounded strangled. "You say he loves her—that witch?"

"I know how you feel," Mabrey replied softly. "But love does not always go only to the worthy, nor is it always reciprocated."

"She knows he loves her—a man like that, yet she'd sacrifice him if she knew he was lying here like this?" Banner asked indignantly.

Mabrey put down his glass. "I don't know," he said, deliberating on the subject. "I've promised him not to tell her. And frankly I don't know what good she could do now even if she came here. I've a feeling it's too late—for all of us. I'm sorry, Jake."

The old seaman rose and took up his cap. His mouth was grim, his jaw rock-hard with determination.

"Nevertheless, she shall know, sir. I'll go and tell her myself. You may have made him a promise not to bother the lady, but I didn't!"

Mabrey watched him stride toward the door. There was an urgency in his movements, and his voice carried the full length of the ship as he stepped on deck.

"Avast there! Lower the longboat, and look lively or I'll cat the lot of ye from here to Cape Hatteras!"

The rush of footsteps on deck attested to the crew's belief in the mate's flat declaration.

Mabrey's eyes rested sadly on his patient's face.

Under his breath he said softly, "I shall never believe in justice again if my future has been purchased at the expense of your life, my boy."

He rose and went to Bart's side. He took his wrist in one hand and began counting the faint rise and fall of the pulse.

CHAPTER 39

Tarifa sat alone in her bedroom in front of the dressing table. Any moment now Luis, Don Tiburcio, and Judah's lawyer, Trumble, would arrive with the papers she had agreed to sign. There was a cold sickness inside her. She would have mounted Guindilla and fled far across the hills if she dared.

For some reason that she could not fathom, she had dressed herself in her old Romany costume. Now she combed her hair out loosely upon her shoulders and tied her amulet about her neck over the gold cross Ygnacio had given her.

She was so engrossed in her own thoughts that she did not even hear Penti when she entered the room and stood regarding her for a moment from the open doorway.

"*Miri pen?*"

Tarifa scowled at the old woman's reflection in the mirror.

"What do you want?"

"I must tell you. He is dead—the captain."

Tarifa whirled to face her.

"You lie!"

The old *gitana* shook her head.

"It is the truth. If he is not dead this minute he soon will be. I have seen it in the cards. I warned him when he left."

"Fortune-telling! What truth is there in that?" Tarifa said scornfully.

"Do not jest about the beliefs of your people, *miri pen*. I gave him my amulet to protect him. But he will not keep it on him and so he will die."

Tarifa's eyes widened. A Gypsy did not give away his amulet, his own protection against evil.

"What makes you think he will die?" she asked guardedly.

"So much blood—and the long darkness following."

Tarifa stood up. She was displeased. There was enough on her mind tonight without adding the old Gypsy's superstitious fears to her worries.

"Once before everyone thought him dead," she said by way of dismissal.

"You did not believe it," answered Penti, "nor did I, or Dr. Mabrey."

"Then what *gitana* nonsense makes you believe it now?"

"Look in your own heart, *miri pen*, and you will know it as well as I do. He will never return to this house. I knew that when he left. I warned him, but like all *gorgios* he refused to believe the words of a *gitana*."

Tarifa shivered for no reason that she could account for, and something deeper than her sense of reason took possession of her. She knew suddenly that what Penti had just said was true. Bart would never return. He had gone from her life for good. She felt a moment of stark loneliness; then it was gone as quickly as it had come. If she had loved him the news the Gypsy brought would have left her desolate. But tonight her ruling passion, Loma de Oro, was uppermost in her mind.

"Why do you upset me with such tales when you know that I have urgent business on my mind? If you were idiot enough to give away your amulet and so have lost it, that is your own worry. I cannot get it back for you." She hesitated for a moment and then added, "Here, take mine."

She tore it from her neck and stretched out her hand toward Penti.

The old Gypsy shrank back.

"No! It is cursed now. You wear it with the cross. You have no true belief in it anymore."

"You are a demented old witch!" Tarifa cried in disgust. "Why in heaven's name did you give him your amulet in the first place, since you set such store by it?"

"To protect him. And because he has given you much. His love. Now even his life. But you do not care, do you? It has always been a curse to you, the cold, calculating Moorish blood that flows in your veins! You do not even care that such a man went to his death because of you!"

"Primita Undebē! Because of me? I think you have lost your senses. And who is supposed to have killed him, my all-seeing friend?"

"Capitán Judah."

"Judah?" Her eyes widened in surprise.

"He went in search of him with Dr. Mabrey. He once made you a promise to deal with Capitán Judah, because of Soledad. And he was afraid for you, *miri pen,* afraid you would try to kill Judah yourself."

Tarifa shook her head impatiently. "I have spoken with Capitán Judah, you know that. I have decided to do as Luis wishes and deed him the piece of land he demands, for Soledad's sake. The arrangements have been made. It is no longer of concern to Bart Kinkaid what happens on Loma de Oro."

There was harshness and condemnation in Penti's short laughter, "You think that would have stopped him? How little you know the man you have married. When he left the rancho it was clearly written on his face, only you were too engrossed in your own affairs to see it."

"What are you talking about?" Tarifa shouted. "What was written on his face?" She was becoming unnerved by the old woman's foolish talk. Yet to her bewildered brain, it seemed as if the old *gitana* had grown in stature until she towered there in the doorway like some gigantic figure of doom.

"Death, *miri pen.* The death wish. He had offered you everything else. It was plain that he had made up his mind to die, honorably as only such a man can die, at the hands of an enemy. I have known others like him who have done the same thing."

"You are making up all this nonsense! I will not listen to anymore!"

"I am telling you the truth. My own luck is gone; I gave it away, I cannot afford to lie. Nor can you, *miri pen.* You have thrown your luck away also. The road we stand upon runs in only two directions. Which will you choose, life or death?"

Tarifa turned away from her and walked to the window facing on the front of the hacienda. Three horsemen were riding up the drive. Luis, Don Tiburcio, and Trumble. She trembled, realizing that for the first time a piece of Loma de Oro would be split from the whole. It was unbearable, like standing by and watching while a loved one was dismembered.

"I cannot do it!" she cried fiercely, whirling to face Penti.

"Do what, *miri pen?*"

"Let them break up the rancho! I cannot give a piece of it to Titus Judah."

"He will fight you in the courts; he will force you to do it."

"Let him fight then! It will take money, and time."

"And in the end," Penti asked, "will you go on fighting till you drop for this cursed land that has brought you nothing but misery? That has robbed you of everything worthwhile in life? What is there you have not sacrified for its sake—your liberty, your beliefs, your child, and now the man who loves you? And to what end? Perhaps the other Alvarjos will now demand their shares, too, under the Americano law. What answer will you make to them?"

Tarifa shook her head. She had to have time to think, the old *gitana*'s words beat at her brain like a mallet, driving her own thoughts out of her head.

"Give it up!" the old woman cried. "Go, before you have lost everything. Before you are damned by the gods for your own selfish greed."

"No!"

There was bitterness and defeat on Penti's face as she turned to leave the room.

"Where are you going?" demanded Tarifa.

"To pack my things. I will be leaving this house soon."

"Leaving?"

"Word will come soon and I will go."

"I think you have lost what little wits you had left. Word from where, from whom?"

Penti shrugged. "It does not matter who brings it. But it will come, word of the capitán's death, and I will go. I shall not return."

Tarifa let her go, but she did not go at once to greet her guests. Instead she instructed a maid to tell the gentlemen that she would be delayed. When the girl had gone, she picked up her amulet thoughtfully and went out into the starless night. Her bare arms were cold as she walked across the patio and entered the chapel.

It was damp inside, dark except for the vigil light winking like a small red eye on the altar. She went forward slowly and laid the amulet on the floor.

She knelt down and clasped her hands.

"I give you this, because it is no longer of any use to me." She wasn't sure whether she fully meant the words but she tried to. For an instant it seemed as if Padre Cazon were beside her, pleased with her speech.

It gave her an odd feeling of warm satisfaction. Penti did not realize that she had found peace and a certain contentment in the beliefs of Padre Cazon. The proof of it was that she was kneeling here now, of her own free will.

Random thoughts ran through her head. Penti's brooding predictions, the strange coldness that had come over her when the old Gypsy had declared Bart was dead or soon would be. She would not allow herself to believe it. Bart was indestructible—Mabrey had told her that. Until now, she did not realize how much she had counted upon the knowledge that he was alive somewhere in the world, despite their separation, able to come to her if she needed him. But she had never needed anyone! No, that was not quite true. Here, alone in the chapel, she was forced to be honest with herself. In these last years she had grown to depend on others—Padre Cazon, Bart, Luis, Santos, even Tía Isabella.

She was not aware of another nagging thought until it leaped at her full blown out of the darkness. Some words, nonsensical to her then, that Padre Cazon had told her or read to her when first he began instructing her for baptism: "Therefore, if thou art offering thy gift at the altar, and there rememberest that thy brother has anything against thee, leave thy gift before the altar and go first to be reconciled to thy brother, and then come and offer thy gift."

It was absurd that such a thought should come to her at this moment. It frightened her. It was as if the Padre's voice spoke again in her ear. She covered both ears with her hands to shut out the thought.

Suddenly she got up and ran from the chapel, climbing the low graveyard wall, and ran up the hill toward Loma de Oro, memories pursuing her like baying hounds. Memories of Bart's face the night he had swooped down on her in the patio, and carried her half-naked to her room. Of his voice telling her solemnly as they stood face-to-face in the study, "I married you for one reason, and one reason only. Because I love you. I have never stopped loving you. But I knew I could never tell you of my love if I hoped to keep you. You would have thrown it back in my face, as you have thrown aside the feelings of every person who has come your way." And Mabrey asking her bluntly, "Is it enough? Is Loma de Oro enough for you forever? Don't you want anything else?" Padre Cazon arguing sadly with her over Luis, "When will you learn, Tarifa, that you cannot compete with God?" And Penti's last dire words: "He has given you his love, even his life, but you do not care that he went to his death because of you. . . ."

She reached the cabaña and slammed the door on her own fears. She lay panting against the wood, fingers pressed hard against it as if to hold it between herself and the world, both temporal and spiritual. She was trembling violently, whether from the cold or her own seething emotions she wasn't sure.

When the paroxysm had passed, she found a candle and lighted it and started the fire in the little fireplace.

The room looked familiar and yet odd somehow as if she were seeing it for the first time. It remained Ygnacio's room. The books, the pictures, the hunting trophies all attested to that. But there were other ghosts here. She could still see Lasho, bound in his grave ribbons, his tiny cheeks and lips painted to look lifelike, lying on the floor at her feet while she danced out her wild grief above him. And she could see the tall dark figure of Kinkaid, wrestling with her in the shadows while they tried to kill each other. She saw once more the terrible look on his face when he discovered Lasho's body, the way he had staggered over to demand that she use his own pistol on him. She recalled the wildness in both their eyes as they stared at each other in that silent room of half-shadows. And later, when he lay in a pool of his own blood at her feet, she could not recall why she had not shot him that mad night.

She moved to the table and took up the tambourine that had lain there gathering dust for so long a time. It sounded dull and flat to her ears. As she began to dance, her legs were stiff and unwilling, but gradually as the rhythm began to absorb her attention, her muscles relaxed, and she moved in and out of the shadows, oblivious to her surroundings.

She was aware that her dancing was the same as it had always been, effortless, exhilarating. But just as the cabaña had seemed both familiar and yet strange to her when she entered it, so did the rhythm of her movements.

Always before the dance had been able to absorb her completely, to wash away all doubts and fears. Now it was as if her brain were detached from her flashing body, watching her from afar with a coolly critical eye.

After a moment she tossed the tambourine aside in angry defeat. She knelt down on the floor in front of the fire, feeling the heat of the flames on her face and breasts.

Perhaps Penti had been right. She should have been content to remain a simple Gypsy, not laughed at their ways and tried to make herself different. Now it was too late. Now she was caught in a trap of her own making. There was no place for her. The people of Loma de Oro did not want her. Penti would leave, for whatever obscure Gypsy reasons she had concocted. There was nothing, no one left for her to turn to.

John Mabrey's words came back to her, superimposed on her own brooding thoughts. "Someday you may find that you want something more even than Loma de Oro." And her own brash reply, "If that time ever comes, Dr. Mabrey, you will know that I have also given up being a Gypsy, and forsaken the gods of my people forever. And such a thing can never happen until I am dead and have gone to join Lasho."

But it had happened, in spite of her every effort to stop

it. She had just left her amulet in the chapel, forsaking her Romany gods forever. She could no longer find solace in either the beliefs or the dances of her people.

She had ceased being a *gitana!*

It was as if she were one of those bewitched creatures in a fairy tale, who changes shape before the naked eye as the spell is lifted.

What would be left of the old Tarifa? What good would she be to herself or anyone else from now on? A greater curse than any *chovihani* could have wished upon her had enveloped her like a suffocating mantle.

She covered her face with her hands and wept. The long, body-wracking sounds of those unused to weeping, the ragged sobbing of stark hopelessness, of complete abandonment to wretchedness.

When at last she lay down, exhausted and still before the fire, she was aware of a strange feeling of release, of peace.

Later, outside, she heard a dog barking somewhere near the kitchen, then footsteps approaching the cabaña.

She got up swiftly and went to bolt the door.

"Tarifa?"

It was Luis' voice.

"Have you forgotten that Don Tiburcio and Señor Trumble are waiting to see you?"

She heard him try the door. "No, I have no forgotten. Tell them I am ill. I will sign the papers in the morning. Give them rooms and ask them to spend the night, *por favor?*"

Luis hesitated.

"You are not seriously ill?"

"No. It is a slight indisposition, nothing more. But I do not wish to see them till morning. *Primita Undebē!* Do as I tell you!"

At the flash of her old temper he seemed relieved.

"Very well. I will send Penti or one of the maids to you."

"Send no one! I want to be alone."

She listened at the door until she heard his footsteps leaving the veranda, then she sank down upon the cot.

She curled up like a cat, her head on the pillow where Bart's had lain when he had wished for death and she had goaded and tricked him into living. She was not certain, even now, why she had done it.

And now was he finally dead, as Penti said, because of her? She sat up and tossed back her hair with both hands. Her small breasts, pointed and firm under the flimsy bodice of her dress, rose and fell with a new excitement.

Death had always held a morbid fascination for her even as a child when she had first encountered it in the bullring. She had hated its easy victory, hated the finality of it. The inexorable challenge of it was what fascinated her. The winner-take-all stakes that made up the wager.

All Gypsies had a fatalistic, Oriental attitude toward life and death, yet in Tarifa there burned another, a different emotion. The driving desire to dominate, to win, even over death itself.

That was why I saved Bart's life, she thought with sudden flashing insight. And it pleased her to have the fact settled in her mind.

She lay down again and presently she fell asleep.

It was late when she awoke. Below her she was aware of the bustling activity of the kitchen yard, and of the hacienda beyond.

She went out onto the veranda and stood for a time surveying the scene below. Her eyes swept over the kitchen square to the red tiles of the hacienda roof, and beyond, to the pastures containing the palominos. Then her gaze wandered to the valley dotted with the herds of Loma de Oro cattle and horses. All this had become her life, her love, her world. She had cherished and protected it as a mother guards a beloved child. But now there was a stillness in her eyes as she watched it, a look of inner speculation.

What could ever mean more to her than Loma de Oro? What ever had? Lasho? Yes, she had loved Lasho as much as she did Loma de Oro. She would have given it to him, all of it, if he had lived. But had she loved her child more than the rancho? Now she would never know.

She closed her eyes for a moment. Down below Judah's lawyer was waiting for her. She could no longer put off the meeting. The strange lassitude that had enveloped her as she surveyed the rancho left her as quickly as it had come. In its place she felt a surge of her old power.

Without hesitation she turned and went back inside the cabaña. She walked swiftly to the desk where once she had written her letters to Bart, and took up the pen and a sheet

of paper. She wrote hurriedly for several moments, then
without pausing to read what she had written, folded the
paper and put it inside her blouse.

She returned to the hacienda the way she had come,
hoping to meet no one until she had completed her errand.
She climbed over the wall, through the graveyard where
she paused briefly at Lasho's grave, past the chapel and
into the patio. She walked briskly along the veranda past
her own room and on to Tía Isabella's, meeting no one on
the way.

The old woman answered her tap at once much to her
relief.

"*Sí?*"

"I must speak to you," Tarifa said.

"Come in."

Isabella was seated in an armchair by the window with
her prayer book in her long hands. She glanced up at Tarifa questioningly.

Then, before Tarifa could speak, she said, "Luis has
told me what you are doing for Soledad's sake. I want you
to know that we are all very grateful." There was mere
politeness in the words, Tarifa noted with amusement, no
warmth. They had never liked each other, the old Castilian
and the Gypsy, yet there was a truce of long standing between them, as well as a grudging mutual admiration that
neither bothered to disguise.

Tarifa took the paper from her blouse. "I wanted to
give you this before I go."

Isabella raised her eyes in quick suspicion.

"Go?"

"Yes. I am leaving."

"You—plan a long trip?"

"A very long one. I am not coming back to—Loma de
Oro."

"But I don't understand," Isabella Alvarjo said slowly.

Tarifa squared her shoulders, forcing her lips to say the
words coldly without a tremor. "I have decided it is time
to give Loma de Oro back to its rightful owners, the Alvarjos. The boys can run the rancho now, with Santos' help.
There is more land than their father left them, including
what I purchased with Bart's money. I believe that you
can persuade them to keep the rancho undivided as Ygnacio

wished them to do, and as I wish it. In these uncertain times it will be better for all concerned. As for Judah, he deserves nothing. Let him go to the courts. Time will be against him, and as long as there is any hope of his getting the land, no harm will come to Soledad. She is the sole pawn in his game."

Tía Isabella looked in bewilderment at the sheet of paper Tarifa had put unfolded into her hand. Her eyes scanned the writing. To all appearances it was a quitclaim to all of Tarifa's share in Loma de Oro. Her eyes came up to meet the Gypsy's.

"This—is very splendid of you, Tarifa. But—where will you go?"

"I don't know yet."

"But why should you do this now? At least part of the rancho should remain yours. Ygnacio would have wanted that. And you have worked so hard. Loma de Oro is your life, why should you give it up?" Her Castilian sense of honor demanded that she ask it.

Tarifa lowered her head for a moment, then raised her chin in protective defiance.

"Is it your right to ask why I do something? I have given the rancho certain things, but Loma de Oro has paid me back a thousandfold. We are even. I ask nothing more."

"I do not understand this—change in you."

Tarifa shrugged her shoulders. "You know that Gypsies are changeable. If my son had lived perhaps I would have made a different decision. Be content that I have made this one in your favor."

Isabella glanced again at the paper in her hand.

"I don't understand why you have brought this to me—"

"You are Don Ygnacio's sister," Tarifa broke in. "You are the logical one to take over these matters. All you have to do is show that paper to Luis and the authorities in Los Angeles. Don Tiburcio can advise you."

Isabella's voice was guarded. "I see that you have also left the family most of the ten thousand dollars you brought from the mines."

"Yes. I will keep the rest to pay my way wherever I am going."

The old woman raised her head and her proud eyes were suddenly filmed with tears.

"I see now what Ygnacio saw in you. Strength and stature. We have not deserved you at Loma de Oro, but you must not leave us." She took a deep breath and added with a tremulous smile, "You must not go from Loma de Oro—my sister."

Not since Encarnacion's death had she spoken that word to another human being. She had never felt until this moment that Tarifa had really been her sister-in-law, even in the eyes of God. Now she recalled Padre Cazon's words asking her to be charitable to the Gypsy, and her heart was filled with bitter self-condemnation that the charity had been shown her instead, by the one she had always despised.

"I must go," Tarifa said. The most difficult part was over; she could leave now without a backward glance. But before she could move, a maid tapped at the door and entered the room.

"Por favor, Dona Tarifa, I did not know that you were here? There, is an Americano seaman asking to see you. He says that it is very urgent. The other gentlemen are waiting for you in the study, so I have shown him into the *sala."*

As the maid spoke Tarifa had felt her heart give an unaccountable and sickening lurch.

"Capitán Kinkaid?"

"No, it is not Don Bartolomeo."

Tarifa's lips set in a grim line. Then it could only be Judah, come to claim his reward, and she felt in a perfect frame of mind to deal with him. She was glad that he had come, glad of the opportunity to lock horns with him at last.

"Tell him I will come at once."

"Sí, Dona Tarifa."

"Shall I go for you?" Tía Isabella inquired.

"No. But you may come with me. I will settle this matter with Judah once and for all, and you may as well be a witness to what passes between us."

As the two women walked down the veranda together there seemed to be a new bond between them.

In the *sala,* a burly blue-clad back was turned toward them as the man stared out the front windows with his hands clasped behind his back.

Tarifa recognized Jake Banner with a start of apprehension. In a flash she knew that everything Penti had predicted was true. A suffocating dread came over her and she realized she had missed the old sailor's first words.

"—speak to you alone about the captain, señora."

"I will go," Isabella said.

Tarifa nodded. "Perhaps it is as well."

Isabella glanced at Tarifa's white face with concern as she left the room.

Tarifa called after her, "Send Penti to me."

"*Sí.*"

"Please sit down," Tarifa told Banner through stiff lips. She was puzzled. He looked as if he hated her enough to kill her then and there.

Banner told his story starkly, without embellishment, watching her as he spoke.

"You think he will die?" she asked in a low voice when he had finished.

"Not while I can help it! No matter what Dr. Mabrey says. He'd promised Bart not to send word to ye. But I made no such promise!"

"But what can I do?"

Banner swerved his eyes to the window and said uncomfortably. "He's in love with ye, Mabrey claims. Whether it's true or not I don't know—nor care. But I ain't seein' him die because of it! If ye've got the power to save him, I'm takin' ye aboard the *Celestial Queen* if I have to tie ye fore 'n' aft an' swing ye on deck in a lubber's chair!"

Tarifa's eyes were hard and flat like a snake that is ready to strike. "You could no more take me from the rancho against my will, Señor Banner, than you could fly from here to San Diego."

Banner knew the truth in her words. The hacienda and rancho were filled with men. One cry and she could surround herself with them, but he reached resolutely for the dirk in his belt.

"More killing?" she asked bitterly. "Is that what you want? What Bart would want? While you have been away from him he may already have died. You should never have left him."

"I came to get you," Banner said stubbornly. His hand

still rested on the dirk. She was a witch, a very demon of a creature, going about half-clad at this hour like some harlot. Not so many years ago in his native Salem, they would have hanged her and rightly so. Mabrey must be wrong. Bart couldn't love a woman like this. He turned away from her in despair and was surprised to hear her saying softly:

"It would be useless if I went with you, señor. There is nothing I could do to help Bart. But I will send someone with you who may help him."

Banner turned around in astonishment at her sudden show of sympathy and interest. The old Gypsy woman who had saved Bart's life long ago was standing in the doorway holding the same bundle of black stuff he remembered from the past.

Tarifa opened her mouth but the old Gypsy spoke first.

"You see, *miri pen,* it is just as I told you it would be. Blood—and darkness."

"Go with Señor Banner," Tarifa replied, ignoring her words of foreboding, "and see what you can do for my husband."

Penti's lips drew back in a sneer.

"Yes, you would throw me into the breech because you are afraid to go yourself? I will go, never fear. Not because you ask it, but because the capitán means something to me. I am a *gitana,* but there is something in my heart besides coldness and fear."

"You lie. I have never feared anything!"

"You are afraid now; I can see it in your eyes. I told you last night you must choose either of two directions of the road in which you stand. I see you insist on choosing the wrong one." She shrugged her shoulders. "It is no longer any affair of mine. I will go to the capitán, but it will do no good. He will be dead by the time I get there."

"He'll not be dead, ye lyin' black-hearted old witch!" Banner had jumped to his feet in his wrath. He'd have liked to strangle the pair of them. But he was sensible enough to realize that once before, between them, they had saved Bart's life. If it was within their power to do so again, he would not stand in their way.

"Pay no attention to her," said Tarifa. "If he is alive, she will know what to do when she gets there."

As if there were no disputing this fact, Penti addressed

the sailor calmly, "Come, we waste valuable time. You have horses outside?"

He nodded.

Tarifa stood by the door and watched them go. Penti mounted and rode off without a backward glance.

Tarifa returned to the *sala*. She had begun to tremble and she made her way into the dining room and splashed brandy into a glass, wetting her hand and blouse in the process.

All the emotional tumult of the past day and night seemed to be taking their toll at last. She felt as if she were losing her mind, her identity. She had not known that Penti's leaving would affect her so profoundly.

When she raised her glass the liquor spilled down the front of her dress. She did not hear Luis enter the room, and his voice startled her when he spoke softly at her elbow.

"Tarifa, I have just been with Tía Isabella. It is a splendid and generous thing you are doing, but you must not think of leaving Loma de Oro. We would not know what to do without you."

She was powerless to reply and she saw the look of shocked concern that came into his dark eyes.

"What is it; what is the matter?" He came to put his arm around her shoulders and she leaned her head wearily against his chest. She told him then of Penti's predictions and of Banner and Mabrey's belief that Bart needed her. When she had finished she asked suddenly, "Do you think I should have gone?"

"Not unless you wanted to go," he said slowly. "Bart would not have wanted you to come to him unless you came willingly. That was why he demanded that promise from the doctor not to send for you." Luis stroked her hair gently. "He is wise and kind, this husband of yours. He does not ask what he knows you are unable to give."

Tarifa stirred restlessly. "And you think I am cold and heartless because of it?"

He shook his head and smiled at her. "I have reason to know, better than others, how generous your heart can be. And today I have seen a measure of its greatness. I think Capitán Kinkaid has known this about you also for a long time, and he will understand whatever you do."

She stood away from him and he noted that the tension

had left her face. "You have always understood me the best, Luis, next to your father and Padre Cazon. I no longer know clearly how I feel or what I am. Does that surprise you? But I think I know now what I must do. Tell Santos to saddle Guindilla for me and bring his own horse. I will need him. Go quickly."

His eyes opened in surprise. "You are going to San Diego? But you must let me come with you."

She shook her head. "Tía Isabella will need you. *Adiós,* Luis." She brushed his cheek with her lips, flashed him a brief smile and was gone like a breeze that had passed him by.

Tarifa waited for Santos alone on the veranda. She had not said good-bye to anyone but Tía Isabella and Luis. Her nerves, stretched to the breaking point, could bear no more.

When they were mounted Santos asked quietly, "Which direction do we take, Patróna?"

"Toward San Diego."

She put spurs to Guindilla and did not speak again, and Santos wondered at her preoccupied silence and the swiftness of the pace she set. There was a strange concentration about her, an immobility in her features that he had never seen before. She did not even glance at the Mission as they passed San Luis Rey.

In a small valley just outside the pueblo, they came upon two horses and saw figures huddled on the ground.

As they halted the man rose and came forward but the woman lay where she was. Santos was surprised to recognize Capitán Kinkaid's mate, Señor Banner.

Tarifa said nothing, but she leaped from her horse and threw herself down beside the woman stretched on the ground.

"Penti!"

"*Miri pen*—"

"What happened?" Tarifa demanded.

"Her horse fell with her as we rounded the corner," said Banner unhappily. "I think she's badly hurt. I didn't like leavin' her alone, but I was just goin' for help."

"No use," sighed Penti. "My back is broken. I told you my luck—was out, *miri pen?*"

"No!" cried Tarifa. "It is not true. We will take you to Dr. Mabrey in San Diego. It isn't far."

"No—listen to me—I have not long." She moistened her lips. "You have been—like my own child, since you were born. I—know your weaknesses—your strengths—better than anyone else—except the capitán." Her eyes were dark with pain, but there was an unmistakable pleading in their depths. "Go to him. Go to the capitán—"

"I was on my way."

Penti nodded with satisfaction and closed her eyes.

"Penti!"

The old Gypsy opened her eyes and they were warm with affection. "My death—for his, if he still lives. If his luck is in. Not—a bad trade, eh, *miri pen?* Do not—be afraid. You have found—the truth. Your salvation lies— away from here." She sighed deeply. *"Kushto, miri pen . . ."*

Tarifa felt her face, her wrist. There was no response. She sobbed as she shook her by the shoulders. Penti could not have left her like this forever in the twinkling of an eye.

"She was a brave woman and a truthful one," said Santos as he stood beside her, his sombrero in his rope-scarred hands.

Tarifa knelt gazing at the old Gypsy who had attended her so faithfully for so long, and she knew the dull ache of a love that has been acknowledged too late. The dread finality of death was in every line of Penti's figure.

How often had death robbed and cheated her, thought Tarifa bitterly. First of Ygnacio, then Lasho and Padre Cazon, and now Penti. Death whose victories were so easily won, so final, remained her enemy.

As she got slowly to her feet there rose in her the old anger and rage. She would not, could not, bend meekly to fate as the Padres had tried to teach her to do. It was not in her to accept defeat without a struggle. She squared her shoulders and turned toward Banner.

"Señor, will you stay here with her until I can send someone back from San Diego? I am going to Bart, and I have need of my mayordomo."

Banner measured her for a moment, then nodded silently.

She mounted Guindilla, looked down once more upon Penti's crumpled form, and sank her spurs into the stallion's sides. Santos followed after her on Marca.

The boat crew from the *Celestial Queen* had been waiting on the shore near the hide houses ever since Banner had left that morning.

Tarifa paused a short way from them and dismounted. Santos got down from his saddle stiffly and stood in the sand at her side, waiting for he knew not what. There was a strangeness about the Patróna today.

Tarifa's eyes wandered out to the big clipper swinging at anchor. She had arrived on these shores with nothing. She was leaving with nothing but the small amount of gold she had kept out of the money she had gotten at the mines. She took a pouch from her sash now and pressed it into Santos' hands.

Her voice was low as she spoke, her eyes never left his worn face. "I will not be coming back, Santos."

"Dona Tarifa!" Pain followed amazement in his gaze.

"Take this," she said hurriedly. "Part of it is to see that Penti is properly buried. At Loma de Oro—near Lasho."

"*Si*, Patróna."

"And the rest is for Salvador and the Indians at Pala. Tell Salvador that Tía Isabella and Don Luis will see that he gets some money and cattle each year from what would have been my share of Loma de Oro."

"*Sí*, Dona Tarifa."

Tears coursed down his leathery face and suddenly he fell to his knees in the sand.

"Señora—do not leave us!"

She came to put her arms around him. "I must go, *amigo mío*, for many reasons. But I will remember you always, and the palominos. You will take care of Guindilla for me until he dies? And bury him on Loma de Oro, near the cabaña?"

"*Sí, sí*. With a little wooden cross to mark the spot," sobbed the mayordomo.

"*Gracias*."

She went to Guindilla, threw her arms about his neck and buried her face in his thick white mane. She felt as if her heart were being torn out of her. She touched his face, his ears, put his soft muzzle against her cheek and heard the questioning nicker and turned back to Santos.

"Take Penti's body back to Loma de Oro yourself."

"*Sí. Lo prometo,* Patróna."

She stood for a moment looking at him.

"*Adiós, amigo mío.*"

"*Adiós,* Dona Tarifa. *Vaya con Dios.*"

He watched her walk through the loose sand toward the boat, then tears dimmed his sight and her image blurred and disappeared.

All the way to the ship Tarifa kept her eyes turned resolutely from the shore. Whatever lay ahead, she had chosen it of her own free will and there could be no looking back.

She climbed up the side of the ship, as nimble as a monkey. Mr. Middleton, whom she remembered from her previous trip from Monterey on the *Celestial Queen,* met her on deck.

"How is the captain?" she asked.

"He is still alive, ma'am. It is a miracle. Will you come to his cabin?"

She nodded and followed him across the deck.

Middleton opened the door for her and she saw Mabrey seated by the bunk, his hand on Bart's wrist. The injured man lay with his eyes closed. His drawn face looked gray and moist under the swinging lantern.

Mabrey stood up looking astonished and relieved at the sight of her.

"Thank God you've come. He's been out of his head. Calling your name. But he made me promise not to send for you."

"I know. Mr. Banner told me."

She approached the bed and put her hand lightly on Bart's forehead under his damp hair. His head moved and he murmured something unintelligible under his breath.

She took the chair Mabrey gave her, keeping her eyes on Bart's face.

"How is he?"

He told her, warning her, as he had warned Banner, that his chances for recovery were slim, and why he thought Bart had planned it this way.

Her eyes met his squarely but there was a tinge of color in her cheeks. She rose and went to the desk.

"Leave us alone for a moment, John."

"I can't do that. At any moment he might—"

"Please. You wanted me to come because you thought I might save him where you could not?"

"Yes. Well—only for a moment then. I will be just outside."

She watched him leave and then went to the bunk and stood for a moment looking down into Bart's face. Death was there, she thought, ugly and cruel. It siphoned away the best of everything, leaving only an empty husk in its place. She took his hand in hers wondering at its limp weakness.

"Bart? Bart, it's Tarifa."

She waited, holding her breath, but the line of his lashes did not move. And then, half-fearful, she spoke his name again and he opened his eyes.

"Tarifa?" It was only a thread of sound, and there was wonderment, puzzlement, disbelief in it.

In spite of his weakness and helplessness, she felt embarrassed; it made her voice grow rough and noncommittal, and she did not say what she had meant to say.

"I came when I heard. I have given Loma de Oro back to the Alvarjos."

His eyes widened.

"Given—"

"Yes. All of it, and the money as well. I am never going back."

He tried to reach up to touch her cheek but his hand held more weight than he could manage and it fell back. She watched him sharply as he closed his eyes and a deep sigh escaped his lips. He had gone beyond her again.

Suddenly, as she studied the worn planes of his face, the signs of suffering etched so sharply there now, she knew with a violent churning clarity what he meant to her, what he must always have meant to her, and she covered her face with her hands and rocked back and forth while the pain and shock of realization surged through her like knife thrusts.

Now God could indeed be cruel, could indeed rob her of everything, she thought wildly. She had turned her back on everything good He had ever sent her, thrown it away with both hands. In her blind fear of losing her precious freedom, she had made herself the worst kind of prisoner. She had become her own jailer, willing herself to live on her sterile emotions, forcing her mind to rule her heart. And in doing so, had she, as Penti claimed, lost everything, even sacrificed Bart's life?

She moved closer to the bunk and stood looking down at him, a terrible longing and hunger in her long eyes, while wetness washed down her face. She was not even aware of it. She took his hand in both of hers and pressed it to her cheek. She knelt down with his slack hand still in hers and bent her head. She thought steadily, "If I have faith, I cannot lose him now." And she said the words Padre Cazon had taught her. Her lips moving, silently, slowly, meaning them with every fiber of her being.

When Mabrey returned, he found Tarifa with her head resting lightly against Bart's arm. His eyes were shut but there was a look of contentment on his worn face.

"Is he—"

"He is asleep," whispered Tarifa. She smiled up at him. "I think he is going to live, John, to be best man at your wedding."

Unbelieving, Mabrey felt his patient's wrist and face.

"He's still got a long way to go," he said cautiously, "but you know, I think you may be right."

During the long weeks that followed, Tarifa seldom left the cabin unless it was to take a short walk on deck while Mabrey examined his patient.

Mabrey's delight and amazement at Bart's recovery was little short of awe.

"By all rights he shouldn't be alive," he told Tarifa privately one evening. "He owes it all to you. You wouldn't let him give up. Time and time again I've seen you drag him back from the brink. I've never seen anything like it."

She watched him calmly with her long eyes as they stood on deck.

"You think he will be well soon? There is no longer any danger?"

"He will be fully recovered, thanks to you."

"Then will you say good-bye to him for me?"

"Good-bye! Tarifa, you can't leave him now."

"He will live; you have said so. I must go my own way."

"But why? Where will you go? This is madness!"

"Back to Spain, I think."

"But he loves you—he needs you. This is an unnecessarily cruel thing you are doing, running away from him."

"I am not running away! I can be no good to him from now on. I have changed. I am no longer the woman he loved. You do not understand."

"I understand that you will ruin his life all over again if you leave him now," Mabrey said harshly. "I can't let you do it!"

Her eyes were guarded and a trifle sad. "You do not understand me, Doctor; do not try to."

In the morning she was gone. Later they learned she had asked two of the sailors to row her ashore. A man in San Diego had sold her a horse. But from there, there was no trace of her. She had vanished as completely as a puff of smoke in the breeze.

Mabrey was left with the ticklish business of informing Bart. He was surprised that he accepted the news as well as he did. Only for a moment did his eyes show the naked pain of his loss.

"She loved me," he said quickly. "She told me so, and I don't think she lied."

"That's why I can't understand it. I tried to stop her—"

"It would have done no good if you had, John. She has to have her freedom. That's what she was afraid of losing with me. She can't understand that I would never jeopardize her independence. I want her to be what she must be, the only thing she can be. Call Banner for me," he said with sudden decision.

"What are you going to do?"

"Set sail for San Francisco. She'll go there first or I miss my guess. It's the quickest place to get a ship leaving California."

"But you're in no condition to be up. I can't allow it."

Kinkaid gave him a level look and swung his legs over the side of the bunk.

"Call Banner, John."

The doctor did as he was told. When he returned, Bart was dressed and seated at his desk looking pale but determined.

"I haven't time to put you ashore, John. But I'll see you get back from San Francisco by the first ship coming south."

"Dammit, Bart, I don't give a bloody curse in hades about my coming or going! All that interests me at the moment is your health! You're in no condition to sail yet. Even if you were, how in heaven's name do you expect to persuade Tarifa—"

Kinkaid stood up and reached for his cap. Mabrey noted how loosely his clothing hung on his big frame since his illness. But there was a quiet determination on his face.

Yankee resolve, thought Mabrey, that intrepid quality that had driven men like Kinkaid to the far ports of the world, in ships thrashing to windward off the Horn, sweeping northward through the trades, in spite of disease, mutiny, or vessels half-dismantled by the elements. Going on nerve and determination alone. Could even Tarifa's independent spirit withstand Kinkaid's roused Yankee intrepidity?

He was betting on the captain.

CHAPTER 40

Tarifa had never cared much for northern California, and she liked it even less after spending the last few days and nights in a dirty, rattletrap boardinghouse in San Francisco. The streets of the pueblo were filled with mud at this time of the year, and the conglomeration of speech, dress, and nationalities made her feel that she was in a foreign country.

When she had boarded the brig the night before, she had not noticed the big clipper that now lay moored some distance away, flying the American flag. It looked a little, she thought, like the *Celestial Queen*. But since leaving San Diego, she had seen several clippers that reminded her of Bart's ship. She had not allowed herself to think much of him or of what lay in the future. She had only decided that returning to Spain would be best. Bandonna was no doubt dead by now, but she had a desire to mingle with her own people again. There was a longing, a hunger in her for something she could not name, something of her own. Her love for Bart, she had put into a separate compartment of her heart where she kept her love for Ygnacio and Lasho, Padre Cazon, and Penti.

She had turned to face the mountains beyond the southern tip of the bay, the direction in which Loma de Oro lay. She did not hear the footsteps on the deck until two hands seized her roughly and whirled her about.

She looked up in astonishment into Bart's gray eyes.

The look on his face made her shrink back from him. "Bart—"

"Why did you leave me?" he asked bleakly.

"I could not stay. I knew you would be all right."

"I needed you, you knew that?" His voice was harsh and his fingers bit into her arms.

Her lashes fell to cover her long eyes.

He shook her. "No, damn it! Look at me!"

Her eyes widened in surprise at the naked violence in his tone. She obeyed him.

"Then why did you go?"

"Because I cannot live like other women. I cannot be bound—even by love."

"I don't want to bind you, damn it! I want you to be free. As free as the air if you must. But I can't let you leave me. You dragged me back from the grave, not once but twice. You owe me something. And by heaven, I'm going to see that I get it!"

She gave him a fleeting smile. He was like the aloof, ruthless *gitanos* of the Sacro Monte whom the women admired so much and pretended to honor and obey. Only she could not pretend. She told him so and heard him laugh.

"Do you think I want your obedience, your homage? Hell, all I want is you at my side for as long as you're happy there."

She studied his face, and something like a rush of fear

left her heart and she knew that it would never return. He meant what he said. She was convinced of that.

"It is not enough," she said. "You deserve more, and I can never give it to you."

"To the devil with what I deserve! It's you I want, always have wanted, and I'll count myself lucky to get you any way you choose to come to me. I told you that before."

He drew her closer and his eyes were bright with resolve. "I don't intend to let you go," he said, "not if I have to clap you in irons till we clear port."

She laughed suddenly, the sharp clear laugh of freedom.

He felt her arms go around his neck as she arched her body and threw her head back to look up at him.

"It was an evil day when you came into my life. I knew it then," she said. "That day when you came into the *monjeria* at San Diego."

"Evil?"

"Yes. You have swept away all my beliefs, the things I trusted in. You make a mockery of the words of my people, and force me to, and yet there is still truth in them." Softly, almost inaudibly, she whispered to him in Romany: "*Kushto, me kamāva tut.*"

"And what does that mean?"

"You see—you mock me! But since you will be satisfied with nothing but the truth, it means my own sweetheart, my darling, upon this heart of mine I love you."

He lifted her face in his hands but before their lips met he said hoarsely. "You must teach me the words, because it is a part of you that I love, the mystery, the passion, and truth of your Gypsy blood. If we have a daughter she must be named Tarifa."

"No," she said, and there was a darkness in her eyes that made his blood leap. "Penti. She was the best that is in my people. Honest with herself, free and courageous."

"And aren't you all of those things?" he asked gently.

"I was never a true Gypsy. I wanted Loma de Oro. I sacrificed my freedom for it. I would have sacrificed your life. Now I want you not as a Gypsy wants her lover, until the newness wears off and she is ready to go on to other adventures, but forever—for the rest of our lives."

"Then I thank God you are not all Gypsy," he said solemnly.

She melted into his arms like a flame igniting banked embers, and his thoughts were swept away into a fiery vortex that left him giddy and shaken. He knew then that he had been right. He would have preferred death to living the rest of his life without her.

"I was afraid," she whispered against his cheek, "so afraid. You threatened everything in me I had built to protect myself."

"But you are not afraid now?"

She kissed him with a wild abandon that even he had believed her incapable of. Her lips trembled with the passion of her words, "*Kushto. Me kamāva tut.* These are the words of my people. I know no better ones."

Later, when they stood arm in arm on the deck of the *Celestial Queen,* with the sea breeze in their faces as the crew swung into a halliard shanty, Kinkaid asked, "Are you going to be happy now that you have given up so much?"

"I am happy with you and the *Celestial Queen.*"

They both looked aloft into the towering tops of the clipper.

"You wouldn't prefer a ranch?"

"No. We will begin a new life, and I will learn all about these big sailing ships of yours."

"We will build a new clipper," he said, "the finest ever designed. And we'll name her the *Tarifa.*"

"No," she smiled up at him, "the *Gitana.* That is the proper name for a fine proud ship. One free to roam the world—free as the wind that will fill her sails."

"Yes," he laughed, "if it pleases you best. And we'll wander with her?"

"To the farthest ports of the world!"

He pulled her into his arms. "Do you have any idea how much you mean to me—how very much I love you?"

Her long eyes were as deeply mysterious as the Sphinx.

"I only know what is in my own heart. For me, love has grown drop by drop, slowly, not like other people's. That is perhaps why I could not recognize it for so long. The seed of affection was planted by Ygnacio, in his kindness to me. It was watered by Guindilla and the palominos, sprouted because of Lasho, and Loma de Oro made it grow into a sturdy tree."

"And I had no part in the growth of this tree of love?" Kinkaid asked lightly.

She gazed deep into his eyes. "You made it blossom," she said simply. "I stood under it and smelled the fragrance, and was afraid to lift my hands to pick the flowers. Can you understand what I am trying to say?"

He raised her hands to his lips and said softly, "I knew it long before you did." Then he bent his head to claim what was his.

A sob broke in her throat and she threw herself beside him, turning her face against his shoulder. His arms went around her.

"I love you. I love you, Bart." A spasm of emotion shook her whole body. The words were said. The words she had never been able to say.

Above her head, his eyes closed slowly as if in benediction.

When she raised her tearstained face he was smiling at her gently. "It was worth waiting for."

*A tumultuous drama
of misplaced love
and betrayal*

Scarlet Shadows

by Emma Drummond

Sweet, innocent, beautiful Victoria Castledon loved her dashing
and aristocratic husband, Charles Sanford. Or at least she thought
she did, until she met the notorious Captain Esterly. He alone
could awaken Victoria to the flaming desires within her, and she
would not be happy until she yielded to love's sweet torment . . .

From London to Constantinople Victoria pursues Captain Esterly
only to find out that this man she so desperately loves is her
husband's brother. Her scandalous desire blazed across continents
—setting brother against brother, husband against husband, lover
against lover . . .

A DELL BOOK $2.25

*The irresistible love story
with a happy ending.*

THE PROMISE

A novel by
DANIELLE STEEL

Based on a screenplay by
GARRY MICHAEL WHITE

After an automobile accident which left Nancy McAllister's beautiful face a tragic ruin, she accepted the money for plastic surgery from her lover's mother on one condition: that she never contact Michael again. She didn't know Michael would be told that she was dead.

Four years later, Michael met a lovely woman whose face he didn't recognize, and wondered why she hated him with such intensity .

A Dell Book $1.95

Dell Bestsellers